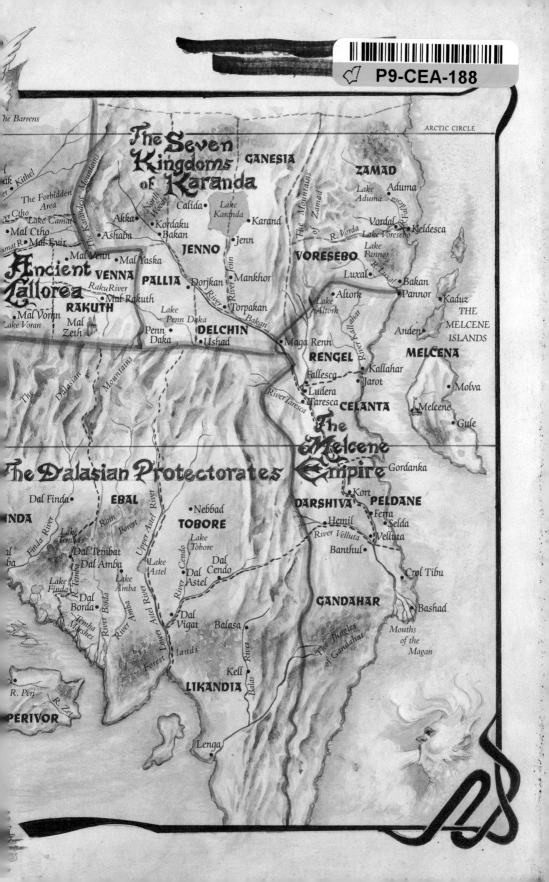

BELGARATH
THE SORCERER

By David Eddings
Published by Ballantine Books:

THE BELGARIAD

Book One: Pawn of Prophecy
Book Two: Queen of Sorcery
Book Three: Magician's Gambit
Book Four: Castle of Wizardry
Book Five: Enchanter's End Game

THE MALLOREON

Book One: Guardians of the West
Book Two: King of the Murgos
Book Three: Demon Lord of Karanda
Book Four: Sorceress of Darshiva
Book Five: The Seeress of Kell

THE ELENIUM

Book One: The Diamond Throne
Book Two: The Ruby Knight
Book Three: The Sapphire Rose

THE TAMULI

Book One: Domes of Fire
Book Two: The Shining Ones
Book Three: The Hidden City

HIGH HUNT

THE LOSERS

BELGARATH
THE SORCERER

DAVID AND LEIGH
EDDINGS

DEL REY

A DEL REY® BOOK
BALLANTINE BOOKS
NEW YORK

For Owen

We have all been at this since April of 1982. Your friendship, guidance, and faith in us has been greatly cherished.
One more to go!

Leigh and David

A note to the reader:

We're sure that the reader has noticed a slight modification of the authorial attribution on the cover of this slender volume. The reader is now privy to one of the worst-kept secrets in contemporary fiction. There are two names on the cover because it took two of us to write this book, and this has been going on from the very beginning. The recognition (finally) of the hitherto unacknowledged coauthor of these assorted works is no more than simple justice—if justice can ever be called simple. It's time to give credit where credit is due, so let's make it official, shall we?

It was well past midnight and very cold. The moon had risen, and her pale light made the frost crystals lying in the snow sparkle like carelessly strewn diamonds. In a peculiar way it seemed to Garion almost as if the snow-covered earth were reflecting the starry sky overhead.

"I think they're gone now," Durnik said, peering upward. His breath steamed in the icy, dead-calm air. "I can't see that rainbow any more."

"Rainbow?" Belgarath asked, sounding slightly amused.

"You know what I mean. Each of them has a different-colored light. Aldur's is blue, Issa's is green, Chaldan's is red, and the others all have different colors. Is there some significance to that?"

"It's probably a reflection of their different personalities," Belgarath replied. "I can't be entirely positive, though. My Master and I never got around to discussing it." He stamped his feet in the snow. "Why don't we go back?" he suggested. "It's cold out here."

They turned and started back down the hill toward the cottage, their feet crunching in the frozen snow. The farmstead at the foot of the hill looked warm and comforting. The thatched roof of the cottage was thick with snow, and the icicles hanging from the eaves glittered in the moonlight. The outbuildings Durnik had constructed were dark, but the windows of the cottage were all aglow with golden lamplight that spread softly out over the mounded snow in the yard. A column of blue-grey woodsmoke rose straight and unwavering from the chimney, rising, it seemed, to the very stars.

1

It probably had not really been necessary for the three of them to accompany their guests to the top of the hill to witness their departure, but it was Durnik's house, and Durnik was a Sendar. Sendars are meticulous about proprieties and courtesies.

"Eriond's changed," Garion noted as they neared the bottom of the hill. "He seems more certain of himself now."

Belgarath shrugged. "He's growing up. It happens to everybody—except to Belar, maybe. I don't think we can *ever* expect Belar to grow up."

"Belgarath!" Durnik sounded shocked. "That's no way for a man to speak about his God!"

"What are you talking about?"

"What you just said about Belar. He's the God of the Alorns, and you're an Alorn, aren't you?"

"Whatever gave you that peculiar notion? I'm no more an Alorn than you are."

"I always thought you were. You've certainly spent enough time with them."

"That wasn't my idea. My Master gave them to me about five thousand years ago. There were a number of times when I tried to give them back, but he wouldn't hear of it."

"Well, if you're not an Alorn, what are you?"

"I'm not really sure. It wasn't all that important to me when I was young. I *do* know that I'm not an Alorn. I'm not crazy enough for that."

"Grandfather!" Garion protested.

"You don't count, Garion. You're only half Alorn."

They reached the door of the cottage and carefully stamped the snow off their feet before entering. The cottage was Aunt Pol's domain, and she had strong feelings about people who tracked snow across her spotless floors.

The interior of the cottage was warm and filled with golden lamplight that reflected from the polished surfaces of Aunt Pol's copper-bottomed pots and kettles and pans hanging from hooks on either side of the arched fireplace. Durnik had built the table and chairs in the center of the room out of oak, and the lamplight enhanced the golden color of the wood.

The three of them immediately went to the fireplace to warm their hands and feet.

The door to the bedroom opened, and Poledra came out. "Well," she said, "did you see them off?"

"Yes, dear," Belgarath replied. "They were going in a generally northeasterly direction the last time I looked."

"How's Pol?" Durnik asked.

"Happy," Garion's tawny-haired grandmother replied.

"That's not exactly what I meant. Is she still awake?"

Poledra nodded. "She's lying in bed admiring her handiwork."

"Would it be all right if I looked in on her?"

"Of course. Just don't wake the babies."

"Make a note of that, Durnik," Belgarath advised. "Not waking those babies is likely to become your main purpose in life for the next several months."

Durnik smiled briefly and went into the bedroom with Poledra.

"You shouldn't tease him that way, Grandfather," Garion chided.

"I wasn't teasing, Garion. Sleep's very rare in a house with twins. One of them always seems to be awake. Would you like something to drink? I think I can probably find Pol's beer barrel."

"She'll pull out your beard if she catches you in her pantry."

"She isn't going to catch me, Garion. She's too busy being a mother right now." The old man crossed the room to the pantry and began rummaging around.

Garion pulled off his cloak, hung it on a wooden peg, and went back to the fireplace. His feet still felt cold. He looked up at the latticework of rafters overhead. It was easy to see that Durnik had crafted them. The smith's meticulous attention to detail showed in everything he did. The rafters were exposed over this central room, but there was a loft over the bedroom and a flight of stairs reaching up to it along the back wall.

"Found it," Belgarath called triumphantly from the pantry. "She tried to hide it behind the flour barrel."

Garion smiled. His grandfather could probably find a beer cask in the dark at the bottom of a coal mine.

The old man came out with three brimming tankards, set them down on the table, and moved a chair around until it faced the fireplace. Then he took one of the tankards, sat, and stretched his feet out toward the fire. "Pull up a chair, Garion," he invited. "We might as well be comfortable."

Garion did that. "It's been quite a night," he said.

"That it has, boy," the old man replied. "That it has."

"Shouldn't we say good night to Aunt Pol?"

"Durnik's with her. Let's not disturb them. This is a special sort of time for married people."

"Yes," Garion agreed, remembering that night two weeks ago when his daughter had been born.

"Will you be going back to Riva soon?"

"I probably should," Garion replied. "I think I'll wait a few days, though—at least until Aunt Pol's back on her feet again."

"Don't wait too long," Belgarath advised with a sly grin. "Ce'Nedra's sitting on the throne all by herself right now, you know."

3

"She'll be all right. She knows what to do."

"Yes, but do you *want* her doing things on her own?"

"Oh, I don't think she'll declare war on anybody while I'm gone."

"Maybe not, but with Ce'Nedra you never really know, do you?"

"Quit making fun of my wife, Grandfather."

"I'm not making fun of her. I love her dearly, but I *do* know her. All I'm saying is that she's a little unpredictable." Then the old sorcerer sighed.

"Is something the matter, Grandfather?"

"I was just chewing on some old regrets. I don't think you and Durnik realize just how lucky you are. I wasn't around when *my* twins were born. I was off on a business trip."

Garion knew the story, of course. "You didn't have any choice, Grandfather," he said. "Aldur ordered you to go to Mallorea. It was time to recover the Orb from Torak, and you had to go along to help Cherek Bear-shoulders and his sons."

"Don't try to be reasonable about it, Garion. The bald fact is that I abandoned my wife when she needed me the most. Things might have turned out very differently if I hadn't."

"Are you still feeling guilty about that?"

"Of course I am. I've been carrying that guilt around for three thousand years. You can hand out all the royal pardons you want, but it's still there."

"Grandmother forgives you."

"Naturally she does. Your grandmother's a wolf, and wolves don't hold grudges. The whole point, though, is that *she* can forgive me, and *you* can forgive me, and you can get up a petition signed by everybody in the known world that forgives me, but I *still* won't forgive myself. Why don't we talk about something else?"

Durnik came back out of the bedroom. "She's asleep," he said softly. Then he went to the fireplace and stacked more wood on the embers. "It's a cold night out there," he noted. "Let's keep this fire going."

"I should have thought of that," Garion apologized.

"Are the babies still asleep?" Belgarath asked the smith.

Durnik nodded.

"Enjoy it while you can. They're resting up."

Durnik smiled. Then he too pulled a chair closer to the fire. "Do you remember what we were talking about earlier?" he asked, reaching for the remaining tankard on the table.

"We talked about a lot of things," Belgarath told him.

"I mean the business of the same things happening over and over again. What happened tonight isn't one of those, is it?"

"Would it come as a surprise to you if I told you that Pol isn't the first to give birth to twins?"

"I know that, Belgarath, but this seems different somehow. I get the feeling that this isn't something that's happened before. This seems like something new to me. This has been a very special night. UL himself blessed it. Has that ever happened before?"

"Not that I know of," the old sorcerer conceded. "Maybe this *is* something new. If it is, it's going to make things a little strange for us."

"How's that?" Garion asked.

"The nice thing about repetitions is that you sort of know what to expect. If everything did stop when the 'accident' happened, and now it's all moving again, we'll be breaking into new territory."

"Won't the prophecies give us some clues?"

Belgarath shook his head. "No. The last passage in the Mrin Codex reads, 'And there shall come a great light, and in that light shall that which was broken be healed, and interrupted Purpose shall proceed again, as was from the beginning intended.' All the other prophecies end in more or less the same way. The Ashabine Oracles even use almost exactly the same words. Once that light reached Korim, we were on our own."

"Will there be a new set of prophecies now?" Durnik asked.

"Next time you see Eriond, why don't you ask him? *He's* the one in charge now." Belgarath sighed. "I don't think we'll be involved in any new ones, though. We've done what we were supposed to do." He smiled just a bit wryly. "To be perfectly frank about it, I'm just as glad to pass it on. I'm getting a little old to be rushing out to save the world. It was an interesting career right at first, but it gets exhausting after the first six or eight times."

"That'd be quite a story," Durnik said.

"What would?"

"Everything you've been through—saving the world, fighting Demons, pushing the Gods around, things like that."

"Tedious, Durnik. Very, very tedious," Belgarath disagreed. "There were long periods when nothing was happening. You can't make much of a story out of a lot of people just sitting around waiting."

"Oh, I'm sure there were enough lively parts to keep it interesting. Someday I'd really like to hear the whole thing—you know, how you met Aldur, what the world was like before Torak cracked it, how you and Cherek Bear-shoulders stole the Orb back—all of it."

Belgarath laughed. "If I start telling *that* story, we'll still be sitting here a year from now, and we won't even be halfway through by then. We've all got better things to do."

"Do we really, Grandfather?" Garion asked. "You just said that our part of this is over. Wouldn't this be a good time to sum it all up?"

"What good would it do? You've got a kingdom to run, and Durnik's got this farm to tend. You've got more important things to do than sit around listening to me tell stories."

"Write it down, then." The notion suddenly caught fire in Garion's mind. "You know, Grandfather, the more I think about it, the more I think you ought to do just that. You've been here since the very beginning. You're the only one who knows the whole story. You really *should* write it down, you know. Tell the world what really happened."

Belgarath's expression grew pained. "The world doesn't care, Garion. All I'd do is offend a lot of people. They've got their own preconceptions, and they're happy with them. I'm not going to spend the next fifty years scribbling on scraps of paper just so that people can travel to the Vale from the other side of the world to argue with me. Besides, I'm not a historian. I don't mind *telling* stories, but writing them down doesn't appeal to me. If I took on a project like that, my hand would fall off after a couple of years."

"Don't be coy, Grandfather. Durnik and I both know that you don't have to do it by hand. You can *think* the words onto paper without ever picking up a pen."

"Forget it," Belgarath said shortly. "I'm not going to waste my time on something as ridiculous as that."

"You're lazy, Belgarath," Durnik accused.

"Are you only just noticing that? I thought you were more observant."

"You won't do it then?" Garion demanded.

"Not unless somebody comes up with a better reason than you two have so far."

The bedroom door opened, and Poledra came out into the kitchen. "Are you three going to talk all night?" she demanded in a quiet voice. "If you are, go do it someplace else. If you wake the babies . . ." She left it hanging ominously.

"We were just thinking about going to bed, dear," Belgarath lied blandly.

"Well, do it then. Don't just sit there and talk about it."

Belgarath stood up and stretched—perhaps just a bit theatrically. "She's right, you know," he said to his two friends. "It'll be daylight before long, and the twins have been resting up all night. If we're going to get any sleep, we'd better do it now."

Later, after the three of them had climbed up into the loft and rolled themselves into blankets on the pallets Durnik kept stored up there, Garion lay looking down at the slowly waning firelight and the flickering shadows in the room below. He thought of Ce'Nedra and his own children, of course, but then he let his mind drift back over the events of this most special of nights. Aunt Pol had always been at the very center of his life, and with the birth of her twins, her life was now fulfilled.

Near to sleep, the Rivan King found his thoughts going back over the conversation he had just had with Durnik and his grandfather. He was honest enough with himself to admit that his desire to read Belgarath's history of the world was not entirely academic. The old sorcerer was a very strange and complex man, and his story promised to provide insights into his character that could come from no other source. He'd have to be pushed, of course. Belgarath was an expert at avoiding work of any kind. Garion, however, thought he knew of a way to pry the story out of his grandfather. He smiled to himself as the fire burned lower and lower in the room below. He knew he could find out how it all began.

And then, because it was really quite late, Garion fell asleep, and, perhaps because of all the familiar things in Aunt Pol's kitchen down below, he dreamed of Faldor's farm, where *his* story had begun.

PART
ONE

THE VALE

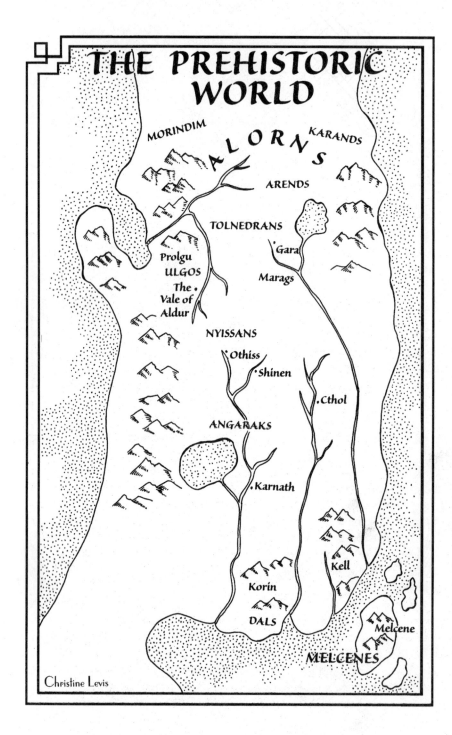

CHAPTER
ONE

The problem with any idea is the fact that the more it gets bandied about, the more feasible it seems to become. What starts out as idle speculation—something mildly entertaining to wile away a few hours before going to bed—can become, once others are drawn into it, a kind of obligation. Why can't people understand that just because I'm willing to *talk* about something, it doesn't automatically follow that I'm actually willing to *do* it?

As a case in point, this all started with Durnik's rather inane remark about wanting to hear the whole story. You know how Durnik is, forever taking things apart to see what makes them work. I can forgive him in this case, however. Pol had just presented him with twins, and new fathers tend to be a bit irrational. Garion, on the other hand, should have had sense enough to leave it alone. I curse the day when I encouraged that boy to be curious about first causes. He can be so tedious about some things. If he'd have just let it drop, I wouldn't be saddled with this awful chore.

But no. The two of them went on and on about it for day after day as if the fate of the world depended on it. I tried to get around them with a few vague promises—nothing specific, mind you—and fervently hoped that they'd forget about the whole silly business.

Then Garion did something so unscrupulous, so underhanded, that it shocked me to the very core. He told Polgara about the stupid idea, and when he got back to Riva, he told Ce'Nedra. That would have been bad enough, but would you believe that he actually encouraged those two to bring *Poledra* into it?

I'll admit right here that it was my own fault. My only excuse is that I was a little tired that night. I'd inadvertently let something slip that I've kept buried in my heart for three eons. Poledra had been with child, and I'd gone off and left her to fend for herself. I've carried the guilt over that for almost half of my life. It's like a knife twisting inside me. Garion knew that, and he coldly, deliberately, used it to force me to take on this ridiculous project. He *knows* that under these circumstances, I simply *cannot* refuse anything my wife asks of me.

Poledra, of course, didn't put any pressure on me. She didn't have to. All she had to do was suggest that she'd rather like to have me go along with the idea. Under the circumstances, I didn't have any choice. I hope that the Rivan King is happy about what he's done to me.

This is most certainly a mistake. Wisdom tells me that it would be far better to leave things as they are, with event and cause alike half buried in the dust of forgotten years. If it were up to me, I would leave it that way. The truth is going to upset a lot of people.

Few will understand and fewer still accept what I am about to set forth, but as my grandson and son-in-law so pointedly insisted, if *I* don't tell the story, somebody else will; and since I alone know the beginning and middle and end of it, it falls to me to commit to perishable parchment, with ink that begins to fade before it even dries, some ephemeral account of what really happened—and why.

Thus, let me begin this story as all stories are begun, at the beginning.

I was born in the village of Gara, which no longer exists. It lay, if I remember it correctly, on a pleasant green bank beside a small river that sparkled in the summer sun as if its surface were covered with jewels— and I'd trade all the jewels I've ever owned or seen to sit again beside that unnamed river.

Our village was not rich, but in those days none were. The world was at peace, and our Gods walked among us and smiled upon us. We had enough to eat and huts to shelter us from the weather. I don't recall who our God was, nor his attributes, nor his totem. I was very young at the time, and it was, after all, long ago.

I played with the other children in the warm, dusty streets, ran through the long grass and the wildflowers in the meadows, and paddled in that sparkling river that was drowned by the Sea of the East so many years ago that they are beyond counting.

My mother died when I was quite young. I remember that I cried about it for a long time, though I must honestly admit that I can no longer even remember her face. I remember the gentleness of her hands and the warm smell of fresh-baked bread that came from her garments, but I can't remember her face. Isn't that odd?

The people of Gara took over my upbringing at that point. I never knew my father, and I have no recollection of having any living relatives in that place. The villagers saw to it that I was fed, gave me cast-off clothing, and let me sleep in their cow sheds. They called me Garath, which meant "of the town of Gara" in our particular dialect. It may or may not have been my real name. I can no longer remember what name my mother had given me, not that it really matters, I suppose. Garath was a serviceable enough name for an orphan, and I didn't loom very large in the social structure of the village.

Our village lay somewhere near where the ancestral homelands of the Tolnedrans, the Nyissans, and the Marags joined. I *think* we were all of the same race, but I can't really be sure. I can only remember one temple—if you can call it that—which would seem to indicate that we all worshiped the same God and were thus of the same race. I was indifferent to religion at that time, so I can't recall if the temple had been raised to Nedra or Mara or Issa. The lands of the Arends lay somewhat to the north, so it's even possible that our rickety little church had been built to honor Chaldan. I'm certain that we didn't worship Torak or Belar. I think I'd have remembered had it been either of those two.

Even as a child I was expected to earn my keep; the villagers weren't very keen about maintaining me in idle luxury. They put me to work as a cowherd, but I wasn't very good at it, if you must know the truth. Our cows were scrubby and quite docile, so not *too* many of them strayed off while they were in my care, and those that did usually returned for milking in the evening. All in all, though, being a cowherd was a good vocation for a boy who wasn't all that enthusiastic about honest work.

My only possessions in those days were the clothes on my back, but I soon learned how to fill in the gaps. Locks had not yet been invented, so it wasn't too difficult for me to explore the huts of my neighbors when they were out working in the fields. Mostly I stole food, although a few small objects did find their way into my pockets from time to time. Unfortunately, I was the natural suspect when things turned up missing. Orphans were not held in very high regard at that particular time. At any rate, my reputation deteriorated as the years went by, and the other children were instructed to avoid me. My neighbors viewed me as lazy and generally unreliable, and they also called me a liar and a thief—often right to my face! I won't bother to deny the charges, but it's not really very nice to come right out and say it like that, is it? They watched me closely, and they pointedly told me to stay out of town except at night.

13

I largely ignored those petty restrictions and actually began to enjoy the business of creeping about in search of food or whatever else might fall to hand. I began to think of myself as a very clever fellow.

I guess I was about thirteen or so when I began to notice girls. That *really* made my neighbors nervous. I had a certain rakish celebrity in the village, and young people of an impressionable age find that sort of thing irresistibly attractive. As I said, I began to notice girls, and the girls noticed me right back. One thing led to another, and on a cloudy spring morning one of the village elders caught me in his hay barn with his youngest daughter. Let me hasten to assure you that nothing was *really* going on. Oh, a few harmless kisses, perhaps, but nothing any more serious. The girl's father, however, immediately thought the worst of me and gave me the thrashing of my life.

I finally managed to escape from him and ran out of the village. I waded across the river and climbed the hill on the far side to sulk. The air was cool and dry, and the clouds raced overhead in the fresh young wind. I sat there for a very long time considering my situation. I concluded that I'd just about exhausted the possibilities of Gara. My neighbors, with some justification, I'll admit, looked at me with hard-eyed suspicion most of the time, and the incident in the hay barn was likely to be blown all out of proportion. A certain cold logic advised me that it wouldn't be too long before I'd be asked pointedly to leave.

Well, I certainly wasn't going to give them *that* satisfaction. I looked down at the tiny cluster of dun-colored huts beside a small river that didn't sparkle beneath the scudding clouds of spring. And then I turned and looked to the west at a vast grassland and white-topped mountains beyond and clouds roiling in the grey sky, and I felt a sudden overwhelming compulsion to go. There was more to the world than the village of Gara, and I suddenly wanted very much to go look at it. There was nothing really keeping me, and the father of my little playmate would probably be laying in wait for me—with cudgel—every time I turned around. I made up my mind at that point.

I visited the village one last time, shortly after midnight. I certainly didn't intend to leave empty-handed. A storage shed provided me with as much food as I could carry conveniently, and, since it's not prudent to travel unarmed, I also took a fairly large knife. I'd fashioned a sling a year or so previously, and the tedious hours spent watching over other people's cows had given me plenty of time for practice. I wonder whatever happened to that sling.

I looked around the shed and decided that I had everything I really needed, and so I crept quietly down that dusty street, waded across the river again, and went from that place forever.

When I think back on it, I realize that I owe that heavy-handed villager an enormous debt of gratitude. Had he not come into that barn when he did, I might never have climbed that hill on such a day to gaze to the west, and I might very well have lived out my life in Gara and died there. Isn't it odd how the little things can change a man's entire life?

The lands of the Tolnedrans lay to the west, and by morning I was well within their borders. I had no real destination in mind, just that odd compulsion to travel westward. I passed a few villages, but saw no real reason to stop.

It was two—or perhaps three—days after I left Gara when I encountered a humorous, good-natured old fellow driving a rickety cart. "Where be ye bound, boy?" he asked me in what seemed to me at the time to be an outlandish dialect.

"Oh," I replied with a vague gesture toward the west, "that way, I guess."

"You don't seem very certain."

I grinned at him. "I'm not," I admitted. "It's just that I've got a powerful urge to see what's on the other side of the next hill."

He evidently took me quite literally. At the time I thought he was a Tolnedran, and I've noticed that they're all very literal-minded. "Not much on the other side of that hill up ahead but Tol Malin," he told me.

"Tol Malin?"

"It's a fair-size town. The people who live there have a puffed-up opinion of themselves. Anybody else wouldn't have bothered with that 'Tol,' but they seem to think it makes the place sound important. I'm going that way myself, and if you're of a mind, you can ride along. Hop up, boy. It's a long way to walk."

I thought at the time that all Tolnedrans spoke the way he did, but I soon found out that I was wrong. I tarried for a couple of weeks in Tol Malin, and it was there that I first encountered the concept of money. Trust the Tolnedrans to invent money. I found the whole idea fascinating. Here was something small enough to be portable and yet of enormous value. Someone who's just stolen a chair or a table or a horse is fairly conspicuous. Money, on the other hand, can't be identified as someone else's property once it's in your pocket.

Unfortunately, Tolnedrans are very possessive about their money, and it was in Tol Malin that I first heard someone shout "Stop, thief!" I left town rather quickly at that point.

I hope you realize that I wouldn't be making such an issue of some of my boyhood habits except for the fact that my daughter can be very tiresome about my occasional relapses. I'd just like for people to see *my* side of it for a change. Given my circumstances, did I really have any choice?

Oddly enough, I encountered that same humorous old fellow again about five miles outside Tol Malin. "Well, boy," he greeted me. "I see that you're still moving along westward."

"There was a little misunderstanding back in Tol Malin," I replied defensively. "I thought it might be best for me to leave."

He laughed knowingly, and for some reason his laughter made my whole day seem brighter. He was a very ordinary-looking old fellow with white hair and beard, but his deep blue eyes seemed strangely out of place in his wrinkled face. They were very wise, but they didn't seem to be the eyes of an old man. They also seemed to see right through all my excuses and lame explanations. "Well, hop up again, boy," he told me. "We still both seem to be going in the same direction."

We traveled across the lands of the Tolnedrans for the next several weeks, moving steadily westward. This was before those people developed their obsession with straight, well-maintained roads, and what we followed were little more than wagon tracks that meandered along the course of least resistance across the meadows.

Like just about everybody else in the world in those days, the Tolnedrans were farmers. There were very few isolated farmsteads out in the countryside, because for the most part the people lived in villages, went out to work their fields each morning, and returned to the villages each night.

We passed one of those villages one morning about the middle of summer, and I saw those farmers trudging out to work. "Wouldn't it be easier if they'd just build their houses out where their fields are?" I asked the old man.

"Probably so," he agreed, "but then they'd be peasants instead of townsmen. A Tolnedran would sooner die than have others think of him as a peasant."

"That's ridiculous," I objected. "They spend all day every day grubbing in the dirt, and that means that they *are* peasants, doesn't it?"

"Yes," he replied calmly, "but they seem to think that if they live in a village, that makes them townsmen."

"Is that so important to them?"

"Very important, boy. A Tolnedran always wants to keep a good opinion of himself."

"I think it's stupid, myself."

"Many of the things people do are stupid. Keep your eyes and ears open the next time we go through one of these villages. If you pay attention, you'll see what I'm talking about."

I probably wouldn't even have noticed if he hadn't pointed it out. We passed through several of these villages during the next couple of weeks, and I got to know the Tolnedrans. I didn't care too much for them, but I got to know them. A Tolnedran spends just about every waking minute trying to determine his exact rank in his community, and the higher he perceives his rank to be, the more offensive he becomes. He treats his servants badly—not out of cruelty, but out of a deep-seated need to establish his superiority. He'll spend hours in front of a mirror practicing a haughty, superior expression. Maybe that's what set my teeth on edge. I don't like having people look down their noses at me, and my status as a vagabond put me at the very bottom of the social ladder, so *everybody* looked down his nose at me.

"The next pompous ass who sneers at me is going to get a punch in the mouth," I muttered darkly as we left yet another village as summer was winding down.

The old man shrugged. "Why bother?"

"I don't care for people who treat me like dirt."

"Do you really care what they think?"

"Not in the slightest."

"Why waste your energy then? You've got to learn to laugh these things off, boy. Those self-important villagers are silly, aren't they?"

"Of course they are."

"Wouldn't hitting one of them in the face make you just as silly—or even sillier? As long as *you* know who you are, does it really matter what other people think about you?"

"Well, no, but—" I groped for some kind of explanation, but I didn't find one. I finally laughed a bit sheepishly.

He patted my shoulder affectionately. "I thought you might see it that way—eventually."

That may have been one of the more important lessons I've learned over the years. Privately laughing at silly people is much more satisfying in the long run than rolling around in the middle of a dusty street with them, trying to knock out all of their teeth. If nothing else, it's easier on your clothes.

The old man didn't really seem to have a destination. He had a cart, but he wasn't carrying anything important in it—just a few half full sacks of grain for his stumpy horse, a keg of water, a bit of food, and several shabby old blankets that he seemed happy to share with me. The better we grew acquainted, the more I grew to like him. He seemed to see his way straight to the core of things, and he usually found something to laugh about in what he saw. In time, I began to laugh too, and I realized that he was the closest thing to a friend I'd ever had.

He passed the time by telling me about the people who lived on that broad plain. I got the impression that he spent a great deal of his time traveling. Despite his humorous way of talking—or maybe because of it—I found his perceptions about the various races to be quite acute. I've spent thousands of years with those people, and I've never once found those first impressions he gave me to be wrong. He told me that the Alorns were rowdies, the Tolnedrans materialistic, and the Arends not quite bright. The Marags were emotional, flighty, and generous to a fault. The Nyissans were sluggish and devious, and the Angaraks obsessed with religion. He had nothing but pity for the Morindim and the Karands, and, given his earthy nature, a peculiar kind of respect for the mystical Dals. I felt a peculiar wrench and a sense of profound loss when, on another one of those cool, cloudy days, he reined in his horse and said, "This is as far as I'm going, boy. Hop on down."

It was the abruptness more than anything that upset me. "Which way are you heading?" I asked him.

"What difference does it make, boy? You're going west, and I'm not. We'll come across each other again, but for right now we're going our separate ways. You've got more to see, and I've already seen what lies in that direction. We can talk about it the next time we meet. I hope you find what you're looking for, but for right now, hop down."

I felt more than a little injured by this rather cavalier dismissal, so I wasn't very gracious as I gathered up my belongings, got out of his cart, and struck off toward the west. I didn't look back, so I couldn't really say which direction he took. By the time I *did* throw a quick glance over my shoulder, he was out of sight.

He had given me a general idea of the geography ahead of me, and I knew that it was late enough in the summer to make the notion of exploring the mountains a very bad idea. The old man had told me that there was a vast forest ahead of me, a forest lying on either side of a river that, unlike other rivers, ran from south to north. From his description I knew that the land ahead was sparsely settled, so I'd be obliged to fend for myself rather than rely on pilferage to sustain me. But I was young and confident of my skill with my sling, so I was fairly sure that I could get by.

As it turned out, however, I wasn't obliged to forage for food that winter. Right on the verge of the forest, I found a large encampment of strange old people who lived in tents rather than huts. They spoke a language I didn't understand, but they made me welcome with gestures and weepy smiles.

Theirs was perhaps the most peculiar community I've ever encountered, and believe me, I've seen a lot of communities. Their skin was strangely colorless, which I assumed to be a characteristic of their race, but the truly odd thing was that there didn't seem to be a soul among them who was a day under seventy.

They made much of me, and most of them wept the first time they saw me. They would sit by the hour and just look at me, which I found disconcerting, to say the very least. They fed me and pampered me and provided me with what might be called luxurious quarters—if a tent could ever be described as luxurious. The tent had been empty, and I discovered that there were many empty tents in their encampment. Within a month or two I was able to find out why. Scarcely a week went by when at least one of them didn't die. As I said, they were all very old. Have you any idea of how depressing it is to live in a place where there's a perpetual funeral going on?

Winter was coming on, however, and I had a place to sleep and a fire to keep me warm, and the old people kept me well fed, so I decided that I could stand a little depression. I made up my mind, though, that with the first hint of spring, I'd be gone.

I made no particular effort to learn their language that winter and picked up only a few words. The most continually repeated among them were "Gorim" and "UL," which seemed to be names of some sort and were almost always spoken in tones of profoundest regret.

In addition to feeding me, the old people provided me with clothing; my own hadn't been very good in the first place and had become badly worn during the course of my journey. This involved no great sacrifice on their part, since a community in which there are two or three funerals every few weeks is bound to have spare clothes lying about.

When the snow melted and the frost began to seep out of the ground, I quietly began to make preparations to leave. I stole food—a little at a time to avoid suspicion—and hid it in my tent. I filched a rather nice wool cloak from the tent of one of the recently deceased and picked up a few other useful items here and there. I scouted the surrounding area carefully and found a place where I could ford the large river just to the west of the encampment. Then, with my escape route firmly in mind, I settled down to wait for the last of winter to pass.

As is usual in the early spring, we had a couple of weeks of fairly steady rain, so I still waited, although my impatience to be gone was becoming almost unbearable. During the course of that winter, that peculiar compulsion that had nagged at me since I'd left Gara had subtly altered. Now I seemed to be drawn southward instead of to the west.

The rains finally let up, and the spring sun seemed warm enough to make traveling pleasant. One evening I gathered up the fruits of my pilferage, stowed them in the rude pack I'd fashioned during the long winter evenings, and sat in my tent listening in almost breathless anticipation as the sounds of the old people gradually subsided. Then, when all was quiet, I crept out of my temporary home and made for the edge of the woods.

The moon was full that night, and the stars seemed very bright. I crept through the shadowy woods, waded the river, and emerged on the other side filled with a sense of enormous exhilaration. I was free!

I followed the river southward for the better part of that night, putting as much distance as I possibly could between me and the old people—enough certainly so that their creaky old limbs wouldn't permit them to follow.

The forest seemed incredibly old. The trees were huge, and the forest floor, all overspread by that leafy green canopy, was devoid of the usual underbrush, carpeted instead with lush green moss. It seemed to me an enchanted forest, and once I was certain there would be no pursuit, I found that I wasn't really in any great hurry, so I strolled—sauntered if you will—southward with no real sense of urgency, aside from that now-gentle compulsion to go someplace, and I hadn't really the faintest idea of where.

And then the land opened up. What had been forest became a kind of vale, a grassy basin dotted here and there with delightful groves of trees verged with thickets of lush berry bushes, centering around deep, cold springs of water so clear that I could look down through ten feet of it at trout, which, all unafraid, looked up curiously at me as I knelt to drink.

And deer, as placid and docile as sheep, grazed in the lush green meadows and watched with large and gentle eyes as I passed.

All bemused, I wandered, more content than I had ever been. The distant voice of prudence told me that my store of food wouldn't last forever, but it didn't really seem to diminish—perhaps because I glutted myself on berries and other strange fruits.

I lingered long in that magic vale, and in time I came to its very center, where there grew a tree so vast that my mind reeled at the immensity of it.

I make no pretense at being a horticulturist, but I've been nine times around the world, and so far as I've seen, there's no other tree like it anywhere. And, in what was probably a mistake, I went to the tree and laid my hands upon its rough bark. I've always wondered what might have happened if I had not.

The peace that came over me was indescribable. My somewhat prosaic daughter will probably dismiss my bemusement as natural laziness, but she'll be wrong about that. I have no idea of how long I sat in rapt communion with that ancient tree. I know that I must have been somehow nourished and sustained as hours, days, even months drifted by unnoticed, but I have no memory of ever eating or sleeping.

And then, overnight, it turned cold and began to snow. Winter, like death, had been creeping up behind me all the while.

I'd formulated a rather vague intention to return to the camp of the old people for another winter of pampering if nothing better turned up, but it was obvious that I'd lingered too long in the mesmerizing shade of that silly tree.

And the snow piled so deep that I could barely flounder my way through it. My food was gone, and my shoes worn out, and I lost my knife, and it suddenly turned very, very cold. I'm not making any accusations here, but it seemed to me that this was all just a little excessive.

In the end, soaked to the skin and with ice forming in my hair, I huddled behind a pile of rock that seemed to reach up into the very heart of the snowstorm that swirled around me, and I tried to prepare myself for death. I thought of the village of Gara, and of the grassy fields around it, and of our sparkling river, and of my mother, and—because I was still really very young—I cried.

"Why weepest thou, boy?" The voice was very gentle. The snow was so thick that I couldn't see who spoke, but the tone made me angry for some reason. Didn't I have reason to cry?

"Because I'm cold and I'm hungry," I replied, "and because I'm dying and I don't want to."

"Why art thou dying? Art thou injured?"

"I'm lost," I said a bit tartly, "and it's snowing and I have no place to go." Was he *blind*?

"Is this reason enough amongst thy kind to die?"

"Isn't it enough?"

"And how long dost thou expect this dying of thine to persist?" The voice seemed only mildly curious.

"I don't know," I replied through a sudden wave of self-pity. "I've never done it before."

The wind howled and the snow swirled more thickly around me.

"Boy," the voice said finally, "come here to me."

"Where are you? I can't see you."

"Walk around the tower to thy left. Knowest thou thy left hand from thy right?"

He didn't have to be so insulting! I stumbled angrily to my half-frozen feet, blinded by the driving snow.

"Well, boy? Art thou coming?"

I moved around what I thought was only a pile of rocks.

"Thou shalt come to a smooth grey stone," the voice said. "It is somewhat taller than thy head and as broad as thine arms may reach."

"All right," I said through chattering teeth when I reached the rock he'd described. "Now what?"

"Tell it to open."

"What?"

"Speak unto the stone," the voice said patiently, ignoring the fact that I was congealing in the gale. "Command it to open."

"Command? Me?"

"Thou art a man. It is but a rock."

"What do I say?"

"Tell it to open."

"I think this is silly, but I'll try it." I faced the rock. "Open," I commanded halfheartedly.

"Surely thou canst do better than that."

"Open!" I thundered.

The rock slid aside.

"Come in, boy," the voice said. "Stand not in the weather like some befuddled calf. It is quite cold." Had he only just now noticed that?

I went inside what appeared to be some kind of vestibule with nothing in it but a stone staircase winding upward. Oddly, it wasn't dark, though I couldn't see exactly where the light came from.

"Close the door, boy."

"How?"

"How didst thou open it?"

I turned to face that gaping opening, and, quite proud of myself, I commanded, "Close!" At the sound of my voice, the rock slid shut with a grinding sound that chilled my blood even more than the fierce storm outside. I was trapped! My momentary panic passed as I suddenly realized that I was dry for the first time in days. There wasn't even a puddle around my feet! Something strange was going on here.

"Come up, boy," the voice commanded.

What choice did I have? I mounted the stone steps worn with countless centuries of footfalls and spiraled my way up and up, only a little bit afraid. The tower was very high, and the climbing took me a long time.

At the top was a chamber filled with wonders. I looked at things such as I'd never seen before. I was still young and not, at the time, above thoughts of theft. Larceny seethed in my grubby little soul. I'm sure that Polgara will find that particular admission entertaining.

Near a fire—which burned, I observed, without fuel of any kind—sat a man who seemed most incredibly ancient, but somehow familiar, though I couldn't seem to place him. His beard was long and full and as white as the snow that had so nearly killed me—but his eyes were eternally young. I think it might have been the eyes that seemed so familiar to me. "Well, boy," he said, "hast thou decided not to die?"

"Not if it isn't necessary," I said bravely, still cataloging the wonders of the chamber.

"Dost thou require anything?" he asked. "I am unfamiliar with thy kind."

"A little food, perhaps," I replied. "I haven't eaten for two days. And a warm place to sleep, if you wouldn't mind." I thought it might not be a bad idea to stay on the good side of this strange old man, so I hurried on. "I won't be much trouble, Master, and I can make myself useful in payment." It was an artful little speech. I'd learned during my months with the Tolnedrans how to make myself agreeable to people in a position to do me favors.

"Master?" he said, and laughed, a sound so cheerful that it made me almost want to dance. Where *had* I heard that laugh before? "I am not thy Master, boy," he said. Then he laughed again, and my heart sang with the splendor of his mirth. "Let us see to this thing of food. What dost thou require?"

"A little bread perhaps—not too stale, if it's all right."

"Bread? Only bread? Surely, boy, thy stomach is fit for more than bread. If thou wouldst make thyself useful—as thou hast promised—we must nourish thee properly. Consider, boy. Think of all the things thou hast eaten in thy life. What in all the world would most surely satisfy this vast hunger of thine?"

I couldn't even say it. Before my eyes swam the visions of smoking roasts, of fat geese swimming in their own gravy, of heaps of fresh-baked bread and rich, golden butter, of pastries in thick cream, of cheese and dark-brown ale, of fruits and nuts and salt to savor it all. The vision was so real that it even seemed that I could smell it.

And he who sat by the glowing fire that burned, it seemed, air alone, laughed, and again my heart sang. "Turn, boy," he said, "and eat thy fill."

I turned, and there on a table, which I hadn't even seen before, lay everything I had imagined. No wonder I could smell it! A hungry boy doesn't ask where the food comes from—he eats. And so I ate. I ate until my stomach groaned. Through the sound of my eating I could hear the laughter of the aged one beside his fire, and my heart leaped within me at each strangely familiar chuckle.

And when I'd finished and sat drowsing over my plate, he spoke again. "Wilt thou sleep now, boy?"

"A corner, Master," I said. "A little out-of-the-way place by the fire, if it isn't too much trouble."

He pointed. "Sleep there, boy," he said, and all at once I saw a bed that I had no more seen than I had the table—a great bed with huge pillows and comforters of softest down. I smiled my thanks and crept into the bed, and, because I was young and very tired, I fell asleep almost at once without even stopping to think about how very strange all of this had been.

But in my sleep I knew that he who had brought me in out of the storm and fed me and cared for me was watching through the long, snowy night, and I slept even more securely in the comforting warmth of his care.

Amd that began my servitude. At first the tasks my Master set me to were simple ones—"Sweep the floor," "Fetch some firewood," "Wash the windows"— that sort of thing. I suppose I should have been suspicious about many of them. I could have sworn that there hadn't been a speck of dust anywhere when I first mounted to his tower room, and, as I think I mentioned earlier, the fire burning in his fireplace didn't seem to need fuel. It was almost as if he were somehow *making* work for me to do.

He was a good Master, though. For one thing, he didn't command in the way I'd heard the Tolnedrans command their servants, but rather made suggestions. "Thinkest thou not that the floor hath become dirty again, boy?" Or "Might it not be prudent to lay in some store of fire-wood?" My chores were in no way beyond my strength or abilities, and the weather outside was sufficiently unpleasant to persuade me that what little was expected of me was a small price to pay in exchange for food and shelter. I *did* resolve, however, that when spring came and he began to look farther afield for things for me to do, I might want to reconsider our arrangement. There isn't really very much to do when winter keeps one housebound, but warmer weather brings with it the opportunity for heavier and more tedious tasks. If things turned *too* unpleasant, I could always pick up and leave.

There was something peculiar about that notion, though. The compulsion that had come over me at Gara seemed gone now. I don't know that I really thought about it in any specific way. I just seemed to notice that it was gone and shrugged it off. Maybe I just thought I'd outgrown it. It seems to me that I shrugged off a great deal that first winter.

I paid very little attention, for example, to the fact that my Master seemed to have no visible means of support. He didn't keep cattle or sheep or even chickens, and there were no sheds or outbuildings in the vicinity of his tower. I couldn't even find his storeroom. I knew there had to be one *somewhere*, because the meals he prepared were always on the table when I grew hungry. Oddly, the fact that I never once saw him cooking didn't seem particularly strange to me. Not even the fact that I never once saw him *eat* anything seemed strange. It was almost as if my natural curiosity—and believe me, I can be *very* curious—had been somehow put to sleep.

I had absolutely no idea of what he did during that long winter. It seemed to me that he spent a great deal of time just looking at a plain round rock. He didn't speak very often, but I talked enough for both of us. I've always been fond of the sound of my own voice—or had you noticed that?

My continual chatter must have driven him to distraction, because one evening he rather pointedly asked me why I didn't go read something.

I knew about reading, of course. Nobody in Gara had known how, but I'd seen Tolnedrans doing it—or pretending to. It seemed a little silly to me at the time. Why take the trouble to write a letter to somebody who lives two houses over? If it's important, just step over and tell him about it. "I don't know how to read, Master," I confessed.

He actually seemed startled by that. "Is this truly the case, boy?" he asked me. "I had thought that the skill was instinctive amongst thy kind."

I *wished* that he'd quit talking about "my kind" as if I were a member of some obscure species of rodent or insect.

"Fetch down that book, boy," he instructed, pointing at a high shelf.

I looked up in some amazement. There seemed to be several dozen bound volumes on that shelf. I'd cleaned and dusted and polished the room from floor to ceiling a dozen times or more, and I'd have taken an oath that the shelf hadn't been there the last time I looked. I covered my confusion by asking "Which one, Master?" Notice that I'd even begun to pick up some semblance of good manners?

"Whichever one falls most easily to hand," he replied indifferently.

I selected a book at random and took it to him.

"Seat thyself, boy," he told me. "I shall give thee instruction."

I knew nothing whatsoever about reading, so it didn't seem particularly odd to me that under his gentle tutelage I was a competent reader within the space of an hour. Either I was an extremely gifted student—

which seems highly unlikely—or he was the greatest teacher who ever lived.

From that hour on I became a voracious reader. I devoured his bookshelf from one end to another. Then, somewhat regretfully, I went back to the first book again, only to discover that I'd never seen it before. I read and read and read, and every page was new to me. I read my way through that bookshelf a dozen times over, and it was always fresh and new. That reading opened the world of the mind to me, and I found it much to my liking.

My newfound obsession gave my Master some peace, at least, and he seemed to look approvingly at me as I sat late into those long, snowy, winter nights reading texts in languages I could not have spoken, but that I nonetheless clearly understood when they seemed to leap out at me from off the page. I also noticed dimly—for, as I think I've already mentioned, my curiosity seemed somehow to have been blunted—that when I was reading, my Master tended to have no chores for me, at least not at first. The conflict between reading and chores came later. And so we passed the winter in that world of the mind, and with few exceptions, I've probably never been so happy.

I'm sure it was the books that kept me there the following spring and summer. As I'd suspected they might, the onset of warm days and nights stirred my Master's creativity. He found all manner of things for me to do outside—mostly unpleasant and involving a great deal of effort and sweat. I do *not* enjoy cutting down trees, for example—particularly not with an axe. I broke that axe handle eight times that summer—quite deliberately, I'll admit—and it miraculously healed itself overnight. I *hated* that cursed, indestructible axe!

But strangely enough, it wasn't the sweating and grunting I resented but the time I wasted whacking at unyielding trees that I could more profitably have spent trying to read my way through that inexhaustible bookshelf. Every page opened new wonders for me, and I groaned audibly each time my Master suggested that it was time for me and my axe to go out and entertain each other again.

And almost before I had turned around twice, winter came again. I had better luck with my broom than I had with my axe. After all, you can pile only so much dust in a corner before you start becoming obvious about it, and my Master was never obvious. I continued to read my way again and again along the bookshelf and was probably made better by it, although my Master, guided by some obscure, sadistic instinct, always seemed to know exactly when an interruption would be most unwelcome. He inevitably selected that precise moment to suggest sweeping or washing dishes or fetching firewood.

Sometimes he would stop what he was doing to watch my labors, a bemused expression on his face. Then he would sigh and return to the things he did that I didn't understand.

The seasons turned, marching in their stately, ordered progression as I labored with my books and with the endless and increasingly difficult tasks my Master set me. I grew bad-tempered and sullen, but never once did I even think about running away.

Then perhaps three—or more likely it was five—years after I'd come to the tower to begin my servitude, I was struggling one early winter day to move a large rock that my Master had stepped around since my first summer with him, but that he now found it inconvenient for some reason. The rock, as I say, was quite large, and it was white, and it was very, very heavy. It would not move, though I heaved and pushed and strained until I thought my limbs would crack. Finally, in a fury, I concentrated my strength and all my will upon the boulder and grunted one single word. "Move!" I said.

And it moved! Not grudgingly with its huge inert weight sullenly resisting my strength, but quite easily, as if the touch of one finger would have been sufficient to send it bounding across the vale.

"Well, boy," my Master said, startling me by his nearness, "I had wondered how long it might be ere this day arrived."

"Master," I said, very confused, "what happened? How did the great rock move so easily?"

"It moved at thy command, boy. Thou art a man, and it is only a rock." Where had I heard *that* before?

"May other things be done so, Master?" I asked, thinking of all the hours I'd wasted on meaningless tasks.

"*All* things may be done so, boy. Put but thy will to that which thou wouldst accomplish and speak the word. It shall come to pass even as thou wouldst have it. Much have I marveled, boy, at thine insistence upon doing all things with thy back instead of thy will. I had begun to fear for thee, thinking that perhaps thou wert defective."

Suddenly all the things I had ignored or shrugged off or been too incurious even to worry about fell into place. My Master had indeed been creating things for me to do, hoping that eventually I'd learn this secret. I walked over to the rock and laid my hands on it again. "Move," I commanded, bringing my will to bear on it, and the rock moved as easily as before.

"Does it make thee more comfortable touching the rock when thou wouldst move it, boy?" my Master asked, a note of curiosity in his voice.

The question stunned me. I hadn't even considered *that* possibility. I looked at the rock. "Move," I said tentatively.

"Thou must command, boy, not entreat."

"Move!" I roared, and the rock heaved and rolled off with nothing but my Will and the Word to make it do so.

"Much better, boy. Perhaps there is hope for thee yet."

Then I remembered something. Notice how quickly I pick up on these things? I'd been moving the rock that formed the door to the tower with only my voice for some five years now. "You knew all along that I could do this, didn't you, Master? There isn't really all that much difference between this rock and the one that closes the tower door, is there?"

He smiled gently. "Most perceptive, boy," he complimented me. I was getting a little tired of that "boy."

"Why didn't you just tell me?" I asked accusingly.

"I had need to know if thou wouldst discover it for thyself, boy."

"And all these chores and tasks you've put me through for all these years were nothing more than an excuse to force me to discover it, weren't they?"

"Of course," he replied in an offhand sort of way. "What is thy name, boy?"

"Garath," I told him, and suddenly realized that he'd never asked me before.

"An unseemly name, boy. Far too abrupt and commonplace for one of thy talent. I shall call thee Belgarath."

"As it please thee, Master." I'd never "thee'd" or "thou'd" him before, and I held my breath for fear that he might be displeased, but he showed no sign that he'd noticed. Then, made bold by my success, I went further. "And how may I call *thee*, Master?" I asked.

"I am called Aldur," he replied, smiling.

I'd heard the name before, of course, so I immediately fell on my face before him.

"Art thou ill, Belgarath?"

"Oh, great and most powerful God," I said, trembling, "forgive mine ignorance. I should have known thee at once."

"Don't do that!" he said irritably. "I require no obeisance. I am not my brother Torak. Rise to thy feet, Belgarath. Stand up, boy. Thine action is unseemly."

I scrambled up fearfully and clenched myself for the sudden shock of lightning. Gods, as all men knew, could destroy at their whim those who displeased them. That was a quaint notion of the time. I've met a few Gods since then, and I know better now. In many respects, they're even more circumscribed than we are.

"And what dost thou propose to do with thy life now, Belgarath?" he asked. That was my Master for you. He always asked questions that stretched out endlessly before me.

"I would stay and serve thee, Master," I said, as humbly as I could.

"I require no service," he said. "These past few years have been for *thy* benefit. In truth, Belgarath, what canst *thou* do for *me?*"

That was a deflating thing to say—true, probably, but deflating all the same. "May I not stay and worship thee, Master?" I pleaded. At that time I'd never met a God before, so I was uncertain about the proprieties. All I knew was that I would die if he sent me away.

He shrugged. You can cut a man's heart out with a shrug, did you know that? "I do not require thy worship either, Belgarath," he said indifferently.

"May I not stay, Master?" I pleaded with actual tears standing in my eyes. He was breaking my heart!—quite deliberately, of course. "I would be thy disciple and learn from thee."

"The desire to learn does thee credit," he said, "but it will not be easy, Belgarath."

"I am quick to learn, Master," I boasted, glossing over the fact that it had taken me five years to learn his first lesson. "I shall make thee proud of me." I actually meant that.

And then he laughed, and my heart soared, even as it had when that old vagabond in the rickety cart had laughed. I had a few suspicions at that point.

"Very well, then, Belgarath," he relented. "I shall accept thee as my pupil."

"And thy disciple, also, Master?"

"That we will see in the fullness of time, Belgarath."

And then, because I was still very young and much impressed with my recent accomplishment, I turned to a winter-dried bush and spoke to it fervently. "Bloom," I said, and the bush quite suddenly produced a single flower. It wasn't much of a flower, I'll admit, but it was the best that I could do at the time. I was still fairly new at this. I plucked it and offered it to him. "For thee, Master," I said, "because I love thee." I don't believe I'd ever used the word "love" before, and it's become the center of my whole life. Isn't it odd how we make these simple little discoveries?

And he took my crooked little flower and held it between his hands. "I thank thee, my son," he said. It was the first time he'd ever called me that. "And this flower shall be thy first lesson. I would have thee examine it most carefully and tell me all that thou canst perceive of it. Set aside thine axe and thy broom, Belgarath. This flower is now thy task."

And that task took me twenty years, as I recall. Each time I came to my Master with the flower that never wilted nor faded—how I grew to hate that flower!—and told him what I'd learned, he would say, "Is that *all*, my son?" And, crushed, I'd go back to my study of that silly little flower.

In time my distaste for it grew less. The more I studied it, the better I came to know it, and I eventually grew fond of it.

Then one day my Master suggested that I might learn more about it if I burned it and studied its ashes. I refused indignantly.

"And why not, my son?" he asked me.

"Because it is dear to me, Master," I said in a tone probably more firm than I'd intended.

"Dear?" he asked.

"I *love* the flower, Master! I will *not* destroy it!"

"Thou art stubborn, Belgarath," he noted. "Did it *truly* take thee twenty years to admit thine affection for this small, gentle thing?"

And that was the *true* meaning of my first lesson. I still have that little flower somewhere, and although I can't put my hands on it immediately, I think of it often and with great affection.

It was not long after that when my Master suggested that we journey to a place he called Prolgu, since he wanted to consult with someone there. I agreed to accompany him, of course, but to be quite honest about it, I didn't *really* want to be away from my studies for that long. It was spring, however, and that's always a good season for traveling. Prolgu is in the mountains, and if nothing else, the scenery was spectacular.

It took us quite some time to reach the place—my Master never hurried—and I saw creatures along the way that I had never imagined existed. My Master identified them for me, and there was a peculiar note of pain in his voice as he pointed out unicorns, Hrulgin, Algroths, and even an Eldrak.

"What troubles thee, Master?" I asked him one evening as we sat by our fire. "Are the creatures we have encountered distasteful to thee?"

"They are a constant rebuke to me and my brothers, Belgarath," he replied sadly. "When the earth was all new, we dwelt with each other in a cave deep in these mountains, laboring to bring forth the beasts of the fields, the fowls of the air, and the fish of the sea. It seemeth me I have told thee of that time, have I not?"

I nodded. "Yes, Master," I replied. "It was before there was such a thing as man."

"Yes," he said. "Man was our last creation. At any rate, some of the creatures we brought forth were unseemly, and we consulted and decided to unmake them, but UL forbade it."

"UL?" The name startled me. I'd heard it quite often in the encampment of the old people the winter before I went to serve my Master.

"Thou hast heard of him, I see." There was no real point in my trying to hide anything from my Master. "UL, as I told thee," he continued, "forbade the unmaking of things, and this greatly offended several of us. Torak in particular was put much out of countenance. Prohibitions or restraints of any kind do not sit well with my brother Torak. It was at his urging, methinks, that we sent such unseemly creatures to UL, telling them that *he* would be their God. I do sorely repent our spitefulness, for what UL did, he did out of a Necessity that we did not at the time perceive."

"It is UL with whom thou wouldst consult at Prolgu, is it not, Master?" I asked shrewdly. You see? I'm not *totally* without some degree of perception.

My Master nodded. "A certain thing hath come to pass," he told me sadly. "We had hoped that it might not, but it is another of those Necessities to which men and Gods alike must bow." He sighed. "Seek thy bed, Belgarath," he told me then. "We still have far to go ere we reach Prolgu, and I have noted that without sleep, thou art a surly companion."

"A weakness of mine, Master," I admitted, spreading my blankets on the ground. My Master, of course, required sleep no more than he required food.

In time we reached Prolgu, which is a strange place on the top of a mountain that looks oddly artificial. We had no more than started up its side when we were greeted by a very old man and by someone who was quite obviously *not* a man. That was the first time I met UL, and the overpowering sense of his presence quite nearly bowled me over. "Aldur," he said to my Master, "well met."

"Well met indeed," my Master replied, politely inclining his head. The Gods, I've noted, have an enormous sense of propriety. Then my Master reached inside his robe and took out that ordinary, round grey rock he'd spent the last couple of decades studying. "Our hopes notwithstanding," he announced, holding the rock out for UL to see, "it hath arrived."

UL nodded gravely. "I had thought I sensed its presence. Wilt thou accept the burden of it?"

My Master sighed. "If I must," he said.

"Thou art brave, Aldur," UL said, "and wiser far than thy brothers. That which commands us all hath brought it to *thy* hand for a purpose. Let us go apart and consider our course."

I learned that day that there was something very strange about that ordinary-looking stone.

The old man who had accompanied UL was named Gorim, and he and I got along well. He was a gentle, kindly old fellow whose features were the same as those of the old people I'd met some years before. We went up into the city, and he took me to his house. We waited there while my Master—and his—spoke together for quite some time. To pass the long hours, he told me the story of how he had come to enter the service of UL. It seemed that his people were Dals, the ones who had somehow been left out when the Gods were selecting the various races of man to serve them. Despite my peculiar situation, I've never been a particularly religious man, so I had a bit of difficulty grasping the concept of the spiritual pain the Dals suffered as outcasts. The Dals, of course, traditionally live to the south of the cluster of mountains known only as Korim, but it appeared that quite early in their history, they divided themselves into various groups to go in search of a God. Some went to the north to become Morindim and Karands; some went to the east to become Melcenes; some stayed south of Korim and continued to be Dals; but Gorim's people, Ulgos, he called them, came west.

Eventually, after the Ulgos had wandered around in the wilderness for generations, Gorim was born, and when he reached manhood, he volunteered to go alone in search of UL. That was long before I was born, of course. Anyway, after many years he finally found UL. He took the good news back to his people, but not too many of them believed him. People are like that sometimes. Finally he grew disgusted with them and told them to follow him or stay where they were, he didn't much care which. Some followed, and some didn't. As he told me of this, he grew pensive. "I have oft times wondered whatever happened to those who stayed behind," he said sadly.

"I can clear that up for you, my friend," I advised him. "I happened across them some twenty-five or so years ago. They had a large camp quite a ways north of my Master's Vale. I spent a winter with them and then moved on. I doubt that you'd find any of them still alive, though. They were all very old when I saw them."

He gave me a stricken look, and then he bowed his head and wept.

"What's wrong, Gorim?" I exclaimed, somewhat alarmed.

"I had hoped that UL might relent and set aside my curse on them," he replied brokenly.

"Curse?"

"That they would wither and perish and be no more. Their women were made barren by my curse."

"It was still working when I was there," I told him. "There wasn't a single child in the entire camp. I wondered why they made such a fuss over me. I guess they hadn't seen a child in a long, long time. I couldn't get any details from them, because I couldn't understand their language."

"They spoke the old tongue," he told me sadly, "even as do my people here in Prolgu."

"How is it that you speak my language then?" I asked him.

"It is my place as leader to speak for my people when we encounter other races," he explained.

"Ah," I said. "That stands to reason, I guess."

My Master and I returned to the Vale not long after that, and I took up other studies. Time seemed meaningless in the Vale, and I devoted years of study to the most commonplace of things. I examined trees and birds, fish and beasts, insects and vermin. I spent forty-five years on the study of grass alone. In time it occurred to me that I wasn't aging as other men did. I'd seen enough old people to know that aging is a part of being human, but for some reason I seemed to be breaking the rules.

"Master," I said one night high in the tower as we both labored with our studies, "why is it that I do not grow old?"

"Wouldst thou grow old, my son?" he asked me. "I have never seen much advantage in it, myself."

"I don't really miss it all that much, Master," I admitted, "but isn't it customary?"

"Perhaps," he said, "but not mandatory. Thou hast much yet to learn, and one or ten or even a hundred lifetimes would not be enough. How old art thou, my son?"

"I think I am somewhat beyond three hundred years, Master."

"A suitable age, my son, and thou has persevered in thy studies. Should I forget myself and call thee 'boy' again, pray correct me. It is not seemly that the disciple of a God should be called 'boy.'"

"I shall remember that, Master," I assured him, almost overcome with joy that he had finally called me his disciple.

"I was certain that I could depend on thee," he said with a faint smile. "And what is the object of thy present study, my son?"

"I would seek to learn why the stars fall, Master."

"A proper study, my son."

"And thou, Master," I said. "What is thy study—if I be not overbold to ask."

"Even as before, Belgarath," he replied, holding up that fatal round stone. "It hath been placed in my care by UL himself, and it is therefore upon me to commune with it that I may know it—and its purpose."

"Can a stone *have* a purpose, Master—other than to be a stone?" The piece of rock, now worn smooth, even polished, by my Master's patient hand, made me apprehensive for some reason. In one of those rare presentiments that I don't have very often, I sensed that a great deal of mischief would come about as a result of it.

"This particular jewel hath a great purpose, Belgarath, for through it the world and all who dwell herein shall be changed. If I can but perceive that purpose, I might make some preparations. That necessity lieth heavily upon my spirit." And then he lapsed once more into silence, idly turning the stone over and over in his hand as he gazed deep into its polished surface with troubled eyes.

I certainly wasn't going to intrude upon his contemplation of the thing, so I turned back to my study of the inconstant stars.

CHAPTER THREE

In time, others came to us, some seemingly by accident, as I had come, and some by intent, seeking out my Master that they might learn from him. Such a one was Zedar.

I came upon him near our tower one golden day in autumn after I'd served my Master for five hundred years or so. This stranger had built a rude altar and was burning the carcass of a goat on it. That got us off on the wrong foot right at the outset. Even the wolves knew enough not to kill things in the Vale. The greasy smoke from his offering was fouling the air, and he was prostrated before his altar, chanting some outlandish prayer.

"What are you doing?" I demanded—quite abruptly, I'll admit, since his noise and the stink of his sacrifice distracted my mind from a problem I'd been considering for the past half century.

"Oh, puissant and all-knowing God," he said, groveling in the dirt, "I have come a thousand leagues to behold thy glory and to worship thee."

"Puissant? Quit trying to show off your education, man. Now get up and stop this caterwauling. I'm no more a God than you are."

"Art thou not the great God Aldur?"

"I'm his disciple, Belgarath. What *is* all this nonsense?" I pointed at his altar and his smoking goat.

"It is to please the God," he replied, rising and dusting off his clothes. I couldn't be sure, but he looked rather like a Tolnedran—or possibly an Arend. In either case, his babble about a thousand leagues was clearly a self-serving exaggeration. He gave me a servile, fawning sort of look. "Tell me truly," he pleaded. "Dost thou think he will find this poor offering of mine acceptable?"

I laughed. "I can't think of a single thing you could have done that would offend him more."

The stranger looked stricken. He turned quickly and reached out as if he were going to grab up the animal with his bare hands to hide it.

"Don't be an idiot!" I snapped. "You'll burn yourself!"

"It must be hidden," he said desperately. "I would rather die than offend mighty Aldur."

"Just get out of the way," I told him.

"What?"

"Stand clear," I said, irritably waving him off, "unless you want to take a trip with your goat." Then I looked at his grotesque little altar, willed it to a spot five miles distant, and translocated it with a single word, leaving only a few tatters of confused smoke hanging in the air.

He collapsed on his face again.

"You're going to wear out your clothes if you keep doing that," I told him, "and my Master won't find it very amusing."

"I pray thee, mighty disciple of most high Aldur," he said, rising and dusting himself off again, "instruct me so that I offend not the God." He must have been an Arend. No Tolnedran could possibly mangle the language the way he did.

"Be truthful," I told him, "and don't try to impress him with false show and flowery speech. Believe me, friend, he can see straight into your heart, so there's no way you can deceive him. I'm not sure which God you worshiped before, but Aldur's like no other God in the whole world." What an asinine thing *that* was to say. No two Gods are *ever* the same.

"And how may I become his disciple, as thou art?"

"First you become his pupil," I replied, "and that's not easy."

"What must I do to become his pupil?"

"You must become his servant." I said it a bit smugly, I'll admit. A few years with an axe and a broom would probably do this pompous ass some good.

"And then his pupil?" he pressed.

"In time," I replied, "if he so wills." It wasn't up to *me* to reveal the secret of the Will and the Word to him. He'd have to find that out for himself—the same as I had.

"And when may I meet the God?"

I was getting tired of him anyway, so I took him to the tower.

"Will the God Aldur wish to know my name?" he asked as we started across the meadow.

I shrugged. "Not particularly. If you're lucky enough to prove worthy, he'll give you a name of his own choosing." When we reached the tower, I commanded the grey stone in the wall to open, and we went inside and on up the stairs.

My Master looked the stranger over and then turned to me. "Why hast thou brought this man to me, my son?" he asked me.

"He besought me, Master," I replied. "I felt it was not my place to say him yea or nay." I could mangle language as well as Zedar could, I guess. "*Thy* will must decide such things," I continued. "If it turns out that he doesn't please thee, I'll take him outside and turn him into a carrot, and that'll be the end of it."

"That was unkindly said, Belgarath," Aldur chided.

"Forgive me, Master," I said humbly.

"*Thou* shalt instruct him, Belgarath. Should it come to pass that he be apt, inform me."

I groaned inwardly, cursing my careless tongue. My casual offer to vegetablize the stranger had saddled *me* with him. But Aldur was my Lord, so I said, "I will, Master."

"What is thy current study, my son?"

"I examine the reason for mountains, Master."

"Lay aside thy mountains, Belgarath, and study man instead. It may be that the study shall make thee more kindly disposed toward thy fellow creatures."

I knew a rebuke when I heard one, so I didn't argue. I sighed. "As my Master commands," I submitted regretfully. I'd almost found the secret of mountains, and I didn't want it to escape me. But then I remembered how patient my Master had been when I first came to the Vale, so I swallowed my resentment—at least right there in front of him.

I was not nearly so agreeable once I got Zedar back outside, though. I put that poor man through absolute hell, I'm ashamed to admit. I degraded him, I berated him, I set him to work on impossible tasks and then laughed scornfully at his efforts. To be quite honest about it, I secretly hoped that I could make his life so miserable that he'd run away.

But he didn't. He endured all my abuse with a saintly patience that sometimes made me want to scream. Didn't the man have any spirit at *all*? To make matters even worse—to my profoundest mortification—he learned the secret of the Will and the Word within six months. My Master named him Belzedar and accepted him as his pupil.

In time Belzedar and I made peace with each other. I reasoned that as long as we were probably going to spend the next dozen or so centuries together, we might as well learn to get along. Actually, once I ground away his tendency toward hyperbole and excessively ornamental language, he wasn't such a bad fellow. His mind was extraordinarily quick, but he was polite enough not to rub my nose in the fact that mine really wasn't.

The three of us, our Master, Belzedar, and I, settled in and learned to get along with a minimum of aggravation on all sides.

And then the others began to drift in. Kira and Tira were twin Alorn shepherd boys who had become lost and wandered into the Vale one day—and stayed. Their minds were so closely linked that they always had the same thoughts at the same time and even finished each other's sentences. Despite the fact that they're Alorns, Belkira and Beltira are the gentlest men I've ever known. I'm quite fond of them, actually.

Makor was the next to arrive, and he came to us from so far away that I couldn't understand how he had ever heard of my Master. Unlike the rest of us, who'd been fairly shabby when we'd arrived, Makor came strolling down the Vale dressed in a silk mantle, somewhat like the garb currently in fashion in Tol Honeth. He was a witty, urbane, well-educated man, and I took to him immediately.

Our Master questioned him briefly and decided that he was acceptable—with all the usual provisos.

"But, Master," Belzedar objected vehemently, "he cannot become one of our fellowship. He is a Dal—one of the Godless ones."

"Melcene, actually, old boy," Makor corrected him in that ultra-civilized manner of his that always drove Belzedar absolutely wild. Now do you see why I was so fond of Makor?

"What's the difference?" Belzedar demanded bluntly.

"All the difference in the world, old chap," Makor replied, examining his fingernails. "We Melcenes separated from the Dals so long ago that we're no more like them than Alorns are like Marags. It's not really up to you, however. I was summoned, the same as the rest of you were, and that's an end on it."

I remembered the odd compulsion that had dragged me out of Gara, and I looked sharply at my Master. Would you believe that he actually managed to look slightly embarrassed?

Belzedar spluttered for a while, but, since there was nothing he could do about it anyway, he muffled his objections.

The next to join us was Sambar, an Angarak. Sambar—or Belsambar as he later became—was not his real name, of course. Angarak names are so universally ugly that my Master did him a favor when he renamed him. I felt a great deal of sympathy for the boy—he was only about fifteen when he joined us. I have never seen anyone so abject. He simply came to the tower, seated himself on the earth, and waited for either acceptance or death. Beltira and Belkira fed him, of course. They *were* shepherds, after all, and shepherds won't let *anything* go hungry. After a week or so, when it became obvious that he absolutely would *not* enter the tower, our Master went down to *him*. Now *that* was something I had never seen Aldur do before. He spoke with the lad at some length in a hideous language—old Angarak, I've since discovered—and turned him over to Beltira and Belkira for tutelage. If anyone ever needed gentle handling, it was Belsambar.

In time, the twins taught him to speak a normal language that didn't involve so much spitting and snarling, and we learned his history. My distaste for Torak dates from that point in time. It may not have been entirely Torak's fault, however. I've learned over the years that the views of any priesthood are not necessarily the views of the Gods they serve. I'll give Torak the benefit of the doubt in this case—the practice of human sacrifice *might* have been no more than a perversion of his Grolim priests. But he did nothing to put a stop to it, and that's unforgivable.

To cut all this windy moralizing short, Belsambar's parents—both of them—had been sacrificed, and Belsambar had been required to watch as a demonstration of his faith. It didn't really work out that way, though. Grolims can be so stupid sometimes. Anyway, at the tender age of nine, Belsambar became an atheist, rejecting not only Torak and his stinking Grolims, but *all* Gods.

That was when our Master summoned him. In his particular case, the summoning must have been a bit more spectacular than the vague urge that had turned *my* face toward the Vale. Belsambar was clearly in a state of religious ecstasy when he reached us. Of course he *was* an Angarak, and they're always a little strange in matters of religion.

It was Belmakor who first raised the notion of building our own towers. He was a Melcene, after all, and they're obsessed with building things. I'll admit that our Master's tower *was* starting to get a bit crowded, though.

The construction of those towers took us several decades, as I recall. It was actually more in the nature of a hobby than it was a matter of any urgency. We did use what you might call our advantages in the construction, of course, but squaring off rocks is a tedious business, even if you don't have to use a chisel. We did manage to clear away a lot of rock, though, and building material got progressively scarcer as the years rolled by.

I think it was late summer one year when I decided that it was time to finish up my tower so that I wouldn't have it hanging over my head nagging at me. Besides, Belmakor's tower was almost finished, and I *was* first disciple, after all. I didn't think it would really be proper for me to let him outstrip me. We sometimes do things for the most childish of reasons, don't we?

Since my brothers and I had virtually denuded the Vale of rocks, I went up to the edge of the forest lying to the north in search of building materials. I was poking around among the trees looking for a streambed or an outcropping of stone when I suddenly felt a baleful stare boring into the back of my neck. That's an uncomfortable feeling that's always irritated me for some reason. "You might as well come out," I said. "I know you're there."

"Don't try anything," an awful voice growled at me from a nearby thicket. "I'll rip you to pieces if you do."

Now that's what I call an unpromising start. "Don't be an idiot," I replied. "I'm not going to hurt you."

That evoked the ugliest laugh I've ever heard. *"You?"* the voice said scornfully. *"You?* Hurt *me?"* And then the bushes parted and the most hideous creature I've ever seen emerged. He was grotesquely deformed, with a huge hump on his back; gnarled, dwarfed legs; and long, twisted arms. This combination made it possible—even convenient—for him to go on all fours like a gorilla. His face was monumentally ugly, his hair and beard were matted, he was unbelievably filthy, and he was partially dressed in a ratty-looking fur of some kind. "Enjoying the view?" he demanded harshly. "You're not so pretty yourself, you know."

"You startled me, that's all," I replied, trying to be civil.

"Have you seen an old man in a rickety, broken-down cart around here anywhere?" the creature demanded. "He told me he'd meet me here."

I stared at him in absolute astonishment.

"You'd better close your mouth," he advised me in that raspy growl. "You'll catch flies if you don't."

All sorts of things clicked into place. "This old man you're looking for," I said. "Did he have a humorous way of talking?"

"That's him," the dwarf said. "Have you seen him?"

"Oh, yes," I replied with a broad grin. "I've known him for longer than you could possibly imagine. Come along, my ugly little friend. I'll take you to him."

"Don't be too quick to throw the word 'friend' around," he growled. "I don't *have* any friends, and I *like* it that way."

"You'll get over that in a few hundred years," I replied, still grinning at the little monster.

"You don't sound quite right in the head to me."

"You'll get used to *that*, too. Come along. I'll introduce you to your Master."

"I don't *have* a master."

"I wouldn't make any large wagers on that."

And that was our introduction to Din. My brothers thought at first that I'd come across a tame ape. Din rather quickly disabused them of that notion. He had by far the foulest mouth I've ever come across, even when he wasn't trying to be insulting, and I honestly believe he could swear for a day and a half without once repeating himself. He was even ungracious to our Master. His very first words to him were "What did you do with that stupid cart of yours? I tried to follow the tracks, but they just disappeared on me."

Aldur, with that inhuman patience of his, simply smiled. Would you believe that he actually *liked* the foul-mouthed little monster? "Is that what took thee so long?" he asked mildly.

"Of *course* that's what took me so long!" Din exploded. "You didn't leave me a trail to follow! I had to reason out your location!" Din had turned losing his temper into an art form. The slightest thing could set him off. "Well?" he said then. "Now what?"

"We must see to thine education."

"What does somebody like me need with an education? I already know what I need to know."

Aldur gave him a long, steady look, and even Din couldn't face *that* for long. Then our Master looked around at the rest of us. He obviously dismissed Beltira and Belkira out of hand. They hadn't the proper temperament to deal with our newest recruit. Belzedar was in a state verging on inarticulate rage. Belzedar may have had his faults, but he wouldn't tolerate any disrespect for our Master. Belmakor was too fastidious. Din was filthy, and he smelled like an open sewer. Belsambar, for obvious reasons, was totally out of question. Guess who that left.

I wearily raised my hand. "Don't trouble thyself, Master," I said. "I'll take care of it."

"Why, Belgarath," he said, "how gracious of thee to volunteer thy service."

I chose not to answer that.

"Ah, Belgarath?" Belmakor said tentatively.

"What?"

"Could you possibly wash him off before you bring him inside again?"

Despite my show of reluctance, I wasn't *quite* as displeased with the arrangement as I pretended to be. I still wanted to finish my tower, and this powerful dwarf seemed well suited to the task of carrying rocks. If things worked out the way I thought they might, I wouldn't have to strain my creativity in the slightest to find things for my ugly little servant to do.

I took him outside and showed him my half-finished tower. "You understand the situation here?" I asked him.

"I'm supposed to do what you tell me to do."

"Exactly." This was going to work out just fine. "Now, let's go back to the edge of the woods. I've got a little chore for you."

It took us quite some time to return to the woods. When we got there, I pointed at a dry streambed filled with nice round rocks of a suitable size. "See those rocks?" I asked him.

"Naturally I can see them, you dolt! I'm not blind!"

"I'm so happy for you. I'd like for you to pile them all beside my tower—neatly, of course." I sat down under a shady tree. "Be a good fellow and see to it, would you?" I was actually enjoying this.

He glowered at me for a moment and then turned to glare at the rocky streambed.

Then, one by one, the rocks began to vanish! I could actually feel him doing it! Would you believe it? Din already *knew* the secret! It was the first case of spontaneous sorcery I had ever seen. "Now what?" he demanded.

"How did you learn to do that?" I demanded incredulously.

He shrugged. "Picked it up somewhere," he replied. "Are you trying to tell me that you can't?"

"Of course I can, but—" I got hold of myself at that point. "Are you sure you translocated them to the right spot?"

"You wanted them piled up beside your tower, didn't you? Go look, if you want. *I* know where they are. Was there anything else you wanted me to do here?"

"Let's go back," I told him shortly.

It took me awhile to regain my composure. We were about halfway back before I could trust myself to start asking questions. "Where are you from?" It was banal, but it was a place to start.

"Originally, you mean? That's sort of hard to say. I move around a lot. I'm not very welcome in most places. I'm used to it, though. It's been going on since the day I was born."

"Oh?"

"I gather that my mother's people had a fairly simple way to rid themselves of defectives. As soon as they laid eyes on me, they took me out in the woods and left me there to starve—or to provide some wolf with a light snack. My mother was a sentimentalist, though, so she used to sneak out of the village to nurse me."

And I thought *my* childhood had been hard.

"She stopped coming a year or so after I'd learned to walk, though," he added in a deliberately harsh tone. "Died, I suppose—or they caught her sneaking out and killed her. I was on my own after that."

"How did you survive?"

"Does it really matter?" There was a distant pain in his eyes, however.

"There are all sorts of things to eat in a forest—if you're not too partic-ular. Vultures and ravens manage fairly well. I learned to watch for them. I found out early on that anyplace you see a vulture, there's probably something to eat. You get used to the smell after a while."

"You're an animal!" I exclaimed.

"We're all animals, Belgarath." It was the first time he'd used my name. "I'm better at it than most, because I've had more practice. Now, do you suppose we could talk about something else?"

CHAPTER
FOUR

And now we were seven, and I think we all knew that for the time being there wouldn't be any more of us. The others came later. We were an oddly assorted group, I'll grant you, but the fact that we lived in separate towers helped to keep down the frictions to some degree.

The addition of Beldin to our fellowship was not as disruptive as I'd first imagined it might be. This is not to say that our ugly little brother mellowed very much, but rather that we grew accustomed to his irascible nature as the years rolled by. I invited him to stay in my tower with me during what I suppose you could call his novitiate—that period when he was Aldur's pupil before he achieved full status. I discovered during those years that there was a mind lurking behind those bestial features, and what a mind it was! With the possible exception of Belmakor, Beldin was clearly the most intelligent of us all. The two of them argued for years about points of logic and philosophy so obscure that the rest of us hadn't the faintest idea of what they were talking about, and they both enjoyed those arguments enormously.

It took me a while, but I finally managed to persuade Beldin that an occasional bath probably wouldn't be harmful to his health and that if he bathed, the fastidious Belmakor might be willing to come close enough to him that they wouldn't have to shout during their discussions. As my daughter's so fond of pointing out, I'm not an absolute fanatic about bathing, but Beldin sometimes carries his indifference to extremes.

During the years that we lived and studied together, I came to know

Beldin and eventually at least partially to understand him. Mankind was still in its infancy in that age, and the virtue of compassion hadn't really caught on as yet. Humor, if you want to call it that, was still quite primitive and brutal. People found any sort of anomaly funny, and Beldin was about as anomalous as you can get. Rural folk would greet his entry into their villages with howls of laughter, and after they had laughed their fill, they'd normally stone him out of town. It's not really very hard to understand his foul temper, is it? His own people tried to kill him the moment he was born, and he'd spent his whole life being chased out of every community he tried to enter. I'm really rather surprised that he didn't turn homicidal. *I* probably would have.

He had lived with me for a couple hundred years, and then on one rainy spring day, he raised a subject I probably should have known would come up eventually. He was staring moodily out the window at the slashing rain, and he finally growled, "I think I'll build my own tower."

"Oh?" I replied, laying aside my book. "What's wrong with this one?"

"I need more room, and we're starting to get on each other's nerves."

"I hadn't noticed that."

"Belgarath, you don't even notice the seasons. When you're facedown in one of your books, I could probably set fire to your toes, and you wouldn't notice. Besides, you snore."

"*I* snore? You sound like a passing thunderstorm every night, all night."

"It keeps you from getting lonesome." He looked pensively out the window again. "There's another reason, too, of course."

"Oh?"

He looked directly at me, his eyes strangely wistful. "In my whole life, I've never really had a place of my own. I've slept in the woods, in ditches, and under haystacks, and the warm, friendly nature of my fellow man has kept me pretty much constantly on the move. I think that, just once, I'd like to have a place that nobody can throw me out of."

What could I possibly say to that? "You want some help?" I offered.

"Not if my tower's going to turn into something that looks like this one," he growled.

"What's wrong with this tower?"

"Belgarath, be honest. This tower of yours looks like an ossified tree stump. You have absolutely no sense of beauty whatsoever."

This, coming from *Beldin*?

"I think I'll go talk with Belmakor. He's a Melcene, and they're natural builders. Have you ever seen one of their cities?"

"I've never had occasion to go into the East."

"Naturally not. You can't pull yourself out of your books long enough to go anyplace. Well? Are you coming along, or not?"

How could I turn down so gracious an invitation? I pulled on my cloak, and we went out into the rain. Beldin, of course, didn't bother with cloaks. He was absolutely indifferent to the weather.

When we reached Belmakor's somewhat overly ornate tower, my stumpy little friend bellowed up, "Belmakor! I need to talk with you!"

Our civilized brother came to the window. "What is it, old boy?" he called down to us.

"I've decided to build my own tower. I want you to design it for me. Open your stupid door."

"Have you bathed lately?"

"Just last month. Don't worry, I won't stink up your tower."

Belmakor sighed. "Oh, very well." He gave in. His eyes went slightly distant, and the latch on his heavy iron-bound door clicked. The rest of us had taken our cue from our Master and used rocks to close the entrances to *our* towers, but Belmakor felt the need for a proper door. Beldin and I went in and mounted the stairs.

"Have you and Belgarath had a falling out?" Belmakor asked curiously.

"Is that any business of yours?" Beldin snapped.

"Not really. Just wondering."

"He wants a place of his own," I explained. "We're starting to get under each other's feet."

Belmakor was very shrewd. He got my point immediately. "What did you have in mind?" he asked the dwarf.

"Beauty," Beldin said bluntly. "I may not be able to share it, but at least I'll be able to look at it."

Belmakor's eyes filled with sudden tears. He always was the most emotional of us.

"Oh, *stop* that!" Beldin told him. "Sometimes you're so gushy you make me want to spew. I want grace. I want proportion, I want something that soars. I'm tired of living in the mud."

"Can you manage that?" I asked our brother.

Belmakor went to his writing desk, gathered his papers, and inserted them in the book he'd been studying. Then he put the book up on a top shelf, spun a large sheet of paper and one of those inexhaustible quill pens he was so fond of out of air itself, and sat down. "How big?" he asked Beldin.

"I think we'd better keep it a little lower than the Master's, don't you?"

"Wise move. Let's not get above ourselves." Belmakor quickly sketched in a fairy castle that took my breath away—all light and delicacy with flying buttresses that soared out like wings and towers as slender as toothpicks.

"Are you trying to be funny?" Beldin accused. "You couldn't house butterflies in that piece of gingerbread."

"Just a start, brother mine," Belmakor said gaily. "We'll modify it down to reality as we go along. You have to do that with dreams."

And that started an argument that lasted for about six months and ultimately drew us all into it. Our own towers were, for the most part, strictly utilitarian. Although it pains me to admit it, Beldin's description of my tower was probably fairly accurate. It did look somewhat like a petrified tree stump when I stepped back to look at it. It kept me out of the weather, though, and it got me up high enough so that I could see the horizon and look at the stars. What else is a tower supposed to do?

It was at that point that we discovered that Belsambar had the soul of an artist. The last place in the world you would look for beauty would be in the mind of an Angarak. With surprising heat, given his retiring nature, he argued with Belmakor long and loud, insisting on *his* variations as opposed to the somewhat pedestrian notions of the Melcenes. Melcenes are builders, and they think in terms of stone and mortar and what your material actually will let you get away with. Angaraks think of the impossible and then try to come up with ways to make it work.

"Why are you doing this, Belsambar?" Beldin once asked our normally self-effacing brother. "It's only a buttress, and you've been arguing about it for weeks now."

"It's the curve of it, Beldin," Belsambar explained, more fervently than I'd ever heard him say anything else. "It's like this." And he created the illusion of the two opposing towers in the air in front of them for comparison. I've never known anyone else who could so fully build illusions as Belsambar. I think it's an Angarak trait; their whole world is built on an illusion.

Belmakor took one look and threw his hands in the air. "I bow to superior talent," he surrendered. "It's beautiful, Belsambar. Now, how do we make it work? There's not enough support."

"I'll support it, if necessary." It was *Belzedar*, of all people! "I'll hold up our brother's tower until the end of days, if need be." What a soul that man had!

"You still didn't answer my question—any of you!" Beldin rasped. "Why are you all taking so much trouble with all of this?"

"It is because thy brothers love thee, my son," Aldur, who had been standing in the shadows unobserved, told him gently. "Canst thou not accept their love?"

Beldin's ugly face suddenly contorted grotesquely, and he broke down and wept.

"And that is *thy* first lesson, my son," Aldur told him. "Thou wilt warily *give* love, all concealed beneath this gruff exterior of thine, but thou must also learn to *accept* love."

It all got a bit sentimental after that.

And so we all joined together in the building of Beldin's tower. It didn't really take us all that long. I hope Durnik takes note that it's not *really* immoral to use our gift on mundane things, Sendarian ethics notwithstanding.

I missed having my grotesque little friend around in my own tower, but I'll admit that I slept better. I wasn't exaggerating in the least in my description of his snoring.

Life settled down in the Vale after that. We continued our studies of the world around us and expanded our applications of our peculiar talent. I think it was one of the twins who discovered that it was possible for us to communicate with each other by thought alone. It *would* have been one—or both—of the twins, since they had been sharing their thoughts since the day they were born. I do know that it was Beldin who discovered the trick of assuming the forms of other creatures. The main reason I can be so certain is that he startled several years' growth out of me the first time he did it. A large hawk with a bright band of blue feathers across its tail came soaring in, settled on my window ledge, and blurred into Beldin. "How about that?" he demanded. "It works after all."

I was drinking from a tankard at the time, and I dropped it and went into an extended fit of choking while he pounded me on the back.

"What do you think you're *doing?*" I demanded after I got my breath.

He shrugged. "I was studying birds," he explained. "I thought it might be useful to look at the world from their perspective for a while. Flying's not as easy as it looks. I almost killed myself when I threw myself out of the tower window."

"You *idiot!*"

"I managed to get my wings working before I hit the ground. It's sort of like swimming. You never know if you can do it until you try."

"What's it like? Flying, I mean?"

"I couldn't even begin to describe it, Belgarath," he replied with a look of wonder on his ugly face. "You should try it. I wouldn't recommend jumping out of any windows, though. Sometimes you're a little careless with details, and if you don't get the tail feathers right, you'll break your beak."

Beldin's discovery came at a fortuitous time. It wasn't very long afterward that our Master sent us out from the Vale to see what the rest of mankind had been up to. As closely as I can pinpoint it, it seems to have been about fifteen hundred years since that snowy night when I first met him.

Anyway, flying is a much faster way to travel than walking. Beldin coached us all, and we were soon flapping around the Vale like a flock of migrating ducks. I'll admit right at the outset that I don't fly very well. Polgara's made an issue of that from time to time. I think she holds it in reserve for occasions when she doesn't have anything else to carp about. Anyway, after Beldin taught us how to fly, we scattered to the winds and went out to see what people were up to. With the exception of the Ulgos, there wasn't really anybody to the west of us, and I didn't get along too well with their new Gorim. The original one and I had been close friends, but the latest one seemed just a bit taken with himself.

So I flew east instead and dropped in on the Tolnedrans. They had built a number of cities since the last time I had seen them. Some of those cities were actually quite large, though their habit of using logs for constructing walls and thatch for roofs made me just a little wary of entering those free-standing firetraps. As you might expect, the Tolnedran fascination with money hadn't diminished in the fifteen hundred years since I'd last seen them. If anything, they'd grown even more acquisitive, and they seemed to spend a great deal of time building roads. What *is* this thing with Tolnedrans and roads? They were generally peaceful, however, since war's bad for business, so I flew on to visit the Marags.

The Marags were a strange people—as I'm sure our friend Relg has discovered by now. Perhaps their peculiarities are the result of the fact that there are many more women in their society than there are men. Their God, Mara, takes what is in *my* view an unwholesome interest in fertility and reproduction. Their society is matriarchal, which is unusual—although the Nyissans tend in that direction as well.

Despite its peculiarities, Marag culture was functional, and they had not yet begun the practice of ritual cannibalism that their neighbors found so repugnant and that ultimately led to their near extinction. They were a generous people—the women particularly, and I got along quite well with them. I don't know that I need to go into *too* much detail. This book will almost certainly fall into Polgara's hands eventually, and she has strong opinions about some things that aren't really all that important.

After several years, we all returned to the Vale and gathered once more in our Master's tower to report on what we had seen.

With a certain delicacy, our Master had sent Belsambar north to see what the Morindim and the Karands were doing. It really wouldn't have been a good idea to send him back into the lands of the Angaraks. He had very strong feelings about the Grolim priesthood, and our journeys were supposed to be fact-finding missions. We weren't out there to right wrongs or to impose our own notions of justice. In retrospect, though, we probably could have saved the world a great deal of pain and suffering if we'd simply turned Belsambar loose on the Grolims. It would have caused bad blood between Torak and our Master, though, and that came soon enough anyway.

It was Belzedar who went down to the north side of Korim to observe the Angaraks. Isn't it funny how things turn out? What he saw in those mountains troubled him very much. Torak always had an exaggerated notion of his significance in the overall scheme of things, and he encouraged his Angaraks to become excessive in their worship. They'd raised a temple to him in the High Places of Korim where the Grolim priesthood ecstatically butchered their fellow Angaraks by the hundreds while Torak looked on approvingly.

The religious practices of the various races of man were really none of our business, but Belzedar found cause for alarm in the beliefs of the Angaraks. Torak made no secret of the fact that he considered himself several cuts above his brothers, and he was evidently encouraging his people to feel the same way about themselves. "It's just a matter of time, I'm afraid," Belzedar concluded somberly. "Sooner or later, they're going to try to impose their notion of their own superiority on the rest of mankind, and that won't work. If someone doesn't persuade Torak to stop filling the heads of the Angaraks with that obscene sense of superiority, there's very likely going to be war in the South."

Then Belsambar told us that the Morindim and the Karands had become demon-worshipers but that they posed no real threat to the rest of mankind, since the demons devoted themselves almost exclusively to eating the magicians who raised them.

Beldin reported that the Arends had grown even more stupid—if that's possible—and that they all lived in a more or less perpetual state of war.

Belmakor had passed through the lands of the Nyissans on his way to Melcena, and he reported that the Snake People were still fearfully primitive. No one's ever accused the Nyissans of being energetic, but you'd think they might have at least *started* building houses by now. The Melcenes, of course, *did* build houses—probably more than they really needed—but it kept them out of mischief. On his way back, he passed through Kell, and he told us that the Dals were much involved in arcane studies—astrology, necromancy, and the like. The Dals spend so much of their time trying to look into the future that they tend to lose sight of the present. I *hate* mystics! The only good part of it was that they were so fuzzy-headed that they didn't pose a threat to anybody else.

The Alorns, of course, were an entirely different matter. They're a noisy, belligerent people who'll fight at the drop of a hat. Beltira and Belkira looked in on their fellow Alorns. Fortunately for the sake of world peace, the Alorns, like the Arends, spent most of their time fighting each other rather than doing war on other races, but the twins strongly suggested that we keep an eye on them. I have been doing just that for the past five thousand years. It was probably that more than anything else that turned my hair white. Alorns can get into more trouble by accident than other people can on purpose—always excepting the Arends, of course. Arends are perpetually a catastrophe waiting to explode.

Our Master considered our reports carefully and concluded that the world outside the Vale was generally peaceful and that only the Angaraks were likely to cause trouble. He told us that he'd have a word with his brother Torak about *that* particular problem, pointing out to him that if any kind of general war broke out, the Gods themselves would inevitably be drawn in, and that would be disastrous. "Methinks I can make him see reason," Aldur told us. Reason? Torak? Sometimes my Master's optimism got the better of him.

As I recall, he had been absently fondling that strange grey stone of his as we made our reports. He'd had the thing for so long that I don't think he even realized that it was in his hand. Over the years since he'd spoken with UL about it, I don't think he'd once put it down, and it somehow almost became a part of him.

Naturally it was Belzedar who noticed it. I wonder how everything might have turned out if he hadn't. "What is that strange jewel, Master?" he asked. Better far that his tongue had fallen out before he asked that fatal question.

"This Orb?" Aldur replied, holding it up for all of us to see. "In it lies the fate of the world." It was then for the first time that I noticed that the stone seemed to have a faint blue flicker deep inside of it. It was, as I think I've mentioned before, polished by a thousand years or more of our Master's touch, and it was now, as Belzedar had so astutely noticed, more a jewel than a piece of plain, country rock.

"How can so small an object be so important, Master?" Belzedar asked. That's another question I wish he'd never thought of. If he'd just been able to let it drop, none of what's happened *would* have happened, and he wouldn't be in his present situation. Despite all of our training, there are some questions better left unanswered.

Unfortunately, our Master had a habit of answering questions, and so things came out that might better have been left buried. If they had, I might not currently be carrying a load of guilt that I'm not really strong enough to bear. I'd rather carry a mountain than carry what I did to Belzedar. Garion might understand that, but I'm fairly sure none of the rest of my savage family would. Regrets? Yes, of course I have regrets. I've got regrets stacked up behind me at least as far as from here to the moon. But we don't die from regret, do we? We might squirm a little, but we don't die.

And our Master smiled at my brother Belzedar, and the Orb grew brighter. I seemed to see images flickering dimly within it. "Herein lies the past," our Master told us, "and the present, and the future, also. This is but a small part of the virtue of the Orb. With it may man—or earth herself—be healed or destroyed. Whatsoever man or God would do, though it be beyond even the power of the Will and the Word, with this Orb may it come to pass."

"Truly a wondrous thing, Master," Belzedar said, looking a bit puzzled, "but still I fail to understand. The jewel is fair, certainly, but in fine it is yet but a stone."

"The Orb hath revealed the future unto me, my son," our Master replied sadly. "It shall be the cause of much contention and great suffering and vast destruction. Its power reaches from where it now lies to blow out the lives of men yet unborn as easily as thou wouldst snuff out a candle."

"It's an evil thing then, Master," I said, and Belsambar and Belmakor agreed.

"Destroy it, Master," Belsambar pleaded, "before it can bring its evil into the world."

"That may not be," our Master replied.

"Blessed be the wisdom of Aldur," Belzedar said, his eyes glittering strangely. "With us to aid him, our Master may wield this wondrous jewel for good instead of ill. It would be monstrous to destroy so precious a thing." Now that I look back at everything that's happened, I suppose I shouldn't really blame Belzedar for his unholy interest in the Orb. It was a part of something that absolutely *had* to happen. I shouldn't blame him for it—but I do.

"I tell ye, my sons," our Master continued, "I would not destroy the Orb even were it possible. Ye have all just returned from looking at the world in its childhood and at man in his infancy. All living things must grow or they will die. Through this jewel shall the world be changed and man shall achieve that state for which he was made. The Orb is not of itself evil. Evil is a thing that lies only in the hearts and minds of men—and of Gods, also." And then our Master fell silent, and he sighed, and we went away and left him in his sad communion with the Orb.

We saw little of our Master in the centuries that followed. Alone in his tower he continued his study of the Orb, and he learned much from it, I think. We were all saddened by his absence, and our work had little joy in it.

I think it was about twenty centuries after I came to serve my Master when a stranger came into the Vale. He was beautiful as no being I have ever seen, and he walked as if his foot spurned the earth.

As was customary, we went out to greet him.

"I would speak with my brother, thy Master, Aldur," he told us, and we knew that we were in the presence of a God.

As the eldest, I stepped forward. "I shall tell my Master you have come," I said politely. I wasn't certain which God he was, but something about this overpretty stranger didn't sit very well with me.

"That is not needful, Belgarath," he told me in a tone that irritated me even more than his manner. "My brother knows I am here. Convey me to his tower."

I turned and led the way without trusting myself to answer.

When we reached the tower, the stranger looked me full in the face. "A bit of advice for thee, Belgarath," he said, "by way of thanks for thy service. Seek not to rise above thyself. It is not *thy* place to approve or to disapprove of *me*. For thy sake I hope that when next we meet, thou wilt remember this instruction and behave in a more seemly manner." His eyes seemed to bore directly into me, and his voice chilled me.

But, because I was still who I was and not even the two thousand years and more I had lived in the Vale had entirely put the wild, rebellious boy in me to sleep, I answered him somewhat tartly. "Thank you for the advice," I told him. "Will you require anything else?" It wasn't up to *me* to tell him where the door was or how to open it. I waited, watching hopefully for some hint of confusion.

"Thou art pert, Belgarath," he observed. "Perhaps one day I shall give myself leisure to instruct thee in proper behavior and customary respect."

"I'm always eager to learn," I replied. As you can see, Torak and I got off on the wrong foot almost immediately. You'll notice that I'd deduced his identity by now.

He turned and gestured, and the stone door of the tower opened. Then he went inside.

We never knew exactly what passed between our Master and his brother. They spoke together for hours, then a summer storm broke above our heads, so we were forced to take shelter and thus missed Torak's departure.

When the storm had cleared, our Master called us to him, and we went up into his tower. He sat at the table where he had labored so long over the Orb. There was a great sadness in his face, and my heart wept to see it. There was also a reddened mark on his cheek that I didn't understand.

But Belzedar saw what I hadn't almost at once. "Master!" he said with a note of panic in his voice. "Where is the jewel? Where is the Orb of power?" I *wish* I'd paid closer attention to the sound of his voice. I might have been able to avert a lot of things if I had.

"Torak, my brother, hath taken it away with him," our Master replied, and *his* voice had almost the sound of weeping in it.

"Quickly!" Belzedar exclaimed. "We must pursue him and reclaim the Orb before he escapes us! We are many, and he is but one!"

"He is a God, my son," Aldur said. "Numbers mean nothing to him."

"But, Master," Belzedar said desperately, "we *must* reclaim the Orb! It *must* be returned to us!" And I *still* didn't realize what was going on in Belzedar's mind. My brains must have been asleep.

"How did thy brother obtain thine Orb from thee, Master?" Beltira asked.

"Torak conceived a desire for the jewel," Aldur said, "and he besought me that I should give it to him. When I would not, he smote me and took the Orb and ran."

That did it! Though the jewel was wondrous, it was still only a stone. The fact that Torak had struck my Master, however, brought flames into my brain. I threw off my cloak, bent my will into the air before me, and forged a sword with a single word. I seized the sword and leapt to the window.

"No!" my Master said, and the word stopped me as if a wall had been placed before me.

"Open!" I commanded, slashing at that unseen wall with the sword I'd just made.

"No!" my Master said again, and the wall wouldn't let me through.

"He hath struck thee, Master!" I raged. "For that I will kill him though he be ten times a God!"

"No. Torak would crush thee as easily as thou wouldst crush an insect that annoyed thee. I love thee much, mine eldest son, and I would not lose thee so."

"There must be war, Master," Belmakor said. That should give you some idea of how seriously we took the matter. The word "war" was the last I'd have ever expected to hear coming from the ultra-civilized Belmakor. "The blow and the theft must not go unpunished. We will forge weapons, and Belgarath shall lead us. We will make war on this thief who calls himself a God."

"My son," Aldur said with a kind of gentle sorrow, "there will be war enough to glut thee of it before thy life ends. Gladly would I have given the Orb to Torak, save that the Orb itself hath told me that one day it would destroy him. I would have spared him had I been able, but his lust for the jewel was too great, and he would not listen." He sighed and then straightened. "There *will* be war, Belmakor. It is unavoidable now. My brother hath the Orb in his possession, and with its power he can do great mischief. We must reclaim it or alter it before Torak can subdue it and bend it to his will."

"Alter?" Belzedar said, aghast. "Surely, Master, surely thou wouldst not *weaken* this precious thing!" It seemed that was all he could think about, and I *still* didn't understand.

"It may not be weakened, Belzedar," Aldur replied, "but will retain its power even unto the end of days. The purpose of our war shall be to press Torak into haste, that he will attempt to use it in a way that it *will* not be used."

Belzedar stared at him. He evidently had thought that the Orb was a passive object. He hadn't counted on the fact that it had its own ideas about things.

"The world is inconstant, Belzedar," our Master explained, "but good and evil are immutable and unchanging. The Orb is an object of good and not merely some bauble or toy. It hath understanding, not such as thine, but understanding nonetheless. And it hath a will. Beware of it, for its will is the will of a stone. It is, as I say, a thing of good. If it be raised to do evil, it will strike down whoever would so use it—be he man or be he God." Aldur obviously saw what I did not, and this was his way to try to warn Belzedar. I don't think it worked, though.

Our Master sighed, then he rose to his feet. "We must make haste," he told us. "Go ye, my disciples. Go ye even unto mine other brothers and tell them that I bid them come to me. I am the eldest, and they will come out of respect, if not love. The war we propose will not be ours alone. I do fear me that all of mankind shall be caught up in it. Go, therefore, and summon my brothers that we may consider what must be done."

CHAPTER FIVE

"A word with you, Belgarath?" Belmakor said when we reached the foot of our Master's tower.

"Of course."

"I really don't think we should leave the Master alone," he suggested gravely.

"You think Torak might come back and hit him again?"

"I rather doubt it, and I'm fairly certain that the Master could take care of himself if that happened."

"He didn't the last time," I replied bleakly.

"That was probably because Torak took him by surprise. You don't normally expect a brother to hit you."

"Why all this concern, then?"

"Didn't you feel the Master's grief? And I'm not just talking about the loss of the Orb. Torak betrayed him and hit him, and now there's going to be a war. I think a couple of us should stay here to comfort the Master and to care for him."

"Do you want to stay?"

"Not me, old boy. I'm at least as angry about this as you are. Right now I'm so angry that I could bite rocks and spit sand."

I considered it. There were seven of us, and we had to reach only five Gods, so we could certainly afford to leave a couple behind. "How about the twins, then?" I suggested. "Neither one of them could function if we separated them anyway, and they don't have the temperament to deal with any confrontations that might turn up."

"Excellent suggestion, old boy," he approved. "Of course, that means that someone else will have to go north to speak with Belar."

"I'll do that," I volunteered. "I think I can probably deal with the Alorns."

"I'll go to Nedra, then. I've met him before, and I know how to get his attention. I'll bribe him if I have to."

"Bribe? He's a God, Belmakor."

"You've never met him, I gather. The Tolnedrans come by their peculiarities honestly."

"Take Belzedar with you," I suggested. "He's obsessed with the Orb, so I don't think we should just turn him loose. He might decide to go after Torak on his own. When you get to the lands of the Tolnedrans, send him up into Arendland to talk with Chaldan. If he tries to argue with you, tell him that I ordered him to do it. I'm the eldest, so that might carry some weight with him. Don't let him go south. I don't want him getting himself killed. Our Master's got enough grief to deal with already."

He nodded gravely. "I'll take the others along as well. We'll split up once we reach the Tolnedrans. Belsambar can go talk with Mara, and Beldin should be able to find Issa."

"That's probably the best plan. Warn Beldin and Belsambar about Belzedar. Let's all keep an eye on him. Sometimes he's a little impulsive."

"Do we want to involve the Dals or the Melcenes?"

I squinted up at the sky. The summer storm had blown off, and only a few puffy white clouds remained. "The Master didn't mention them," I replied a little dubiously. "You might want to warn them, though. They probably wouldn't care to participate in a religious war—considering the fact that they don't have a God—but you should probably suggest that they stay out of the way."

He shrugged. "Whatever you think best. Will you talk with the twins?"

"Why don't you do that? I've got a long way to go, and the Alorns are spread out all over the north. It might take me quite a little while to find Belar."

"Good hunting," he said with a faint smile.

"Very funny, Belmakor," I replied dryly.

"One does one's best, old boy. I'll go speak with the twins." And he sauntered off in the direction of the twins' tower. Not much ever ruffled Belmakor—at least not on the surface.

Since speed was important, I decided to change into the form of an eagle and fly north, which proved to be a mistake. I think I've already mentioned the fact that I don't fly very well. I've never really been able to get the hang of it. For one thing, I'm not all that comfortable with feathers, and for another—wings or not—the sight of all that empty air under me makes me decidedly uncomfortable, so I flap a great deal more than is really necessary, and that can become very tiring after a while.

The major problem, however, lay in the fact that the longer I remained in the form of an eagle, the more the character of the eagle became interwoven with my own. I began to be distracted by tiny movements on the ground, and I had fierce urges to swoop down and kill things.

This obviously wasn't working, so I settled back to earth, resumed my own form, and sat for a time to catch my breath, rest my arms, and consider alternatives. The eagle, for all his splendor, is really a stupid bird, and I didn't want to be continually distracted from my search for Belar by every mouse or rabbit on the ground beneath me.

I considered the possibility of the horse. A horse can run very fast for short periods, but he soon tires, and he's not very much brighter than the eagle. I decided against taking the form of a horse and moved on to other possibilities. An antelope can run for days without tiring, but the antelope is a silly creature, and too many other animals on this vast plain looked upon him as a food source. I didn't really have the time to stop to persuade every passing predator to go find something else to eat. I needed a form with speed and stamina and a sufficiently intimidating reputation to keep other creatures at a distance.

After a while it occurred to me that all the traits I was looking for were to be found in the wolf. Of all the creatures of the plain and forest, the wolf is the most intelligent, the swiftest, and the most tireless. Not only that, no sane animal crosses a wolf if he can possibly avoid it.

It took me a while to get it right. Beldin had taught us all to assume the form of a bird, but I was on my own when it came to putting on fur and paws.

I'll admit that I botched it the first few times. Have you ever seen a wolf with feathers and a beak? You really wouldn't want to. I finally managed to put all thoughts of birds out of my mind and came much closer to my idealized conception of what a wolf ought to look like.

It's a strange sort of process, this changing of form. First you fill your mind with the image of the creature you want to become, and then you direct your will inward and sort of melt yourself into the image. I wish Beldin were around. He could explain it far better than I can. The important thing is just to keep trying—and to change back quickly if you get it wrong. If you've left out the heart, you're in trouble.

After I'd made the change, I checked myself over rather carefully to make sure I hadn't left anything out. I'd imagine that I looked just a bit ridiculous groping at my head and ears and muzzle with my paws, but I wanted to be certain that other wolves wouldn't laugh at me when they saw me.

Then I started across the grassland. I soon realized that my choice had been a good one. As soon as I got used to the idea of running on all fours, I found the shape of the wolf quite satisfactory and the mind of the wolf most compatible with my own. After an hour or so, I was pleased to note that I was covering the ground at least as fast as I had when floundering through the air as an eagle. I quickly discovered that it's a fine thing to have a tail. A tail helps you to keep your balance, and it acts almost like a rudder when you're making quick turns. Not only that, when you have a fine, bushy tail, you can wrap it around yourself at night to ward off the chill. You really ought to try it sometime.

I ran north for a week or so, but I still hadn't come across any Alorns. Then on one golden afternoon in late summer I encountered a young she-wolf who was feeling frolicsome. She had, as I recall, fine haunches and a comely muzzle.

"Why so great a hurry, friend?" she said to me coyly in the way of wolves. Even in my haste, I was startled to find that I could understand her quite clearly. I slowed, and then I stopped.

"What a splendid tail you have," she complimented me, quickly following up on her advantage, "and what excellent teeth."

"Thank you," I replied modestly. "Your own tail is also quite fine, and your coat is truly magnificent." I admired her openly.

"Do you really think so?" she said, preening herself. Then she nipped playfully at my flank and dashed off a few yards, trying to get me to chase her.

"I would gladly stay a while so that we might get to know each other better," I told her, "but I have a most important errand."

"An errand?" she scoffed, with her tongue lolling out in amusement. "Whoever heard of a wolf with any errand but his own desires?"

"I am not really a wolf," I explained.

"Really? How remarkable. You look like a wolf, and you talk like a wolf, and you certainly smell like a wolf, but you say that you are not a wolf. What are you, then?"

"I am a man." I said it rather deprecatingly. Wolves have strong opinions about certain things, I discovered.

She sat, a look of amazement on her face. She had to accept what I said as the truth, since wolves are incapable of lying. "You have a tail," she pointed out, "and I have never seen a man with a tail before. You have a fine coat. You have four feet. You have long, pointed teeth, sharp ears, and a black nose, and yet you say you are a man."

"It is very complicated."

"It must be," she conceded. "I think I will run with you for a while, since you *must* attend to this errand of yours. Perhaps we can discuss it as we go along, and you can explain this complicated thing to me."

"If you wish." I rather liked her and was glad by then for any company. It's lonely being a wolf sometimes. "I must warn you though, that I run very fast," I cautioned her.

She sniffed. "All wolves run very fast."

And so, side by side, we ran off over the endless grassland in search of the God Belar.

"Do you intend to run both day and night?" she asked me after we had gone several miles.

"I will rest when I grow tired."

"I am glad of that." Then she laughed in the way of wolves, nipped at my shoulder, and scampered off.

I began to consider the morality of my situation. Though my companion looked quite delightful to me in my present form, I was almost positive that she would seem less so once I resumed my proper shape. Further, while it's undoubtedly a fine thing to be a father, I was fairly certain that a litter of puppies might prove to be an embarrassment when I returned to my Master. Not only that, the puppies would not be entirely wolves, and I didn't really want to father a race of monsters. But finally, since wolves mate for life, when I left my companion—as I would eventually be compelled to do—she would be abandoned, left alone with a litter of fatherless puppies, and subject to the scorn and ridicule of the other members of her pack. Propriety is very important to wolves. Thus, I resolved to resist her advances on our journey in search of Belar.

I wouldn't have devoted so much time and space to this incident except to help explain how insidiously the personalities of the shapes we assume come to dominate our thinking. Before we had gone very far, I was as much or more a wolf as my little friend. If you should ever decide to practice this art, be careful. To remain in a shape *too* long is to invite the very real possibility that when the time comes to go back to your own form, you may not want to. I'll quite candidly admit that by the time the young she-wolf and I reached the realms of the Bear God, I'd begun to give long thoughts to the pleasures of the den and the hunt, the sweet nuzzlings of puppies, and the true and steadfast companionship of a mate.

At length we found a band of hunters near the edge of that vast primeval forest where Belar, the Bear God, dwelt with his people. To the amazement of my companion, I resumed my own shape and approached them. "I have a message for Belar," I told them.

"How may we know this to be true?" one burly fellow demanded truculently. Why *is* it that Alorns will go out of their way to pick a fight?

"You know it's true because I say it's true," I told him bluntly. "The message is important, so quit wasting time flexing your muscles and take me to Belar at once."

Then one of the Alorns saw my companion and threw his spear at her. I didn't have time to make what I did seem natural or to conceal it from them. I stopped the spear in midflight.

They stood gaping at that spear stuck quivering in the air as if in the trunk of a tree. Then, because I was irritated, I flexed my mind and broke the spear in two. "Sorcery!" one of them gasped.

"Amazing level of perception there, old boy," I said sarcastically, imitating Belmakor at his best. "Now, unless you'd all like to live out the rest of your lives as cabbages, take me to Belar at once. Oh, incidentally, the wolf's with me. The next one of you who tries to hurt her is going to spend the rest of his life carrying his entrails around in a bucket." You have to be graphic to get an Alorn's attention sometimes. I beckoned to the wolf, and she came to my side, baring her fangs at them. She had lovely fangs, long and curved and as sharp as daggers. Her display of them got the Alorns' immediate and undivided attention. "Nicely done," I snarled admiringly to her. She wagged her tail, her lip still curled menacingly at those thick-witted barbarians.

"Shall we go talk to Belar, gentlemen?" I suggested in my most civilized manner on the theory that sometimes you have to beat Alorns over the head.

We found the God Belar in a rude encampment some miles deeper into the forest. He appeared to be very young—scarcely more than a boy, though I knew that he was very nearly as old as my Master. I have my suspicions about Belar. He was surrounded by a bevy of busty, blonde-braided Alorn maidens, who all seemed enormously fond of him. Well, he *was* a God, after all, but the admiration of those girls didn't seem to be entirely religious.

All right, Polgara, just let it lie, will you?

The Alorns in that crude encampment in the woods were rowdy, undisciplined, and—by and large—drunk. They joked boisterously with their Master with absolutely no sense of decorum or dignity.

"Well met, Belgarath," Belar greeted me, though we'd never met before and I hadn't told any of those belligerent hunters my name. "How goes it with my beloved elder brother?"

"Not well, my Lord," I replied rather formally. Despite the tankard he held in one hand and the blonde he held in the other, he was still a God, so I thought it best to mind my manners. "Thy brother Torak came unto my Master and smote him and bore away a particular jewel that he coveted."

"*What?*" the young God roared, springing to his feet and spilling both tankard and blonde. "Torak hath the Orb?"

"I greatly fear it is so, my Lord. My Master bids me entreat thee to come to him with all possible speed."

"I will, Belgarath," Belar assured me, retrieving his tankard and the pouty-looking blonde. "I will make preparations at once. Hath Torak used the Orb as yet?"

"We think not, my Lord," I replied. "My Master says we must make haste, ere thy brother Torak hath learned the full power of the jewel he hath stolen."

"Truly," Belar agreed. He glanced at the young she-wolf sitting at my feet. "Greetings, little sister," he said in flawless wolfish. "Is it well with thee?" Belar had his faults, certainly, but you could never criticize his manners.

"Most remarkable," she said with some amazement. "It appears that I have fallen in with creatures of great importance."

"Thy companion and I must make haste," he told her. "Otherwise I would make suitable arrangements for thy comfort. May I offer thee to eat?" You see what I mean about Belar's courtesy?

She glanced at the ox turning on a spit over an open fire. "That smells interesting," she said.

"Of course." He took up a very long knife and carved off a generous portion for her. He handed it to her, being careful to snatch his fingers back out of the range of those gleaming fangs.

"My thanks," she said, tearing off a chunk and downing it in the blink of an eye. "This one—" She jerked her head at me "—was in so much hurry to reach this place that we scarce had time to catch a rabbit or two along the way." She daintily gulped the rest of the meat down in two great bites. "Quite good," she noted, "though one wonders why it was necessary to burn it."

"A custom, little sister," he explained.

"Oh, well, if it is a custom—" She carefully licked her whiskers clean.

"I will return in a moment, Belgarath," Belar said, and moved away to speak with his Alorns.

"That one is nice," my companion told me pointedly.

"He is a God," I told her.

"That means nothing to me," she said indifferently. "Gods are the business of men. Wolves have little interest in such things." Then she looked at me critically. "One would be more content with you if you would keep your eyes where they belong," she added.

"One does not understand what you mean."

"I think you do. The females belong to the nice one. It is not proper for you to admire them so openly." Regardless of *my* reservations about the matter, it was fairly obvious that *she* had made some decisions. I thought it might be best to head that off.

"Perhaps you would wish to return to the place where we first met so that you may rejoin your pack?" I suggested delicately.

"I will go along with you for a while longer." She rejected my suggestion. "I was ever curious, and I see that you are familiar with things that are most remarkable." She yawned, stretched, and curled up at my feet—being careful, I noticed, to place herself between me and those Alorn girls.

The return to the Vale where my Master waited took far less time than my journey to the land of the Bear God had. Although time is normally a matter of indifference to them, when there's need for haste, the Gods can devour distance in ways that hadn't even occurred to me. We set out at what seemed no more than a leisurely stroll with Belar asking me questions about my Master and our lives in the Vale while the young she-wolf padded along sedately between us. After several hours of this, my impatience made me bold enough to get to the point. "My Lord," I said, "forgive me, but at this rate, it'll take us almost a year to reach my Master's tower."

"Not nearly so long, Belgarath," he disagreed pleasantly. "I believe it lies just beyond that next hilltop."

I stared at him, not believing that a God could be so simple, but when we crested the hill, there lay the Vale spread before us with my Master's tower in the center.

"Most remarkable," the wolf murmured, dropping to her haunches and staring down into the Vale with her bright yellow eyes. I had to agree with her about that.

My brothers had returned by now, and they were waiting at the foot of our Master's tower as we approached. The other Gods were already with my Master, and Belar hastened into the tower to join them.

When my brothers saw my companion, they were startled. "Belgarath," Belzedar objected, "is it wise to bring such a one here? Wolves are not the most trustworthy of creatures, you know."

The she-wolf bared her fangs at him for that. How in the world could she possibly have understood what he'd said?

"What is her name?" the gentle Beltira asked me.

"Wolves don't need names, brother," I replied. "They know who they are without such appendages. Names are a human conceit, I think."

Belzedar shook his head and moved away from the wolf.

"Is she quite tame?" Belsambar asked me. Taming things was a passion with Belsambar. I think he knew half the rabbits and deer in the Vale by their first names, and the birds used to perch on him the way they would have if he had been a tree.

"She isn't tame at all, Belsambar," I told him. "We met by chance while I was going north, and she decided to tag along."

"Most remarkable," the wolf said to me. "Are they always so full of questions?"

"How did you know they were asking questions?"

"You, too? You are as bad as they are." That was a maddening habit of hers. If she considered a question unimportant, she simply wouldn't answer it.

"It's the nature of man to ask questions," I said a bit defensively.

"Curious creatures," she sniffed, shaking her head. She could also be a mistress of ambiguity.

"What a wonder," Belkira marveled. "You've learned to converse with the beasts. I pray you, dear brother, instruct me in this art."

"I wouldn't exactly call it an art, Belkira. I took the form of a wolf on my journey to the north. The language of wolves came with the form and remained even after I changed back. It's no great thing."

"I think you might be wrong there, old chap," Belmakor said with a thoughtful expression. "Learning foreign languages is a very tedious process, you know. I've been meaning to learn Ulgo for several years now, but I haven't gotten around to it. If I were to take the form of an Ulgo for a day or so, it might save me months of study."

"You're lazy, Belmakor," Beldin told him bluntly. "Besides, it wouldn't work."

"And why not?"

"Because an Ulgo's still a man. Belgarath's wolf doesn't form words the way we do because she doesn't think the way we do."

"I don't think the way an Ulgo does, either," Belmakor objected. "I think it *would* work."

"You're wrong, it wouldn't."

That particular argument persisted off and on for about a hundred years. The notion of trying it and finding out one way or the other never occurred to either of them. Now that I think of it, though, it probably did. Neither of them was so stupid that he wouldn't have thought of it. But they both enjoyed arguing so much that they didn't want to spoil the fun by settling the issue once and for all.

The wolf curled up and went to sleep while the rest of us waited for the decision of our Master and his brothers about the wayward Torak. When the other Gods came down from the tower, their faces were somber, and they left without speaking to us.

Then Aldur summoned us, and we went upstairs. "There will be war," our Master told us sadly. "Torak must not be permitted to gain full mastery of the Orb. They are of two different purposes and must not be joined, lest the fabric of creation be rent asunder. My brothers have gone to gather their people. Mara and Issa will circle to the east through the lands of the Dals that they might come at Torak from the south of Korim. Nedra and Chaldan will encircle him from the west, and Belar will come at him from the north. We will lay waste his Angaraks until he returns the Orb. Though it rends my heart, it must be so. I will set tasks for each of thee that thou must accomplish in mine absence."

"Absence, Master?" Belzedar asked.

"I must go even unto Prolgu to consult with UL. The Destinies that drive us all are known, though imperfectly, to him. He will provide guidance for us, that we do not overstep certain limits in our war upon our brother."

The wolf, quite unnoticed, had gone to him and laid her head in his lap. As he spoke to us, he absently—or so I thought at the time—stroked her with an oddly affectionate hand. I knew it was improbable, but I got the strong impression that they somehow already knew each other.

Our Master was a long time at Prolgu, but we had more than enough to keep us occupied, and I'm certain the peoples of the other Gods were just as busy. With the possible exception of the Alorns and the Arends, war was an alien concept to most of the rest of mankind, and even those belligerent people were not very good at the kind of organization necessary to build an army. By and large, the world had been peaceful, and such fights as occasionally broke out tended to involve just a few men pounding on each other with assorted weapons that weren't really very sophisticated. Fatalities occurred, of course, but I like to think they were accidental most of the time.

This time was obviously going to be different. Whole races were going to be thrown at each other, and nothing had prepared us for that. We relied rather heavily on Belsambar's knowledge of the Angaraks in the early stages of our planning. That elevated opinion of themselves which Torak had instilled in his people had made them aloof and secretive, and strangers or members of other races were not welcome in their cities. To emphasize that, Angaraks had traditionally walled in their towns. It was not so much that they anticipated war—although Torak himself probably did—but rather that they seemed to feel the need for some visible sign that they were separate from and superior to the rest of mankind.

Beldin sat scowling at the floor after Belsambar had described the wall surrounding the city where he'd been born over a thousand years before. "Maybe they've discontinued the practice," he growled.

"They hadn't when I went down to have a look at them five centuries ago," Belzedar told him. "If anything, the walls around their cities were higher—and thicker."

Beltira shrugged. "What one man can build, another man can tear down."

"Not when it's raining spears and boulders and boiling oil, he can't," Beldin disagreed. "I think we can count on the Angaraks to pull back behind those walls when we go after them. They breed like rabbits, but they're still going to be outnumbered, so they won't want to meet us in open country. They'll go into their cities, close the gates, and make us come to them. That's an excellent way for us to get a lot of people killed. We've got to come up with some way to tear those walls down without throwing half of mankind at them."

"We could do it ourselves," Belkira suggested. "As I recall, *you* translocated a half acre or so of rocks when you helped Belgarath build his tower."

"Those were *loose* rocks, brother," Beldin told him sourly, "and it was all I could do to walk the next day. Belsambar says that the Angaraks stick their walls together with mortar. We'd have to take them apart stone by stone."

"And they'd be rebuilding them as fast as we tore them down," Belmakor added. He looked thoughtfully up at the ceiling of Belsambar's tower where we'd gathered. Then, naturally, considering the fact that it was Belmakor, he reverted to logic. "First off, Beldin's right. We can't just swarm their cities under. The casualties would be unacceptable." He looked around at the rest of us. "Do we agree on that?"

We all nodded.

"Splendid," he said dryly. "Second, if we try to take down their walls with the Will and the Word, we'll exhaust ourselves and we won't really accomplish all that much."

"What does that leave us?" Belzedar asked him crossly. I'd picked up a few hints from the others that Belzedar and Belmakor had argued extensively when they had reached the lands of the Tolnedrans. Belzedar, as second disciple, had assumed that *he* was in charge. Belmakor, borrowing *my* authority, had contested that, and Beldin had backed him. Belzedar was mightily offended, I guess, and he seemed to be looking for some way to get back at Belmakor for what he felt to be his humiliation. "We can't strike at Torak directly, you realize," he went on. "The only way we can hurt him enough to force him to give back the Orb is to hurt his people, and we won't be able to hurt them if they're hiding behind those walls."

"The situation would seem to call for something mechanical then, wouldn't you say, old chap?" Belmakor responded in his most urbanely offhand tone.

"Mechanical?" Belzedar looked baffled.

"Something that doesn't bleed, old boy. Something that can reach out from beyond the range of the Angarak spears and knock down those walls."

"There isn't any such thing," Belzedar scoffed.

"Not yet, old chap, not yet, but I rather think Beldin and I can come up with something that'll turn the trick."

I'd like to set the record straight at this point. All manner of people have tried to take credit for the invention of siege engines. The Alorns claim it; the Arends claim it; and the Malloreans certainly claim it; but let's give credit where credit's due. It was my brothers, Belmakor and Beldin, who built the first ones.

This is not to say that all of their machines worked the way they were supposed to. Their first catapult flew all to pieces the first time they tried to shoot it, and their mobile battering ram was an absolute disaster, since they couldn't come up with a way to steer it. It tended to wander away from its intended target and mindlessly bang on unoffending trees— but I digress.

It was at that point in the discussion that our mystical brother, Belsambar, suggested something so horrible that we were all taken aback. "Belmakor," he said in that self-effacing tone of his, "do you think you can really devise something that would throw things long distances?"

"Of course, old boy," Belmakor replied confidently.

"Why should we throw things at the walls, then? We have no quarrel with the walls. Our quarrel's with Torak. I'm an Angarak, and I know the mind of Torak better than any of the rest of you. He encourages his Grolims to sacrifice people because it's a sign that they love him more than they love their fellow man. The more the victim on the altar suffers, the greater he views it as a demonstration of love for him. It's the specific, *individualized* pain of the sacrificial victim that satisfies him. We can hurt him best if we make the pain general."

"Exactly what did you have in mind, brother?" Belmakor asked him with a puzzled look.

"Fire," Belsambar told him with dreadful simplicity. "Pitch burns, and so does naphtha. Why should we waste our time and the lives of our soldiers attacking walls? Use your excellent engines to loft liquid fire over the walls and into the cities. Trapped by their own walls, the Angaraks will be burned alive, and there won't be any need for us even to enter their cities, will there?"

"*Belsambar!*" Beltira gasped. "That's horrible!"

"Yes," Belsambar admitted, "but as I said, I know the mind of Torak. He fears fire. The Gods can see the future, and Torak sees fire in his. Nothing we could do would cause him more pain. And isn't that our purpose?"

In the light of what happened later, Belsambar was totally correct, though how he knew is beyond explanation. Torak *did* fear fire—and with very good reason.

Although Belsambar's suggestion was eminently practical, we all tried to avoid it. Belmakor and Beldin went into an absolute frenzy of creativity, and the twins no less so. *They* experimented with weather. They spun hurricanes and tornadoes out of clear blue skies, hoping thereby to blow down the Angarak cities and towns. I concentrated my efforts on assorted illusions. I'd fill the streets of the walled cities of Angarak with unimaginable horrors. I'd drive them out from behind their walls before their mystical kinsman could roast them alive.

Belzedar worked at least as hard as the rest of us. He seemed obsessed with the Orb, and his labor on means to reclaim it was filled with a kind of desperate frenzy. Through it all, Belsambar sat, patiently waiting. He seemed to know that once the fighting started, we'd return to his hideous solution.

In addition to our own labors, we frequently traveled to the lands of our allies to see what progress they were making. Always before, the various cultures had been rather loose-knit, with no single individual ruling any of the five proto-nations. The war with Torak changed all that. Military organization is of necessity pyramidal, and the concept of one leader commanding an entire race carried over into the various societies after the war was over. In a way, I suppose you could give Torak credit—or blame—for the idea of kings.

I guess that *I'm* the one who was ultimately responsible for the royal house of the Alorns. By general consensus, my brothers and I had continued to serve as liaisons between the various races, and we more or less automatically assumed responsibility for the people of whichever God we had personally invited to that conference in the Vale after Torak stole the Orb. I think that my entire life has been shaped by the fact that I had the misfortune to be saddled with the Alorns.

Our preparations for war took several years. The assorted histories of the period tend to gloss over that fact. There were border clashes with the Angaraks, of course, but no really significant battles. Finally the Gods decided that their people were ready—if anybody in those days actually could be called ready for war. The war against the Angaraks was like no other war in human history in that our deployment involved a general migration of the various races. The Gods were so intimately involved with their people in those days that the notion of leaving the women and children and old people behind while the men went off to fight simply didn't occur to them.

Mara and Issa took their Marags and Nyissans and started their trek southeasterly into the lands of the Dals, even as the Tolnedrans and Arends began their swing toward the west. The Alorns, however, didn't move. It was perhaps the only time I ever saw my Master truly vexed about anything. He instructed me with uncharacteristic bluntness to go north and find out what was holding them up.

So I went north again, and, as always by now, I didn't go alone. I don't know that we'd ever actually discussed it, but the young she-wolf had sort of expropriated me. Since she was along, I once again chose the shape of a wolf for the journey. She approved of that, I suppose. She never was totally satisfied with my real form, and she seemed much happier with me when I had four feet and a tail.

We found out what was holding up the Alorns almost before we reached the lands of the Bear God. Would you believe that they were *already* fighting—*with each other?*

Alorn society—such as it was in those days—was clannish, and the bickering was over which Clan-Chief was going to take command of the entire army. The other Gods had encountered similar problems and had simply overruled the urges toward supremacy of the various factions and selected one leader to run things. Belar, however, wouldn't do that. "I'm sure you can see my position, Belgarath," he said to me when I finally found him. He said it just a little defensively, I thought.

I took a very deep breath, suppressing my urge to scream at him. "No, my Lord," I said in as mild a tone as I could manage. "Actually, I don't."

"If I select *one* Clan-Chief over the others, it might be construed as favoritism, don't you see? They're simply going to have to settle it for themselves."

"The other races are already on the march, my Lord," I reminded him as patiently as I could.

"We'll be along, Belgarath," he assured me, "eventually."

By then I knew Alorns well enough to realize that Belar's "eventually" would quite probably stretch out for several centuries.

The she-wolf at my side dropped to her haunches with her tongue lolling out. Her laughter didn't improve my temper very much, I'll confess.

"Would you be open to a suggestion, my Lord?" I asked the Bear God in a civil tone.

"Why, certainly, Belgarath," he replied. "To be honest with you, I've been racking my brains searching for a solution to this problem. I'd hate to disappoint my brothers, and I really don't want to miss the war entirely."

"It wouldn't be the same without you, my Lord," I assured him. "Now, as for your problem. Why don't you just call all your Clan-Chiefs together and have them draw lots to decide which of them will be the leader of the Alorns?"

"You mean just leave it all in the hands of pure chance?"

"It *is* a solution, my Lord, and if you and I both promise not to tamper in any way, your Clan-Chiefs won't have any cause for complaint, will they? They'll all have an equal chance at the position, and if you order them to abide by the way the lot falls, it should put an end to all this . . ." I choked back the word "foolishness."

"My people *do* like to gamble," he conceded. "Did you know that we invented dice?"

"No," I said blandly. "I didn't know that." To my own certain knowledge, every other race made exactly the same claim. "Why don't we summon your Clan-Chiefs, my Lord? You can explain the contest—and the rules—to them, and we can get on with it. We certainly wouldn't want to keep Torak waiting, would we? He'll miss you terribly if you're not there when the fighting starts."

He grinned at me. As I've said before, Belar has his faults, but he *was* a likable young God. "Oh, by the way, my Lord," I added, trying to make it sound like an afterthought, "if it's all right with you, I'll march south with your people." *Somebody* had to keep an eye on the Alorns.

"Certainly, Belgarath," he replied. "Glad to have you."

And so the Alorn Clan-Chiefs drew lots, and regardless of what Polgara may think, I did *not* tamper with the outcome. In my view, one Clan-Chief was almost the same as any other, and I really didn't care who won—just as long as *somebody* did. As luck had it, the Clan-Chief who won was Chaggat, the ultimate great-grandfather of Cherek Bear-shoulders, the greatest king the Alorns have ever had. Isn't it odd how those things turn out? I've since discovered that while *I* didn't tamper and neither did Belar, something else *did*. The talkative friend Garion carries around in his head took a hand in the game. *He* was the one who selected Cherek's ancestor to be the first king of the Alorns. But I'm getting ahead of myself—or had you noticed that?

Once the question of leadership had been settled, the Alorns started moving in a surprisingly short time—although it's *not* all that surprising, if you stop and think about it. The Alorns of that era were seminomadic in the first place, so they were always ready to move on—largely, I think, because of their deep-seated aversion to orderliness. Prehistoric Alorns kept messy camps, and they found the idea of moving on to be far more appealing than the prospect of tidying up.

Anyway, we marched south, passing through the now-deserted lands of the Arends and the Tolnedrans. It was about midsummer when we reached the country formerly occupied by the Nyissans. We began to exercise a certain amount of caution at that point. We were getting fairly close to the northern frontier of the Angaraks, and it wasn't very long before we began to encounter small, roving bands of the Children of Torak.

Alorns have their faults—lots of them—but they *are* good in a fight. It was there on the Angarak border that I first saw an Alorn berserker. He was a huge fellow with a bright red beard, as I recall. I've always meant to find out if he might have been a distant ancestor of Barak, Earl of Trellheim. He *looked* a lot like Barak, so there probably was some connection. At any rate, he outran his fellows and fell single-handedly on a group of about a dozen Angaraks. I considered the odds against him and started to look around for a suitable grave site. As it turned out, however, it was the Angaraks who needed burying after he finished with them. Shrieking with maniacal laughter and actually frothing at the mouth, he annihilated the whole group. He even chased down and butchered the two or three who tried to run away. The children of the Bear God, of course, stood there and cheered.

Alorns!

The frothing at the mouth definitely disconcerted my companion, though. It took me quite some time to persuade her that the red-bearded berserker wasn't really rabid. Wolves, quite naturally, try to avoid rabid creatures, and my little friend was right on the verge of washing her paws of the lot of us.

Our encounters with the Children of the Dragon God grew more frequent as we drew nearer and nearer to the High Places of Korim, which at that time was the center of Angarak power and population. We managed to obliterate a fair number of walled Angarak towns on our way south, and the reports filtering in from our flanks indicated that the other races involved in our assault on Torak's people were also destroying towns and villages as we converged on Korim.

The engines devised by Belmakor and Beldin worked admirably, and our customary practice when we came on one of those walled towns was to sit back and lob boulders at the walls for a few days while my brothers and I raked the place with tornadoes and filled the streets with illusory monsters. Then, when the walls had been reduced to rubble and the inhabitants to gibbering terror, we'd charge in and kill all the people. I tried my best to convince Chaggat that it was really uncivilized to slaughter all those Angaraks and that he ought to give some consideration to taking prisoners. He gave me that blank, uncomprehending stare that all Alorns seem born with and said, "What for? What would I do with them?"

Unfortunately, the barbarians we accompanied took to Belsambar's notion of burning people alive enthusiastically. In their defense, I'll admit that they were the ones who actually had to do the fighting, and somebody who's on fire has trouble concentrating on the business at hand. Quite often Chaggat's Alorns would batter down a wall and rush into a town where all the inhabitants had already burned to death. That always seemed to disappoint the Alorns.

In his defense, I must say that Torak finally *did* mount a counterattack. His Angaraks came swarming out of the mountains of Korim like a plague, and we met them on all four sides. I don't like war; I never have. It's the stupidest way imaginable to resolve problems. In this case, however, we didn't have much choice.

The outcome was ultimately a foregone conclusion. We outnumbered the Angaraks by about five to one or better, and we annihilated them. Go someplace else to look for the details of that slaughter. I don't have the stomach to repeat what I saw during those awful two weeks. In the end, we drove them back into the mountains of Korim and began our inexorable advance on Torak's ultimate stronghold, that city-temple that surmounted the highest peak. Our Master frequently exhorted his brother to return the Orb, pointing out to him that his Angaraks verged on extinction and that without his children, Torak was nothing. The Dragon God wouldn't listen, however.

The ruggedness of the terrain on the eastern slopes of the mountains of Korim had forced the Marags and Nyissans to make their approach from the south. Had it not been for that, the disaster that followed would have been far worse.

It was the prospect of losing all of his children that ultimately drove the Dragon God over the line into madness. Faced with the choice of either surrendering the Orb or losing all of his worshipers, Torak, to put it bluntly, went crazy. The madness of man is bad enough, but the madness of a God? Horrible!

Driven to desperation, my Master's brother took that ultimate step that only his madness would have suggested to him. He knew what would happen. There is no way that he could not have known. Nonetheless, faced with the extermination of all of Angarak, he raised the Orb. His control of my Master's Orb was tenuous at best, but he raised it all the same.

And with it, he cracked the world.

The sound was like no sound I had ever heard before—or have heard since. It was the sound of tearing rock. To this very day I still start up from a sound sleep, sweating and trembling, as the memory of that dreadful sound echoes down to me through five millennia.

The Melcenes, who are quite competent geologists, described what really happened to the world when Torak broke it apart. My own studies confirm their theories. The core of the world is still molten, and that primeval protocontinent, which we all thought so firm, actually floated on that seething underground sea of liquid rock, not unlike a raft.

Torak used the Orb to break the strings that held the raft together. In his desperation to save his Angaraks, he split the crust of that huge landmass apart so that the rest of mankind could not complete the destruction of his children. The crack he made was miles wide, and the molten rock from far below began to spurt up through that awful chasm. In itself, that would have been catastrophic enough—but then the sea poured into the newly created fissure. Believe me, you *don't* want to spill cold water on boiling rock!

The whole thing exploded!

I would not even venture to guess how many people died when that happened—half of mankind at the very least, and probably far more. Had the geography of eastern Korim been more gentle, in all probability the Marags and Nyissans would have drowned or wound up living in Mallorea. At any rate, the world we had known ended in that instant.

Torak paid a very dear price for what he had done, however. The Orb was not at all happy to be used in the way he used it. Belsambar had been right: Torak had seen fire in his future, and the Orb gave him fire. As it happened, he raised the Orb with his left hand, and after he cracked the world, he didn't have a left hand any more. The Orb burned it down to cinders. Then, as if to emphasize its discontent, it boiled out his left eye and melted down the left side of his face just for good measure. I was ten miles away when it happened, and I could hear his shrieks as clearly as if he'd been standing next to me.

The really dreadful part of the whole business lies in the fact that, unlike humans, the Gods don't heal. *We* expect a few cuts, bruises, and abrasions as we go through life; they don't. Healing is built into us. The Gods aren't supposed to need it.

After he cracked the world, Torak definitely needed healing. It's entirely probable that he felt that first searing touch of fire from the moment he cracked the world until that awful night some five thousand years later when, stricken, he cried out to his mother.

The earth shrieked and groaned as the power of the Orb and the will of Torak burst the plain asunder, and, with a roar like ten thousand thunders, the sea rushed in to explode and seethe in a broad, foaming band between us and the Children of the Dragon God. The cracked land sank beneath our feet, and the mocking sea pursued us, swallowing the plain and the villages and the cities that lay upon it. Then it was that Gara, the village of my birth, was lost forever, and that fair, sparkling river I so loved was drowned beneath the endlessly rolling sea.

A great cry went up from the hosts of mankind, for indeed the lands of most of them were swallowed up by the sea that Torak had let in.

"How remarkable," the young she-wolf at my side observed.

"You say that overmuch," I told her sharply, stung by my own griefs. Her casual dismissal of the catastrophe we'd just witnessed seemed a little understated and more than a little cold-blooded.

"Do you not find it remarkable?" she asked me quite calmly. How are you going to argue with a wolf?

"I do," I replied, "but one should not say that too often, lest one be thought simple." It was a spiteful thing to say, I'll grant you, but her calm indifference to the death of over half my species offended me. Over the years I've come to realize that my helpless irritation with her quirks is one of the keystones of our relationship.

She sniffed. That's a maddening trait of hers. "I will say as I wish to say," she told me with that infuriating superiority of all females. "You need not listen if it does not please you, and if you choose to think me simple, that is your concern—and your mistake."

And now we were confounded. The broad sea stood between us and the Angaraks, and Torak stood on one shore and we upon the other.

"What do we do, Master?" I demanded of Aldur.

"We can do nothing," he replied. "It is finished. The war is over."

"Never!" Belar cried. "My people are Alorns. I shall teach them the ways of the sea. If we cannot come upon the traitor Torak by land, my Alorns shall build a great fleet, and we shall come upon him by sea. The war is *not* done, my brother. Torak hath smote thee, and he hath stolen away that which was thine, and now he hath drowned this fair land in the death-cold sea. Our homes and our fields and forests are no more. This I tell thee, my beloved brother, and my words are true. Between Alorn and Angarak there shall be endless war until the traitor Torak be punished for his iniquities—yea, even if it prevail so until the end of days!" Oh, Belar could be eloquent when he set his mind to it. He loved his beer tankard and his adoring Alorn girls, but he'd set all that aside for the chance to make a speech.

"Torak *is* punished, Belar," my Master said to his enthusiastic younger brother. "He burns even now—and will burn forever. He hath raised the Orb against the earth, and the Orb hath requited him for that. Moreover, now is the Orb awakened. It came to us in peace and love. Now it hath been raised in hate and war. Torak hath betrayed it and turned its gentle soul to stone. Now its heart shall be as ice and iron-hard, and it *will* not be used so again. Torak hath the Orb, but small pleasure shall he find in the having. He may no longer touch it, neither may he look upon it, lest it slay him."

My Master, you'll note, was at least as eloquent as Belar.

"Nonetheless," Belar replied, "I will make war upon him until the Orb be returned to thee. To this I pledge all of Aloria."

"As thou wouldst have it, my brother," Aldur said. "Now, however, we must raise some barrier against this encroaching sea, lest it swallow up all the dry land that is left to us. Join, therefore, thy will with mine, and let us put limits upon this new sea."

Until that day I had not fully realized to what degree the Gods differed from us. As I watched, Aldur and Belar joined their hands and looked out over the broad plain and the approaching sea.

"Stay," Belar said to the sea, raising one hand. His voice wasn't loud, but the sea heard him and stopped. It built up, angry and tossing, behind the barrier of that single word, and a great wind tore at us.

"Rise up," Aldur said just as softly to the earth. My mind was staggered by the immensity of that command. The earth, so newly wounded by Torak, groaned and heaved and swelled. And then, before my very eyes, it rose up. Higher and higher it rose as the rocks beneath cracked and shattered. Out of the plain there shouldered up mountains that hadn't been there before, and they shuddered away the loose earth the way a dog shakes off water, to stand as an eternal barrier to the sea that Torak had let in.

Have you ever stood about a half mile from the center of that sort of thing? Don't, if you can possibly avoid it. We were all hurled to the ground by the most violent earthquake I've ever been through. I lay clutching at the ground while the tremors actually rattled my teeth. The freshly broken earth groaned and even seemed to howl. And she wasn't alone. My companion crouched at my side, raised her face to the sky, and also howled. I put my arms about her and held her tightly against me—which probably wasn't a very good idea, considering how frightened she was. Oddly, she didn't try to bite me—or even growl at me. She licked my face instead, as if *she* were trying to comfort *me*. Isn't *that* peculiar?

When the shaking subsided, we all regained our composure somewhat and stared first at that new range of mountains and then toward the East, where Torak's new sea was sullenly retreating.

"Remarkable," the wolf said as calmly as if nothing had happened.

"Truly," I could not but agree.

And then the other Gods and their peoples came to the place where we were and marveled at what Belar and my Master had done to hold back the sea.

"Now is the time of sundering," my Master told them sadly. "This land that was once so fair and sustained our children in their infancy is no more. That which remains here on this shore is bleak and harsh and will no longer support your people. This then is mine advice to ye, my brothers. Let each take his own people and journey into the west. Beyond the mountains wherein lies Prolgu ye shall find another fair plain—not so broad perhaps, nor so beautiful as that which Torak hath drowned this day, but it will sustain the races of man."

"And what of thee, my brother?" Mara asked him.

"I shall take my disciples and return even unto the Vale," Aldur replied. "This day hath evil been unloosed in the world, and its power is great. The Orb hath revealed itself to *me*, and through its power hath the evil been unloosed. Upon *me*, therefore, falls the task of preparation for the day when good and evil shall meet in that final battle wherein shall be decided the fate of the world."

"So be it then," Mara said. "Hail and farewell, my brother." And he turned and with Issa and Chaldan and Nedra and all their people, they went away toward the West.

But Belar lingered. "Mine oath and my pledge bind me still," he declared. "I will not go to the West with the others, but will take my Alorns to the unpeopled lands of the Northwest instead. There we will seek a way by which we may come again on Torak and his children. Thine Orb *shall* be returned unto thee, my brother. I shall not rest until it be so." And then he turned and put his face to the north, and his tall warriors followed after him.

My master watched them go with a great sadness on his face, and then he turned westward, and my brothers and I followed after him as, sorrowing, we began our journey back to the Vale.

PART
TWO

THE APOSTATE

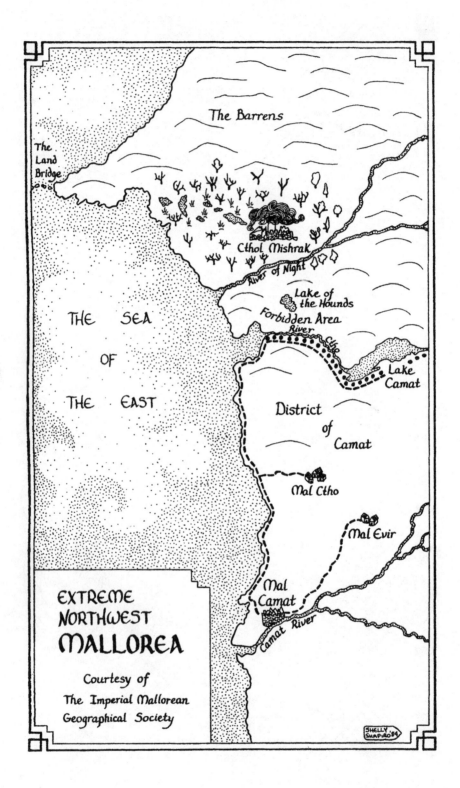

The Barrens

The Land Bridge

Cthol Mishrak

River of Night

THE SEA

OF

THE EAST

Lake of the Hounds

Forbidden Area

River Cthb

Lake Camat

District

of

Camat

Mal Ctho

Mal Evir

Mal Camat

Camat River

EXTREME NORTHWEST MALLOREA

Courtesy of
The Imperial Mallorean
Geographical Society

SHELLY SHAPIRO 84

CHAPTER
SEVEN

My brothers and I were badly shaken by the outcome of our war with the Angaraks. We certainly hadn't anticipated Torak's desperate response to our campaign, and I think we all felt a gnawing personal guilt for the death of half of mankind. We were a somber group when we reached the Vale. We had ongoing tasks, of course, but we took to gathering in our Master's tower in the evenings, seeking comfort and reassurance in his presence and the familiar surroundings of the tower.

Each of us had his own chair, and we normally sat around a long table, discussing the events of the day and then moving on to more wide-ranging topics. I don't know that we solved any of the world's problems with those eclectic conversations, but that's not really why we held them. We needed to be together during that troubled time, and we needed the calm that always pervaded that familiar room at the top of the tower. For one thing, the light there was somehow different from the light in our own towers. The fact that our Master didn't bother with firewood might have had something to do with that. The fire on his hearth burned because he wanted it to burn, and it continued to burn whether he fed it or not. Our chairs were large and comfortable and made of dark, polished wood, and the room was neat and uncluttered. Aldur stored his things in some unimaginable place, and they came to him when he called them rather than lying about collecting dust.

Our evening gatherings continued for six months or so, and they helped us to gather our wits and to ward off the nightmares that haunted our sleep.

Sooner or later, one of us was bound to ask the question, and as it turned out, it was Beltira. "What started it all, Master?" he asked reflectively. "This goes back much farther than what's been happening recently, doesn't it?"

You'll notice that Durnik wasn't the first to be curious about beginnings.

Aldur looked gravely at the gentle Alorn shepherd. "It doth indeed, Beltira—farther back then thou canst possibly imagine. Once, when the universe was all new and long before my brothers and I came into being, an event occurred that had not been designed to occur, and it was that event which divided the purpose of all things."

"An accident then, Master?" Beldin surmised.

"A most apt term, my son," Aldur complimented him. "Like all things, the stars are born; they exist for a certain time; and then they die. The 'accident' of which we speak came about when a star died in a place and at a time that were not a part of the original design of all creation. The death of a star is a titanic event, and the death of this particular star was made even more so by its unfortunate proximity to other stars. Ye have all studied the heavens, and therefore ye know that the universe is comprised of clusters of stars. The particular cluster of which we speak consisted of so many suns that they were beyond counting, and the wayward sun that died in their very midst ignited others, and they in turn ignited more. The conflagration spread until the entire cluster exploded."

"Was that anywhere near where we are now, Master?" Belsambar asked him.

"Nay, my son. The EVENT took place on the far side of the universe—so far in fact that the light of that catastrophe hath not yet reached this world."

"How is that possible, Master?" Belsambar looked confused.

"Sight isn't instantaneous, brother," Beldin explained. "There's a lag between the time when something happens and the time when we see it. There are a lot of things we see in the night sky that aren't really there any more. Someday when we've both got some time, I'll explain it to you."

"How could so remote an event have any meaning here, Master?" Belzedar asked, his tone baffled.

Aldur sighed. "The universe came into being with a Purpose, Belzedar," he replied with a strange kind of wonder in his voice. "The accident divided that Purpose, and what was once one became two. Awareness came out of that division, and the two Purposes have contended with each other since that EVENT took place. In time, the two agreed that this world—which did not even exist as yet—would be their final battleground. That is why my brothers and I came into existence, and that is why we made this world. It is *here* that the division of the Purpose of the universe will be healed. A series of EVENTS, some great and some very small, have been leading up to the final EVENT, and that EVENT shall be a Choice."

"Who's supposed to make that choice?" Beldin asked.

"We are not permitted to know that," Aldur replied.

"Oh, fine!" Beldin exploded with heavy sarcasm. "It's all a game, then! When's this supposed to happen?"

"Soon, my son. Very soon."

"Could you be a little more specific, Master? I know how long you've been around, and you and I might have very different ideas about what the word 'soon' means."

"The Choice must be made when the light of that exploding star cluster reaches this world."

"And that could happen at any time, couldn't it? It could come popping out of the sky sometime after midnight this very night, for all we know."

"Curb thine impatience, Beldin," Aldur told him. "There will be signs to advise us that the moment of the Choice draws nigh. The cracking of the world was one such sign. There will be others as well."

"Such as?" Beldin pressed. Once he grabbed hold of an idea, Beldin couldn't let go of it.

"Before the light comes, there will be a time—a moment—of utter darkness."

"I'll watch for it," Beldin said sourly.

"As I understand it, there are two possible Destinies out there," Belmakor observed. "Torak's one of them, isn't he?"

"My brother is a part of one of them, yes. Each of the Destinies is comprised of innumerable parts, and each hath a consciousness that doth exceed the awareness of any of those parts."

"Which one came first, Master?" Belkira asked.

"We do not know. We are not permitted to know."

"More games," Beldin said in a tone of profoundest disgust. "I *hate* games."

"We must all play this one, however, gentle Beldin. The rules may not be to our liking, but we must abide by them, for they are laid down by the contending Purposes."

"Why? It's *their* fight. Why involve the rest of us? Why don't they just pick a time and place, meet, and have it out once and for all?"

"That they may not do, my son, for should they ever confront each other directly, their struggle would destroy the whole of the universe."

"I don't think we'd want that," Belkira said mildly. The twins *are* Alorns, after all, and Alorns take a childish delight in gross understatement.

"*You* are the other Destiny, aren't you, Master?" Belsambar asked. "Torak is the one, and you are the other."

"I am a part of it, my son," Aldur conceded. "We are all parts of it. That is why what we do is so important. One will come in the fullness of time, however, who will be even more important. It is *he* who will meet Torak and prepare the way for the Choice."

And that was the very first time I ever heard of Belgarion. Aldur knew he was coming, though, and he'd been patiently preparing for him since he and his brothers had built the world. If you want to put it in the simplest terms, I suppose you could say that the Gods created this world to give Belgarion something to stand on while he set things right again. It was a lot of responsibility for somebody like Garion, but I suppose he was up to it. Things *did* turn out all right—more or less.

Our Master's explanation of what we were doing laid a heavy responsibility on us, as well, and we felt it keenly. Even in the midst of our labors, however, we all noticed that the world had been enormously changed by what Torak had done to it. The presence of a new ocean in what had been the center of the continent had a profound effect on the climate, and the mountain range our Master and Belar had raised to confine that ocean changed it even more. Summers became dryer and hotter for one thing, and the winters became longer and colder. That's one of the reasons that I tend to get very angry when someone starts playing around with the weather. I've seen what happens when something or someone tampers with normal weather patterns. Garion and I had a very long talk about that on one occasion, as I recall—that is, *I* talked. He listened. At least I *hope* he did. Garion has enormous power, and sometimes he turns it loose before he thinks his way completely through a given course of action.

With the change of climate there also came a gradual alteration of the world around us. The vast primeval forest on the northern edge of the Vale began to thin out, for one thing, and it was replaced by grassland. I'm sure the Algars approve of that, but I preferred the trees myself.

There was also a rather brutal alteration of the climate of the Far North. Belar, however, persisted in his plan to find some way to close with the Angaraks again, and his Alorns were obliged to endure truly savage winters.

There in the Vale, however, we had more on our minds than the weather. The cracking of the world set a lot of things in motion, and Aldur kept the seven of us very busy making sure that things that were supposed to happen did happen. We surmised that the Angaraks were doing the same thing. The two contending Purposes undoubtedly were maneuvering for position.

About twenty years after the cracking of the world, our Master summoned us all to his tower and suggested that one of us ought to go to what's now Mallorea to find out what Torak and his people were up to.

"I'll go," Beldin volunteered. "I fly better than the rest of you, and I can move around among the Angaraks without attracting any attention."

"Somehow your reasoning there escapes me, old boy," Belmakor said. "You're a rather remarkable-looking fellow, you know."

"That's the whole point. When people look at me, all they can see is this hump on my back and the fact that my arms are longer than my legs. They don't bother to look at my face to find out what my race is. There's a kind of anonymity that goes with being deformed."

"Do you want me to go with you?" Belsambar offered. "I'm an Angarak, after all, and I know the customs."

"Thanks, brother, but no. You've got some fairly strong opinions about Grolims. We wouldn't be anonymous for very long if you started turning every single priest of Torak inside out. I'm just going there to look, and I'd rather that Torak didn't know that I'm around."

"I wouldn't interfere, Beldin."

"Let's not take the chance. I love you too much to risk your life."

"You really shouldn't go alone, Beldin," Belzedar told him, his eyes strangely intent. "I think perhaps I'd better go, too."

"I'm not a child, Belzedar. I can take care of myself."

"I'm sure of it, but we can cover more ground if there are two of us. The other continent's quite large, and the Angaraks have probably spread out by now. The Master wants information, and two of us can get it faster than one."

Now that I think back about it, Belzedar's arguments were just a bit thin. Angarak society was the most tightly controlled in the world. Torak was *not* going to let his people spread out; he would keep them under his thumb. Belzedar had his own reasons for wanting to go to Mallorea, and I should have realized that helping Beldin wasn't one of them.

The two of them argued for a while, but Beldin finally gave in. "I don't care," he said. "Come along if it means so much to you."

And so the next morning the two of them took the forms of hawks and flew off toward the east.

We all dispersed not long after that. The Master had some fairly extensive tasks for me in Arendia and Tolnedra.

The young she-wolf went with me, of course. I hadn't even considered leaving her behind, and it probably wouldn't have done me any good if I had. When we'd first met, she'd said, "I will go along with you for a while." Evidently, we hadn't come to the end of that "while" yet. I didn't really mind, though. She was good company.

The shortest route to northern Arendia lay across Ulgoland, so the wolf and I went up into those mountains and proceeded in a generally northwesterly direction. I made us a proper camp every night. Fire had made her nervous right at first, but now she rather liked having a fire in the evening.

After a few days I realized that we were going to be passing fairly close to Prolgu. I didn't really like the current Gorim very much; this particular successor seemed to feel that Ulgos were better than the rest of mankind. I reluctantly concluded that it'd be bad manners to bypass Prolgu without paying a courtesy call, so I veered slightly north in order to reach the city.

The route I chose to reach Prolgu ran up through a thickly wooded gorge with a tumbling mountain stream running down the middle of it. It was about midmorning, and the sunlight had just reached the damp bottom of the gorge. I was wool-gathering, I suppose. A kind of peace and serenity comes over me when I'm in the mountains.

Then the wolf laid her ears back and growled warningly.

"What's the problem?" I asked her, speaking in the language of men without even thinking about it.

"Horses," she replied in wolvish. "But perhaps they are not really horses. They smell of blood and of raw meat."

"Do not be concerned," I told her, lapsing into wolvish. "One has encountered them before. They are Hrulgin. They are meat-eaters. What you smell is the blood and meat of a deer."

"One thinks that you are wrong. The smell is not that of deer. What one smells is the blood and meat of man."

"That is impossible." I snorted. "The Hrulgin are not man-eaters. They live in peace with the Ulgos here in these mountains."

"One's nose is very good," she told me pointedly. "One would not confuse the smell of man-blood and meat with the smell of a deer. These flesh-eating horses have been killing and eating men, and they are hunting again."

"Hunting? Hunting what?"

"One thinks that they are hunting you."

I sent out a probing thought. The minds of the Hrulgin aren't really very much like the minds of horses. Horses eat grass, and about the only time they're aggressive is during the breeding season. The Hrulgin *look* a great deal like horses—if you discount the claws and fangs—but they don't eat grass. I'd touched the minds of Hrulgin before at various times when I'd been traveling in the mountains of Ulgoland. I knew that they were hunters and fairly savage, but the peace of UL had always put restraints on them before. The minds I touched this time seemed to have shrugged off those restraints.

The wolf was right. The Hrulgin were hunting me.

I'd been hunted before. A young lion stalked me for two days once before I'd finally chased him off. There's no real malice in the mind of a hunting animal. He's just looking for something to eat. What I encountered *this* time, however, was a cruel hatred and, much worse, to my way of looking at it, an absolute madness. These particular Hrulgin were much more interested in the killing than they were in the eating. I was in trouble here.

"One suggests that you do something about your shape," the she-wolf advised. She dropped to her haunches, her long, pink tongue lolling out of the side of her mouth. In case you've never noticed, that's the way canines laugh.

"What is so funny?" I demanded of her.

"One finds the man-things amusing. The hunter puts all his thought on the thing he hunts. If it is a rabbit he hunts, he will not turn aside for a squirrel. These meat-eating horses are hunting a man—you. Change your shape, and they will ignore you."

I was actually embarrassed. Why hadn't *I* thought of that? For all our sophistication, the instinctive reaction that seizes you when you realize that something wants to kill and eat you is sheer panic.

I formed the image in my mind and slipped myself into the shape of the wolf. "Much better," my companion said approvingly. "You are a handsome wolf. Your other shape is not so pleasing. Shall we go?"

We angled up from the streambed and stopped at the edge of the trees to watch the Hrulgin. The sudden disappearance of my scent confused them, and it seemed also to infuriate them. The herd stallion reared, screaming his rage, and he shredded the bark of an unoffending tree with his claws while flecks of foam spattered out from his long, curved fangs. Several of the mares followed my scent down the gorge, then back, moving slowly and trying to sniff out the place where I'd turned aside and slipped away.

"One suggests that we move along," the she-wolf said. "The flesh-eating horses will think that we have killed and eaten the man-thing they were hunting. This will make them angry with us. They may decide to stop hunting the man-thing and start hunting wolves."

We stayed just back of the edge of the trees so that we could watch the baffled Hrulgin near the edge of the mountain stream in case they decided to start hunting wolves instead of men. After about a half hour, we were far enough out in front of them that the chances that they could catch up with us were very slim.

The change in the Hrulgin had me completely baffled. The peace of UL had always been absolute before. What had driven the Hrulgin mad?

As it turned out, the Hrulgin weren't the only monsters that had lost their wits.

My automatic use of the word "monster" there isn't an indication of prejudice. It's just a translation of an Ulgo word. The Ulgos even refer to the Dryads as monsters. Ce'Nedra was somewhat offended by that term, as I recall.

Anyway, I decided not to revert to my own form once we had evaded the Hrulgin. Something very strange was going on here in Ulgoland. My companion and I reached that peculiarly shaped mountain upon which Prolgu stands, and we started up.

About halfway to the top, we encountered a pack of Algroths, and they were just as crazy as the Hrulgin had been. Algroths are not among my favorite creatures anyway. I'm not sure what the Gods were thinking of when they created them. A blend of ape, goat, and reptile seems a bit exotic to me. The Algroths were also hunting for people to kill and eat. Whether I liked him or not, I definitely needed to have words with the Gorim.

The only problem was the fact that Prolgu was totally deserted. There were some signs of a hasty departure, but the abandoning of the city had happened some time back, so my companion and I couldn't pick up any hint of a scent that might have told us which way the Ulgos had gone. We came across some mossy human bones, however, and I didn't care for the implications of that. Was it possible that the Ulgos had all been killed? Had UL changed his mind and abandoned them?

I didn't really have time to sort it out. Evening had fallen over the empty city, and my companion and I were still sniffing around in the empty buildings when a sudden bellow shattered the silence, a bellow that was coming from the sky. I went to the doorway of the building we'd been searching and looked up.

The light wasn't really very good, but it was good enough for me to see that huge shape outlined against the evening sky.

It was the dragon, and her great wings were clawing at the sky and she was belching clouds of sooty fire with every bellow.

Notice that I speak of her in the singular and the feminine. This is no indication of any great perception on my part, since there was only one dragon in the entire world, and she was female. The two males the Gods had created had killed each other during the first mating season. I had always felt rather sorry for her, but not this time. She, like the Hrulgin and the Algroths, was intent on killing things, but she was too stupid to be selective. She'd burn anything that moved.

Moreover, Torak had added a modification to the dragons when he and his brothers were creating them. They were totally immune to anything I might have been able to do to them with the Will and the Word.

"One would be more content if you would do something about that," the wolf told me.

"I am thinking about it," I replied.

"Think faster. The bird is returning."

Her faith in me was touching, but it didn't help very much. I quickly ran over the dragon's characteristics in my mind. She was invulnerable, she was stupid, and she was lonely. Those last two clicked together in my mind. I loped to the edge of the city, focused my will on a thicket a few miles south of the mountain, and set fire to it.

The dragon screeched and swooped off toward my fire, belching out her own flames as she went.

"One wonders why you did that."

"Fire is a part of the mating ritual of her kind."

"How remarkable. Most birds mate in the spring."

"She is not exactly a bird. One thinks that we should leave these mountains immediately. There are strange things taking place here that one does not understand, and we have errands to attend to in the lowlands."

She sighed. "It is always errands with you, isn't it?"

"It is the nature of the man-things," I told her.

"But you are not a man-thing right now."

I couldn't dispute her logic, but we left anyway, and we reached Arendia two days later.

The tasks my Master had set for me involved certain Arends and some Tolnedrans. At the time, I didn't understand why the Master was so interested in weddings. I understand now, of course. Certain people needed to be born, and I was out there laying groundwork for all I was worth.

I'd rather thought that the presence of my companion might complicate things, but as it turned out, she was an advantage, since you definitely get noticed when you walk into an Arendish village or a Tolnedran town with a full-grown wolf at your side, and her presence *did* tend to make people listen to me.

Arranging marriages in those days wasn't really all that difficult. The Arends—and to a somewhat lesser degree the Tolnedrans—had patriarchal notions, and children were supposed to obey their fathers in important matters. Thus, I was seldom obliged to try to convince the happy couple that they ought to get married. I talked with their fathers instead. I had a certain celebrity in those days. The war was still fresh in everybody's mind, and my brothers and I *had* played fairly major roles in that conflict. Moreover, I soon found that the priesthood in both Arendia and Tolnedra could be very helpful. After I'd been through the whole business a couple of times, I began to develop a pattern. When the wolf and I went into a town, we'd immediately go to the temple of either Chaldan or Nedra. I'd identify myself and ask the local priests to introduce me to the fathers in question.

It didn't *always* go smoothly, of course. Every so often I'd come across stubborn men who for one reason or another didn't care for my choice of spouses for their children. If worse came to worst, though, I could always give them a little demonstration of what I could do about things that irritated me. That was usually enough to bring them around to my way of thinking.

"One wonders why all of this is necessary," my companion said to me as we were leaving one Arendish village after I'd finally persuaded a particularly difficult man that his daughter's happiness—and his own health—depended on the girl's marriage to the young fellow we had selected for her.

"They will produce young ones," I tried to explain.

"What an amazing thing," she responded dryly. A wolf can fill the simplest statement with all sorts of ironic implications. "Is that not the usual purpose of mating?"

"*Our* purpose is to produce *specific* young ones."

"Why? One puppy is much like another, is it not? Character is developed in the rearing, not in the blood line."

We argued about that off and on for centuries, and I strongly suspect her of arguing largely because she knew that it irritated me. Technically, I was the leader of our odd little pack, but she wasn't going to let me get above myself.

Arendia was a mournful sort of place in those days. The melancholy institution of serfdom had been well established among the Arends even before the war with the Angaraks, and they brought it with them when they migrated to the West. I've never understood why anyone would submit to being a serf in the first place, but I suppose the Arendish character might have had something to do with it. Arends go to war with each other on the slightest pretext, and an ordinary farmer needs *someone* around to protect him from belligerent neighbors.

The lands the Arends had occupied in the central part of the continent had been open, and the fields had long been under cultivation.

Their new home was a tangled forest, so they had to clear away the trees before they could plant anything. This was the work that fell to the serfs. The wolf and I soon became accustomed to seeing naked people chopping at trees. "One wonders why they take off their fur to do this," she said to me on one occasion. There's no word in wolfish for "clothing," so she had to improvise.

"It is because they only have one of the things they cover their bodies with. They put them aside while they are hitting the trees because they do not want them to be wounded while they work." I decided not to go into the question of the poverty of the serfs or of the expense of a new canvas smock. The discussion was complicated enough already. How do you explain the concept of ownership to a creature that has no need for possessions of any kind?

"This covering and uncovering of their bodies that the man-things do is foolishness," she declared. "Why do they do it?"

"For warmth when it is cold."

"But they also do it when it is not cold. Why?"

"For modesty, I suppose."

"What is modesty?"

I sighed. I wasn't making much headway here. "It is just a custom among the man-things," I told her.

"Oh. If it is a custom, it is all right." Wolves have an enormous respect for customs. Then she immediately thought of something else. She was *always* thinking of something else. "If it is the custom among man-things to cover their bodies sometimes but not others, it is not much of a custom, is it?"

I gave up. "No," I said. "Probably not."

She dropped to her haunches in the middle of the forest path we were following with her tongue lolling out in wolfish laughter.

"Do you *mind?*" I demanded.

"One is merely amused by the inconsistencies of the man-side of your thought," she replied. "If you would take your true form, your thought would run more smoothly." She was still convinced that I was really a wolf and that my frequent change of form was no more than a personal idiosyncrasy.

In the forests of Arendia, we frequently encountered the almost ubiquitous bands of outlaws. Not *all* of the serfs docilely accepted their condition. I don't like having people point arrows at me, so after the first time or two, I went wolf as soon as we were out of sight of the village we'd just left. Even the stupidest runaway serf isn't going to argue with a couple of full-grown wolves. That's one of the things that's always been a trial to me. People are *forever* interfering with me when I've got something to attend to. Why can't they just leave me alone?

We went down into Tolnedra after a number of years, and I continued my activities as a marriage broker, ultimately winding up in Tol Nedrane.

Don't bother trying to find it on a map. The name was changed to Tol Honeth before the beginning of the second millennium.

I know that most of you have seen Tol Honeth, but you wouldn't have recognized it in its original state. The war with the Angaraks had taught the Tolnedrans the value of defensible positions, and the island in the center of the Nedrane—"the River of Nedra"—seemed to them to be an ideal spot for a city. In may very well be *now*, but there were a lot of drawbacks when they first settled there. They've been working on it for five thousand years now, and I suppose they've finally ironed out most of the wrinkles.

When the wolf and I first went there, however, the island was a damp, marshy place that was frequently inundated by spring floods. They've built a fairly substantial wall of logs around the island, and the houses inside were also built of logs and had thatched roofs—an open invitation to fire, in my opinion. The streets were narrow, crooked, and muddy; and quite frankly, the place smelled like an open cesspool. My companion found that particularly offensive, since wolves have an extremely keen sense of smell.

My major reason for being in Tolnedra was to oversee the beginnings of the Honethite line. I've never really liked the Honeths. They've an exalted opinion of themselves, and I've never much cared for people who look down their noses at me. My distaste for them may have made me a little abrupt with the prospective bridegroom's father when I told him that his son was required to marry the daughter of an artisan whose primary occupation was the construction of fireplaces. The Honeth family absolutely *had* to have some hereditary familiarity with working in stone. If it didn't, the Tolnedran Empire would never come into existence, and we were going to need the empire later on. I wouldn't bore you with all of this except to show you just how elemental our arrangements in those days really were. We were setting things in motion that wouldn't come to fruition for thousands of years.

After I'd bullied the bridegroom's father into accepting the marriage I'd proposed for his son, the wolf and I left Tol Nedrane—by ferry, since they hadn't gotten around to building bridges yet. The ferryman overcharged us outrageously, as I recall, but he was a Tolnedran, after all, so that was to be expected.

I'd finally finished the various tasks my Master had given me, and so the wolf and I went eastward toward the Tolnedran Mountains. It was time to go home to the Vale, but I wasn't going to go back through Ulgoland. I wasn't going to go *near* Ulgoland until I found out what had happened there. We tarried for a while once we got into the mountains, however. My companion entertained herself chasing deer and rabbits, but I spent my time looking for that cave our Master had told us about on several occasions. I knew it was in these mountains somewhere, so I took some time to do a little exploring. I didn't plan to do anything about it if I found it, but I wanted to see the place where the Gods had lived while they were creating the world.

To be honest about it, that wasn't the only time I looked for that cave. Every time I passed through those mountains, I'd set aside a week or so to look around. The original home of the Gods would be something to see, after all.

I never found it, of course. It took Garion to do that—many, many years later. Something important was going to happen there, and it didn't involve me.

Beldin had returned from Mallorea when the wolf and I got back to the Vale, but Belzedar wasn't with him. I'd missed my ugly little brother during the century or so that he'd been in Mallorea. There were certain special ties between us, and though it may seem a bit odd, I enjoyed his company.

I reported my successes to our Master, and then I told him about what we had encountered in Ulgoland. He seemed to be as baffled as I'd been.

"Is it possible that the Ulgos did something to offend their God, Master?" I asked him. "Something so serious that he decided to wash his hands of the lot of them and turn the monsters loose again?"

"Nay, my son," Aldur replied, shaking that silvery head of his. "He would not—could not—do that."

"He changed his mind once, Master," I reminded him. "He didn't want any part of mankind when the original Gorim went to Prolgu, as I recall. Gorim had to badger him for years before he finally relented. It's probably uncharitable of me to mention it, but the current Gorim isn't very lovable. He offends *me* with a single look. The heavens only know how offensive he could be once he started talking."

Aldur smiled faintly. "It is uncharitable of thee, Belgarath," he told me. Then he actually laughed. "I must confess that I find myself in full agreement with thee, however. But no, Belgarath, is most patient. Not even the one who is currently Gorim could offend him so much. I will investigate this troubling matter and advise thee of my findings."

"I thank thee, Master," I said, taking my leave. Then I stopped by

Beldin's place to invite him to come by for a few tankards and a bit of talk. I prudently borrowed a keg of ale from the twins on my way home.

Beldin came stumping up the stairs to the room at the top of my tower and drained off his first tankard without stopping for breath. Then he belched and wordlessly handed it back to me for a refill.

I dipped more ale from the keg, and we sat down across the table from each other. "Well?" I said.

"Well what?" That was Beldin for you.

"What's happening in Mallorea?"

"Can you be a little more specific? Mallorea's a big place." The wolf had come over and laid her chin in his lap. She'd always seemed fond of Beldin for some reason. He scratched her ears absently.

"What's Torak doing?" I asked with some asperity.

"Burning, actually." Beldin grinned that ugly, crooked grin of his. "I think our Master's brother's going to burn for a long, long time."

"Is that still going on?" I was a little surprised. "I'd have thought the fire would have gone out by now."

"Not noticeably. You can't see the flames any more, but Old Burnt-face is still on fire. The Orb was very discontented with him, and it *is* a stone, after all. Stones aren't noted for their forgiveness. Torak spends a lot of his time screaming."

"Isn't that a shame?" I said with a vast insincerity.

Beldin grinned at me again. "Anyway," he went on, "after he broke the world apart, he had his Angaraks put the Orb in an iron box so that he wouldn't have to look at it. Just the sight of it makes the fire hotter, I guess. That ocean he'd built was chasing the Angaraks just as fast as it was chasing us, so they ran off to the East with the waves lapping at their heels. All their holy places got swallowed up when the water came in, and they either had to sprout gills or find high ground."

"I find that I can bear their discomfort with enormous fortitude," I said smugly.

"Belgarath, you've been spending too much time with the Alorns. You're even starting to sound like one."

I shrugged. "Alorns aren't really all that bad—once you get used to them."

"I'd rather not. They set my teeth on edge."

"What happened next?"

"That explosion we saw when the water hit the lava boiling up out of the crack in the earth's crust rearranged the geography off to the East rather significantly. There's an impressive new swamp between where Korim used to be and where Kell is."

"Is Kell still there?"

"Kell's always been there, Belgarath, and it probably always will be.

There was a city at Kell before the rest of us came down out of the trees. This new swamp hasn't been there long, but the Angaraks managed to slog through. Torak himself was busy screaming, so his army commanders were obliged to take charge. It didn't take them very long to realize that all that muck wasn't exactly suitable for human habitation."

"I'm surprised that it bothered them. Angaraks adore ugliness."

"Anyway, there was a big argument between the generals and the Grolims, I understand. The Grolims were hoping that the sea would re-cede so that they could all go back to Korim. The altars were there, after all. The generals were more practical. They knew that the water wasn't going to go down. They stopped wasting time arguing and ordered the army to march off toward the northwest and to take the rest of Angarak with them. They marched away and left the Grolims standing on the beach staring longingly off toward Korim." He belched again and held out his empty tankard.

"You know where it is," I told him sourly.

"You're not much of a host, Belgarath." He rose, stumped over to the keg, and scooped his tankard full, slopping beer all over my floor. Then he stumped back. "The Grolims weren't very happy about the generals' decision. They wanted to go back, *but* if they went back all alone, there wouldn't be anybody to butcher but each other, and they're not quite *that* devout. They went chasing after the horde, haranguing them to turn around. That irritated the generals, and there were a number of ugly in-cidents. I guess that's what started the break-up of Angarak society."

"The *what?*" I said, startled.

"I speak plainly, Belgarath. Is your hearing starting to fail? I've heard that happens to you old people."

"What do you mean, 'the breakup of Angarak society'?"

"They're coming apart at the seams. As long as Torak was function-ing, the Grolim priesthood had everything their way. During the war, the generals got a taste of power, and they liked it. With Torak incapacitated, the Grolims really don't have any authority; most Angaraks feel the same way about Grolims as Belsambar does. Anyway, the generals led the Angaraks up through the mountains, and they came down on a plain that was more or less habitable. They built a large military camp at a place they call Mal Zeth, and they put guards around it to keep the Grolims out. Eventually the Grolims gave up and took *their* followers north and built another encampment. They call it Mal Yaska. So now you've got two different kinds of Angaraks in Mallorea. The soldiers at Mal Zeth are like soldiers everywhere; religion isn't one of their highest priorities. The zealots at Mal Yaska spend so much time praying to Torak that they haven't gotten around to building houses yet."

"I wouldn't have believed that could ever happen," I said, "not to

Angaraks. Religion's the only thing they've ever been able to think about." Then I thought of something. "How did Belsambar react when you told him about this?"

Beldin shrugged. "He didn't believe me. He can't accept the fact that Angarak society disintegrated. Our brother's having a lot of trouble right now, Belgarath. I think he's feeling some obscure racial guilt. He *is* an Angarak, after all, and Torak *did* drown more than half of mankind. Maybe you'd better have a talk with him—persuade him that it's not really his fault."

"I'll see what I can do," I promised. "Is that the way things stand in Mallorea right now?"

He laughed. "Oh, no. It gets better. About twenty years ago, Torak stopped feeling sorry for himself and came to his senses. Back in the old days, he'd have simply stamped Mal Zeth into a mud puddle and let it go at that, but now he's got his mind on other things. He stole the Orb, but he can't do anything with it. The frustration's making him more than a little crazy. He winnowed through Mal Zeth and Mal Yaska, took the most fanatic of his worshipers, and went to the Far Northeast coast—up near the lands of the Karands. When they got there, he ordered his followers to build him a tower—out of iron."

"Iron?" I said incredulously. "An iron tower wouldn't last ten years. It would start to rust before you even got it put together."

"He ordered it not to, I guess. Torak's fond of iron for some reason. Maybe he got the idea from that iron box he keeps the Orb in. I think he's got some strange notion that if he piles enough iron around the Orb, he can weaken it to the point that he can control it."

"That's pure nonsense!"

"Don't blame me. It's Torak's idea, not mine. The people he took with him built a city up there, and Torak covered it with clouds— gloomiest place you ever saw. The Angaraks call it Cthol Mishrak—the City of Endless Night. Torak's not nearly as pretty as he used to be—not with half of his face gone—so maybe he's trying to hide. Ugly people do that sometimes. I was born ugly, so I'm used to it. That's pretty much it, Belgarath. The Angaraks have three cities now, Cthol Mishrak, Mal Yaska, and Mal Zeth, and they're going in three different directions. Torak's so busy trying to subdue the Orb that he's not paying any attention to what's going on in Mal Zeth and Mal Yaska. Angarak society's disintegrating, and it couldn't happen to a nicer bunch of people. Oh, one other thing. Evidently Torak was quite impressed with us. He's decided to take disciples of his own."

"Oh? How many?"

"Three so far. There may be more later on. I guess the war taught Torak that disciples are useful people to have around. Before the war, he wasn't interested in sharing power, but that seems to have changed. Did you know that an ordinary priest is powerless once he gets past the boundaries of his own country?"

"I don't quite follow you."

"The Gods aren't above a little cheating now and then. They've each invested their priests with certain limited powers. It helps to keep the faithful in line. An ordinary Grolim—or one of the priests of Nedra or Chaldan, and Salmissra certainly—has *some* ability to do the kinds of things we do. Once they leave the region occupied by the worshipers of their own God, though, that ability goes out the window. A *disciple*, on the other hand, carries it with him wherever he goes. That's the reason we could do things at Korim. Torak saw the value of that and started gathering disciples of his own."

"Any idea of who they are?"

"Two of them used to be Grolims—Urvon and Ctuchik. I couldn't find anything out about the third one."

"Where was Belzedar during all of this?"

"I haven't got the slightest idea. After we flew in and went back to our own shapes, he gave me a few lame excuses about wanting to survey the whole continent and then went off toward the East. I haven't seen him since then. I have no idea of what he's been doing. I'll tell you one thing, though."

"Oh? What's that?"

"Something's definitely gnawing on his bowels. He couldn't wait to get away from me."

"You have that effect on some people, my brother."

"Very funny, Belgarath. Very funny. How much beer have you got left?"

"Just what's in the keg. You've been hitting it fairly hard."

"I've managed to build up a thirst. Have you ever tasted Angarak beer?"

"Not that I recall, no."

"Try to avoid it if you can. Oh, well, if we run out here, we can always go pay a call on the twins, I suppose." And he belched, rose, and lurched back to the beer keg again.

CHAPTER EIGHT

He came in from the west, and at first we thought he was a blind man because he had a strip of cloth covering his eyes. I could tell by his clothes that he was an Ulgo. I'd seen those hooded leather smocks in Prolgu. I was a little surprised to see him, since as far as I knew, the Ulgos had been exterminated. I went out to greet him in his own language. "*Yad ho, groja UL,*" I said. "*Vad mar ishum.*"

He winced. "That is not necessary," he told me in normal speech. "The Gorim has taught me your tongue."

"That's fortunate," I replied a bit ruefully. "I don't speak Ulgo very well."

"Yes," he said with a slight smile, "I noticed that. You would be Belgarath."

"It wasn't entirely my idea. Are you having trouble with your eyes?"

"The light hurts them."

I looked up at the cloudy sky. "It's not really all that bright today."

"Not to you, perhaps," he said. "To me it is blinding. Can you take me to your Master? I have some information for him from Holy Gorim."

"Of course," I agreed quickly. Maybe now we'd find out what was really going on in Ulgoland. "It's this way," I told him, pointing at the Master's tower. I did it automatically, I suppose. He probably couldn't see the gesture with his eyes covered. Then again, maybe he could; he seemed to have no trouble following me.

Belsambar was with our Master. Our mystic Angarak brother had grown increasingly despondent in the years since the cracking of the world. I'd tried to raise his spirits from time to time without much success, and I'd finally suggested to our Master that perhaps it might be a good idea if *he* were to try cheering Belsambar up.

Aldur greeted the Ulgo courteously. "*Yad ho, groja UL.*" His accent was much better than mine.

"*Yad, ho, groja UL,*" the Ulgo responded. "I have news from Gorim of Holy UL."

"I hunger for the words of your Gorim," Aldur replied. Ulgos tend to be a stiff and formal people, and Aldur knew all the correct responses. "How fares it with my father's servants?"

"Not well, Divine Aldur. A catastrophe has befallen us. The wounding of the earth maddened the monsters with whom we had lived in peace since the first Gorim led us to Prolgu."

"So *that's* what it was all about!" I exclaimed.

He gave me a slightly puzzled look.

"I went through Holy Ulgo a few years back, and the Hrulgin and Algroths were trying to hunt me down. Prolgu was deserted, and the she-dragon was sort of hovering over it. What happened, friend?"

He shrugged. "I didn't see it personally," he replied. "It was before my time, but I've spoken with our elders, and they told me that the wounding of the earth shook the very mountains around us. At first they thought that it was no more than an ordinary earthquake, but Holy UL spoke with the old Gorim and told him of what had happened at Korim. It was not long after that that the monsters attacked the people of Ulgo. The old Gorim was slain by an Eldrak—a fearsome creature."

Aldur sighed. "Yes," he agreed. "My brothers and I erred when we made the Eldrakyn. I sorrow for the death of your Gorim." It was a polite thing to say, but I don't think my Master had been any fonder of the previous Gorim than I'd been.

"I didn't know him, Divine One," the Ulgo admitted with a slight shrug. "Our elders have told me that the earth had not yet finished her trembling when the monsters fell on us. Even the Dryads turned savage. The people of Ulgo retreated to Prolgu, thinking that the monsters would fear the holy place, but it was not so. They pursued the people even there. Then it was that UL revealed the caverns to us."

"The caverns," Aldur mused. "Of course. Long have I wondered at the import of those caverns beneath Prolgu. Now it is clear to me. I have also wondered why I could not reach my father's mind when Belgarath told me of his strange adventures in the mountains of Ulgo. I was misdirecting my thought if he is in the caverns with thy people. I marvel at his wisdom. Are the servants of UL safe in those caves?"

"Completely, Divine One. Holy UL placed an enchantment upon the caves, and the monsters feared to follow us there. We have lived in those caverns since the earth was wounded."

"Your brother's curse reaches very far, Master," Belsambar said somberly. "Even the pious people of Ulgo have felt its sting."

Aldur's face grew stern. "It is even as thou hast said, my son," he agreed. "My brother Torak hath much to answer for."

"And his people, as well, Master," Belsambar added. "All of Angarak shares his guilt."

I wish I'd paid closer attention to what Belsambar was saying and to that lost look in his eyes. It was too easy to shrug off Belsambar's moods. He was a thoroughgoing mystic, and they're always a little strange.

"My Gorim has commanded me to advise thee of what has come to pass in Holy Ulgo," our visitor continued. "He asked me to entreat thee to convey this news to thy brethren. Holy Ulgo is no longer safe for mankind. The monsters rage through the mountains and forests, slaying and devouring all who come into their sight. The people of Ulgo no longer venture to the surface, but remain in our caverns where we are safe."

"That's why the light hurts your eyes, isn't it?" I asked him. "You were born and reared in almost total darkness."

"It is even as you say, Ancient Belgarath," he replied. That was the first time anybody ever called me that. I found it just slightly offensive. I wasn't really all *that* old—was I?

"Thus have I completed the task laid upon me by my Gorim," the Ulgo said to my Master. "Now I beg thy permission to return to the caves of my people, for truly, the light of this upper world is agony to me. Mine eyes, like twin knives, do stab into my very brain." He was a poetic rascal; I'll give him that.

"Abide yet a time," Aldur told him. "Night will soon descend, and then mayest thou begin thy journey in what to us would be darkness, but which to thee will be only a more gentle light."

"I shall be guided by thee, Divine One," the Ulgo agreed.

We fed him—that's to say that the twins fed him. Beltira and Belkira have an obsessive compulsion to feed things.

Anyway, our Ulgo left after the sun went down, and he was a half hour gone before I realized that he hadn't even told us his name.

Belsambar and I said good night to the Master, and I walked my Angarak brother back to his tower in the gathering twilight. "It goes on and on, Belgarath," he said to me in a melancholy voice.

"What does?"

"The corruption of the world. It'll never be the same as it was before."

"It never has been, Belsambar. The world changes every day. Somebody dies every night, and somebody's born every morning. It's always been that way."

"Those are natural changes, Belgarath. What's happening now is evil, not natural."

"I think you're exaggerating, brother. We've hit bad stretches before. The onset of winter isn't all that pleasant when you get right down to it, but spring comes back eventually."

"I don't think it will this time. This particular winter's just going to get worse as the years roll by." A mystic will turn *anything* into a metaphor. Metaphors are useful sometimes, but they can be carried too far.

"Winter always passes, Belsambar," I told him. "If we weren't sure of that, there wouldn't really be much point to going on with life, would there?"

"*Is* there a point to it, Belgarath?"

"Yes, there is. Curiosity, if nothing else. Don't you want to see what's going to happen tomorrow?"

"Why? It's just going to be worse." He sighed. "This has been going on for a long time, Belgarath. The universe broke apart when that star exploded, and now Torak's broken the world apart. The monsters of Ulgoland have been maddened, but I think mankind's been maddened, too. Once, a long time ago, we Angaraks were like other people. Torak corrupted us when he gave the Grolims sway over us. The Grolims made us proud and cruel. Then Torak himself was corrupted by his unholy lust for our Master's Orb."

"He found out that was a mistake, though."

"But it didn't change him. He still hungers for dominion over the Orb, even though it maimed him. His hunger brought war into the world, and war corrupted all of the rest of us. You saw me when I first came to the Vale. Could you have believed then that I'd be capable of burning people alive?"

"We had a problem, Belsambar. We were *all* looking for solutions."

"But *I* was the one who rained fire on the Angaraks. *You* wouldn't have; not even *Beldin* would have; but *I* did. And when we started burning my kinsmen, Torak went mad. He wouldn't have broken the world and drowned all those people if I hadn't driven him to it."

"We *all* did things he didn't like, Belsambar. You can't take all the credit."

"You're missing my point, Belgarath. We were *all* corrupted by events. The world turned cruel, and that made *us* cruel as well. The world's no longer fair. It's no more than a rotten, wormy husk of what it once was. Eternal night is coming, and nothing we can do will hold it back."

We'd reached the foot of his tower. I put my hand on his shoulder. "Go to bed, Belsambar," I told him. "Things won't look so bad in the morning when the sun comes up."

He gave me a faint, melancholy smile. "*If* it comes up." Then he embraced me. "Good-bye, Belgarath," he said.

"Don't you mean good night?"

"Perhaps." Then he turned and went into his tower.

It was just after midnight when I was awakened by a thunderous detonation and a great flash of intense light. I leaped from bed and dashed to the window—to stare in total disbelief at the ruins of Belsambar's tower. It was no more than a stump now, and a great column of seething fire was spouting upward from it. The noise and that fire were bad enough, but I also felt a great vacancy as if something had been wrenched out of my very soul. I knew what it was. I no longer had the sense of Belsambar's presence.

I really can't say how long I stood frozen at that window staring at the horror that had just occurred.

"Belgarath! Get down here!" It was Beldin. I could see him clearly, standing at the foot of my tower.

"What happened?" I shouted down to him.

"I *told* you to keep an eye on Belsambar! He just willed himself out of existence! He's gone, Belgarath! Belsambar's gone!"

The world seemed to come crashing down around me. Belsambar had been a little strange, but he was still my brother. Ordinary people who live ordinary lives can't begin to understand just how deeply you can become involved with another person over the course of thousands of years. In a peculiar sort of way, Belsambar's self-obliteration maimed me. I think I'd have preferred to lose an arm or a leg rather than my mystic Angarak brother, and I know that my other brothers felt much the same. Beldin wept for days, and the twins were absolutely inconsolable.

That sense of vacancy that had come over me when Belsambar ended his life echoed all across the world. Even Belzedar and Belmakor, who were both in Mallorea when it happened, felt it, and they came soaring in, a week or so afterward, although I'm not sure what they thought they could do. Belsambar was gone, and there was no way we could bring him back.

We comforted our Master as best we could, although there wasn't really anything we could do to lessen his suffering and sorrow.

You wouldn't have thought it to look at him, but Beldin *did* have a certain sense of delicacy. He waited until he got Belzedar outside the Master's tower before he started to berate him for his behavior in Mallorea. Belmakor and I happened to be present at the time, and we were both enormously impressed by our distorted brother's eloquence. "Irresponsible" was perhaps the kindest word he used. It all went downhill from there.

Belzedar mutely accepted his abuse, which wasn't really at all like him. For some reason, the death of Belsambar seemed to have hit him harder even than it had the rest of us. This is not to say that we all didn't grieve, but Belzedar's grief seemed somehow excessive. With uncharacteristic humility, he apologized to Beldin—not that it did any good. Beldin was in full voice, and he wasn't about to stop just because Belzedar admitted his faults. He eventually started repeating himself, and that was when Belmakor stepped in rather smoothly. "What *have* you been doing in Mallorea, old boy?" he asked Belzedar.

Belzedar shrugged. "What else? I've been attempting to recover our Master's Orb."

"Isn't that just a little dangerous, dear chap? Torak's still a God, you know, and if he catches you, he'll have your liver for breakfast."

"I think I've come up with a way to get around him," Belzedar replied.

"Don't be an idiot," Beldin snapped. "The Master's got enough grief already without your adding to it by getting yourself obliterated following some half-baked scheme."

"It's thoroughly baked, Beldin," Belzedar replied coolly. "I've taken plenty of time to work out all the details. The plan *will* work, and it's the only way we'll ever be able to get the Orb back."

"Let's hear it."

"No, I don't think so. I don't need help, and I definitely don't need any interference." And with that he turned on his heel and walked off toward his tower with Beldin's curses chasing after him.

"I wonder what he's up to," Belmakor mused.

"Something foolish," Beldin replied sourly. "Belzedar's not always the most rational of men, and he's been absolutely obsessed with the Master's Orb since he first laid eyes on it. Sometimes you'd almost think it was something of his own that Torak stole."

"You've noticed that, too, I see," Belmakor said with a faint smile.

"*Noticed* it? How could anyone *miss* it? What were *you* doing in Mallorea?"

"I wanted to see what had happened to my people, actually."

"Well? What did?"

"Torak didn't do them any favors when he cracked the world."

"I don't think he was trying to. What happened?"

"I can't be entirely positive. Melcena was an island kingdom off the east coast, and when Torak started rearranging the world's geography, he managed to sink about half of those islands. That inconvenienced folks just a bit. Now they're all jammed together in what little space they've got left. They appointed a committee to look into it."

"They did *what?*"

"That's the first thing a Melcene thinks of when a crisis of any kind crops up, old boy. It gives us a sense of accomplishment—and we can always blame the committee if things don't work out."

"That's the most ridiculous thing I've ever heard in my life."

"Of course it is. We Melcenes are a ridiculous people. It's part of our charm."

"What did the committee come up with?" I asked him.

"They studied the problem from all angles—for about ten years, actually—and then they filed their report to the government."

"And what were their findings?" I asked.

"The report was five hundred pages long, Belgarath. It'd take me all night to repeat it."

"Boil it down."

"Well, the gist of it was that the Melcene Empire needed more land."

"It took them ten years to come up with *that?*" Beldin demanded incredulously.

"Melcenes are very thorough, old boy. They went on to suggest expansion to the mainland."

"Isn't it already occupied?" I asked him.

"Well, yes, but all of the people along the east coast are of Dallish extraction anyway—until you get farther north into the lands of the Karands—so there's a certain kinship. The Emperor sent emissaries to our cousins in Rengel and Celanta to explore possible solutions to our predicament."

"When did the war start?" Beldin asked bluntly.

"Oh, there wasn't any war, old boy. We Melcenes are far too civilized for that. The emperor's emissaries simply pointed out to the petty kinglets the advantages of becoming a part of the Melcene Empire—and the *disadvantages* of refusing."

"Threats, you mean?" Beldin suggested.

"I wouldn't actually call them threats, dear boy. The emissaries were very polite, of course, but they did manage to convey the notion that the Emperor would be terribly disappointed if he didn't get what he wanted. The little kings got the point almost immediately. Anyway, after the Melcenes established footholds in Rengel and Celanta, they annexed Darshiva and Peldane. Gandahar's giving them some trouble, though. The people in the jungles of Gandahar have domesticated the elephant, and elephant cavalry's a little difficult to cope with. I'm sure they'll work things out, though."

"Do you think they'll expand into the lands of the Dals?" I asked him.

Belmakor shook his head. "That wouldn't be a good idea at all, Belgarath."

"Why? I've never heard that the Dals are a particularly warlike people."

"They aren't, but no one in his right mind crosses the Dals. They're scholars of the arcane, and they've discovered all sorts of things that could make life unpleasant for anybody who blundered into their territory. Have you ever heard of Urvon?"

"He's one of Torak's disciples, isn't he?"

"Yes. He more or less controls the Grolims at Mal Yaska, and Ctuchik runs things in Cthol Mishrak. Anyway, a few years ago Urvon wanted a survey of the native people of Mallorea, so he sent his Grolims out to have a look. The ones he sent to Kell didn't come back. They're still wandering around in the shadow of that huge mountain down there— blind and crazy. Of course, you can't always tell if a Grolim's crazy; they aren't too rational to begin with."

Beldin barked that ugly laugh of his. "You can say that again, brother."

"What *are* the Dals at Kell up to?" I asked curiously.

"All sorts of things—wizardry, necromancy, divining, astrology."

"Don't tell me that they're still into *that* tired old nonsense."

"I'm not entirely positive that it is nonsense, old boy. Astrology's the province of the Seers, and they're more or less at the top of the social structure at Kell. Kell's been there forever, and it doesn't really have what you could call a government. They all just do what the Seers tell them to do."

"Have you ever met one of these Seers?" Beldin asked.

"One—a young woman with a bandage over her eyes."

"How could she read the stars if she's blind?"

"I didn't say that she was blind, old boy. Evidently she only takes the bandage off when she wants to read the Book of the Heavens. She was a strange girl, but the Dals all listened to her—not that what she said made much sense to me."

"That's usually the case with people who pretend to be able to see the future," Beldin noted. "Talking in riddles is a very good way to keep from being exposed as a fraud."

"I don't think they're frauds, Beldin," Belmakor disagreed. "The Dals tell me that no Seer has ever been wrong about what's going to happen. The Seers think in terms of Ages. The Second Age began when Torak broke the world apart."

"It *was* a sort of memorable event," I said. "The Alorns started their calendar that day. I think we're currently in the year one hundred and thirty-eight—or so."

"Foolishness!" Beldin snorted.

"It gives them something to think about beside picking fights with their neighbors."

The she-wolf came loping across the meadow. "One wonders when you are coming home," she said to me pointedly.

"She's almost as bad as a wife, isn't she?" Beldin observed.

She bared her fangs at him. I could never really be sure just how much she understood of what we were saying.

"Are you going back to Mallorea?" I asked Belmakor.

"I don't think so, old boy. I think I'll look in on the Marags instead. I rather like the Marags."

"Well, *I am* going back to Mallorea," Beldin said. "I still want to find out who Torak's third disciple is, and I'd like to keep an eye on Belzedar—if I can keep up with him. Every time I turn around, he's given me the slip." He looked at me. "What are you going to do?"

"Right now I'm going home—before my friend here sinks her fangs into my leg and drags me there."

"I meant it more generally, Belgarath."

"I'm not entirely sure. I think I'll stay around here for a while—until the Master thinks of something else for me to do."

"Well," the wolf said to me, "are you coming home or not?"

"Yes, dear." I sighed, rolling my eyes upward.

It was lonely in the Vale after Belsambar left us. Beldin and Belzedar were off in Mallorea, and Belmakor was down in Maragor, entertaining Marag women, I'm sure. That left only the twins and me to stay with our Master. There was a sort of unspoken agreement among us that the twins would always stay close to Aldur. That particular custom had started right after Torak stole our Master's Orb. I moved around quite a bit during the next several centuries, however. There were still marriages to arrange— and an occasional murder.

Does that shock you? It shouldn't. I've never made any pretense at being a saint, and there *were* people out there in the world who were inconvenient. I didn't tell the Master what I was doing—but he didn't ask, either. I'm not going to waste my time—or yours—coming up with lame excuses. I was driven by Necessity, so I did what was necessary.

The years rolled on. I would have passed my three thousandth birthday without even noticing it if my companion hadn't brought it to my attention. For some reason she always remembered my birthday, and that was very odd. Wolves watch the seasons, not the years, but she never once forgot that day that no longer had any real meaning for me.

I stumbled rather bleary-eyed from my bed that morning. The twins and I had been celebrating something or other the night before. She sat watching me with that silly tongue of hers lolling out. Being laughed at is not a good way to start out the day. "You smell bad," she noted.

"Please don't," I said. "I'm not feeling well this morning."

"Remarkable. You felt very well last night."

"That was then. This is now."

"One is curious to know why you do this to yourself. You know that you will be unwell in the morning."

"It is a custom." I had found over the years that shrugging things off as "a custom" was the best approach with her.

"Oh. I see. Well, if it is a custom, I suppose it is all right. You are older today, you know."

"I feel much, *much* older today."

"You were whelped on this day a long time ago."

"Is it my birthday again? Already? Where *does* the time go?"

"Behind us—or in front. It depends on which way you are look-ing." Can you believe the complexity of that thought coming from a wolf?

"You have been with me for quite some time now."

"What is time to a wolf? One day is much like another, is it not?"

"As I recall it, we first met on the grasslands to the north before the world was broken."

"It was about then, yes."

I made a few quick mental calculations. "A thousand or so of my birthdays have passed since then."

"So?"

"Do wolves normally live so long?"

"You are a wolf—sometimes—and *you* have lived this long."

"That is different. You are a very unusual wolf."

"Thank you. One had thought that you might not have noticed that."

"This is really amazing. I cannot believe that a wolf would live so long."

"Wolves live as long as they choose to live." She sniffed. "One would be more content with you if you would do something about your smell," she added.

You see, Polgara, you weren't the first to make that observation.

———

It was several years later when I had occasion to change my form for some reason that I've long since forgotten. I can't even remember what form I took, but I do remember that it was early summer, and the sun was streaming golden through the open window of my tower, bathing all the clutter of half-forgotten experiments and the heaps of books and scrolls piled against the walls in the pellucid light of that particular season. I'd thought that the wolf was asleep when I did it, but I probably should have known better. Nothing I did ever slipped past her.

She sat up with those golden eyes of hers glowing in the sunlight. "So *that's* how you do it," she said to me. "What a simple thing."

And she promptly turned herself into a snowy white owl.

CHAPTER
NINE

I knew little peace after that. I never knew when I turned around what might be staring at me—wolf or owl, bear or butterfly. She seemed to take great delight in startling me, but as time wore on more and more she appeared to me in the shape of an owl.

"What is this thing about owls?" I growled one day.

"I like owls," she explained, as if it were the simplest thing in the world. "During my first winter, when I was a young and foolish thing, I was chasing a rabbit, floundering around in the snow like a puppy, and a great white owl swooped down and snatched my rabbit almost out of my jaws. She carried it to a nearby tree and ate it, dropping the scraps to me. I thought at the time that it would be a fine thing to be an owl."

"Foolishness." I snorted.

"Perhaps," she replied blandly, preening her tail feathers, "but it amuses me. It may be that one day a different shape will amuse me even more."

Those of you who know my daughter will see how she came by her affinity for that particular shape. Neither Polgara nor my wife will tell me how they communicated with each other during those terrible years when I thought I'd lost Poledra forever, but they obviously did, and Poledra's fondness for owls quite obviously rubbed off. But I'm getting ahead of myself here.

Things went along quietly in the Vale for the next several centuries. We'd set most of the things in motion that needed to be ready for us later, and now we were just marking time.

As I'd been almost sure that it would, Tol Nedrane had burned to the ground, and my badgering of that patriarch of the Honethite family finally paid off. One of his descendants, a minor public official at the time, had that affinity for masonry I'd so carefully bred into his family, and after he'd surveyed the ashes of the city, he persuaded the other city fathers that stone doesn't burn quite as fast as logs and thatch. It's heavier than wood, though, so before they could start erecting stone buildings, they had to fill in the marshy places on the island in the Nedrane. Over the shrill objections of the ferrymen, they built a couple of bridges, one to the south bank of the Nedrane and the other to the north one.

After they'd filled the swamps with rubble, they got down to business. To be quite honest about it, we didn't care if the citizens of Tol Honeth lived in stone houses or in paper shacks. It was the work gangs that were important. They provided the basis for the legions, and we were going to need those legions later. Building stone is too heavy for one man to carry—unless he has the sort of advantages my brothers and I have. The standard work gang of ten men ultimately became the elemental squad. When they had to move larger stones, they'd combine into ten gangs of ten—the typical company. And when they had to install those huge foundation blocks, they'd gather up a hundred gangs of ten—a legion, ob-viously. They had to learn how to cooperate with each other to get the job done, and they learned to take orders from their overseers. I'm sure you get the picture. My Honethite became the general foreman of the whole operation. I'm still sort of proud of him—even though he was a Honeth.

Tolnedra at that time was not nearly as civilized as it is now—if you can call Ce'Nedra civilized. There are always people in any society who'd rather take what they want from others instead of working for it, and Tolnedra was no exception. There were bands of marauding brigands out in the countryside, and when one of those bands attempted to cross the south bridge in order to loot Tol Nedrane, my stonemason ordered his work gangs to drop their tools and take up their weapons. The rest, as they say, is history. My protégé immediately realized what he'd created, and the dream of empire was born.

After the Honethite stonemason had extended his control of the sur-rounding countryside for about twenty leagues in all directions, he changed the name of his native city to Tol Honeth and dubbed himself

Ran Honeth I, Emperor of all Tolnedra—a slightly grandiose title for a man whose "empire" was only about four hundred square leagues, I'll grant you, but it was a start. I felt rather smug about the way it all turned out.

I didn't have time to sit around congratulating myself, though, because it was about then that the Arendish civil wars broke out. I'd invested a lot of effort in Arendia, and I didn't want those families I'd founded getting wiped out in the course of the festivities. The three major cities in Arendia, Vo Mimbre, Vo Wacune, and Vo Astur, had been established fairly early on, and each city, along with its surrounding territory, was ruled by a duke. I'm not certain that the idea of a single king would have occurred to the Arends if the example of the First Honethite Dynasty hadn't existed to the South. It wasn't until much later, however, that the duke of Vo Astur formalized the internal conflict by proclaiming himself king of Arendia.

The informal civil war was trouble enough, though. I'd established families in each of the three duchies, and my major concern at the time was keeping them from encountering each other on the battlefield. If Mandorallen's ancestor had killed Lelldorin's, for example, I'd never have been able to make peace between the two of them.

To add to the confusion in Arendia, herds of Hrulgin and packs of Algroths periodically made forays into eastern Arendia to look for something—somebody—to eat. The Ulgos were down in the caves, so the favorite food of those monsters was in short supply in their home range.

I saw this at firsthand once when I was supposedly guiding the baron of Vo Mandor, Mandorallen's ancestor, toward a battlefield. I didn't want him to reach that field, so I was taking him the long way around. We were near the Ulgo frontier when the Algroths attacked.

Mandorin, the baron, was a Mimbrate to the core, and he and his vassals were totally encased in armor, which protected them from the venomous claws of the Algroths.

Mandorin shouted the alarm to his vassals, clapped down his visor, set his lance, and charged.

Some traits breed very true.

Algroths' courage is a reflection of the pack, not the individual, so when Mandorin and his cohorts began killing Algroths, the courage of the pack diminished. Finally they ran back into the forest.

Mandorin was grinning broadly when he raised his visor. "A frolicsome encounter, Ancient Belgarath," he said gaily. "Their lack of spirit, however, hath deprived us of much entertainment."

Arends!

"You'd better pass along word of this incident, Mandorin," I told him.

"Let everybody in Arendia know that the monsters of Ulgoland are coming down into this forest."

"I shall advise all of Mimbre," he promised. "The safety of the Wacites and Asturians doth not concern me."

"They're your countrymen, Mandorin. That in itself should oblige you to warn them."

"They are mine enemies," he said stubbornly.

"They're still human. Decency alone should spur you to warn them, and you *are* a decent man."

That got his attention. His face was troubled for a moment or so, but he finally came around. "It shall be as you say, Ancient One," he promised. "It shall not truly be necessary, however."

"Oh?"

"Once we have concluded our business with the Asturians, I shall myself, with some few companions, mount an expedition into the mountains of Ulgo. Methinks it will be no great chore to exterminate these troublesome creatures."

Mandorallen himself would not have said it any differently.

It was about fifteen hundred years after the cracking of the world when Beldin came back from Mallorea to fill us in on Torak and his Angaraks. Belmakor left his entertainments in Maragor to join us, but there was still no sign of Belzedar. We gathered in the Master's tower and took our usual chairs. The fact that Belzedar's chair was empty bothered us all, I think.

"It was absolute chaos in Mallorea for a while," Beldin reported. "The Grolims from Mal Yaska were selecting their sacrificial victims almost exclusively from the officer corps of the army, and the generals were arresting and executing every Grolim they could lay their hands on, charging them with all sorts of specious crimes. Finally Torak got wind of it, and he put a stop to it."

"Pity," Belmakor murmured. "What did he do?"

"He summoned the military high command and the Grolim hierarchy to Cthol Mishrak and delivered an ultimatum. He told them that if they didn't stop their secret little war, they could all just jolly well pick up and move to Cthol Mishrak where he could keep an eye on them. That got their immediate attention. They could live in at least semiautonomy in Mal Zeth and Mal Yaska, and the climate in those two cities isn't all that bad. Cthol Mishrak's like a suburb of Hell. It's on the southern edge of an arctic swamp, and it's so far north that the days are only about two hours long in the wintertime—if you can call what comes after dawn up there 'day.' Torak's put a perpetual cloud bank over the place, so it never really gets light. 'Cthol Mishrak' means 'the City of Endless Night,' and that comes fairly close to describing it. The sun never touches the ground, so the only thing that grows around there is fungus."

Beltira shuddered. "Why would he do that?" he asked, his expression baffled.

Beldin shrugged. "Who knows why Torak does anything? He's crazy. Maybe he's trying to hide his face. I think that what finally brought the generals and the Grolims to heel, though, was the fact that the disciple Ctuchik runs things in Cthol Mishrak. I've met Urvon, and he can chill the blood of a snake just by looking at it. Ctuchik's reputed to be even worse."

"Have you found out who the third disciple is yet?" I asked.

Beldin shook his head. "Nobody's willing to talk about him. I get the impression that he's not an Angarak."

"That is very unlike my brother," Aldur mused. "Torak doth hold the other races of man in the profoundest of contempt."

"I could be wrong, Master," Beldin admitted, "but the Angaraks themselves seem to believe that he's not one of them. Anyway, the threat of being required to return to Cthol Mishrak brought out the peaceful side of Urvon's nature, and Urvon rules in Mal Yaska. He started making peace overtures to the generals almost immediately."

"Does Urvon really have that much autonomy?" Belkira asked.

"Up to a point, yes. Torak concentrates on the Orb and leaves the administrative details to his disciples. Ctuchik's absolute master in Cthol Mishrak, and Urvon sits on a throne in Mal Yaska. He adores being adored. The only other power center in Angarak Mallorea is Mal Zeth. Logic suggests that Torak's third disciple is there—probably working behind the scenes. Anyway, once Urvon and the generals declared peace on each other, Torak told them to behave themselves and sent them home. They hammered out the details later. The Grolims have absolute sway in Mal Yaska, and the generals in Mal Zeth. All the other towns and districts are ruled jointly. Neither side likes it very much, but they don't have much choice."

"Is that the way things stand right now?" Belkira asked.

"It's moved on a bit from there. Once the generals got the Grolims out of their hair, they were free to turn their attention to the Karands."

"Ugly brutes," Belmakor observed. "The first time I saw one, I couldn't believe he was human."

"They've been sort of humanized now," Beldin told him. "The Angaraks started having trouble with the Karands almost as soon as they came up out of the Dalasian Mountains. The Karands have a sort of loose confederation of seven kingdoms in the northeast quadrant of the continent. Torak's new ocean did some radical things to the climate up there.

They'd been in the middle of an ice age in Karanda—lots of snow, glaciers, and all that, but all the steam that came boiling out of the crack
in the world melted it off almost overnight. There used to be a little
stream called the Magan that meandered down out of the Karandese
Mountains in a generally southeasterly direction until it emptied out into
the ocean down in Gandahar. When the glaciers melted all at once, it
stopped being so gentle. It gouged a huge trench three-quarters of the way
across the continent. That sent the Karands off in search of high ground.
Unfortunately, the high ground they located just happened to be in lands
claimed by the Angaraks."

"I wouldn't call it all that unfortunate," Belmakor said. "If the
Angaraks are busy with the Karands, they won't come pestering us."

"The unfortunate part came later," Beldin told him. "As long as the
generals were squabbling with the Grolims, they didn't have time to deal
with the Karands. Once Torak settled *that* particular problem, the generals moved their army up to the borders of the Karandese Kingdom of Pallia, and then they invaded. The Karands were no match for them, and
they crushed Pallia in about a month. The Grolims started sharpening
their gutting knives, but the generals wanted to leave Pallia intact—
paying tribute, of course. They suggested that the Karands in Pallia be
converted to the worship of Torak. That made the Grolims crazy. So far
as *they* were concerned, the other races of mankind were good only as
slaves or sacrifices. Anyway, to keep it short, Torak thought it over and
eventually sided with the military. Their solution gives him more worshipers, for one thing, and it'll give him a much bigger army just in case
Belar ever finds a way to lead his Alorns onto the Mallorean continent.
Alorns seem to make Torak nervous, for some reason."

"You know," Belmakor said, "they have the same effect on me. Maybe
it has something to do with their tendency to go berserk at the slightest
provocation."

"Torak took the whole idea one step further," Beldin went on. "He
wasn't satisfied with just Pallia. He ordered the Grolims to go out and
convert *all* of Karanda. 'I will have them all,' he told the Grolims. 'Any
man who liveth in all of boundless Mallorea shall bow down to me, and
if any of ye shirk in this stern responsibility, ye shall feel my displeasure
most keenly.' That got the Grolims' attention, and they went out to convert the heathens."

"This is troubling," Aldur said. "So long as my brother had only his
Angaraks, we could easily match his numbers. His decision to accept
other races alters our circumstances."

"He's not having all that much success, Master," Beldin advised him.
"He succeeded in converting the Karands, largely because his army's supe-

rior to those howling barbarians, but when the generals got to the borders of the Melcene Empire, they ran head-on into elephant cavalry. It was very messy, I'm told. The generals pulled back and swept down into Dalasia instead." He looked at Belmakor. "I thought you said that the Dals had cities down there."

"They used to—at least they did the last time I was there."

"Well, there aren't any there now—except for Kell, of course. When the Angaraks moved in, there wasn't anything there but farming villages with mud-and-wattle huts."

"Why would they do that?" Belmakor asked in bafflement. "They had beautiful cities. Tol Honeth looks like a slum by comparison."

"They had reasons," Aldur assured him. "The destruction of their cities was likely a subterfuge to keep the Angaraks from realizing how sophisticated they really are."

"They didn't look all that sophisticated to me," Beldin said. "They still plow their fields with sticks, and they've got almost as much spirit as sheep."

"Also a subterfuge, my son."

"The Angaraks didn't have any trouble converting them, Master. The idea of having a God after all these eons—even a God like Torak—brought them in by the thousands. Was that a pretense, too?"

Aldur nodded. "The Dals will go to any lengths to conceal their real tasks from the unlearned."

"Did the generals ever try to go back into the Melcene Empire?" Belmakor asked.

"Not after that first time, no," Beldin replied. "Once you've seen a few battalions trampled by elephants, you start to get the picture. There's a bit of trade between the Angaraks and Melcenes, but that's about as far as their contacts go."

"You said you'd met Urvon," Belkira said. "Was that in Cthol Mishrak or Mal Yaska?"

"Mal Yaska. I stay clear of Cthol Mishrak because of the Chandim."

"Who are the Chandim?" I asked him.

"They used to be Grolims. Now they're dogs—as big as horses. Some people call them 'the Hounds of Torak.' They patrol the area around Cthol Mishrak, sniffing out intruders. They'd have probably picked me out rather quickly. I was on the outskirts of Mal Yaska, and I happened to see a Grolim coming in from the east. I cut his throat, stole his robe, and slipped into the city. I was snooping around in the temple when Urvon surprised me. He knew right off that I wasn't a Grolim—recognizin' me unspeakable talent almost immediately, don't y' know." For some unaccountable reason he lapsed into a brogue that was common among Wacite serfs in northern Arendia. Maybe he did it because he knew it would irritate me, and Beldin never misses an opportunity to tweak my nose.

Never mind. It'd take far too long to explain.

"I was a bit startled by the man's appearance," my dwarfed brother continued. "He's one of those splotchy people you see now and then. Angaraks are an olive-skinned race—sort of like Tolnedrans are—but Urvon's got big patches of dead-white skin all over him. He looks like a piebald horse. He blustered at me a bit, threatening to call the guards, but I could almost smell the fear on him. *Our* training is much more extensive than the training Torak gave *his* disciples, and Urvon knew that I outweighed him—metaphorically speaking, of course. I didn't like him very much, so I overwhelmed him with my charm—*and* with the fact that I picked him up bodily and slammed him against the wall a few times. Then, while he was trying to get his breath, I told him that if he made a sound or even so much as moved, I'd yank out his guts with a white-hot hook. Then, to make my point, I showed him the hook."

"Where did you get the hook?" Beltira asked.

"Right here." Beldin held out his gnarled hand, snapped his fingers, and a glowing hook appeared in his fist. "Isn't it lovely?" He shook his fingers and the hook disappeared. "Urvon evidently believed me— although it's a bit hard to say for sure, since he fainted right there on the spot. I gave some thought to hanging him from the rafters on my hook, but I decided that I was there to observe, not to desecrate temples, so I left him sprawled on the floor and went back out into the countryside where the air was cleaner. Grolim temples have a peculiar stink about them." He paused and scratched vigorously at one armpit. "I think I'd better stay out of Mallorea for a while. Urvon's got my description posted on every tree. The size of the reward he's offering is flattering, but I guess I'll let things cool down a bit before I go back."

"Good thinking," Belmakor murmured, and then he collapsed in helpless laughter.

My life changed rather profoundly a few weeks later. I was bent over my worktable when my companion swooped in through the window she'd finally convinced me to leave open for her, perched sedately on her favorite chair, and shimmered back into her proper wolf-shape. "I think I will go away for a while," she announced.

"Oh?" I said cautiously.

She stared at me, her golden eyes unblinking. "I think I would like to look at the world again."

"I see."

"The world has changed much, I think."

"It is possible."

"I might come back some day."

"I would hope so."

"Good-bye, then," she said, blurred into the form of an owl again, and with a single thrust of her great wings she was gone.

Her presence during those long years had been a trial to me sometimes, but I found that I missed her very much. I often turned to show her something, only to realize that she was no longer with me. I always felt strangely empty and sad when that happened. She'd been a part of my life for so long that it had seemed that she'd always be there.

Then, about a dozen years later, my Master summoned me and instructed me to go to the Far North to look in on the Morindim. Their practice of raising demons had always concerned him, and he very definitely didn't want them to get *too* proficient at it.

The Morindim were—still are, I guess—far more primitive than their cousins, the Karands. They both worship demons, but the Karands have evolved to the point where they're able to live in at least a semblance of a normal life. The Morindim can't—or won't. The clans and tribes of Karanda smooth over their differences for the common good, largely because the chieftains have more power than the magicians. The reverse is true among the Morindim, and each magician is a sublime egomaniac who views the very existence of other magicians as a personal insult. The Morindim live in nomadic, primitive tribalism, and the magicians keep their lives circumscribed by rituals and mystic visions. To put it bluntly, a Morind lives in more or less perpetual terror.

I journeyed through Aloria to the north range of mountains in what is now Gar og Nadrak. Belsambar had filled us all in on the customs of those savages after his long-ago survey of the area, so I knew more or less how to make myself look like a Morind. Since I wanted to discover what I could about their practice of raising demons, I decided that the most efficient way to do it was to apprentice myself to one of the magicians.

I paused long enough at the verge of their vast, marshy plain to disguise myself, darkening my skin and decorating it with imitation tattoos. Then, after I'd garbed myself in furs and ornamented myself with feathers, I went looking for a magician.

I'd been careful to include quest-markings—the white fur headband and the red-painted spear with feathers dangling from it—as a part of my disguise, since the Morindim usually consider it unlucky to interfere with a quester. On one or two occasions, though, I had to fall back on my own particular form of magic to persuade the curious—or the belligerent—to leave me alone.

I happened across a likely teacher after about a week in those barren wastes. A quester is usually an aspiring magician anyway, and a burly fellow wearing a skull-surmounted headdress accosted me while I was crossing one of the innumerable streams that wander through that arctic waste. "You wear the marks of a quester," he said in a challenging sort of way as the two of us stood hip deep in the middle of an icy stream.

"Yes," I replied in a resigned sort of way. "I didn't ask for it. It just sort of came over me." Humility and reluctance are becoming traits in the young, I suppose.

"Tell me of your vision."

I rather quickly evaluated this big-shouldered, hairy, and somewhat odorous magician. There wasn't really all that much to evaluate. "All in a dream," I said. "I saw the king of Hell squatting on the coals of infernity, and he spoke to me and told me to go forth across the length and breadth of Morindicum and to seek out that which has always been hidden. This is my quest." It was pure gibberish, of course, but I think the word "infernity"—which I made up on the spur of the moment—got his attention.

I've always had this way with words.

"Should you survive this quest of yours, I will accept you as my apprentice—and my slave."

I've had better offers, but I decided not to negotiate. I was here to learn, not to correct bad manners.

"You seem reluctant," he observed.

"I'm not the wisest of men, Master," I confessed, "and I have little skill with magic. I would be more happy if this burden had been placed on another."

"It is yours to bear, however," he roared at me. "Behold the gift that is mine to give." He quickly sizzled out a design on the top of the water with a burning forefinger, evidently not observing that the swift current of the stream carried it off before he'd even finished his drawing.

He raised a Demon Lord, one of the Disciples of the king of Hell. Now that I think back on it, I believe it was Mordja. I met Mordja many years later, and he did look a bit familiar to me. "What is this thou hast done?" Mordja demanded in that awful voice of his.

"I have summoned thee to obey me," my prospective tutor declared, ignoring the fact that his protective design was a half-mile downstream by now.

Mordja—if it was Mordja—laughed. "Behold the face of the water, fool," he said. "There is no longer protection for thee. And therefore—"

He reached out one huge, scaly hand, picked up my prospective "Master," and bit off his head. "A bit thin," he observed, crushing the skull and brains with those awful teeth. He negligently tossed away the still-quivering carcass and turned those baleful eyes on me.

I left rather hurriedly at that point.

I eventually found a less demonstrative magician who was willing to take me on. He was very old, which was an advantage, since the apprentice to a magician is required to become his "Master's" slave for life. He lived alone in a dome-shaped tent made of musk-ox hides on a gravel bar beside one of those streams. His tent was surrounded by a kitchen midden, since he had the habit of throwing his garbage out of the front door of his tent rather than burying it. The bar was backed by a thicket of stunted bushes that were enveloped by clouds of mosquitoes in the summertime.

He mumbled a lot and didn't make much sense, but I gathered that his clan had been exterminated in one of those wars that are always breaking out among the Morindim.

My contempt for "magic" as opposed to what *we* do dates from that period in my life. Magic involves a lot of meaningless mumbo-jumbo, cheap carnival tricks, and symbols drawn on the ground. None of that is really necessary, of course, but the Morindim believe that it is, and their belief makes it so.

My smelly old "Master" started me out on imps—nasty little things about knee high. When I'd gotten that down pat, I moved up to fiends and then up again to afreets. After a half-dozen years or so, he finally decided that I was ready to try my hand on a full-grown demon. In a rather chillingly offhand manner, he advised me that I probably wouldn't survive my first attempt. After what had happened to my first "Master," I had a pretty good idea of what he was talking about.

I went through all that nonsensical ritual and raised a demon. He wasn't a very *big* demon, but he was as much as I wanted to try to cope with. The whole secret to raising demons is to confine them in a shape of *your* imagining rather than their natural form. As long as you keep them locked into your conception of them, they have to obey you. If they manage to break loose and return to their *real* form, you're in trouble.

I rather strongly advise you not to try it.

Anyway, I managed to keep my medium-size demon under control so that he couldn't turn on me. I made him perform a few simple tricks—turning water into blood, setting fire to a rock, withering an acre or so of grass—

you know the sort of tricks I'm talking about—and then, because I was getting *very* tired of hunting food, I sent him out with instructions to bring back a couple of musk-oxen. He scampered off, howling and growling, and came back a half-hour or so later with enough meat to feed my "Master" and me for a month. Then I sent him back to Hell.

I *did* thank him, though, which I think confused him more than just a little.

The old magician was very impressed, but he fell ill not long afterward. I nursed him through his last illness as best I could and gave him a decent burial after he died. I decided at that point that I'd found out as much as we needed to know about the Morindim, and so I discarded my disguise and went back home again.

On my way back to the Vale I came across a fair-sized, neatly thatched cottage in a grove of giant trees near a small river. It was just on the northern edge of the Vale, and I'd passed that way many times over the years. I'll take an oath that the house had never been there before. Moreover, to my own certain knowledge, there was not another human habitation within five hundred leagues, except for our towers in the Vale itself. I wondered who might have built a cottage in such a lonely place, so I went to the door to investigate these hardy pioneers.

There was only one occupant, though, a woman who seemed young, and yet perhaps not quite so young. Her hair was tawny and her eyes a curious golden color. Oddly, she didn't wear any shoes, and I noticed that she had pretty feet.

She stood in the doorway as I approached—almost as if she'd been expecting me. I introduced myself, advising her that we were neighbors—which didn't seem to impress her very much. I shrugged, thinking that she was probably one of those people who preferred to be alone. I was on the verge of bidding her good-bye when she invited me in for supper. It's the oddest thing. I hadn't been particularly hungry when I'd approached the cottage, but no sooner did she mention food than I found myself suddenly ravenous.

The inside of her cottage was neat and cheery, with all those little touches that immediately identify a house in which a woman lives as opposed to the cluttered shacks where men reside. It was quite a bit larger than the word "cottage" implies, and even though it was none of my business, I wondered why she needed so much room.

She had curtains at her windows—naturally—and earthenware jars filled with wildflowers on her windowsills and on the center of her glowing oak table. A fire burned merrily on her hearth, and a large kettle bubbled and hiccuped over it. Wondrous smells came from that kettle and from the loaves of freshly baked bread on the hearth.

"One wonders if you would care to wash before you eat," she suggested with a certain delicacy.

To be honest, I hadn't even thought about that.

She seemed to take my hesitation for agreement. She fetched me a pail of water, warm from the hearth, a cloth, a towel of sorts, and a cake of brown country soap. "Out there," she told me, pointing at the door.

I went back outside, set the pail on a stand beside the door, and washed my hands and face. Almost as an afterthought, I pulled off my tunic and soaped down my upper torso, as well. I dried off with the towel, pulled my tunic back on, and went inside again.

She sniffed. "Much better," she said approvingly. Then she pointed at the table. "Sit," she told me. "I will bring you food." She fetched an earthenware plate from a cupboard, padding silently barefooted over her well-scrubbed floor. Then she knelt on her hearth, ladled the plate full, and brought me a meal such as I had not seen in years.

Her easy familiarity seemed just a bit odd, but it somehow stepped over that awkwardness that I think we all feel when we first meet strangers.

After I'd eaten—more than I should have, probably—we talked, and I found this strange, tawny-haired woman to have the most uncommon good sense. This is to say that she agreed with most of my opinions.

Have you ever noticed that? We base our assessment of the intelligence of others almost entirely on how closely their thinking matches our own. I'm sure that there are people out there who violently disagree with me on most things, and I'm broad-minded enough to concede that they might possibly not be *complete* idiots, but I much prefer the company of people who agree with me.

You might want to think about that.

I enjoyed her company, and I found myself thinking up excuses not to leave. She was a remarkably handsome woman, and there was a fragrance about her that made my senses reel. She told me that her name was Poledra, and I liked the sound of it. I found that I liked almost everything about her. "One wonders by what name *you* are called," she said after she had introduced herself.

"I'm Belgarath," I replied, "and I'm first disciple of the God Aldur."

"How remarkable," she noted, and then she laughed, touching my arm familiarly as if we'd known each other for years.

I lingered in her cottage for a few days, and then I regretfully told her that I had to go back to the Vale to report what I'd found out in the north to my Master.

"I will go along with you," she told me. "From what you say, there are remarkable things to be seen in your Vale, and I was ever curious." Then she closed the door of her house and returned with me to the Vale.

Strangely, my Master was waiting for us, and he greeted Poledra courteously. I can never really be sure, but it seemed to me that some mysterious glance passed between them as if they knew each other and shared some secret that I was not aware of.

All right. I'm not stupid. Naturally I had some suspicions, but as time went by, they became less and less important, and I quite firmly put them out of my mind.

Poledra simply moved into my tower with me. We never actually discussed it; she just took up residence. That raised a few eyebrows among my brothers, to be sure, but I'll fight anyone who has the bad manners to suggest that there was anything improper about our living arrangements. It put my willpower to the test, I'll admit, but I behaved myself. That always seemed to amuse Poledra for some reason.

I thought my way through our situation extensively that winter, and I finally came to a decision—a decision Poledra had obviously made a long time ago. She and I were married the following spring. My Master himself, burdened though he was, blessed our union.

There was joy in our marriage, and a kind of homey, familiar comfort. I never once thought about those things that I had prudently decided not to think about, so they in no way clouded the horizon. But that, of course, is another story.

Don't rush me. We'll get to it—all in good time.

CHAPTER
TEN

I'm sure you can understand that I wanted peace in the world at that particular time. A newly married man has better things to do than to dash off to curb the belligerence of others. Unfortunately, it was no more than a couple of years after Poledra and I were married when the Alorn clan wars broke out. Aldur summoned the twins and me to his tower as soon as word of that particular idiocy reached us. "Ye must go there," he told us in a tone that didn't encourage disagreement. Our Master seldom commanded us, so we paid rather close attention to him when he did. "It is essential that the current royal house of Aloria remain in power. One will descend from that line who will be vital to our interests."

I wasn't *too* thrilled at the prospect of leaving Poledra behind, but I certainly wasn't going to take her into the middle of a war. "Wilt thou look after my wife, Master?" I asked him. It was a foolish question, of course. Naturally he'd look after her, but I wanted him to understand my reluctance to go to Aloria and my reasons for it.

"She will be safe with me," he assured me.

Safe, perhaps, but not happy about being left behind. She argued with me about it at first, but I led her to believe that it was Aldur's command—which wasn't *exactly* a lie, was it? "I won't be all that long," I promised her.

"Don't be," she replied. "One would have you understand that one is discontented about this."

Anyway, the twins and I left the Vale and started north the first thing the next morning. When we reached the cottage where I'd met Poledra, the she-wolf was waiting for us. The twins were somewhat surprised, but I don't think I really was. "Another of those errands?" she asked me.

"Yes," I replied flatly, "and one does not require company."

"Your requirements are none of my concern," she told me, her tone just as flat as mine. "I will go along with you whether you like it or not."

"As you wish." I surrendered. I'd learned a long time ago just how useless it was to give her orders.

And so we were four when we reached the southern border of Aloria and began looking for Belar. I think he was avoiding us, though, because we weren't able to find him. He could have stopped the clan wars at any time, of course, but Belar had a stubborn streak in him that was at least a mile wide. He absolutely would not take sides when his Alorns started bickering with each other. Even-handedness is probably a good trait in a God, but this was ridiculous. We finally gave up our search for him and went on to the mouth of the river that bears our Master's name and looked out across what has come to be known as the Gulf of Cherek. We saw ships out there, but they didn't look all that seaworthy to me. A flat-bottomed scow with a squared-off front end isn't my idea of a corsair that skims the waves. The twins and I talked it over and decided to change form and fly across rather than hail one of those leaky tubs.

"One notes that you still have not learned to fly well," the snowy owl ghosting along at my side observed.

"I get by," I told her, clawing at the air with my wings.

"But not well." She *always* had to get in the last word, so I didn't bother trying to answer, but concentrated instead on keeping my tail feathers out of the water.

After what seemed an interminable flight, we reached the crude sea-port that stood on the site of what's now Val Alorn and went looking for King Chaggat's direct descendant, King Uvar Bent-beak. We found him splitting wood in the stump-dotted clearing outside his log house. Ran Vordue IV, the then-current Emperor of Tolnedra, lived in a palace. Uvar Bent-beak ruled an empire at least a dozen times the size of Tolnedra, but he lived in a log shack with a leaky roof, and I don't think it ever oc-curred to him to order one of his thralls to chop his firewood for him. Thralldom never really worked in Aloria, since Alorns don't make good slaves. The institution was never actually abolished. It just fell into dis-use. Anyway, Uvar was stripped to the waist, sweating like a pig, and chopping for all he was worth.

"Hail, Belgarath," he greeted me, sinking his axe into his chopping block and mopping the sweat off his bearded face. I always kept in touch with the Alorn kings, so he knew me on sight.

"Hail, Bent-beak," I replied. "What's going on up here?"

"I'm cutting wood," he told me, his face very serious.

"Yes," I said, "I noticed that almost immediately, but that wasn't what I was talking about. We heard that you've got a war on your hands."

Uvar had little piglike eyes, and he squinted at me around that huge broken nose of his. "Oh," he said, "that. It's not much of a war really. I can deal with it."

"Uvar," I told him as patiently as I could, "if you plan to deal with it, don't you think it's time you got started? It's been going on for a year and a half now."

"I've been sort of busy, Belgarath," he said defensively. "I had to patch my roof, and winter's coming on, so I have to lay in a store of firewood."

Can you *believe* that this man was a direct ancestor of King Anheg?

To hide my exasperation with him, I introduced the twins.

"Why don't we all go inside?" Uvar suggested. "I've got a barrel of fairly good ale, and I'm a little tired of splitting wood anyway."

The twins, with an identical gesture, concealed the grins that came to their faces, and we went into Uvar's "palace," a cluttered shack with a dirt floor and the crudest furniture you can imagine.

"What started this war, Uvar?" I asked the King of Aloria after we had all pulled chairs up to his wobbly table and sampled his ale.

"Religion, Belgarath," he replied. "Isn't that what starts every war?"

"Not always, but we can talk about that some other time. How could religion start a war in Aloria? You people are all fully committed to Belar."

"Some are a little more committed than others," he said, making a sour face. "Belar's idea of going after the Angaraks is all very well, I suppose, but we can't get at them because there's an ocean in the way. There's a priest in a place off to the east somewhere who's just a little thick-witted." *This?* Coming from *Uvar?* I shudder to think of how stupid that priest must have been for Uvar to notice!

"Anyway," the king went on, "this priest has gathered up an army of sorts, and he wants to invade the kingdoms of the South."

"Why?"

Uvar shrugged. "Because they're there, I suppose. If they weren't there, he wouldn't want to invade them, would he?"

I suppressed an urge to grab him and shake him. "Have they done anything to offend him?" I asked.

"Not that I know of. You see, Belar's been away for a while. He gets homesick for the old days sometimes, so he takes some girls, a group of warriors, several barrels of beer, and goes off to set up a camp in the woods. He's been gone for a couple of years now. Anyway, this priest has decided that the southern kingdoms ought to join us when we go to make war on the Angaraks and that it'd probably be more convenient if we all worshiped the same God. He came to me with his crazy idea, and I ordered him to forget about it. He didn't, though, and he's been out preaching to the other clans. He's managed to persuade about half of them to join him, but the other half is still loyal to me. They're fighting each other off there a ways." He made a vague gesture toward the east. "I don't think the clans that went over to him are so interested in religion as they are in the chance to loot the southern kingdoms. The really religious ones have formed what they call the Bear-cult. I think it's got something to do with Belar—except that Belar doesn't know anything about it." He drained off his tankard and went into the pantry for more ale.

"He's not going to move until he finishes cutting firewood," Belkira said quietly.

I nodded glumly. "Why don't you two see what you can do to speed that up?" I suggested.

"Isn't that cheating?" Beltira asked me.

"Maybe, but we've got to get him moving before winter settles in."

They nodded and went back outside again.

Uvar was a little startled by how much his woodpile had grown when he and I went back outside again. "Well," he said, "now that that's been taken care of, I guess maybe I'd better go do something about that war."

The twins and I cheated outrageously in the next several months, and we soon had the breakaway clans on the run. There was a fairly large battle on the eastern plains of what is now Gar og Nadrak. Uvar might have been a little slow of thought, but he was tactician enough to know the advantage of taking and holding the high ground and concealing the full extent of his forces from his enemies. We quietly occupied a hill during the middle of the night. Uvar's troops littered the hillside with sharpened stakes until the hillside looked like a hedgehog, and his reserves hunkered down on the back side of the hill.

The breakaway clans and Bear-cultists who had camped on the plain woke up the next morning to find Uvar staring down their throats. Since they were Alorns, they attacked.

Most people fail to understand the purpose of sharpened stakes. They aren't there to skewer your opponent. They're there to slow him down enough to give you a clean shot at him. Uvar's bowmen got lots of practice that morning. Then, when the rebels were about halfway up the hill, Uvar blew a cow's-horn trumpet, and his reserves swept out in two great wings from behind the hill to savage the enemy's rear.

It worked out fairly well. The clansmen and the cultists didn't really have any options, so they kept charging up the hill, slashing at the stakes with their swords and axes. The founder of the Bear-cult, a big fellow with bad eyesight, came hacking his way up toward us. I think the poor devil had gone berserk, actually. He was frothing at the mouth by the time he got through all the stakes, anyway.

Uvar was waiting for him. As it turned out, the months the King of Aloria had spent splitting wood paid off. Without so much as changing expression, Bent-beak lifted his axe and split the rebellious priest of Belar from the top of his head to his navel with one huge blow. Resistance more or less collapsed at that point, and the Bear-cult went into hiding, while the rebellious clans suddenly became very fond of their king and renewed their vows of fealty.

Now do you see why war irritates me? It's always the same. A lot of people get killed, but in the end, the whole thing is settled at the conference table. The notion of having the conference first doesn't seem to occur to people.

The she-wolf's observations were chilling. "One wonders what they plan to do with the meat," she said. That raised the hackles on the back of my neck, but I rather dimly perceived a way to end wars forever. If the victorious army had to *eat* the fallen, war would become much less attractive. I'd gone wolf enough to know that meat is flavored by the diet of the eatee, and stale beer isn't the best condiment in the world.

Uvar was clearly in control now, so the twins, the wolf, and I went back to the Vale. The wolf, of course, left us when we reached Poledra's cottage, and my wife was in my tower when I got there, looking for all the world as if she'd been there all along.

Belmakor had returned during our absence, but he'd locked himself in his tower, refusing to respond when we urged him to come out. The Master told us that our Melcene brother had gone into a deep depression for some reason, and we knew him well enough to know that he wouldn't appreciate any attempts to cheer him up. I've always been somewhat suspicious about Belmakor's depression. If I could ever confirm those suspicions, I'd go back to where Belzedar is right now and put him someplace a lot more uncomfortable.

This was a painful episode, so I'm going to cut it short. After several years of melancholy brooding about the seeming hopelessness of our endless tasks, Belmakor gave up and decided to follow Belsambar into obliteration.

I think it was only the presence of Poledra that kept me from going mad. My brothers were dropping around me, and there was nothing I could do to prevent it.

Aldur summoned Belzedar and Beldin back to the Vale, of course. Beldin had been down in Nyissa keeping an eye on the Serpent People, and we all assumed that Belzedar had still been in Mallorea, although it didn't take him long to arrive. He seemed peculiarly reluctant to join us in our sorrow, and I've always thought less of him because of his attitude. Belzedar had changed over the years. He still refused to give us any details about his scheme to retrieve the Orb—not that we really had much opportunity to talk with him, because he was quite obviously avoiding us. He had a strangely haunted look on his face that I didn't think had anything to do with our common grief. It seemed too personal somehow. After about a week, he asked Aldur for permission to leave, and then he went back to Mallorea.

"One notes that your brother is troubled," Poledra said to me after he'd gone. "It seems that he's trying to follow two paths at once. His mind is divided, and he doesn't know which of the paths is the true one."

"Belzedar's always been a little strange," I agreed.

"One would suggest that you shouldn't trust him too much. He's not telling you everything."

"He's not telling me *anything*," I retorted. "He hasn't been completely open with us since Torak stole the Master's Orb. To be honest with you, love, I've never been so fond of him that I'm not going to lose any sleep over the fact that he wants to avoid us."

"Say that again," she told me with a warm smile.

"Say what again?"

"Love. It's a nice word, and you don't say it very often."

"You know how I feel about you, dear."

"One likes to be told."

"Anything that makes you happy, love." I will *never* understand women.

Beldin and I spoke together at some length about Belzedar's growing aloofness, but we ultimately concluded that there wasn't very much we could do about it.

Then Beldin raised another issue that was of more immediate concern. "There's trouble in Maragor," he told me.

"Oh?"

"I was on my way back form Nyissa when I heard about it. I was in a hurry, so I didn't have time to look into it very deeply."

"What's going on?"

"Some idiot misread one of their sacred texts. Mara must have been about half asleep when he dictated it. Either that, or the scribe who was writing it down misunderstood him. It hinges on the word 'assume.' The

Marags are taking the word quite literally, I understand. They've taken to making raids across their borders. They capture Tolnedrans or Nyissans and take them back to Mar Amon. They have a big religious ceremony, and the captives are killed. Then the Marags eat them."

"They do *what?*"

"You heard me, Belgarath. The Marags are practicing ritual cannibalism."

"Why doesn't Mara put a stop to it?"

"How should I know? I'm going back down there as soon as the Master allows me to leave. I think one of us had better have a long talk with Mara. If word of what's going on gets back to Nedra or Issa, there's going to be big trouble."

"What *else* can go wrong?" I exploded in exasperation.

"Lots of things, I'd imagine. Nobody ever promised you that life was going to be easy, did they? I'll go to Mar Amon and see what I can do. I'll send for you if I need any help."

"Keep me posted."

"If I find out anything meaningful. How are you and Poledra getting along?"

I smirked at him.

"That's disgusting, Belgarath. You're behaving like some downy-cheeked adolescent."

"I know, and I'm enjoying every minute of it."

"I'm going to go call on the twins. I'm sure they'll be able to put their hands on a barrel of good alc. I've been in Nyissa for the past few decades, and the Nyissans don't believe in beer. They have other amusements."

"Oh?"

"Certain leaves and berries and roots make them *sooo* happy. Most Nyissans are in a perpetual fog. Are you coming to visit the twins with me?"

"I don't think so, Beldin. Poledra doesn't like the smell of beer on my breath."

"You're hen-pecked, Belgarath."

"It doesn't bother me in the slightest, brother." I smirked at him again, and he stumped away muttering to himself.

The Alorn clan wars reerupted several times over the next few hundred years. The Bear-cult was still agitating the outlying clans, but the kings of Aloria were able to keep things under control, usually by attacking cult strongholds and firmly trampling cult members into the ground. There's a certain direct charm about the Alorn approach to problems, I suppose.

I think it was about the middle of the nineteenth century when I received an urgent summons from Beldin. The Nyissans had been making slave raids into Maragor, and the Marags responded by invading the lands of the Serpent People. I spoke extensively with Poledra and told her in no uncertain terms that I wanted her to stay in the Vale while I was gone. I asserted what minimal authority a pack leader might have at that point, and she *seemed* to accept that authority—although with Poledra you could never really be entirely sure. She sulked, of course. Poledra could be absolutely adorable when she sulked. Garion will probably understand that, but I doubt that anyone else will.

I kissed my wife's pouty lower lip and left for Maragor—although I'm not sure exactly what Beldin thought I might be able to do. Attempting to rein in the Marags was what you might call an exercise in futility. Marag men were all athletes who carried their brains in their biceps. The women of Maragor encouraged that, I'm afraid. They want stamina, not intelligence.

All right, Polgara, don't beat it into the ground. I liked the Marags. They had their peculiarities, but they *did* enjoy life.

The Marag invasion of Nyissa turned out to be an unmitigated disaster. The Nyissans, like the snakes they so admired, simply slithered off into the jungle, but they left a few surprises behind to entertain the invaders. Pharmacology is an artform in Nyissa, and not all of the berries and leaves that grow in their jungles make people feel good. Any number of them seem to have the opposite effect—although it's sort of hard to say for sure. It's entirely possible that the thousands of Marags who stiffened, went into convulsions, and died as the result of eating an apparently harmless bit of food were made ecstatic by the various poisons that took them off.

Grimly the Marags pressed on, stopping occasionally to roast and eat a few prisoners of war. They reached Sthiss Tor, the Nyissan capital, but Queen Salmissra and all of the inhabitants had already melted into the jungles, leaving behind warehouses crammed to the rafters with food. The dim-witted Marags feasted on the food—which proved to be a mistake.

Why am I *surrounded* by people incapable of learning from experience? *I* wouldn't have to see too many people die from "indigestion" to begin to have some doubts about my food source. Would you believe that the Nyissans even managed to poison their cattle herds in such a subtle way that the cows looked plump and perfectly healthy, but when a Marag ate a steak or roast or chop from one of those cows, he immediately turned black in the face and died frothing at the mouth? Fully half of the males of the Marag race died during that abortive invasion.

Things were getting out of hand. Mara wouldn't just sit back and watch the Nyissans exterminate his children for very long before he'd decide to intervene, and once he did that, torpid Issa would be obliged to wake up and respond. Issa was a strange God. After the cracking of the world, he'd simply turned the governance of the Snake People over to his High Priestess, Salmissra, and had gone into hibernation. I guess it hadn't occurred to him to do anything to prolong her life, and so in time she died. The Serpent People didn't bother to wake him when she did. They simply selected a replacement.

Beldin and I went looking for the then-current Queen Salmissra so that we could offer to mediate a withdrawal of the Marags. We finally found her in a house deep in the jungles, a house almost identical to her palace in Sthiss Tor. She's probably got those houses scattered all over Nyissa.

We presented ourselves to her eunuchs, and they took us to her throne room, where she lounged, admiring her reflection in a mirror. Salmissra—like all the other Salmissras—absolutely adored herself.

"I think you've got a problem, your Majesty," I told her bluntly when Beldin and I were ushered into her presence. "Do you want my brother and me to try to end this war?"

The Serpent Woman didn't seem to be particularly interested. "Do not expend thine energy, Ancient Belgarath," she said with a yawn. All of the Salmissras have been virtually identical to the first one. They're selected because of their resemblance to her and trained from early childhood to have that same chill, indifferent personality. Actually it makes them easier to deal with. Salmissra—any one of the hundred or so who've worn the name—is always the same person, so you don't have to adjust your thinking.

Beldin, however, managed to get her attention. "All right," he told her with an indifference that matched her own, "it's the dry season. Belgarath and I'll set fire to your stinking jungles. We'll burn Nyissa to the ground. Then the Marags will *have* to go home."

That was the only time I've ever seen any of the Salmissras display any emotion other than sheer animal lust. Her pale eyes widened, and her chalk-white skin turned even whiter. "Thou wouldst *not!*" she exclaimed.

Beldin shrugged. "Why not? It'll end this war, and if we get rid of all the assorted narcotics, maybe your people can learn to do something productive. Don't toy with me, Snake Woman, you'll find that I play rough. Let the Marags go home, or I'll burn Nyissa from the mountains to the sea. There won't be a berry or a leaf left—not even the ones that sustain *you.* You'll get old almost immediately, Salmissra, and all those pretty boys you're so fond of will lose interest in you almost as fast."

She glared at him, and then her colorless eyes began to smolder. "You interest me, ugly one," she told him. "I've never coupled with an ape before."

"Forget it," he snarled. "I like my women fat and hot-blooded. You're too cold for me, Salmissra." That was my brother for you. He was never one to beat around the bush. "Do we agree then?" he pressed. "If you let the Marags go home, I won't burn your stinking swamp."

"The time will come when you'll regret this, Disciple of Aldur."

"Ah, me little sweetie," he replied in that outrageous Wacite brogue. "I've regretted many things in me long, long life, don't y' know, but I'll be after tellin' y' one thing, darlin'. Matin' with a snake ain't likely t' be one of 'em." Then his face hardened. "This is the last time I'm going to ask you, Salmissra. Are you going to let the Marags go, or am I going to start lighting torches?"

And that more or less ended the war.

"You were moderately effective there, old boy," I complimented my brother as we left Salmissra's jungle hideout. "I thought her eyes were going to pop out when you offered to burn her jungle."

"It got her attention." Then he sighed. "It might have been very interesting," he said rather wistfully.

"What might have?"

"Never mind."

We nursed the limping Marag column back to their own borders, leaving thousands of dead behind us in those reeking swamps, and then Beldin and I returned to the Vale.

When we got there, our Master sent me back to Aloria. "The Queen of the Alorns is with child," he told me. "The one for whom we have waited is about to be born. I would have thee present at this birth and at diverse other times during his youth."

"Are we sure he's the right one, Master?" I asked him.

He nodded. "The signs are all present. Thou wilt know him when first thou seest him. Go thou to Val Alorn, therefore. Verify his identity and then return."

And that's how I came to be present when Cherek Bear-shoulders was born. When one of the midwives brought the red-faced, squalling infant out of the queen's bedroom, I knew immediately that my Master had been right. Don't ask me how I knew, I just did. Cherek and I had been linked since the beginning of time, and I recognized him the moment I laid eyes on him. I congratulated his father and then went back to the Vale to report to my Master and, I hoped, to spend some time with my wife.

I went back to Aloria a number of times during Cherek's boyhood, and we got to know each other quite well. By the time he was ten, he was as big as a full-grown man, and he kept on growing. He was over seven feet tall when he ascended the throne of Aloria at the age of nineteen. We gave him some time to get accustomed to his crown, and then I went back to Val Alorn and arranged a marriage for him. I can't remember the girl's name, but she did what she was supposed to do. Cherek was about twenty-three when his first son, Dras, was born, and about twenty-five when Algar came along. Riva, his third son, was born when the King of Aloria was twenty-seven. My Master was pleased. Everything was happening the way it was supposed to.

Cherek's three sons grew as fast as he had. Alorns are large people anyway, but Dras, Algar, and Riva took that tendency to extremes. Walking into a room where Cherek and his sons were was sort of like walking into a grove of trees. The word "giant" is used rather carelessly at times, but it was no exaggeration when it was used to describe those four.

As I've suggested several times, my Master had at least some knowledge of the future, but he shared that knowledge only sparingly with us. I knew that Cherek and his sons and I were supposed to do *something*, but my Master wouldn't tell me exactly what, reasoning, I suppose, that if I knew too much about it, I might in some way tamper with it and make it come out wrong.

I'd gone to Aloria during the summer when Riva turned eighteen. That was a fairly significant anniversary in a young Alorn's life back then, because it was on his eighteenth birthday that a description of him was added to his name. Four years previously, Riva's older brother had become Dras Bull-neck, and two years after that, Algar had been dubbed Algar Fleet-foot. Riva, who had huge hands, became Iron-grip. I honestly believe that he could have crushed rocks into powder in those hands of his.

Poledra had a little surprise for me when I returned to the Vale. "One wonders if you have finished with these errands for a time," she said when I got home to our tower.

"One hopes so," I replied. We didn't *exactly* speak to each other in wolvish when we were alone, but we came close. "One's Master will decide that, however," I added.

"One will speak with the Master," she told me. "It is proper that you stay here for a time."

"Oh?"

"It is a custom, and customs should be observed."

"Which custom is that?"

"The one that tells us that the sire should be present at the births of his young."

I stared at her. "Why didn't you tell me?" I demanded.

"I just did. What would you like for supper?"

CHAPTER
ELEVEN

Poledra largely ignored her pregnancy. "It's a natural process," she told me with a shrug. "There's nothing very remarkable about it." She continued attending to what she felt were her duties even as her waistline expanded and her movements became increasingly awkward, and nothing I could do or say could persuade her to change her set routine.

Over the centuries, she'd made some significant alterations to my tower. As you may have heard, I'm not the neatest person in the world, but that's never bothered me very much. A bit of clutter gives a place that lived-in look, don't you agree? That all changed after Poledra and I were married. There weren't any interior walls in my tower, largely because I like to be able to look out all of my windows when I'm working. I sort of haphazardly arranged my living space—this area for cooking and eating, that for study, and the one over there for sleeping. It worked out fairly well while I was alone. My location in the various parts of the tower told me what I was supposed to be doing.

Poledra didn't like it that way. I think she wanted greater definition. She started adding furniture—tables, couches, and brightly colored cushions. She loved bright colors for some reason. The rugs she'd scattered about on the stone floor gave me some trouble—I was forever tripping over them. All in all, though, her little touches made that rather bleak tower room a more homey sort of place, and homeyness seems to be important to females of just about any species. I'd suspect that even female snakes add a few decorations to their dens. I was tolerant of these peculiarities, but one thing drove me absolutely wild. She was forever putting things away—and I usually couldn't find them afterward. When I'm working on something, I like to keep it right out in plain sight, but no sooner would I lay something down than she'd pick it up and stick it on a shelf. I think putting up those shelves had been a mistake, but she'd insisted, and during the early years of our marriage I'd been more than willing to accommodate her every whim.

We *had* argued extensively about curtains, however. What *is* this thing women have about curtains? All they really do is get in the way. They don't hold in any appreciable heat in the wintertime, nor keep it out in the summer, and they get in the way when you want to look out. For some reason, though, women don't feel that a room is complete without curtains.

She may have gone through that period of morning sickness that afflicts most pregnant women, but if she did, she didn't tell me about it. Poledra's always up and about at first light, but I tend to be a late riser if I don't have something important to attend to. Regardless of what my daughter may think, that's not a symptom of laziness. It's just that I like to talk, and evenings are the time for talk. I usually go to bed late and get up late. I don't sleep any longer than Polgara does, it's just that we keep different hours. At any rate, Poledra may or may not have endured that morning nausea, but she didn't make an issue of it. She *did* develop those peculiar appetites, though. The first few times she asked for strange foods, I tore the Vale apart looking for them. Once I realized that she was only going to take a few bites, however, I started cheating. I *wasn't* going to sprout wings and fly to the nearest ocean just because she had a sudden craving for oysters. A *created* oyster tastes almost the same as a real one, so she pretended not to notice my subterfuge.

Then, when she was about five months along, we got into the business of cradles. I was a little hurt by the fact that she asked the twins to make them instead of having me do it. I protested, but she bluntly told me, "You're not good with tools." She put her hand on my favorite chair and shook it. I'll concede that it wobbled a bit, but it hadn't collapsed under me in the thousand or so years I'd been sitting in it. That's sturdy enough, isn't it?

The twins went all out in building those cradles. When you get right down to it, a cradle's just a small bed with rockers on it. The ones the twins built, however, had elaborately curled rockers and intricately carved headboards.

"Why two?" I asked my wife after Beltira and Belkira had proudly delivered their handiwork to our tower.

"It doesn't hurt to be prepared for any eventuality," she replied. "It's not uncommon for several young to be born at the same time." She laid one hand on her distended belly. "Soon I'll be able to count the heart-beats. Then I'll know if two cradles will be enough."

I considered the implications of that and chose not to pursue the matter any further. There were some things I'd decided that I wouldn't even *think* about, much less bring out into the open.

Poledra's pregnancy may not have been remarkable to her, but it certainly was to *me*. I was so swollen up with pride that I was probably unbearable to be around. My Master accepted my boasting with fondly amused tolerance, and the twins were quite nearly as ecstatic as I was. Shepherds get all moony at lambing time, so I suppose their reaction was only natural. Beldin, however, soon reached the point where he couldn't stand to be around me, and he went off to Tolnedra to keep watch over the second Honethite Dynasty. The Tolnedrans were establishing trade relations with the Arends and the Nyissans, and the Honeths have always been acquisitive. We definitely didn't want them to start getting ideas about annexation. One war between the Gods had been quite enough, thank you.

Winter came early that year, and it seemed much more severe than usual. Trees were exploding in the cold in the Far North, and the snow was piling up to incredible depths. Then on a bitterly cold day when the sky was spitting pellets of snow as hard as pebbles, four Alorns bundled to the ears in fur came down into the Vale. I was able to recognize them from a considerable distance because of their size.

"Well met, Ancient Belgarath," Cherek Bear-shoulders greeted me when I went out to meet him and his sons. I *wish* people wouldn't call me that.

"You're a long way from home, Cherek," I noted. "Is there some sort of problem?"

"Just the opposite, Revered One," Dras Bull-neck rumbled at me. Dras was even bigger than his father, and his voice came up out of his boots. "My brothers have found a way to reach Mallorea."

I looked quickly at Iron-grip and Fleet-foot. Riva was nearly as tall as Dras, but leaner. He had a fierce black beard and piercing blue eyes. Algar, the silent brother, was clean-shaven, and he had the rangy limbs of a coursing hound. "We were hunting," Riva explained. "There are white bears in the Far North, and Mother's birthday is in the spring. Algar and I wanted to give her a white fur cape as a present. She'd like that, wouldn't she?" There was a strange, boyish innocence about Riva. It's not that he was stupid or anything. It was just that he was eager to please and always enthusiastic. Sometimes he almost seemed to bubble.

Algar, of course, didn't say anything. He almost never did. He was the most close-mouthed man I've ever known.

"I've heard about those white bears," I said. "Isn't hunting them just a little dangerous?"

Riva shrugged. "There were two of us," he said—as if that would make a difference to a fourteen-foot bear weighing almost a ton. "Anyway, the ice is very thick in the northern reaches of the Sea of the East this year. We'd wounded a bear, and he was trying to get away from us. We were chasing him, and that's when we found the bridge."

"What bridge?"

"The one that crosses over to Mallorea." He said it in the most offhand way imaginable, as if the discovery of something that Alorns had been trying to find for two thousand years wasn't really all that important.

"I don't suppose you'd care to give me a few details about this bridge?" I suggested.

"I was just getting to that. There's a point that juts out to the east up in Morindland, and another that juts toward the west out of the lands of the Karands over in Mallorea. There's a string of rocky little islets that connects the two. The bear had gotten away from us somehow. It was sort of foggy that day, and it's very hard to see a white bear in the fog. Algar and I were curious, so we crossed the ice, following that string of islands. About midafternoon a breeze came up and blew off the fog. We looked up, and there was Mallorea. We decided not to go exploring, though. There's no point in letting Torak know that we've discovered the bridge, is there? We turned around and came back. We ran across a tribe of Morindim and they told us that they've been using that bridge for centuries to visit the Karands. A Morind will give you anything he owns for a string of glass beads, and Karandese traders seem to know that. The Morinds will trade ivory walrus tusks and priceless sea-otter skins and the hides of those dangerous white bears for a string of beads you can buy in any country fair for a penny." His eyes narrowed. "I hate it when people cheat other people, don't you?" Riva definitely had opinions.

Bear-shoulders gave me a rueful smile. "We could have found out about this years ago if we'd taken the trouble to spend some time with the Morindim. We've been tearing the north apart for two thousand years trying to find some way to cross over to Mallorea and pick up the war with the Angaraks where we left off, and the Morindim knew the way all along. We've *got* to learn to pay more attention to our neighbors."

As nearly as I can recall, that's fairly close to the way the conversation went. Those of you who've read the *Book of Alorn* will realize that the priest of Belar who wrote those early passages took a great deal of liberty with his material. It just goes to show you that you should never trust a priest to be entirely factual.

———

I gave Cherek Bear-shoulders a rather hard look. I could see where this was going. "This is all very interesting, Cherek, but why are you bringing it to me?"

"We thought you'd like to know, Belgarath," he said with an ingenuously feigned look of innocence. Cherek was a very shrewd man, but he could be terribly transparent sometimes.

"Don't try to be coy with me, Cherek," I told him. "Exactly what have you got on your mind?"

"It's not really all that complicated, Belgarath. The boys and I thought we might drift over to Mallorea and steal your Master's Orb back from Torak One-eye." He said it as if he were proposing a stroll in the park. "Then we got to thinking that you might want to come along, so we decided to come down here and invite you."

"Absolutely out of the question," I snapped. "My wife's going to have a baby, and I'm *not* going to leave her here alone."

"Congratulations," Algar murmured. It was the only word he spoke that whole afternoon.

"Thank you," I replied. Then I turned back to his father. "All right, Cherek. We know that this bridge of yours is there. It'll still be there next year. I might be willing to discuss this expedition of yours then—but not now."

"There might be a problem with that, Belgarath," he said seriously. "When my sons told me about what they'd found, I went to the priests of Belar and had them examine the auguries. *This* is the year to go. The ice up there won't be as thick again for years and years. Then they cast my *own* auguries, and from what they say, *this* could be the most fortunate year in my whole life."

"Do you actually *believe* that superstitious nonsense?" I demanded. "Are you so gullible that you think that somebody can foretell the future by fondling a pile of sheep guts?"

He looked a little injured. "This was *important*, Belgarath. I certainly wouldn't trust sheep's entrails for something like this."

"I'm glad to hear that."

"We used a horse instead. Horse guts never lie."

Alorns!

"I wish you all the luck in the world, Cherek," I told him, "but I won't be going with you."

A pained look came over his massive, bearded face. "There's a bit of a problem there, Belgarath. The auguries clearly state that we'll fail if you don't go along."

"You can gut a dragon if you want to, Cherek, but I'm staying right here. Take the twins—or I'll send for Beldin."

"It wouldn't be the same, Belgarath. It has to be *you*. Even the stars say that."

"Astrology, too? You Alorns *are* branching out, aren't you? Do the priests of Belar sprinkle stars on the gut pile?"

"*Belgarath!*" he said in a shocked tone of voice. "That's sacrilegious!"

"Tell me," I said sarcastically, "have your priests tried a crystal ball yet? Or tea leaves?"

"*All right, Belgarath, that's enough.*" It was one of the very few times I've ever heard that voice. Garion's been hearing it since he was a child, but it seldom had occasion to speak to *me*. Needless to say, I was just a bit startled. I even looked around to see where it was coming from, but there wasn't anybody there. The voice was inside my head.

"*Are you ready to listen?*" it demanded.

"*Who are you?*"

"*You know who I am. Stop arguing. You WILL go to Mallorea, and you WILL go now. It's one of those things that has to happen. You'd better go talk with Aldur.*" And then the sense of that other presence in my mind was gone.

I was more than a little shaken by this visitation. I suppose I tried to deny it, but I *did* know who had been talking to me. "Wait here," I bluntly told the King of Aloria and his sons. "I have to go talk with Aldur."

"I can see that thou art troubled, my son," our Master said to me after I'd entered his tower.

"Bear-shoulders and those overgrown sons of his are out there," I reported. "They've found a way to get to Mallorea, and they want me to go with them. It's a very bad time for me, Master. Poledra's due sometime in the next couple of months, and I really should be here. Cherek's very insistent, but I told him that they'd have to go without me."

"And?" My Master knew that there was more.

"I had a visitation. I was told in no uncertain terms that I had to go along."

"That is most rare, my son. The Purpose doth not often speak to us directly."

"I was afraid you'd look at it that way," I admitted glumly. "Can't this be put off?"

"Nay, my son. The TIME is part of the EVENT. Once missed, it will not return, and in the loss of this opportunity, we might well fail. This entails a great sacrifice for thee, my son—greater than thou canst ever know—but it must be made. We are compelled by Necessity, and Necessity will brook no opposition."

"Somebody's *got* to stay with Poledra, Master," I protested.

"*Mayhap one of thy brothers will agree to stand in thy stead. Thy task, however, is clear. If the voice of Necessity hath told thee to go, thou must surely go.*"

"I don't like this, Master," I complained.

"*That is not required, my son. Thou art required to go, not to like the going.*"

He was a lot of help. Grumbling under my breath, I went back outside and hurled my thought in the general direction of Tolnedra. "*I need you!*" I bellowed at Beldin.

"*Don't scream!*" he shouted back. "*You made me spill a tankard of fine ale.*"

"*Quit thinking about your belly and get back here.*"

"*What's wrong?*"

"*I have to leave, and somebody's got to look after Poledra.*"

"*I'm not a midwife, Belgarath. Have the twins do it. They're the experts at this sort of thing.*"

"*With sheep, you clot! Not with people! Get back here right now!*"

"*Where are you going?*"

"*To Mallorea. Cherek's sons have found a way to get there that doesn't involve sprouting feathers. We're going to Cthol Mishrak to take back the Orb.*"

"*Are you crazy? If Torak catches you trying that, he'll roast you over a slow fire.*"

"*I don't intend to let him catch me. Are you coming back or not?*"

"*All right. Don't get excited; I'm coming.*"

"*I'll be gone by the time you get here. No matter what she says or tries to do, don't let Poledra follow me. Keep her inside that tower. Chain her to the wall if you have to, but keep her at home.*"

"*I'll take care of it. Give my best to Torak.*"

"*Very funny, Beldin. Now get started.*"

As you might have noticed, I wasn't exactly in a good humor at that point. I went back to where I'd left the King of Aloria and his sons stamping their feet in the snow. "All right," I told them, "this is what we're going to do. We're going to my tower, and you're *not* going to say anything at all about this insane notion of yours to my wife. I want her to believe that you're just passing through and stopped by to pay a courtesy call. I *don't* want her to know what we're up to until we're a long way away from here."

"I take it you've had a change of heart," Cherek noted blandly.

"Don't push your luck, Bear-shoulders," I told him. "I've been overruled, and I'm not very happy about it."

I can't be entirely sure how much Poledra really knew, and to this day she won't tell me. She greeted the Alorns politely and told them that supper was already cooking. That was a fair indication that she knew *something*. Cherek and his boys and I hadn't been in sight of the tower when we'd held our little get-together. I've often wondered just exactly how far my wife's "talents" go. The fact that she'd lived for three hundred years—that I was willing to admit that I knew about—was a fair indication that she wasn't what you'd call ordinary. If she did have what we refer to as "talent," she never exercised it while I was around. That was a part of our unspoken agreement, I suppose. I didn't ask certain questions, and she didn't surprise me by doing unusual things. Every marriage has its little secrets, I guess. If married people knew *everything* about each other, life would be terribly dull, I guess.

As I think I've indicated, Bear-shoulders was probably one of the world's worst liars. After he'd eaten enough roast pork to glut a regiment, he leaned back in his chair expansively. "We have business in Maragor," he told my wife, "and we stopped by to see if your husband would be willing to show us the way." *Maragor?* What possible interest could Alorns have in Maragor?

"I see," Poledra replied in a noncommittal sort of way.

Now I was stuck with Cherek's lie, so I had to try to make the best of it. "It's not really very far, dear," I told my wife. "It shouldn't take me more than a week or so to get them through the mountains to Mar Amon."

"Unless it snows again," she added. "It must be very important if you're willing to go through those mountains in the wintertime."

"Oh, it *is*, Lady Poledra," Dras Bull-neck assured her. "Very, very important. It has to do with trade."

Trade? I know it sounds impossible, but Dras was an even worse liar than his father. The Marags have no seacoast. How could Alorns even *get* to Maragor to trade with them? Not to mention the fact that Marags had absolutely no interest whatsoever in commerce—and they were cannibals besides! What a dunce Cherek's oldest son was! I shuddered. This idiot was the Crown Prince of Aloria!

"We've heard some rumors that the streams in Maragor are absolutely awash with gold," Riva added. At least Riva had a *little* good sense. Poledra knew enough about Alorns to know that the word "gold" set their hearts on fire.

"I'll try to mediate for you, Bear-shoulders," I said, pulling a long face, "but I don't think you'll have very much luck with the Marags. They aren't interested enough in the gold even to bend over to pick it up, and I don't think you could offer them anything that'd make them willing to take the trouble."

"I think your trip will take longer than a week," Poledra told me. "Be sure to take warm clothing."

"Of course," I assured her.

"Perhaps I should go with you."

"Absolutely not—not when you're this close."

"You worry too much about that."

"No. You stay here. I've sent for Beldin. He's coming back to stay with you."

"Not unless he bathes first, he won't."

"I'll remind him."

"When will you be leaving?"

I cast a spuriously inquiring look at Cherek. "Tomorrow morning?" I asked him.

He shrugged, overdoing it a bit. "Might as well," he agreed. "The weather in those mountains isn't going to get any better. If we're going to have to wade through snow, we'd better get to wading."

"Stay under the trees," Poledra advised. "The snow isn't as deep in thick woods." If she did know, she was taking it very calmly.

"We'd better get some sleep," I said, standing up abruptly. I didn't need any more lies to try to talk my way around.

Poledra was very quiet in our bed that night. She clung to me fiercely, however, and along toward morning she said, "Be very careful. The young and I will be waiting when you come back." Then she said something she rarely ever said, probably because she felt it was unnecessary to say it. "I love you," she told me. Then she kissed me, rolled over, and immediately went to sleep.

The Alorns and I left early the next morning, ostentatiously going off toward the south and Maragor. When we were about five miles south of my tower, however, we circled back, staying well out of sight, and proceeded on toward the northeast.

CHAPTER
TWELVE

This all happened about three thousand years ago, long before the Algars and the Melcenes had begun their breeding experiments with domestic animals, so what passed for horses in those days were hardly more than ponies—which wouldn't have worked out very well for a group of seven-foot-tall Alorns. So we walked. That's to say *they* walked, I ran. After trying to keep up with them for a couple of days, I called a halt. "This isn't working," I told them. "I'm going to do something, and I don't want you getting excited about it."

"What have you got in mind, Belgarath?" Dras rumbled at me a little nervously. I had quite a reputation in Aloria back then, and the Alorns had exaggerated notions about the kinds of things I could do.

"If I'm going to have to run just to keep up, I'm going to run on all four feet."

"You don't have four feet," he objected.

"I'm going to fix that right now. After I do, I won't be able to talk to you—at least not in a language you'll understand—so if you've got any questions, ask them now."

"Our friend here is the most powerful sorcerer in the world," Cherek told his sons sententiously. "There's absolutely nothing he can't do." I think he really believed that.

"No questions?" I asked, looking around at them. "All right then," I said, "now it's your turn to try to keep up." I formed the image in my mind and slipped myself into the familiar form of the wolf. I'd done it often enough before that it was almost automatic by now.

"Belar!" Dras swore, jumping back from me.

Then I ran off a hundred yards toward the northeast, stopped, turned, and sat down on my haunches to wait for them. Even Alorns could understand the meaning of that.

The priest of Belar who wrote the early sections of the *Book of Alorn* was quite obviously playing fast and loose with the truth when he described our journey. He was either drunk when he wrote it, or he didn't have the facts straight. Then again, he may have thought that what really happened was too prosaic for a writer of his vast talent. He declares that Dras, Algar, and Riva were waiting for us a thousand leagues to the north, which simply wasn't true. He then announces that my hair and beard were turned white by the frost of that bitter winter, which was also a lie. My hair and beard had turned white long before that—largely because of my association with the children of the Bear-God.

I still wasn't too happy about this trip, and I placed the blame for it squarely on the shoulders of my traveling companions. I ran those four to the verge of exhaustion day after day. I'd resume my own form every evening, and I usually had enough time to get a fire going and supper started before they came wheezing and staggering into camp. "We're in a hurry," I'd remind them somewhat maliciously. "We've got a long way to go to reach this bridge of yours, and we want to get there before the ice starts to break up, don't we?"

We continued in a northeasterly direction across the snow-covered plains of what's now Algaria until we hit the eastern escarpment. I had no intention of climbing that mile-high cliff, so I turned slightly and led my puffing companions due north onto the moors of present-day eastern Drasnia. Then we cut across the mountains to that vast emptiness where the Morindim live.

My spiteful efforts to run Cherek and his sons into the ground every day accomplished two things. We reached Morindland in less than a month, and my Alorn friends were in peak condition when we got there. *You* try running as fast as you can all day every day for a month and see what it does to you. Assuming that you don't collapse and die in the first day or so, you'll be in very good shape before the month is out. If there was any fat left on my friends by the time we'd reached Morindland, it was under their fingernails. As it turned out, that was very useful.

When we came down out of the north range of mountains that marks the southern boundaries of Morindland, I resumed my own form and called a halt. It was the dead of winter, and the vast arctic plain where the Morindim lived was covered with snow and darkness. The long northern night had set in, although as luck had it, we had reached Morindland early enough in the lunar month that a half-moon hung low over the southern horizon, providing sufficient light to make travel possible—unpleasant, but possible. "I don't know that we need to go out there," I told my fur-clad friends, gesturing at the frozen plain. "There's not much point in holding extended conversations with every band of Morindim we come across, is there?"

"Not really," Cherek agreed, making a face. "I don't care that much for the Morindim. They spend weeks talking about their dreams, and we don't really have time for that."

"When Algar and I were coming back from the land bridge, we stuck to these foothills," Riva told us. "The Morindim don't like hills, so we didn't see very many of them."

"That's probably the best way to do it," I agreed. "I could deal with an occasional band of them if I had to, but it'd just be a waste of time. Do you know how to make curse-markers? And dream-markers?"

Iron-grip nodded gravely. "A combination of those two would sort of make them keep their distance, wouldn't it?"

"I don't understand," Dras rumbled with a puzzled look.

"You would if you'd come out of the taverns in Val Alorn once in a while," Algar suggested to him.

"I'm the eldest," Bull-neck replied a bit defensively. "I have responsibilities."

"Of course you do," Riva said sardonically. "Let's see if I can explain it. The Morindim live in a different kind of world—and I'm not just talking about all this snow. Dreams are more important to them than the real world, and curses are very significant. Belgarath just suggested that we carry a dream-marker to let the Morindim know that we're obeying a command that came to us in a dream. We'll also carry a curse-marker that'll tell them that anybody who interferes with us will have to deal with our demon."

"There's no such thing as a demon," Dras scoffed.

"Don't get your mind set in stone on that, Dras," I warned him.

"Have you ever seen one?"

"I've raised them, Dras. Aldur sent me up here to learn what I could about these people. I apprenticed myself to one of their magicians and learned all the tricks. Riva's got it fairly close. If we carry dream-markers and curse-markers, the Morindim will avoid us."

"Pestilence-markers?" Algar suggested. Algar never used more words

143

than he absolutely had to. I've never fully understood what he was saving them for.

I considered it. "No," I decided. "Sometimes the Morindim feel that the best way to deal with pestilence is to stand off and shoot the infected people full of arrows."

"Inconvenient," Algar murmured.

"We won't encounter very many Morindim this far south anyway," I told them, "and the markers should make them keep their distance."

As it turned out, I was wrong on that score. Riva and I fashioned the markers, and we set out toward the east, staying well up in the foothills. We hadn't traveled for more than two days—nights, actually, since that was when the moon was out—when suddenly there were Morindim all around us. The markers kept them away, but it was only a matter of time until some magician would come along to take up the challenge.

I didn't sleep very much during the course of our journey along those foothills. The north range is riddled with caves, and I'd hide the Alorns in one of them and then go out to scout around. I very nearly froze my paws off. Lord, it was cold up there!

It wasn't too long until I started coming across countermarkers. For every curse, there's a countercurse, and the presence of those counter-markers told me louder than words that magicians were starting to converge on us. This was puzzling, because Morind magicians are all insanely jealous of each other and they almost never cooperate. Since the magicians control all aspects of the lives of their assorted clans, a gathering such as we were seeing was a virtual impossibility.

The moon, of course, ignored us and continued her inevitable course, waxing fuller and fuller every night until she reached that monthly fulfillment of hers. Cherek and his sons couldn't understand why the moon kept coming up even though the sun didn't. I tried to explain it to them, but when I got to the part about the real orbit of the moon and the apparent orbit of the sun, I lost them. Finally I just told them, "They follow different paths," and let it go at that. All they really had to know was that the moon would be in the arctic sky for about two weeks out of every month during the winter. Anything more would have just confused them. To be honest about it, I'd have been just as happy if the sun's baby sister had dropped below the horizon before her pregnancy started to show. Once she became full, it was as bright as day up there. A full moon over a snow-covered landscape really puts out a lot of light, and that was terribly inconvenient. I suppose that was what the Morindim had been waiting for.

I'd hidden Cherek and the boys in a cave just before moon-set, as usual, and then I went out to scout around. No more than a mile to the east of the cave, I saw Morindim—thousands of them.

I dropped to my haunches and started to swear—no mean trick for a wolf. The unnatural gathering of what appeared to be every clan in Morindland had completely blocked us off. We were in deep trouble.

When I finished swearing, I turned, loped back to the cave where the Alorns were sleeping, and resumed my own form. "You'd better wake up," I told them.

"What's the matter?" Cherek asked, throwing off his fur robe.

"All of Morindim is stretched across our path no more than a mile from here."

"They don't *do* that," Riva protested. "The clans *never* gather together in the same place."

"Evidently the rules have changed."

"What are we going to do?" Dras demanded.

"Could we slip around them?" Cherek asked.

"Not hardly," I told him. "They're stretched out for miles."

"What are we going to do?" Dras said again. Dras tended to repeat himself when he got excited.

"I'm working on it." I started thinking very fast. One thing was certain. Somebody was tampering with the Morindim. Riva was right; the clans *never* cooperated with each other. Someone had found a way to change that, and I didn't think it was a Morind who'd done it. I cudgeled my brain, but I couldn't come up with any way to get out of this. Each of the clans had a magician, and each magician had a pet demon. When the moon rose again, I was very likely to be up to my ears in creatures who normally lived in Hell. I was definitely going to need some help.

I have no idea of where the notion came from—

Let me correct that. Now that I think about it, I *do* know where it came from.

"*Are you in there?*" I asked silently.

"*Of course.*"

"*I've got a problem here.*"

"*Yes, probably so.*"

"*What do I do?*"

"*I'm not permitted to tell you.*"

"*That didn't seem to bother you back in the Vale.*"

"*That was different. Think, Belgarath. You know the Morindim, and you know how hard it is to control one of their demons. The magician has to con-*"

centrate very hard to keep his demon from turning on him. What does that suggest to you?"

"I do something to break their concentration?"

"Is that a question? If it is, I'm not allowed to answer."

"All right, it's not a question. What do you think of the idea—just speculatively? Do your rules allow you to tell me if an idea is a bad one?"

"Just speculatively? I think that's allowed."

"It'll make things a little awkward, but I think we can work around it."

I suggested any number of possible solutions, and that silent voice inside my head rejected them one after another. I started to grow more and
more exotic at that point. To my horror, that bodiless voice seemed to
think that my most outrageous and dangerous notion had some possibilities. You should always try to curb your creativity in situations like that.

"Are you mad?" Riva exclaimed when I told the Alorns what I had
in mind.

"Let's all hope not," I told him. "There isn't any other way out, I'm
afraid. I'm going to have to do it this way—unless we want to turn around
and go home, and I don't think that's permitted."

"When are you going to do this?" Cherek asked me.

"Just as soon as the moon comes up again. I want to pick the time,
I don't want some tattooed magician out there picking it for me."

"Why wait?" Dras demanded. "Why not do it now?"

"Because I'll need light to draw the symbols in the snow. I definitely
don't want to leave anything out. Try to get some sleep. It might be quite
a while before we get the chance again." Then I went back outside to
keep watch.

It was a nervous night—day, actually, since your days and nights get
turned around during the arctic winter. When I'd suggested the plan to
that voice of Necessity that seemed to have taken up residence inside my
head for a time, I'd been grasping at straws, since I wasn't really sure I
could pull it off. Worrying isn't a good way to spend any extended period
of time.

When I judged that the moon was about ready to come up, I went
back into the cave and woke up my friends. "I don't want you standing
too close to me," I advised them. "There's no point in all of us getting
killed."

"I thought you knew what you were doing!" Dras objected. Dras was
an excitable sort of fellow despite his size, and his normally deep voice
sounded a little squeaky.

"In theory, yes," I told him, "but I've never tried it before, so things
could go wrong. I'll have to wait until the magicians raise their demons
before I do anything, so it might be sort of touch-and-go for a while. Just
be ready to run. Let's go."

We came out of the cave, and I looked off toward the east. The pale glow along the horizon told me that it was very close to moon-rise, so we struck off in that direction, moving steadily toward the waiting Morindim. We topped a rise just as they were waking up. It's an eerie thing to watch Morindim getting up in the winter. It resembles nothing quite so much as a suddenly animated graveyard, since they customarily bury themselves in snow before they go to sleep. The snow's cold, of course, but the outside air is much colder. It's a chilling thing to see them rising up out of the snow like men climbing up out of their graves.

The magicians probably hadn't gotten any more sleep than I had. They had their own preparations to make. Each of them had stamped out the symbols in the snow and taken up positions inside those protective designs. They were already muttering the incantations when we came over the hill. And let me tell you, those Morind magicians are very careful not to speak too clearly when summoning demons. Those incantations are what you might call trade secrets, and the magicians guard them very jealously.

I decided that the hilltop was probably as good a place as any to make my stand, so I trampled my own design into the snow and stepped inside.

It was about then that several of the tribesmen in the valley below saw us, and there was a lot of pointing and shouting. Then the magicians began hurling challenges at me. That's a customary thing among primitive people. They spend more time boasting and threatening each other than they do actually fighting. I didn't waste my breath shouting back.

Then the demons started to appear. They were of varying sizes, depending on the skills of the magicians who summoned them. Some were no bigger than imps, and some were as big as houses. They were all hideous, of course, but that was to be expected. The one thing they all had in common was the fact that they steamed in the cold. They come from a much hotter climate, you realize.

I waited. Then, when I judged that all but a few of the demons were present, I began to gather in my Will. It was surprisingly easy, since I was bent on creating an illusion rather than actually doing anything in a physical sense. I didn't speak the Word yet, though. I didn't want to spring my surprise on them until the last possible moment.

You have no idea of how hard it is to keep your Will buttoned in like that. I could feel my hair rising as if it wanted to stand on end, and I felt as if I were about to explode.

Then somewhere in that mob below us somebody blew a horn. I gather that was supposed to be a signal of some kind. All the magicians began barking commands, and the howling demons started toward us, the imps skittering across the snow and the big ones lumbering up the hill like burning garbage scows, melting down the snowdrifts as they came.

"Behold!" I thundered—augmenting my voice, I'll admit—and I pointed dramatically toward the south. I didn't want the moon or the northern lights lessening the impact of what I was going to do.

Then, posing like a charlatan in a country fair, I spoke the words that released my Will in a voice they probably heard in Kell.

"Rise up!" I roared—and the sun came up.

Oh, *come* now. You know better than that. *Nobody* can order the sun around. Don't be so gullible.

It *looked* like the sun, though. It was a very good illusion, even if I do say so myself.

The Morindim were thunderstruck, to say the very least. My clever fakery quite literally bowled them over. Would you believe that a sizable number of them actually fainted?

The demons faltered, and most of them sort of shimmered like heat waves rising off hot rocks as they resumed their real forms. The shimmering ones turned around and went back to eat the magicians who'd enslaved them. That created a sort of generalized panic down in the valley. I expect that some of those Morindim were still running a year later.

There were still eight or ten magicians who'd kept their grip on their slaves though, and those fiery demons kept plowing up through the snow toward me. I'll admit that I'd desperately hoped that the panic my imitation sun would cause would be universal. I *didn't* want to have to take the next step.

"*I hope you're right about this,*" I muttered to the uninvited guest inside my skull.

"*Trust me.*"

I *hate* it when people say that to me.

I didn't bother to mutter. Nobody in his right mind would attempt to duplicate what *I* was about to do. I spoke the incantation quite precisely. This wasn't a good time for blunders. I was concentrating very hard, and my illusion flickered and went out, leaving me with nothing but the moon to work with.

There was another shimmering in the air, much too close to me for my comfort—and this particular shimmering glowed a sooty red. Then it congealed and became solid. I'd decided not to try to be exotic. Most Morind magicians get very creative when they devise the shape into which they plan to imprison their demon. I didn't bother with tentacles or scales or any of that nonsense. I chose to use a human shape, and about all I did to modify the thing was to add horns. I *really* concentrated on those horns, since my very life hung on them.

It was shaky there for a while. I hadn't realized how big the thing was going to be. It *was* a Demon Lord, though, and size is evidently an indication of rank in the hierarchy of Hell.

It struggled against me, naturally, and icicles began to form up in my beard as the sweat rolling down my face froze in the bitter cold. "Stop it!" I commanded the thing irritably. "Just do what I tell you to do, and then I'll let you go back to where it's warm."

I can't believe I said that!

Oddly, it might have saved my life, though. The Demon Lord was steaming in the cold. *You* try jumping out of Hell into the middle of an arctic winter and see how *you* like it. My Demon Lord was rapidly turning blue, and his fangs were chattering.

"Go down there and run off those other demons coming up the hill," I commanded.

"You are Belgarath, aren't you?" It was the most awful voice I've ever heard. I was a bit surprised to discover that my reputation extended even into Hell. That sort of thing could go to a man's head.

"Yes," I admitted modestly.

"Tell *your* Master that *my* Master is not pleased with what you are doing."

"I'll pass that along. Now get cracking before your horns freeze off."

I can't be entirely sure what it was that turned the trick. It might have been the cold, or it might have been that the King of Hell had ordered the Demon Lord to go along with me so that I could carry his message back to Aldur. Maybe the presence of the Necessity intimidated the thing. Or perhaps I was strong enough to control that huge beast—though that seems unlikely. For whatever reason, however, the Demon Lord drew himself up to his full height—which was *really* high—and bellowed something absolutely incomprehensible. The other demons vanished immediately, and the magicians who had raised them all collapsed, convulsing in the snow in the throes of assorted seizures.

"Nicely done," I complimented the Demon Lord. "You can go home now. Sleep warm." As I've tried so many times to explain to Garion, these things have to be done with a certain style. I learned that from Belmakor.

Cherek and his sons had been standing some distance away, and after

I'd dismissed the Demon Lord, they began to increase that distance. "Oh, stop that!" I snapped at them. "Come back here."

They seemed very reluctant, and a great deal of white was showing in their eyes, but they approached me apprehensively. "I've got something to attend to," I told them. "Keep going east. I'll catch up with you."

"Ah—what have you got in mind?" Cherek asked in an awed sort of voice.

"Riva had it right," I explained. "This little gathering was totally out of character for the Morindim. Somebody's out there playing games. I'm going to go find out who he is and tell him to stop. East is that way." I pointed toward the newly risen moon.

"How long do you think it's going to take?" Riva asked me.

"I have no idea. Just keep going." Then I changed back into my wolf-shape and loped off toward the south. I'd been getting, well, a prickling sensation for several days, and it seemed to come from that general direction.

Once I got out of the range of the thoughts of my Alorns and the confused babble of the still-convulsing Morind magicians, I stopped and very carefully pushed out a searching thought.

The sense that came back to me was very familiar. It should have been: it was Belzedar.

I immediately pulled my thought back in. What was he *doing*? Evidently he'd been following us, but why? Was he coming along to lend a hand? If that was what he had in mind, why didn't he just catch up and join us? Why all this sneaking through the snow?

I hadn't really understood Belzedar since the day Torak stole the Orb. He'd grown more and more distant and increasingly secretive. I could have simply sent my voice to him and invited him to join us, but for some reason I didn't. I wanted to see what he was doing first. I'm not normally a suspicious man, but Belzedar had been acting strangely for about two thousand years, and I decided that I'd better find out why before I let him know that I was aware of his presence.

I had his general location pinpointed, and as I loped higher up into the mountains of the north range, I periodically sent my thought out in short, searching little spurts.

Try to remember that. When you go looking for somebody with your mind, and you stay in contact with him for too long, he'll know you're there. The trick is just to brush him. Don't give him time to realize that somebody's looking for him. It takes a lot of practice, but if you work on it, you'll get it down pat.

I was narrowing it down when I saw the fire. Of all the idiotic things! Here he was, trying to sneak along behind me and he goes and lights a beacon! My tongue lolled out. I couldn't help laughing. I stopped running and slowed to a crawl, inching through the snow on my belly toward that fire.

Then I saw him standing by that ridiculous fire of his, and he wasn't alone. There was a Morind with him. The Morind was a stringy old man dressed in furs, and the skull-surmounted staff he held proclaimed him to be a magician.

I crept closer, inch by inch. Sneaking up on somebody in the snow isn't as easy as it sounds. The snow muffles any noise you might make, but if it's cold enough, your whole body steams. Fortunately, I'd cooled off a bit, so my fur kept the heat of my body from reaching the outside air. Belly down, I lay under a snow-clogged bush and listened.

"He made the sun come up!" The magician was telling my brother in a shrill voice. "Then he raised a Demon Lord! My clan will have no further part in this!"

"They *must*!" Belzedar urged. "Belgarath must not be permitted to reach Mallorea! We *must* stop him!"

What was this? I crept a few inches closer.

"There's nothing I can do," the magician said adamantly. "My clan is scattered to the winds. I could not gather them together again even if I wanted to. Belgarath is too powerful. I will not face him again."

"Think of what you're giving up, Etchquaw," Belzedar pleaded. "Will you be the slave of the king of Hell for the rest of your life?"

"Morindland is cold and dark, Zedar," the magician replied. "I do not fear the flames of Hell."

"But you could have a God! My Master will accept you if you will do only this one small thing for him!" Belzedar's voice was desperate.

The skinny Morind straightened, his expression resolute. "You have my final word, Zedar. I will have nothing more to do with this Belgarath. Tell your Master what I have said. Tell Torak to find someone else to contest with your brother Belgarath."

CHAPTER
THIRTEEN

In retrospect, it was probably for the best that I was a wolf when I made that discovery. The personality of the wolf had become so interwoven with my own during the past month that my reactions were not entirely my own. A wolf is incapable of hatred—rage, yes; hatred, no. Had I been in my own form, I probably would have done something precipitous.

As it was, I simply lay there in the snow with my ears pricked forward, listening as Zedar pleaded with the Morind magician. That gave me enough time to pull my wits together. How could I have been so blind? Zedar had given himself away hundreds of times since Torak had cracked the world, but I'd been too inattentive to notice . . . I'd have more than likely wasted a great deal of time berating myself, but once again the wolf that enclosed me shrugged that useless activity aside. But now that I knew the truth about my sometime brother, what was I going to do about it?

The simplest thing, of course, would be to lay in wait until the Morind left and then dash into the clearing and rip Zedar's throat out with my teeth. I was tempted; the Gods know that I was tempted. There was a certain wolfish practicality about that notion. It was quick; it was easy; and it would remove a clear and present danger once and for all.

Unfortunately, it would also leave a thousand questions unanswered, and curiosity is a trait common to both men and wolves. I knew what Zedar had done. Now I wanted to know why. I did know one thing, though. I had just lost another brother. I didn't even think of him as "Belzedar" any more.

There was a more practical reason for my restraint, however. The gathering of the Morindim had obviously been at Zedar's instigation. He'd overcome their reluctance to join together by offering them a God. To my way of thinking, there wasn't really all that much difference between Torak and the king of Hell, but the Morindim obviously saw it otherwise. Zedar had planted *that* particular trap in my path. How many others were out there besides? That's what I *really* needed to know. A trap, once set, can lay there waiting long after the man who set it is dead. The situation seemed to call for subterfuge, and I've always been fairly good at that.

"You're just wasting your breath, Zedar," the Morind was saying. "I'm not going to confront a magician as powerful as your brother. If you want to fight him, do it yourself. I'm sure your Master will help you."

"He *can't*, Etchquaw. It is forbidden. *I* must be the instrument of Necessity during this particular EVENT."

What was this?

"If you are Necessity's tool, why did you come to us?" It's easy to dismiss the Morindim. You don't normally expect anything remotely resembling intelligence from demon-worshipers, but this Etchquaw fellow was surprisingly perceptive. "I think you are afraid of this Belgarath," he went on, "and I think you are afraid of *his* Necessity. Well, I won't stick my head into the fire for you, Zedar. I've learned to live with demons. I don't really need a God—particularly not a God as powerless as Torak. My demon can do anything I tell him to do. Your Torak seems to be quite limited."

"*Limited?*" Zedar objected. "He cracked the world, you idiot!"

"And what did it get him?" The Morind's tone was scornful. "It got him fire, Zedar. That's what it got him. If all I want is fire, I can wait until I get to Hell."

Zedar's eyes narrowed. "You won't have to wait that long, Etchquaw," he said firmly.

I suppose I could have stopped him. I could feel his Will building, but to be honest with you, I didn't really believe he'd do it.

But he did. I was fairly close, so the sound when he spoke the Word that released his Will was thunderous.

Etchquaw quite suddenly caught on fire.

I'm sorry to open old wounds, Garion, but you weren't the first to do it. There was a difference, though. You had plenty of reason for what you did in the Wood of the Dryads. Zedar, however, set fire to the Morind out of pure viciousness. There's also the fact that you felt guilty, but I'm sure that Zedar didn't.

This was all coming at me a little too fast, so I inched my way back out from under that snowy bush and left Zedar to his entertainments.

The one thing that kept flashing in my mind was Zedar's use of the word "EVENT." This was one of those incidents that our Master had warned us about. I'd been fairly sure that something important was going to happen, but I'd thought that it was going to happen at Cthol Mishrak. Evidently I'd been wrong. There might be another EVENT later, but we had to get by this one first. I decided that it was time for another consultation.

"Can we talk?" I asked the presence inside my head.

"Was there something?"

I think that's the thing that irritated me the most about my uninvited guest—he thought he was funny. I didn't bother to make an issue of it. Considering his location, he probably already knew how I felt. "This is one of those little confrontations that keep happening, isn't it?"

"Obviously."

"An important one?"

"They're all important, Belgarath."

"Zedar said that he's the instrument of the other Necessity this time. I thought it was Torak."

"It was. It changes from time to time, though."

"Then Zedar was telling the truth."

"If you choose to believe him, yes."

"Will you stop doing that?" I said it aloud. Fortunately, it came out in wolfish, so I don't think anyone could hear it.

"You're in a testy humor today."

"Never mind that. If Zedar's the instrument of the other one, who's yours?"

There was a long silence, and I could feel the amusement dripping from it.

"You're not serious!"

"I have every confidence in you."

"What am I supposed to do?"

"I'm sure it'll come to you."

"Aren't you going to tell me?"

"Of course not. We have to play by the rules."

"I need some directions here. If I make it up as I go along, I'm bound to make mistakes."

"We sort of take those into account. You'll do just fine."

"I'm going to kill Zedar." It was an empty threat, of course. Once I had gotten past my initial rage, my homicidal instincts had cooled. Zedar had been my brother for over three thousand years, so I wasn't going to kill him. I might set his beard on fire or tie his entrails into a very complicated knot, but I wouldn't kill him. In spite of everything, I still loved him too much for that.

There's that word again. It always keeps cropping up, for some reason.

"*Try to be serious, Belgarath,*" the voice in my head told me. "*You're incapable of killing your brother. All you have to do is neutralize him. Don't get carried away. We're going to need him again on down the line.*"

"You're not going to tell me what to do, are you?"

"*It isn't permitted this time. You and Zedar are going to have to work out the details for yourselves.*"

And then the silly thing was gone.

I spent several minutes swearing. Then I loped back to where Zedar had been warming himself by the cheerily burning Morind. As I ran along, I began to formulate a plan. I could confront Zedar right now and get it over with, but there were a lot of holes in that idea. Now that I knew how things stood, there was no way he could take me by surprise, and without the element of surprise, he was no match for me. I could take him with one hand, but that would still leave the question of traps hanging up in the air. I reasoned that my best course would be to follow him for a few days to see if he was in contact with others—Morindim or anybody else. I knew Zedar well enough to know that he'd much prefer to let others do his dirty work for him.

Then I stopped and dropped to my haunches. Zedar was fully aware of the fact that my favorite alternative form was that of a wolf. If he saw a wolf—or even wolf tracks in the snow—he'd immediately know that I was around. I was going to have to come up with something else.

Given the rules of this particular encounter, I think I can take credit for the idea that came to me. My visitor had told me that he wasn't permitted to make suggestions, so I was entirely on my own.

I ran back over the last couple thousand years in my mind. Zedar had spent almost the entire time in Mallorea, so there were a lot of things that had happened in the Vale that he didn't know about. He knew that the she-wolf had stayed with me in my tower, but he *didn't* know about her abilities. If a wolf started following him, he might get suspicious, but an owl? I didn't think so—at least he wouldn't unless I let him see how inept I was at flying.

I remembered the owl very well, of course, so it wasn't too hard to form the image in my mind. It was only *after* I had merged myself into the image that I realized my mistake. The image was *female!*

It didn't really make any difference, of course, but it definitely confused me right at first. How is it possible for women to keep their heads on straight with all those additional internal organs—and all those exotic substances floating around in their blood?

I don't think it would be a good idea for me to pursue this line of thought any further.

Considering my irrational nervousness about flying too high, it's fortunate that owls have no real reason to go very far up in the air. An owl's interested in what's on the ground, not what's up among the stars. I ghosted low over the snow-covered earth back toward where I had left Zedar.

Have you any idea of how well an owl can see in the dark? I was absolutely amazed by how good my eyes were. My feathers, of course, were very soft, and I found that I could fly in absolute silence. I concentrated on that, and would you believe that my flying improved? I smoothed out my frantic flapping and actually managed to achieve a certain grace.

Etchquaw had burned down to a heap of charred, smoking rubble by now, and Zedar was gone. His tracks, however, weren't. They angled back up the hillside toward the edge of the stunted evergreens at the tree-line, and then they turned east. That made things even easier for me. It's a little hard to follow someone inconspicuously when you're flying out in the open. As an owl, though, I was able to drift silently from tree to tree until I caught up with him. He seemed to be heading due east, parallel to the course I'd set for Cherek and his sons, and I began to entertain myself by zigzagging back and forth across his path, now ahead of him, now off to one side, and now behind. He wasn't really hard to follow, since he'd conjured up a dim, greenish light to see by—and to hold off the boogiemen. Did I ever tell you that Zedar's afraid of the dark? That adds another dimension to his present situation, doesn't it?

He was bundled to the ears in furs, and he was muttering to himself as he floundered along through the snow. Zedar talks to himself a lot. He always has.

I could not for the life of me figure out what he was up to. If he thought that he could keep up with those long-legged Alorns, he was sadly mistaken. I was sure that Cherek and his boys were at least ten miles ahead of him by now. He was still angling slightly up hill, and by the time the moon set again he'd reached the crest of the north range. Then he stopped.

I drifted to a nearby tree and watched him—owlishly.

Sorry. I couldn't resist that.

"*Master!*" His thought almost knocked me off the limb I was perched on. Lord, Zedar could be clumsy when he got excited.

"*I hear thee, my son.*" I recognized the voice. I was a bit astounded to discover that Torak was almost as clumsy as Zedar was. He was a God! Was that the best he could do? Maybe that was the problem. Maybe Torak's divinity had made him so sure of himself that he got careless.

"*I have failed, Master.*" Zedar's silent voice was trembling. Torak was not the sort to accept the failure of his underlings graciously.

"*Failed?*" There were all sorts of unpleasant implications in the maimed God's tone. "*I will not accept that, Zedar. Thou must not fail.*"

"*Our plan was flawed, Master. Belgarath is far more powerful than we had anticipated.*"

"*How did this come to pass, Zedar? He is thy brother. How is it that thou wert ignorant of the extent of his might?*"

"*He seemed me but a foolish man, Master. His mind is not quick nor his perceptions acute. He is, moreover, a drunken lecher with scant morality and little seriousness.*"

You rarely hear anything good about yourself when you eavesdrop. Have you ever noticed that?

"*How did he manage to thwart thee, my son?*" There was a steely accusation in Torak's voice.

"*He hath in some manner unknown to me gained knowledge of the techniques by which the magicians of the Morindim raise and control the demons that are their slaves. I tell thee truly, Master, he doth far surpass those savages.*"

Naturally he didn't know how I'd learned Morind magic. He'd been in Mallorea when I'd gone to Morindland to take lessons.

"*What did he do, Zedar?*" Torak demanded. "*I must know the extent of his capabilities ere I consult with the Necessity that guides us.*"

It took me a moment to realize what I'd just heard. The other Necessity—the opposite of the one that had taken up residence in my head—was not in direct communication with Zedar. Torak stood between them! He was too jealous to permit *anyone* to have access to that spirit—or whatever you want to call it. There was my edge! I'd be told if I made a mistake; Zedar wouldn't. I suddenly wanted to flap my wings and crow like a rooster.

I listened very carefully while Zedar described my confrontation with the Morindim and their demons. He exaggerated a bit. Zedar's language was always a bit excessive, but he had a very good reason for it this time. His continued good health depended on his persuading Torak that I was well-nigh invincible.

There was a long silence after Zedar had finished his extravagant description of my Demon Lord.

"*I will consider this and consult with the Necessity,*" Torak said finally. "*Dog the steps of thy brother whilst I devise some new means to delay him. We need not destroy him. The TIME of the EVENT is as important as the EVENT itself.*"

The implications there were clear. There *weren't* any other traps out there. They'd hung everything on the Morindim. I felt like grinning, but that's a little hard to do with a hooked beak. Now there was no need to wait any longer; I knew what I had to know. I decided to put Zedar out of action right here and now. I could fly over the top of him, change back to my own form, and fall on him like a collapsing roof.

"Not yet," the voice told me. "It isn't time yet."

"When then?"

"*Just a few more minutes, and you might want to reconsider your plan. I think it might have some holes in it.*"

After a moment's thought, I realized that the voice was right. Falling on top of Zedar wasn't a very good idea. I'd have just as much chance of knocking myself senseless as I would him. Besides, I wanted to talk with him a little first.

The sense of Torak's somewhat nebulous presence was gone now. The maimed God in Cthol Mishrak was busy consulting with that other awareness. Zedar started down the hill through the evergreens, angling back to pick up the trail.

I flew on and landed in the snow several hundred yards in front of him. Then I changed back into my own form and waited, leaning rather casually against a tree.

I could see that greenish light of his bobbing through the trees as he came toward me, and I took advantage of the time to put a lid on my towering anger. It's not a good idea to let your emotions run away with you when you're involved in a confrontation.

Then he came out of the trees on the other side of the clearing where I'd stationed myself.

"What kept you?" I asked him in a calm, run-of-the-mill tone of voice.

"Belgarath!" he gasped.

"You must be half asleep, Belzedar. Couldn't you *feel* my presence? I wasn't trying to hide it."

"Thank the Gods you're here," he said with feigned enthusiasm. He was quick on his feet; I'll give him that. "Weren't you listening? I've been trying to get in touch with you."

"I've been running as a wolf. That might have dulled my perceptions. What are you doing here?"

"I've been trying to catch up with you. You and the Alorns are running into an unnecessary danger."

"Oh?"

"There's no need for you to go to Mallorea. I've already retrieved the Orb. This absurd quest of yours is just a waste of time."

"What an amazing thing. Let's see it."

"Ah—I didn't think it was safe to bring it up here with me. I wasn't positive I could catch up with you, and I didn't want to take it back to Mallorea, so I put it in a safe place."

"Good idea. How did you manage to get it away from Torak?" As long as he was being so creative, I thought I'd give him a chance to expand on his wild story.

"I've been at this for two thousand years, Belgarath. I've been working on Urvon all this time. He's still a Grolim, but he's afraid of the power of our Master's jewel. He distracted Torak, and I was able to slip into that iron tower at Cthol Mishrak and steal the Orb."

"Where did Torak keep it?" That particular bit of information might be very useful later on.

"It was in a room adjoining the one where he spends all his time. He didn't want that iron box in the same room with him. The temptation to open it might have been too great for him."

"Well," I said blandly, "I guess that takes care of all of that, then. I'm glad you came along when you did, brother. I wasn't really too eager to go to Mallorea. I'll go fetch Cherek and his sons while you go pick up the Orb. Then we can all go back to the Vale." I waited for a little bit to give him a moment to exult over his success in deceiving me. "Isn't that sort of what you'd expect from a drunken lecher with scant morality and little seriousness?" I added, throwing his own words back in his teeth. Then I sighed with genuine regret. "Why, Belzedar?" I asked him. "Why have you betrayed our Master?"

His head came up sharply, and his look was stricken.

"You ought to pay more attention, old boy," I told him. "I've been almost on top of you for the past ten hours. Did you really think it was necessary to set fire to Etchquaw?" I'll admit that I was goading him. He was still my brother, and I didn't want to be the one to strike the first blow. I bored in inexorably. "You're Torak's third disciple, aren't you, Zedar? You've gone over to the other side. You've sold your soul to that one-eyed monster in Cthol Mishrak. What did he offer you, Zedar? What is there in this whole world that was worth what you've done?"

He actually broke down at that point. "I had no choice, Belgarath," he sobbed. "I thought that I could deceive Torak—that I could pretend to accept him and serve him—but he put his hand on my soul and tore it out of me. His touch, Belgarath! Dear God, his touch!"

I braced myself. I knew what was coming. Zedar always overreacted. It was his one great weakness.

He started by throwing fire into my face. Between one spurious sob and the next, his arm whipped back and then flashed forward with a great blob of incandescent flame nestled in his palm.

I brushed it aside with a negligent gesture. "Not good enough, brother," I told him. Then I knocked him cartwheeling through the snow with my fist. It was tactically sound. He'd have felt my Will building anyway, and I got an enormous satisfaction out of punching him in the mouth.

He came up spitting blood and teeth and trying to gather his wits. I didn't give him time for that, however. He spent the next several minutes dancing in the snow, dodging the lightning bolts I threw at him. I still didn't want to kill him, so I gave him an instant of warning before I turned each bolt loose. It *did* keep him off balance, though, and the sizzling noise when the bolts hit the snow really distracted him.

Then he enveloped himself in a cloud of absolute darkness, trying to hide. I dissolved his cloud and kept shooting lightning at him. He *really* didn't like that. Zedar's afraid of a lot of things, and lightning's one of them. My thunderclaps and the sizzle and steam *definitely* upset him.

He tried more fire, but I smothered each of his flames before he even got it well started. I suppose I might have toyed with him longer, but by now he fully understood that I had the upper hand. There was no real point in grinding his face in that any more, so I jumped on him and quite literally beat him into the ground with my bare hands. I could have done it any number of other ways, I guess, but his betrayal seemed to call for a purely physical chastisement. I hammered on him with my fists for a while, and right at first he gave as good as he got. We banged on each other for several minutes, but I was enjoying it far more than he was. I had a great deal of pent-up anger, and hitting him felt very, very good.

I finally gave him a good solid punch on the side of his head, and his eyes glazed over, and he slumped senseless into the snow.

"That'll teach you," I muttered to him, rising and standing over his unconscious body. It was a silly thing to say, but I had to say *something*.

I had a little problem, though. What was I going to do with him *now*? I wasn't going to kill him, and the blow I'd given him wouldn't keep him unconscious for very long. I was certain that the rules of this encounter prohibited the voice inside my head from making any suggestions, so I was on my own.

I considered the inert form at my feet. In his present condition, Zedar posed no threat to anyone. All I really had to do was keep him in that condition. I took him by the shoulders and dragged him back in among the trees. Then I piled branches over him. In spite of everything, I didn't want him to freeze to death or get smothered by a sudden snow squall. Then I reached my hand in under the branches, found his face, and gathered my Will. "This all must have been exhausting for you, Zedar," I told him. "Why don't you see if you can catch up on your sleep?"

Then I released my Will. I smiled and stood up. I'd gauged it rather carefully. Zedar would sleep for at least six months, and that would keep him out of my hair while the Alorns and I went to Cthol Mishrak to finish what we'd set out to do.

I felt quite pleased with myself as I resumed the form of the wolf.

Then I went looking for Cherek and his boys.

CHAPTER
FOURTEEN

Evidently the word of my Demon Lord had gotten around, because we didn't encounter any more of the Morindim as we crossed the southern edge of their range. The moon had gone off to the south, but the northern lights illuminated the sky well enough, and we made good time. We soon reached the shore of Torak's Sea.

Fortunately the beach was littered with huge piles of driftwood. Otherwise, I don't think we'd have been able to tell where the land stopped and the sea began. The ground along that beach was nearly as flat as the frozen sea, and both were covered with knee-deep snow.

"We go north along the beach from here," Riva told us. "After a while it swings east. The bridge is off in that direction."

"Let's stay clear of your bridge," I told him.

"What?"

"Torak knows we're coming, and by now he knows that Zedar wasn't able to stop us. He might have a few surprises waiting for us if we follow that string of islands. Let's cross the ice instead."

"There aren't any landmarks out there, Belgarath," he objected, "and we can't even take our bearings on the sun. We'll get lost."

"No, we won't, Riva. I've got a very good sense of direction."

"Even in the dark?"

"Yes." I looked around, squinting into the bitterly cold wind sweeping down out of the northwest. "Let's get behind that pile of driftwood," I told them. "We'll build a fire, have a hot meal, and get some sleep. The next several days aren't going to be very pleasant."

Crossing open ice in the dead of winter is one of the more uncomfortable experiences you'll ever have, I expect. Once you get out a ways from shore, the wind has total access to you, and the arctic wind blows continually. Of course, it sweeps the ice clear of snow, so at least you don't have to wade through snowdrifts. There are enough other problems to make up for the absence of drifts, though. When people talk about crossing ice, they're usually talking about a frozen lake, which is normally as flat as a tabletop. Sea ice isn't like that because of the tides. The continual rising and falling of the water during the autumn and early winter keeps breaking up the ice before it gets thick enough to become stable, and that creates ridges and deep cracks that make crossing a stretch of sea ice almost as difficult as crossing a range of mountains. I didn't enjoy it very much.

The sun had long since abandoned the north, and the moon had wandered away, so I can't really give you any idea of how long it took us to make it across—probably not as long as it seemed, since I reverted to the form of the wolf and I could keep going for a long time without slowing down. Moreover, my malicious running of the Alorns had conditioned them to the point that they could almost keep up with me.

Anyway, we finally reached the coast of Mallorea—just in time, as it turned out, because a three-day blizzard came up almost as soon as we hit the beach. We took shelter under a mountainous pile of driftwood to wait out the storm. Dras turned out to be very useful at that point. He took his battle-axe to that jumble of logs and limbs and hollowed us out a very comfortable den near the center of the pile. We built a fire and gradually thawed out.

During one of his visits to the Vale, Beldin had sketched me out a rough map of Mallorea, and I spent a great deal of time hunched over that map while the blizzard was busy drifting about eight feet of snow over our shelter. "How far is your bridge up the coast from where we crossed?" I asked Riva when the wind began to subside.

"Oh, I don't know. Fifty leagues or so, I guess."

"You're a lot of help, Riva," I told him sourly. I stared at the map again. Beldin hadn't known about the bridge, of course, so he hadn't drawn it in, and he also hadn't included a scale, so all I could do was guess. "As closely as I can make it out, we're approximately due west of Cthol Mishrak," I told my friends.

"Approximately?" Cherek asked.

"This map isn't all that good. It gives me a general idea of where the city is, but that's about all. When the wind dies down a bit more, we'll scout around. Cthol Mishrak's on a river, and there's a swamp north of that river. If we find a swamp inland, we'll know that we're fairly close."

"And if we don't?"

"Then we'll have to go looking for it—or the river."

Cherek squinted at my map. "We could be north of the swamp, Belgarath," he objected. "Or south of the river, for that matter. We could end up wandering around up here until summertime."

"Have you got anything better to do?"

"Well, no, but—"

"Let's not start worrying until we find out what's lying inland. Your auguries say this is your lucky year, so maybe we've come ashore in the right place."

"But you don't believe in auguries."

"No, but you do. Maybe that's all it takes. If you *think* you're lucky, you probably are."

"I suppose I didn't think of that," he said, his face suddenly brightening. You can convince an Alorn of almost anything if you talk fast enough.

We rolled up in our furs and slept at that point. There really wasn't anything else to do, unless we wanted to sit around and watch Dras play with his dice—Drasnians love to gamble, but I got much more entertainment from dreaming about my wife.

I can't be sure how long I slept, but some time later, Riva shook me awake. "I think you'd better reset that sense of direction of yours, Belgarath," he said accusingly.

"What's the matter?"

"I just went outside to see if the wind had died. The sun's coming up."

I sat up quickly. "Good," I said. "Go wake up your father and brothers. We've got a little light for a while. Let's take advantage of it to have a look inland. Tell them not to bother breaking down our camp. We'll go take a look and then come back. I want it to be dark again before we start out."

There were rounded mounds backing the beach where we'd sat out the storm, and once we got to them, Dras negligently hit the snow-covered side of one of them with his axe. "Sand," he reported. That sounded promising.

We topped the dunes and gazed out over a scrubby forest that looked almost like a jungle dotted here and there with broad clearings.

"What do you think?" Cherek asked me. "It looks sort of boggy. It's frozen, of course, and knee-deep in snow, but those clearings would be open water in the summer if it *is* that swamp."

"Let's go look," I said, squinting nervously at the fading "dawn" along the southern horizon. "We'd better hurry if we want to reach it before it gets dark again."

We trotted down the back-side of the dune and out among the gnarled, stunted trees. When we got to one of those clearings, I kicked the snow out of the way and had a look. "Ice," I said with a certain satisfaction. "Chop a hole in it, Dras. I need to have a look at the water."

"You're dulling the edge of my axe, Belgarath," he complained.

"You can sharpen it again. Start chopping."

He muttered a few choice oaths, bunched those enormous shoulders, and began to chop ice.

"Harder, Dras," I urged him. "I want to get down to water before the light goes."

He began to chop harder and faster, sending splinters and chunks of ice in all directions. After several minutes, water began to seep up from the bottom of the hole.

I suppressed an urge to dance with glee. The water was brown. "That's enough," I told the huge man. I knelt, scooped up a handful of water, and tasted it. "Brackish," I announced. "It's swamp water, all right. It looks as if your auguries were right, Cherek. This is your lucky year. Let's go back to the beach and have some breakfast."

Algar fell in beside me as we started back. "I'd say it's your lucky year, too, Belgarath," he murmured quietly. "Father would have been a little grumpy if we'd missed that swamp."

"I can't possibly lose, Algar," I replied gaily. "When we get back to the beach, I'll borrow your brother's dice and roll the main all day long."

"I don't play dice. What are you talking about?"

"It's a game called hazard," I explained. "You're supposed to call a number before your first roll. If it comes up, you win. That number's called the 'main.'"

"And if it doesn't come up, you lose?"

"It's a little more complicated than that. Have Dras show you."

"I've got better things to do with my money, Belgarath, and I've heard stories about my brother's dice."

"You don't think he'd cheat you, do you? You are his brother."

"If there was money involved, Dras would cheat our own mother."

You see what I mean about Drasnians?

We returned to our den, and Riva cooked an extensive breakfast. Cooking is a chore that nobody really likes—except for my daughter, of course—so it usually fell to the youngest. Oddly, Riva wasn't a bad cook.

———

You didn't know that, did you, Pol?

"Will you recognize this place when you see it?" Dras rumbled around a mouthful of bacon.

"It shouldn't be too hard," I replied blandly, "since it's the only city north of the river."

"Oh," he said. "I didn't know that."

"It'll sort of stand out," I continued. "It's got a perpetual cloud bank over it."

He frowned. "What causes that?"

"Torak, from what Beldin says."

"Why would he do that?"

I shrugged. "Maybe he hates the sun." I didn't want to get too exotic in my explanation. Little things confused Dras. A big one might have unraveled his whole brain.

I apologize to the entire Drasnian nation for that last remark. Dras was brave and strong and absolutely loyal, but sometimes he was just a little slow of thought. His descendants have *more* than overcome that. If anyone doesn't believe that, I invite him to try having business dealings with Prince Kheldar.

"All right then," I told them after we'd eaten. "Torak's mind is very rigid. Once he gets hold of an idea, he won't let go of it. He almost certainly knows about that bridge—particularly since the Karands use it to go over to trade with the Morindim, and the Karands are Torak-worshipers now. They probably use the bridge only in the summer when there isn't any ice, though. I don't think Torak would even take the ice into account."

"Where are we going with this?" Cherek asked.

"I'm sure Torak's expecting us, *but* he's expecting us to come at him from the north—from the direction of the bridge. If he's put people out there to stop us, that's where they'll be."

Riva laughed delightedly. "But we won't be coming from the north, will we? We'll be coming from the west instead."

"Good point," Algar murmured with an absolutely straight face. He concealed it very well, but Algar was much brighter than his brothers—or his father, for that matter. Maybe that's why he didn't waste his breath trying to talk to them.

"I can do certain things to keep the Angaraks facing north," I continued. "Now that the blizzard's blown off, I'll decorate the snowbanks up there near your bridge with footprints and perfume the bushes with our scent. That should throw the Chandim off."

"Chandim?" Dras gave me that blank stare.

"The Hounds of Torak. They'll be trying to sniff us out. I'll give them enough clues to make them do their sniffing north of here. If we're half-way careful, we should be able to reach Cthol Mishrak without being noticed."

"You knew this all along, didn't you, Belgarath?" Riva said. "That's why you made us cross the ice where we did instead of going up to the bridge."

I shrugged. "Naturally," I replied modestly. It was a bare-faced lie, of course; I'd only just put it all together myself. But a reputation for infal-lible cleverness doesn't hurt when you're dealing with Alorns. The time might come very soon when I'd be making decisions based on hunches, and I wouldn't have time for arguments.

It was dark again by the time we crawled out of our den and struck out across the snowy dunes toward the frozen bog to the east. We soon discovered that not *all* of the Chandim had gone north to lay in wait for us. We came across tracks as large as horses' hooves in the fresh snow from time to time, and we could hear them baying off in the swamp now and again.

I'll make a confession here. Despite my strong reservations about it, for once I *did* tamper with the weather—just a bit. I created a small por-table fog bank for us to hide in and a very docile little snow-cloud that followed us like a puppy, happily burying our tracks in new snow. It doesn't really take much to make a cloud happy. I kept both the fog and the cloud tightly controlled, though, so their effects didn't alter any major weather patterns. Between the two of them, they kept the Chandim from finding us with their eyes, and the new-fallen snow muffled the sound of our passage. Then I summoned a cooperative family of civet cats to trail along behind us. Civet cats are nice little creatures related to skunks, ex-cept that they have spots instead of stripes. Their means of dealing with creatures unlucky enough to offend them are the same, though—as one of Torak's Hounds discovered when he got too close. I don't imagine he was very popular in his pack for the next several weeks.

We crept unobserved through that frozen swamp for several days, hid-ing in thickets during the brief daylight hours and traveling during the long arctic nights.

Then one morning our fog bank turned opalescent. I let it dissipate so that we could take a look, but it really wasn't necessary. I knew what was lighting up the fog. The sun had finally cleared the horizon. Winter was wearing on, and it was time for us to hurry. As the fog thinned, we

saw that we were nearing the eastern edge of the swamp. A low range of
hills rose a few miles ahead, and just beyond those hills was an inky black
cloud bank. "That's it," I told Cherek and his boys, speaking very quietly.

"That's what?" Dras asked me.

"Cthol Mishrak. I told you about the clouds, remember?"

"Oh, yes. I guess I'd forgotten."

"Let's take cover and wait for dark. We have to start being very careful now."

We burrowed our way into a thicket growing out of a low hummock,
and I passed my snow-cloud over our tracks once or twice and then sent
it home with my thanks. As an afterthought, I also released the civet cats.

"You have a plan?" Riva asked me.

"I'm working on it," I replied shortly. Actually, I *didn't* have a plan.
I hadn't really thought we'd live long enough to get this far. I decided that it might be a good time to have a chat with my friend in the
attic.

"*Are you still there?*" I asked tentatively.

"*No, I'm off somewhere chasing moonbeams. Where else would I be,
Belgarath?*"

"*Silly question, I guess. Are you permitted to give me a description of the
city?*"

"*No, but you've already got one. Beldin told you everything you need to
know. You know that Torak's in the iron tower and that the Orb's there with
him.*"

"*Should I get ready for anything? I mean, is there going to be another one
of those meetings here in Cthol Mishrak? The notion of getting into a wrestling
match with Torak doesn't appeal to me very much.*"

"*No. That was all settled when you met Zedar.*"

"*We actually won one?*"

"*We win about half of them. Don't get overconfident, though. Pure chance
could trip you up. You know what to do when you get there, don't you?*"

And suddenly I *did* know. Don't ask me how, I just did. "*Maybe I'd
better scout on ahead,*" I suggested.

"*Absolutely not. Don't give yourself away by wandering around aimlessly.
Take the Alorns, do what you came to do, and get out.*"

"*Are we on schedule?*"

"*Yes—if you get it done tonight. After tonight, you're in trouble. Don't try
to talk to me again—not until you're clear of the city. I won't be permitted to
answer you. Good luck.*" Then he was gone again.

The light lasted for about three hours—which only seemed like about
three years to me. When the lingering twilight finally faded, I was *very*
jumpy. "Let's go," I told the Alorns. "If we come across any Angaraks, put

them down quickly, and don't make any more noise than you absolutely have to."

"What's the plan?" Cherek asked me.

"I'm going to make it up as we go along," I replied. Why should *I* be the only one with bad nerves?

He swallowed hard. "Lead the way," he told me. Say what you like about Alorns—and I usually do—but no one can fault their bravery.

We crept out of the thicket and waded through the snow until we reached the edge of the swamp. I wasn't particularly worried about tracks, since the Grolims had been patrolling this part of the swamp regularly, and their tracks were everywhere, mingled with the occasional tracks of one of the Hounds. A few more wouldn't mean anything.

Our luck was holding. A blizzard had come in out of the west, and the screaming wind had scoured all the snow off the hillsides facing the swamp. It was no more than an hour until we reached the top of the hill we were climbing, and then we got our first look at the City of Endless Night.

I could see Torak's iron tower, of course, but that wasn't what concerned me. The light wasn't good, naturally, but it was good enough to reveal the fact that Cthol Mishrak had a wall around it. I swore.

"What's wrong?" Dras asked me.

"You see that wall?"

"Yes."

"That means we'll have to go through a gate, and you don't look all that much like a Grolim."

He shrugged. "You worry too much, Belgarath," he rumbled. "We'll just kill the gate-guards and then walk in like we own the place."

"I think we might be able to come up with something a little better than that," Algar said quietly. "Let's see how high the wall is."

As I think I mentioned, the wind of that blizzard had swept the west side of the hills bare of snow—and drifted it all on the *east* side. We stared at those six-foot drifts. This wasn't going at all well.

"There's no help for it, Belgarath," Cherek told me gravely. "We're going to have to follow that road." He pointed at a narrow track that wound up the hill from the gate of the city.

"Cherek," I replied in a pained tone, "that path's as crooked as a broken-backed snake, and the snow's piled up so high on both sides that we won't be able to see anybody coming toward us. We'll be right on top of him before we even know he's there."

He shrugged. "But we'll be expecting him," he said. "He won't be expecting us. That's all the advantage we really need, isn't it?"

It was sheer idiocy, of course, but for the life of me, I couldn't think of anything better—short of wading through the drifts, and we didn't have time for that. We had an appointment in Cthol Mishrak, and I didn't want to be late. "We'll try it," I gave in.

We did encounter one Grolim on our way down to the city, but Algar and Riva jumped him before he could even cry out, and they made quick work of him with their daggers. Then they picked him up, swung him a few times, and threw him up over the top of the snow bank to the left while Dras kicked snow over the pool of blood in the middle of the trail.

"My sons work well together, don't they?" Cherek noted with fatherly pride.

"Very well," I agreed. "Now, how are we going to get off this trail before we reach the gate?"

"We'll get a little closer, and then we'll burrow through the snow off to one side. The last one through can kick the roof of our tunnel down. Nobody'll ever know we've been here."

"Clever. Why didn't *I* think of that?"

"Probably because you're not used to living in snow country. When I was about fifteen, there was a married woman in Val Alorn that sort of took my eye. Her husband was old, but very jealous. I had a snow tunnel burrowed all the way around his house before the winter was over."

"What an absolutely fascinating sidelight on your boyhood. How old was she?"

"Oh, about thirty-five or so. She taught me all sorts of things."

"I can imagine."

"I could tell you about them, if you'd like."

"Some other time, maybe. I've got a lot on my mind right now."

I'll wager you never read about *that* conversation in the *Book of Alorn.*

Algar moved on slightly ahead of us, carefully peeking around each bend in that winding path. Finally he came back. "This is far enough," he said shortly. "The gate's just around the next turn."

"How high's the wall?" his father asked.

"Not bad," Algar replied. "Only about twelve feet."

"Good," Cherek said. "I'll lead out. You boys know what to do when you come along behind."

They all nodded, taking no offense at being called "boys." Cherek lived to be over ninety, and he still called them "boys."

Tunneling through snow isn't nearly as difficult as it sounds, if you've got some help. Cherek clawed his way through, angling slightly upward as he swam through toward a point some fifty feet or so to the left of the gate. Dras followed behind him, raising up every few inches to compress the snow above him. Riva went next, pushing at the sides with his shoulders to compress the snow there. "You next," Algar told me. "Bounce up and down on your belly to flatten the floor of the tunnel."

"This isn't a permanent structure, Algar," I protested.

"We *do* sort of plan to leave, don't we, Belgarath?"

"Oh. I guess I hadn't thought that far ahead."

He was polite enough not to make an issue of that. "I'll come last," he told me. "I know how to close up the entrance so that nobody'll see it."

Despite my sense of urgency, I knew that we still had at least fifteen hours until the sun would peek briefly over the southern horizon again. We burrowed like moles for a couple of hours, and then I bumped into Riva's feet. "What's wrong?" I asked. "Why are we stopping?"

"Father's reached the wall," he replied. "You see? That wasn't so bad, was it?"

"Where did you fellows come up with this?"

"We do it sometimes when we're hunting, and it's a very good way to sneak up on enemies."

"How are we going to get over the wall?"

"I'll stand on Dras' shoulders, and Algar'll stand on Father's. We'll hoist ourselves up on top of the wall and then pull the rest of you up. It probably wouldn't work if we were shorter. We came up with the idea during the last clan war." He peered on ahead. "We can move on now. Father's out of the tunnel."

We inched our way forward, and we were soon standing beside the wall. Cherek and Dras braced their hands against the stones, and Algar and Riva clambered up their backs, reached up, grabbed the top of the wall, and pulled themselves up.

"Belgarath first," Riva whispered down. "Hold him up so I can reach his hand."

Dras took me by the waist and lifted me up in the air. That's how I found out how strong Riva's hands were. I halfway expected to see blood come spurting out of the ends of my fingers when he seized my outstretched hand.

And then we were inside the city. Beldin had described Cthol Mishrak as a suburb of Hell, and I saw no reason to dispute that description. The buildings were all jammed together, and the narrow, twisting alleyways were covered over by the jutting second storeys that butted tightly together overhead. The idea made some sense in a city so far north, I'll grant you. At least the streets weren't buried in snow, but the total lack of any windows in the buildings made the streets resemble hallways in some dungeon. They were poorly lighted by widely spaced torches that guttered and gave off clouds of pitchy smoke. It was depressing, but my friends and I didn't really *want* brightly lit boulevards. We were sneaking, and that's an activity best performed in the dark.

I'm not certain if those narrow, smoky corridors were unpopulated by the arrangement between my friend in the attic and his opposite, or if it was a custom here in the City of Endless Night—which stands to reason, since the Hounds were out—but we didn't encounter a soul as we worked our way deeper and deeper into the very heart of Angarak.

We finally emerged in the unlovely square in the middle of the city and looked through the perpetually murky air at the iron tower Beldin had described. It was—naturally, when you take Torak's personality into account—even higher than Aldur's tower. It was absolutely huge and monumentally ugly. Iron doesn't make for very pretty buildings. It was black, of course, and even from a distance it looked pitted. It *had* been there for almost two thousand years, after all. The Alorns and I weren't really looking at that monument to Torak's ego, however. We were looking at the pair of huge Hounds guarding the rivet-studded door.

"Now what?" Algar whispered.

"Nothing simpler," Dras said confidently. "I'll just walk across the square and bash out their brains with my axe."

I had to head *that* off immediately. The other Alorns might very well see nothing at all wrong with his absurd plan. "It won't work," I said quickly. "They'll start baying as soon as they see you, and that'll rouse the whole city."

"Well, how *are* we going to get past them then?" he demanded truculently.

"I'm working on it." I thought very fast, and it suddenly came to me. I knew it'd work, because it already had once. "Let's pull back into this alley," I muttered. "I'm going to change again."

"You're not as big as they are when you're a wolf, Belgarath," Cherek pointed out.

"I'm not going to change myself into a wolf," I assured him. "You'd better all step back a ways. I might be a little dangerous until I get it under control."

They backed nervously away from me.

I didn't turn myself into a wolf, or an owl, or an eagle, or even a dragon.

I became a civet cat.

The Alorns backed away even farther.

The idea probably wouldn't have worked if Torak's Hounds had been real dogs. Even the stupidest dog knows enough to avoid a civet cat or a skunk. The Chandim weren't really dogs, though. They were Grolims, and they looked on the wild creatures around them with contempt. I flared out my spotted tail and, chittering warningly, I started across the snow-covered plaza toward them. When I got close enough for them to see me, one of them growled at me. "Go away," he said in a hideous voice. He actually seemed to chew on the words.

I ignored him and kept moving toward them. Then, when I judged that they were in range, I turned around and pointed the dangerous end of my assumed form at them.

I don't think I need to go into the details. The procedure's a little disgusting, and I wouldn't want to offend any ladies who might read this.

When a *real* dog has a brush with a skunk or a civet cat, he does a lot of yelping and howling to let the world know how sorry he feels for himself, but the pair at the door weren't real dogs. They did a lot of whining, though, and they rolled around, digging their noses into the snow and pawing at their eyes.

I watched them clinically over my shoulder, and then I gave them another dose, just for good measure.

The last I saw of them, they were blundering blindly across the open square, stopping every few yards to roll in the snow again. They didn't bark or howl, but they *did* whimper a lot.

I resumed my own form, waved Cherek and the boys in, and then set my fingertips to that pitted iron door. I could sense the lock, but it wasn't a very good one, so I clicked it open with a single thought and began to inch the door open very slowly. It still made noise. It sounded very loud in that silent square, but I don't imagine that the sound really carried all that far.

When Cherek and his sons got to within a few yards of me, they stopped. "Well, come on," I whispered to them.

"Ah—that's all right, Belgarath," Cherek whispered back. "Why don't you go on ahead? We'll follow you." He seemed to be trying to hold his breath.

"Don't be an idiot," I snapped at him. "The smell's out here where the Hounds were. None of it splashed on me—not in this form anyway."

They still seemed very reluctant to come any closer.

I muttered a few choice oaths and slipped sideways through the doorway into the absolute darkness beyond it. I fumbled briefly in the pouch at my waist, brought out a stub of a candle, and touched fire to it with my thumb.

Yes, it *was* a little risky, but I'd been told that Torak wouldn't be able to interfere. I wanted to make sure of that before we went any farther.

The Alorns edged through the doorway and looked around the chamber at the bottom of the tower nervously. "Which way?" Cherek whispered.

"Up those stairs, I'd imagine," I replied, pointing at the iron stairway spiraling up into the darkness. "There's not much point to building a tower if you don't plan to live at the top of it. Let me check around down here first, though."

I shielded my candle and went around the interior wall of the room. When I got behind the stairs, I came to a door I hadn't seen before. I put my fingertips to it and I could sense the stairs on the other side. They were going down. This was one of the things that I was supposed to do when I got inside the tower. I didn't know why I was supposed to do it, but I *had* to know where those stairs were. I kept the memory of their location in my head for over three thousand years. Then, when I came back to Cthol Mishrak with Garion and Silk, I finally understood why.

Now, though, I went back around to the foot of those iron stairs that wound upward. "Let's go up," I suggested.

Cherek nodded, took my candle, and then drew his sword. He started up the stairs with Riva and Algar close behind him while Dras and I brought up the rear.

It was a long climb. Torak's tower was very high. It didn't really have to be that high, but you know how Torak was. When you get right down to it, I'm about half surprised that his tower didn't reach up to the stars.

Eventually, we reached the top, where there was another one of those iron doors.

"What now?" Cherek whispered to me.

"You might as well open it," I told him. "Torak isn't supposed to be able to do anything about us, but we'll never know until we go in. Try to be quiet, though."

He drew in a deep breath, handed the candle to Algar, and put his hand on the latch.

"Slowly," I cautioned.

He nodded and turned the handle with excruciating caution.

As Beldin had surmised, Torak had done something to the iron of his tower to keep it from rusting, so the door made surprisingly little noise as Bear-shoulders inched it open.

He looked inside briefly. "He's here," he whispered to us. "I think he's asleep."

"Good," I grunted. "Let's move right along. This night isn't going to last forever."

We filed cautiously into that chamber behind the iron door. I immediately saw that among his other faults, Torak was a plagiarist. His tower room closely resembled my Master's room at the top of *his* tower—except that everything in Torak's tower was made of iron. It was dimly illuminated by the fire burning on his hearth.

The Dragon God lay tossing and writhing on his iron bed. That fire was still burning, I guess. He'd covered his ruined face with a steel mask that very closely resembled his features as they had originally appeared. It was a beautiful job, but the fact that a replica of that mask adorns every Angarak temple in the world makes it just a little ominous in retrospect. Unlike those calm replicas, though, the mask that covered Torak's face actually moved, and the expression on those polished features wasn't really very pretty. He was clearly in torment. It's probably cruel, but I didn't have very much sympathy for him. The chilling thing about the mask was the fact that the left eye slit was open, and Torak's left eye was the one thing that was still visibly burning.

As the maimed God twisted and turned, bound in his pain-haunted slumber, that burning eye seemed to follow us, watching, watching, even though Torak himself was powerless to prevent what we were going to do.

Dras went to the side of the bed, tentatively hefting his war-axe. "I could save the world an awful lot of trouble here," he suggested.

"Don't be absurd," I told him. "Your axe would only bounce off him, and it *might* just wake him up." I looked around the room and immediately saw the door directly opposite the one we'd entered. Since those were the only two doors in the room, it narrowed down the search considerably. "Let's go, gentlemen," I told the towering Alorns. "It's time to do what we came to do." It *was* time. Don't ask me how I knew, but it was definitely the right time. I crossed Torak's room and opened the door, with that burning eye watching my every step.

The room beyond that door wasn't very big—hardly more than a closet. An iron table sat in the precise center of it, a table that was really no more than a pedestal, and an iron box of not much more than a hand's-breadth high sat on the exact center of that pedestal. The box was glowing as if it had just been removed from a forge, but it was not the cherry red of heated iron.

The glow was blue.

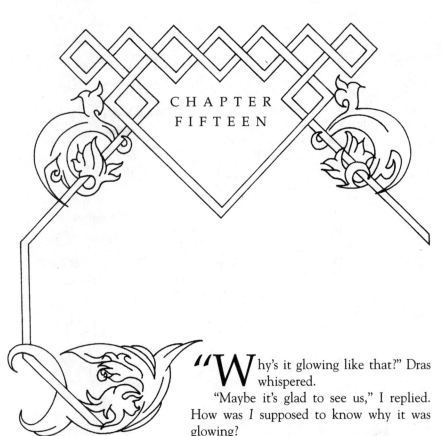

CHAPTER
FIFTEEN

"W hy's it glowing like that?" Dras whispered.

"Maybe it's glad to see us," I replied. How was *I* supposed to know why it was glowing?

"Is it safe to touch that box?" Algar asked shrewdly.

"I'm not sure," I replied. "The Orb itself is dangerous, but I don't know about the box."

"One of us is going to have to open it," Algar said. "Torak could have put it here to trick us. For all we know, the box could be empty, and the Orb's someplace else."

I knew who was supposed to open the box and take out the Orb. The Purpose that had brought us to this place had planted that piece of information in my head before we got here, but I *also* knew that it was going to have to be voluntary. I was going to have to nudge them a bit.

"The Orb knows you, Belgarath," Cherek told me. "You do it."

I shook my head. "I'm not supposed to. There are other things I have to do, and whoever takes up the Orb will spend the rest of his life guarding it. One of you gentlemen is going to have to do it."

"*You* decide who it's going to be," Cherek said.

"I'm not permitted to do that."

"It's really very simple, Belgarath," Dras told me. "We'll take turns trying to open the box. Whichever one of us doesn't die is the right one."

"No," I told him flatly. "You've *all* got things you're supposed to do, and dying here in Cthol Mishrak isn't one of them." I squinted at the glowing box. "I want you gentlemen to be absolutely honest about this. The Orb's the most powerful thing in the world. Whichever one of you picks it up will be able to do *anything*, but the Orb doesn't *want* to do just anything. It's got its own agenda, and if anybody tries to use it for something outside that agenda, it won't be happy. Torak already found that out. Examine your hearts, gentlemen. I need somebody who's *not* ambitious. I need somebody who'll be willing to devote his whole life to guarding the Orb without ever trying to use it. If the notion of having infinite power at your fingertips appeals to you in the slightest, you're not the one."

"That lets me out," Cherek said with a slight shrug. "I'm a king, and kings are *supposed* to be ambitious. The first time I got drunk, I'd *have* to try to do something with it." He looked at his sons. "It's going to have to be one of you boys."

"I could probably keep a grip on my ambition," Dras said, "but I think it ought to be somebody whose mind's quicker than mine. I can handle a fight, but thinking too much makes my head hurt." It was a brutally candid admission, and it raised my opinion of Dras considerably.

Riva and Algar looked at each other. Then Riva shrugged and smiled that boyish smile of his. "Oh, well," he said. "I haven't really got anything better to do anyway." And he reached out, opened the box, and took out the Orb.

"*Yes!*" the voice in my head exulted.

"Well, now," Algar said casually, "since we've settled that, why don't we go?"

That's what *really* happened in Torak's tower. All that blather about "evil intent" in the *Book of Alorn* was made up out of whole cloth by somebody who got carried away by his own creativity. I shouldn't really blame him for it, I guess. I do it all the time myself. The real facts behind any story always seem sort of prosaic to me.

"Stick it inside your clothes someplace," I told Riva. "It's a little excited right now, and that glow's awfully conspicuous."

"Won't I glow, too?" Riva asked dubiously. "The way the box did, I mean?"

"Try it and find out." I suggested.

"Does glowing hurt?" he asked.

"I don't think so. Don't worry, Riva. The Orb's very fond of you. It's not going to hurt you."

"Belgarath, it's a rock. How can it be fond of anything?"

"It's not an ordinary rock. Just put it away, Riva, and let's get out of here."

He swallowed hard and tucked the Orb inside his fur tunic. Then he held out one of his huge hands and examined it closely. "No glow yet," he noted.

"See? You're going to have to learn to trust me, boy. You and I have a long way to go together, and it'll be difficult for both of us if you're going to ask me silly questions every time we turn around."

"*Silly?*" he objected. "After what it did to Torak, I don't think my questions were silly."

"Poor choice of terms, perhaps. Let's go."

I had a bad moment when we were retracing our steps and Torak cried out. It was a howl of utter desolation; somewhere in his sleep the Dragon God knew that we were taking the Orb. He was powerless to stop us, but that shout almost made me jump out of my skin.

I don't like being startled like that, which may account for what I did then. "Go back to sleep, Torak," I told him. Then I threw his own words back in his teeth. "A word of advice for thee, brother of my Master, by way of thanks for thine unintended service to me this day. Don't come looking for the Orb. My Master's very gentle. I'm not. If you come anywhere near the Orb, I'll have you for lunch."

It was sheer bravado, of course, but I had to say *something* to him, and my little display of spitefulness may have served some purpose. When he finally did wake up, he was in a state of inarticulate rage, and he wasted a great deal of time punishing the Angaraks who'd been supposed to prevent me from reaching his tower. That gave the Alorns and me a fairly good head start.

We crept back down the stairs to the foot of the tower, listening tensely for Grolims, but finding only an eerie silence. When we got to the bottom, I looked out into the snowy square. It had remained deserted. My luck was holding.

"Let's go!" Dras said impatiently. Prince Kheldar and I had a long discussion about that some years back, and he told me that burglars always suffer from that same impatience and that it makes getting away almost more dangerous than breaking in. Your natural instinct after you steal something is to take to your heels; but if you don't want to get caught, you'd better suppress that instinct.

The residual odor from my encounter with the Hounds was still very strong on Torak's doorstep, and the five of us were careful to breathe shallowly until we reached the shelter of that dark alleyway from which we'd emerged when we first got to the square.

"What do you think?" Cherek whispered to me as we followed that twisting, smoky alley back toward the city wall. "Will it be safe to go back the way we came?"

I was already working on that, and I hadn't come up with an answer yet. No matter how careful we'd been on our way here from the coast, there were bound to be traces of our passage. I knew Torak well enough to be fairly certain that he wouldn't personally lead the search. He'd leave that to underlings, and that meant Urvon or Ctuchik. Based on Beldin's description of him, I wasn't particularly worried about Urvon. Ctuchik was an unknown, though. I had no idea of what Torak's other disciple was capable of, and this probably wasn't a good time to find out.

Going north was obviously out of the question. Torak already had people in place at the land-bridge, and I didn't want to have to fight my way through them—assuming we could. Going west was probably quite nearly as dangerous. I had to operate on the theory that Ctuchik could do almost anything I could do, and I'd certainly be able to sense those traces I mentioned before. I didn't even consider going east. There wasn't much point in going deeper into Mallorea when safety lay in the other direction.

That left only south. "Are you gentlemen feeling up to a bit of a scuffle?" I asked Cherek and his sons.

"What did you have in mind?" Cherek asked me.

"Why don't we go pick a fight with the guards at the north gate?"

"I can think of a dozen reasons why we shouldn't," Riva said dubiously.

"But I can think of a better one why we should. We don't know how long it's going to be until Torak wakes up, and he's not going to take the loss of the Orb philosophically. As soon as his feet hit the floor, he's going to be organizing a pursuit."

"That stands to reason, I suppose," Iron-grip conceded.

"We want those pursuers to go off in the wrong direction if we can possibly arrange it. A pile of dead Grolims at the north gate would probably suggest that we went that way, wouldn't you say?"

"It would to me, I guess."

"Let's go kill some Grolims, then."

"Wait a minute." Cherek objected. "If we're going to go back the way we came, we won't want to draw attention to that gate."

"But we aren't going back the way we came."

"Which way are we going then?"

"South, actually—well, southwest would probably be closer."

"I don't understand."

"Trust me."

He started to swear. Evidently hearing that remark irritated him as much as it always irritated me.

There were six black-robed Grolims at the north gate, and we made quick work of them. There were a few muffled cries, of course, and some fairly pathetic groaning, but the fact that there weren't any windows in the houses of Cthol Mishrak kept any people inside from hearing them.

"All right," Dras said, wiping his bloody axe on a fallen Grolim, "now what?"

"Let's go back to your tunnel."

"Belgarath," he objected, "we want to get *away* from the city."

"We'll go out through the gate, crawl through your tunnel, and circle around the city until we come to the river on the south side of it."

"There's a trail around the outside of the wall," Riva pointed out. "Why use the tunnel at all?"

"Because the Hounds would pick up our scent. We want them to think we've gone north. We'll need some time to get out ahead of them."

"Very clever," Algar murmured.

"I don't understand," Dras said.

"The river's probably frozen, isn't it?" Algar asked him.

"I suppose so."

"Wouldn't that make it sort of like a highway—without any trees or hills to slow us down?"

Dras considered it. Then comprehension slowly dawned on his big face. "You know, Algar," he said, "I think you're right. Belgarath *is* a very clever old man."

"Do you suppose we could congratulate him some other time?" Riva said to them. "I'm the one who's carrying the loot, and I'd like to put some distance between this place and my backside."

I saw that I was going to have to rearrange Riva's thinking. "Loot" wasn't really a proper term to use when he was referring to my Master's Orb.

We hurried out past the sprawled bodies of the gate-guards, rounded the bend in the path, and plunged back into the snowbank on the left side. It wasn't too long until we came out of the tunnel at the city wall. There was a sort of beaten pathway in the snow along the outside of the wall where Grolims or ordinary Angaraks had been patrolling, and we followed that eastward until we reached the corner. Then we turned and followed it south through the drifts toward the river. Altogether, I'd imagine that it took us about two hours to reach the riverbank.

As I'd been fairly sure it would be, the frozen river was clear of snow. It wound like a wide black ribbon through the snow-clogged countryside.

"That's lucky," Dras noted. "We won't leave any tracks."

"That was sort of the idea," I told him just a bit smugly.

"How did you know that there wouldn't be about three feet of snow on top of the ice?" he asked me.

"That blizzard came in out of the west. There's nothing out there in that river for the wind to pile snow up behind, so it swept the ice clean for us. The snow's probably all stacked up against the mountains of western Karanda."

"You think of everything, don't you, Belgarath?"

"I try. Let's get out on the ice and head down to the coast. I'm starting to get homesick."

We rather carefully brushed out the tracks we made going down the riverbank. Then we crossed the ice to the far side to avoid the light of the torches atop the city wall and started downriver.

We didn't exactly skate along, but there was a certain amount of sliding. After about three hours, the murky clouds hovering over the region began to lighten along the southern horizon.

"The sun's coming up," Algar noted. "Is that going to wake Torak up?"

I wasn't certain about that. "I'll check," I replied. The passenger riding along between my ears had told me not to try to talk to him until we were clear of the city. Well, we were clear now, so I chanced it. *"Do you want to wake up?"* I asked.

"Don't be insulting."

"I didn't do it on purpose. The question of someone waking up is looming rather large right now. We've got what we came for. Is that the end of this particular EVENT?"

"More or less. It's not completely over until you get back across the Sea of the East."

"Can you tell me when Torak's going to wake up?"

"No. You'll know when it happens."

"A hint or two would help."

"Sorry, Belgarath. Just keep going. You're doing well so far."

"Thanks." I didn't say it very graciously.

"I liked the way you dealt with those two Hounds. It never would have occurred to me. Where did you come up with the idea?"

"I came out second best in an encounter with a skunk when I was a boy. It's the sort of thing you remember."

"I can imagine. Keep going, and keep your ears open." Then it was gone again.

It was perhaps a quarter of an hour later when I found out what he meant by keeping my ears open—although I don't think I would have missed it even if I'd been asleep. There's a version of the *Book of Torak* that describes what the Dragon God did when he woke up—and Algar had shrewdly put his finger on when it was going to happen. Evidently a part of the arrangement between the voice in my head and the one in Torak's had been the length of time Torak would remain comatose. Sunrise is a natural transition, and it was then that old One-eye finally woke up. We were ten miles away from the city by then, but we could still hear him as he screamed his fury and then wrecked the entire city—even going so far as to knock down his own tower. It was one of the more spectacular temper tantrums in the history of the world.

"Why don't we run for a while?" Algar suggested as the awful sound of the destruction of Cthol Mishrak knocked all the snow off the trees along the riverbank.

"We *are* running," Dras told him.

"Why don't we run faster?" That was when I found out why Algar was called Fleet-foot. Lord, that boy could run!

The *Book of Alorn* tells the story of what happened there in Mallorea. It's a very good story, filled with drama, excitement, and mythic significance. I've recited it myself on any number of occasions. It's related to what really happened only by implication, but it's still a good story. The fellow who wrote it was an Alorn, after all, and he overstated the significance of the land-bridge—largely, I suspect, because a pair of Alorns discovered it. In actuality, I didn't even *see* the land-bridge during that journey—mainly because there were probably several hundred Angaraks standing on each one of those rocky islets waiting for us. We had traveled to Mallorea across the frozen Sea of the East, and we went back home the same way.

Torak's outburst—for which I'll take partial credit, since my goading as we were leaving his tower undoubtedly contributed to his rage—completely demoralized the Grolims, Chandim, and ordinary Angaraks who'd lived in Cthol Mishrak. Beldin has since discovered that it was ultimately Ctuchik who restored order—with his customary brutality. It still took him several hours, however, and even then our ruse diverted him. The Angaraks found the six butchered Grolims at the north gate, and Ctuchik sent the Hounds off to the north and the west without stopping to consider the possibility of trickery.

The day up there didn't last very long, but nightfall didn't slow the Alorns and me. We followed Algar on downriver, moving as fast as we possibly could.

When the sun put in its brief appearance the following day, however, the Hounds returned to the ruins of Cthol Mishrak and reported to

Ctuchik that they'd found no trace of us. That's when Torak's disciple expanded his search. Inevitably, some sharp-nosed Hound picked up our scent. Then the chase was on. Ctuchik crammed several hundred ordinary Grolims into the shape of Hounds, killing about half of them in the process, and that huge, ravening pack came galloping down the river after us.

"What are we going to do, Belgarath?" Cherek gasped. "The boys and I are starting to get winded. I'm not sure how much longer we'll be able to run."

"I'm going to try something," I told him. "Let's stop and catch our breath here while I work out the details." I went over it in my mind again. Riva had ultimate power tucked inside his tunic, but he wasn't supposed to use it. If my reasoning was correct, though, he wouldn't have to. "All right," I said, "this is how we'll work it. Riva, when those Hounds behind us come into sight, I want you to take out the Orb and hold it up so that they can see it."

"I thought you said I wasn't supposed to."

"I didn't say that you were going to use it. I just told you to hold it up. I want the Chandim to be able to see it—*and* I want *it* to be able to see *them*."

"What good's that going to do?"

Actually, I wasn't really sure, but I had a strong hunch about what would happen. "It'd take too long to explain. Have I been wrong yet?"

"Well—I suppose not."

"Then you'll just have to trust me when I tell you that I know what I'm doing." I was praying rather fervently that I *did*, in fact, know what I was doing.

It wasn't very long before several dozen Hounds came loping around a bend in that frozen river. "All right, Riva," I said. "Now's the time. Raise up the Orb. Don't give it any orders, just hold it up. Don't squeeze it. I know how strong your hands are. If you get excited and crush the Orb, we're in trouble."

"I thought we already were," Cherek muttered somewhere behind me.

"I heard that," I threw back over my shoulder at him.

Riva sighed, took out the Orb, and held it over his head. "Good-bye, father," he said mournfully.

The Hounds running after us skidded to a stop on the slippery river as they caught sight of the glowing Orb in Riva's upraised hand.

Then the Orb stopped glowing. It flickered and then went dark.

Riva groaned.

Then the Orb woke up again, and it didn't glow blue this time. The light that blazed forth from it was pure white, and it was about three times brighter than the sun.

The Chandim fled, howling in pain, stumbling, bumping into each other, and with their toenails shrieking across the ice.

I don't know if any of those Grolims ever regained their sight, but I *do* know that they were all totally blind when they ran back up the river.

"Well," I said with a certain astonishment, "what do you know? It worked after all. What an amazing thing!"

"*Belgarath!*" There was a note of anguish in Cherek's voice. "Are you saying that you didn't *know?*"

"It was theoretically sound," I replied, "but you never really know about theories until you try them out."

"What happened?" Dras demanded.

I shrugged. "Riva's forbidden to use the Orb. That's why the Orb permits him to touch it. *He* couldn't do anything, but the Orb could—and it did. The Orb doesn't like Torak—or the Angaraks. It *does* like Riva, though. I deliberately put him in danger, and that forced the Orb to take matters into its own hands. It worked out rather well, don't you think?"

They stared at me in absolute horror. "Remind me never to play dice with you, Belgarath," Dras said in a trembling voice. "You take too many chances."

With Ctuchik and Torak both to drive them, more of the Hounds came back down the river after us, and a fair number of Grolims, as well. There were mounted men following along behind the Grolims, helmeted men in mail shirts and carrying assorted weapons. Those were the first Murgos I ever saw. I didn't like them then, and my opinion of them hasn't improved over the years. Their horses were somewhat bigger than the scrubby little ponies found on the other side of the Eastern Sea, but the Murgos were still too big for their mounts.

All right, I'll be mentioning Murgos and Nadraks and Thulls from time to time as we go along, so I'm going to sort them out for you. The three Angarak tribes that migrated to the western continent after the destruction of Cthol Mishrak were not, in fact, tribes at all. They were all Angaraks, but the almost two thousand years that they had lived in the City of Endless Night had modified them. The differences between them were not racial nor tribal, but rather were based on class. The word "Murgo" in old Angarak meant warrior; the word "Nadrak" meant townsman; and the word "Thull" meant peasant or serf. Murgos are built like soldiers, broad shouldered, narrow-waisted, and generally athletic. Nadraks tend to be leaner. Thulls are built like oxen. Torak had been so intent on trying to subdue the Orb that he hadn't paid any attention to what was happening to the inhabitants of Cthol Mishrak as a result of two thousand years of what might be called selective breeding, and he assumed that they differed from each other because they were of different tribes. That's one of the reasons that the Angarak societies he exported to the West didn't work very well. Murgos felt that work was beneath their dignity; Thulls were too stupid to set up anything even resembling a government; and Nadraks had nobody to swindle but each other.

Have you got all that straight? Try to remember it. I don't want to have to go through it all again. I repeat myself often enough as it is.

The Hounds had been made wary by what had happened to their packmates, so they held back while the Murgos and Grolims rushed to the attack. I didn't even have to tell Riva what to do this time. He took out the Orb and held it up over his head.

Once again the Orb flickered and went out, and once again it took fire. It went a little further this time, however. It was probably the first time in its history that Cthol Mishrak had been fully illuminated, and the western slopes of the Karandese Mountains and the Eastern Sea as far north as the pole and as far west as the shores of Morindland were engulfed in a light that was at least as bright as the light that reached us at Korim three thousand years later.

The charging Murgos and Grolims were instantly incinerated by that awful light. I discovered something about the Orb in that moment. It had a certain innate sense of decency. It warned people before it unleashed its power on them. That's what the blinding of the Hounds had been—a warning. There was only one, though. If people chose to ignore the Orb's first warning, they didn't get a second.

The Alorns and I were stunned by the enormity of what had just happened. The Hounds took advantage of our momentary confusion to circle around along the riverbanks to get ahead of us, and that made it possible for them to slow us down. That single flash of brilliant light had temporarily blinded *us*, too, and we floundered along in the darkness after it subsided. Our near blindness, coupled with the periodic suicidal charges of individual Hounds, slowed us to the point that we continued downriver at a crawl.

"How much farther to the coast?" Cherek panted.

"I have no idea," I admitted.

"This isn't turning out well, Belgarath."

"You worry too much." I turned teary eyes at his youngest son. "Keep holding it up in the air, Riva. Let it see what's coming after us."

We kept going down the river, our trip punctuated by a series of bright flashes and what sounded like thunderclaps as the Orb exploded the Hounds that came rushing at us from the riverbanks.

"They're coming up from behind us, Belgarath!" Dras called from the rear. "Torak's with them!"

I swore. I hadn't expected this. It's not like the Gods to take a hand in these skirmishes. *"Is he supposed to do that?"* I threw the question into the echoing vaults of my mind.

"No, he's not!" My passenger sounded suddenly very angry. *"He's cheating!"*

"Does that mean that the rules have been suspended?"

"I think it does. Be careful though. We don't want to blow up this whole side of the universe."

I choked a little on that. *"Do you want me to do it?"*

"Absolutely not! If you take up the Orb, it'll attach itself to you, and you'll never be able to get rid of it. You'd have to become its guardian, and you don't have time for that. Tell Riva what to do. Don't let him destroy Torak, whatever happens. He's not the one who's supposed to do that."

"Cherek!" I said sharply. "Take Dras and Algar! Hold those people back while I talk to Riva!"

The king of Aloria nodded grimly, and the three of them spread out on the ice, their weapons ready. The Murgo skirmishers in the forefront of the advancing Angaraks got a quick lesson in the virtue of prudence at that point. It's *not* a good idea to try to attack large Alorns when they're ready for you.

"Listen very carefully, Riva," I told Iron-grip. "I want you to concentrate on your hand."

"What?"

"You don't have to understand. Just look at the Angaraks and think about what you'd like to do to them, but think about your hand at the same time. The Orb's a weapon, but you don't have to swing it. Just be aware of it, and it'll do what you want it to do."

"I thought you said that I wasn't supposed to do that," he objected.

"The rules have changed. The other side's cheating, so we're going to cheat a little, too. *Don't* try to hurt Torak, though. You'll destroy the world if you do."

"I'll do *what*?"

"You heard me. Concentrate on obliterating the Angaraks instead. Torak's clever enough to get the point—eventually. He probably won't cheat again."

"I'll do what I can." Riva didn't sound too sure of himself. He raised the Orb, though, and I could feel his Will building as he concentrated on the advancing Angaraks.

But nothing happened.

"You've got to release it!" I shouted at him.

"What?"

"You've got the thought right, but you've got to turn it loose!"

"How?"

"Say something!"

"What do I say?"

"I don't care! Try 'now,' or 'burn,' or 'kill!' Just say *something!*"

"Go." He said it rather tentatively.

I controlled myself with a certain amount of effort. "You're giving orders here, Riva," I told him. "Don't make it sound like a question."

"*Go!*" he thundered.

It wasn't the Word I'd have used, but it turned the trick. The advancing Angaraks began exploding. Whole strings of them blew up one after another—bright flashes and sharp detonations running in sequence from one riverbank to the other. Cherek's youngest son obliterated the front rank. Then he went back and methodically destroyed the second rank, then the third.

"Can't you do more than one at a time?" I asked him.

"Do you want to do this?" he demanded from between clenched teeth.

"No. It's not allowed."

"Then do you want to shut up and let me do it?"

Now do you see how Garion comes by his short temper? Riva was normally the most even-tempered Alorn I've ever come across, but you didn't want to irritate him.

After he'd turned the first five or six ranks of Angaraks into puffs of smoke and floating ashes, the rest of them got the message. They turned and fled, giving the raging Torak a wide berth.

Torak may have been raging, but I noticed that he was covering his steel-encased face with his remaining hand. He *definitely* didn't want to lose his other eye. Finally, even he turned and fled howling.

"You can turn it off now," I suggested to Riva.

"I could go after them," he offered eagerly. "I could chase down every Angarak on the whole continent. Torak wouldn't have a single worshiper left."

"Never mind," I told him. "You've gone as far as you're supposed to. Put the Orb away."

Cherek, Dras, and Algar came back. "Nice little fight," the King of Aloria noted. "That Orb's a handy thing to have along, isn't it?"

Alorns!

It seems to me I've said that before. You might as well get used to it. I've been rolling my eyes up at the sky and sighing *"Alorns!"* for so long now that I don't even know I'm doing it any more.

We went down to the mouth of the river and started slogging out across the ice. The Hounds were keeping their distance now, but they *were* still following us.

"Are they going to be a problem?" I asked my friend.

"Not for long. They'll have to turn back when we get about halfway across."

"Why?"

"They're Grolims, Belgarath. They don't have any power on your side of the Sea of the East."

"Zedar did."

"That's because he's a disciple. Different rules apply to disciples. Ctuchik or Urvon could keep coming, but ordinary Grolims can't."

"Why not?"

"Beldin explained it to you once, remember?"

"Oh, now that you mention it, I guess I do. Grolims don't have any power in a place where there aren't any Angaraks?"

"Amazing. You remembered after all."

"What now?"

"Pick up one foot and put it in front of the other one. I'll let you decide which foot. Don't try to pick them both up at the same time, though."

"Very funny."

We continued across that awful broken sea ice for the next couple of days with the Hounds still not too far behind us.

There was no boundary line out there, of course, but I knew when we had reached the halfway point, because the Hounds suddenly broke off their pursuit. They lined up along an ice-ridge and sat howling in frustration.

"Our luck's still holding," I told the Alorns.

"How's that?" Cherek asked me.

"That's as far as the Hounds can come. We're home free now."

That turned out to be premature, because suddenly there was a Hound directly in front of us—a Hound twice the size of the ones howling behind us. It seemed to emanate a reddish glow.

"Don't bother," I told Riva as his hand dug into the neck of his tunic. "The dog's an illusion. It's not really there."

"You haven't heard the last of this, Belgarath," the monstrous creature growled at me, seeming almost to chew on the words with its long fangs.

"You would be Urvon," I said calmly, "or possibly Ctuchik."

"I'll let *you* worry about that. You and I are going to meet again, old man; you've got my promise on that. You've won this time. Next time you won't be so lucky."

And then it vanished.

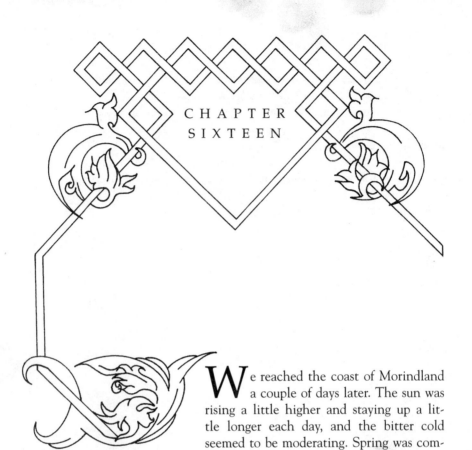

CHAPTER
SIXTEEN

We reached the coast of Morindland a couple of days later. The sun was rising a little higher and staying up a little longer each day, and the bitter cold seemed to be moderating. Spring was coming to the north.

We decided not to retrace our steps and cross the arctic wastes of Morindland again. We went south instead. We weren't in any danger now, and we all wanted to find a warmer climate. We followed the shoreline until we reached present-day Gar og Nadrak, which in those days was eastern Aloria. Cherek was king there, but he didn't have very many subjects in that part of his kingdom—unless you count the deer. The Alorns who were there were all members of the Bear-cult anyway, so we avoided them. Bear-cultists have wanted to get their hands on the Orb since their order was founded, and Cherek and the rest of us weren't very eager for any more confrontations.

Once we were beyond the North Range, we turned west again and proceeded through that vast forest, crossed the mountains, and reached the Drasnian moors. Then we turned southwesterly, passed Lake Atun, and eventually reached the banks of the Aldur River on a fine spring morning.

There was someone waiting for us there.

"Well, boy," the humorous old man in the rickety cart said to me, "I see you're still headed west."

"I guess it's sort of a habit by now," I replied in as casual a way as I could manage.

"You two know each other, I take it," Cherek noted.

"We've run across each other a few times," I replied. I assumed that my Master had reasons for wanting to remain anonymous, so I didn't give him away.

"Have you had breakfast yet?" the old man asked.

"If you want to call it that," Dras replied. "A few chunks of dried beef is hardly what I'd call breakfast."

"I've got a camp set up a mile or so downriver," the old man told us, "and I've had an ox roasting all night. You're welcome to join me, if you're of a mind. Are you thirsty, too? I've got a barrel of good ale chilling in the river back at camp."

That settled it, of course. The Alorns followed along behind the cart like a litter of happy puppies as the old man and I led them to breakfast. "Let's feed your friends first," the old man told me quietly. "Then you and I need to talk."

"If that's the way you want it," I replied.

Cherek and his sons fell on the roasted ox like a pack of hungry wolves and plunged into the ale barrel like a school of fish. After an hour or so of eating and drinking, they all became very sleepy and decided to take a little nap. The old man and I strolled down to the riverbank and stood looking out across the water. The spring runoff had begun in the Tolnedran Mountains, and the river ran bank-full and muddy brown.

"Is there any particular reason for the disguise?" I asked, getting right to the point.

"Probably not," my Master replied. "I use it when I have occasion to leave the Vale. People tend not to notice me when I'm plodding along in the cart. My brothers and I had a meeting in the cave."

"Oh?"

"We're going to have to leave, Belgarath."

"*Leave?*"

"We don't have any choice. If we stay, sooner or later we'll have to confront Torak directly, and that would destroy the world. This world's too important for us to let that happen. The Child of Light is going to need it."

"Who's the Child of Light?"

"It varies. *You* were, while you and Zedar were scuffling up in Morindland. The Necessities can't meet directly, so they have to function through agents. I think I've explained this to you before."

I nodded glumly. I wasn't happy about this particular turn of events.

"There's going to be an ultimate Child of Light, however," he went on, "and an ultimate Child of Dark. They're the ones who're going to set-tle everything once and for all. It's your job to prepare for the coming of the Child. Keep an eye on Riva. The Child will descend from him."

"Won't I ever see you again?"

He smiled faintly. "Of course you will. I've spent too much time rais-ing you to turn you loose. Pay close attention to your dreams, Belgarath. I won't be able to come back directly—at least not very often—so I'll talk with you while you're asleep."

"That's something, anyway. Is that how you're going to guide us, through our dreams?"

"You'll be guided by the Necessity. The Second Age that the Dals talk about is over now. This is the Third Age, the Age of Prophecy. The two Necessities are going to inspire certain people to predict the future."

I saw the flaw in that immediately. "Isn't that sort of dangerous?" I asked. "That's not the sort of information we'd want just anybody to get his hands on."

"That's already been taken care of, my son. The rest of mankind won't understand what the predictions mean. They'll be obscure enough so that most people will think that they're just the ravings of assorted madmen. Tell your Alorns to watch for them and to write down what they say if it's at all possible. There'll be hidden messages in them."

"It's a cumbersome way to do business, Master."

"I know, but it's part of the rules."

"I'm not so sure that the rules are holding, Master. The other side started cheating when we were in Cthol Mishrak."

"That was Torak. His Necessity apologized for that. Torak's being punished for it."

"Good. What am I supposed to do now? I really ought to get back to Poledra, you know."

He sighed. "That's going to have to wait, I'm afraid. I'm sorry, Belgarath—more sorry than you could possibly know—but you haven't finished yet. You still have to divide up Aloria."

"I have to do *what?*"

He explained it to me—at some length.

It's my story, and I'll tell it the way I want to. If you don't like the way I'm telling it, tell it yourself.

After he'd given me my instructions, the old man fed his horse and then drove his cart off toward the south, leaving me with only the snoring Alorns for company. I didn't bother to wake them, and they slept straight on through until the following morning.

"Where's your friend?" Cherek asked when they finally woke up.

"He had something to attend to," I replied.

"Well, it's all over then, isn't it?" Dras said. "It'll be good to get back to Val Alorn."

"You aren't going to Val Alorn, Dras," I told him.

"What?"

"You're going back up to those moors we just came across."

"Why would I want to do that?"

"Because I'm telling you to do it." I was a little blunt about it. I wasn't in a very good humor that morning. I looked at Bear-shoulders. "I'm sorry, Cherek," I told him, "but I'm going to have to split up your kingdom. The Angaraks aren't just going to let this slide, so we're going to have to get ready for them. Riva's guarding the Orb, so the rest of you are going to have to guard *him*. I'm going to spread you out so that Torak's people can't slip up on Riva and steal back the Orb."

"How long's that likely to take?" Cherek asked me. "How long until I can put my kingdom back together again?"

"You're not going to be able to do that, I'm afraid. The division of Aloria's going to be permanent."

"Belgarath!" He said it plaintively, almost like a child protesting the removal of his favorite toy.

"It's out of my hands, Cherek. You're the one who came up with the idea of stealing the Orb. Now you're going to have to live with the consequences. Dras has to establish his own kingdom on the north moors. Algar's going to have his down here on these grasslands. You're going back to Val Alorn. Your kingdom's going to be that peninsula."

"*Kingdom?*" he exploded. "That's hardly bigger than a clothes closet!"

"Don't worry about it. Your kingdom's the ocean now. Call your ship-builders together. Those scows they've been building aren't good enough. I'll draw up some plans for you. The king of the Ocean's going to need war boats, not floating bathtubs."

His eyes narrowed speculatively. "The king of the Ocean," he mused. "That's got a nice ring to it, doesn't it? Can you really make war with boats, though?"

"Oh, yes," I assured him. "And the nice part of it is that you don't have to walk to get to the battlefield."

"Where do you want me to go, Belgarath?" Riva asked me.

"I'll show you myself. I'm supposed to go with you to help you get set up."

"Thanks, but where are we going?"

"To the Isle of the Winds."

"That's nothing but a rock out in the middle of the Great Western Sea!" he objected.

"I know, but it's *your* rock. You're going to take a sizable number of Alorns and go there. You volunteered to pick up the Orb. Now it's your responsibility. When we get to the Isle, you're going to build a fortress, and you and your people are going to spend the rest of your lives guarding the Orb. Then you're going to turn the responsibility for guarding the Orb over to your children, and then they'll take over."

"How long's this going to last?"

"I haven't got the faintest idea—centuries, probably, maybe even eons. Your father's going to build war boats, and he's not going to let *any-body* near the Isle of the Winds."

"This isn't what I had in mind when we started, Belgarath," Cherek complained.

"Life's just filled with these little disappointments, isn't it? Play-time's over, gentlemen. It's time to grow up. We've got work to do."

I probably didn't really have to run roughshod over them like that, but my Master hadn't been very gentle with *me*, and the sniveling of Cherek and his boys was making me tired. They'd set off on the most important mission in the history of their race as if it had been some kind of lark. Now that the consequences of their little romp in the snow were coming home to roost, all they could do was stand around and complain about it.

Alorns are such babies at times.

I hammered the details of the division into them with that same callousness. I didn't give them time to get all weepy and sentimental. I told Cherek in precise terms just how many warriors he was going to send to each of his sons to help with the founding of the new kingdoms. His expression grew mournful when he realized that I was usurping over half of his subjects. Every time he started to protest, I reminded him pointedly that the retrieval of the Orb had been his idea in the first place. *I* hadn't wanted to leave my pregnant wife at the time, so I didn't have much sympathy for him now.

"All right," I concluded that evening, "that's the way we're going to do it. Any questions?"

"What are we supposed to do when we get set up?" Dras asked sullenly. "Just stand around and wait for the Angaraks?"

"You'll get further instructions from Belar," I told him. "The Gods are involved in this, too, you know."

"Belar doesn't like me," Dras said. "I beat him at dice most of the time."

"Don't play dice with him, then. Try to stay on the good side of him."

"This is awfully open country around here," Algar said, looking out at the vast grassland. "I'm going to have to do a lot of walking."

"There are wild horses out there. Chase them down and ride."

"My feet drag on the ground when I try to sit on a horse."

"Chase down a bigger one, then."

"There aren't any bigger ones."

"Breed some."

"The weather on the Isle of the Winds is really miserable," Riva complained.

"Build houses with thick walls and stout roofs."

"The wind'll blow thatch roofs right off the houses."

"Make your roof out of slate, then, and nail it down."

Cherek finally got as tired of it as I was getting. "You've got your instructions," he told his sons. "Now go do as you're told. You might be kings now, but you're still my sons. Don't make me ashamed of you."

That put the starch back in their spines.

The farewells the following morning were tearful, however. Then we scattered to the winds, leaving Algar standing forlornly on the bank of the Aldur River.

Riva and I went west until we reached the mountains, and then we swung off slightly northwesterly to avoid the northern reaches of Ulgoland. I'd gotten all the entertainment I wanted out of our skirmishes with the Angaraks. I didn't feel much like playing with Algroths or Eldrakyn.

We came down out of the mountains and crossed the fertile plains of modern-day Sendaria until we reached the shore of the Great Western Sea. We stopped there to wait for the warriors Cherek had promised to send—and their women, of course. I was establishing new countries, and I needed breeding stock.

Yes, I know that's a blunt way to put it, and it'll probably offend Polgara, but that's just too bad. If she doesn't have that to be offended about, she'll probably just find something else.

Got you that time, didn't I, Pol?

While Riva and I were waiting for his people to arrive from Val Alorn, I amused myself by cheating. There was a sizable forest near the beach, and I utilized my talents to fell trees and saw them into boards. Riva had seen me do all sorts of things with the Will and the Word, but for some reason, the sight of a log spewing out unprovoked sawdust seemed to unnerve him. He finally refused entirely to watch, but sat instead staring out at the sea and muttering the word "unnatural"—usually loud enough for me to hear. I tried to explain to him that we were going to need boats to get to the Isle of the Winds, and that boats implied lumber, but he refused to listen to me. It wasn't until I had stacks of lumber spread out for a quarter of a mile along the beach that he finally came up with what came fairly close to a reasonable objection. "If you make boats out of those green boards, they'll sink. They'll have to cure for at least a year."

"Oh, not that long," I disagreed. Then, just to show him who was in charge, I looked at a nearby stack, concentrated, and said, "Hot."

The stack started to smoke immediately. Riva had irritated me, and I had gone a bit too far. I reduced the heat, and the smoke was replaced by steam as the green boards began to sweat out their moisture.

"They're warping," he pointed out triumphantly.

"Of course they are," I replied calmly. "I want them to warp."

"Warped lumber's no good."

"It depends on what you want to build with it," I disagreed. "We want ships, and ships have curved sides. Something with flat sides is called a barge, and it doesn't sail very well."

"You've got an answer for everything, haven't you, Belgarath? Even for your mistakes."

"Why are you being so cross with me, Riva?"

"Because you've torn my life apart. You've separated me from my family, and you're taking me to the most wretched place on earth to spend the rest of my life. Stay away from me, Belgarath. I don't like you very much right now." And he stalked off up the beach.

I started after him.

"Leave him alone, Belgarath." It was my friend again.

"If I'm going to have his cooperation, I'm going to have to make peace with him."

"He's a little upset right now. He'll settle down. Don't weaken your position by going to him. Make him come to you."

"What if he doesn't?"

"He has to. You're the only one who can tell him what to do, and he knows it. He's got an enormous sense of responsibility. That's why I chose him. Dras is bigger, and Algar's smarter, but Riva sticks to something once he starts it. Go back to baking boards. It'll keep your mind off your troubles."

Somehow he always knew what the most insulting thing he could say would be. *Baking boards!* I still get hot around the ears when I remember that particular expression.

Two days later, Riva came to me apologetically. "I'm sorry, Belgarath," he said contritely.

"What for? You didn't say anything that wasn't true. I *have* torn your life apart, I *have* separated you from your family, and I *am* going to take you to the Isle of the Winds to spend the rest of your life. The only thing you left out was the fact that none of it's been my idea. You're the Keeper of the Orb now, and somebody has to tell you what to do. I'm your teacher. Neither one of us asked for the jobs, but we got them anyway. We might as well make the best of it. Now come over here, and I'll show you the plans I've drawn up for your boats."

"Ships," he corrected absently.

"Any way you want it, Orb-keeper."

The Alorns began drifting in the next afternoon. Alorns don't march. They don't even stay together when they're traveling, and their direction is pretty indeterminate, since small groups of them periodically break off to go exploring.

Riva put them to work building ships immediately, and that lonely beach turned into an impromptu shipyard. There were a number of arguments about my design for those ships, and some of the objections raised by various Alorns were even valid. Most of them were silly, however. Alorns love to argue, probably because arguments in their culture are usually preludes to fights.

I drifted up and down the beach, cheating wherever it was necessary, and we finished about ten of those ships in just under six weeks. Then Riva left his cousin Anrak in charge and we took an advance party out into the Sea of the Winds toward the Isle.

If you've never seen the Isle of the Winds, you might think that the descriptions of it you've heard are exaggerations. Believe me, they aren't. In the first place, the island has only one beach, a narrow strip of gravel about a mile long at the head of a deeply indented bay on the east side. The rest of the shoreline is comprised of cliffs. There are woods inland, dark evergreen forests such as you'll find in any northern region, and some fairly extensive meadows in the mountain valleys to the north. It probably wouldn't be so bad, except that the wind blows all the time, and it can—and frequently does—rain for six straight months without let up. Then, when it gets tired of raining, it snows.

We rowed around the Isle twice, but we didn't find any other beaches, so we rowed up that bay I mentioned and came ashore on the island's only beach.

"Where am I supposed to build this fort?" Riva asked me when the two of us finally got our feet on solid ground again.

"That's up to you," I replied. "What's the most logical place to build it?"

"Right here, I suppose, since this is the only place where anybody can come ashore. If I've got my fort here, I'll be able to see them coming, at least."

"Sound thinking." I looked at him rather closely. That boyish quality was starting to fade. The responsibility he'd so lightly accepted back in Cthol Mishrak was starting to sit heavily on him.

He looked at the steep valley running down out of the mountains to the head of the bay. "The fort's going to have to be a little bigger than I'd thought," he mused. "I'll need to block that whole valley with it. I guess I'll have to build a city here."

"You might as well. There won't be much to do on this island except make babies, so your population's going to expand. You'll need lots of houses."

He suddenly blushed.

"You *do* know what's involved in that, don't you? Making babies, I mean?"

"Of course I do."

"I just wanted to be sure that you weren't going to be out turning over cabbage leaves or trying to chase down storks looking for them."

"Don't be insulting." He looked up the valley again. "There are enough trees to build a city, I guess."

"No," I told him flatly. "Don't build a wooden city. The Tolnedrans tried that at Tol Honeth, and they no sooner got it finished than it burned to the ground. Use rock."

"That'll take a long time, Belgarath," he objected.

"Have you got anything better to do? Set up a temporary camp here on the beach and put signal fires on those headlands at the mouth of the bay to guide the rest of your people here. Then you and I are going to spend some time designing a city. I don't want this place just growing here like a weed. Its purpose is to protect the Orb, and I want to be certain that there aren't any holes in the defenses."

Over the next several weeks the rest of Riva's ships rowed in, six or eight at a time, and by then Iron-grip and I had completed the layout of the city.

"What do you think I ought to call it—the city, I mean?" he asked me when we were finished.

"What difference does it make?"

"A city ought to have a name, Belgarath."

"Call it anything you like. Name it after yourself, if you want."

"Val Riva?"

"Isn't that a little ostentatious? Just call it Riva and let it go at that."

"That doesn't really sound like a city, Belgarath."

"It will, once people get used to it."

Finally Anrak arrived. "That's the last of us, Riva," he bellowed as he waded ashore. "We're all here now. Have you got anything to drink?"

The party there on the beach got rowdy that night, and after I'd had a few tankards, the noise began to make my head hurt, so I climbed up the steep valley to get away from the carousing and to think a bit. I still had a number of things to do before I could go home, and I considered various ways to get them all taken care of in a hurry. I *really* wanted to get back to the Vale and to Poledra. I was undoubtedly a father by now, and I sort of wanted to have a look at my offspring.

It was probably a couple of hours past midnight when I glanced down toward the beach. I jumped to my feet swearing. All the ships were on fire!

I ran back down the valley to the beach and found Riva and his cousin standing at the water's edge singing an Alorn drinking song. They were bleary-eyed and swaying back and forth, as drunk as lords.

"What are you doing?" I screamed at them.

"Oh, there you are Belgarath," Riva said, blinking owlishly at me. "We looked all over for you." He gestured out at the burning ships. "Nice fire, isn't it?"

"It's a splendid fire. Why did you set it?"

"That lumber you made for us is nice and dry, so it burns very well."

"Riva, why are you burning the ships?"

He looked at his cousin. "Why *are* we burning the ships, Anrak? I forget."

"It's to keep people from getting bored and running off," Anrak replied.

"Oh, yes. Now I remember. Isn't that a good idea, Belgarath?"

"It's a rotten idea!"

"What's wrong with it?"

"How am *I* supposed to get home now?"

"Oh," he said. "I hadn't thought of that, I guess." His eyes brightened. "Would you like something to drink?" he asked me.

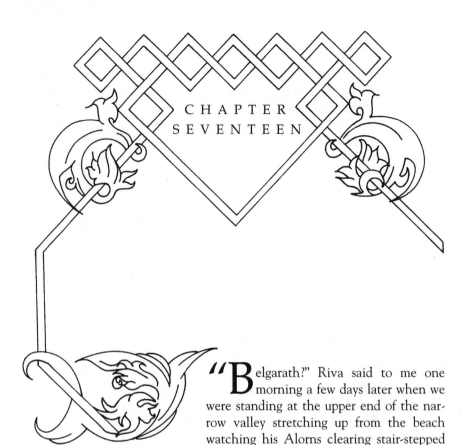

CHAPTER
SEVENTEEN

"Belgarath?" Riva said to me one morning a few days later when we were standing at the upper end of the narrow valley stretching up from the beach watching his Alorns clearing stair-stepped terraces across the steep valley floor.

"Yes, Riva?"

"Am I supposed to have a sword?"

"You've already got one."

"No, I mean a special sword."

"Yes," I replied. Where had he found out about *that*?

"Where is it then?"

"It doesn't exist yet. You're supposed to make it."

"I can do that, I guess. What am I supposed to make it from?"

"Stars, as I understand it."

"How am I going to get my hands on any stars?"

"They'll fall out of the sky."

"I guess it *was* Belar who talked to me last night, then."

"I don't follow you."

"I had a dream—at least I thought it was a dream. I seemed to hear Belar's voice. I recognized it because I used to watch him play dice with Dras. He used to swear a lot while he was playing, because Dras always won. Isn't that odd? You'd think a God could make the dice come up any way he wanted them to, but Belar doesn't even think about cheating. Dras does, though. Dras could roll a ten with only one die."

I tried to stay calm. "Riva, you're straying. You started to tell me about your dream. If Belar spoke to you, it might be sort of important."

"He used a lot of 'thees' and 'thous.'"

"The Gods do that. What did he say?"

"I'm not sure if I got the first part of it right. I was dreaming about something else, and I didn't want to be interrupted."

"Oh? What were you dreaming about?"

He actually blushed. "It's not really important," he said evasively.

"You never know about dreams. What was it about?"

He blushed even redder. "Well—there was a girl involved in it. That wouldn't be too significant, would it?"

"Ah—no, I suppose not. Did Belar finally manage to get your attention?"

"He had to talk to me pretty loudly. I was *really* interested in that girl."

"I'm sure you were."

"She had the blondest hair I've ever seen, and would you believe that she didn't have any clothes on?"

"*Riva!* Forget about the girl! What did Belar say?"

"You don't have to get excited, Belgarath," he said in a slightly injured tone. "I'm getting to it." He frowned. "Let me see now. It seems to me that he said something like, 'Behold, Guardian of the Orb, I will cause two stars to fall from the sky, and I will show thee where they lie, and thou shalt take up the two stars and shall place them in a great fire and forge them. And the one star shall be a blade, and the other a hilt, and it shall be a sword that shall guard the Orb of my brother, Aldur.' Or something like that."

"We'll have to put out watchmen at night, then."

"Oh? What for?"

"To keep an eye on the sky, of course. We have to know where the stars come down."

"Oh, I already know where they came down, Belgarath. Belar took me to the front of my tent and pointed at the sky. The two stars came down side by side, and I saw them hit the ground. Then Belar went away, and I went back to bed to see if I could find that girl again."

"*Will* you forget about that girl?"

"No, I don't think I ever will. She was the most beautiful girl I've ever seen."

"Do you happen to remember where the stars came down?"

"Up there." He gestured vaguely at the snow-covered mountain peak rearing up at the head of the valley.

"Let's go get them."

"Shouldn't I stay here? I'm sort of in charge, I guess. Doesn't that mean that I'm supposed to supervise the work?"

"Is your cousin sober?"

"Anrak? Probably—more or less, anyway."

"Why don't you call him and let him take over here? We'd better go find those stars before it snows again and buries them."

"Oh, we'd still be able to find them. A little snow wouldn't hide them."

I gave him a puzzled look

"They're *stars*, Belgarath, and stars shine. We'll be able to see the light even if they're completely covered."

You see what I mean about Riva's innocence? He was far from being simpleminded, but he just couldn't bring himself to believe that anything could go wrong. He bellowed down the hill to his cousin, and then the two of us started up that narrow valley. There had evidently been a stream or river running down along the bottom of it at some time in the past, because there were rounded boulders at the bottom, but the stream was gone now. It had probably changed course when Torak rearranged the world.

Riva entertained me while we climbed by describing the girl he'd dreamed about. For some reason, he couldn't seem to think about anything else.

The fallen stars weren't really all that hard to find, of course. They'd been white-hot when they hit the mountain, and they'd melted huge craters in the snow.

"Those aren't stars, Belgarath," Riva objected when I picked them up triumphantly. "They're nothing but a couple of lumps of iron."

"The snow put out their light," I told him. It wasn't entirely true, but it was easier than trying to explain.

"You can't put out the light of a star," he scoffed.

"These are special stars, Riva." I was digging myself in deeper, but I didn't feel like arguing with him.

"Oh. I hadn't thought of that, I guess. What do we do now?"

"We follow Belar's instructions. Let's build a fire."

"Up here? In the snow?"

"There's something else you have to do up here. You've still got the Orb with you, haven't you?"

"Of course. I've always got it." He patted the lump under his tunic. "What are we going to use for a hammer? And an anvil?"

"I'll take care of it. I don't think ordinary tools would work. These stars seem to be a little harder than ordinary iron."

We went into a nearby grove of trees, and I built a fire. I cheated quite a bit with that fire. You won't get the kind of heat we were going to need out of green wood. "Throw them in the fire, Riva," I instructed him.

"Anything you say," he agreed, tossing the two lumps of celestial iron into the flames.

Then I focused my Will and constructed the hammer and anvil and tongs. I suspect that if you went to that mountain behind the Hall of the Rivan King, you'd find that they're still there. They're so dense that they probably haven't rusted down yet.

Riva hefted the hammer. "It's heavier than it looks," he noted.

"That's because it's a magic hammer." It was easier than getting into the business of comparative density.

"I thought it might be," he said quite calmly.

We sat on a log by that roaring fire waiting for the lumps of iron to heat up. When they were finally white-hot, Riva raked them out of the coals and got down to work. Somewhere along the way, he'd picked up any number of skills. He wasn't as good a smith as Durnik is, but he was competent.

After about ten minutes, he stopped hammering and looked rather closely at the glowing lump he had been beating on.

"What's wrong?" I asked him.

"These stars must be magic, too—just like the hammer. If they were just ordinary iron, they'd have cooled by now."

No, Durnik, I didn't cheat. I think Belar did, though.

There are a number of versions of the *Book of Alorn* that rather blandly state that I assumed the shape of a fox to advise Riva while he was forging the sword. That's sheer nonsense, of course. I've never taken the form of a fox in my entire life. What *is* it about priests that drives them to embellish a good story with improbable details? If they're *that* hungry for magic, why don't they just spend a little time and pick up the skills for themselves? Then they'll be able to play with magic to their heart's content.

Riva continued to hammer on those two glowing lumps of iron until he'd roughed out the shape of the blade and the hilt. Then I made a file for him, and he started to smooth them out. He suddenly stopped and started to swear.

"What's the matter?" I asked him.

"I've made a mistake," he said sourly.

"I don't see anything wrong."

"I've got two pieces, Belgarath. How am I going to put them together?"

"We'll get to that. Keep polishing."

After he'd dressed off the blade, he set it aside and started on the massive, two-handed hilt. "Does it need a pommel?" he asked me.

"We'll get to that, too."

He kept working. His face was streaming sweat from the heat of the iron, and he finally threw down the file and laid the hilt on the anvil with the tongs. "That's probably as good as I can get it," he said. "I'm not a goldsmith. Now what?"

I willed a barrel of water into existence. "Quench them," I told him.

He picked up that huge blade with his tongs and plunged it into the water. The cloud of steam was really quite spectacular. Then he dropped the hilt in. "I still don't think we'll be able to put them together."

"Trust me."

It took quite some time for the submerged pieces of iron to stop glowing. I had to refill the barrel twice before they started to turn black.

Riva tentatively stuck his hand into the water and touched the blade. "I think they're cool enough now."

"Take out the Orb," I told him.

He looked around quickly. "I don't see any Angaraks," he said.

"No. This is something else."

He reached inside his tunic and took out the glowing Orb. It looked very small in that massive hand of his.

"Now fish out the hilt," I instructed.

He plunged his arm into the barrel and brought out that huge hilt.

"Put the Orb where the pommel ought to be."

"Why?"

"Just do it. You'll see."

He held up the hilt in one hand and put the Orb against the bottom of the handle. The click that came when they adhered together was clearly audible. Riva gasped.

"It's all right," I told him. "That was supposed to happen. Now pick up the blade and put the bottom of it against the top of the hilt."

He did that. "Now what?"

"Push."

"Push? What do you mean, push?"

"You know what the word means. Push the blade into the hilt."

"That's ridiculous, Belgarath. They're both solid steel."

I sighed. "Just try it, Riva. Don't stand around arguing with me. This is magic, and I'm the expert. Don't push too hard, or you'll shove the blade all the way through."

"Have you been drinking?"

"Do it, Riva!"

The blade made a strange singing sound as it slowly slid into the hilt, and the sound shuddered all the snow off nearby trees. When it was fully inserted, Riva tentatively wiggled the two pieces. Then he wrenched at them. "What an amazing thing!" he said. "It's all one piece now!"

"Naturally. Grab the hilt and hold your sword up." *This* was the real test.

He took hold of the two-handed hilt and lifted that huge sword a foot or so. "It hardly weighs anything!" he exclaimed.

"The Orb's carrying the weight," I explained. "Remember that when you have to take the Orb off. If you're holding the sword in one hand when you do that, the weight of it'll probably break your wrist. Raise the sword, Iron-grip."

He lifted it easily over his head, and, as I'd hoped, it burst joyously into blue flame, shearing off the rough edges and polishing the sword to mirror brightness. "Nice job," I complimented him. Then I howled with delight and danced a little jig of pure joy.

Riva was gaping at his flaming sword. "What happened?" he asked.

"You did it right, boy!" I exulted.

"You mean this was *supposed* to happen?"

"Every time, Riva! Every time! The sword's part of the Orb now. That's why it's on fire. Every time you raise it up like that, it'll take fire, and if I understand it right, it'll do the same thing when your son picks it up—and his son—and *his* son, as well."

"I don't have a son."

"Wait a while, he'll be along. Bring your sword. We're supposed to go up to the summit now."

He spent a fair amount of time swishing that sword through the air as we climbed the rest of the way to the top. I'll admit that it was impressive, but the screeching whistle it made as it carved chunks off the air began to get on my nerves after a while. He was having fun, though, so I didn't say anything to him about it.

There was a boulder at the top of the peak that was about the size of a large house. I looked at it when we got there, and I began to have some doubts about what we were supposed to do. It was an awfully big rock.

"All right," Riva said, "now what?"

"Get a firm grip on your sword and split that rock."

"That'll shatter the blade, Belgarath."

"It's not supposed to."

"Why am I supposed to split rocks with my sword? Wouldn't a sledge-hammer work better?"

"You could pound on that boulder with a hammer for a year and not even dent it."

"More magic?"

"Sort of. There used to be a river running down the valley. It got dammed up when Torak cracked the world. It's still there, though—under that boulder. Your family's going to repair the world, and this is where you're going to start. Break the rock, Riva. Free the river. You're going to need fresh water in your city anyway."

He shrugged. "If you say so, Belgarath."

Garion, I want you to notice the absolute trust that boy had. You might want to think about that the next time you feel like arguing with me.

Riva raised up that enormous flaming sword and delivered a blow that probably would have broken a lesser rock down into rubble. I'm sure that the sound startled all the deer in Sendaria.

The boulder split evenly down the middle, and the two sides fell ponderously out of the way.

The river came gushing out like a breaking wave.

Riva and I got very wet at that point. We struggled out of the water and stood looking at our river with a certain sense of accomplishment.

"Oops," Riva said after a moment.

"Oops what?"

"Maybe I should have warned the fellows working down below," he replied. "I don't think they'll be too happy about this."

"They aren't down in the streambed, Riva. That's where they've been dumping the excess dirt and rock they're scraping off those terraces."

"I hope you're right. Otherwise, they'll probably get washed out to sea, and they'll probably swear at me for a week after they swim back."

As it turned out, our newly released river saved those Alorns months of work. There were natural terraces under all the accumulated debris they'd been moving, and that first rush of water washed those terraces clean. The Alorns who *were* washed out to sea were so pleased with that turn of events that they didn't even swear at Riva—at least not very much.

Now that Riva had his sword, I was finished with the things I was supposed to do on the Isle of the Winds. I could finally go home. I spent a day or so giving Riva and his cousin Anrak their instructions. Anrak was a little too fond of good brown ale, but he was a good-natured fellow, popular with the other Alorns. He was the perfect second-in-command. Some of the orders Riva was going to have to give his people wouldn't go down very well. Anrak, with his boisterous, good-humored laughter, was the perfect one to make them palatable. I sketched in Riva's throne room for him and told him how to fasten his sword to the wall behind the throne. It was a little difficult to keep his attention, since he wanted to talk about the girl in his dream. Then I wished them good luck and went off down the beach until I was out of sight. There was no real point in upsetting Riva's people any more than they already were.

I chose the form of an albatross for my return to the mainland. A seven-foot wingspan is very useful when you fly as badly as I do. After I was a few miles out to sea and had picked up some altitude, I learned the trick of simply locking those great wings out and coasting along on the air. What a joy that was! No flapping. No floundering. No panic. I even got to the point where I liked it. I think I could have soared like that for a solid month. I actually took a few short naps on my way.

It was almost with regret that I saw the coast of what's now Sendaria on the horizon.

You wouldn't believe how different Sendaria was in those days. What's now farmland was an untamed forest of huge trees, and just about the only part of it that was inhabited was a stretch along the north bank of the Camaar River that was occupied by the Wacite Arends. Because I was really in a hurry to get back to the Vale, I took the familiar form of the wolf and loped off through the forest.

This time I didn't have to wait periodically for any Alorns to catch up with me, so I made very good time. It was summer by now, so I had good weather. I angled down across Sendaria in a southeasterly direction and soon reached the mountains.

After a bit of consideration, I decided not to waste time with a tiresome detour, but to cut straight across the northern end of Ulgoland. I didn't really think that the monsters would be a problem. They were interested in men, not wolves; even Algroths and Hrulgin avoided wolves.

I gave some thought to swinging by Prolgu to advise the current Gorim of what had happened in Mallorea, but I decided against it. My Master knew about it, and he'd certainly have advised UL before he and his brothers had departed.

That was something I didn't really want to think about. My Master had been the central fact of my life for four thousand years, and his departure left a very large hole in my concept of the world. I couldn't imagine the Vale without him.

Anyway, I bypassed Prolgu and continued southeasterly toward the Vale. I saw a few Algroths lurking near the edge of the trees, and once a herd of Hrulgin, but they wisely chose not to interfere with me. I was in a hurry, and I wasn't in any mood for interruptions.

I loped across a ridge-line and descended into a river gorge. Since all the rivers on this side of the mountains of Ulgo flowed eastward to empty into the Aldur River, the quickest way to reach the Vale would be simply to follow the river until it reached the plains of Algaria.

Notice that I was already thinking of that vast grassland in those terms.

I can't exactly remember why I chose to resume my own form when I reached the river. Maybe I thought I needed a bath. I'd been on the go for six months now, and I certainly didn't want to offend Poledra by showing up in our tower smelling like a goat. Perhaps it was because I wanted a hot meal. As a wolf, I was quite satisfied with a diet of raw rabbit or uncooked deer or even an occasional fieldmouse, but I was not entirely a wolf, and periodically I grew hungry for cooked food. I pulled down a deer, anyway, resumed my own form, and set to work building a fire. I spitted a haunch, set it to roasting over the fire, and bathed in the river while it cooked.

I probably ate too much. A wolf on the move doesn't really spend too much time eating—usually no more than a few bites before he's off again—so I'd definitely managed to build up quite an appetite.

Anyway, after I'd eaten, I dozed by my fire. I really don't know how long I slept, but I was awakened quite suddenly by a kind of mindless hooting that sounded almost like laughter. I cursed my inattentiveness. Somehow a pack of rock-wolves had managed to creep up on me.

The term "rock-wolf" is really a misnomer. They aren't really wolves but are more closely related to hyenas. They're scavengers, and they'd probably caught scent of my deer. It would have been a simple thing to change back into a wolf and outrun them. I was comfortable, though, and I certainly didn't feel like running on a full stomach. I was also feeling just a little pugnacious. I'd been sleeping very well, and being awakened that way irritated me. I built up my fire and settled my back against a tree to wait for them. If they pushed me *too* far, there'd be one less pack of rock-wolves in the morning.

I saw a few of the ugly brutes slinking along at the edge of the trees, but they were afraid of my fire, so they didn't come any closer. That went on for the rest of the night. The fact that they neither attacked nor went off to find food somewhere else was a bit puzzling. This was not the way rock-wolves normally behaved.

Dawn was just touching the eastern sky when I found out why.

I'd just piled more wood on my fire when I caught a movement at the edge of the trees out of the corner of my eye. I thought it was another rock-wolf, so I took hold of a stick that was burning quite well, turned, and drew back my arm to throw the burning brand at the beast.

It wasn't a rock-wolf, however. It was an Eldrak.

I'd seen Eldrakyn before, of course, but always from a distance, so I hadn't realized just how big they are. I silently berated myself for not going wolf while I had the chance. Changing form takes a *little* while, and the huge creature wasn't very far away from me. If he were totally mad, as the Hrulgin and Algroths had been, he wouldn't give me nearly enough time.

He was shaggy and about eight feet tall. He didn't have what you'd really call a nose, and his lower jaw stuck out. He had long yellow tusks like a wild boar, and they jutted upward out of that protruding lower jaw. He had little, piglike eyes sunk deep under a heavy brow ridge, and those eyes burned red. "Why man-thing come to Grul's range?" He growled at me.

That was a surprise. I knew that the Eldrakyn were more intelligent than Algroths or Trolls, but I didn't know that they could talk.

I recovered quickly. The fact that he could talk raised the possibility of a peaceful solution here. "Just passing through, old boy," I replied urbanely. "I didn't mean to trespass, but I didn't realize that this range belongs to you."

"*All* know," His voice was hideous. "*All* know this is Grul's range."

"Well, not everybody, actually. I'm a stranger here, and you don't have the boundaries of your range clearly marked."

"You eat Grul's deer." He said it accusingly. This wasn't going too well. Being careful to conceal what I was doing, I slipped my long Alorn dagger out of its sheath and hid it in my left sleeve, handle down.

"I didn't eat it all," I told him. "You're welcome to the rest of it."

"How are you called?"

"The name's Belgarath." Maybe he'd heard of me. The Demon-Lord in Morindland had, after all. If my reputation extended all the way to Hell, maybe it'd penetrated these mountains, as well.

" 'Grat?" he said.

"Belgarath," I corrected.

" 'Grat." He said it with a certain finality. Evidently the shape of his jaw made it impossible for him to come any closer to the correct pronunciation. "It is good that Grul know this. Grul keep names of all man-things he eats in here." He banged the side of his head with the heel of his hand. " 'Grat want to fight before Grul eat him?" he asked hopefully.

I have had more congenial offers from time to time. I stood up. "Go away, Grul," I told him. "I don't have time to play with you."

A hideous grin distorted his shaggy face. "*Take* time, 'Grat. First we play. Then Grul eat."

This was *really* going downhill. I looked at him rather closely. He had huge arms that hung down to his knees. I definitely didn't want him wrapping those arms around me, so I carefully put my back against the tree. "You're making a mistake, Grul," I told him. "Take the deer and go away. The deer won't fight. I will." It was sheer bravado, of course. I

wouldn't have much chance against this huge monster in a purely physical struggle, and he was so close to me by now that any alternative would
have been very chancy. What a silly way this was for a man like me to
end his career.

"'Grat too small to fight Grul. 'Grat not too smart if he not see this.
'Grat is brave, though. Grul will remember how brave 'Grat was, after
Grul eat him."

"You're *too* kind," I murmured to him. "Come along then, Grul. Since
you've got your heart set on this, we may as well get going. I've got better
things to do today." I was gambling. The fact that this huge, shaggy monster could speak was an indication that he could also think—minimally.
My bluster was designed to make him a little wary. I didn't want him simply to rush me. If I could make him hesitate, I might have a chance.

My apparent willingness to fight him had the desired effect. Grul
wasn't accustomed to having people shrug off his huge size, so he was just
a bit cautious as he approached. That was what I'd been hoping for.
When he reached out with both huge hands to grasp me, I ducked under
them and stepped forward, smoothly pulling my knife out of my sleeve.
Then, with one quick swipe, I sliced him across the belly. I wasn't certain
enough of his anatomy to try stabbing him in the heart. As big as he was,
his ribs were probably as thick as my wrist.

He stared at me in utter amazement. Then he looked down at the entrails that came boiling out of the gaping wound that ran from hip to hip
across his lower belly.

"I think you dropped something there, Grul," I suggested.

He clutched at his spilling entrails with both hands, a look of consternation on his brutish face. "'Grat cut Grul's belly," he said. "Make
Grul's insides fall out."

"Yes, I noticed that. Did you want to fight some more, Grul? I think
you could spend your time better by sewing yourself back together. You're
not going to be able to move very fast with your guts tangled around your
feet."

"'Grat is not nice," he accused mournfully, sitting down and holding
his entrails in his lap.

For some reason, that struck me as enormously funny. I laughed for a
bit, but when two great tears began to run down his shaggy face, I felt a
little ashamed of myself. I held out my hand, willed a large, curved needle
into existence, and threaded it with deer sinew. I tossed it to him. "Here,"
I told him. "Sew your belly back together, and remember this if we ever
run across each other again. Find something else to eat, Grul. I'm old and
tough and stringy, so I really wouldn't taste too good—and I think you've
already discovered that I'm very expensive."

The dawn had progressed far enough along to give me sufficient light to travel, so I left him sitting by my fire trying to figure out how to use the needle I had given him.

Oddly, the incident brightened my disposition enormously. I'd actually pulled it off. What an amazing thing that was! I savored that last comment of his. By now, half the world agreed with him. 'Grat is *definitely* not nice.

I reached the western edge of the Vale two days later. It was early summer, one of the loveliest times of year. The spring rains have passed, and the dusty heat that comes later hasn't yet arrived. Even though our Master was gone, I don't think I've ever seen the Vale more beautiful. The grass was bright green, and many of the fruit trees that grew wild there were in bloom. The berries were out, although they weren't really ripe yet. I rather like the tart taste of half-ripe berries anyway. The sky was very blue, and the puffy white clouds seemed almost to dance aloft. The roiling grey clouds and stiff winds of early spring are dramatic, but early summer is lush and warm and filled with the scent of urgent growth. I was home, and I don't know that I've ever been any happier.

I was in a peculiar sort of mood. I was eager to get back to Poledra, but for some reason I was enjoying the sense of anticipation. I discarded my traveling form and almost sauntered across the gentle hills and valleys of the Vale. I knew that Poledra would sense my approach, and, as she always did, she'd probably be fixing supper. I didn't want to rush her.

It was just evening when I reached my tower, and I was a little surprised not to see lights in the windows. I went around to the far side, opened the door and went on in. "Poledra," I called up the stairs to her.

Strangely, she didn't answer.

I went on up the stairs.

It was dark in my tower. Poledra's curtains may not have kept out the breeze, but they definitely kept out the light. I twirled a tongue of flame off my index finger and lit a candle.

There wasn't anybody there, and the place had that dusty, unused look. What was going on here?

Then I saw a square of parchment in the precise center of my work-table, and I recognized Beldin's crabbed handwriting immediately. "Come to my tower." That was all it said.

I raised my candle and saw that the cradles were gone. Evidently Beldin had transferred my wife and offspring to *his* tower. That was odd. Poledra had a very strong attachment to *this* tower. Why would Beldin have moved her? As I remembered, she didn't particularly like his tower. It was a little too fanciful for her taste. Puzzled, I went back downstairs.

It was only about a five minute-walk to Beldin's tower, and I didn't really hurry. But my sense of anticipation was fading toward puzzlement.

"Beldin!" I shouted up to him. "It's me. Open your door."

There was quite a long pause, and then the rock that formed his door slid open.

I started on up the stairs. Now I *did* hurry.

When I reached the top of the stairs, I looked around. Beltira, Belkira, and Beldin were there, but Poledra wasn't. "Where's my wife?" I asked.

"Don't you want to meet your daughters?" Beltira asked me.

"Daughters? More than one?"

"That's why we made two cradles, brother," Belkira said. "You're the father of twins."

Beldin reached into one of the cradles and gently lifted out a baby. "This is Polgara," he introduced her. "She's your eldest." He handed me the blanket-wrapped baby. I turned back the corner of the blanket and looked into Pol's eyes for the very first time. Pol and I didn't get off to a very good start. Those of you who know her know that my daughter's eyes change color, depending on her mood. They were steel grey when I first looked into them and as hard as agates. I got the distinct impression that she didn't care much for me. Her hair was very dark, and she seemed not to have the characteristic chubbiness babies are supposed to have. Her face was expressionless, but those steely eyes of hers spoke volumes. Then I did something that had been a custom back in the village of Gara. Pol was my firstborn, whether she liked me or not, so I laid my hand on her head in benediction.

I felt a sudden jolt in that hand, and I jerked it back with a startled oath. It's a bit unfortunate that the first word Polgara heard coming from my mouth was a curse. I stared at this grim-faced baby girl. A single lock at her brow had turned snowy white at my touch.

"What a wonder!" Beltira gasped.

"Not really," Beldin disagreed. "She's his firstborn, and he just marked her. Unless I miss my guess, she's going to grow up to be a sorcerer."

"Sorceress," Belkira corrected.

"What?"

"A sorcerer is a man. She's a girl, so the right word would be sorceress."

Sorceress or not, my firstborn was wet, so I put her back in her cradle.

My younger daughter was the most beautiful baby I've ever seen— and that's not just fatherly pride. Everybody who saw her said exactly the same thing. She smiled at me as I took her from Beldin, and with that one sunny little smile, she reached directly into my heart and claimed me.

"You still haven't answered my question, Beldin," I said, cuddling Beldaran in my arms. "Where's Poledra?"

"Why don't you sit down and have a drink, Belgarath?" He went quickly to an open barrel and dipped me out a tankard of ale.

I sat down at the table with Beldaran on my knee. I probably shouldn't mention it, but *she* wasn't wet. I took a long drink, a little puzzled by the evasiveness of my brothers. "Quit playing around, Beldin," I said, wiping the foam off my lips. "Where's my wife?"

Beltira came to me and took Beldaran.

I looked at Beldin and saw two great tears in his eyes. "I'm afraid we've lost her, Belgarath," he told me in a sorrowing voice. "She had a very hard labor. We did everything we could, but she slipped away."

"What are you talking about?"

"She died, Belgarath. I'm sorry, but Poledra's dead."

PART
THREE

THE TIME OF WOE

SEA OF
THE WINDS

Peat
Bogs

Pasturelands

of Wild

Riva

THE
ISLE OF
THE WINDS

SHELLY.
SHAPIRO·83

The Hook
of Arendia

CHAPTER
EIGHTEEN

I won't be able to give you a coherent ac-
count of the next several months, be-
cause I don't really remember them. I had
a few rational interludes, but they jump
out at me with stark clarity, totally discon-
nected from what happened before or after. I try very hard to suppress
those memories, since disinterring a period of madness isn't a particularly
pleasant way to pass the time.

If Aldur hadn't left us, things might have been easier for me, but Necessity had taken him from me at the worst possible time. So it seemed
to me that I was alone with only my unbearable grief for company.
There's no real point in beating this into the ground. I know now that
what happened was necessary. Why don't we just let it go at that?

I seem to remember long periods of being chained to my bed with
Beldin and the twins taking turns watching over me and ruthlessly crushing every attempt I made to gather my Will. They were *not* going to let
me follow the examples set by Belsambar and Belmakor. Then, after my
suicidal impulses had lessened to some degree, they unchained me—not
that it meant anything particularly. I seem to remember sitting and staring at the floor for days on end with no real awareness of the passage of
time.

Since the presence of Beldaran seemed to calm me, my brothers frequently brought her to my tower and even allowed me to hold her. I
think it was probably Beldaran who finally brought me back from the
brink of total madness. How I loved that baby girl!

Beldin and the twins did *not* bring Polgara to me, however. Those icy grey eyes of hers cut large holes in my soul, and Polgara's eyes would turn from deep blue to steel grey at the very mention of my name. There was no hint of forgiveness in Pol's nature whatsoever.

Beldin had shrewdly watched my slow ascent from the pit of madness, and I think it was late summer or early autumn when he finally broached a subject of some delicacy. "Did you want to see the grave?" he asked me. "I hear that sometimes people do."

I understand the theory, of course. A grave's a place to visit and to decorate with flowers. It's supposed to help the bereaved put things into perspective. Maybe it works that way for some people, but it didn't for me. Just the word brought my sense of loss crashing down around my ears all over again.

I *knew* that setting all this down was going to be a mistake.

I more or less returned to sanity again by the time winter was winding down, and after the twins had questioned me rather closely, they unchained me and let me move around. Beldin never mentioned that "grave" again.

I took to walking vigorously through the slushy snow that covered the Vale. I walked fast because I wanted to be exhausted by nightfall. I made sure that I was too tired to dream. The only trouble with that plan lay in the fact that everything in the Vale aroused memories of Poledra. Have you any idea how many snowy owls there are in this world?

I think I probably came to a decision during that soggy tail end of winter. I wasn't fully aware of it, but it was there all the same.

In furtherance of that decision, I began to put my affairs in order. On one raw, blustery evening I went to Beldin's tower to look in on my daughters. They were just over a year old by then, so they were walking— sort of. Beldin had prudently gated the top of his stairs to prevent accidents. Beldaran had discovered how much fun it was to run, although she fell down a lot. For some reason that struck her as hilarious, and she'd always squeal with delighted laughter when it happened.

Polgara, of course, never laughed. She still doesn't very often. Sometimes I think Polgara takes life a little too seriously.

Beldaran ran to me with her arms outstretched, and I swept her up and kissed her.

Polgara wouldn't even look at me, but concentrated instead on one of her toys, a curiously gnarled and twisted stick—or perhaps it was the root of some tree or bush. My eldest daughter was frowning as she turned it over and over in her little hands.

"I'm sorry about that," Beldin apologized when he saw me looking at the peculiar toy. "Pol's got a very penetrating voice, and she doesn't bother to cry when she's unhappy about something. She screams instead. I had to give her something to keep her mind occupied."

"A stick?" I asked.

"She's been working on it for six months now. Every time she starts screaming, I give it to her, and it shuts her up immediately."

"A *stick?*"

He threw a quick look at Polgara and then leaned toward me to whisper, "It's only got one end. She still hasn't figured that out. She keeps trying to find the other end. The twins think I'm being cruel, but at least now I can get some sleep."

I kissed Beldaran again, set her down, went over to Polgara, and picked her up. She stiffened up immediately and started trying to wriggle out of my hands. "Stop that," I told her. "You may not care much for the idea, Pol, but I'm your father, and you're stuck with me." Then I quite deliberately kissed her. Those steely eyes softened for just a moment, and they were suddenly the deepest blue I have ever seen. Then they flashed back to grey, and she hit me on the side of the head with her stick. "Spirited, isn't she?" I observed to Beldin. Then I set her down, turned her around, and gave her a little spank on the bottom. "Mind your manners, miss," I told her.

She turned and glared at me.

"Be well, Polgara," I said. "Now go play."

That was the first time I ever kissed her, and it was a long time before I did it again.

Spring came grudgingly that year, spattering us with frequent rain showers and an occasional snow squall, but things eventually began to dry out, and the trees and bushes started tentatively to bud.

It was on a cloudy, blustery spring day when I climbed a hill on the western edge of the Vale. The air was cool, and the clouds roiled overhead. It was a day very much like that day when I had decided to leave the village of Gara. There's something about a cloudy, windy spring day that always stirs a wanderlust in me. I sat there for a long time, and that unrealized decision I'd made toward the end of winter finally came home to roost. Much as I loved the Vale, there were far too many painful memories here. I knew that Beldin and the twins would care for my daughters, and Poledra was gone, and my Master was gone, so there was nothing really holding me here.

I looked down into the Vale, where our towers looked like so many carelessly dropped toys and where the herds of browsing deer looked like ants. Even the ancient tree at the center of the Vale was reduced by distance. I knew that I'd miss that tree, but it'd always been there, so it probably still would be when I came back—if I ever *did* come back.

Then I rose to my feet, sighed, and turned my back on the only place I'd ever really called home.

I skirted the eastern edge of Ulgoland. I hadn't exercised my gift since that dreadful day, and I wasn't really sure if I still could. Grul had probably healed by now, and I was fairly sure that he'd be nursing a grudge—*and* that he wouldn't let me get close enough to knife him again. It would have been terribly embarrassing to try to gather my Will only to discover that it just wasn't there anymore. There were also Hrulgin, Algroths, and an occasional Troll up in those mountains, so prudence suggested that I go around them.

My brothers tried to make contact with me, of course. I dimly heard their voices calling me from time to time, but I didn't bother to answer. It would just have been a waste of time and effort. I wasn't going back, no matter what they said to me.

I went up through western Algaria and didn't encounter anyone. When I judged that I was well past the northern edge of Ulgoland, I turned westward, crossed the mountains, and came down onto the plains around Muros.

There was a sleepy little village of Wacite Arends where Muros now stands, and I stopped there for supplies. Since I didn't have any money with me, I reverted to the shady practices of my youth and stole what I needed.

Then I went downriver, ultimately ending up in Camaar. Like all seaports, there was a certain cosmopolitanism about Camaar. The city was nominally subject to the duke of Vo Wacune, but the waterfront dives I frequented had as many Alorns and Tolnedrans and even Nyissans in them as they did Wacites. The locals were mostly sailors, and sailors out on the town after a long voyage are a good-natured and generous lot, so it wasn't all that hard to find people willing to stand me to a few tankards of ale.

As is usually the case in a preliterate society, the fellows in the taverns loved to listen to stories, and I could make up stories with the best. And that was how I made my way in Camaar. I've done that fairly frequently over the years. It's an easy way to make a living, and you can usually do it sitting down, which was a good thing in this case, since most of the time I was in no condition to stand. To put it quite bluntly, I became a common drunkard. I apparently also became a public nuisance, since I seem to remember being thrown out of any number of low waterfront dives, places that are notoriously tolerant of little social gaffes.

I really couldn't tell you how long I stayed in Camaar—two years at least, and possibly more. I drank myself into insensibility each night, and I never knew where I'd wake up in the morning. Usually it was in a gutter or some smelly back alley. People are not particularly interested in listening to stories first thing in the morning, so I took up begging on streetcorners as a sideline. I became fairly proficient at it—proficient enough at any rate to be roaring drunk by noon every day.

I started seeing thing that weren't there and hearing voices nobody else could hear. My hands shook violently all the time, and I frequently woke up with the horrors.

But I didn't dream, and I had no memories of anything that had happened more than a few days ago. I wouldn't go so far as to say that I was happy, but at least I wasn't suffering.

Then one night while I was comfortably sleeping in my favorite gutter, I *did* have a dream. My Master probably had to shout to cut through my drunken stupor, but he finally managed to get my attention.

When I woke up, there was no question in my mind at all that I'd been visited. I hadn't had a real dream for years. Not only that, I was stone-cold sober, and I wasn't even shaking. What really persuaded me, though, was the fact that the heavenly perfume wafting from the tavern I'd probably been thrown out of the previous evening turned my stomach inside out right there on the spot. I amused myself by kneeling over my gutter and vomiting for a half hour or so, much to the disgust of everyone who happened by. I soon discovered that it wasn't so much the stink of that tavern that set my stomach all achurn, but the stale, sour reek exuding from the rags I wore and from my very skin. Then, still weakly retching, I lurched to my feet, stumbled out onto a wharf, and threw myself into the bay with the rest of the garbage.

No, I wasn't trying to drown myself. I was trying to wash off that dreadful smell. When I came out of the water, I reeked of dead fish and the various nasty things that people dump into a harbor—usually when nobody's watching—but it was a definite improvement.

I stood on the wharf for a time, shivering violently and dripping like a downspout, and I made up my mind to leave Camaar that very day. My Master obviously disapproved of my behavior, and the next time I weakened, he'd probably arrange to have me vomit up my shoe soles. Fear isn't the best motivation for embarking on a life of sobriety, but it gets your attention. The taverns of Camaar were too close at hand, and I knew most of the tavernkeepers by name, so I decided to go down into Arendia to avoid temptation.

I stumbled through the streets of the better parts of town, offending the residents mightily, I'm sure, and along about noon I reached the upstream edge of the city. I didn't have any money to pay a ferryman, so I swam across the Camaar River to the Arendish side. It took me a couple of hours, but I wasn't really in any hurry. The river was bank-full of fresh, running water, and it washed off a multitude of sins.

I walked back to the ferry landing to ask a few questions. There was a rude hut on the riverbank, and the fellow who lived there was sitting on a tree stump at the water's edge with a fishing pole in his hands. "An' would y' be wantin' t' cross over t' Camaar, friend?" he asked in that brogue that immediately identified him as a Wacite peasant.

"No, thanks," I replied. "I just came from there."

"Yer a wee bit on the damp side. Surely y' didn't swim across?"

"No," I lied. "I had a small boat. It overturned on me while I was trying to beach it. What part of Arendia have I landed in? I lost my bearings while I was crossing the river."

"Ah, it's a lucky one y' are t' have come ashore here instead of a few miles downriver. Yer in the lands of his Grace, the duke of Vo Wacune. Off t' the west be the lands of the duke of Vo Astur. I shouldn't say it— them bein' our allies and all—but the Asturians are a hard an' treacherous people."

"Allies?"

"In our war with the murderin' Mimbrates, don't y' know."

"Is that still going on?"

"Ah, t' be sure. The duke of Vo Mimbre fancies himself king of all Arendia, but our duke an' th' duke of the Asturians ain't about t' bend no knees t' him." He squinted at me. "If y' don't mind me sayin' it, yer lookin' a bit seedy."

"I've been sick for a while."

He started back from me. "It ain't catchin', is it?"

"No. I got a bad cut, and it didn't heal right."

"That's a relief. We've already got enough trouble on this side o' the river without some traveler bringin' in a pestilence, don't y' know."

"Which way do I go to hit the road to Vo Wacune?"

"Back up the river a few miles. There's another ferry landin' right where the road starts. Y' can't miss it." He squinted at me again. "Would y' be after wantin' a drop or two of somethin' t' brace y' up fer yer journey? 'Tis a cruel long way t' walk, don't y' know, and y'll find me prices t' be the most reasonable on this side o' the river."

"No thanks, friend. My stomach's a little delicate. The illness, you understand."

" 'Tis a shame. Y' look t' be a jolly sort, an' I wouldn't mind the company, don't y' know."

A jolly sort? Me? This fellow *really* wanted to sell me some beer. "Well," I said, "I'm not getting any closer to Vo Wacune just standing here. Thanks for the information, friend, and good luck with your fishing." I turned and went back up the river.

By the time I reached Vo Wacune, I'd more or less shaken off the lingering aftereffects of my years in Camaar, and I was starting to think coherently again. The first order of business was to find some decent clothing to replace the rags I was wearing and a bit of money to get me by. I suppose I could have stolen what I needed, but my Master might not have cared for that, so I decided to behave myself. The solution to my little problem lay no further away than the nearest temple of Chaldan, Bull God of the Arends. I *was* something of a celebrity in those days, after all.

I can't say that I really blame the priests of Chaldan for not believing me when I announced my name to them. In their eyes I was probably just another ragged beggar. Their lofty, disdainful attitude irritated me, though, and without even thinking about it, I gave them a small demonstration of the sort of things I was capable of, just to prove that I was really who I'd told them I was. Actually, I was almost as surprised as they were when it really worked, but neither my madness nor the years of concentrated dissipation in Camaar had eroded my talent.

The priests fell all over themselves apologizing, and they pressed new clothing and a well-filled purse on me by way of recompense for their failure to take me at my word. I accepted their gifts graciously, though I realized that I didn't really need them now that I knew that my "talent" hadn't deserted me. I could have spun clothes out of air and turned pebbles into coins if I'd really wanted to. I bathed, trimmed my shaggy beard, and put on my new clothes. I felt much better, actually.

What I needed more than clothes or money or tidying up was information. I'd been sorely out of touch with things during my stay in Camaar, and I was hungry for news. I was surprised to find that our little adventure in Mallorea was now common knowledge here in Arendia, and the priests of the Bull God assured me that the story was well-known in Tolnedra and had even penetrated into Nyissa and Maragor. I probably shouldn't have been surprised, now that I think about it. My Master had met with his brothers in their cave, and their decision to leave had been based largely on our recovery of the Orb. Since this was undoubtedly the most stupendous event since the cracking of the world, the other Gods would certainly have passed it on to their priests before they departed.

The story had been greatly embellished, of course. Any time there's a miracle involved, you can trust a priest to get creative. Since their enhancement of the bare bones of the story elevated me to near Godhood, I decided not to correct them. A reputation of that kind can be useful now and then. The white robe the priests had given me to replace the dirty rags I'd been wearing gave me a dramatic appearance, and I cut myself a long staff to fill out the characterization. I didn't plan to stay in Vo Wacune, and if I wanted the cooperation of the priesthood in the various towns I'd pass through, I was going to have to dress the part of a mighty sorcerer. It was pure charlatanism, of course, but it avoided arguments and long explanations.

I spent a month or so in the temple of Chaldan in Vo Wacune, and then I hiked to Vo Astur to see what the Asturians were up to—no good, as it turned out, but this *was* Arendia, after all. The Asturians held the balance of power during the long, mournful years of the Arendish civil wars, and they'd change sides at the drop of a hat.

Frankly, the Arendish civil wars bored me. I wasn't interested in the spurious grievances the Arends were constantly inventing to justify atrocities they were going to commit anyway. I went to Asturia because Asturia had a seacoast and Wacune didn't. The last thing I'd done before I left Cherek and his sons had been to break the Kingdom of Aloria all to pieces, and I was moderately curious about how it was working out.

Vo Astur was situated on the south bank of the Astur River, and Alorn ships frequently sailed upriver to call there. I stopped by the temple, and the priests directed me to several riverfront taverns where I might reasonably expect to find Alorn sailors. I wasn't happy about the prospect of testing my willpower in a tavern, but there was no help for it. If you want to talk to an Alorn, you're going to have to go where the beer is.

As luck had it, I came across a burly Alorn sea captain in the second tavern I visited. His name was Haknar, and he'd sailed down to Arendia from Val Alorn. I introduced myself, and the white robe and staff helped to convince him that I was telling the truth. He offered to buy me a tankard or six of Arendish ale, but I politely declined. I didn't want to get started on that again. "How are the boats working out?" I asked him.

"Ships," he corrected. Sailors always make that distinction. "They're fast," he conceded, "but you have to pay close attention to what you're doing when the wind comes up. King Cherek told me that *you* designed them."

"I had a little help," I replied modestly. "Aldur gave me the basic plan. How *is* Cherek?"

"A little mournful, really. I think he misses his sons."

"It couldn't be helped. We had to protect the Orb. How are the boys doing in their new kingdoms?"

"They're getting by, I guess. I think you rushed them, Belgarath. They were a little young when you sent them off into the wilderness like that. Dras calls his kingdom Drasnia, and he's starting to build a city at a place he calls Boktor. I think he misses Val Alorn. Algar calls *his* kingdom Algaria, and he *isn't* building cities. He's got his people rounding up horses and cattle instead."

I nodded. Algar probably wouldn't have been interested in cities. "What's Riva doing?" I asked.

"He's *definitely* building a city. The word 'fort' would probably come closer, though. Have you ever been to the Isle of the Winds?"

"Once," I said.

"Then you know where the beach is. That valley that runs down out of the mountains sort of stair-steps its way down to the beach. Riva had his people build stone walls across the front of each step. Now he's got them building their houses up against the backs of those walls. If somebody tried to attack the place, he'd have to fight his way over a dozen of those walls. That could get *very* expensive. I stopped by the Isle on my way here. They're making good progress."

"Has Riva started building his Citadel yet?"

"He's got it laid out, but he wants to get his houses built first. You know how Riva is. He's awfully young, but he *does* look out for his people."

"He'll make a good king, then."

"Probably so. His subjects are a little worried, though. They really want him to get married, but he keeps putting them off. He seems to have somebody special in mind."

"He does. He dreamed about her once."

"You can't marry a dream, Belgarath. The Rivan throne has to have an heir, and that's something a man can't do all by himself."

"He's still young, Haknar. Sooner or later some girl's going to take his eye. If it starts to look like it's going to be a problem, I'll go to the Isle and have a talk with him. Is Cherek still calling what's left of his kingdom Aloria?"

"No. Aloria's gone now. That took a lot of the heart out of Bear-shoulders. He hasn't even gotten around to putting a name to that peninsula you left him. The rest of us just call it 'Cherek' and let it go at that. That's whenever he lets us come home. We spend a lot of time at sea patrolling the Sea of the Winds. Cherek's very free with titles of nobility, but there's a large fishhook attached to them. I was about half drunk when he made me Baron Haknar. It wasn't until I sobered up that I realized that I'd volunteered to spend three months out of every year for the rest of my life sailing around in circles up in the Sea of the Winds. It's really unpleasant up there, Belgarath—particularly in the winter. I get ice a half-foot thick on my sails every night. My deckhands talk about the 'Haknar jig.' That's when the morning breeze shakes the ice off the sails and drops it down on the deck. My sailors have to dance out of the way or get brained. Are you sure I can't offer you something to drink?"

"Thanks all the same, Haknar, but I think I'd better be moving on.

Vo Astur depresses me. You can't get an Asturian to talk about anything but politics."

"Politics?" Haknar laughed. "The only thing I've ever heard an Asturian talk about is who he's going to go to war with next week."

"That's what passes for politics here in Asturia," I told him, rising to my feet. "Give my best to Cherek the next time you see him. Tell him that I'm still keeping an eye on things."

"I'm sure that'll make him sleep better at night. Are you coming to Val Alorn for the wedding?"

"What wedding?"

"Cherek's. His wife died while he was off in Mallorea. Since you stole all his sons, he's going to need a new heir. His bride-to-be is a real beauty—about fifteen or so. She's pretty, but she's not really very bright. If you say 'good morning' to her, it takes her ten minutes to think up an answer."

I felt a sudden wrench. I wasn't the only one who'd lost a wife. "Give him my apologies," I told Haknar shortly. "I don't think I'll be able to make it. I'd better be going now. Thanks for the information."

"Glad to be of help, Belgarath." Then he turned and bellowed, "Innkeeper! More ale!"

I went back out into the street and walked slowly back toward the temple of Chaldan, being careful not to think about Cherek's bereavement. I had my own, and that filled my mind. I didn't really want to dwell on it, since there was nobody around to chain me to a bed.

I'd received a few tentative invitations to visit the duke in his palace, but I'd put them off with assorted vague excuses. I hadn't visited the Duke of Vo Wacune, and I definitely didn't want to show any favoritism. Given my probably undeserved celebrity, I decided not to have anything to do with *any* of those three contending dukes. I had no desire to get involved in the Arendish civil wars—not even by implication.

That might have been a mistake. I probably could have saved Arendia several eons of suffering if I'd just called those three imbeciles together and rammed a peace treaty down their throats. Considering the nature of Arends, however, they'd more than likely have violated the treaty before the ink was dry.

Anyway, I'd found out what I needed to know in Vo Astur, and the invitations from the Ducal Palace were becoming more and more insistent, so I thanked the priests for their hospitality and left town before daybreak the following morning. I've been leaving town before daybreak for longer than I care to think about.

I was almost certain that the Duke of Vo Astur would take my departure as a personal affront, so when I was a mile or so south of town, I went back into the woods a ways and took the form of the wolf.

Yes, it *was* painful. I wasn't even certain that I could bring myself to do it, but it was time to find out. I'd been doing a number of things lately that pushed at the edges of my pain. I was *not* going to live out my life as an emotional cripple. Poledra wouldn't have wanted that, and if I went mad, so what? One more mad wolf in the Arendish forest wouldn't have made that much difference.

My assessment of the duke of Vo Astur turned out to be quite accurate. I was ghosting southward along the edge of the woods about an hour later when a group of armed horsemen came pounding along that twisting road. The Asturian duke *really* wanted me to pay him a visit. I drifted back in under the trees, dropped to my haunches, and watched the duke's men ride by. Arends were a much shorter people in those days than they are now, so they didn't look *too* ridiculous on those stunted horses.

I traveled down through the forest and ultimately reached the plains of Mimbre. Unlike the Wacites and the Asturians, the Mimbrates had cleared away the woods of their domain almost completely. Mimbrate horses were larger than those of their northern cousins, and the nobles of that southern duchy already had begun to develop the armor that characterizes them today. A mounted knight needs open ground to work on, so the trees had to go. The open farmland that resulted was rather peripheral to Mimbrate thinking.

When we think of the Arendish civil wars, we normally think of the three contending duchies, but that wasn't the full extent of it. Lesser nobles also had their little entertainments, and there was hardly a district in all of Mimbre that didn't have its own ongoing feuds. I'd resumed my own form, although I'll admit that I gave some serious consideration to living out the rest of my life as a wolf, and I was going south toward Vo Mimbre when I came across one of those feuds in full flower.

Unfortunately, the dimwitted Arends absolutely loved the idea of siege engines. Arends have a formal turn of mind, and the prospect of a decades-long standoff appeals to them enormously. The besiegers could set up camp around the walls of a fortress and mindlessly throw boulders at the walls for years, while the besieged could spend those same years happily piling rocks against the inside of those walls. Stalemates get boring after a while, though, and every so often, somebody felt the need to commit a few atrocities to offend his opponent.

In this particular case, the besieging baron decided to round up all the local serfs and behead them in plain view of the defender's castle.

That's when *I* took a hand in the game. As it happened, I was stand-

ing on a hilltop, and I posed dramatically there with my staff outstretched. "Stop!" I roared, enhancing my voice to such an extent that
they probably heard me in Nyissa. The baron and his knights wheeled to
gawk; the knight who was preparing to chop off a serf's head paused momentarily, and then he raised his sword again.

He dropped it the next instant, however. It's a little hard to hold
onto a sword when the hilt turns white-hot in your hands. He danced
around, howling and blowing on his burned fingers.

I descended the hill and confronted the murderous Mimbrate baron.
"You will *not* perpetrate this outrage!" I told him.

"What I do is none of thy concern, old man," he replied, but he
didn't really sound very sure of himself.

"I'm *making* it my concern! If you even *attempt* to harm these people,
I'll tear out your heart!"

"Kill this old fool," the baron told one of his knights.

The knight dutifully reached for his sword, but I gathered my Will,
leveled my staff, and said, "Swine."

The knight immediately turned into a pig.

"Sorcery!" the baron gasped.

"Precisely. Now pack up your people and go home—and turn those
serfs loose."

"My cause is just," he asserted.

"Your methods aren't. Now get out of my sight, or you'll grow a snout
and a curly tail right where you stand."

"The practice of sorcery is forbidden in the realm of the Duke of Vo
Mimbre," he told me—as if that made any difference.

"Oh, really? How are you going to stop me?" I pointed my staff at a
nearby tree stump and exploded it into splinters. "You're pressing your
luck, my Lord Baron. That could just as easily have been you. I told you
to get out of my sight. Now do it before I lose my temper."

"Thou wilt regret this, Sorcerer."

"Not as much as you will if you don't start moving right now." I gestured at the knight I'd just converted into ambulatory bacon, and he returned to his own form. His eyes were bulging with horror. He took one
look at me and fled screaming.

The stubborn baron started to say something, but he evidently
changed his mind. He ordered his men to mount up and then sullenly led
them off toward the south.

"You can go back to your homes," I told the serfs. Then I went back
up to my hilltop to watch and to make sure that the baron didn't try to
circle back on me.

I suppose I could have done it differently. There hadn't really been
any need for that direct confrontation. I could have driven the baron and

his knights off without ever revealing myself, but I'd lost my temper. I get into trouble that way fairly often.

Anyway, two days later I began to see lurid descriptions of a "foul sorcerer" nailed to almost every tree I passed. The descriptions of me were fairly accurate, but the reward offered for my capture was insultingly small.

I decided at that point to go directly on to Tolnedra. I was certain that I could deal with any repercussions resulting from my display of bad temper, but why bother? Arendia was starting to bore me anyway, and I've been chased out of a lot of places in my time, so one more wasn't going to make that much difference.

CHAPTER NINETEEN

I crossed the River Arend, the traditional border between Arendia and Tolnedra, early one morning in late spring. The north bank of the river was patrolled by Mimbrate knights, of course, but that wasn't really any problem. I *do* have certain advantages, after all.

I paused for a time in the Forest of Vordue to give some thought to my situation. When my Master had roused me from my drunken stupor back in Camaar, he hadn't really given me any instructions, so I was more or less on my own. There wasn't anyplace I really had to go, and no particular urgency about getting there. I still felt my responsibilities, however. I suppose I was what you might call a disciple emeritus, a vagabond sorcerer wandering around poking my nose into things that were probably none of my business. If I happened to come across anything significant, I could pass it on to my brothers back in the Vale. Aside from that, I was free to wander wherever I chose. My grief hadn't really diminished, but I was learning to live with it and to keep it rather tightly controlled. The years in Camaar had taught me the futility of trying to hide from it.

And so, filled with a kind of suppressed melancholy, I set off toward Tol Honeth. As long as I was here anyway, I thought I might as well find out what the empire was up to.

There was a certain amount of political maneuvering going on in the Grand Duchy of Vordue as I passed through on my way south. The Honeths were in power again, and the Vordue family always took that as a personal affront. There were abundant signs that the Second Honethite

Dynasty was in its twilight. That's a peculiar thing about dynasties in any of the world's kingdoms. The founder of a dynasty is usually vigorous and gifted, but as the centuries roll by, his successors become progressively less so. The fact that they almost invariably marry their cousins might have something to do with it. Controlled inbreeding might work out all right with horses and dogs and cattle, but when it comes to humans, keeping it in the family's not a good idea. Bad traits will breed true the same as good ones will, and stupidity seems to float to the surface a lot faster than courage or brilliance.

At any rate, the Honethite Emperors had been going downhill for the past century or so, and the Vorduvians were slavering with anticipation, feeling that their turn on the throne was just around the corner.

It was early summer when I reached Tol Honeth. Since it was their native city, the Honethite Emperors had devoted much of their time— and most of the imperial treasury—to improving the capital. Any time the Honeths are in power in Tolnedra, an investment in marble quarries will yield handsome returns.

I crossed the north bridge to the city and paused at the gate to answer the perfunctory questions of the legionnaires standing guard there. Their armor was very impressive, but they weren't. I made a mental note of the fact that the legions seemed to be getting badly out of condition. Somebody was going to have to do something about that.

The streets were crowded. The streets of Tol Honeth always are. Everybody in Tolnedra who thinks he's important gravitates to the capital. Proximity to the seat of power is very important to certain kinds of people.

In a roundabout sort of way I was a religious personage, so, as I had in Arendia, I went looking for a church. The main temple of Nedra had been moved since I'd last been in Tol Honeth, so I had to ask directions. I knew better than to ask any of the richly dressed merchant princes passing by with perfumed handkerchiefs held to their noses and haughty expressions on their faces. Instead, I found an honest man replacing broken cobblestones. "Tell me, friend," I said to him, "which way should I go to reach the Temple of Nedra?"

"It's over on the south side of the Imperial Palace," he replied. "Go on down to the end of this street and turn left." He paused and squinted at me. "You'll need money to get in," he advised me.

"Oh?"

"It's a new custom. You have to pay the priest at the door to get inside—and pay another priest to get near the altar."

"Peculiar notion."

"This is Tol Honeth, friend. Nothing's free here, and the priests are just as greedy as everybody else."

"I think I can come up with something they'd rather have than money."

"I wouldn't make any large wagers on that. Good luck."

"I think you dropped something there, friend," I told him, pointing at the large copper Tolnedran penny I'd just conjured up and dropped on the stones by his left knee. He *had* been helpful, after all.

He quickly snatched up the penny—probably the equivalent of a day's wages—and looked around furtively.

"Be happy in your work," I told him, and moved off down the street.

The Temple of Nedra was like a palace, an imposing marble structure that exuded all the warmth of a mausoleum. The common people prayed outside in little niches along the wall. The inside was reserved for the people who could afford to pay the bribes. "I need to talk with the High Priest," I told the clergyman guarding the huge door.

He looked me up and down disdainfully. "Absolutely out of the question. You should know better than even to ask."

"I *didn't* ask. I told you. Now go fetch him—or get out of my way and I'll find him myself."

"Get away from here."

"We're not getting off to a good start here, friend. Let's try it again. My name's Belgarath, and I'm here to see the High Priest."

"Belgarath?" He laughed sardonically. "There's no such person. Go away."

I translocated him to a spot several hundred yards up the street and marched inside. I was definitely going to have words with the High Priest about this practice of charging admission to a place of worship; not even Nedra would have approved of that. The temple was crawling with priests, and each one seemed to have his hand out. I avoided confrontations by the simple expedient of creating a halo, which I cocked rather rakishly over one ear. I'm not certain if Tolnedran theology includes a calendar of saints, but I *did* get the attention of the priests—*and* their wholehearted cooperation. And I didn't even have to pay for it.

The High Priest's name was Arthon, and he was a paunchy man in an elaborately jeweled robe. He took one look at my halo and greeted me with a certain apprehensive enthusiasm. I introduced myself, and he became *very* nervous. It wasn't really any of *my* business that he was violating the rules, but I saw no reason to let him know that. "We've heard about your adventures in Mallorea, Holy Belgarath," he gushed at me. "Did you really kill Torak?"

"Somebody's been spinning moonbeams for you, Arthon," I replied. "I'm not the one who's supposed to do that. We just went there to recover something that'd been stolen."

"Oh." He sounded disappointed. "To what do we owe the honor of your visit, Ancient One?"

I shrugged. "Courtesy. I was passing through, and I thought I ought to look in on you. Has anyone heard from Nedra?"

"Our God has departed, Belgarath," he reminded me.

"*All* the Gods have departed, Arthon. They *do* have ways to keep in touch, though. Belar spoke to Riva in a dream, and Aldur came to me the same way no more than a couple of months ago. Pay attention to your dreams. They might be significant."

"I did have a peculiar dream about six months ago," he recalled. "It seemed that Nedra spoke to me."

"What did he say?"

"I forget now. I think it had something to do with money."

"Doesn't it always?" I thought about it for a moment. "It probably involved this new custom of yours. I don't think Nedra would approve of the practice of charging admission to the temple. He's the God of *all* Tolnedrans, not just the ones who can afford to buy their way into your church."

A wave of consternation crossed his face. "But—" he started to protest.

"I've seen some of the creatures who live in Hell, Arthon," I told him quite firmly. "You *don't* want to spend any time with them. It's up to you, though. What's happening here in Tolnedra?"

"Oh, not too much, Belgarath." He said it just a bit evasively, and I could almost smell what he was trying to hide.

I sighed. "Don't be coy, Arthon," I told him wearily. "The Church is not supposed to get involved in politics. You've been taking bribes, haven't you?"

"How did you know that?" His voice was a little shrill.

"I can read you like a book, Arthon. Give the money back and keep your nose out of politics."

"You must pay a call on the Emperor," he said, skillfully sidestepping the issue.

"I've met members of the Honeth family before. One's pretty much the same as the others."

"His Majesty will be offended if you don't call on him."

"Spare him the anguish then. Don't tell him that I've been here."

He wouldn't hear of that, of course. He definitely didn't want me to start probing into the question of who was bribing him, nor of how large his share of the admission fees was, so he escorted me to the palace, which was teeming with members of the Honeth family. Patronage is the absolute soul of Tolnedran politics. Even the toll-takers at the most remote bridges in the empire change when a new dynasty comes into power.

The current Emperor was Ran Honeth the Twenty-something or other, and he'd discarded imbecility in favor of the unexplored territory of idiocy. As is usually the case in such situations, an officious relative had assumed his defective kinsman's authority, scrupulously prefacing each of his personal decrees with "The Emperor has decided . . ." or some other absurdity, thus maintaining the dignity of the cretin on the throne. The relative, a nephew in this case, kept Arthon and me cooling our heels in an anteroom for two days while he escorted all manner of high-ranking Tolnedrans immediately into the imperial presence.

Eventually I got tired of it. "Let's go, Arthon," I told Nedra's priest. "We both have better things to do."

"We *cannot!*" Arthon gasped. "It would be considered a mortal insult!"

"So? I've insulted *Gods* in my time, Arthon. I'm not going to worry about hurting the feelings of a halfwit."

"Let me talk with the Lord High Chamberlain again." He jumped to his feet and hurried across the room to speak with the imperial nephew.

The nephew was a typical Honeth. His first response was to look down his nose at me. "You will await his Imperial Majesty's pleasure," he told me in a lofty tone.

Since he was feeling so lofty, I stood him on a vacant patch of empty air up near the rafters so that he could *really* look down on people. I'll grant you that it was petty, but then so was he. "Do you think that his Imperial Majesty's pleasure might have worked its way around to us yet, old boy?" I asked him in a pleasant tone. I left him up there for a little while to make sure that he got my point, and then I brought him down again.

We got in to see the Emperor immediately.

This particular Ran Honeth was sitting on the Imperial Throne sucking his thumb. The bloodline had deteriorated even further than I'd imagined. I nudged at the corner of his mind and didn't find anything in there. He haltingly recited a few imperial pleasantries—I shudder to think of how long it must have taken him to memorize them—and then he regally gave Arthon and me permission to withdraw. His entire performance was somewhat marred by the fact that forty some-odd years of sucking his thumb had grossly misaligned his front teeth. He looked like a rabbit, and he lisped outrageously.

I assessed the mood of the imperial nephew as Arthon and I bowed our way out of the throne room, and I decided that it might be a good time for me to leave Tol Honeth. As soon as the fellow regained his composure, the trees in the neighborhood were almost certainly going to flower with more of those posters. This was getting to be a habit.

I thought about that as I made my way toward Tol Borune. Ever since I'd abandoned my career as a common drunk, I'd been misusing my gift. The Will and the Word is a fairly serious thing, and I'd been turning it into a bad joke. Despite my grief, I was still my Master's disciple, not some itinerant trickster. I suppose I could excuse myself by pointing to my emotional state during those awful years, but I don't think I will. I'm supposed to know better.

I bypassed Tol Borune, largely to avoid any more opportunities to turn offensive people into pigs or to stick them up in the air just for fun. That was probably a good idea; I'm sure the Borunes would have irritated me. I've got a fair amount of respect for the Borune family, but they can be awfully pig-headed sometimes.

Sorry, Ce'Nedra. Nothing personal intended there.

At any rate, I traveled through the lands of the Anadile family and finally reached the northern edge of the Wood of the Dryads. The passing centuries have altered the countryside down there to some degree, but now that I think back on it, I followed almost exactly the same route as I did three thousand years later when a group of friends and I were going south on the trail of the Orb. Garion and I have talked about "repetitions" any number of times, and this may have been another of those signals that the purpose of the universe had been disrupted. Then again, the fact that I followed the same route might have been due to the fact that it was the natural way south and also that I was familiar with it. Once you get a theory stuck in your head, you'll go to almost any lengths to twist things around to make them fit.

Even in those days the Wood of the Dryads was an ancient oak forest with a strange kind of serene holiness about it. Humans have a tendency to compartmentalize their religion to keep it separate from everyday life. The Dryads live in the center of *their* religion, so they don't even have to think—or talk—about it. That's sort of refreshing.

I'd been in their wood for more than a week before I even saw a Dryad. They're timid little creatures, and they don't really care to come into contact with outsiders—except at certain times of the year. Dryads are all females, of course, so they're obliged to have occasional contacts with the males—of various species—in order to reproduce.

I'm sure you get the picture.

I didn't really make an effort to find any Dryads. Technically, they're "monsters," though certainly not as dangerous as the Eldrakyn or Algroths, but I still didn't want any incidents.

Evidently, though, it was "that time of year" for the first Dryad I encountered, because she'd laid aside her customary shyness and was aggressively trying to track me down. When I first saw her, she was standing in the middle of the forest path I was following. She had flaming red hair, and she was no bigger than a minute. She was, however, holding a fully drawn bow, and her arrow was pointed directly at my heart. "You'd better stop," she advised me.

I did that—immediately.

Once she was certain that I wasn't going to try to run, she became very friendly. She told me that her name was Xana, and that she had plans for me. She even apologized for the bow. She explained it by telling me that travelers were rare in the Wood, and that a Dryad with certain things on her mind had to take some precautions to prevent escapes.

I tried to explain to her that what she was proposing was wildly inappropriate, but I couldn't seem to get through to her. She was a very determined little creature.

I think I'll just let it go at that. What happened next isn't central to the story I'm telling, and there's no point in being deliberately offensive.

Dryads customarily share things with their sisters, so Xana introduced me to other Dryads, as well. They all pampered me, but there was no getting around the fact that I was a captive—a slave, if we want to be blunt about it—and my situation was more than a little degrading. I didn't make an issue of it, though. I smiled a lot, did what was expected of me, and waited for an opportunity. As soon as I had a moment alone, I slipped into the form of the wolf and loped off into the wood. They searched for me, of course, but they didn't know what they were looking for, so I had no trouble evading them.

I reached the north bank of the River of the Woods, swam across, and shook the water out of my fur. You might want to keep that in mind: if you take the form of a furred creature and you happen to get wet before you change back, always shake off the excess water first. Otherwise, your clothes will be dripping when you resume your real form.

I was in Nyissa now, so I didn't have to worry about Dryads any more. I started keeping a sharp eye out for snakes instead. Normal humans make some effort to keep the snake population under control, but the snake is a part of the Nyissan religion, so they don't. Their jungles are literally alive with slithering reptiles—all venomous. I managed to get bitten three times during my first day in that stinking swamp, and that made me *extremely* cautious. It wasn't hard to counteract the venom, fortunately, but being bitten by a snake is never pleasant.

The war with the Marags had seriously altered Nyissan society. Before the Marag invasion, the Nyissans had cleared away large plots of jungle and built cities and connecting highways. Highways provide invasion routes, however, and a city, by its very existence, proclaims the presence of large numbers of people and valuable property. You might as well *invite* attack. Salmissra realized that, and she ordered her subjects to disperse and to allow the jungle to reclaim all the towns and roads. This left only the capital at Sthiss Tor, and since I'd sort of drifted into the self-appointed task of making a survey of the Kingdoms of the West, I decided to pay a call on the Serpent Queen.

The Marag invasion had occurred almost a hundred years earlier, but there were still abundant signs of the devastation it had caused. The abandoned cities, choked in vines and bushes, still showed evidence of fire and of the kind of destruction siege engines cause. Now the Nyissans themselves scrupulously avoided those uninviting ruins. When you get right down to it, Nyissa is a theocracy. Salmissra is not only queen, but also the High Priestess of the Serpent God. Thus, when she gives an or-der, her people automatically obey her, and she'd ordered them to go live out in the brush with the snakes.

I was a little footsore when I reached Sthiss Tor, and very hungry. You have to be careful about what you eat in Nyissa. Virtually every plant and a fair number of the birds and animals are either narcotic or poisonous, or both.

I located a ferry landing and crossed the River of the Serpent to the garish city of Sthiss Tor. The Nyissans are an inspired people. The rest of the world likes to believe that inspiration is a gift from the Gods, but the Nyissans have found a simpler way to achieve that peculiar ecstasy. Their jungles abound with various plants with strange properties, and the Snake People are daring experimenters. I knew a Nyissan once who was addicted to nine different narcotics. He was the happiest fellow I've ever known. It's probably not a good idea to have your house designed by an architect with a chemically augmented imagination, however. Assuming that it doesn't collapse on the workmen during construction, it's likely to have any number of peculiar features—stairways that don't go anyplace, rooms that there's no way to get into, doors that open out into nothing but air, and assorted other inconveniences. It's also likely to be painted a color that doesn't have a name and has never appeared in any rainbow.

I knew where Salmissra's palace was, since Beldin and I had been in Sthiss Tor during the Marag invasion, so I wasn't obliged to ask directions of people who didn't even know where *they* were, much less where anything else was.

The functionaries in the palace were all shaved-headed eunuchs. There's probably a certain logic there. From puberty onward, the assorted Salmissras are kept on a regimen of various compounds that slow the normal aging process. It's very important that Salmissra forever looks the same as the original handmaiden of Issa. Unfortunately, one of the side effects of those compounds is a marked elevation of the Queen's appetite—and I'm not talking about food. Salmissra does have a kingdom to run, and if her servants were functional adult males, she'd probably never get anything done.

Please, I'm trying to put this as delicately as possible.

The queen knew that I was coming, of course. One of the qualifications for the throne of Nyissa is the ability to perceive things that others can't. It's not exactly like *our* peculiar gift, but it serves its purpose. The eunuchs greeted me with genuflections and various other fawning gestures of respect and immediately escorted me to the throne room. The current Salmissra, naturally, looked the same as all her predecessors, and she was reclining on a divanlike throne, admiring her reflection in a mirror and stroking the bluntly pointed head of a pet snake. Her gown was diaphanous, and it left very little to the imagination. The huge stone statue of Issa, the Serpent God, loomed behind the dais where his current handmaiden lay.

"Hail, Eternal Salmissra," the eunuch who was escorting me intoned, prostrating himself on the polished floor.

"The Chief Eunuch approaches the throne," the dozen red-robed functionaries intoned in unison.

"What is it, Sthess?" Salmissra replied in an indifferent sort of voice.

"Ancient Belgarath entreats audience with the Beloved of Issa."

Salmissra turned her head slowly and gazed at me with those colorless eyes of hers. "The Handmaiden of Issa greets the Disciple of Aldur," she proclaimed.

"Fortunate the Disciple of Aldur, to be received by the Serpent Queen," the chorus intoned.

"You're looking well, Salmissra," I responded, cutting across about a half hour of tedious formality.

"Do you really think so, Belgarath?" She said it with a kind of girlish ingenuousness which suggested that she was quite young—probably no more than two or three years on the throne.

"You always look well, dear," I replied. The little endearment was probably a violation of all sorts of rules, but I felt that, considering her age, I could get away with it.

"The honored guest greets Eternal Salmissra," the chorus announced.

"Do you suppose we could dispense with that?" I asked, jerking my thumb over my shoulder at the kneeling eunuchs. "You and I need to talk, and all that singing distracts my attention."

"A *private* audience, Belgarath?" she asked me archly.

I winked at her with a sly smirk.

"It is our pleasure that the Ancient One shall divulge his mind to us in private," she announced to her worshipers. "You have our permission to withdraw."

"Well, *really*!" I heard one of them mutter in an outraged tone.

"Remain if you wish, Kass," Salmissra said to the protestor in an in-different tone of voice. "Know, however, that no one living will hear what passes between me and the disciple of Aldur. Go and live—or stay and die." She had style, I'll give her that. Her offer cleared the throne room immediately.

"Well," she said, her colorless eyes smoldering, "now that we're alone—" She left it hanging suggestively.

"Ah, don't y' be after temptin' me, darlin'," I said, grinning. Beldin had gotten away with that; why couldn't I?

She actually laughed. That was the only time I *ever* heard one of the hundred or more Salmissras do that.

"Let's get down to business, Salmissra," I suggested briskly. "I've been conducting a survey of the western kingdoms, and I think we might profitably exchange some information."

"I hunger for your words, Ancient One," she said, her face taking on an outrageously vapid expression. This one had a very sharp mind and a highly developed sense of humor. I quickly altered my approach. An in-telligent Salmissra was a dangerous novelty.

"You know what happened in Mallorea, of course," I began.

"Yes," she replied simply. "Congratulations."

"Thank you."

"Would you like to sit here?" she invited, rising to a half-sitting po-sition and patting the seat of the divan beside her.

"Ah—thanks, but I think better on my feet. Aloria's been divided into four separate kingdoms now."

"Yes, I know. How did you ever browbeat Cherek into permitting that?"

"I didn't. Belar did."

"Is Cherek really that religious?"

"He didn't like it, but he saw the necessity for it. Riva's got the Orb now, and he's on the Isle of the Winds. You might want to warn your sea captains to stay away from the Isle. Cherek's got a fleet of war-boats, and they'll sink any ship that goes within fifty leagues of Riva's island."

Her colorless eyes grew speculative. "I just had a very interesting thought, Belgarath."

"Oh?"

"Is Riva married yet?"

"No. He's still a bachelor."

"You might tell him that *I'm* not married, either. Doesn't that suggest something rather interesting to you? It certainly does to me."

I almost choked on that one. "You're not really serious, are you?"

"It's something worth exploring, don't you think? Nyissa's a small nation, and my people don't make very good soldiers. The Marag invasion taught us that. If Riva and I were to marry, it'd form a very interesting alliance."

"Don't the rules say that you're not supposed to marry?"

"Rules are tiresome, Belgarath. People like you and me can ignore them when it suits us. Let's be honest here. I'm the figurehead ruler of a weak nation, and I don't like that very much. I think I'd like to take real power instead. An alliance with the Alorns might just make that possible."

"You'd be flying in the face of tradition, you know."

"Traditions are like rules, Belgarath. They're made to be ignored. Issa's been dormant for a long time now. The world's changing, and if Nyissa doesn't change, too, we'll be left behind. We'll be a small, primitive backwater. I think I might just be the one to change that."

"It wouldn't work, Salmissra," I told her.

"My sterility, you mean? I can take care of that. All I have to do is stop taking those drugs, and I'll be as fertile as any young woman. I'll be able to give Riva a son to rule his island, and he can give me a daughter to rule here. We could alter the balance of power in this part of the world."

I laughed. "It'd send the Tolnedrans into hysterics, if nothing else."

"That in itself would be worth the trouble."

"It would indeed, but I'm afraid it's out of the question. Riva's already been spoken for."

"Oh? Who's the lucky girl?"

"I haven't any idea. It's one of those marriages made in Heaven. The Gods have already selected Riva's bride."

She sighed. "Pity," she murmured. "Ah, well. Riva's still only a boy. I suppose I could educate him, but that's sort of tiresome. I prefer experienced men."

I moved on rather quickly. This was a *very* dangerous young lady. "The Arendish civil war's heating up. Asturia and Wacune are currently allied against Mimbre—at least they were when I was there. It was two whole months ago, though, so the situation might have changed by now."

"Arends," she sighed, rolling her eyes upward.

"Amen to *that*. The Second Honethite Dynasty's winding down in Tolnedra. They might be able to squeeze out one or two more emperors, but that well's almost dry. The Vorduvians are waiting in the wings—not very patiently."

"I *hate* the Vorduvians," she said.

"Me, too. We'll have to endure them, though."

"I suppose." She paused, her pale eyes hooded. "I heard about your recent bereavement," she said tentatively. "You have my sincerest sympathy."

"Thank you." I even managed to say it in a level tone.

"Another possibility occurs to me," she said then. "You and I are both currently at liberty. An alliance between *us* might be even more interesting than one between Riva and me. Torak isn't going to stay in Mallorea forever, you know. He's already sent scouting parties across the land-bridge. It's just a matter of time until there's an Angarak presence on *this* continent, and that'll bring in the Grolims. Don't you think we should start to get ready?"

I got *very* careful at that point. I was obviously dealing with a political genius here. "You're tempting me again, Salmissra." I was lying, of course, but I think I managed to convince her that I was interested in her obscene suggestion. Then I sighed. "Unfortunately, it's forbidden."

"Forbidden?"

"By my Master, and I wouldn't even consider crossing him."

She sighed. "What a shame. I guess that still leaves me with the Alorns. Maybe I'll invite Dras or Algar to pay a visit to Sthiss Tor."

"They have responsibilities in the North, Salmissra, and you have yours here. It wouldn't be much of a marriage, no matter which of them you chose. You'd seldom see each other."

"Those are the best kind of marriages. We wouldn't have so much chance to bore each other." She brought the flat of her hand sharply down on the arm of her throne. "I'm not talking about love, Belgarath. I need an alliance, not entertainment. I'm in a very dangerous situation here. I was foolish enough to let a few things slip when I first came to the throne. The eunuchs know that I'm not just a silly girl consumed by her appetites. I'm sure that the candidates for my throne are already in training. As soon as one's chosen, the eunuchs will poison me. If I can't find an Alorn to marry, I'll have to take a Tolnedran—or an Arend. My life depends on it, old man."

Then I finally understood. It wasn't ambition that was driving her so much as it was her instinct for self-preservation. "You *do* have an alternative, you know," I told her. "Strike first. Dispose of your eunuchs before they're ready to dispose of you."

"I already thought of that, but it won't work. They all dose themselves with antidotes to every known poison."

"As far as I know, there's no antidote for a knife-thrust in the heart, Salmissra."

"We don't do things that way in Nyissa."

"Then your eunuchs won't be expecting it, will they?"

Her eyes narrowed. "No," she agreed, "they wouldn't." She suddenly giggled. "I'd have to get them all at once, of course, but a bloodbath of those dimensions would be quite an object lesson, wouldn't it?"

"It'd be a long time before anybody ever tried to cross you again, dear."

"What a wonderful old man you are," she said gratefully. "I'll have to find some way to reward you."

"I don't really have any need for money, Salmissra."

She gave me a long, smoldering look. "I'll have to think of something else, then, won't I?"

I thought it might be a good idea to change the subject at that point. "What's happening to the South?" I asked her.

"You tell *me*. The people down there are western Dals. *Nobody* knows what the Dals are doing. Somehow they're in contact with the Seers at Kell. I think we'd all better keep an eye on the Dals. In many ways they have a more dangerous potential than the Angaraks. Oh, I almost forgot to tell you. Torak's left the ruins of Cthol Mishrak. He's in a place called Ashaba in the Karandese Mountains now. He's passing orders on to the Grolims through Ctuchik and Urvon. Nobody knows where Zedar is." She paused. "Are you sure you wouldn't like to sit here beside me?" she offered again. "We wouldn't *really* have to get married, you know. I'm sure Aldur wouldn't object to a more informal arrangement. Come sit beside me, Belgarath, and we can talk about that reward I mentioned. I'm sure I'll be able to think of *something* you'd like."

CHAPTER
TWENTY

When you consider all the trouble I've had with a long string of Salmissras, my feelings about that particular one were just a bit unusual, but then so was she. The selection of each new Queen of Nyissa is based almost entirely on physical appearance. At a certain point in the life of a reigning queen, twenty candidates for the succession are chosen. The palace eunuchs have a painting of the original Salmissra, and they go through the kingdom comparing that painting to the faces of all the twelve-year-old girls they can find. Twenty are selected and are taken to country estates lying in the vicinity of Sthiss Tor for training. When the old queen dies, the twenty are closely examined, and one of them is elevated to the throne. The other nineteen are killed. It's brutal, but it is politically sound. Appearance and manner are the deciding factors in the election. Intelligence is not taken into consideration. In that kind of random selection, however, you have as much chance of choosing a genius as an idiot. Quite clearly, they got a bright one this time. She was beautiful, of course. Salmissra always is. She had all of the proper mannerisms, naturally, since her very life had depended on learning those mannerisms. She had, however, been clever enough to conceal her intelligence, her sense of humor, and the sheer force of her personality—until after she'd ascended the throne. Once she'd been crowned queen, she thought she was safe. I imagine that the palace eunuchs were *very* upset when they discovered her true nature—upset enough, at any rate, to start planning her assassination.

I liked her. She was an intelligent young woman making the best of a bad situation. As she'd mentioned, the various drugs she took to maintain her appearance made her infertile, but she'd already come up with a solution to that problem. I've always sort of wondered what might have happened if she *had* married. It might have changed the course of history in that part of the world.

I lingered in her palace for a couple of weeks, and then I rather regretfully moved on. My hostess was generous enough to lend me her royal barge, and I went up the River of the Serpent to the rapids in style for a change.

When the barge reached the rapids, I went ashore on the north bank and took the trail that wound up into the mountains toward Maragor.

It was a relief to get up out of the Nyissan swamps. For one thing, I didn't have to keep a constant eye out for snakes anymore, and for another, I wasn't continually trailing a cloud of mosquitoes. I'm not really sure which of them is worse. The air grew cooler as I ascended into that spur of mountains, and the forests thinned out. I've always rather liked mountains.

There was a bit of trouble at the border of Maragor. The Marags were still practicing that ritual cannibalism Beldin had told me about, and the border guards tended to look upon travelers as a food source. I didn't have too much trouble persuading them that I probably wouldn't taste good, though, and then I went northeast toward the capital at Mar Amon.

I believe I've hinted at some of the peculiarities of the Marag culture before, but I suspect I'll have to be a little more specific at this point. The God Mara was just a bit overly enthusiastic about physical beauty. For a woman, this presents no particular problem; she either has it or she hasn't. A man, however, has to work on it. Masculine beauty involves muscle development, so Marag men spent a great deal of time lifting heavy things over their heads. That gets boring after a while, though, and there's not much point in having bushel baskets full of muscles if you don't use them for something. The men of Maragor devised contests of various sorts—running, jumping, throwing things, swimming, and the like. Unfortunately, if you develop enough muscles, they'll eventually start to squeeze your head and reduce the size of your brain. In time, most of the men of Maragor were all as beautiful as marble statues—and almost as intelligent. They were totally incapable even of taking care of themselves, and so the women had to take over. They owned all the property, and they housed their childlike heroes in dormitories and arranged various athletic competitions that kept those beautiful specimens of manhood happy.

There were far more women among the Marags than there were men, but that didn't really cause any problems, since Marag men wouldn't really have made good husbands anyway. The Marags got along very well without marriage. They were happy, they enjoyed life, and they were kind and generous to each other. They seemed to be incapable of the jealousy and irrational possessiveness that mars other cultures.

I think that covers everything. For various reasons, Polgara's always had a low opinion of the Marags, and if I take this too much further, it'll just give her another excuse to scold me.

Oh, one last thing. The Marags didn't have a single ruler. They had a "Council of Matriarchs" instead—nine middle-age and presumably wise women who made all the decisions. It was a little unusual, but it worked out fairly well.

Maragor lay in a pleasant, fertile basin in the southern part of the Tolnedran Mountains. There are extensive mineral deposits in those mountains, and the turbulent streams that run down into the basin where the Marags lived pass through those deposits and carry with them assorted minerals and a fair number of gemstones. Unless you know what to look for, diamonds, sapphires, and emeralds appear to be no more than common pebbles. Gold, however, is plainly visible on the bottom of every brook in Maragor. The Marags ignored it. They had a barter economy and were largely self-sufficient, so they had no real interest in trade with other nations. Thus, they didn't need money. Their idea of beauty leaned in the direction of personal physical attractiveness, so they didn't bother with jewelry. Once you've eliminated money and jewelry, gold becomes largely meaningless. It's too soft and too heavy to have any real practical use.

It did get *my* attention, however. I dallied a bit on my journey from the border to the capital and managed to pick up a fairly large pouchful of gold nuggets. It's hard to walk away when there are lumps of gold lying in plain sight.

It was autumn when I reached Mar Amon, a beautiful city that lay a few leagues to the west of the large lake in the center of Maragor. I went to the Temple of Mara and introduced myself to the High Priestess. There were priests, of course, but as was the case in the rest of Marag society, men played a decidedly minor role in their religion. The High Priestess was a tall, handsome woman in her mid-forties, and her name was Terell. I talked with her for a while, and I soon realized that she had no interest at all in the outside world. That was probably the fatal flaw in the Marag culture. No place is so isolated that you can safely ignore the rest of mankind—particularly when your streambeds are cluttered with free gold.

Despite the fact that I don't have rippling biceps and a neck like a tree trunk, the women of Mar Amon found me attractive. My celebrity may have played a part in that. The average Marag male's sole claim to fame was most likely the fact that he'd won a footrace some years back, and his conversation tended to be a little elemental. Women, as you may have noticed, like to talk. You may have also noticed that I do, too.

I drifted around Mar Amon, and many a conversation that I struck up by saying "good morning" to a Marag lady who might be out sweeping off her doorstep lasted for several weeks. The women of Maragor were generous and friendly, so I always had something to eat and a place to sleep.

There are all manner of things that a man can do to take his mind off his troubles. I'd tried one of them in Camaar, and that didn't turn out too well. The one I tried in Mar Amon wasn't nearly as self-destructive, but the end result was probably the same. Extensive sensuality can erode your mind almost as much as extensive drinking can. It's not as hard on your liver, though.

Let's not take this any further, shall we?

I spent nine years in Mar Amon, drifting along in a sort of haze, and after the first few years I was on a first-name basis with every lady in town.

Then one spring, Beldin came looking for me. I was having breakfast in the kitchen of a lovely young woman when he came stumping through the door with a face that looked like a thundercloud. "What do you think you're doing, Belgarath?" he demanded.

"Having breakfast at the moment. What does it look like?"

"It looks to me like you're living in sin."

"You sound like an Ulgo, Beldin. The definition of sin varies from culture to culture. The Marags don't consider these informal arrangements sinful. How did you manage to find me?"

"It wasn't too hard," he growled. "You left a very wide trail." He came over to the table and sat down. Wordlessly my hostess brought him some breakfast. "You're a legend in Camaar, you know," he continued, still scowling at me. "They've never seen *anybody* who could get as drunk as you used to."

"I don't do that any more."

"No. I noticed that you've found other entertainments instead. You disgust me. The very sight of you sickens me."

"Don't look, then."

"I *have* to. This wasn't my idea. For all I care, you can drown yourself in cheap beer and roll around with every woman you come across. I came after you because I was *sent* after you."

"Give Aldur my apologies. Tell him that I've retired."

"Oh, really? You *can't* retire, you clot. You signed on willingly, and you can't go back on that just because you're feeling sorry for yourself."

"Go away, Beldin."

"Oh, no, Belgarath. Our Master sent me to take you back to the Vale, and I'm going to obey him, even if you aren't. We can do it the easy way, or we can do it the hard way. It's entirely up to you. You can come along peacefully—all in one piece—or I'll *take* you back in chunks."

"That might take a little doing, brother mine."

"Not really. If all the childish tricks you played on your way here are any indication, you don't have enough of your talent left to blow out a candle. Now stop wallowing in self-pity and come back home where you belong." He stood up.

"No." I also stood up.

"You're disgusting, Belgarath. Do you *really* think that this past twelve years of dissipation and debauchery have changed anything? Poledra's still dead, your daughters are still in the Vale, and you still have responsibilities."

"I'll pass them on to you, brother. Enjoy them."

"I guess we'd better get started, then."

"Started with what?"

"Fighting." And he promptly punched me in the belly.

Beldin is enormously strong, and his blow knocked me completely across the room. I lay on the floor gasping and trying to get my breath back. He stumped after me and kicked me in the ribs. "We can do this all week, if you want," he growled. Then he kicked me again.

My principles had been eroded by the years of what he chose to call dissipation and debauchery, but not so much that I was going to elevate our discussion from a physical one to something more serious, and he knew that. As long as he stuck to kicks and punches, I couldn't respond with anything *except* kicks and punches. I finally got to my feet, and we pounded on each other for a while. Peculiarly, it made me feel better, and I rather think Beldin knew that it would.

Finally we both collapsed on the floor, half exhausted.

With a great effort, he rolled his gnarled and twisted body over and hit me. "You've betrayed our Master!" he bellowed at me, then hit me again. "You've betrayed Poledra!" He blackened one of my eyes. "You've betrayed your daughters!" In a remarkable display of agility for a man lying on the floor, he kicked me in the chest. "You've betrayed the memories of Belsambar and Belmakor! You're no better than Zedar!" He drew back that massive fist again.

"Hold it," I told him, weakly raising one hand.

"Have you had enough?"

"Obviously."

"Are you coming back to the Vale with me?"

"All right—if it's *that* important to you."

He sat up. "Somehow I knew you'd see it my way. Have you got anything to drink around here?"

"Probably. I couldn't vouch for it, though. I haven't had a drink since I left Camaar."

"You've probably worked up quite a thirst, then."

"I don't think I should, Beldin."

"Don't worry, you're not like other drunks. You were drinking in Camaar for a specific reason. That part of it's past now. Just don't let it get ahead of you again."

The Marag lady whose kitchen we'd just wrecked brought us each a tankard of ale. It tasted awful to me, but Beldin seemed to like it. He liked it enough to have three more, at any rate. I didn't even finish the first one. I didn't want to go down *that* road again. Just in passing, I'd like to let you know that over the centuries I've spent far more time *holding* tankards than I have drinking from them. People can believe what they want to, but I've slept in enough gutters for one lifetime, thanks all the same.

The next morning we apologized to my hostess for all the damage we'd done, and left for the Vale. The weather was fine, so we decided to walk rather than assume other forms. There was no particular urgency about getting home.

"What's been going on?" I asked Beldin when we were about a mile out of Mar Amon.

"The Angaraks have been coming across the land-bridge," he replied.

"Yes, so I understand. Salmissra told me about those scouting parties."

"It's gone a little further than that. As closely as I've been able to tell, the entire population of Cthol Mishrak has been coming across. The soldiers came over to this side first, and they moved down the coast. They've been building a fortress at the mouth of one of those rivers that runs down to the Sea of the East. They call their fort Rak Goska, and they refer to themselves as Murgos. They're still Angaraks, but they seem to feel a need to distinguish themselves from the people who stayed in Mallorea."

"Not exactly. Have you ever gotten around to learning Old Angarak?"

"I don't waste my time on dead languages, Belgarath."

"It's not entirely dead. The people at Cthol Mishrak spoke a corrupted version of it. Anyway, the word 'Murgo' meant nobleman or warrior in Old Angarak. Evidently these Murgos are the people who were the aristocrats in Cthol Mishrak."

"What does 'Thull' mean?"

"Serf—or maybe peasant. The distinction's a little vague in Angarak society. You should know that, Beldin. You've spent more time in Mallorea than I have."

"I wasn't there to socialize. The second wave of Angaraks settled to the north of the Murgos. They call themselves Thulls, and they're sup-plying the Murgos with food. The third wave's moving into what used to be eastern Aloria—that big forest up there. They've been calling them-selves Nadraks."

"Townsmen," I translated for him. "The merchant class. Are the Alorns doing anything about this?"

"Not really. You spread them a little thin. Bull-neck *talks* about expe-ditions in the East, but he doesn't have the manpower. Algar probably couldn't do very much about it, because the Eastern Escarpment blocks his access to that part of the continent."

"We'd better see if we can make contact with the Master when we get back to the Vale. This migration's got a very specific reason behind it. As long as the Angaraks stayed in Mallorea, they weren't any problem. They're establishing a presence on this side of the Sea of the East so that they can bring in the Grolims. We might want to chase those Murgos, Nadraks, and Thulls back to where they came from."

"Another war?"

"If we have to. I don't think we want Grolims on this continent if we can prevent it."

"Astonishing," he said.

"What is?"

"Your mind still works. I thought that maybe you'd broken it during the course of the last dozen years."

"I came close. Another few years in Camaar probably would have turned the trick. I was drinking everything in sight."

"So I heard. What finally persuaded you to dry out?"

"The Master paid me a call. I sobered up in a hurry after that and left Camaar. I went down through Arendia and Tolnedra—you know about all that if you've been trailing me. Did the Dryads cause you any problems when you went through their woods?"

"I didn't see a one of them."

"Maybe it's the wrong time of year. They *definitely* interrupted my trip."

"Oh?"

"It was during their breeding season."

"That must have been exciting."

"Not really. Did you talk with Salmissra at all when you went through Sthiss Tor?"

"Briefly. There was a lot of turmoil in Sthiss Tor when I passed through there. Somebody'd just butchered all the high-level palace eunuchs."

I laughed delightedly. "Good girl!"

"What are you talking about, Belgarath?"

"This particular Salmissra's actually got a mind. She made the mistake of letting the palace eunuchs find out about it, though. They were planning to assassinate her, and I suggested a way for her to remove that particular danger. Did she get them all?"

"From what I heard, she did."

"That's probably why it too her so long. She's a very thorough young lady. Now, what's Torak doing at Ashaba? Salmissra told me that he'd gone there."

"From what I hear, he's having religious experiences. He's been caught up in a kind of ecstasy for the past ten years or so. He's babbling all sorts of obscure pronouncements. Urvon's got a team of Grolims at Ashaba taking down every word. They're calling those ravings 'the Ashabine Oracles.' In fact, there's been an outbreak of lunacy lately. Bullneck's got a crazy man chained to a post a few miles to the west of Boktor, with scribes copying down the poor fellow's every word."

"Good. I told him to do that. Just before the Master left, he told me that we were going to be getting our instructions from prophecy now instead of receiving them directly. This is the Age of Prophecy."

"You sound like a Dal when you talk about ages that way."

"Evidently the Dals know something we don't. I think we'll need a copy of that transcription Dras is having set down, and we'd better pass the word to the other kingdoms to start paying attention to crazy people." I paused. "How are the girls?" I asked, trying to make it sound casual.

"Older. You've been gone for quite a while."

"They must be about ten years old by now."

"Thirteen, actually. Their birthday was just this past winter."

"It'll be good to see them again."

"Don't get your heart set on a warm reunion, Belgarath. Beldaran might be happy to see you, but you're not one of Pol's favorite people."

That turned out to be a gross understatement.

Beldin and I traveled out of Maragor and crossed the Tolnedran Mountains to the Vale. We didn't particularly hurry. My grotesque little brother's observations about Polgara had made me slightly apprehensive about meeting her—fully justified, as it turned out.

I had missed the serenity of the Vale during those vagabond years, and a profound sense of peace came over me as we came down out of the mountains and looked once more upon our home. The painful memories were still there, of course, but the passage of time had muted and softened them, although every so often I'd see something that twisted inside me like a knife.

My daughters had moved in with the twins during Beldin's absence. The promise Beldaran had exhibited when she was a baby had been more than fulfilled. Though she was only thirteen, she was breathtakingly beautiful. Her hair was the color of flax, and it was full and very long. Her face could quite literally stop your heart, and she was as graceful as a gazelle.

"Father!" she exclaimed when I reached the top of the stairs. Her voice was rich and vibrant, the kind of voice that makes you hold your breath to listen. She flew across the floor and threw herself into my arms. I cursed that wasted twelve years when she did that, and all of my love for her came back, almost overwhelming me. We stood locked in an embrace with tears streaming down our faces.

"Well, Old Wolf," another voice said acidly, "I see you've finally decided to come back to the scene of the crime."

I winced. Then I sighed, took my arms from around Beldaran's slender shoulders, and turned to face Polgara.

Beldaran was probably the most beautiful girl I've ever seen, but Polgara, to put it kindly, was no prize. Her dark hair was a tangled wreck with twigs and leaves snarled in it. She was tall and skinny and quite nearly as dirty as Beldin. She had knobby knees—usually skinned up—and her dirty fingernails were ragged and chewed off close. It took her years to train herself not to bite her nails. The white lock at her brow was scarcely visible, since her hair was absolutely filthy. I got the strong impression that it was all quite deliberate. Polgara's got very good eyes, and I'm certain that she could see that she was no match for her sister when it came to sheer physical beauty. For some obscure reason, she seemed to be going out of her way to make herself as ugly as she possibly could. She was succeeding admirably.

Yes, I know. We'll get to her transformation all in good time. Don't rush me.

It wasn't her physical appearance that made our reunion so unpleasant, though. Beldin had raised Polgara and Beldaran. Somehow my younger daughter had avoided picking up his speech patterns, but Polgara hadn't. She had them all—with bells on.

"It's good to see you again, Polgara," I greeted her, trying to sound as if I meant it.

"Really? Why don't we see if we can fix that? Did they stop making beer in Camaar? Is that why you left?"

I sighed. This promised to be moderately ugly. "Do you suppose we should kiss each other before we get into all that?" I suggested.

"It's not going to pay you to get that close to me, Old Man. I didn't like you when I first saw you, and you haven't done anything lately to change my opinion."

"That's all over now."

"Of *course* it is—right up until the moment you get a sniff of beer or see a passing skirt."

"Have you been telling tales?" I asked Beldin.

"Not me," he replied. "Pol has her own ways to keep track of what you've been up to."

"Shut up, uncle," she snapped at him. "This drunken fool doesn't need to know about that."

"You're wrong, Pol," I told her. "This drunken fool *does* need to know about it. If you're gifted, you're going to need training."

"Not from you, father. I don't need *anything* from you. Why don't you go back to Camaar? Or the Wood of the Dryads? It's almost mating season there again. Beldaran and I'd just *adore* having a horde of half-human baby sisters."

"Watch your mouth, Pol."

"Why? We're father and daughter, old man. We should always be completely open with each other. I wouldn't want you to have any misconceptions about my opinion of you. Have you dallied with a Troll yet? Or an Eldrak? That would *really* be exciting, wouldn't it?"

I gave up and sat down in a chair. "Go ahead, Pol," I told her. "Enjoy yourself."

I'm sure she did. She'd spent years polishing some of those cutting remarks, and she delivered them with a certain flair. Leaving the girls in Beldin's custody may have been a mistake, because Polgara at least had been a very apt pupil. Some of the names she called me were truly hair-raising. Oddly, Beldaran didn't seem to be the slightest bit offended by her sister's choice of language. I'm sure she knew what the words meant, but they didn't seem to bother her. For all I knew, she may have shared Pol's views, but she forgave me. Polgara obviously didn't.

I sat there looking out the window at the sunset while my daughter continued her diatribe. After an hour or so, she started to repeat herself. There are only so many insults in any language. She *did* lapse into Ulgo once or twice, but her accent wasn't very good. I corrected her, of course;

correcting the children is a father's first responsibility. Pol didn't take correction very graciously.

Finally I stood up. "This isn't really getting us anywhere," I told her. "I think I'll go home now. As soon as I get things straightened up in the tower, you girls can move in with me."

"You're not serious!"

"Oh, yes I am, Pol. Start packing. Like it or not, we *are* going to be a family." I smiled at her. "Sleep well, Polgara." Then I left.

I could still hear her screaming when I got to my tower.

The girls moved in the following week. Beldaran was an obedient child, and she accepted my decision without question. That, of course, forced Pol to obey, as well, since she loved her sister so much that she couldn't bear to be separated from her. We didn't see very much of her, but at least her things were in my tower.

She spent most of her time for the rest of that summer in the branches of the tree in the center of the Vale. At first I assumed that eventually hunger would bring her down out of the tree and back to my tower, but I had overlooked the twins' habit of feeding things. They saw to it that Polgara didn't go hungry.

I decided to wait her out. If nothing else, winter would bring her inside. Beldaran, however, started moping. That must have been a very difficult time for my blonde daughter. She loved us both, and our dislike for each other obviously caused her a great deal of distress. She begged me to try to make peace with her sister. I knew it was a mistake, but I couldn't refuse Beldaran anything she asked of me, so I sighed and went down the Vale to give it one more try.

It was a warm, sunny morning in late summer, and it seemed to me that there were an unusual number of birds flying around as I walked through the tall grass toward the tree.

There were even more of them about when I got there. The air around the tree was alive with them—and it wasn't just one variety. There were robins and bluebirds and sparrows and finches and larks, and the sound of all that chirping and singing was almost deafening.

Polgara was lounging in the fork of a huge branch about twenty feet up with birds all around her, and she watched my approach with cold, unfriendly eyes. "What is it, father?" she demanded when I reached the foot of the tree.

"Don't you think this has gone on long enough?" I asked her.

"This what?"

"You're being childish, Pol."

"I'm entitled to be childish. I'm only thirteen. We'll have a *lot* more fun when I grow up."

"You're breaking Beldaran's heart with this foolishness, you know. She misses you very much."

"She's stronger than she looks. She can endure almost as much as I can." She absently shooed a warbling lark off her shoulder. The birds around her were singing their hearts out in a kind of ecstatic adoration.

I decided to try another tack. "You're missing a splendid opportunity, Pol," I told her.

"Oh?"

"I'm sure you've spent the summer composing new speeches. You can't very well try them out on me when you're perched on a limb sharpening your beak."

"We'll get to that later, father. Right now the sight of you makes me nauseous. Give me a few dozen years to get used to you." She smiled at me, a smile with all the warmth of an iceberg. "Then we'll talk. I have many, many things to say to you. Now go away."

To this day I don't know how she did it. I didn't hear or feel a thing, but the sounds those thousands of birds were making suddenly became angry, threatening, and they descended on me like a cloud, stabbing at me with their beaks and flogging me with their wings. I tried to beat them off with my hands, but you can't really drive off that many birds. About all the songbirds could do was peck at me and pull out tufts of my hair and beard, but the hawks were a whole different matter. I left in a hurry with Polgara's mocking laughter following me.

I was more than a little grumpy when I reached Beldin's tower. "How far has she gone?" I demanded of him.

"How far has who gone with what?"

"Polgara. Just how much is she capable of?"

"How should I know? She's a female, Belgarath. They don't think the way we do, so they do things differently. What did she do to you?"

"She turned every bird in the Vale loose on me."

"You *do* look a bit mussed. What did you do to irritate her so much?"

"I went down to the tree and told her to come home."

"I take it she refused the invitation?"

"And then some. How long has she been doing this sort of thing?"

"Oh, I don't know—a couple of years, I guess. That'd be consistent."

"I didn't follow that."

He gave me a surprised look. "Do you mean you don't *know?* Haven't you ever been the least bit curious about the nature of our gift?"

"I had other things on my mind."

He rolled his eyes upward. "Have you ever seen a child who could do the sort of things we do?"

"I hadn't thought about it, but now that you mention it—"

"How've you managed to live this long with your head turned off? The talent doesn't show up until we reach a certain age. Usually girls pick it up a little sooner than boys."

"Oh?"

"It's related to puberty, you dunce!"

"What's puberty got to do with it?"

He shrugged. "Who knows? Maybe the gift is glandular."

"That doesn't make any sense, Beldin. What have glands got to do with the Will and the Word?"

"Maybe it's a built-in safety precaution. A gifted two-year-old might be a little dangerous. The gift has to be controlled, and that implies a certain maturity. You should be glad that it works that way. Polgara's not very fond of you, and if she'd had the gift when she was a toddler, she might have turned you into a toad."

I started to swear.

"What's the trouble?"

"I'm going to have to get her down out of that tree. She's going to need training."

"Leave her alone. She's not going to hurt herself. The twins and I explained the limitations to her. She isn't experimenting. About all she does is talk to birds."

"Yes. I noticed that."

"You might think about rolling around in the creek before you go home."

"Why would I want to do that?"

"You've got bird droppings all over you, and Beldaran might find you just a bit offensive."

The Master paid me a visit that night, and he gave me some very peculiar instructions. He seemed to think they were important, but they didn't make very much sense to me.

As Poledra had pointed out, I'm not really very good with tools, and the task my Master set me involved some very tiny, meticulous work. Fortunately, I had a fair number of Tolnedran silver imperials in my purse, so I didn't have to go up into the mountains in search of ore deposits. Free gold isn't too hard to find, but refining silver is a lot of work.

The sculpture itself wasn't too hard—once I got used to using those tiny little tools—but making the chains was very tedious.

It was autumn by the time I finished, and then one evening I completed the last clasp. "Beldaran," I called my blonde daughter.

"Yes, father?" she replied, looking up from her sewing. I had taught her to read, of course, but she preferred sewing.

"I have something for you."

She came over eagerly. "What is it?"

"Here." I held out the silver amulet I'd made for her.

"Oh, father! It's lovely!"

"Try it on."

She draped it around her neck, fastened the clasp, and flew to the mirror. "Oh," she said. "That's exquisite!" She peered at the reflection a little more closely. "It's Polgara's tree, isn't it?"

"That's what it's supposed to be."

"It means something, doesn't it?"

"Probably. I'm not sure exactly what, though. The Master told me to make them, but he didn't bother to explain."

"Shouldn't this one be for Pol? It's *her* tree, after all."

"The tree was there a long time before Polgara was, Beldaran." I held up another of the amulets. "This one's hers."

She looked at it. "An owl? What a peculiar thing to give to Pol."

"It wasn't my idea." I'd suffered a great deal sculpting that owl. It raised a lot of memories.

Yes, Durnik, I know I could have cast them, but the Master told me to sculpt them instead.

I knew what *my* amulet meant, and it was easy. I'd taken the form of a wolf so often that I could have carved that one with my eyes closed. I put it on, sighed, and snapped the clasp.

"Ah—father?" Beldaran said, her hands at the back of her neck.

"Yes, dear?"

"Something's wrong with the clasp. It won't come undone."

"It isn't supposed to, Beldaran. You're not supposed to take it off."

"Not *ever?*"

"Not ever. The Master wants us to wear them always."

"That might be a little awkward sometimes."

"Oh, I think we can manage. We're a family, Beldaran. The amulets are supposed to remind us of that—among other things."

"Does Polgara's amulet lock, too?"

"I hope so. I built it to lock."

She giggled.

"What's so funny?"

"I don't think she's going to like that, father. If you lock something around her neck, she's probably going to be *very* unhappy about it."

I winked at her. "Maybe we'd better wait to tell her until *after* she's got it locked in place, then."

"Why don't we?" she said, rolling her eyes roguishly. Then she giggled again, threw her arms around my neck, and kissed me.

Beldaran and I went down to the tree the next morning to give Polgara her amulet.

"What am I supposed to do with this?" she demanded.

"You're supposed to wear it," I told her.

"Why?"

I was getting a little tired of this. "It's not my idea, Pol," I told her. "I made the amulets because Aldur told me to make them. Now put it on and stop all this foolishness. It's time for us all to grow up."

She gave me a peculiar look and fastened her amulet about her neck.

"And now we are three," Beldaran said warmly.

"Amazing," Polgara said tartly. "You *do* know how to count."

"Don't be nasty," Beldaran told her. "I know that you're more clever than I am, Polgara. You don't have to hit me over the head with it. Now come back home where you belong."

I could have berated Pol for months on end about that, and she probably would have ignored me. When Beldaran said it, though, she agreed without any argument. And so we went back to the tower and set up housekeeping.

Things were relatively peaceful, oddly enough. Beldaran managed to keep Polgara and me from each others' throats, at least—and could persuade her to wear her amulet, when Pol found a way to circumvent my lock. My blonde daughter had been right. Polgara was much more intelligent than she was. This is not to say that Beldaran was stupid. It was just that Pol's one of the most intelligent people I have ever known— bad-tempered, of course, but extremely intelligent.

I'm sorry, Pol, but you are. It's nothing to be ashamed of.

As soon as she got to the tower, Pol took over in the kitchen. Beltira and Belkira had taught her how to cook, and she absolutely loved the business of preparing food. She was very good at it, too. I've never really paid all that much attention to what I eat, but when every meal that's set before you is a banquet, you start to notice it.

This is not to say that everything was all sweetness and light. Pol and I *did* have an occasional spat.

You know, that's one of the silliest words in any language. Spat: it sounds like something gooey hitting the floor.

This all went on for about three years, and during that time Polgara and I began to develop a pattern that we've more or less faithfully followed for over three thousand years now. She makes clever comments about my various habits, and I generally ignore them. We don't scream at each other, and we seldom swear. It's not so much that we don't *want* to on occasion, but we learned to behave ourselves out of consideration for Beldaran.

It was not long after the girls' sixteenth birthday when Aldur paid me another visit. Pol and I had gotten into a fairly serious argument that evening. In passing, I'd mentioned the fact that it was about time for her to learn how to read. You wouldn't *believe* how much that offended her.

"Are you calling me stupid?" she demanded in that rich voice of hers, and things went rapidly downhill from there. To this day I don't know why it made her so angry.

Anyway, I went to bed in a foul temper, and I slept fitfully.

"Belgarath, my son," I knew the voice, of course.

"Yes, Master?"

"I would have thine house joined with the house of the guardian of the Orb."

"Is it a Necessity, Master?"

"Yea, my beloved disciple. This, however, is the gravest task I have ever called upon thee to perform. From the joining of thine house with the house of the Rivan King shall descend the ultimate Child of Light. Choose, therefore, which of thy daughters thou shalt give to the Rivan King to be his wife, for in the joining of the two houses shall a line invincible be forged that shall join my Will with the Will of my brother, Belar, and Torak himself may not prevail against us."

I was tempted. Lord knows I was tempted, but I already knew who was going to be Riva's wife. He'd described her to me in great detail on that day when we'd forged his sword, and she did *not* have dark hair.

Beldaran was ecstatic when I told her of my decision. "A king?" she exclaimed.

"Well, technically, I guess. I don't know that Riva thinks of himself that way, though. He's not very interested in ceremony or show."

"What does he look like?"

I shrugged. "Tall, dark hair, blue eyes." I went over to the washstand and filled the basin with water. "Here," I said to her. "I'll show you." And I put the image of Riva's face on the surface of the water.

"He's *gorgeous*!" she squealed. Then her eyes narrowed slightly. "Does he have to wear that beard?"

"He's an Alorn, Beldaran. Most Alorn men wear beards."

"Maybe I can talk to him about that."

Polgara's reaction was a bit peculiar. "Why did you choose Beldaran?" she asked.

"Actually I didn't," I replied. "Riva did—or he had the choice made for him. He's been dreaming about her ever since he landed on the Isle of the Winds. It was probably Belar who put Beldaran's face in Riva's dreams. Belar's partial to blonde girls."

"This is ridiculous, father. You're going to marry my sister off to a complete stranger."

"They'll have plenty of time to get to know each other."

"How old is this Alorn?"

"Oh, I don't know—probably in his late thirties."

"You're going to marry Beldaran to an old man?"

"I'd hardly call thirty-five or forty old, Pol."

"Naturally you wouldn't, since you're thirty-five or forty thousand yourself."

"No. Four, actually."

"What?"

"I'm *four* thousand, Pol, not forty thousand. Don't make it any worse than it already is."

"When is this absurdity going to take place?"

"We have to go to the Isle of the Winds first. It shouldn't be too long after that. Alorns don't believe in long engagements."

She stormed out of the tower muttering curses.

"I'd sort of hoped she'd be happy for me." Beldaran sighed.

"She'll come around, dear." I tried to sound hopeful about it, but I had some fairly serious doubts. Once Polgara got something in her mind, it was *very* hard to get her to turn around.

CHAPTER
TWENTY-
TWO

Things might have gone a little better if we'd been able to start out immediately, but it was still winter, and I had no intention of dragging my daughters out in bad weather. Beldaran put the time to good use sewing on her wedding gown. Polgara, however, took up residence in the tree again, and she steadfastly refused even to talk to us.

It was about a month after I'd made the decision when Riva's cousin Anrak showed up in the Vale with another Alorn. "Ho, Belgarath!" the boisterous Anrak greeted me. "Why are you still here?"

"Because it's still winter."

"Oh, it's not all that bad. Riva's getting impatient to meet the girl he's going to marry."

"How did *he* find out about it?"

"He had another one of those dreams."

"Oh. Who's your friend?"

"His name's Gelheim. He's a sort of an artist. Riva wants a picture of his bride."

"He knows what she looks like. He's been dreaming about her for the last fifteen years."

Anrak shrugged. "He just wants to be sure you've picked the right one, I guess."

"I don't think Belar and Aldur would have let me make a mistake, do you?"

"You never know. Sometimes the Gods are a little strange. Have you got anything to drink?"

"I'll introduce you to the twins. They make fairly good beer. They're Alorns, so they know how it's done."

Beldaran and Anrak hit it off immediately, but Polgara was a different matter. It started out innocently enough one morning when Anrak came by just after breakfast. "I thought you had two daughters," Riva's cousin said to me.

"Yes," I told him. "Polgara's a little unhappy with me right now; she's living in a tree."

"It doesn't sound to me as if she's quite right in the head. Does she look like her sister?"

"Not too much, no."

"I thought they were twins."

"That doesn't always mean that they look alike."

"Where's this tree of hers?"

"Down in the center of the Vale."

"I think I'll go down and have a look at her. If Riva's going to get married, maybe I should, too."

Beldaran giggled.

"What's so funny, Pretty?" he asked her. It was his favorite nickname for her.

"I don't think my sister's the marrying kind, Anrak. You can suggest it to her, if you'd like, but leave yourself plenty of running room when you do."

"Oh, she can't be *that* bad."

Beldaran concealed a smirk and give him directions to the tree.

His eyes still looked a bit startled when he came back to the tower. "Unfriendly, isn't she?" he noted mildly. "Is she always that dirty?"

"My sister doesn't believe in bathing," Beldaran replied.

"She doesn't particularly believe in good manners, either. I could probably clean her up, but that mouth of hers might cause some problems. I'm not even sure what some of those words mean."

"What did you say to her to set her off?" Beldaran asked him.

"I was honest," Anrak replied with a shrug. "I told her that Riva and I usually did things together, and that as long as he was going to get married, I might as well, too—and since she wasn't attached ..." He scratched at his beard. "That's about as far as I got, actually." He looked slightly injured. "I'm not used to having people laugh at me. It was a perfectly honorable suggestion. It wasn't as if I'd made an improper proposal." He went across the room to look into Beldaran's mirror. "Is there something the matter with my beard?" he asked. "It looks all right to *me*."

"Polgara's not particularly partial to beards, Anrak," I explained.

"She didn't have to be so insulting though, did she? Do I *really* look like a rat hiding in a clump of bushes?"

"Polgara exaggerates sometimes," Beldaran told him. "She takes a little getting used to."

"I don't think it'd work out," he decided. "I'm not trying to insult you, Belgarath, but you left a lot of the bark on that one when you were raising her. If I decide that I *really* want to get married, I think I'll choose a nice Alorn girl. Sorcerese girls are a little too complicated for me."

"Sorcerese?"

"Isn't that what your race is called?"

"It's a profession, Anrak, not a race."

"Oh. I didn't know that."

Gelheim drew several pictures of Beldaran, and then he left. "Tell Riva that we'll be along in the spring," Anrak told him.

Gelheim nodded, then started out through the dreary tag end of winter. He was almost as close-mouthed as Algar was.

Anrak spent much of his time at the twins' tower, but he came by one day to tell me about Riva's progress on the hall he was building at the upper end of the city. "Actually, it's a little showy for my taste," he said somewhat critically. "Not that it's got all that many frills or anything, but it's awfully big. I didn't think Riva was that full of himself."

"He's following instructions," I explained. "The Hall of the Rivan King is there to protect the Orb, not the people who live inside. We definitely don't want Torak to get his hands on it again."

"There isn't much danger of that, Belgarath. He'd have to get past Dras and Algar first, and Bear-shoulders has a fleet of war boats patrolling the Sea of the Winds. One-eye might start out with a big army, but there wouldn't be very many of them left by the time they reached the Isle."

"It doesn't hurt to take a few extra precautions."

The weather finally broke about a month later, and we started making preparations for the trip.

"Are we almost ready to leave?" Beldaran asked one fine spring afternoon.

"I don't think we need to bring the furniture," Beldin said a bit sourly. Beldin believed in traveling light.

"I'll go get Polgara, then," she said.

"She won't come, Beldaran," I said.

"Oh, she'll come, all right." There was an uncharacteristic hint of steel in my younger daughter's voice.

"She doesn't approve of this wedding, you know."

"That's her problem. She *is* going to attend, whether she likes it or not." It was easy to underestimate Beldaran because of her sweet, sunny disposition. She rarely asserted any kind of authority, largely because she didn't have to. We all loved her so much that she usually got what she wanted without making any fuss about it. When one of us crossed her, however, she could be *very* firm. She'd been a bit disappointed that the twins wouldn't be going with us, but somebody had to stay in the Vale, and the twins weren't really comfortable in the presence of strangers.

I think I'd have given a great deal to have heard the conversation between my daughters when Beldaran went to the tree to fetch Pol. Neither of them would talk about it afterward. But though Polgara was a bit sullen, she did come with us.

We skirted the eastern border of Ulgoland, of course, but that was standard practice in those days. Beldin scouted ahead. We weren't really expecting any trouble, but Beldin never missed an opportunity to fly.

I wonder how he and Vella are getting along. She doesn't have her daggers any more, but I'd imagine that her beak and talons sort of make up for that.

The weather was particularly fine that year, and the snow had largely melted in the passes through the Sendarian Mountains. When we reached Muros, Anrak went on ahead. "Riva's instructions," he explained. "As soon as I get to the coast, I'm supposed to send word to him. He'll bring a ship and meet us in Camaar."

"Do we really think it's safe to take father back to Camaar?" Polgara said with just a hint of spitefulness. But both the girls were a little nervous in Muros. Sometimes I forgot about the fact that they'd never been out of the Vale before, and strangers made them uncomfortable. Muros wasn't much of a town in those days, but it still had more people in it than my daughters were used to.

We hired a carriage there and rode downriver in style. When we reached Camaar, I did not revisit the waterfront. We took lodgings in one of the better inns in the main part of town, and I let Beldin go find Anrak.

"Riva's on the way," Anrak assured us when Beldin brought him to our inn. "He's probably crowded on several acres of sail. He *really* wants to meet you, Pretty."

Beldaran blushed.

"Disgusting," Polgara muttered. I knew that this was all going to come to a head eventually. Polgara's discontent about her sister's impending wedding was probably quite natural. There were ties between my daughters that I couldn't even begin to understand. Polgara seemed to be the dominant twin, but she was the one who automatically spoke in plurals—which is usually the sign of the submissive sister. To this very day, if you're impolite enough to ask Polgara how old she is, she'll probably say something like "We're about three thousand—or so." Beldaran's been gone for a long time, but she still looms very large in Polgara's conception of the world.

I think that someday I'll have a long talk with Pol about that. The worldview of someone who's never really been alone might be very interesting.

And then Riva arrived in Camaar. I'm sure that the citizens noticed him. It wasn't so much the fact that he was seven feet tall that got their attention. I think it might have had something to do with the way he tried to walk straight through anything or anyone standing between him and Beldaran. I've seen people who were in love before, but *nobody* has ever taken it to such extremes as Riva did.

When he came into the room at the inn—Beldin was quick enough to get the door open for him before he walked right through it—he took one look at my blonde daughter, and that was it for him.

Beldaran had been practicing a pretty little speech, but when she saw Riva's face, she lost it entirely.

They didn't *say* anything to each other! Have you ever spent an entire afternoon in the room with two people who don't talk at all, but just sat gazing into each others' faces?

It finally got to the point that it was embarrassing, so I spent the afternoon looking at Polgara instead. Now, *there* was a study for you. There was so much naked emotion in that room that the air almost seemed to crackle with it. At first Polgara looked at Iron-grip with open and undisguised hostility. Here was her rival, and she absolutely hated him. Gradually, however, the sheer force of the absolute adoration with which Riva and Beldaran gazed at each other began to impress itself upon her. Polgara can keep her emotions from showing on her face, but she can't control her eyes. I watched those glorious eyes of hers flicker back and forth from steely grey to deepest lavender as her conflicting emotions struggled within her. It took her a long time. Polgara isn't one to give up easily. Finally, however, she sighed a long, quavering sigh, and two great tears welled up in those eyes. She quite obviously realized that she had lost. There was no way she could compete with the love between her sister and the Rivan King.

I felt a sudden wave of sympathy for her at that point, so I went over to where she was sitting and took her dirty hand in mine. "Why don't we step outside, Pol?" I suggested gently. "Get a bit of air?"

She gave me a quick, grateful look, nodded mutely, and rose to her feet. We left the room with dignity.

There was a balcony at the end of the hallway outside the room, and we went there. "Well," she said in an almost neutral tone of voice, "I guess that settles that, doesn't it?"

"It was settled a long time ago, Pol," I told her. "This is one of those Necessities. It *has* to happen."

"It always comes back to that, doesn't it, father?"

"Necessity? Of course, Pol. It has to do with who we are."

"Does it ever get any easier?"

"Not that I've noticed."

"Well, I just hope that they'll be happy." I was so proud of her at that moment that my heart almost burst.

Then she suddenly turned to me. "Oh, father!" she cried with a broken-hearted wail. She clung to me in a sudden storm of weeping.

I held her, saying "There, there." That's one of the stupidest things a man can possibly say, but under the circumstances, it was the best I could manage.

In time she got it under control, and she sniffed, a particularly unlovely sound.

"Use your handkerchief," I told her.

"I forgot to bring one."

I made one for her—right there on the spot—and offered to her.

"Thank you." She blew her nose and dabbed at her eyes. "Is there a bathhouse in this place?" she asked then.

"I think so. I'll ask the innkeeper."

"I'd appreciate it. I think it's time I got cleaned up. I don't really have any reason to be dirty any more, do I?"

Somehow that one escaped me.

"Why don't you go out and buy me a decent gown, father?" she suggested then.

"Of course, Pol. Anything else?"

"A comb and brush, perhaps." She took hold of one tangled lock, pulled it forward, and looked at it critically. "I suppose I really ought to do something about my hair, too."

"I'll see what I can find. Would you like a ribbon, as well?"

"Don't be ridiculous, father. I'm not a maypole. I don't need decorations. Go talk to the innkeeper. I *really* want to take a bath. Oh, incidentally, just a plain dress. This is Beldaran's party, not mine. I'll be in my room." And she went off down the hallway.

I located the bathhouse for her, and then I went looking for Anrak. I found him and Beldin in the taproom on the main floor of the inn. "Go find me a dressmaker," I told him.

"A *what?*"

"Polgara wants a new dress."

"What's wrong with the one she's got?"

"Just do it, Anrak, don't argue with me. Oh, she wants a comb and brush, too. The dressmaker should be able to tell you where to find them."

He looked mournfully into his half-full tankard.

"*Now*, Anrak."

He sighed and went on out.

"What's this all about?" Beldin asked me.

"Polgara's had a change of heart. She doesn't want to look like an abandoned bird's nest any more."

"What brought that on?"

"I haven't got any idea, and I'm not going to ask. If she wants to look like a girl instead of a haystack, that's up to her."

"You're in a peculiar humor."

"I know." Then I jumped into the air and crowed exultantly.

We were all stunned when Polgara came into the room the next morning. The plain dress she wore was blue, of course. Pol almost always wears blue. Her long, dark hair was pulled back rather severely and tied at the nape of her neck. Now that she was clean, we saw that her skin was very fair, much like her sister's, and she was startlingly beautiful. It was her manner, however, that took us all by surprise. Even at sixteen, Pol was as regal as any queen.

Riva and Anrak both rose to their feet and bowed to her. Then Anrak sighed lustily.

"What's the matter?" his cousin asked him.

"I think I've made a mistake."

"There's nothing new about that."

"I think I'm going to regret this one, though. I might have had a chance with Lady Polgara if I'd pressed the issue. The Vale's pretty isolated, so she didn't have any other suitors. I'm afraid it's too late now, though. As soon as we get her to Riva, every young man on the Isle's going to pay court to her."

Pol gave him a warm look.

"Why did you let her get away?" Riva asked him.

"You saw how she looked yesterday, didn't you?"

"No, not really. I had my mind on other things."

Beldaran blushed. They'd both had their minds on other things.

"Please don't be offended, Lady Polgara," Anrak said to my eldest daughter.

"Not at all, Anrak," she replied. She seemed quite taken with the idea of being called "Lady Polgara." Just about everybody in the world calls her that now, but I think she still gets a warm glow every time she hears it.

"Well," Anrak said, choosing his words carefully, "Lady Polgara was just a little indifferent to appearances when I first saw her. I think she's a sorceress—like her father. Of course, he's a sorcerer, not a sorceress, but you know what I mean. Anyway, all sorcerers are very deep, you know, and she'd probably been thinking about something for several million years, and—"

"I'm only sixteen, Anrak," Pol corrected him gently.

"Well, yes, I know, but time doesn't mean the same thing to you people as it does to us. You can make time stop and start again any time you want, can't you?"

"Can we do that, father?" she asked me with some curiosity.

"I don't know." I looked at Beldin. "Can we?"

"Well, theoretically, I suppose," he replied. "Belmakor and I discussed the possibility once, but we decided that it wouldn't be a good idea. You might get time all mixed up—one time in one place and a different time in another. It'd probably be very hard to get it all put back together right again, and you couldn't just leave it that way."

"Why not?"

"Because you'd be in two places at the same time."

"What's wrong with that?"

"It'd be a paradox, Belgarath. Belmakor and I weren't sure what that might do to the universe—rip it to pieces, maybe, or just make it vanish."

"It wouldn't do that."

"I wasn't going to try it to find out."

"You see what I mean about how deep these people are?" Anrak said to his cousin. "Anyway, the Lady Polgara had flown up into a tree, and she was doing sorceress things. I sort of suggested that I might consider marrying her—since her sister was going to marry you, and twins always like to do things together. She didn't think too much of the idea, I guess, so I didn't press the issue. To be honest about it, she wasn't very tidy when I first saw her." He stopped, looking at Pol with a certain consternation.

"I was in disguise, Anrak," she helped him out.

"Really? Why was that?"

"It was one of those sorceress things you mentioned."

"Oh, one of those. It was a very good disguise, Lady Polgara. You were an absolute mess."

"I wouldn't push that too much further, Anrak," Beldaran advised. "Why don't we have some breakfast and start packing instead? I really want to see my new home."

We set sail later on that same day, and we arrived at Riva's city two days afterward. His people were all down at the beach waiting for us—well, for Beldaran, actually. I don't imagine that the Rivans were very interested in looking at Beldin and me, but they really wanted to get a look at their new queen. Riva hovered protectively over her. He didn't want anybody admiring her *too* much.

I'm sure they got his point—at least where Beldaran was concerned. There were other things to be admired, however.

"You'd better get yourself a club," Beldin muttered to me.

"What?"

"A club, Belgarath—a stout stick with a big end."

"What do I need with a club?"

"Use your eyes, Belgarath. Take a long, hard look at Polgara and then look at the faces of all those young Alorns standing on the beach. Believe me, you're going to need a club."

I didn't, exactly, but I made a special point of not letting Pol out of my sight while we were on the Isle of the Winds. I suspect that I might have been more comfortable if Pol had held off on emerging from her cocoon for a while. I was proud of her, of course, but her altered appearance made me *very* nervous. She was young and inexperienced, and the young men on the Isle were obviously very much taken with her.

My strategy was quite simple. I sat in plain view and scowled. I was wearing one of those ridiculous white robes people are always trying to foist off on me, and I carried a long staff—much as I had in Arendia and Tolnedra. I had quite a reputation among Alorns, and those absurd trappings enhanced it and got my point across. The young Rivans were polite and attentive—which was fine. But they didn't lure Polgara off into dark corners—which *wouldn't* have been.

Pol, of course, was having the time of her life. She didn't exactly *encourage* that crowd of suitors, but she smiled a great deal and even laughed now and then. It's a cruel thing to suggest, but I suspect that she even enjoyed the fact that young Rivan girls frequently left the room where she was holding court so that they could go someplace private. Gnawing on your own liver isn't the sort of thing you want to do in public.

We'd been in the Hall of the Rivan King for about a week when a fleet of Cherek war boats sailed into the harbor. The other Alorn kings had arrived for Riva's wedding.

It was good to see Cherek and his sons again, although we didn't really have much chance to talk. Pol assured me that she could take care of herself, but I didn't feel like taking chances.

Yes, Polgara, I was jealous. Aren't fathers *supposed* to be jealous? I knew what those young men had on their minds, and I was *not* going to leave you alone with them.

A couple of days after Cherek and the boys had arrived, Beldin came looking for me. I was in my usual place wearing my usual scowl, and Polgara was busy breaking hearts. "I think you'd better have a talk with Bear-shoulders," he told me.

"Oh?"

"Riva's wedding's starting to give Dras and Algar some ideas."

"What kind of ideas?"

"Grow up, Belgarath. Regardless of how Riva and Beldaran feel about each other, this *is* a political marriage."

"Theological, actually."

"It means the same thing. Dras and Algar are starting to think about the advantages that might be involved in a marriage to Polgara."

"That's ridiculous!"

"I'm not the one who's thinking about it, so don't blame me if it's ridiculous. Sooner or later, one of them's going to go to Cherek and ask him to speak with you about it. Then he'll come to you with some kind of proposal. You'd better head that off before he embarrasses himself. We still need the Alorns on our side."

I swore and stood up. "Can you keep an eye on Polgara for me?"

"Why not?"

"Watch out for that tall one with the blond hair. Pol's paying a little too much attention to him for my comfort."

"I'll take care of it."

"Don't do anything permanent to him. He's the son of a Clan-Chief, and this Isle's a little too confined for a clan war." Then I went looking for Cherek Bear-shoulders.

I stretched the truth just a bit when I told him that Aldur had instructed me to keep Pol with me in the Vale and that she wasn't supposed to get married for quite some time. Once I'd headed off their father, Dras and Algar could make all the proposals to him they wanted to. He wouldn't act as their go-between.

Bear-shoulders had aged since we'd gone to Mallorea. His hair and beard were shot with grey now, and a lot of the fun seemed to have gone out of his eyes. He told me that the Nadraks had been scouting along Bull-neck's eastern border and that the Murgos had been coming down the Eastern Escarpment and probing into Algaria.

"We probably ought to discourage that," I told him.

"Dras and Algar are taking care of it," he replied. "Technically speaking, there's still a state of war between us and the Angaraks, so we could probably justify a certain amount of firmness if the issue ever came up in court."

"Cherek, we're talking about international politics here. There aren't any laws, and there aren't any courts."

He sighed. "The world's getting more civilized all the time, Belgarath," he said mournfully. "The Tolnedrans are always trying to come up with picky little restrictions."

"Oh?"

"They've been trying to get me to agree to outlaw what they call 'piracy.' Isn't that the most ridiculous thing you ever heard of? There aren't any laws on the high seas. What happens out there isn't anybody's business. Why drag judges and lawyers into it?"

"Tolnedrans are like that sometimes. Tell Dras and Algar to find wives someplace else, would you please? Polgara's not available at the moment."

"I'll mention it to them."

The Alorn calendar was a little imprecise in those days. The Alorns kept a count of years, but they didn't bother attaching names to the months the way the Tolnedrans did. Alorns just kept track of the seasons and let it go at that, so I can't really give you the precise date of the wedding of Beldaran and Riva. It was three weeks or so after the arrival of Riva's father and brothers, though. About ten days before the wedding, Polgara set aside her campaign to break every heart on the Isle of the Winds, and she and Beldaran went into an absolute frenzy of dressmaking. With the help of several good-natured Alorn girls, they rebuilt Beldaran's wedding dress from the ground up, and then they turned their attention to a suitable gown for the bride's sister. Beldaran had always enjoyed sewing, but Pol's fondness for that activity dates from that period in her life. Sewing keeps a lady's fingers busy, but it gives her plenty of time to talk. I'm not really sure what those ladies talked about during those ten days, because they always stopped whenever I entered the room. Evidently it was the sort of thing ladies prefer not to share with men. Polgara apparently gave her sister all sorts of advice about married life—although how *she* found out about such things is beyond me. How much information could she have picked up sitting in a tree surrounded by birds?

Anyway, the happy day finally arrived. Riva was very nervous, but Beldaran seemed serene. The ceremony took place in the Hall of the Rivan King—Riva's throne room. A throne room probably isn't the best place to hold a wedding, but Riva insisted, explaining that he wanted to be married in the presence of the Orb and that it might have been a little inappropriate for him to wear his sword into the Temple of Belar. That was Riva for you.

There are all sorts of obscure little ceremonies involved in weddings, the meanings of which have long since been lost. The bridegroom is supposed to get there first, for example, and he's supposed to be surrounded by burly people who are there to deal firmly with anyone who objects. Riva had plenty of those, of course. His father, his brothers, and his cousin, all in bright-burnished mail shirts, bulked large around him as he stood at the front of the hall. I'd firmly taken Bull-neck's axe away from him and made him wear a sheathed sword instead. Dras was an enthusiast, and I didn't want him to start chopping up wedding guests just to demonstrate how much he loved his younger brother.

Once they'd settled down and the clinking of their mail had subsided, Beldin provided a fanfare to announce the bride's arrival. Beldin absolutely adored Beldaran, and he got a bit carried away. I'm almost positive that the citizens of Tol Honeth, hundreds of leagues to the south, paused in the business of swindling each other to remark "What was that?" when the sound of a thousand silver trumpets shattered the air of the Rivan throne room. That fanfare was followed by an inhumanly suppressed choir of female voices—a few hundred or so, I'd imagine—whispering a hymn to the bride. Beldin had studied music for a couple of quiet centuries once, and that hymn was very impressive, but eighty-four-part harmony is just a little complicated for my taste.

Armored Alorns swung the great doors of the Hall of the Rivan King open, and Beldaran, all in white, stepped into the precise center of that doorway. I knew it was the precise center because I'd measured it eight times and cut a mark into the stones of the floor that's probably still there. Beldaran, pale as the moon, stood in that framing archway while all those Alorns turned in their seats to crane their necks and look at her.

Somewhere, a great bell began to peal. After the wedding, I went looking for that bell, but I never found it.

Then my youngest daughter was touched with a soft white light that grew more and more intense.

Polgara, wrapped in a blue velvet cloak, stepped forward to take my arm. "Are you doing that?" she asked me, inclining her head toward the shaft of light illuminating her sister.

"Not me, Pol," I replied. "I was just going to ask if *you* were doing it."

"Maybe it's Uncle Beldin." She slightly shrugged her shoulders, and her cloak softly fell away to reveal her gown. I almost choked when I saw it.

Beldaran was all in white, and she glowed like pale flame in that shaft of light that I'm almost certain was a wedding gift from the funny old fellow in the rickety cart. Polgara was all in blue, and her gown broke away from her shoulders in complex folds and ruffles trimmed with snowy lace. It was cut somewhat daringly for the day, leaving no question that she was a girl. That deep-blue gown was almost like a breaking wave, and Polgara rose out of it like a Goddess rising from the sea.

I controlled myself as best I could. "Nice dress," I said from between clenched teeth.

"Oh, this old thing?" she said deprecatingly, touching one of the ruffles in an offhand way. Then she laughed a warm, throaty laugh that was far older than her years, and she actually kissed me. She'd never willingly done that before, and it startled me so much that I barely heard the alarm bells ringing in my head.

We separated and took the glowing bride, one on either arm, and, with stately, measured pace and slow, delivered up our beloved Beldaran to the adoring King of the Isle of the Winds.

I had quite a bit on my mind at that point, so I more or less ignored the wedding sermon of the High Priest of Belar. Anyway, if you've heard one wedding sermon, you've heard them all. There came a point in the ceremony, though, when something a little out of the ordinary happened.

My Master's Orb began to glow a deep, deep blue that almost perfectly matched the color of Polgara's gown. We were all terribly happy that Beldaran and Riva were getting married, but it seemed to me that the Orb was far more impressed with Polgara than with her sister. I'll take an oath that I really saw what happened next, although no one else who was there will admit that he saw it, too. That's probably what half persuaded me that I'd been seeing things that weren't really there. The Orb, as I say, began to glow, but it always did that when Riva was around, so there was nothing really unusual about that.

What *was* unusual was the fact Polgara began to glow, as well. She seemed faintly infused with that same pale-blue light, but the absolutely white lock at her brow was *not* pale. It was an incandescent blue.

And then I seemed to hear the faint flutter of ghostly wings coming from the back of the hall. *That* was the part that made me question the accuracy of my own senses.

It seemed, though, that Polgara heard it, too, because she turned around.

And with profoundest respect and love, she curtsied with heart-stopping grace to the misty image of the snowy white owl perched in the rafters at the back of the Hall of the Rivan King.

PART
FOUR

POLGARA

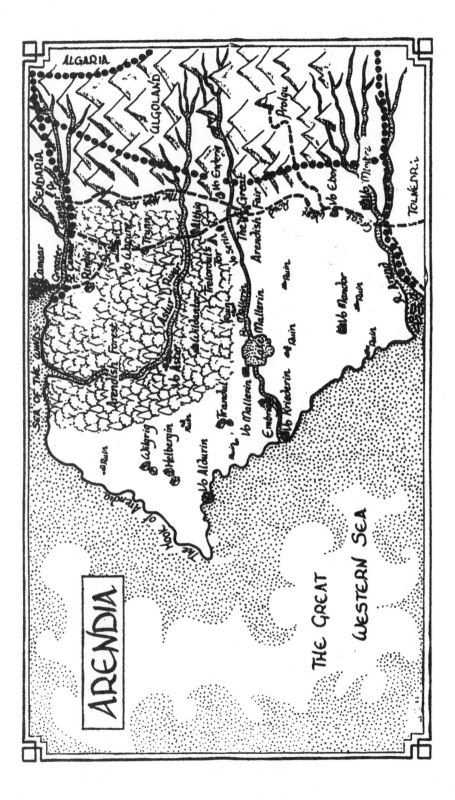

CHAPTER TWENTY-THREE

All right, don't beat me over the head with it. Of *course* I should have realized that something very peculiar was going on. But if you'll just stop and think about it for a moment, I believe you'll understand. You'll recall that Poledra's apparent death had driven me quite mad. A man who has to be chained to his bed has problems. Then I'd spent two or three years pickling my brains in the waterfront dives in Camaar and another eight or nine entertaining the ladies of Mar Amon, and during all that time I saw a *lot* of things that weren't really there. I'd grown so accustomed to that sort of thing that whenever I saw something unusual, I just shrugged it off as another hallucination. The incident at Beldaran's wedding *wasn't* a hallucination, but how was *I* supposed to know that? Try to be a little more understanding. It'll make a better person of you.

And so Beldaran and Riva were married, and they were both deliriously happy. There were other things afoot in the world, however, and since the Alorn kings were all on the Isle of the Winds anyway, Beldin suggested that we might want to seize the opportunity to discuss matters of state. All sorts of nonsense has been written about the origins of the Alorn Council, but that's how it really started. The Tolnedrans have been objecting to this rather informal yearly gathering for centuries now—largely because they aren't invited. Tolnedrans are a suspicious people, and any time they get word of a conference of any kind, they're absolutely certain that there's a plot against them at the bottom of it.

Polgara sat in on our conference. She didn't particularly want to, right at first, but I insisted. I wasn't going to give her an opportunity to wander about the citadel unsupervised.

I'm not sure that our impromptu conference really accomplished very much. We spent most of the time talking about the Angaraks. None of us were happy about their presence on this side of the Sea of the East, but for the moment there wasn't much we could do about it. The distances were simply too great.

"I could probably go into that forest to the east of the moors and burn down those cities the Nadraks are building there," Dras rumbled in that deep voice of his, "but there wouldn't be much point to it. I don't have the manpower to occupy all that wilderness. Sooner or later I'd have to pull out, and then the Nadraks would just come back out of the woods and rebuild."

"Have there been any contacts with them?" Pol asked.

He shrugged. "A few skirmishes is about all. Every so often they come out of the mountains, and then we chase them back. I don't think they're very serious about it. They're probably just testing our defenses."

"I meant peaceful contacts."

"There's no such thing as peaceful contacts between Alorns and Angaraks, Polgara."

"Perhaps there should be."

"I think that's against our religion."

"Maybe you should reconsider that. I understand that the Nadraks are merchants. They might be interested in trade."

"I don't think they've got anything I'd want."

"Oh, yes they do, Dras. They've got information about the Murgos, and *they're* the ones we're really interested in. If anyone's going to cause us trouble, it'll be the Murgos. If we can find out from the Nadraks what they're doing, we won't have to go down to Rak Goska to investigate for ourselves."

"She's got a point, Dras," Algar told his brother. "My people have had a few contacts with the Thulls, but you can't get very much information out of a Thull. From what I hear, the Nadraks don't care very much for the Murgos, so they probably wouldn't mind passing information along."

"Can you actually climb the Eastern Escarpment to get to Mishrak ac Thull?" Cherek asked him with a certain surprise.

"There are some ravines that cut down through the escarpment, father," Algar replied. "They're steep, but they're passable. The Murgos patrol the western frontier of Mishrak ac Thull, and every so often one of those patrols comes down onto the plains of Algaria—usually to steal horses. We'd rather they didn't do that, so we chase them back." He smiled faintly. "It's easier to let *them* find those ravines for us than to go looking for them ourselves."

"There's a thought," Dras noted. "If the Murgos want horses, couldn't we interest them in trade, too?"

Algar shook his head. "Not Murgos, no. Their minds don't work that way. One of my Clan-Chiefs questioned a Thull who actually knew his right hand from his left. The Thull said that Ctuchik's at Rak Goska. As long as *he's* dominating Murgo society, there won't be any peaceful contacts with them."

"Pol's right, then," Beldin said. "We're going to have to try to work through the Nadraks." He squinted at the ceiling. "I don't think this Angarak migration poses much of a threat—at least not yet. There weren't all *that* many people in Cthol Mishrak to begin with, and Ctuchik's got them spread out fairly thin. The real threat is still Mallorea. I think I'll go back there and keep an eye on things. The Angaraks on this continent are just an advance party. They're probably here to build supply dumps and staging areas. You won't have to start sharpening your swords until the Malloreans begin coming across. I'll keep my ear to the ground over there and let you know when the military moves north out of Mal Zeth toward the bridge."

Polgara pursed her lips. "I think we might want to establish closer ties with the Tolnedrans and the Arends."

"Why's that, dear sister?" Riva asked her. He was her brother-in-law now, and he automatically used that form of address. Family's an important thing to Alorns.

"We might need their help with the Malloreans."

"The Tolnedrans wouldn't help unless we paid them to," Cherek disagreed, "and the Arends are too busy fighting with each other."

"They live here, too, Bear-shoulders," she pointed out, "and I don't think they'd want Malloreans on this continent any more than we would. The legions could be very helpful, and the Arends have been training for war since before Torak split the world. Besides, Chaldan and Nedra probably would be offended if we all went off to war and didn't invite them to come along."

"Excuse me, Polgara," Dras rumbled, "but how did you learn so much about politics? As I understand it, this is the first time you've ever been out of the Vale."

"Uncle Beldin keeps me posted," she replied, shrugging slightly. "It's always nice to know what the neighbors are up to."

"Is there any point to involving the Nyissans or the Marags?" Riva asked.

"We should probably make the offer," I said. "The current Salmissra's a fairly intelligent young woman, and she's as concerned about the Angaraks as we are. The Marags wouldn't be of much use. There aren't that many of them, and the fact that they're cannibals might make everybody else nervous."

Beldin laughed that ugly laugh of his. "Tell them to start eating Angaraks. Let the Murgos get nervous."

"I think maybe we'd all better start thinking about going home," Cherek suggested, rising to his feet. "The wedding's over now, and if the Malloreans *are* coming, we'd better start getting ready for them."

And that was more or less the extent of the first Alorn Council.

"Is it always that much fun?" Polgara asked me as we were returning to our quarters.

"Fun? Did I miss something?"

"Politics, father," she explained. "All this business of trying to guess what the other side's going to do."

"I've always rather enjoyed it."

"I guess you really *are* my father, then. That was much more fun than leading young men around by their noses or turning their knees to water just by fluttering my eyelashes at them."

"You're a cruel woman, Polgara."

"I'm glad you realize that, father. It wouldn't be much fun at all to catch you unawares." She gave me one of those obscure little smiles. "Watch out for me, father," she warned. "I'm at least as dangerous as you are or Torak is."

You *did* say it, Pol, so don't try to deny it.

Our parting from Beldaran wasn't one of the happier moments in our lives. My love for my blonde daughter had been the anchor that had hauled me back to sanity, and Polgara's ties to her twin sister were so complex that I couldn't even begin to understand them.

Beldin and I talked at some length before we separated. He promised to keep me advised about what was going on in Mallorea, but I had a few suspicions about his motives for going back there. I had the feeling that he wanted to continue his discussion of white-hot hooks with Urvon, and there was always the chance of coming across Zedar in some out-of-the-way place. There are nicer people in the world than Beldin.

I wished him the best of luck—and I meant it. There are nicer people than me out there, as well. 'Grat is not nice, after all.

My brother left from the headland just south of the harbor at Riva, spiraling upward on lazy wings. Pol and I, however, left by more conventional means. Bear-shoulders took us to the Sendarian coast in that dangerously narrow war boat of his. Even though I'd helped to design them, I don't like Cherek war boats. There's no denying that they're fast, but it always feels to me whenever I board one that it's right on the verge of capsizing. I'm sure Silk understands that, but Barak never will.

Pol and I took our time returning to the Vale. There was no real hurry, after all. In a curious sort of way, Beldaran's marriage made peace between Polgara and me. We didn't talk about it, we just closed ranks to fill in the gap that had suddenly appeared in our lives. Pol still made those clever remarks, but a lot of the bite had gone out of them.

It was midsummer by the time we got home, and we spent the first week or so giving the twins a full description of the wedding and of Pol's conquests. I'm sure they noticed the change in her appearance, but they chose not to make an issue of it.

Then we settled back in. It was after dinner one evening when Polgara raised something I'd been cudgeling my brains to find a way to bring up myself. As I remember, we were doing the dishes at the time. I don't particularly like to dry dishes, since they'll dry themselves if you just leave them alone, but Polgara seems to feel a kind of closeness in the business, and if it made her happy, I wasn't going to disturb the uneasy peace between us by objecting.

She handed me the last dripping plate, dried her hands, and said, "I guess it's time for me to start my education, father. The Master's been harping on that for quite some time now."

I almost dropped the plate. "Aldur talks to you, too?" I asked her as calmly as I could.

She gave me a quizzical look. "Of course." Then the look became offensively pitying. "Oh, *come* now, father. Are you trying to say that you didn't *know?*"

I know now that I shouldn't have been so surprised, but I'd been raised in a society in which women were hardly more than servants. Poledra had been an entirely different matter, of course, but for some reason the implications of what Polgara had just told me were profoundly shocking. The fact that Aldur had come to her in the same way that he came to me was an indication of a certain status, and I simply wasn't ready to accept the idea of a female disciple. I guess that sometimes I'm just a little too old-fashioned.

Fortunately, I had sense enough to keep those opinions to myself. I carefully finished drying the plate, put it on the shelf, and hung up the dishtowel.

"Where's the best place to begin?" she asked me.

"The same place I did, I suppose. Try not to be offended, Pol, but you're going to have to learn how to read."

"Can't you just tell me what I need to know?"

I shook my head.

"Why not?"

"Because I don't *know* everything you'll need to learn. Let's go sit down, Pol, and I'll try to explain it." I led her over to that part of the tower that I devoted to study. I'd never even considered building interior walls in the tower, so it was really just one big room with certain areas devoted to certain activities. We sat down at a large table littered with books and scrolls and obscure pieces of machinery. "In the first place," I began, "we're all different."

"What an amazing thing. How is it that I never noticed that?"

"I'm serious, Pol. This thing we call 'talent' shows up in different ways in each of us. Beldin can do things I wouldn't even attempt, and the others also have certain specialities. I can give you the basics, but then you'll be on your own. Your talent's going to develop along lines that'll be dictated by the way your mind works. People babble about 'sorcery,' but most of what they say is pure nonsense. All it is—all it *can* be—is thought, and each of us thinks differently. That's what I meant when I said you're on your own."

"Why do I need to read, then? If I'm so unique, what can your books tell me that'll be of any use?"

"It's a shortcut, Pol. No matter how long you live, you're not going to have time to rethink every thought that's ever occurred to everyone who's ever lived. That's why we read—to save time."

"How will I know which thoughts are right and which ones aren't?"

"You won't—at least not at first. You'll get better at recognizing fallacies as you go along."

"But that'll only be my opinion."

"That's sort of the way it works, yes."

"What if I'm wrong?"

"That's the chance you have to take." I leaned back in my chair. "There aren't any absolutes, Pol. Life would be simpler if there were, but it doesn't work that way."

"Now I've got you, Old Man," she said it with a certain disputational fervor. Polgara *loves* a good argument. "There *are* things we know for certain."

"Oh? Name one."

"The sun's going to come up tomorrow morning."

"Why?"

"It always has."

"Does that really mean that it always will?"

A faint look of consternation crossed her face. "It *will*, won't it?"

"Probably, but we can't be *absolutely* certain. Once you've decided that something's absolutely true, you've closed your mind on it, and a closed mind doesn't go anywhere. Question everything, Pol. That's what education's all about."

"This might take longer than I thought."

"Probably so, yes. Shall we get started?"

Pol needs reasons for the things she does. Once she understood why reading was so important, she learned how in a surprisingly short time, and she got better at it as she went along. Perhaps it was something to do with her eyes. I probably can read faster than most because I can grasp the meaning of an entire line at a single glance. Pol picks up whole paragraphs in the same way. If you ever have occasion to watch my daughter reading, don't be deceived by the way she seems to be idly leafing through a book. She isn't. She's reading every single word. She went through my entire library in slightly more than a year. Then she went after Beldin's— which was a bit more challenging, since Beldin's library at that time was probably the most extensive in the known world.

Unfortunately, Polgara argues with books—out loud. I was engaged in my own studies at the time, and it's very hard to concentrate when a steady stream of "Nonsense!" "Idiocy!" and even "Balderdash!" is echoing off the rafters.

"Read to yourself!" I shouted at her one evening.

"But, father dear," she said sweetly, "you directed me to this book, so you must believe what it says. I'm just trying to open your mind to the possibility of an alternative opinion."

We argued about philosophy, theology, and natural science. We haggled about logic and law. We screamed at each other about ethics and comparative morality. I don't know when I've ever had so much fun. She crowded me at every turn. When I tried to pull in the wisdom of ages to defend my position, she neatly punctured all my windy pomposity with needle-sharp logic. In theory, I was educating *her*, but I learned almost as much as she did in the process.

Every so often, the twins came by to complain. Pol and I are vocal people, and we tend to get louder and louder as an argument progresses. The twins didn't really live all *that* far away, so they got to listen to our discussions—although they'd have preferred not to.

I was enormously pleased with her mind, but I was somewhat less pleased with the wide streak of vanity that was emerging in her. Polgara tends to be an extremist. She'd spent her young girlhood being militantly indifferent to her appearance. Now she went completely off the scale in the opposite direction. She absolutely *had* to bathe at least once a day— even in the wintertime. I've always been of the opinion that bathing in the winter is bad for your health, but Pol scoffed at that notion and immersed herself up to the eyebrows in warm, soapy water at every opportunity. More to the point, though, she also suggested that I should bathe more frequently. I think she had some sort of mental calendar ticking away inside her head, and she could tell me—and frequently did—exactly how long it had been since my last bath. We used to have long talks about that.

So far as I was concerned, if she wanted to bathe five times a day, that was up to her. But she also insisted on washing her hair each time! Pol has a full head of hair, and our tower seemed to be filled with a perpetual miasma. Damp hair is not one of my favorite fragrances. It wasn't so bad in the summertime when I could open the windows to air the place out, but in the winter I just had to live with it.

I think the last straw was when she moved Beldaran's standing mirror into a position where she could watch herself reading. All right, Polgara had grown up to be at least as pretty as Beldaran, but really—

She did things to her eyebrows that looked terribly painful to me.

I know as a matter of fact that they were painful, since I woke up one morning with her leaning placidly over me plucking out mine—hair by hair. Then, still not content, she started on my ears. Neatness is nice, I guess, but I drew the line there. The hair in a man's ears is there for a reason. It keeps out bugs, and it insulates the brain from the chill of winter. Polgara's mother had never objected to the fact that I had furry ears. Of course, Poledra looked at the world differently.

Pol spent inordinate amounts of time with her hair.

She combed.

She brushed.

She made me crazy with all that fussing. Yes, I know that Polgara has beautiful hair, but it crackles when the weather turns cold. Try it sometime. Let your hair grow until you can sit on it; then stroke it with a brush on a chill winter morning. There were times when she looked like a hedgehog, and bright sparks flew from her fingers whenever she touched anything even remotely metallic.

She used to swear about that a lot. Polgara doesn't really approve of swearing, but she does know all the words.

I think it was during the late spring of her eighteenth year when she finally stepped over the line and demonstrated her talent while I was watching. It's an obscure sort of modesty with Pol. She doesn't like to have anyone around to see what she's doing when she unleashes it. I suspect that it may have something to do with nakedness. Nobody—and I do mean nobody—has ever seen Polgara step all dripping from her bath wearing nothing but that dreamy smile. She conceals her gift in that self-same way—except in an emergency.

It wasn't actually an emergency. Pol had been deep into a Melcene philosophical tract, and she was concentrating on it very hard. I sort of suggested that it had been two days since we'd eaten. It was the end of winter, and I suppose I could have gone wolf and chased down a field-mouse or two, but I *really* wanted something to eat. Fieldmice are nice, but they're all fur and bones, and that's not really very satisfying for a full-grown animal.

"Oh, bother," she said, and made a negligent sort of gesture—without even looking up from her book—and there was quite suddenly a hind-quarter of beef smoking on the kitchen table, without benefit of platter.

I looked at it with a certain amount of chagrin. It was dripping gravy all over my floor, for one thing, and it wasn't quite fully done, for another. Polgara had provided cow. Cooking and seasoning to taste was *my* problem.

I bit down very hard on my lower lip. "Thanks awfully," I said to her in my most acid tone.

"Don't mention it," she replied without raising her eyes from her book.

CHAPTER
TWENTY-
FOUR

The world outside the Vale was changing. There's nothing particularly remarkable about that; the world is always
changing. About the only difference this
time lay in the fact that we noticed it. The
open grasslands to the north of us had always been uninhabited before—
unless you count the wild horses and cattle. But now the Algars lived
there.

I always rather liked Algar Fleet-foot. He was clearly the most intelligent of Cherek's sons. The fact that he never missed an opportunity to
keep his mouth shut was an indication of that. I suspect that if he'd been
Cherek's first son, it might not have been necessary to break up Aloria.
This is not intended to throw rocks at Dras Bull-neck. Dras was unques-
tionably one of the bravest men I've ever known, but he was just a bit on
the impetuous side. Maybe his sheer physical size had something to do
with that.

Fleet-foot's breeding program was beginning to produce larger horses,
and more and more of his people were mounted now. He'd also began to
cross-breed the rather scrubby Alorn cattle with the wild cows of the
plain to produce animals of a significant size that were at least marginally
tractable.

The Algars were fairly good neighbors—which is to say that they
didn't pester us. Fleet-foot periodically sent messengers to the Vale to
bring us news, but otherwise his people left us alone.

It was about two years after Beldaran's wedding—late spring I think it was—when Algar himself came down into the Vale with his cousin Anrak. "Good news, Belgarath," Anrak called up to my tower. "You're going to become a grandfather."

"It's about time," I called down. "Come on up, both of you." I went to the head of the stairs and told the door to open to admit them.

"When's Beldaran due?" I asked as they started up the stairs.

"A month or so, I suppose," Anrak replied. "She wants you and her sister to come to the Isle. Ladies like to have family around for the birth of their first child, I guess." They reached the top of the stairs, and Anrak looked around. "Where's Lady Polgara?" he asked.

"She's visiting the twins," I told him. "She'll be back in a bit. Sit down, gentlemen. I'll bring some ale. I think this calls for a little celebration."

We sat and talked for most of the rest of the afternoon, and then Polgara returned. She took the news quite calmly, which rather surprised me. "We'll need to pack a few things" was about all she said before she started supper. I strongly suspect that she already knew about her sister's condition.

"I brought horses," Algar said quietly.

"Good," Pol replied. "It's a long trip."

"Have you ridden very often?" he asked her.

"Not really."

"It'll take a little getting used to," he cautioned.

"I think I can manage, Algar."

"We'll see."

I probably should have paid more attention to the warning note in his voice. I'd never had much experience with horses. They'd been around, of course, but until the breeding program of the Algars, they'd been quite small, and I'd always felt that I could get from place to place almost as fast by walking. We left early the next morning, and by noon I began to wish that I *had* walked. Algarian saddles are probably the best in the world, but they're still very hard, and the steady, ground-eating trot that was Algar's favorite pace tended to make me bounce up and down, and every bounce grew more and more painful. I took my meals standing up for the first couple of days.

As we rode farther north, we began to encounter small herds of cattle. "Is it really a good idea to let them wander around loose that way?" Anrak asked Algar.

"Where are they going to go?" Algar replied. "This is where the grass and water are."

"Isn't it a little hard to keep track of them?"

"Not really." Algar pointed at a lone horseman on top of a nearby hill.

"That looks to be a very dull job."

"Only if you're lucky. When you're tending cattle, you don't *want* the job to be exciting."

"What do you plan to do with all these cows?" I asked him.

"Sell them, I suppose. There should be a market for them somewhere."

"Maybe," Anrak said a little dubiously, "but how do you plan to get them there?"

"That's why they have feet, Anrak."

The following day we came across an encampment of one of the Algarian clans. Most of their wagons were like farm wagons everywhere in the world—four wheels and an open bed. A few, however, were enclosed, looking strangely boxlike. "Is that something new?" I asked Algar, pointing at one of them.

He nodded. "We move around a lot, so we decided to take our houses with us. It's more practical that way."

"Do you think you'll ever get around to building a city?" Anrak asked him.

"We already have," Algar replied. "Nobody really lives there, but we've got one. It's off to the east a ways."

"Why build a city if you don't plan to live in it?"

"It's for the benefit of the Murgos."

"The Murgos?"

"It gives them a place to visit when they come to call." Algar smiled faintly. "It's much more convenient for us that way."

"I don't understand."

"We're herdsmen, Anrak. We go where the cows go. The Murgos can't really comprehend that. Most of their raiding parties are quite small. They come down the ravines in the escarpment to steal horses and then try to get back before we catch them. Every so often, though, a larger party comes down looking for a fight. We built what looks like a city so that they'll go there instead of wandering all over Algaria. It makes them easier to find."

"It's just bait, then?"

Algar considered that. "I suppose you could put it that way, yes."

"Wasn't building it a lot of work?"

Algar shrugged. "We didn't really have much else to do. The cows feed themselves, after all."

We spent the night in the Algarian encampment and rode west the following morning.

The main pass through the mountains was clear of snow by now, and I noticed that Fleet-foot was paying rather close attention to it as we rode up into the foothills. "Good grass," he noted, "and plenty of water."

"Are you thinking of expanding your kingdom?" I asked him.

"Not really. A couple of the clans are occupying the area up around

Darine, but there are too many trees west of the mountains to make the country good for cows. Doesn't this road lead to a town someplace up ahead?"

I nodded. "Muros," I told him. "The Wacite Arends built it."

"Maybe after Riva's son is born, I'll drop on down to Vo Wacune and have a talk with the duke. It shouldn't be too hard to drive cows through this pass, and if word got around that we were bringing herds through here, cattle-buyers might start gathering at Muros. I'd hate to have to go looking for them."

And that's what started the yearly cattle fair at Muros. In time it became one of the great commercial events in all the west.

But I'm getting ahead of myself here.

I hired a carriage again in Muros, and I was very happy to get out of the saddle. Pol and I rode inside while Algar and his cousin stayed on horseback. We reached Camaar without incident and boarded the ship Anrak had waiting there. Rivan ships are broader than Cherek war boats, so the two-day voyage to the Isle of the Winds was actually pleasant.

You can't really sneak up on the city Riva had built on the Isle, so he knew we were coming long before we arrived, and he was waiting on the wharf when we reached it.

"Are we in time?" Polgara called to him as the sailors were throwing ropes to men on the wharf.

"Plenty of time, I think," he replied. "At least that's what the midwives tell me. Beldaran wanted to come down to meet you, but I told her no. I'm not sure if climbing all those stairs would be good for her."

"I see you've shaved off your beard," I said.

"It was easier than arguing about it. My wife has opinions about beards."

"You look younger without it," Pol noted approvingly.

The sailors ran out the gangplank, and we all went ashore.

Polgara embraced her brother-in-law warmly, and we started the long climb up the hill to the citadel.

"How's the weather been?" Anrak asked his cousin.

"Unusual," Riva replied. "It hasn't rained for almost a week now. The streets are even starting to dry out."

Beldaran was waiting for us in the gateway to the Citadel, and she was *very* pregnant.

"You seem to be putting on a bit of weight, dear," Pol teased after they had embraced.

"You noticed." Beldaran laughed. "I think I'll be losing most of it before very long, though. At least I hope so." She laid one hand on her distended stomach. "It's awkward and uncomfortable, but I suppose it's worth it." Then she waddled over and kissed me. "How have you been, father?" she asked me.

"About the same," I replied.

"Oh, yes," Pol agreed. "Nothing changes our father."

"Why don't we go inside?" Riva suggested. "We don't want Beldaran taking a chill."

"I'm perfectly fine, Riva," she told him. "You worry too much."

Beldaran's pregnancy raised all sorts of emotions in me. Strangely, the memories of her mother weren't all that painful. Poledra's pregnancy had made her very happy, and I remembered that rather than what happened later.

I'd been a little uneasy about returning Polgara to the scene of her previous triumphs, but she evidently felt that she'd already broken enough hearts there, so she largely ignored the young men who flocked to the Citadel when word of her arrival got around. Pol enjoys being the center of attention, but she had other things on her mind this time. The young men sulked, but I don't think that bothered her much. I know it didn't bother *me*.

She spent most of her time with her sister, of course, but she did have long conferences with the midwives. I think her interest in the healing arts dates from that time. I suppose that birth is a logical place to begin the study of medicine.

The rest of us were redundant. If there's ever a time in a man's life when he's redundant, it's when his women-folk are delivering babies. Pol made that abundantly clear to us, and we wisely chose not to argue with her about it. Young as she was, Polgara had already begun to take charge of things. There have been times—many times—when I'd have been happier if she weren't quite so forceful, but that's the way she is.

Riva had set aside a room high up in one of the towers that served him as a kind of study, not that he was really all that studious. I'm not trying to imply that he was stupid, by any means, but he didn't have that burning interest in books that characterizes the scholar. I think his major concern at that time had to do with the tax code.

Fleet-foot, Anrak, and I took to joining him in that tower room— largely to stay out from underfoot, I think.

"Have you heard from Beldin?" Algar asked me one morning after we'd settled in for one of those random day-long discussions.

"Not for several months," I replied. "I guess things are quiet in Mallorea."

"Is Torak still at Ashaba?" Riva asked.

"So far as I know. From what Beldin told me the last time we talked, that ecstasy is still on him."

"I don't quite understand that," Anrak confessed. "Exactly what's happening to him?"

"Have you heard about the two Destinies?"

"Vaguely. The priest of Belar talks about them in church sometimes. It usually puts me to sleep."

"Try to stay awake this time," I told him. "To put it in the simplest terms, the universe came into existence with a Purpose."

"I understand that part."

"Good. Anyway, something happened that wasn't supposed to happen, and it divided that Purpose. Now there are two possibilities where there used to be only one."

"This is the place where I usually go to sleep," he said.

"Fight it. Always before, we got our instructions directly from the Gods, but they've left now, so we're supposed to be instructed by one or the other of the two Necessities. Torak follows one, and we follow the other. Certain people get touched by those Necessities, and they start to talk. Most people think they're just crazy, but they're not. They're passing instructions on to us."

"Isn't that a cumbersome way to do it?"

I shrugged. "Yes, but it has to be that way."

"Why?"

"I haven't the faintest idea. Anyway, Torak's been raving for years now, and Urvon's got scribes taking down his every word. There are instructions and hints about the future in those ravings. As soon as Torak comes to his senses again, he'll try to figure out what they mean." I suddenly remembered something. "Does Dras still have that maniac chained to a post near Boktor?" I asked Riva.

"So far as I know he does—unless the fellow's chewed his chain in two and run off into the fens by now. There's one in Darine, as well, you know. He's not *quite* as crazy as the one Dras has, but he's close."

I looked at Algar. "You've got clans near Darine, don't you?"

"Yes."

"Can you get word to one of your Clan-Chiefs? I want scribes to start taking down that fellow's ravings. They're probably important."

"I've already taken care of that, Belgarath."

"I think I'll take the long way around when I go home," I mused. "I want to have a look at these two prophets—and talk to them. Maybe I can say something that'll set them off. Has Dras made any contacts with the Nadraks?"

"Not personally," Riva replied. "Dras has prejudices where Angaraks are concerned. There are merchants in Boktor, though, and there's a little bit of trade going on along the border. The merchants have been picking up quite a bit of information."

"Anything useful?"

"It's hard to say. Things have a way of getting garbled after they've passed through six or eight people. From what I understand, the Murgos have been moving south into the lands of the western Dals. They almost had to, I guess. The Thulls have started to lose interest in feeding their former masters, and nothing grows around Rak Goska. The Murgos either had to move or starve."

"Maybe they'll wander off the southern end of the continent," Algar said. "The notion of watching the Murgos marching out to sea sort of appeals to me."

"Has there been any word about Ctuchik?" I asked.

"I think he's left Rak Goska," Riva replied. "They say that he's building a city at a place called Rak Cthol. It's supposed to be on top of a mountain somewhere."

"It'd be consistent," I said. "Ctuchik's a Grolim, and the Grolims have been in mourning ever since Korim sank into the sea. They adore temples on top of mountains, for some reason."

"They wouldn't get too much worship out of me in a place like that," Anrak said. "I'll go to church if it's not too much trouble, but I don't think I'd want to climb a mountain to get there." He looked at me. "Have you ever met this Ctuchik?"

"I think so," I replied. "I think he was the one who was chasing us after we stole the Orb. Ctuchik more or less ran things at Cthol Mishrak. Torak was concentrating all his attention on the Orb, so he left the day-to-day details to Ctuchik. I know that the one leading the pursuit was either Urvon or Ctuchik, and I hear Urvon didn't go to Cthol Mishrak unless Torak summoned him."

"What does Ctuchik look like?"

"A dog, last time I looked," Algar murmured.

"A dog?"

"One of the Hounds of Torak," I explained. "Certain Grolims took on the form of Hounds so that they could guard the place."

"Who'd want to go near a place like Cthol Mishrak?"

"We did," Algar told him. "There was something there we wanted." He looked at me. "Has Beldin heard anything about where Zedar might be?" He asked.

"Not that he mentioned."

"I think maybe we ought to keep an eye out for him. We *know* that Urvon's at Mal Yaska and Ctuchik's at Rak Cthol. We *don't* know where Zedar is, and that makes him dangerous. Urvon and Ctuchik are Angaraks. If either one of them comes after the Orb, he'll come with an army. Zedar's *not* an Angarak, so he might try something different."

I could have saved myself—and a large number of other people—a great deal of trouble if I'd paid closer attention to what Fleet-foot said. We didn't have time to pursue the question, though, because it was just about then that the messenger Pol had sent found us.

"Lord Riva," he said to my son-in-law, "Lady Polgara says that you're supposed to come now."

Riva stood up quickly. "Is everything all right?" he asked.

The messenger was a bearded Alorn warrior, and he seemed a little offended by his errand. Polgara tends to ignore rank, and when she needs something, she'll send the first person she sees to get it. "Everything seems normal to me," the messenger replied, shrugging. "The women are all running around with pails of hot water, and your wife's yelling."

"Yelling?" Riva's eyes got wild.

"Women always yell when they're having babies, my Lord. My wife's had nine, and she still yells. You'd think they'd get used to it after a while, wouldn't you?"

Riva pushed past him and went down the stairs four at a time.

It was the first time that Pol had officiated at a birth, so she was probably just a bit premature about summoning Riva. Beldaran's labor continued for about another four hours, and Iron-grip was *definitely* in the way the whole time. I think my daughter learned a valuable lesson that day. After that, she always invented something for the expectant father to do during his wife's labor—usually something physical and a long way away from the birthing chamber.

In the normal course of time, Beldaran delivered my grandson, a red-faced, squirming boy with damp hair that dried to sandy blond. Polgara emerged from the bedroom with the small, blanket-wrapped bundle in her arms and a strange, almost wistful look on her face. "Behold the heir to the Rivan throne," she said to us, holding out the baby.

Riva stumbled to his feet. "Is he all right?" he stammered.

"He has the customary number of arms and legs, if that's what you mean," Pol replied. "Here." She thrust the baby at his father. "Hold him. I want to help my sister."

"Is she all right?"

"She's fine, Riva. Take the baby."

"Isn't he awfully small?"

"Most babies are. Take him."

"Maybe I'd better not. I might drop him."

Her eyes glinted. "Take the baby, Riva." She said it slowly, emphasizing each word. *Nobody* argues with Polgara when she takes that tone.

Riva's hands were shaking very badly when he reached out to take his son.

"Support his head," she instructed.

Riva placed one of his huge hands behind the baby's head. His knees were visibly trembling.

"Maybe you'd better sit down," she said.

He sank back into his chair, his face very pale.

"*Men!*" Polgara said, rolling her eyes upward. Then she turned and went back into the bedroom.

My grandson looked at his father gravely. He had very blue eyes, and he seemed much calmer than the trembling giant who was holding him. After a few minutes, Iron-grip began that meticulous examination of his newborn offspring that all parents seem to feel is necessary. I'm not sure why people always want to count fingers and toes under those circumstances. "Would you *look* at those tiny little fingernails!" Riva exclaimed. Why are people always surprised about the size of baby's fingernails? Are they expecting claws, perhaps?

"Belgarath!" Riva said then in a choked voice. "He's deformed!"

I looked down at the baby. "He looks all right to me."

"There's a mark on the palm of his right hand!" He carefully opened those tiny fingers to show me.

The mark wasn't very large, of course, hardly more than a small white spot. "Oh, that," I said. "Don't worry about it. It's supposed to be there."

"What?"

"Look at your own hand, Riva," I said patiently.

He opened that massive right hand of his. "But that's a burn mark. I got it when I picked up the Orb for the first time—before it got to know me."

"Did it hurt when it burned you?"

"I don't remember exactly. I was a little excited at the time. Torak was right in the next room, and I wasn't sure he'd stay asleep."

"It's not a burn, Riva. The Orb knew who you were, and it wasn't going to hurt you. All it did was mark you. Your son's marked the same way because he's going to be the next keeper of the Orb. You might as well get used to that mark. It's going to be in your family for a long time."

"What an amazing thing. How did you find out about this?"

I shrugged. "Aldur told me," I replied. It was the easy thing to say, but it wasn't true. I *hadn't* known about the mark until I saw it, but as soon as I did, I knew exactly what it meant. Evidently a great deal of information had been passed on to me while I had been sharing my head with that peculiar voice that had guided us to Cthol Mishrak. The inconvenient part of the whole business lies in the fact that these insights don't rise to the surface until certain events come along to trigger them. Moreover, as soon as I saw that mark on my grandson's palm, I knew there was something I had to do.

That had to wait, however, because Polgara came out of the bedroom just then. "Give him to me," she told Riva.

"What for?" Iron-grip's voice had a possessive tone to it.

"It's time he had something to eat. I think Beldaran ought to take care of that—unless *you* want to do it."

He actually blushed as he quickly handed the baby over.

I wasn't able to attend to my little project until the following morning. I don't think the baby got very much sleep that night. *Everybody* wanted to hold him. He took it well, though. My grandson was an uncommonly good-natured baby. He didn't fuss or cry, but just examined each new face with that same grave, serious expression. *I* even got the chance to hold him once—for a little while. I took him in my hands and winked at him. He actually smiled. That made me feel very good, for some reason.

There was a bit of an argument the next morning, however. "He needs to get some sleep," Polgara insisted.

"He needs to do something else first," I told her.

"Isn't he a little young for chores, father?"

"He's not too young for this one. Bring him along."

"Where are we going?"

"To the throne room. Just bring him, Pol. Don't argue with me. This is one of those things that's supposed to happen."

She gave me a strange look. "Why didn't you say so, father?"

"I just did."

"What's happening here?" Riva asked me.

"I wouldn't want to spoil it for you. Come along."

We trooped through the halls from the royal apartment to the Hall of the Rivan King, and the two guards who were always there opened the massive doors for us.

I'd been in Riva's throne room before, of course, but the size of the place always surprised me just a bit. It was vaulted, naturally. You can't really support a flat roof safely over a room of that size. Massive beams crisscrossed high overhead, and they were held in place by carved wooden buttresses. There were three great stone firepits set at intervals in the floor, and a broad aisle that led down to the basalt throne. Riva's sword hung point-down on the wall behind the throne, and the Orb resting on the pommel was flickering slightly. I'm told that it did that whenever Riva entered the hall.

We marched straight to the throne. "Take down your sword, Iron-grip," I said.

"Why?"

"It's a ceremony, Riva," I told him. "Take down the sword, hold it by the blade, and introduce your son to the Orb."

"It's only a rock, Belgarath. It doesn't care what his name is."

"I think you might be surprised."

He shrugged. "If you say so." He reached up and took hold of the huge blade. Then he lifted down the great sword and held the pommel out to the baby in Polgara's arms. "This is my son, Daran," he said to the Orb. "He'll take care of you after I'm gone."

I might have said it differently, but Riva Iron-grip was a plain-spoken sort of fellow who didn't set much store in ceremonies. I immediately recognized the derivation of my grandson's name, and I was sure that Beldaran would be pleased.

I'm almost certain that the infant Daran had been asleep in his aunt's arms, but something seemed to wake him up. His eyes opened, and he saw my Master's Orb, which his father was holding out to him. It's easy to say that a baby will reach out for any bright thing that's offered to him, but Daran knew exactly what he was supposed to do. He'd known about that before he was even born.

He reached out that small, marked hand and firmly laid it palm-down on the Orb.

The Orb recognized him immediately. It burst joyously into bright blue flame, a blue aura surrounded Pol and the baby, and the sound of millions of exulting voices seemed to echo down from the stars.

I have it on the very best of authority that the sound brought Torak howling to his feet in Ashaba, half a world away.

CHAPTER
TWENTY-
FIVE

Pol and I stayed on the Isle of the Winds for about a month after Daran was born. There wasn't anything urgent calling us back to the Vale, and it was a rather special time in our lives. Beldaran was up and about in a few days, and she and Pol spent most of their time together. I don't think I'd fully understood how painful their separation had been for both of them. Every now and then, I'd catch a glimpse of Polgara's face in an unguarded moment. Her expression was one of obscure pain. Beldaran had inexorably been drawn away from her—first by her husband and now by her baby. Their lives had diverged, and there was nothing either of them could do about it.

Algar Fleet-foot left for Vo Wacune after a week or so to have a talk with the Wacite duke. Evidently, the idea that'd come to him in that mountain pass had set fire to his imagination, and he *really* wanted to explore the possibility of establishing a permanent cattle fair at Muros. Raising cows has its satisfactions, I suppose, but getting rid of them after you've raised them is something else. If I'd paid closer attention to the implications of his notion, I might have realized just how profoundly it would affect history. Revenues from that fair financed the military adventures of the Wacites during the Arendish civil wars, and the profits to be made in Muros almost guaranteed a Tolnedran presence there. Ultimately, I suppose, that cattle fair was responsible for the founding of the Kingdom of Sendaria. I've always felt that an economic theory of history is an oversimplification, but in this case it had a certain validity.

Meanwhile, I hovered on the outskirts of my little family waiting for the chance to get my hands on my grandson. You have no idea of how difficult that was. He was Beldaran's first child, and she treated him like a new appendage. When *she* wasn't holding him, Polgara was. Then it was Riva's turn. Then it was time for Beldaran to feed him again. They passed him around like a group of children playing with a ball, and there wasn't room for another player in their little game.

I was finally obliged to take steps. I waited until the middle of the night, crept into the nursery, and lifted Daran out of his cradle. Then I crept out again. All grandparents have strong feelings about their grandchildren, but my motives went a little further than a simple desire to get all gooey inside. Daran was the direct result of certain instructions my Master had given me, and I needed to be alone with him for a few minutes to find out if I'd done it right.

I carried him out into the sitting room where a single candle burned, held him on my lap, and looked directly into those sleepy eyes. "It's nothing really all that important," I murmured to him. I *refuse* to babble gibberish to a baby. I think it's insulting. I was very careful about what I did, of course. A baby's mind is extremely malleable, and I didn't want to damage my grandson. I probed quite gently, lightly brushing my fingertip—figuratively speaking—across the edges of his awareness. The merger of my family with Riva's was supposed to produce someone very important, and I needed to know something about Daran's potential.

I wasn't disappointed. His mind was unformed, but it was very quick. I think he realized in a vague sort of way what I was doing, and he smiled at me. I suppressed an urge to shout with glee. He was going to work out just fine. "We'll get to know each other better later on," I told him. "I just thought I ought to say hello." Then I took him back to the nursery and tucked him into his cradle.

He watched me a lot after that, and he always giggled when I winked at him. Riva and Beldaran thought that was adorable. Polgara, however, didn't. "What did you do to that baby?" she demanded when she caught me alone in the hall after supper one evening.

"I just introduced myself, Pol," I replied as inoffensively as possible.

"Oh, *really?*"

"You've got a suspicious mind, Polgara," I told her. "I *am* the boy's grandfather, after all. It's only natural for him to like me."

"Why does he laugh when he looks at you, then?"

"Because I'm a very funny fellow, I suppose. Hadn't you ever noticed that?"

She glowered at me, but I hadn't left her any openings. It was one of the few times I ever managed to outmaneuver her. I'm rather proud of it, actually. "I'm going to watch you very closely, Old Man," she warned.

"Feel free, Pol. Maybe if I do something funny enough, I'll even be able to get a smile out of you." Then I patted her fondly on the cheek and went off down the hall, whistling a little tune.

Pol and I left the Isle a few weeks later. Anrak sailed us across the Sea of the Winds to that deeply indented bay that lies just to the west of Lake Sendar, and we landed at the head of the bay where the city of Sendar itself now stands. There wasn't a city there at the time, though, just that gloomy forest that covered all of northern Sendaria until about the middle of the fourth millennium.

"That's not very promising-looking country, Belgarath," Anrak told me as Pol and I prepared to disembark. "Are you sure you wouldn't rather have me sail you around to Darine?"

"No, this is fine, Anrak. Let's not risk the Cherek Bore if we don't have to."

"It's not all *that* bad, Belgarath—or so they tell me."

"You're wrong, Anrak," I said quite firmly. "It *is* that bad. The Great Maelstrom in the middle of it swallows whole fleets just for breakfast. I'd rather walk."

"Cherek war boats go through it all the time, Belgarath."

"This isn't a Cherek war boat, and you aren't crazy enough to be a Cherek. We'll walk."

And so Anrak beached his ship, and Pol and I got off. I wonder when the practice of beaching ships fell into disuse. Sailors used to do it all the time. Now they stand off a ways and send passengers ashore in longboats. It's probably a Tolnedran innovation. Tolnedran sea captains tend to be a bit on the timid side.

My daughter and I stood on that sandy beach watching Anrak's sailors straining to get his ship back out into the water. When she was finally afloat again, they poled her out a ways, raised the sails, and went off down the bay.

"What now, father?" Pol asked me.

I squinted up at the sun. "It's midafternoon," I told her. "Let's set up a camp and get an early start in the morning."

"Are you sure you know the way to Darine?"

"Of course I am." I wasn't, actually. I'd never been there before, but I had a general idea of where it was. Over the years, I've found that it's usually best to pretend that I know what I'm doing and where I'm going. It heads off a lot of arguments in the long run.

We went back from the beach a ways and set up camp in a rather pleasant forest clearing. I offered to do the cooking, but Pol wouldn't hear of it. I even made a few suggestions about cooking over an open campfire, but she tartly told me to mind my own business and she did it her own way. Actually, supper didn't turn out too badly.

We traveled northwesterly through that ancient forest for the next couple of days. The region was unpopulated, so there weren't any paths. I kept our general direction firmly in mind and simply followed the course of least resistance. I've spent a lot of time in the woods over the years, and I've found that to be about the best way to go through them. There's a certain amount of meandering involved, but it gets you to where you're going—eventually.

Polgara, however, didn't like it. "How far have we come today?" she asked me on the evening of the second day.

"Oh, I don't know," I replied. "Probably six or eight leagues."

"I meant in a straight line."

"You don't follow straight lines in the woods, Pol. The trees get in the way."

"There *is* a faster way to do this, father."

"Were you in a hurry?"

"I'm not enjoying this, Old Man." She looked around at the huge, mossy trees with distaste. "It's damp, it's dirty, and there are bugs. I haven't had a bath for four days."

"You don't have to bathe when you're in the woods, Pol. The squirrels don't mind if your face is dirty."

"Are we going to argue about this?"

"What did you have in mind?"

"Why walk when we can fly?"

I stared at her. "How did you know about that?" I demanded.

"Uncle Beldin does it all the time. You're supposed to be educating me, father. This seems to be a perfect time for me to learn how to change my form into one that's more useful. You can suit yourself, of course, but *I'm* not going to plod through this gloomy forest all the way to Darine just so you can look at the scenery." Pol can turn the slightest thing into an ultimatum. It's her one great failing.

There *was* a certain logic to what she was saying, however. Wandering around in the woods is enjoyable, but there were other things I wanted to do, and the art of changing form is one of the more useful ones. I wasn't entirely positive that her talent was that far along yet, though, so I was a little dubious about the whole idea. "We'll try it," I finally gave in. It was easier than arguing with her.

"When?"

"Tomorrow morning."

"Why not now?"

"Because it's getting dark. I don't want you flying into a tree and breaking your beak."

"Whatever you say, father." Her submissive tone was fraudulent, naturally. She'd won the argument, so now she could afford to be gracious about it.

She was up the next morning before it got light, and she'd crammed my breakfast into me before the sun came up. "Now, then," she said, "let's get started." She *really* wanted to try this.

I described the procedure to her at some length, carefully going over all the details while her look of impatience grew more and more pronounced.

"Oh, let's get on with it, father," she said finally.

"All right, Pol," I surrendered. "I suppose you can always change back if you turn yourself into a flying rabbit."

She looked a little startled at that.

"Details, Polgara," I told her. "This is one case when you *really* have to pay attention to details. Feathers aren't that easy, you know. All right. Don't rush. Take it slowly."

And, of course, she ignored me. Her eyebrows sank into a scowl of intense concentration. Then she shimmered and blurred—and became a snowy white owl.

My eyes filled with tears immediately, and I choked back a sob. "Change back!"

She looked a little startled when she resumed her own form.

"Don't *ever* do that again!" I commanded.

"What's wrong, father?"

"Any shape but that one."

"What's wrong with that one? Uncle Beldin says that mother used to do it all the time."

"Exactly. Pick another shape."

"Are you crying, father?" she asked with a certain surprise.

"Yes, as a matter of fact, I am."

"I didn't think you knew how." She touched my face almost tenderly. "Would some other kind of owl be all right?"

"Turn yourself into a pelican if you want to. Just stay away from that shape."

"How about this one?" She blurred into the form of a tufted owl instead. She was a mottled brown color, and the sprigs of feathers sprouting from the sides of her head altered that painful appearance enough so that I could bear to live with it.

I drew in a deep breath. "All right," I told her, "flap your wings and see if you can get up off the ground."

She hooted at me.

"I can't understand you, Pol. Just flap your wings. We can talk about it later."

Would you believe that she did it perfectly the first time? I should have had suspicions at that point, but I was still all choked up, so I didn't think about it. With a few strokes of those soft wings she lifted herself effortlessly off the ground and circled the clearing a few times. Then she landed on a tree branch and began to preen her feathers.

It took me awhile to regain my composure, and then I went over to her tree and looked up at her. "Don't try to change back," I instructed. "You'll fall out of the tree if you do."

She stared down at me with those huge, unblinking eyes.

"We're going in that direction." I pointed northeasterly. "I'm not going to turn myself into a bird because I don't fly very well. I'll take the shape of a wolf instead. I'll probably be able to keep up with you, but don't get out of sight. I want to be close enough to catch you if something goes wrong. Keep an eye on the sun. We'll change back about noon."

She hooted at me again, that strange hollow cry of the tufted owl.

"Don't argue with me, Polgara," I told her. "We're going to do this my way. I don't want you to get hurt." Then, to avoid any further argument, I slipped into the form of the wolf.

Her flights were short at first. She drifted from tree to tree, obediently staying just ahead of me. I didn't have any difficulty keeping up with her. By midmorning, however, she began to extend the distance between perches, and I was obliged to move up from a sedate trot to a lope. By noon I was running. Finally I stopped, lifting my muzzle, and howled at her.

She circled, swooped back, and settled to earth. Then she shimmered back into her own form. "Oh, that was just *fine!*" she exclaimed with a sensuous shudder of pure pleasure.

I was right on the verge of an oration at that point. She'd pushed me fairly hard that morning. It was her smile that cut me off before I even got started, though. Polgara seldom smiled, but this time her face actually seemed to glow, and that single white lock above her forehead was bright as a sun-touched snowbank. Dear Gods, she was a beautiful girl! "You need to use your tail feathers just a bit more" was all I said to her.

"Yes, father," she said, still smiling. "What now?"

"We'll rest a bit," I decided. "When the sun goes down, we'll start out again."

"In the dark?"

"You're an owl, Polgara. Night's the natural time for you to be out flying."

"What about you?"

I shrugged. "Night or day—it doesn't matter to a wolf."

"We had to leave our supplies behind," she noted. "What are we going to eat?"

"That's up to you, Pol—whatever's unlucky enough to cross your path, I'd imagine."

"You mean *raw?*"

"You're the one who wanted to be an owl, dear. Sparrows eat seeds, but owls prefer mice. I wouldn't recommend taking on a wild boar. He might be a little more than you can handle, but that's entirely up to you."

She stalked away from me muttering swear words under her breath.

I'll admit that her idea worked out quite well. It would have taken us two weeks to reach Darine on foot. We managed it the other way in three nights.

The sun was just rising when we reached the hilltop south of the port city. We resumed our natural forms and marched to the city gate. Like just about every other city in the north in those days, Darine was constructed out of logs. A city has to burn down a few times before it occurs to the people who live there that wooden cities aren't really a good idea. We went through the unguarded gate, and I asked a sleepy passerby where I could find Hatturk, the Clan-Chief Algar had told me was in charge here in Darine. He gave me directions to a large house near the waterfront and then stood there rather foolishly ogling Polgara. Having beautiful daughters is nice, I suppose, but they *do* attract a certain amount of attention.

"We'll need to be a little careful with Hatturk, Pol," I said as we waded down the muddy street toward the harbor.

"Oh?"

"Algar says that the clans that have moved here from the plains aren't really happy about the breakup of Aloria, and they're definitely unhappy about that grassland. They migrated here because they got lonesome for trees. Primitive Alorns all lived in the forest, and open country depresses them. Fleet-foot didn't come right out and say it, but I sort of suspect that Darine might just be a stronghold of the Bear-cult, so let's be a little careful about what we say."

"I'll let you do the talking, father."

"That might be best. The people here are probably recidivist Alorns of the most primitive kind. I'm going to need Hatturk's cooperation, so I'm going to have to step around him rather carefully."

"Just bully him, father. Isn't that what you usually do?"

"Only when I can stand over somebody to make sure he does what I tell him to do. Once you've bullied somebody, you can't turn your back on him for very long, and Darine's not so pretty that I want to spend the next twenty years here making sure that Hatturk follows my instructions."

"I'm learning all sorts of things on this trip."

"Good. Try not to forget too many of them."

Hatturk's house was a large building constructed of logs. An Alorn

Clan-Chief is really a sort of miniking in many respects, and he's usually surrounded by a group of retainers who serve as court functionaries and double as bodyguards on the side. I introduced myself to the pair of heavily armed Algars at the door, and Pol and I were admitted immediately. Most of the time being famous is a pain, but it has some advantages.

Hatturk was a burly Alorn with a grey-shot beard, a decided paunch, and bloodshot eyes. He didn't look too happy about being roused before noon. As I'd more or less expected, his clothing was made of bearskins. I've never understood why members of the Bear-cult feel that it's appropriate to peel the hide off the totem of their God. "Well," he said to me in a rusty-sounding voice, "so you're Belgarath. I'd have thought you'd be bigger."

"I could arrange that if it'd make you feel more comfortable."

He gave me a slightly startled look. "And the lady?" he asked to cover his confusion.

"My daughter, Polgara the Sorceress." I think that might have been the first time anyone had ever called her that, but I wanted to get Hatturk's undivided attention, and I *didn't* want him to be distracted by Pol's beauty. It seemed that planting the notion in his mind that she could turn him into a toad might be the best way to head off any foolishness. To her credit, Pol didn't even turn a hair at my somewhat exotic introduction.

Hatturk's bloodshot eyes took on a rather wild look. "My house is honored," he said with a stiff bow. I got the distinct impression that he wasn't used to bowing to anybody. "What can I do for you?"

"Algar Fleet-foot tells me that you've got a crazy man here in Darine," I told him. "Polgara and I need to have a look at him."

"Oh, he's not really all *that* crazy, Belgarath. He just has spells now and then when he starts raving. He's an old man, and old men are always a little strange."

"Yes," Polgara agreed mildly.

Hatturk's eyes widened as he realized what he'd just said. "Nothing personal intended there, Belgarath," he hastened to apologize.

"That's all right, Hatturk," I forgave him. "It takes quite a bit to offend me. Tell me a little bit more about this strange old man."

"He was a berserker when he was younger—an absolute terror in a fight. Maybe that explains it. Anyway, his family's fairly well off, and when he started getting strange, they built a house for him on the outskirts of town. His youngest daughter's a spinster—probably because she's cross-eyed—and she looks after him."

"Poor girl," Pol murmured. Then she sighed rather theatrically. "I imagine I've got that to look forward to, as well. My father here is stranger than most, and sooner or later he's going to need a keeper."

"That'll do, Pol," I said firmly. "If you've got a couple of minutes, Hatturk, we'd like to see this old fellow."

"Of course." He led us out of the room and down the stairs to the street. We talked a bit as we walked through the muddy streets to the eastern edge of town. The idea of paving streets came late to the Alorns, for some reason. I put a few rather carefully phrased questions to Hatturk, and his answers confirmed my worst suspicions. The man was a Bear-cultist to the bone, and it didn't take very much to set him off on a rambling diatribe filled with slogans and clichés. Religious fanatics are *so* unimaginative. There's no rational explanation for their beliefs, so they're free to speak without benefit of logic, untroubled by petty concerns such as truth or even plausibility.

"Are your scribes getting down everything your berserker's saying?" I cut him off.

"That's just a waste of time and money, Belgarath," he said indifferently. "One of the priests of Belar had a look at what the scribes had taken down, and he told me to quit wasting my time."

"King Algar gave you very specific orders, didn't he?"

"Sometimes Algar's not right in the head. The priest told me that as long as we've got *The Book of Alorn*, we don't need any of this other gibberish."

Naturally a priest who was a member of the Bear-cult wouldn't want those prophecies out there. It might interfere with their agenda. I swore under my breath.

The Darine Prophet and his caretaker daughter lived in a neat, well-tended cottage on the eastern edge of town. He was a very old, stringy man with a sparse white beard and big, knobby hands. His name was Bormik, and his daughter's name was Luana. Hatturk's description of her was a gross understatement. She seemed to be intently examining the tip of her own nose most of the time. Alorns are a superstitious people, and physical defects of any kind make them nervous, so Luana's spinsterhood was quite understandable.

"How are you feeling today, Bormik?" Hatturk said, almost in a shout. Why do people feel they have to yell when they're talking to those who aren't quite right in the head?

"Oh, not so bad, I guess," Bormik replied in a wheezy old voice. "My hands are giving me some trouble." He held out those big, swollen hands.

"You broke your knuckles on other people's heads too many times when you were young," Hatturk boomed. "This is Belgarath. He wants to talk with you."

Bornik's eyes immediately glazed over. "Behold!" he said in a thunderous voice. "The Ancient and Beloved hath come to receive instruction."

"There he goes again," Hatturk muttered to me. "All that garbled nonsense makes me nervous. I'll wait outside." And he turned abruptly and left.

"Hear me, Disciple of Aldur," Bormik continued. His eyes seemed fixed on my face, but I'm fairly sure he didn't see me. "Hear my words, for my words are truth. The division *will* end, for the Child of Light is coming."

That was what I'd been waiting to hear. It confirmed that Bormik *was* the voice of prophecy and what he'd been saying all these years had contained vital information—and we'd missed it! I started to swear under my breath and to think up all sorts of nasty things to do to the thick-headed Hatturk. I glanced quickly at Polgara, but she was sitting in a corner of the room speaking intently to Bormik's cross-eyed daughter.

"And the Choice shall be made in the holy place of the children of the Dragon God," Bormik continued, "For the Dragon God is error, and was not intended. Only in the Choice shall error be mended, and all made whole again. Behold, in the day that Aldur's Orb burns hot with crimson fire shall the name of the Child of Dark be revealed. Guard well the son of the Child of Light, for he shall have no brother. And it shall come to pass that those which once were one and now are two shall be rejoined, and in that rejoining shall one of them be no more."

Then Bormik's weary old head drooped, as if the effort of prophecy had exhausted him. I might have tried to shake him awake, but I knew that it'd be fruitless. He was too old and feeble to go on. I stood, picked up a quilt from a nearby bench, and gently covered the drowsing old man. I certainly didn't want him to take a chill and die on me before he'd said what he was supposed to say. "Pol," I said to my daughter.

"In a minute, father," she said, waving me off. She continued to speak with that same low intensity to the cross-eyed Luana. "Agreed, then?" she said to the spindly spinster.

"As you say, Lady Polgara," Bormik's middle-age daughter replied. "A bit of verification first, if you don't mind." She rose, crossed the room, and looked intently at the image of her face in a polished brass mirror. "Done!" was all she said. Then she turned and looked around the room, and her eyes were as straight as any I've ever seen—very pretty eyes, as I recall.

What was going on here?

"All right, father," Pol said in an offhand sort of way. "We can go now." And she walked on out of the room.

"What was that all about?" I asked her as I opened the front door for her.

"Something for something, father," she replied. "You might call it a fair trade."

"There's our problem," I told her, pointing at the brutish Hatturk impatiently waiting in the street. "He's a Bear-cultist, and even if I could dragoon him into transcribing Bormik's ravings, he'd let the priests of the Bear-cult see them before he passed them on to me. Revisionism is the soul of theology, so there's no telling what sort of garbage would filter through to me."

"It's already been taken care of, father," she told me in that offensively superior tone of hers. "Don't strain Hatturk's understanding by trying to explain the need for accuracy to him. Luana's going to take care of it for us."

"Bormik's daughter?"

"Of course. She's closest to him, after all. She's been listening to his ravings for years now, and she knows exactly how to get him to repeat things he's said in the past. All it takes is a single word to set him off." she paused. "Oh," she said, "here's your purse." She held out my much-lighter money pouch, which she'd somehow managed to steal from me. "I gave her money to hire the scribes."

"And?" I said, hefting my diminished purse.

"And what?"

"What's in it for her?"

"Oh, *father*," she said. "You saw her, didn't you?"

"Her eyes, you mean?"

"Of course. As I said, something for something."

"She's too old for it to make any difference, Pol," I objected. "She'll never catch a husband now."

"Maybe not, but at least she'll be able to look herself straight in the eye in the mirror." She gave me that long-suffering look. "You'll never understand, Old Wolf. Trust me, I know what I'm doing. What now?"

"I guess we might as well go on to Drasnia. We seem to have finished up here." I shrugged. "How did you straighten her eyes?"

"Muscles, Old Wolf. Tighten some. Relax others. It's easy if you pay attention. Details, father, you have to pay attention to details. Isn't that what you told me?"

"Where did you learn so much about eyes?"

She shrugged. "I didn't. I just made it up as I went along. Shall we go to Drasnia?"

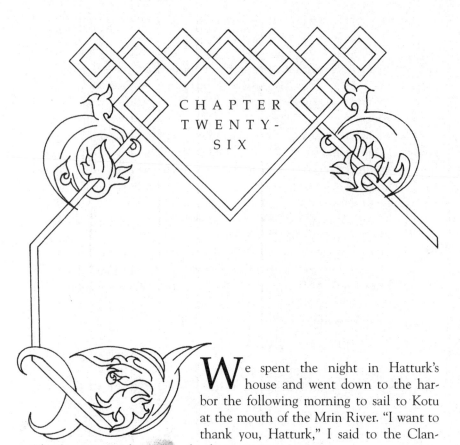

We spent the night in Hatturk's house and went down to the harbor the following morning to sail to Kotu at the mouth of the Mrin River. "I want to thank you, Hatturk," I said to the Clan-Chief as we stood on the wharf.

"My pleasure, Belgarath," he replied.

"I've got a word of advice for you, if you don't mind listening."

"Of course."

"You might want to give some thought to keeping your religious opinions to yourself. The Bear-cult's caused a great deal of trouble in Aloria in the past, and the Alorn Kings aren't particularly fond of it. King Algar's a patient man, but his patience only goes so far. The cult's been suppressed a number of times in the past, and I sort of feel another one coming. I really don't think you want to be on the wrong side when that happens. Algar Fleet-foot can be *very* firm when he sets his mind to it."

He gave me a sullen sort of look. I *did* try to warn him, but I guess he chose not to listen.

"Does Dras know we're coming, father?" Polgara asked me as we were boarding the ship.

I nodded. "I talked with a Cherek sea captain yesterday. He's on the way to Boktor right now. His ship's one of those war boats, so he'll get there long before we reach Kotu."

"It'll be good to see Dras again. He's not quite as bright as his brothers, but he's got a good heart."

"Yes," I agreed. "I guess I should have a talk with him when we get to Kotu. I think it's time that he got married."

"Don't look at me, father," she said primly. "I'm fond of Dras, but not *that* fond."

Kotu is one of the major seaports in the world now, largely because it's the western terminus of the North Caravan Route. When Pol and I went there, however, trade with the Nadraks was very limited, and Kotu was hardly more than a village with only a few wharves jutting out into the bay. It took us two days to make the voyage across the Gulf of Cherek from Darine to the mouth of the Mrin River, and Dras was waiting for us when we arrived. He had a fair number of his retainers with him, but they hadn't come along to see *me*. It was Polgara they were interested in. Evidently, word had filtered into the various Alorn kingdoms about the beautiful daughter of Ancient Belgarath, and the young Drasnians had come downriver from Boktor to have a look for themselves.

I'm sure they weren't disappointed.

When we'd gone to the Isle of the Winds for Beldaran's wedding, the girls had only been sixteen, and they had never been out of the Vale. Polgara had made me *very* nervous during the course of that trip. But she was older now, and she'd demonstrated that she knew how to take care of herself, so I could watch those young men swarming around her with equanimity and even with a certain amusement. Pol enjoyed their attentions, but she wasn't going to do anything inappropriate.

Our ship docked in midafternoon, and we took rooms at a somewhat seedy inn, planning to sail upriver the next morning to the village of Braca, where the Mrin Prophet was kenneled.

Bull-neck and I talked until quite late that evening, which gave Pol the opportunity to break a few hearts.

Dras leaned back in his chair and looked at me speculatively. "Algar's going to get married, you know," he told me.

"It's funny he didn't mention it," I replied. "He went with us to Riva's Island."

"You know how Algar is," Dras said with a shrug. "I suppose I ought to be thinking about that myself."

"I'd been intending to bring that up," I told him. "Ordinary people can get married or not, whichever suits them, but kings have certain responsibilities."

"I don't suppose . . ." He left it hanging tentatively in the air between us.

"No, Dras," I replied firmly. "Polgara's not available. I don't think you'd want to be married to her anyway. She has what you might call a prickly disposition. Pick yourself a nice Alorn girl instead. You'll be happier in the long run."

He sighed. "She *is* pretty, though."

"That she is, my friend, but Pol's got other things to do. The time might come when she'll get married, but that'll be *her* decision, and it's still a long way off. How far is it upriver to Braca?"

"A day or so. We have to go through the fens to get there." He tugged at his beard. "I've been thinking of draining the fens. That region might make good farmland if I could get rid of all the water."

I shrugged. "It's your kingdom, but I think draining the fens might turn into quite a chore. Have you heard from your father lately?"

"A month or so ago. His new wife's going to have another baby. They're hoping for a boy this time. I suppose my half sister *could* take the throne after father dies, but Alorns aren't comfortable with the idea of a queen. It seems unnatural to us."

You have no idea of how long it took me to change *that* particular attitude. Porenn is probably one of the most gifted rulers in history, but back-country Drasnians still don't take her seriously.

I slept a little late the next morning, and it was almost noon before we got under way.

The Mrin River is sluggish at its mouth, which accounts for the fens, I suppose. The fens are a vast marshland lying between the Mrin and the Aldur. It's one of the least attractive areas in the North, if you want my personal opinion. I don't like swamps, though, so that might account for my attitude. They smell, and the air's always so humid that I can't seem to get my breath. And then, of course, there are all those bugs that look upon people as a food source. I stayed in the cabin while we went upriver. Polgara, though, paced around the deck, trailing clouds of suitors. I know she was having fun, but *I* certainly wouldn't have given every mosquito for ten miles in any direction a clear invitation to drink my blood, no matter how much fun I was having.

Bull-neck's ship captain dropped anchor at sundown. The channel was clearly marked by buoys, but it's still not a good idea to wander around in the fens in the dark. There are too many chances for things to go wrong.

Dras and I were sitting in the cabin after supper, and it wasn't too long before Pol joined us. "Dras?" she said as she entered. "Why do your people wiggle their fingers at each other all the time?"

"Oh, that's just the secret language," he replied.

"Secret language?"

"The merchants came up with the notion. I guess there are times

when you're doing business that you need to talk privately with your partner. They've developed a kind of sign language. It was fairly simple right
at first, but it's getting a little more complicated now."

"Do you know this language?"

He held out one huge hand. "With fingers like these? Don't be
ridiculous."

"It might be a useful thing to know. Don't you think so, father?"

"We have other ways to communicate, Pol."

"Perhaps, but I still think I'd like to learn this secret language. I don't
like having people whispering to each other behind my back—even if
they're doing it with their fingers. Do you happen to have someone on
board ship who's proficient at it, Dras?"

He shrugged. "I don't pay much attention to it, myself. I'll ask
around, though."

"I'd appreciate it."

We set out again the following morning and reached the village of
Braca about noon. Dras and I stood at the rail as we approached it. "Not
a very pretty place, is it?" I observed, looking at the collection of rundown shanties huddled on the muddy riverbank.

"It's not Tol Honeth, by any stretch of the imagination," he agreed.
"When we first found out about this crazy man, I was going to take him
to Boktor, but he was born here, and he goes wild when you try to take
him away from the place. We decided that it'd be better just to leave him
here. The scribes don't care much for the idea, but that's what I'm paying
them so much for. They're here to write down what he says, not to enjoy
the scenery."

"Are you sure they're writing it down accurately?"

"How would I know, Belgarath? I can't read. You know that."

"Do you mean you still haven't learned how?"

"Why should I bother? That's what scribes are for. If something's all
that important, they'll read it to me. The ones here have worked out a
sort of system. There are always three of them with the crazy man. Two
of them write down what he says, and the third one listens to him. When
he finishes, they compare the two written versions, and the one who does
the listening decides which one's accurate."

"It sounds a little complicated."

"You made quite an issue of how much you wanted accuracy. If you
can think up an easier way, I'd be glad to hear it."

Our ship coasted up to the rickety dock, the sailors moored her, and
we went ashore to have a look at the Mrin Prophet.

I don't know if I've ever seen anyone quite so dirty. He wore only a
crude canvas loincloth, and his hair and beard were long and matted. He
was wearing an iron collar, and a stout chain ran from the collar to the

thick post set in the ground in front of his kennel—I'm sorry, but that's the only word I can use to describe the low hut where he apparently slept. He crouched on the ground near the post making animal noises and rhythmically jerking on the chain that bound him to the post. His eyes were deep-sunk under shaggy brows, and there was no hint of intelligence or even humanity in them.

"Do you really have to chain him like that?" Polgara asked Dras.

Bull-neck nodded. "He has spells," he replied. "He used to run off into the fens every so often. He'd be gone for a week or two, and then he'd come crawling back. When we found out just who and what he is, we decided we'd better chain him for his own safety. There are sinkholes and quicksand bogs out in the fens, and the poor devil doesn't have sense enough to avoid them. He can't recite prophecy if he's twelve feet down in a quicksand bog."

She looked at the low hut. "Do you really have to treat him like an animal?"

"Polgara, he *is* an animal. He stays in that kennel because he wants to. He gets hysterical if you take him inside a house."

"You said he was born here," I noted.

Dras nodded. "About thirty or forty years ago. This was all part of father's kingdom before we went to Mallorea. The village has been here for about seventy years, I guess. Most of the villagers are fishermen."

I went over to where the three scribes on duty were sitting in the shade of a scrubby willow tree and introduced myself. "Has he said anything lately?" I asked.

"Not for the past week," one of them replied. "I think maybe it's the moon that sets him off. He'll talk at various other times, but he *always* does when the moon's full."

"I suppose there might be some explanation for that. Isn't there some way you can clean him up a little?"

The scribe shook his head. "We've tried throwing pails of water on him, but he just rolls in the mud again. I think he likes being dirty."

"Let me know immediately when he starts talking again. I have to hear him."

"I don't think you'll be able to make much sense out of what he's saying, Belgarath," one of the other scribes told me.

"That'll come later. I've got the feeling that I'm going to spend a lot of time studying what he says. Does he ever talk about ordinary things? The weather or maybe how hungry he is?"

"No," the first scribe replied. "As closely as we're able to determine, he can't talk—at least that's what the villagers say. It was about eight or ten years ago when he started. It makes our job easier, though. We don't have to wade through casual conversation. Everything he says is important."

We stayed on board Bull-neck's ship that night. We needed the co-operation of the villagers, and I didn't want to stir up any resentments by commandeering their houses while we were in Braca.

About noon the following day one of the scribes came down to the dock. "Belgarath," he called to me. "You'd better come now. He's talking."

One of the young Drasnians had been teaching Pol that sign language, and he didn't look *too* happy when she suspended the lesson to accompany Dras and me to the prophet's hovel.

The crazy man was crouched by that post again, and he was still jerking on his chain. I don't think he was actually trying to get loose. The clinking of the chain seemed to soothe him for some reason. Then again, aside from the wooden bowl they fed him from, that chain was his only possession. It was his, so he had a right to play with it, I guess. He was making animal noises when we approached.

"Has he stopped?" I asked the scribe who had come to fetch us.

"He'll start up again," the scribe assured me. "He breaks off and moans and grunts for a while every so often. Then he goes back to talking. Once he starts, he's usually good for the rest of the day. He stops when the sun goes down."

Then the crazy man let go of his chain and looked me directly in the face. His eyes were alert and very penetrating. "Behold!" he said to me in a booming, hollow voice, a voice that sounded almost exactly the same as Bormik's. "The Child of Light shall be accompanied on his quest by the Bear and by the Guide and by the Man with Two Lives. Thou, too, Ancient and Beloved, shall be at his side. And the Horse-Lord shall also go with ye, and the Blind Man, and the Queen of the World. Others also will join with ye—the Knight Protector and the Archer and the Huntress and the Mother of the Race That Died and the Woman who Watches, whom thou hast known before."

He broke off and began to moan and drool and yank on his chain again.

"That should do it," I told Dras. "That's what I needed to know. He's authentic."

"How were you able to tell so quickly?"

"Because he talked about the Child of Light, Dras. Bormik did the same thing back in Darine. You might want to pass that on to your father and brothers. That's the key that identifies the prophets. As soon as someone mentions the Child of Light, you'd better put some scribes nearby, because what he's saying is going to be important."

"How did you find that out?"

"The Necessity and I spent some time together when we were on the way to Mallorea, remember? He talked about the Child of Light extensively." Then I remembered something else. "It might be a little far-fetched, and I don't know if it'll ever happen in our part of the world, but we might come across somebody who talks about the Child of Dark, as well. Have people take down what *he* says, too."

"What's the difference?"

"The ones who talk about the Child of Light are giving *us* instructions. The ones who mention the Child of Dark are telling Torak what to do. It might be useful if we can intercept some of those messages."

"Are you going to stay here and listen?"

"There's no need of that. I've found out what I wanted to. Have your scribes make me a copy of everything they've set down so far and send it to me in the Vale."

"I'll see to it. Do you want to go back to Kotu now?"

"No, I don't think so. See if you can find somebody here with a boat who knows the way through the fens. Pol and I'll go on down to Algaria and then on home from there. There's not much point in backtracking."

"Is there anything you want me to do?"

"Go back to Boktor and get married. You'll need a son to pass your crown to."

"I don't *have* a crown, Belgarath."

"Get one. A crown doesn't really mean anything, but people like to have visible symbols around."

Polgara was scowling at me.

"What?" I asked her.

"The fens, father? You're going to make me go through the *fens?*"

"Look upon it as an educational experience, Pol. Let's go gather up our things. I want to get back to the Vale."

"What's the rush?"

"Let's just say I'm homesick."

She rolled her eyes upward with that long-suffering look she's so fond of.

The fellow with the boat was named Gannik, and he was a talkative, good-natured fellow. His boat was long and slender—more like a canoe than a rowboat. Occasionally he paddled us down through the fens, but most of the time he poled us along. I didn't care much for the idea of having someone standing up in that narrow craft, but he seemed to know what he was doing, so I didn't make an issue of it.

I *did* want to get back to the Vale, but my main reason for leaving Braca so abruptly had been a desire to get Pol away from the young Drasnian who'd been teaching her the secret language. I could retain my equanimity so long as Pol's suitors gathered around her in groups, but seeing her sitting off to one side alone with one of those young men made me nervous. Pol had uncommon good sense, *but*—

I'm sure you get my drift.

I brooded about that as Gannik poled us on south through that soggy marshland. Polgara was eighteen years old now, and it was definitely time for me to have that little talk with her. She and Beldaran had grown up without a mother, so there'd been no one around to explain certain things to her. Beldaran quite obviously *did* know about those things, but I wasn't entirely certain that Pol did. Grandchildren are very nice, but unanticipated ones might be just a little embarrassing.

The border between Drasnia and Algaria wasn't really very well defined when it passed through the fens. The Drasnians called that vast swamp Mrin Marsh, and the Algars referred to it as Aldurfens. It was all the same bog, though. We were about three days south of Braca when Pol saw one of those aquatic creatures that live in such places. "Is that an otter or a beaver?" she asked Gannik when a small, round, sleek head popped above the water ahead of us.

"That's a fenling," he replied. "They're like otters, but a little bigger. They're playful little rascals. Some people trap them for their fur, but I don't think I'd care to do that. It just doesn't seem right to me for some reason. I like to watch them play."

The fenling had very large eyes, and he watched us curiously as Gannik poled his boat through the large pond that appeared to be the creature's home. Then it made that peculiar chittering sound that the fenlings make. It sounded almost as if he were scolding us.

Gannik laughed. "We're scaring the fish," he said, "and he's telling us about it. Sometimes it seems they can almost talk."

Vordai, the witch of the fens, came to that selfsame conclusion some years later, and she dragooned me into doing something about it.

We finally reached that part of the swamp that was fed by the channels at the mouth of the Aldur river, and Gannik poled us to the higher ground lying to the east of the swamp. Pol and I thanked him and went ashore.

It was good to get my feet on dry ground again.

"Are we going to change form again?" Pol asked me.

"In a bit. We've got something to talk about first, though."

"Oh, what's that?"

"You're growing up, Pol."

"Why, do you know, I believe you're right."

"Do you mind? There are some things you need to know."

"Such as?"

That's where I started floundering. Pol stood there with a vapid, wide-eyed expression on her face, letting me dig myself in deeper and deeper. Polgara can be very cruel when she puts her mind to it. Finally I stopped. Her expression was just a little *too* vacant. "You already know about all this, don't you?" I accused her.

"About what, father?"

"Stop that. You know where babies come from. Why are you letting me embarrass the both of us?"

"You mean they don't hatch out under cabbage leaves?" She reached out and patted me on the cheek. "I know all about it, father. I helped to deliver Beldaran's baby, remember? The midwives explained the whole procedure to me. It *did* sort of stir my curiosity, I'll admit."

"Don't get *too* curious, Pol. There are certain customary formalities before you start experimenting."

"Oh? Did you go through those formalities in Mar Amon—every single time?"

I muttered a few swear words under my breath and then slipped into the form of a wolf. At least a wolf can't blush, and my face had been getting redder and redder as I had gone along.

Polgara laughed that deep rich laugh I hadn't heard very often and blurred into the shape of the tufted owl.

CHAPTER TWENTY-SEVEN

Beldin had returned from his visit to Mallorea when Pol and I reached the Vale. I was a bit surprised that he'd made it back so soon. He's normally good for a couple of centuries when he goes there. He was his usual gracious self when he came stumping up the stairs to my tower on the morning after the night Pol and I got home. "Where have you two been?" he snapped at us.

"Be nice, uncle," Pol replied calmly. "We had some things to take care of."

"You're back early," I said. "Is there some sort of emergency?"

"Stop trying to be clever, Belgarath. You don't have the gift for it. The Mallorean Angaraks are just milling around over there. Nothing's going to happen until Torak comes out of seclusion at Ashaba." He suddenly grinned. "Zedar's there with him now, and it's making that piebald Urvon crazy."

"Oh?"

"Urvon's a born toady, and the fact that Zedar's closer to Torak than he is right now is more than he can bear. To make it worse, he can't go to Ashaba to protect his interests because he's afraid to come out of Mal Yaska."

"What's he so afraid of?"

"Me. I guess he has nightmares about that hook I showed him."

"Still? That was over five hundred years ago, Beldin."

"Evidently it made a lasting impression. At least it keeps *one* of Torak's disciples pinned down. What's for breakfast, Pol?"

She gave him a long, steady look.

"You seem to be filling out a bit," he noted, brazenly running his eyes over her. "You might want to try to keep that under control. You're getting a little hippy."

Her eyes narrowed dangerously. "Don't press your luck, uncle," she warned.

"I'd pay attention to her, Beldin," I advised him. "She's started her education, and she's a very apt pupil."

"I sort of thought she might be. What *were* you two up to? The twins told me you'd gone to the Isle."

"There's an heir to the Rivan throne now," I told him. "His name's Daran, and he shows quite a bit of promise. The Master's Orb was very pleased to meet him."

"Maybe I'll drift on over there and have a look at him," Beldin mused. "I might not be related to him the way you are, but Beldaran and I *were* fairly close when she was growing up. What took you so long coming back?"

"Pol and I took a swing through Darine and then went over to Drasnia on our way back. I wanted to take a look at those two prophets. There's no question about their authenticity."

"Good. Torak's having a little difficulty with *his* prophecy."

"What kind of difficulty?"

"He doesn't like what it says. When he came out of his trance and read what Urvon's scribes had taken down, he tore down a couple of mountains, I guess. The Ashabine Oracles seem to have offended him."

"That sounds promising. Is there any way we can get our hands on a copy?"

"Not likely. Torak *definitely* doesn't want that document widely circulated. Urvon *had* a copy, but Torak reached out from Ashaba and set fire to it." He scratched at his beard. "Zedar's at Ashaba, and we both know him well enough to be sure that he'll have a copy. If Torak ever lets him leave, he'll probably take it with him. It's my guess that it's the only copy that isn't under One-eye's direct control. Someday I'll catch up with Zedar and take it off his carcass." He scowled at me. "Why didn't you kill him when you had the chance?"

"I was told not to. I think you'd better restrain *your* homicidal impulses, as well, if you ever happen to come across him. We're going to need him later on."

"I don't suppose you could be any more specific?"

I shook my head. "That's all I was told."

He grunted sourly. "I *might* be able to get hold of a copy of 'The

Mallorean Gospels'—if I could figure out a way to get into Kell and back out again all in one piece."

"What are 'The Mallorean Gospels'?" Pol asked him.

"Another set of prophecies," he replied. "They'll be very obscure, though. The Dals wrote them, and the Dals are absolutely neutral. Oh, incidentally, Belgarath, Ctuchik's moved."

"Yes, I'd heard about that. He's at a place called Rak Cthol now."

He nodded. "I flew over it on my way home. It isn't very inviting. It's built on top of a peak that sticks up out of the middle of a desert. I picked up a few rumors. Evidently this epidemic of prophecy's pretty widespread. Some of Ctuchik's Grolims have come down with it, too. He's got them at Rak Cthol with scribes camped on them. I doubt that *their* prophecies'll be as precise as Torak's, but it might be worth our while to try to get hold of a copy. I'll leave that up to you, though. I think I'd better stay away from Ctuchik. I've brushed up against his mind a few times, and he could probably feel me coming from a hundred leagues off. We want information, not fistfights."

"The Murgos are on the move, you know," Pol told him. "They're moving into the southern half of the continent and enslaving the western Dals in the process."

"I've got a great deal of respect for the Dals' intellectual gifts," he replied, "but they don't have much spirit, do they?"

"I think that's all subterfuge," I told him. "They don't have any trouble keeping Urvon's Grolims away from Kell." I leaned back. "I think maybe I'll visit Rak Cthol and pay a call on Ctuchik," I mused. "He's new in this part of the world, so somebody ought to welcome him—or at least see what he looks like when he isn't a Hound."

"It'd be the neighborly thing to do," Beldin said with an evil grin.

"Are you going back to Mallorea?"

"Not for a while. I want to go look at your grandson first."

"Do you want to keep an eye on Polgara for me while I'm gone?"

"I don't need a keeper, father," she told me.

"Yes, as a matter of fact, you do," I disagreed. "You're at a dangerous stage in your education. You *think* you know more than you really do. I don't want you to start experimenting without supervision."

"I'll watch her," Beldin promised. He looked at her then. "Have we forgotten about breakfast altogether, Pol? Just because you've decided to watch your weight doesn't mean that the rest of us have to start fasting."

I went northeasterly out of the Vale that same morning and changed my form as soon as I reached the Algarian plain. I don't like to pass through the Vale as a wolf. The deer and rabbits there might be alarmed. They're all more or less tame, and it's not polite to frighten the neighbors.

I swam across the Aldur River and reached the Eastern Escarpment the following morning. I followed it for quite some distance until I came to one of those ravines Algar had told us about at Riva's Isle. The Eastern Escarpment's one of the results of what the Master and Belar were obliged to do to contain the ocean Torak created when he cracked the world. The mountain range that came pushing up out of the earth fractured along its western edge, and the result was that imposing, mile-high cliff that forms the natural boundary between Algaria and Mishrak ac Thull.

I considered it as I stood at the mouth of the ravine and decided to wait until nightfall before climbing it. Fleet-foot had told us that Murgos sometimes came down those ravines on horse-stealing expeditions, and I didn't want to meet a chance group of them in tight quarters. Besides, I didn't particularly want Ctuchik to know that I was coming. Zedar knew that my favorite alternative to my own form was that of the wolf, and I couldn't be sure whether he'd shared that knowledge with his fellow disciples. I went a mile or so on along the cliff and bedded down in the tall grass.

As it turned out, my decision was a wise one. About noon, I heard riders picking their way around the rubble at the foot of the cliff. I pricked up my ears and stayed hidden in the tall grass.

"I hope you know what you're doing, Rashag," I heard one of them saying. "I've heard about what the Horse People do to those who try to steal their animals."

"They'll have to catch us before they can do anything to us, Agga," another voice replied.

I very slowly raised my head. The breeze was a bit erratic, but I was fairly sure it wouldn't carry my scent to their horses. I peered intently in the direction from which their voices had been coming. Then I saw them. There were only the two of them. They were wearing chain-mail shirts and conical helmets, and they both had swords belted at their waists. Murgos are not an attractive race to begin with, and the fact that they gash their faces during the ceremony that marks their entry into adulthood doesn't add very much to their appearance. The pair I was watching were fairly typical representatives of their race. They had broad shoulders, of course; you don't spend most of your life practicing swordsmanship without developing a *few* muscles. Aside from those bulky shoulders though, they were fairly lean. They had swarthy skin, prominent cheekbones, and narrow, angular eyes.

I saw immediately why Murgos risked coming down the steep ravines that cut the escarpment. The horses they were riding weren't very good.

"I saw a large herd from the top of the cliff," the one called Rashag told his companion.

"Horses or cows?" Agga asked him.

"It's hard to say for sure. The cliff's very high and the animals were in deep grass."

"I didn't come down that ravine to steal cows, Rashag. If I want a cow, I'll take one from the Thulls. They don't get excited the way the Horse People do. What did that Grolim you were talking with want?"

"What else? He was looking for somebody to butcher. His altar's drying out, and it needs fresh blood."

"He didn't look all that much like a Thullish Grolim."

"He wasn't. He's a southern Grolim from Rak Cthol. Ctuchik's got them spread out along the top of the cliff. He doesn't want any surprises, and the Horse People *do* know about the ravines."

"Alorns," Agga spat. "I *hate* Alorns."

"I don't imagine they're very fond of us, either. The Grolim told me to pass the word that we're all supposed to stay out of the Wasteland of Murgos."

"Who'd want to go there anyway? All that's there is black sand and that stinking lake."

"I'm sure Ctuchik has his reasons. He doesn't confide in me though. Actually, I've never even seen the man."

"I have," Agga said, shuddering. "I had to take a message to Rak Cthol from my general, and Ctuchik questioned me about it. He looks like a man who's been dead for a week."

"What's Rak Cthol like?"

"It's not the sort of place you'd want to visit."

They were almost out of earshot by now, and I decided not to follow them. They were obviously of fairly low rank, so it wasn't likely that their conversation would provide any useful information. I lowered my chin onto my paws and went back to sleep.

I did see them one more time, though. It was starting to get dark, and I rose, arched my back, stretched, and yawned.

Then I heard horses galloping toward me. I sank back down in the grass to watch. Rashag and Agga were coming back, and they didn't have any Algar horses. The only Algar horses I saw had Algars on their backs, and they were in hot pursuit of the two fleeing Murgos. Algar horses were—still are—much better than Murgo horses, so the outcome was fairly predictable. Rashag and Agga didn't make it back to Cthol Murgos.

I waited until the Algars returned to their herd, then loped back to the mouth of the ravine and started up. The going would have been difficult for a horse, but wolves have toenails, so I made it to the top before daylight. I sniffed at the air to make sure that no one was in the vicinity, and then I went off toward the southeast and Ctuchik's fortress in the middle of the Wasteland of Murgos.

The mountains of southern Mishrak ac Thull and northern Cthol Murgos are arid and rocky with hardly any vegetation to provide much in the way of concealment, so I traveled mostly at night. Wolves see well in the dark, but I relied primarily on my nose and my ears to warn me whenever I came near people. Those desiccated wastes held very little in the way of game, so a wolf might have seemed out of place there, and would probably have attracted attention. But I wasn't particularly worried about the Thulls. They were an inattentive people, in the first place, and they built large fires at night—not because it was particularly cold at that time of year. Mainly they built fires because Thulls are afraid of the dark. When you get right down to it, there's not really very much in the world that a Thull *isn't* afraid of.

Once I crossed the border into Cthol Murgos, though, I began to be more careful. Murgos are just the opposite of Thulls. They make some show of not being afraid of anything—even the things they *should* be afraid of.

There were very few people in those mountains, however—either Thulls or Murgos. Every so often I'd see a Murgo outpost, but I didn't have any trouble skirting those places.

It took me a little longer to reach the Wasteland of Murgos than it might have if I'd been traveling through friendly territory, since I spent quite a bit of time hiding or slinking around to stay out of sight. I was certain that no ordinary Murgo would pay very much attention to me, because Murgos are interested in people, not animals. But since wolves weren't common in the region, a Murgo who happened to see me might mention it to the next Grolim he came across. Sometimes the most casual remark will alert a Grolim. I didn't want anybody to spoil the surprise I had planned for Ctuchik.

I finally came down out of the mountains into the area colorfully known as the Wasteland of Murgos. There was some evidence that it'd been a large lake or even an inland sea at some time in the past. I seem to remember that there'd been a sizable body of water lying to the west of the Angarak city of Karnath before Torak cracked the world, and this black-sand–floored desert had obviously been drained all at one time. The skeletons of large aquatic creatures dotted the sand, but the only remnant of that ancient sea was the rancid Tarn of Cthok, some distance to the north of Rak Cthol. I was a little concerned about the fact that I was leaving tracks in that black sand, but the wind out there blew most of the time, so I quit worrying about it.

I finally got within sight of the steep mountain peak that Ctuchik had topped with his city, and I dropped to my haunches to think things over a little bit. Wolves were not unheard of in the mountains of Cthol Murgos and the wasteland, but a wolf padding through the streets of Rak

Cthol definitely would attract attention. I was going to need some other disguise, and since the narrow path angling up around the peak was certain to be patrolled and since the city gates would be guarded, I couldn't see any alternative but feathers.

It was late afternoon, and the heated air rising up off that black sand would help. I went behind a pile of rocks and slipped back into my own form. Then, after giving some consideration to the surrounding terrain, I formed the image of a vulture in my mind and flowed into that particular shape. I'll grant you that there are nicer birds in the world than vultures, but there were whole flocks of the ugly brutes circling in the air over Ctuchik's mountain, so at least I wouldn't be conspicuous.

I caught an updraft and spiraled aloft on the west side of Ctuchik's mountain. The sun was just going down, and its ruddy light stained that basalt peak, making it look peculiarly as if it had been dipped in blood. Considering what was going on at the top of it, that was fairly appropriate, I suppose.

I've made quite an issue of the fact that I don't fly very well, but I'm not a *complete* incompetent, and riding an updraft is a fairly simple process. All you really have to do is lock your wings and let it carry you. Hawks and eagles and vultures do it all the time.

I circled up and up until I was above the city, and then I swooped down and perched on the wall to look things over. At that particular time Rak Cthol was still under construction, and it was not nearly as cluttered as it came to be later on. It was already ugly, though. I think that was a reflection of Ctuchik's mind. Although it really wasn't necessary, he appeared to be consciously trying to duplicate the layout of Cthol Mishrak. The actual work of construction was being performed by slaves, of course, since Murgos and Grolims feel they're above that sort of thing. I watched from my perch atop the wall as the slaves were herded into their cells in those tunnels beneath the city and locked in for the night. Then I patiently waited for it to get dark.

Quite obviously, I was going to need a disguise, but I was fairly sure I could find something that'd get me by. As it turned out, it was even easier than I'd expected. There were Murgo sentries patrolling the top of the wall. There was no need for that, really, since there was a sheer drop of almost a mile to the desert floor, but Murgos tend to be traditionalists. They'd patrolled the top of the wall at Cthol Mishrak, so they patrolled the top of the wall here. I slipped very slowly back into my own form to avoid alerting Ctuchik to the fact that I'd come to pay him a visit, and then I concealed myself in a narrow embrasure to wait for a Murgo.

There were a number of ways I could have done it, I suppose, but I chose the simplest. I waited until the sentry had passed, and then I bashed him on the head with a rock. It was quieter than any of the more exotic things I might have done, and it sufficed. I dragged the Murgo back into the embrasure and peeled off his black robe. I didn't bother with his mail shirt. Chain mail is uncomfortable, and it tends to rattle when you're moving around. I considered dropping my Murgo over the wall but decided against it. I didn't have anything against him personally, and I wasn't entirely sure how much noise he'd make when he hit the ground a mile below.

Yes, I know all about my reputation, but I don't *really* like to kill people unless it's necessary. I've always felt that random murders tend to coarsen one's nature. You might want to think about that when you consider murder as a solution to a problem.

I pulled up the hood of the Murgo robe and went looking for Ctuchik. The simplest way would have been to ask, but I might have had trouble imitating the rasping Murgo dialect, so I listened to a number of random conversations and quite gently probed the thoughts of various sentries and passersby instead. Polgara's much better at that than I am, but I know how it's done. I was fairly careful about it, since everybody in Rak Cthol, Grolim and Murgo, wore those black robes, and that made it hard to tell them apart. It's entirely possible, I suppose, that Murgos think of themselves as a form of minor clergy—or it might just be that Grolims are descendants of the original Murgo tribe. I didn't want to probe the thoughts of a Grolim, since some of them at least are talented enough to recognize that when it happens.

My eavesdropping—both with my ears and with my mind—eventually gave me enough clues to narrow down the search. Ctuchik was somewhere in the Temple of Torak. I'd more or less expected that, but a little verification never hurts.

The Temple was deserted. Even Grolims have to sleep sometime, and it was getting fairly close to midnight. Ctuchik, however, was *not* asleep. I could sense his mind at work as soon as I entered the Temple. That made finding him much easier. I went along the back wall on that balcony that seems to be a standard feature in every major Grolim temple and eventually located the right door. And, naturally, it was locked. A single thought would have unlocked it, but it would probably have also alerted Ctuchik to my presence. Murgo locks aren't very sophisticated, though, so I did it the other way. I might not be as good a burglar as Silk is, but I *have* had some experience in that line of work.

There was a flight of stairs leading downward behind that door, and

I followed them, being very careful not to make any noise. A black painted door stood at the bottom of the stairs, and, oddly, no guards. I think this particular visit of mine persuaded Ctuchik that leaving that door unguarded was a bad idea. I picked the lock and went inside.

The sense of Ctuchik's mind was coming from above me, so I didn't bother to investigate the lower level of his turret. There's a peculiar similarity to the way our minds work. We all feel more comfortable in towers. Ctuchik's tower was hanging off the side of the mountain, though.

I went up the stairs. I ignored the second level and climbed to the top. The door there wasn't locked, and I could sense the presence of the owner of the turret behind it. He seemed to be reading something, and he wasn't particularly alert.

I set myself and opened the door.

An emaciated-looking Grolim with a white beard was sitting at a table near one of the round windows poring over a scroll by the light of a single oil lamp. That Murgo I'd seen at the escarpment—Agga, I think his name was—had described Ctuchik as a man who looked as if he had been dead for a week. I think Agga'd understated it. I've never known anybody who looked more cadaverous than Ctuchik.

"What?" he exclaimed, dropping his scroll and leaping to his feet. "Who gave you permission to come here?"

"It's late, Ctuchik," I told him. "I didn't want to bother anybody, so I let myself in."

"You!" His sunken eyes blazed.

"Don't do anything foolish," I cautioned him. "This is just a social call. If I'd had anything else in mind, you'd already be dead." I looked around. His tower wasn't nearly as cluttered as mine, but he hadn't been here very long. It takes centuries to accumulate really good clutter. "What on earth possessed you to set up shop in this hideous place?" I asked him.

"It suits me," he replied shortly, struggling to get control of himself. He sat back down and retrieved his scroll. "You always manage to show up where you're least expected, don't you, Belgarath?"

"It's a gift. Are you busy right now? I can come back some other time if you're doing something important."

"I think I can spare you a few moments."

"Good." I closed the door, went over to his table, and sat down in the chair directly across from him. "I think we should have a little chat, Ctuchik—as long as we're living so close to each other."

"You've come to welcome me to the neighborhood?" He looked faintly amused.

"Not exactly. I thought we should establish a few ground rules, is all. I wouldn't want you to blunder into anything by mistake."

"I don't make mistakes, Belgarath."

"Oh, really? I can think of a dozen or so you've made already. You didn't exactly cover yourself with glory at Cthol Mishrak, as I recall."

"You know that what happened at Cthol Mishrak had been decided before you even got there," he retorted. "If Zedar had done what he was supposed to, you wouldn't have made it that far."

"Sometimes Zedar's a little undependable—but that's beside the point. I'm not here to talk about the good old days. I'm here to give you a bit of advice. Keep a tight leash on your Murgos. The time isn't right for anything major, and we both know it. A lot of things have to happen yet before we can get down to business. Keep the Murgos out of the Western Kingdoms. They're starting to irritate the Alorns."

He sneered. "My, my, isn't that a shame."

"Don't try to be funny. You're not ready for a war, Ctuchik—particularly not with the Alorns. Iron-grip's got the Orb, and you saw what he can do with it when we had that little get-together at Cthol Mishrak. If you don't get your Murgos under control, he might take it into his head to pay you a call. If you irritate him too much, he'll turn this mountain of yours into a very large pile of gravel."

"He's not the one who's supposed to raise the Orb," Ctuchik objected.

"My point exactly. Let's not push our luck here. We haven't received all our instructions as yet, so we don't even know what we're supposed to do. If you push the Alorns too far, Iron-grip's very likely to lose his temper and do something precipitous. If that happens, it could throw this whole business into the lap of pure, random chance. We could end up with a *third* possibility, and I don't think the other two would like that very much. So let's not complicate things any more than they already are."

He pulled speculatively at his beard. "You might be right," he conceded grudgingly. "We've all got lots of time, I suppose, so there's no great hurry."

"I'm glad you agree." I squinted at him. "Have you managed to get any of your people into the house at Ashaba as yet?"

His eyes suddenly looked startled.

"It's the logical thing for you to do, Ctuchik. Zedar's there taking down Torak's every word. If you and that pinto-spotted Urvon don't get some of your people inside, Zedar's going to have the upper hand."

"I'm working on it," he replied shortly.

"I hope so. One of you'd better get your hands on a copy of the Ashabine Oracles before Torak corrupts them into incomprehensibility."

"Urvon's got a copy. I can always take his away from him."

"Torak burned Urvon's copy. Don't you people even *talk* to each other?"

"I don't have anything to say to Urvon."

"Or to Zedar, either, I gather. This bickering between the three of you is going to make *my* job much, much easier."

"You aren't the important one, Belgarath. You've *had* your turn as the Child of Light, and I think you blundered it away. You should have killed Zedar when you had the chance."

"You *definitely* need instructions, Ctuchik. Zedar's part in all of this isn't over yet. He's still got things to do, and if he *doesn't* do them, we come right back to that third possibility again. Some of your Grolims have been seized by the spirit of *your* Necessity. Get good copies of what they're saying, and don't tamper with them. Torak's erasing whole pages of the Ashabine Oracles, so the Prophecies of your western Grolims might very well end up being all you'll have to work with. This isn't a good area for experimentation. Certain things *have* to happen, and we both have to know about them. I don't have time to come down here every few centuries to educate you."

"I know my responsibilities, Belgarath. You do your work, and I'll do mine."

"I can hold up my end of it," I told him. Then I stood up and smiled benignly at him. "It's been absolutely *wonderful* talking with you, old boy, and we'll have to do it again one of these days."

"My pleasure, old chap," he replied with a thin little smile. "Stop by any time."

"Oh, I *will*, Ctuchik, I *will*. Incidentally, don't try to follow me, and don't send anybody to get in my way—not anybody you care anything about, anyway."

"I don't really care for *anybody*, old man."

"You ought to try it sometime, Ctuchik. It might sweeten your disposition."

Then I went out and closed the door behind me.

CHAPTER
TWENTY-
EIGHT

I flew due west from Rak Cthol, then went wolf and skirted the eastern border of Maragor, climbed up through the Tolnedran Mountains to the southern end of the Vale. All in all, I was rather pleased with myself. Things had gone well at Rak Cthol.

It was early evening when I reached my tower.

"How did it go?" Beldin asked me when I joined him and Pol.

"Not bad." I said it in an offhand sort of way. Boasting's very unbecoming, after all.

"What happened, father?" Pol asked in that suspicious tone she always takes when I have been out of her sight for more than five minutes. I *wish* Polgara would trust me just once. Of course, that would probably stop the sun.

I shrugged. "I went to Rak Cthol."

"Yes, I know. And—?"

"I talked to Ctuchik."

"And—?"

"I didn't kill him."

"Father, get to the point!"

"Actually, I led him down the garden path. I told him a great many things he already knew just as an excuse to get close enough to him to test his capabilities. He's actually not all that good." I sat down in my favorite chair. "Is supper ready yet?" I asked her.

"It's still cooking. Talk, father. What really happened?"

"I slipped into his city and paid him a call in the middle of the night. I made a large issue of telling him to keep his Murgos out of the western kingdoms, and then I raised the possibility that if the Murgos irritated the Alorns *too* much, Riva might use the Orb against them. That can't happen, of course, but I think the notion worried Ctuchik. He seems to be very gullible in some ways. I'm sure he believes that I'm a fussy old windbag who runs around repeating the obvious. Then I raised the possibility that if somebody did something that he wasn't supposed to do, it might just let pure, random chance enter into the picture."

"And he *believed* you?" Beldin asked incredulously.

"He seemed to. At least he considered it enough to worry about it. Then we discussed the Ashabine Oracles. Both Ctuchik and Urvon are trying to slip people into Torak's house at Ashaba to get copies, but I got the impression that Torak's controlling those copies rather jealously, and Zedar's doing his best to keep his brothers' spies away from Ashaba. The three of them hate each other with a passion that's almost holy."

"What's Ctuchik look like?" Beldin asked me. "I've seen that piebald Urvon a few times, but I've never actually seen Ctuchik."

"He's tall, skinny, and he's got a long, white beard. He looks like a walking corpse."

"Peculiar."

"What is?"

"Old Burnt-face seems to be attracted to ugliness. Ctuchik sounds hideous, and that speckled Urvon's no prize. Zedar's not so bad, I guess— unless you want to take the ugliness of his soul into account."

"You're not really in a position to talk, uncle," Pol reminded him.

"You didn't have to say that, Pol. What now, Belgarath?"

I scratched at my beard. "I think we'd better get the twins and see if we can contact the Master. We need some advice here. The Angaraks absolutely *must* have uncorrupted copies of the Oracles, and Torak's doing everything he possibly can to keep that from happening."

"Can we *do* that?" Pol asked me.

"I'm not sure," I admitted, "but I think we'd better try. Zedar might have a clean copy, but I'd hate to hang the fate of the world on a maybe."

As it turned out, it was surprisingly easy to get in touch with Aldur. I think it might have been because we were in an interim stage between the time when we were guided by the Gods and the time when the Prophecies took over. At any rate, a simple "Master, we need you." brought Aldur's presence into my tower. He was a bit filmy and indistinct, but he was there.

He went immediately to Polgara, which shouldn't have surprised me. "My beloved daughter," he said to her, lightly touching her cheek.

Would you *believe* that I felt a momentary surge of jealousy at that point? Polgara was *my* daughter, not *his*. We all get strange when we get older, I guess. I choked back my instinctive protest, and I think I had a little epiphany at that point. Jealousy is a symptom of love, I suppose—a primitive form, but love nonetheless. I *loved* my dark-haired, steely-eyed daughter, and since love—and hate—are at the very core of what I am, Polgara won the whole game right then and there. We argued for another three thousand years or so, but all I was doing was fighting a rearguard action. I'd already lost.

"You know what Torak's doing at Ashaba, don't you, Master?" Beldin asked.

"Yes, my son," Aldur replied sadly. "My brother is distraught, and he thinks to change what must happen by changing the word that tells him of it."

"If he goes too far and changes the Oracles *too* much, his Angaraks won't know what they're supposed to do," I said in a worried tone. "Are we going to have to take steps?"

"Nay, my son," the Master replied. "True copies *do* exist, though my brother might wish otherwise. The Necessity that drives him will not be so thwarted. Belzedar is with my brother, and, though he knows it not, he is still in some measure driven by *our* Necessity. He hath ensured that the words of that other Necessity are safe and whole."

"That's a relief," Beldin said. "If we had to start taking care of *both* sets of instructions, it might get burdensome. I think we're going to have our hands full just taking care of our own."

"Set thy mind at rest, my son," Aldur told him. "The steps that lead to the ultimate meeting unfalteringly proceed."

"We've identified two of the prophets who're giving us *our* instructions, Master," I advised him. "Their words are being faithfully set down."

"Excellent, my son."

Pol looked slightly worried. "Are there others, Master?" she asked. "The Alorns know how important those prophecies are, but I don't think the Tolnedrans or the Arends do. We could be missing something significant. *Are* there other speakers?"

He nodded. "They are of less import, however, my daughter, and are more in the nature of verification. Put thy mind at ease. Failing all else, we may appeal to the Dals for aid. The Seers at Kell are seeking out *all* the prophecies—both the instruction of *our* Necessity and that of Torak's."

"Astonishing," Beldin said. "The Dals are actually doing something useful for a change."

"They must, gentle Beldin, for they, too, have a task in this matter—a task of gravest significance. We must not hinder them. The path they follow is obscure, but it will in the fullness of time bring them to the selfsame place whither our path leads us. All is proceeding as it must, my children. Be not unquiet. We will speak more of this anon."

And then he was gone.

"Evidently we're doing it right," Beldin noted, "at least so far."

"You worry too much, Beldin," Belkira told him. "I don't think we *could* do it wrong."

Beltira, however, was looking at Pol with a kind of wonder on his face. "Dear sister," he said to her.

That came crashing down on me. "Please don't do that, Beltira," I told him.

"But she *is*, Belgarath. She is one of our fellowship."

"Yes, I know, but it puts *me* in a peculiar situation. I know that Pol and I are related, but this turn of events makes it *very* complicated."

"Be not dismayed, dear brother," Pol told me sweetly. "I'll explain it all to you later—in simple terms, of course. Now, if you gentlemen will get out of my kitchen, I'll finish fixing supper."

Things went on quietly in the Vale for the next several years. Polgara continued her education, and I think she startled us all by how rapidly she was progressing. Pol had joined us late, but she was more than making up for lost time. There were levels of subtlety in some of the things she did that were absolutely exquisite. I didn't tell her, of course, but I was terribly proud of her.

It was spring, I think, when Algar Fleet-foot came down into the Vale to deliver copies of the now-completed Darine Codex to us. "Bormik died last autumn," he told us. "His daughter spent the winter putting everything together and then sent word to me that the Codex was finished. I went there to pick it up and to persuade her to come back to Algaria with me."

"Wasn't she happy in Darine?" Pol asked him.

He shrugged. "She may have been, but she's done us a great service, and Darine isn't going to be the safest place in the world later on this summer."

"Oh?" I said.

"The Bear-cult's starting to get out of hand there, so it's time for me to go explain a few things to them. Hatturk's beginning to annoy me. Oh, Dras sent these." He opened another pouch and took out several scrolls. "This isn't complete yet, because the Mrin Prophet's still talking, but these are copies of everything he's said so far."

"That's what I've been waiting for," I told him eagerly.

"Don't get your hopes up too much," he told me. "I looked into them a few times on my way down here. Are you *sure* that fellow who's chained to a post up in Drasnia is really a prophet? That thing you've got in your hands is pure gibberish. I'd hate to see you following instructions that turn out to be no more than the ravings of a genuine madman."

"The Mrin Prophet *can't* rave, Algar," I assured him. "He can't talk."

"He's talked enough to fill up four scrolls so far."

"That's the whole point. Everything that's in these scrolls is pure prophecy, because the poor fellow's incapable of speech *except* when he's passing on the words of the Necessity."

"Whatever you say, Belgarath. Are you coming to the Alorn Council this summer?"

"I think that might be nice, father," Pol said. "I haven't seen Beldaran for quite a while, and you should probably look in on your grandson."

"I really ought to work on these, Pol," I objected, pointing at the scrolls.

"Bring them with you, father," she suggested. "They're not *that* heavy, after all." Then she turned back to Algar. "Send word to Riva," she told him. "Let him know that we're coming. Now, how's your wife?"

And so we went to the Isle of the Winds for the meeting of the Alorn Council—which was more in the nature of a family gathering in those days than it was a formal meeting of heads of state. We had a brief business meeting to get that out of the way, and then we were free to enjoy ourselves.

I was a bit surprised to discover that my grandson was about seven years old now. I tend to lose track of time when I'm working on something, and the years had slipped by without my noticing them.

Daran was a sturdy little boy with sandy-colored hair and a serious nature. We got along well together. He loved to listen to stories, and, though it's probably immodest of me to say it, I'm most likely one of the best storytellers in the world.

"What really happened in Cthol Mishrak, grandfather?" he asked me one rainy afternoon when the two of us were in a room high up in one of the towers feasting on some cherry tarts I had stolen from the pastry kitchen. "Father's started to tell me the story several times, but something always seems to come up just when he's getting to the good part."

I leaned back in my chair. "Well," I said, "let me see—" And then I told him the whole story, embellishing it only slightly—for artistic purposes, you understand.

"Well, then," he said gravely as darkness settled over Riva's Citadel, "I guess that sort of tells me what I'm supposed to do for the rest of my life." He sighed.

"Why so great a sigh, Prince Daran?" I asked him.

"It might have been nice to be just an ordinary person," he said with uncommon maturity for one so young. "I'd kind of like to be able to get up in the morning and go out to look at what's beyond the next hill."

"It's not all that much different from what's on this side," I told him.

"Maybe not, grandfather, but I would sort of like to see it—just once." He looked at me with those very serious blue eyes of his. "But I can't. That stone on the hilt of father's sword won't let me, will it?"

"I'm afraid not, Daran," I replied.

"Why me?"

Dear God! How many times have I heard that? How should I know why him? I wasn't in charge. I took a chance at that point. "It has to do with what we are, Daran. We're sort of special, and that means we've got special responsibilities. If it makes you feel any better, we aren't required to like them." Saying that to a seven-year-old might have been a little brutal, but my grandson wasn't your ordinary child. "This is what we're going to do," I told him then. "We're both going to get a good night's sleep, and we're going to get up early tomorrow morning, and we're going to go out and see what's on the other side of that hill."

"It's raining. We'll get wet."

"We've both been wet before, Daran. We won't melt."

I managed to offend *both* of my daughters with *that* little project.

The boy and I had fun, though, so all the scoldings we got several days later didn't bother either of us all that much. We tramped the steep hills of the Isle of the Winds, and we camped out and fished for trout in deep, swirling pools in mountain streams, and we talked. We talked about many things, and I think I managed to persuade Daran that what he had to do was necessary and important. At least he wasn't throwing that "Why me?" in my face at every turn. I've been talking to a long series of sandy-haired boys for about three thousand years now. I've been obliged to do a lot of things down through those endless centuries, but explaining our rather unique situation to those boys could very well have been the most important.

The Alorn Council lasted for several weeks, and then we all left for home. Pol, Beldin, and I sailed across the Sea of the Winds and made port at Camaar on a blustery afternoon. We took lodgings in the same well-appointed inn in which Beldaran and Riva had first met.

"How old is Beldaran now?" Beldin asked that evening after supper.

"Twenty-five, uncle," Pol told him, "the same age as I am."

"She looks older."

"She's been sick. I don't think the climate on that island agrees with her. She catches cold every winter, and it's getting harder and harder for her to shake them off." She looked at me. "You didn't help her by sneaking off with her son the way you did."

"We didn't sneak," I objected. "I left her a note."

"Belgarath's very good at leaving notes when he sneaks off," Beldin told her.

I shrugged. "It avoids arguments. Daran and I needed to talk. He's reached the age where he has questions, and I'm the best one to answer them. I think we got it all settled—at least for now. He's a good boy, and now that he knows what's expected of him, he'll probably do all right."

It was late summer by the time we got back to the Vale, and I immediately went to work on the Darine Codex, since it was complete. I'd decided to hold off on the Mrin Codex, which was clearly the more difficult of the two. Difficulty is a relative term when you're talking about those two documents, however. The need to conceal the meaning of the prophecy made both of them very obscure.

After several years of intensive study, I began to develop a vague perception of what lay in store for us. I didn't *like* it very much, but at least I had a fuzzy sort of idea about what was coming. The Darine Codex is more general than the Mrin, but it does identify a number of cautionary signals. Each time one of those meetings is about to take place, it'll be preceded by a very specific event. At least that would give us a bit of warning.

It must have been ten years or so later when Dras Bull-neck sent a messenger to the Vale to advise us that the Mrin Prophet had died *and* to deliver copies of the entire Mrin Codex. I laid aside Bormik's prophecy and dug into the ravings of that madman who'd spent most of his life chained to a post. As I just mentioned, the Darine Codex had given me a generalized idea of what was coming, and that made the Mrin Codex at least marginally comprehensible. It was still very rough going, though.

Polgara continued her own studies, and Beldin went back to Mallorea, so I was able to concentrate. As usually happens when I'm deeply into something, I lost track of time, so I can't really tell you exactly when it was that the Master came to me again, only that he had some very specific instructions. I regretfully set my studies aside and left for southern Tolnedra the very next morning.

I stopped by Prolgu to speak with the Gorim, and then I went to Tol Borune to have a few words with the grand duke. He wasn't very happy when I told him of the plans I had for his son, but when I advised him that what I was proposing would prepare the way for his family to ascend the Imperial Throne in Tol Honeth, he agreed to think about it. I didn't think it was really necessary to tell him that the elevation of the Borunes wasn't going to take place for about five hundred years. There's no real point in confusing people with picky little details, is there?

Then I ventured down to the Wood of the Dryads.

It was *that* time of year again, and it wasn't very long before I was accosted on a forest path by a golden-haired Dryad named Xalla. As usual, she had an arrow pointed directly at my heart. "Oh, put that down," I told her irritably.

"You won't try to run away, will you?" she demanded.

"Of course not. I need to talk with Princess Xoria."

"I saw you first. Xoria can have you after I've finished with you."

As I mentioned before, I'd swung by Prolgu on my way to Tolnedra. My long talk with the Gorim had been about the Dryads, so I was prepared. I reached into my pocket and took out a piece of chocolate candy. "Here," I said, holding it out to her.

"What's that?"

"It's something to eat. Try it. You'll like it."

She took the candy and sniffed at it suspiciously. Then she popped it into her mouth.

You wouldn't *believe* how she reacted. There's something about chocolate that does strange things to Dryads. I've seen many women in the throes of passion, but Xalla carried it to such extremes that it actually embarrassed me. Finally I turned my back and went off a little distance so that she could have some privacy.

I don't know that I need to go into any greater detail. I'm sure you get the picture.

Anyway, after the chocolate had run its course through her tiny body, Xalla was very docile—even kittenish. You might want to keep that in mind the next time you're going through the Wood of the Dryads. I know that it's a point of pride among most young men to claim unlimited stamina in that particular area of human activity, but these are the young men who've never encountered a Dryad at *that* time of year.

Take chocolate with you. Trust me.

My affectionate little companion took me through the Wood to Princess Xoria's tree. Xoria was even tinier than Xalla, and she had flaming red hair. Now that I think about it, she very closely resembled her ultimate great-granddaughter. She was comfortably lying on a bed of moss in a fork of her tree about twenty feet up when Xalla led me into the clearing. She looked at me a bit appraisingly. "I appreciate the gift, Xalla." she said critically, "but isn't it a bit old?"

"It has some food in its pocket, Xoria," Xalla replied. "And the food makes you feel *very* nice."

"I'm not hungry," the princess said indifferently.

"You really ought to try some, Xoria," Xalla urged her.

"I just ate. Why don't you take it out into the Wood and kill it? It's probably too old to be much good."

"Just try a piece of its candy," Xalla pressed. "You'll really like it."

"Oh, all right, I guess." The Dryad princess climbed down. "Give me some," she commanded me.

"As your Highness wishes," I replied, reaching into my pocket.

Princess Xoria's reaction to the chocolate was even more intense than Xalla's had been, and when she finally recovered her composure, she seemed to have lost her homicidal impulses. "Why have you come into our Wood, old man?" she asked me.

"I'm supposed to suggest a marriage to you," I replied.

"What's marriage?"

"It's a sort of formalized arrangement that involves mating," I explained.

"With you? I don't think so. You're nice enough, I suppose, but you're very old."

"No," I told her, "not with me, with somebody else."

"What's involved in this marriage business?"

"There's a little ceremony, and then you live together. You're supposed to agree not to mate with anybody else."

"How boring. Why on earth would I want to agree to something like that?"

"To protect your Wood, your Highness. If you marry the young man, his family will keep woodcutters away from your oak trees."

"We can do that ourselves. A lot of humans have come into our Wood with axes. Their bones are still here, but their axes turned to rust a long time ago."

"Those were single woodcutters, Xoria. If they start coming down here in gangs, you and your sisters will run out of arrows. They'll also build fires."

"*Fire!*"

"Humans like fire. It's one of their peculiarities."

"Why are you doing this, old man? Why are you trying to force me to join with somebody I've never even seen?"

"Necessity, Xoria. The young man's a member of the Borune family, and you're going to mate with him because a long time from now your mating's going to produce someone very special. She'll be the mate of the Child of Light, and she'll be called the Queen of the World." Then I sighed and put it to her directly. "You're going to do it, Xoria. You'll argue with me about it, but in the end, you'll do as you're told—just the same as I will. Neither of us has any choice in the matter."

"What does this Borune creature look like?"

I'd looked rather carefully at the young man while I'd been talking to his father, so I cast his image onto the surface of the forest pool at the foot of Princess Xoria's tree so that she could see the face of her future husband.

She gazed at the image with those grass-green eyes of hers, absently nibbling on the end of one of her flaming red locks. "It's not bad-looking," she conceded. "Is it vigorous?"

"All the Borunes are vigorous, Xoria."

"Give me another piece of candy, and I'll think about it."

The son of the grand duke of the Borunes was named Dellon, and he was
a rather pleasant young man who found
the idea of being married to a Dryad intriguing. I went back to Tol Borune to pick
up more candy and to talk with him privately. I cast Princess Xoria's image on the surface of a basin of water for him, and he grew even more interested. Then I went back to the Wood and dosed Xoria with judiciously
spaced out pieces of sugar-laced candy.

You have to be very careful when you're feeding chocolate to a
Dryad. If you give her too much, she'll become addicted, and she won't
be interested in anything else. I wanted Xoria to be docile, not comatose.

The major stumbling block in the whole business turned out to be
Dellon's mother, the grand duchess. The lady was a member of the
Honethite family, and the sole reason the Honeths had arranged her marriage to the grand duke of the Borune family in the first place was to gain
access to the priceless resources of the Wood of the Dryads. There were
forests in the mountains east of Tol Honeth and around Tol Rane, of
course, but those forests were fir, pine, and spruce—all softwoods. The
only significant source of hardwoods in Tolnedra was the forest of Vordue
in the north, and the Vorduvians charged outrageous prices for their lumber. The Honeths had been eyeing the oaks in the Wood of the Dryads
with undisguised greed for centuries.

My promise to the grand duke that this marriage eventually would result in a Borune Dynasty on the Imperial Throne had won *him* over to my

side, but when I casually mentioned that one of the stipulations of the marriage contract would be the inviolability of the Wood, the grand duchess went up in flames.

She was a Honethite to the core, however, so after an initial outburst, she resorted to guile. I knew perfectly well that her objection was based on economics, but she pretended that it was theological. Religion is almost always the last refuge of the scoundrel—and the grand duchess was a scoundrel if I ever met one. It sort of runs in her family. Back before the cracking of the world, the Gods had frowned on interracial marriages. Alorns didn't marry Nyissans, and Tolnedrans didn't marry Arends. Torak, of course, was the one who took it to extremes. My proposal involved an *interspecies* union, and Dellon's mother took her case to the priests of Nedra. Priests are bigots by nature, so she enlisted their aid without much difficulty.

That brought everything to a standstill. I was still shuttling back and forth between the Wood and Tol Borune, so she had plenty of opportunity to sneak around behind my back and gain support in her opposition.

"My hands are tied, Belgarath," the grand duke told me when I returned to Tol Borune after a trip down into the Wood. "The priests absolutely forbid this marriage."

"Your wife's playing politics, your Grace," I told him bluntly.

"I know, but as long as the priests of Nedra are on her side, there's nothing I can do."

I fumed about it for a while, and then I came up with a solution. The grand duchess wanted to play politics, and I was going to show her that I could play, too. "I'll be gone for a while, your Grace," I told him.

"Where are you going? Back to the Wood?"

"No. I have to see somebody in Tol Honeth."

This was during the early years of the second Vorduvian Dynasty, and I knew just the man to see. When I reached Tol Honeth, I went to the Imperial Palace and bullied enough functionaries to get a private audience with the emperor, Ran Vordue II.

"I'm honored, Ancient One," he greeted me.

"Let's skip the pleasantries, Ran Vordue," I told him. "I haven't got much time, and we have some interests that coincide right now. What would you say if I told you that the Honeths are right on the verge of gaining access to an unlimited supply of hardwood?"

"*What?*" he exploded.

"I thought you might feel that way about it. The fortunes of your family are based almost entirely on the Forest of Vordue. If the Honeths gain access to the Wood of the Dryads, you can expect the price of hardwood lumber to head for the cellar. I'm trying to arrange a marriage that'll keep the Honeths out of the Wood—permanently. The Borune grand duchess is a Honethite, though, and she's fighting me on theological grounds. Is the High Priest of Nedra by any chance related to you?"

"My uncle, actually," he replied.

"I thought there might be some connection. I need a dispensation from him to permit the son of the House of Borune to marry a Dryad princess."

"Belgarath, that's an absurdity!"

"Yes, I know, but I need one anyway. The marriage *must* take place."

"Why?"

"I'm manipulating history, Ran Vordue. This marriage really doesn't have much to do with what's going to happen in Tolnedra. It's aimed at Torak, and it's not going to hit him for about three thousand years."

"You can actually see that far into the future?"

"Not really, but my Master can. *Your* interest in this matter is sort of peripheral. We have different reasons for it, but we both want to keep the Honeths out of the Wood of the Dryads."

He squinted thoughtfully at the ceiling. "Would it help if my uncle went to Tol Borune and performed the ceremony in person?" he asked me.

That idea hadn't even occurred to me. "Why, yes, Ran Vordue," I replied with a broad grin, "I think it might."

"I'll arrange it." Then he grinned back at me. "Confusion to the Honeths," he said.

"I might want to drink to that."

And so Dellon and Xoria were married, and the House of Borune was inseparably linked to the Dryads.

Oh, incidentally, the groom's mother didn't attend the wedding. She wasn't feeling very well.

The whole business had taken me almost three years, but considering how important it was, I felt it was time well spent. I was in a smugly self-congratulatory frame of mind when I started back for the Vale. Even now, when I look back on it, I nearly sprain my arm trying to pat myself on the back.

It was late winter when I went through the Tolnedran Mountains, so I made most of the trip as a wolf. Wolves are much better adapted to making their way in snow-covered mountains than men are, so I fall back on my alternative form in those situations almost out of habit.

When I came down out of the mountains into the southern end of the Vale, I resumed my normal form, and the sound of the twins' com-

bined voices was roaring inside my head almost before my tail disappeared. *"Don't shout!"* I shouted back at them.

"Where have you been?" Beltira's voice demanded.

"In Tolnedra. You knew that."

"We've been trying to reach you for a week now."

"I had to cross the mountains, so I went wolf." That had always been
one of the drawbacks involved in taking another form. It interfered with
our peculiar method of communication. If the brother who was trying to
reach you didn't know that you'd changed, his thought was very likely to
miss you entirely. *"What's the matter?"* I sent out the question.

"Beldaran's very ill. Polgara's gone to the Isle to see what she can do." He
paused. *"You'd better get there in a hurry, Belgarath."*

A cold knot of fear settled in my chest. *"I'll cut up across Ulgoland to
Camaar,"* I told them. *"Let Polgara know that I'm coming."*

"We might need to reach you. Are you going wolf again?"

"No. I'll fly—a falcon, I think."

"You don't fly very well, Belgarath."

"Maybe it's time I learned. I'm changing right now."

My concern for Beldaran was so overpowering that I didn't even
think about the things that normally interfere with my flying, and after
about half an hour I was cutting through the air like an arrow shot from
a bow. I even experimented with translocation a time or two, but that
didn't work out very well—largely because I reverted to my own form in
the process and found myself ten miles from where I'd started and trying
to fly without benefit of wings. I gave up on that idea and did it the old-
fashioned way.

I was exhausted by the time I reached Camaar two days later, but I
grimly pressed on across the Sea of the Winds.

I'd made very good time, but I still got there too late. Beldaran had
already died.

Polgara was inconsolable, and Riva was almost in the same condition
as I'd been after Poledra's death. There was no point in trying to talk to
either one of them, so I went looking for my grandson.

I found him atop the highest tower of the Citadel. It appeared that
he had cried himself out, and he was standing, puffy-eyed and somber, at
the battlements. He was full-grown now, and he was very tall.

"All right, Daran," I said to him harshly, "get away from there."

"Grandfather!"

"I said to get away from there." I *wasn't* going to take any chances
with him. A sudden upsurge of despair could very well push him into
doing something foolish. I'd have time for my own grief later on. Right
now I had to concentrate on his.

"What are we going to do, grandfather?" he wept.

"We're going to go on, Daran. It's what we always do. Now tell me what happened."

He pulled himself together. "Mother's been catching cold every winter for years now. Aunt Pol told us that it'd weakened her lungs. This past winter it was much worse. She started coughing up blood. That's when father sent for Aunt Pol. There was nothing she could do, though. She tried everything, but mother was just too weak. Why weren't you here, grandfather? *You* could have done something."

"I'm not a physician, Daran. Your aunt knows far more about that than I do. If *she* couldn't save your mother, no one could have. Does your father have a prime minister? Somebody who takes care of things when he's busy?"

"You mean Brand? He's the Rivan Warder. Father depends on him to handle administration."

"We'd better go talk with him. You're going to have to take over here until your father recovers from this."

"Me? Why me?"

"You're the Crown Prince, Daran, that's why. It's your responsibility. Your father's incapacitated right now, and that drops everything into your lap."

"I don't think that's very fair. I feel just as badly about this as father does."

"Not quite. At least you can still talk—and think. He can't. I'll help you through it, and Brand knows what has to be done."

"Father *will* get better, won't he?"

"We can hope so. It might take him awhile, though. It took *me* twelve years after your grandmother died."

"Nobody's going to pay any attention to me when I tell them to do something, grandfather. I don't even have a full beard yet."

"You're twenty years old, Daran. It's time you grew up. Now, let's go talk with Brand."

I'll admit that it was brutal, but *somebody* here on the Isle had to be able to function. Riva quite obviously couldn't. The Orb absolutely *had* to be protected, and if word of Riva's state got back to Ctuchik—well, I didn't want to think about that.

Brand was one of those solid, dependable men that the world needs more of, and he understood the situation almost immediately. He was unusually perceptive for an Alorn, so he was able to see not only what I told him, but also the things I *couldn't* tell him in front of Daran. There was a distinct possibility that Iron-grip would never really recover, and Daran would have to serve as regent. We were going to have to bury my grandson in details to the point that *his* grief wouldn't incapacitate him, as well. I left the two of them talking and went to Polgara's quarters.

I knocked on her door. "It's me, Pol. Open up."

"Go away."

"Open the door, Polgara. I need to talk to you."

"Get away from me, father."

I shrugged. "It's your door, Pol. If you don't open it right now, you'll have to have it replaced."

Her face was ravaged when she opened the door. "What is it, father?"

"You haven't got time for this, Polgara. You can cry yourself out later. Right now I need you. Riva can't even think, so I've made Daran regent. Somebody's going to have to look after him, and I've got something that absolutely *has* to be done."

"Why me?"

"Not you, *too*, Pol. Why does *everybody* keep saying that to me? You're elected because you're the only one who can handle it. You're going to stay here and help Daran in every way you can. Don't let him sink into melancholia the way his father has. The Angaraks have eyes everywhere, and if there's any sign of weakness here, you can expect a visit from Ctuchik. Now, pull yourself together. Blow your nose and fix your face. Daran's talking with the Rivan Warder right now. I'll take you to where they are, and then I have to leave."

"You're not even going to stay for the funeral?"

"I've got the funeral in my heart, Pol, the same as you have. No amount of ceremony's going to make it go away. Now go fix your face. You look awful."

I'm sorry, Pol, but I had to do it that way. I had to force both you and Daran back from the abyss of despair, and piling responsibilities on you was the only way I could think of to do it.

I left my daughter and my grandson deep in a discussion with Brand, and made some pretense of leaving the Isle. I didn't, however. I went up into the mountains behind Riva's city instead and found a quiet place.

Then I crumpled and wept like a broken-hearted child.

Iron-grip never fully recovered from the loss of his wife. Of course, he was nearing sixty when Beldaran left us, so it was almost time for Daran to take over anyway. It gave me an excuse to compel Pol to stay on the Isle—*and* to keep her busy. Keeping busy is very important during a time of bereavement. If I'd had something vital to attend to at the time of Poledra's death, things might have turned out quite differently.

I suppose I realized that—dimly—when I returned to the Vale, so I buried myself in my study of the Mrin Codex. I went through it from one end to the other looking for some clue that might have warned me about what was going to happen to Beldaran. Fortunately, I didn't find anything. If I had, I'm sure my guilt would have overpowered me.

About six or seven years had passed when Daran's messenger arrived in the Vale to tell me that Riva Iron-grip had died. Bear-shoulders had died the previous winter, and Bull-neck and Fleet-foot were both very old men now. One of the disadvantages of a long life span is the fact that you lose a lot of friends along the way. Sometimes I feel that my life has been one long funeral.

Polgara returned to the Vale a year or so later, and she had a couple of trunks full of medical books with her. There probably wasn't anything in those books that could have helped Beldaran, but I think Pol wanted to make sure. I'm not certain what she'd have done if she'd found some cure that she hadn't known about, but she was as lucky as I'd been.

Things went on quietly in the Vale for about fifty years. Daran got married, had a son, and grew old, while Pol and I continued our studies. Our shared sense of loss brought us closer together. As I delved deeper into the Mrin Codex, my sense of what lay ahead of us grew more troubled, but so far as I could determine, we had everything in place that needed to be there, so we were ready.

Beldin returned from Mallorea near the end of the twenty-first century, and he reported that very little was going on there. "So far as I can tell, nothing's going to happen until Torak comes out of his seclusion at Ashaba."

"It's pretty much the same here," I replied. "The Tolnedrans have found out about the gold in Maragor, and they've built a city at a place called Tol Rane on the Marag border. They've been trying to lure the Marags into trade, but they aren't having much luck. Is Zedar still at Ashaba?"

He nodded. "I guess Burnt-face yearns for his company."

"I can't imagine why."

We quite deliberately didn't talk about Beldaran or about the other friends who'd passed on. We'd all been rather intimately involved with the family of Cherek Bear-shoulders, and we felt the sense of their loss more keenly than we had when other, perhaps more casual acquaintances died.

The rudimentary trade between Drasnia and Gar og Nadrak came to an abrupt halt when the Nadraks began to mount attacks on towns and villages in eastern Drasnia. Bull-neck's son, Khadar, took steps, and the Nadraks retreated back into their forests.

Then in 2115, the Tolnedrans, frustrated by the Marag indifference to trade, took action. If I'd been paying attention, I might have been able to intervene, but I had my mind on other things. The merchant Princes of Tol Honeth started by instigating a nationwide rumor campaign about the Marag practice of ritual cannibalism, and the stories grew wilder and wilder with each retelling. Nobody really likes the idea of cannibalism, but the upsurge of indignation in Tolnedra was largely spurious, I suspect. If there hadn't been all that gold in the streams of Maragor, I don't think the Tolnedrans would have gotten so excited about Marag eating habits.

Unfortunately, Ran Vordue IV had occupied the throne for only about a year when this all came to a head, and his lack of experience contributed significantly to what finally happened. The carefully whipped up hysteria finally crowded him into a corner, and Ran Vordue made the fatal mistake of declaring war on the Marags.

The Tolnedran invasion of Maragor was one of the darker chapters in human history. The legions that swept across the border were not bent on conquest but upon the extermination of the Marag race, and they quite nearly succeeded. The slaughter was ghastly, and in the end only that characteristic greed that infects all Tolnedrans prevented the total extinction of the Marags. Toward the end of the campaign, the legion commanders began taking prisoners—primarily women—whom they sold to the Nyissan slavers who, like vultures, habitually hover around the fringes of almost any battlefield.

The whole business was sickening, but I suppose we owe those barbaric generals a vote of thanks. If they *hadn't* sold their captives the way they did, Taiba would not have been born, and that would have been a catastrophe. The "Mother of the Race That Died," as she's called in the Mrin Codex, absolutely *had* to be there when the time came, or all of our careful preparations would have gone out the window.

Once the legions had wiped out the Marags, the Tolnedran gold hunters rushed into Maragor like a breaking wave. Mara, however, had his own ideas about that. I've never really understood Mara, but I understood his reaction to what the Tolnedrans had done to his people very well, and I wholeheartedly approved, even though it took us to the brink of another war between the Gods. To put it quite simply, Maragor became a haunted place. The spirit of Mara wailed in insupportable grief, and horrors beyond imagination appeared before the eyes of the horde of gold hunters who swept into the basin where Maragor had been. Most of them went mad. The majority of them killed themselves, and the few who managed to stumble back to Tolnedra had to be confined in madhouses for the rest of their lives.

The spirit of Nedra was *not* pleased by the atrocious behavior of his children, and he spoke *very* firmly with Ran Vordue about it. That accounts for the founding of the monastery at Mar Terrin. I was rather pleased about Mar Terrin, since the greedy merchants who'd started the whole thing were, to a man, among the first monks who were sent there to comfort the ghosts of the slaughtered Marags. Forcing a Tolnedran to take a vow of poverty is probably just about the worst thing you can do to him.

Unfortunately, it didn't stop there. Belar and Mara had always been close, and the actions of the children of Nedra offended Belar mightily. *That* was what was behind the Cherek raids along the Tolnedran coast. The war boats swept out of the Great Western Sea like packs of coursing hounds, and the coastal cities of the empire were sacked and burned with tiresome regularity. The Chereks, obviously acting on instructions from Belar, paid particular attention to Tol Vordue, the ancestral home of the Vorduvian family. Ran Vordue IV could only wring his hands in anguish as his native city was ravaged by repeated Cherek attacks.

Ultimately, my Master had to step in and mediate a peace settlement between Belar and Nedra. Torak was still our main concern, and he was quite enough to worry about without *other* family squabbles cropping up to confuse the issue.

CHAPTER
THIRTY

After the destruction of Maragor and after the ensuing punitive raids along the Tolnedran coast by Cherek berserkers had died down a bit, an uneasy peace settled over the western kingdoms— except for Arendia, of course. *That* tedious war went on and on, in some measure perhaps because the Arends couldn't think of any way to stop it. An endless series of atrocities and counteratrocities had turned hatred into a religion in Arendia, and the natives were all very devout.

Pol and I spent the next few centuries in the Vale, quietly pursuing our studies. My daughter accepted without comment the fact that she wasn't going to age. The peculiar thing about the whole business in her case was the fact that she really *didn't*. Beldin and the twins and I had all achieved the appearance of a certain maturity. We picked up wrinkles and grey hair and a distinguished look. Pol didn't. She'd passed her three hundredth birthday, and she still looked much the same as she had at twenty-five. Her eyes were wiser, but that's about as far as it went. I guess a sorcerer is *supposed* to look distinguished and wise, and that implies wrinkles and grey hair. A woman with grey hair and wrinkles is called a crone, and I don't think Pol would have liked that very much. Maybe we all wound up looking the way we thought we ought to look. My brothers and I thought we should look wise and venerable. Pol didn't mind the wise part, but "venerable" wasn't in her vocabulary.

I think I might want to investigate that someday. The notion that we somehow create ourselves is intriguing.

Anyway, I think it was early in the twenty-fifth century when Polgara began going out on her own. I tried to put my foot down the first time, but she rather bluntly told me to mind my own business. "The Master told *me* to take care of this, father. As I recall, *your* name didn't even come up during the conversation."

I found that remark totally uncalled for.

I waited for a half a day after she'd ridden out of the Vale on her Algar horse, and then I followed her. I hadn't been instructed *not* to, and I was still her father. I knew that she had enormous talent, but still—

I had to be very careful, of course. With the exception of her mother, Polgara knows me better than anybody else in the world ever has, and I rather think she could sense my presence from ten leagues away. I expanded my repertoire enormously as I followed her north along the eastern border of Ulgoland. I think I altered my form on an average of once every hour. I even went so far as to take the form of a fieldmouse one evening as I watched her set up camp. A hunting owl quite nearly ended my career that time.

My daughter gave no sign that she knew I was following her, but with Polgara, you never really know. She crossed the mountains to Muros, where she turned south toward Arendia. *That* made me nervous.

As I'd more or less expected, she was accosted by Wacites on the road to Vo Wacune. Arends are usually very polite to ladies, but this particular group appeared to have left its manners at home. They questioned her rather rudely and told her that unless she could produce some kind of safe-conduct, they'd have to take her into custody.

You would not *believe* how smoothly she handled that. She was right in the middle of delivering a blistering remonstrance, and between one outraged word and the next, she simply put them all to sleep. I probably wouldn't even have noticed it if she hadn't made that telltale little gesture with one hand. I've talked with her about that several times, but she still feels the Word that releases her Will is not quite enough. She always seems to want to add a gesture.

The Wacites went to sleep instantly, without bothering to close their eyes. She even put their horses to sleep. Then she rode off, humming softly to herself. After she'd gone a couple of miles, she gathered her Will again, said, "Wake up," and waved her hand once more.

The Wacites were not aware of the fact that they'd just taken a nap, so it appeared to them that she'd simply vanished. Sorcery or magic, or whatever you want to call it, makes Arends nervous, so they chose not to follow her—not that they'd have known which way she'd gone anyway.

She hadn't given me any details about the nature of her little chore in Arendia, so I still had to follow her. After that encounter in the forest, though, I did so more out of curiosity than any real concern for her safety. I knew that she could take care of herself.

She rode on to Vo Wacune, and when she reached the gates of the city, she imperiously demanded to be taken to the palace of the duke.

Of all the cities of ancient Arendia, Vo Wacune was by far the loveliest. The cattle fair at Muros was very profitable for the Wacite Arends, so they had plenty of money to spend on architecture. There were marble quarries in the foothills lying to the east of the city, and marble-sheathed buildings are always prettier than structures made of other kinds of rock. Vo Astur was built of granite, and Vo Mimbre's made with that yellow-colored stone that's so abundant in southern Arendia. It went further than that, though. Vo Astur and Vo Mimbre were fortresses, and they *looked* like fortresses, blocky and unlovely. Marble-clad Vo Wacune, however, looked like a city seen in a dream. It had tall, delicate spires, broad shady avenues, and many parks and gardens. Anytime you read a fairy tale that describes some mythic city of unspeakable beauty, you can be fairly certain that the description is based on Vo Wacune.

I paused in a grove of trees just outside the gates and watched Pol enter the city. Then, after a moment's consideration, I changed form again. Arends are very fond of hunting dogs, so I took the form of a hound and followed along. The duke would assume that I was *her* dog, and she'd assume that I was *his*.

"Your Grace." She greeted the duke with a flowing curtsy. "It is imperative that we speak privately. I must disclose my mind unto thee out of the hearing of others."

"That is not customary, Lady—?" He left it delicately hanging in the air. He *really* wanted to know who this queenly visitor was.

"I will identify myself unto thee when we are alone, your Grace. Unfriendly ears are everywhere in poor Arendia, and word of my visit must not reach Vo Mimbre nor Vo Astur. Thy realm is in peril, your Grace, and I am come to abate that peril. Let us not alert thine enemies to mine advisement of thee, and my name alone would so alert them."

Where *had* she learned to speak in that archaic language?

"Thy manner and bearing are such that I am inclined to give ear unto thee, my Lady," the duke replied. "Let us go apart so that thou mayest give me this vital instruction." He rose from his throne, offered Pol his arm, and led her from the room.

I padded along behind them, my toenails clicking on the floor. Arendish nobles always give their hunting dogs the free run of their houses, so nobody paid any attention to me. The duke, however, shooed me out when he and Pol went into a room just down the hall. That wasn't really any problem, though. I curled up on the floor just outside with my head almost touching the door.

"And now, Lady," the duke said, "prithee divulge thy name to me."

"My name's Polgara," she replied, dropping the flowery speech. "You might have heard of me."

"The daughter of Ancient Belgarath?" He sounded stunned.

"Exactly. You've been receiving some bad advice lately, your Grace. A Tolnedran merchant's been telling you that he speaks for Ran Vordue XVII. He does not. The House of Vordue is *not* offering an alliance. If you follow his advice and invade Mimbrate territory, the legions will *not* come to your aid. If you violate your alliance with the Mimbrates, they'll immediately ally themselves with the Asturians, and you'll be swarmed under."

"The Tolnedran merchant has documents, Lady Polgara," the duke protested. "They bear the Imperial Seal of Ran Vordue himself."

"The imperial seal isn't that difficult to duplicate, your Grace. I can make one for you right here and now, if you'd like."

"If the Tolnedran doth not speak for Ran Vordue, then for whom?"

"He speaks for Ctuchik, your Grace. The Murgos want strife in the west, and Arendia, already torn by this unending civil war, is the best place to set off new fires. Do with the deceitful Tolnedran as you will. I must go to Vo Astur now and then on to Vo Mimbre. Ctuchik's scheme is very complex, and if it succeeds, its ultimate goal will be war between Arendia and Tolnedra."

"That must not be!" the duke exclaimed. "Divided as we are, the legions would crush us!"

"Precisely. And then the Alorns would be drawn in, and general war would break out. Nothing would suit Ctuchik better."

"I will wring confirmation of this foul plot from the Tolnedran, Lady Polgara," he said. "Of that I give thee my pledge."

The door opened, and the duke stepped over me. After your dogs have been underfoot long enough, you don't even see them any more.

Polgara, however, *didn't* step over me. "All right, father," she said to me in withering tones, "you can go home now. I can manage here without you very well."

And, as a matter of fact, she did. I still followed her, though. She went to Vo Astur and spoke with the Asturian duke in much the same way as she had with the duke of Vo Wacune. Then she went on to Vo Mimbre and alerted them, as well. In that one single journey, she dismantled something that had probably taken the cadaverous Ctuchik ten years to build. He'd never met her, and he already had reason to hate her.

She explained it all to me when we got back to the Vale—*after* she'd taken me to task for trailing along behind her. "Ctuchik's got people here in the western kingdoms who don't really look that much like Angaraks," she told me. "Some of them are modified Grolims, but there are others, as well. Have you ever heard of the Dagashi?"

"I can't say that I have," I replied.

"They're a group of paid assassins based somewhere to the south of Nyissa. They're very good spies as well as highly skilled murderers. At any rate, the Murgos have discovered gold in that spine of mountains that runs northeast from Urga to Goska, so Ctuchik can afford to bribe Tolnedrans."

"*Anybody* can bribe Tolnedrans, Pol."

"Possibly, yes. At any rate, his spies have been enlisting various Tolnedrans to present the three duchies here in Arendia with spurious offers of alliance that supposedly come from Ran Vordue. Ran Vordue, of course, doesn't know anything about them. The idea was that when the legions didn't turn up to assist the people who were expecting them, the Arends would attack northern Tolnedra in retaliation. Northern Tolnedra is Vorduvian territory, and the emperor would respond by crushing the Arendish duchies one by one. Once the Alorns heard about it, they'd believe that the empire was trying to expand its borders, and they'd take steps. It was a very clever plan, actually."

"But you put a stop to it."

"Yes, father, I know. We might want to keep an eye on Ctuchik. I think he's planning something. He's not trying to stir up all this mischief just for the fun of it."

"I'll watch him," I promised her.

Beldin returned from one of his periodic trips to Mallorea not long after that, and he told us that nothing much was going on there. "Except that Zedar's left Ashaba," he added, almost as an afterthought.

"Any idea of where he's gone?" I asked.

"Not a clue. Zedar's as slippery as an eel. For all I know, he's hiding out at Kell. What's going on with the Nadraks?"

"I don't follow you."

"I came back from Mallorea that way, and they're massing up about ten leagues east of the Drasnian border. I'd say that they're planning something major."

I started to swear. "*That's* what it was all about!"

"Talk sense, Belgarath. What's been happening?"

"There'd been a certain amount of limited trade back and forth across that border. Then the Nadraks started getting belligerent. They made a few raids into Drasnia, and Bull-neck's son chased them back into the woods. It's been quiet up there for quite some time now."

"I think it might get noisy again fairly soon. The Nadrak cities are almost deserted. Every man who can stand up, see lightning, and hear thunder is camped out in the woods a day's march from the border."

"We'd better warn Rhonar."

"Who's he?"

"The current king of Drasnia. I'll take a run up there and let him know what's happening. Why don't you go up into Algaria and see if you can find Cho-Dan, the Chief of the Clan-Chiefs? Let's get some Algar cavalry just north of Lake Atun."

"Don't the Algars have a king anymore?"

"The title's sort of fallen into disuse. The Algars are nomads, and clan's more important to them than nation. I'll go to Boktor and then over to Val Alorn to warn the Chereks."

Beldin rubbed his hands together. "We haven't had a war in a long time."

"I haven't missed them all that much." I scratched at my beard. "I think maybe I'll run on down to Rak Cthol and have another little chat with Ctuchik as soon as the Alorns are in place. Maybe I can head this off before it gets out of hand."

"Spoilsport. Where's Pol?"

"Over in Arendia—Vo Wacune, I think. Ctuchik's been playing games there, too. Pol's keeping an eye on things. Let's go alert the Alorns."

King Rhonar of Drasnia received my news with a certain amount of enthusiasm. He was as bad or worse than Beldin. Then I went on across the Gulf of Cherek to Val Alorn and talked with King Bledar. He was even worse than Rhonar. His fleet sailed for Kotu the next day. I rather hoped that Beldin could keep a tight leash on the Alorns when they got to the Nadrak border. Pol and I had just spent several centuries trying to keep a lid on open hostilities here in the West, and this incipient confrontation threatened to blow that lid off.

Then I went to Rak Cthol.

I paused in the desert a few leagues to the west of that ugly mountain and considered a number of options. My last visit undoubtedly had convinced Ctuchik that posting sentries wouldn't be a bad idea, so getting through the city unnoticed might have been a little tricky. It was with a certain distaste that I finally came to the conclusion that I didn't really have to go *through* the city. I knew where Ctuchik's turret was, after all, and it *did* have windows.

It was late at night, so there wasn't any warm air rising up off the black sand. This meant that I literally had to claw my way up through the air as I circled the peak up and up. About the only good thing about it was the fact that after I was about fifty feet up, I couldn't see the ground any more.

As luck had it, Ctuchik had fallen asleep over his worktable, and he had his head down on his folded arms when I flapped in through his window. I shed all those vulture feathers and shook him awake. The years hadn't improved his appearance. He still looked like a walking dead man.

He half rose with a startled exclamation, and then he got control of himself. "Good to see you again, old boy," he lied.

"I'm glad you're enjoying it. You'd better get word to your Nadraks. Tell them to call off this invasion. The Alorns know they're coming."

His eyes went flat. "Someday you're going to irritate me, Belgarath."

"I certainly *hope* so. God knows you've irritated *me* enough lately."

"How did you find out about the Nadraks?"

"I've got eyes everywhere, Ctuchik. You can't hide what you're doing from me. Didn't what happened to your scheme in Arendia convince you of that?"

"I'd sort of wondered why that fell apart."

"Now you know." I wasn't actually trying to steal Pol's credit, I just thought it might be a good idea to keep *her* part in that little coup a secret from Ctuchik for a while longer. Pol was good, but I wasn't sure if she was ready for a confrontation with Ctuchik. Besides, I didn't really want him to know about her just yet. You might say that I was holding her in reserve.

"I'm awfully sorry, old chap," he said with a faint sneer. "I'm afraid I won't be able to help you with the Nadraks. It's not really my idea. I'm just following orders from Ashaba."

"Don't try to be clever, Ctuchik. I know you can talk with Torak any time you need to. You'd better do that right now. You weren't around when we invaded the country around Korim. Believe me, Torak gets *very* upset when large numbers of Angaraks get killed, and what's right on the verge of happening on the Drasnian border is very likely to exterminate the Nadraks entirely. I've seen the way Alorns make war. It's entirely up to you, of course; *I'm* not the one who's going to have to answer to Torak." Then, just to twist the knife a bit and add to his confusion, I smirked at him. "You *really* need a copy of the Ashabine Oracles, old boy," I told him spitefully. "The Mrin Codex is giving me *very* good instructions. I knew all about this little game of yours a couple hundred years ago, so I've had lots of time to get ready for you." Then I smiled beatifically at him. "Always nice talking with you, Ctuchik." Then I stepped to the window and jumped.

That little exercise in gross theatricality almost got me killed. I was no more than a hundred feet above the desert floor when I finally got all my feathers in place. Changing form while you're falling is *very* difficult. For some reason, it's hard to concentrate when the ground's coming up at you that fast.

Aside from the opportunity it gave me to add to Ctuchik's confusion, however, my visit to Rak Cthol was largely a waste of time. I should have known that Torak would never back away from something once he'd set it in motion, no matter *how* many things got in his way. His ego simply would not permit it. The Nadraks came howling across the Drasnian border before I even got back from Rak Cthol, and, quite predictably, the Alorns met them head-on and soundly defeated them. A few of them *did* manage to escape, but it was centuries before there were enough Nadraks again even to worry about.

Torak evidently juggled things around in his mind sufficiently that it wasn't *his* fault for ignoring my warning. In commemoration of the event, he ordered his Grolims to quadruple the number of sacrifices. Over the centuries, his Grolims have killed more Angaraks than the Alorns ever have.

After the survivors of that debacle limped back to Gar og Nadrak and hid out in the forest, I went to Arendia to see what Pol was up to. I finally located her in Vo Wacune, living in a splendid house not far from the ducal palace. Like all the rest of Vo Wacune, her house had been constructed of marble, and it positively gleamed. It was quite a large house, and it had wings to it that partially enclosed a well-tended flower garden with paved walks, neatly trimmed hedges, and manicured lawns. "What's all this?" I asked her when her servants finally ushered me into her presence.

She was sitting in an ornate chair by a rose quartz fireplace that glowed pink, wearing a truly stunning blue gown. "I'm moving up in the world, father."

"You found a gold mine somewhere?"

"Something better, actually. My estate is quite large, and the land's very fertile."

"Your estate?"

"It's just to the north of Lake Medalia—over on the other side of the River Camaar. I even have a manor house up there. You have the distinct honor to be addressing her Grace, the duchess of Erat."

"Be serious, Pol."

"I *am* serious, father. The old duke was very grateful for the information I gave him about Ctuchik's scheme, so I've always been welcome at the Ducal Palace."

I gave her a hard look. "He gave you a title just for following the Master's instructions? And you accepted it? Tacky, Pol, very tacky. We aren't supposed to take rewards for obeying orders."

"It went a little further, Old Wolf. You know the situation here in Arendia?"

"Last I heard, the Wacites and the Mimbrates were allied against the Asturians. That alliance seems to be lasting longer than most of the others."

"It's still in effect, father. Anyway, after the old duke died, his son

Alleran took the ducal throne. He and I were quite close, since I'd helped his mother raise him. We married Alleran off—I even persuaded his mother *not* to let him marry his cousin—and in due time, his wife presented him with a son. The duke of Vo Astur saw a chance to muddy the waters here in Arendia when that happened, and he sent a group of his underlings to abduct the little boy. The current duke of Vo Astur is a crude sort of fellow, and the note his hirelings left was very direct. He told Alleran that he'd kill his son unless Wacune abrogated the treaty with Mimbre and stayed strictly neutral. I went to Vo Astur and rescued the little boy. I *also* gave the Asturian duke a lesson in good manners."

"What did you do to him?" I asked the question a bit apprehensively. There are certain rules concerning the use of our gift. "You didn't kill him, did you?"

"Of course not, father. I know better than that. The duke of Vo Astur has an open sore on the lining of his stomach now. It provides him with all sorts of entertainment, and it keeps him out of mischief. That was five years ago, and there hasn't been a major battle in Arendia since I visited Vo Astur."

"You've made peace in Arendia?" I was stunned.

"A temporary peace, father," she corrected. "It's probably too early to tell if it's permanent. I'll ulcerate stomachs from one end of Arendia to the other if I have to in order to put an end to this foolishness, though. Duke Alleran was very grateful, and that's why I'm the duchess of Erat now."

"Why didn't *I* think of that?" I exclaimed. "It's so simple. You ended the Arendish civil wars with a bellyache." I bowed to her. "I'm proud of you, your Grace."

"Why, thank you, father." She beamed. Then she pursed her lips thoughtfully. "The congratulations might be a little premature, though. As soon as there's a new duke in either Vo Mimbre or Vo Astur, hostilities might break out again. I think I'd better stay here in Vo Wacune. These Wacites are the least aggressive of the Arends, and I have a certain amount of authority here because of my friendship with the duke's family. Possibly I can guide them in the right direction. *Somebody* in Arendia is going to have to take the role of peacemaker. Give me a little time here, and I might just be able to establish a custom. *Maybe* I can get the Mimbrates and Asturians into the habit of bringing their disputes to Vo Wacune for mediation instead of trying to solve them on the battlefield."

"That's a lot to hope for in Arendia, Pol."

She shrugged. "It's worth a try. Go get cleaned up, father. There's a grand ball at the ducal palace tonight, and we've been invited—well, *I* have, but you can come along as my personal guest."

"A *what?*"

"A grand ball, father—music, dancing, polite conversation, that sort of thing."

"I don't dance, Pol."

She smiled sweetly at me. "I'm sure you'll pick it up in no time, Old Wolf. You're a very clever fellow. Now go bathe and trim your beard. Don't embarrass me in public."

CHAPTER
THIRTY-
ONE

I moved around quite a bit during the next six hundred years or so, but Polgara remained in Vo Wacune. Her assessment of the Wacite Arends proved to be essentially correct, and with her there to guide them, they were able to keep a tentative peace in Arendia.

The virtual destruction of the Nadraks had persuaded the cadaverous Ctuchik to pull in his horns, so there was even an uneasy peace along the eastern frontier.

As I'd promised Dellon's father, the Borunes ascended the throne of Tolnedra—2537 or so, I believe it was. The Vorduvians and the Honethites had been passing the crown back and forth between them for centuries, so when Ran Vordue XX died without an heir, the Honeths assumed that it was their turn again. There were several Honethite nobles who felt that they were qualified, and the resulting divisions in that family were severe enough to deadlock the Council of Advisors. I've heard that the bribes were astronomical. Ultimately, a southern council member rather tentatively placed the name of the Grand Duke of the Borunes in nomination. The Vorduvians and the Horbites had not been pleased at the prospect of several centuries of Honethite misrule, so they dropped their own candidates and swung their support to the Borunes. Since the Honeths were still divided, they had no single candidate, and the crown went to the Borunes almost by default.

Ran Borune I was a very capable emperor. The major problem in Tolnedra at that time was still the ongoing raids along the coast by

Cherek freebooters. Ran Borune took steps almost as soon as his coronation was over. He pulled the legions out of their garrisons and put them
to work building the highway that now connects Tol Vordue and Tol
Horb. He didn't make the legions happy by doing that, but he remained
firm. He got his highway, but that was more in the nature of a bonus. His
real purpose in the project was to spread his legions out along the coast
to repel the Chereks no matter where they came ashore. All in all, it
worked out rather well. I'd spent quite some time in Val Alorn trying to
talk sense into various Cherek kings, without much success. Inevitably,
they'd piously declare that they were merely following the instructions
Belar had given them after the Tolnedran invasion of Maragor. I'd tried
to point out that Tolnedra had been sufficiently punished by now, but
they'd refused to listen to me. I suspect that the loot they were picking
up in Tolnedran cities might have had something to do with that upsurge
of religious enthusiasm. When their raiding parties started encountering
the legions, however, their piety began to cool, and other parts of the
world became much more interesting.

I think it was about 2940 when I happened to swing by Vo Wacune
to see how Polgara was doing. I may have gotten there just in time. Her
Grace, the duchess of Erat, was in love. I *knew* she'd been spending too
much time in Arendia.

She was in her marble-walled garden tending roses when I arrived.
"Well, Old Wolf," she greeted me, "what have you been up to?"

I shrugged. "This and that," I replied.

"Is the world still in one piece?"

"More or less. I've had to patch it a few times, though."

"Would you look at this?" she said, cutting a rose and handing it to
me. It was a white rose, but not entirely. The tips of the petals were a
pale lavender.

"Very nice," I said.

"That's all you can say? Very nice? It's beautiful, father. Ontrose developed it just for me."

"Who's Ontrose?"

"He's the man I'm going to marry, father—just as soon as he gets up
the nerve to ask me."

What was this? I got very careful at that point. "Interesting idea, Pol.
Send him around and we'll talk about it."

"You don't approve."

"I didn't say that. Have you thought your way completely through the
notion, though?"

"Yes, father, I have."

"And the drawbacks didn't persuade you to think about it a little
more?"

"What drawbacks were those?"

"Well, in the first place, there's quite a difference in your ages, I'd imagine. He's probably not much over thirty, and if I remember correctly, you're about nine hundred and fifty."

"Nine hundred and forty, actually. What's that got to do with it?"

"You'll outlive him, Pol. He'll be old before you've turned around twice."

"I think I'm entitled to a *little* bit of happiness, father—even if it doesn't last very long."

"And were you planning to have children?"

"Of course."

"The chances are very good that they'll have normal life-spans, as well, you know. *You* won't get old. *They* will."

"Don't try to talk me out of this, father."

"I'm not. I'm just pointing out a few realities to you. You remember how you felt when Beldaran died, don't you? Do you really want to go through that again—a half dozen times or so?"

"I can endure it, father. Maybe if I get married, my life will become normal. Maybe I'll get old, as well."

"I wouldn't make any large wagers on that, Pol. You've still got a lot of things to do, and if I'm reading the Mrin Codex correctly, you're going to be around for a long time. I'm very sorry, Pol, but we *aren't* normal. You've been here for almost a thousand years, and I've been kicking around for nearly five."

"*You* got married," she accused.

"I was *supposed* to, and your mother was very different. She lived longer, for one thing."

"Maybe marrying me will extend Ontrose's life, as well."

"I wouldn't count on it. It might *seem* longer to him, though."

"What's that suppose to mean?"

"You're not the easiest person in the world to get along with, Pol."

Her eyes turned cold. "I think we've just about exhausted the possibilities of this conversation, father. Go back to the Vale and keep your nose out of my affairs."

"Don't throw the word 'affair' around like that, Pol. It makes me nervous."

She drew herself up. "That will do, father," she told me. Then she turned and stormed away.

I stayed around for another couple of weeks, and I even met Ontrose. He was a nice enough young fellow, I suppose, and he seemed to understand the situation much better than Pol did. He adored her, of course, but he was fully aware of just how long she'd been in Vo Wacune—about six hundred years, if my arithmetic is correct. I was fairly sure that he was not going to ask her any inappropriate questions, no matter how much she might have wanted him to.

Finally I left and started back for the Vale. I have certain advantages, so I was fairly sure that nothing was going to come of Pol's infatuation. She's frequently mentioned in both the Darine and the Mrin codices, but there's no reference to a husband until much later. Either she was going to come to her senses, or Ontrose would live out his life without ever asking her to marry him. In either case nothing embarrassing was likely to happen.

I went back to my studies, but it was only three years later when Pol called me, rousing me out of a sound sleep in the middle of one blustery night. *"Father!"* Her voice sounded desperate. *"I need you!"*

"What's the matter?"

"The Asturians have betrayed us. They've formed an alliance with the Mimbrates, and they're marching on Vo Wacune. Hurry, father. There isn't much time."

I rolled out of bed, dressed, and picked up my traveling cloak. I did stop for a few moments to look at a certain passage in the Mrin Codex before I left, however. I hadn't been entirely sure what it meant before, but Polgara's urgent summons had suddenly made everything clear.

Fabled Vo Wacune was doomed. The only thing I could do now was try to get Pol out of there before the inevitable happened.

I hurried westward to the edge of the Vale through the tag end of that windy night and went wolf. There wasn't much point in trying to sprout feathers. I wouldn't have made much headway trying to fly into the teeth of that howling gale.

It was two days later and I was about halfway across Ulgoland before the wind finally abated. Then I took wing and was able to make better time.

I reached Vo Wacune about midafternoon of the following day, but I didn't go immediately into the marble city. I circled over the surrounding forest instead, and it didn't take me very long to locate the Asturians. They were no more than a few leagues from the gates of Vo Wacune. They'd be in place by morning, and there was absolutely nothing anybody could do to stop them. I swore and flew on back to the city.

Normally, I'll change back to my own form before I enter any populated place, but this was an emergency. I flew on and settled into a tree in Pol's garden.

As it turned out, she was in the garden, and she wasn't alone. Ontrose was with her. He was wearing chain mail, and he had a sword belted around his waist. "It must needs be, dear lady," he was saying to her. "Thou must go from Vo Wacune to a place of safety. The Asturians are almost at the city gates."

I slid back into my real form and climbed down out of the tree. "He's right, Pol," I said. Ontrose looked a little startled, but Pol was used to that sort of thing.

"Where have you been?" she demanded.

"I ran into some wind. Get your things together. We've got to get you out of here right now."

"I'm not going anywhere. Now that you're here, we can drive off the Asturians."

"No, as a matter of fact, we can't. It's prohibited. I'm sorry, Pol, but this has to happen, and we're not allowed to interfere."

"Is it certain, Ancient One?" Ontrose asked me.

"I'm afraid so, Ontrose. Has Polgara told you about the prophecies?" He nodded gravely.

"The passage in the Mrin Codex is very obscure, but there's not much question now about what it means. You might want to talk with the duke. If you hurry, you *may* be able to get the women and children to safety, but the city's not going to be here in a few days. I saw the Asturians as I was coming in. They're throwing everything they've got at you."

"They will have much less when they return to Vo Astur," he said bleakly.

"I'm not leaving," Polgara said stubbornly.

"Thou art in error, dear Lady," he told her quite firmly. "Thou wilt accompany thy father and go from this place."

"No! I won't leave you!"

"His Grace, the duke, hath placed me in command of the defense of the city, Lady Polgara. It is my responsibility to deploy our forces. There is no place in that deployment for thee. I therefore instruct thee to depart. Go."

"No!"

"Thou art the duchess of Erat, Lady Polgara, and therefore of the Wacite nobility. Thine oath of fealty to his Grace, our duke, demands thine obedience. Do not dishonor thy station by this stubborn refusal. Make ready. Thou shalt depart within the hour."

Her chin came up sharply. "That was unkindly said, my Lord," she accused.

"The truth often *is* unkindly, my Lady. We both have responsibilities. I will not fail mine. Do not fail thine. Now go."

Her eyes suddenly filled with helpless tears. She embraced him fiercely and then fled back into the house.

"Thanks, Ontrose," I said simply, clasping his hand. "I wasn't making very much headway there."

"Care for her, Ancient One. She is the very core of my life."

"I will, Ontrose, and we'll remember you."

"That is, perhaps, the best that one can hope for. Now I must go and see to our defenses. Farewell, Ancient Belgarath."

"Farewell, Ontrose."

And so I took my weeping daughter out of the doomed city. We went north, crossed the River Camaar, and journeyed back through Muros toward the pass that led across the mountains to Algaria. I kept a very close watch on Polgara the whole time—I didn't want any backsliding, but it probably wasn't really necessary. She *was*, as Ontrose had so pointedly reminded her, a member of the nobility. She had her orders, and she was not likely to disobey.

She refused to talk to me, but that was to be expected, I guess. What I *didn't* expect was her adamant refusal to return to the Vale with me. When we reached the tumbled ruin of her mother's cottage, she stopped. "This is as far as I'm going," she told me.

"What?"

"You heard me, father. I'm going to stay here."

"You have work to do, Pol."

"That's too bad. *You'll* have to take care of it. Go back to your tower and snuggle up to your prophecies, but leave me out of it. We're through, father. This is the end of it. Now go away and don't bother me any more."

I could see that there was no point in trying to argue with her. I'd been through my own grief, so I had some idea of what she was enduring. I'd have to keep an eye on her, of course—from a distance. She'd just spent hundreds of years in Arendia, and some of it might have rubbed off. Arendish ladies turn suicidal at the drop of a hat. If the least little disappointment comes along, an Arendish lady immediately starts thinking about knives and poison and rivers and high towers they can jump from. Pol would get over this eventually, but in the meantime, she'd have to be watched.

I went back to the Vale and enlisted the twins. I'd have used Beldin, too, but he'd gone back to Mallorea. We took turns hiding in the bushes near Poledra's cottage for the next five or six years. At first my brokenhearted daughter simply camped out in the ruins, but eventually she started making some minimal repairs. I felt that to be a good sign, and the twins and I started to relax a bit. We still watched her, though.

The First Borune Dynasty was still in power in Tol Honeth during the early centuries of the fourth millennium, and they'd established a professional diplomatic service—largely to keep things stirred up in Arendia. Tolnedra *definitely* didn't want a unified Arendia on her northern border. Tolnedran ambassadors were also dispatched to Val Alorn and Boktor, and trade was soon established. The Drasnians had made some tentative contacts with the Nadraks again, and the fur trade began to flourish. The Chereks were of necessity involved, since they were the only sailors in the world who could negotiate the treacherous currents in the Cherek Bore.

The inviolability of the Isle of the Winds drove the Borunes crazy for some reason. They were positive that the Cherek blockade was in place to hide some vast treasure on the Isle, and they desperately wanted a piece of it. As long as they were so hysterical about it, I decided that the best way to calm them down was to let them take a look for themselves to find out that there wasn't anything of value on the Isle. The isolation of the Rivans was starting to make me nervous. I remembered the lesson of Maragor all too well.

So I went to Val Alorn and told the Chereks to relax their blockade a bit. Tolnedrans want a treaty for everything, so the results were the Accords of Val Alorn—3097, I think. A fleet of Tolnedran merchant vessels set sail for the city of Riva almost immediately.

I'd assumed that the King of Cherek would advise the Rivans of the new arrangement, but he had his mind on the last clan war in Cherek, so he overlooked it. Thus the Rivans weren't expecting company, so they didn't open their gates. The Tolnedran merchants tried to set up shop on the beach, but the wind kept blowing their tents away, and the Rivans refused to come out of their city.

The Borune Dynasty had been going downhill steadily for a hundred years or so, and the last Borune Emperor, clearly an idiot, succumbed to the importunings of the merchant princes and dispatched legions to force the gates of the City of Riva. I'm not an expert on commerce, but it seems to me that trying to drive customers into your shop at sword-point is *not* a good way to do business.

The Rivans responded in a fairly predictable way. They opened the gates of their city, but they *didn't* come out for a shopping spree. They wiped out five Tolnedran legions and then systematically burned every ship in their harbor.

Ran Borune XXIV was incensed. He was preparing to launch the full might of the empire at the Isle of the Winds when a note from the Cherek Ambassador to Tol Honeth brought him up short.

The note is sort of a classic, so I'll repeat it here verbatim:

> Majesty:
> Know that Aloria will permit no attack upon Riva. The fleets of Cherek, whose masts rise as thick as the trees of the forest, will fall upon your flotilla, and the legions of Tolnedra will

feed the fish from the hook of Arendia to the farthest reaches of the Sea of the Winds. The battalions of Drasnia will march south, crushing all in their paths and lay siege to your cities. The horsemen of Algaria shall sweep across the mountains and shall lay waste your empire from end to end with fire and sword.

Know that in the day you attack Riva will the Alorns make war upon you, and you shall surely perish, and your empire also.

And that more or less ended the Tolnedran threat in the North. Borune legal experts immediately dug into the Accords of Val Alorn looking for loopholes, but all they found was a deliberately obscure clause I'd inserted. It read: "—but Aloria shall maintain Riva and keep it whole." Cherek and Drasnia had agreed not to make war on Tolnedra, but *Aloria* hadn't. I've always been rather proud of that little bit of legal trickery.

After I'd explained the situation to the Rivan King, he relaxed his restrictions a bit and permitted the merchants to build a sort of village on the beach. It wasn't very profitable, but it kept the Tolnedrans from the brink of insanity.

The last Borune emperor died childless, and the usual circus erupted in Tol Honeth as the great families contested with each other for the throne. Unfortunately, perhaps, the major houses had been quietly importing poisons from Nyissa, and various candidates for the Imperial Throne *and* assorted members of the Council of Advisors gave ample evidence of the virulence of those poisons.

Eventually the Honeths won out—largely because they had enough money to buy the necessary votes and to pay the exorbitant prices the Nyissans charged for their poisons. The Honethite family had lapsed into almost total incompetence, however, and fortunately they stayed in power only for about three hundred years or so. Then the Borunes came to power again. The Second Borune Dynasty was also a fairly short one, but it accomplished quite a bit. They expanded their highway system in Tolnedra proper, and they dispatched twenty legions "as a gesture of goodwill" to what's now Sendaria to construct the network of highways that linked the city of Sendar and the port at Camaar with Muros in the interior and Darine on the northeast coast.

The Chereks didn't much care for that idea, since it permitted Tolnedran merchants to avoid the Cherek Bore entirely by shipping goods from Kotu to Darine and then overland to Camaar without Cherek hands ever touching them.

The last Emperor of the Second Borune Dynasty, the childless Ran Borune XII, took a direct hand in choosing his successor, and he passed imperial power on to the Horbite family. The Council of Advisors received no bribes, and the Honeths and the Vordues had no chance to muddy the waters by poisoning each other.

The Horbites proved to be a happy choice. Ran Horb I was competent, but his son, Ran Horb II, was probably the greatest emperor in all Tolnedran history. His achievements were staggering. He brought an end to open warfare in Arendia by allying himself with the weaker faction, the Mimbrates. I don't think either Polgara or I grieved very much when, in 3822, Vo Astur was destroyed and the Asturians were chased back into the forest. We both still remembered what the Asturians had done to the beautiful city of Vo Wacune.

Ran Horb II moved right on from there. He built an imperial highway, the Great West Road, up through Arendia, linking northern Tolnedra with the port at Camaar and with the entire highway system in Sendaria. He incidentally established that kingdom in 3827, reasoning that, so long as he controlled the highways, it was more efficient to let the Sendars govern themselves. He concluded a treaty with Cho-Dorn the Old, chief of the Clan-Chiefs of Algaria and built the Great North Road that reached from Muros up across northwestern Algaria to the causeway that ran up through the fens to Boktor, where it connected with the North Caravan Route into Gar og Nadrak.

He normalized trade with the Nyissans, and, in the twilight of his life, he concluded a treaty with the Murgos that established the South Caravan Route to Rak Goska.

There was grumbling in Val Alorn about all of this. Ran Horb II clearly saw that as long as the Chereks controlled the seas, Tolnedra would be more or less at their mercy. Ran Horb's highways bypassed the Chereks. Tolnedrans no longer had to go to sea. They could move their goods overland without ever smelling salt water.

This is not to imply that the highways were all completed during Ran Horb's lifetime. It took the rest of the Horbite Dynasty to complete that task. During the process, the modern world, the world as we currently know it, gradually began to take shape.

The highways made travel easier, of course, but my gratitude to Ran Horb II stems largely from his almost offhand creation of the Kingdom of Sendaria. The Mrin Codex, and to a lesser degree the Darine, told me quite clearly that I was going to need Sendaria later.

Oddly, when you consider their achievements, the Horbite Dynasty lasted for only one hundred fifty years. The son of Ran Horb VI was drowned in a boating accident when his father was quite old, so there was no heir to the imperial throne.

Then the ill-fated Ranite family came to power. The Ranites didn't accomplish anything during their ninety years in power because a hereditary ailment in their line inevitably struck them down in their prime.

They went through seven emperors in ninety years, and most of them were sick all the time. In effect, they were nothing more than caretakers.

Then in 4001 the Vorduvians ascended the throne, and, since Tol Vordue is a seaport, they immediately began to let the Horbite highway system fall into disrepair. I'm not sure how many Vorduvian ships will have to be sunk by Cherek war boats before the Vorduvians begin to come to grips with reality.

I've never really cared all that much for the Vorduvians anyway, and *that* particular idiocy made me throw up my hands in disgust.

There was something nagging at me, though. I seemed to keep remembering a very obscure passage in the Mrin Codex. I went back to my tower and dug out my copy and went looking for it. One of the things that makes the Mrin Codex so difficult lies in the fact that it doesn't have any continuity. The past and the present and the future are all jumbled together, so it doesn't read chronologically. There's no way to know which EVENT is going to come first and which will come next. The scribes who took it all down made no attempt to reset it into anything resembling coherence, so when you go looking for something, you have to start at the beginning and plow your way through the whole incomprehensible mess.

I almost missed it. Maybe if I hadn't been so disgusted with the Vordues, I would have, but I was thinking about roads when I came across it again.

"Behold," it said, "when that which was straight becomes crooked, and that which was sound becomes unsound, it shall be a warning unto thee, Ancient and Beloved." That got my immediate attention. The Tolnedran roads *were* becoming unsound. There were places in Sendaria where they'd turned into deep bogs of soupy mud—and, since they were impassable, people detoured out around them, and the straight *was* becoming crooked. It stretched things a bit, but I had become used to that in reading the Mrin. I read on eagerly. "Beware," it continued, "for there is a serpent abroad in the land, and he shall bring the Guardian low." That didn't seem to mean anything at all. Then I took the scroll to the window and peered closely at it in full sunlight, I could faintly make out the fact that one of the scribes had scrubbed out the word "she" and substituted "he" instead. The three scribes had probably argued about it, and the one who'd written down that "she" probably had been overruled. But what if he'd been right? When you talk about a female snake in our part of the world, you're talking about Salmissra.

I read on. "For the Guardian is weighted down with eld, and the serpent will come upon him unawares, and the venom of the serpent shall chill his heart and the hearts of all his issue besides. Hasten, Ancient and

Beloved. The life of the last issue of the Guardian's line lieth in deadly peril. Save him, lest all be lost, and the darkness reign forever."

I stared at it in horror.

Gorek the Wise, king of Riva and Guardian of the Orb, *was* a very old man, and the Tolnedran roads *were* falling apart, and Salmissra had *never* been the sort you wanted to trust.

I'll grant you that it was very scanty, but the way those words kept screaming inside my head sent me flying down the steps of my tower four at a time.

I absolutely *had* to get to the Isle of the Winds immediately.

CHAPTER
THIRTY-
TWO

I'd begun to form the image of the falcon in my mind before I even hit the foot of the stairs, and as soon as I was outside I started sprouting feathers. Falcons are faster than most other birds, and the screaming inside my head convinced me that speed was essential here. I didn't *like* flying—I still don't—but I've done a lot of things I haven't liked over the years. We do what we have to do, like it or not.

I don't think it ever occurred to me *not* to take Polgara along. I knew that she had something very important to do when we reached the Isle of the Winds. I didn't know exactly what it was, but I *did* know that this would be an absolute catastrophe if she weren't with me.

I think that perhaps I'll go to Riva and have a talk with Garion about that. I'm beginning to develop a theory, and I'd like to check it with him. That peculiar voice has spent much more time with him than it ever did with me, so he's far more familiar with its quirks than I am. Every now and then, though, I get a strong feeling that I've been tampered with. I'll be plodding along about half asleep, and then something will happen— and it doesn't always have to be something out of the ordinary. In fact, it usually isn't. Most of the time it's something so commonplace that no-body else even notices it. But when it *does* happen, something inside my head clicks together, and I'm moving before I'm even aware of it. I sus-pect that certain things were planted in my brain during that trip Cherek and his boys and I took to Cthol Mishrak. I'm not actually aware of them until that unremarkable incident comes along, and then I know immediately what I'm supposed to do.

All right. I'm digressing. So what?

It didn't take me very long to reach Poledra's cottage. It was early spring, but it was already fairly warm, and Polgara was out spading up her kitchen garden. Pol has very fair skin, and she sunburns quite easily. She'd woven herself a ridiculous-looking straw hat to keep the sun off her nose. I probably shouldn't say it, but it made her look just a bit like a mushroom.

I swooped in, thrust down my talons, and had started to change back before they even touched the ground. "I need you, Pol," I told her.

"I needed you once, remember?" she replied coldly. "You didn't seem very interested. Now I get the chance to return the favor. Go away, father."

"We don't have time for this, Polgara. You can make clever remarks later. Right now we have to go to the Isle of the Winds. Gorek's in danger."

"Lots of people are in danger, father. It happens all the time." She paused. "Who's Gorek?"

"Have you had your head turned off for all these centuries? Don't you have any idea at all about what's going in the world?"

"My world ended when you let the Asturians destroy Vo Wacune, Old Man."

"No, as a matter of fact, it didn't. You're still who you are, and you're coming with me to the Isle of the Winds even if I have to pick you up in my talons and *take* you there."

"As badly as you fly? Don't be ridiculous. Who's this Gorek you're so worried about?"

"He's the Rivan king, Pol, the Guardian of the Orb."

"The Chereks are still out there in the Sea of the Winds. They'll protect him."

"You *have* been out of touch, Pol. The Chereks are letting people get through now."

"*What?* Are you insane? Why did you permit that?"

"It's a long story, and we don't have the leisure to go through it. Don't waste time with owls this time, Pol. Go to a falcon instead."

"Not without a good reason, I won't."

I resisted the urge to swear at her. "I just dredged the meaning out of a passage in the Mrin. Salmissra's going to make an attempt on the life of the Rivan king—and his entire family. If she manages to pull it off, Torak wins."

"*Salmissra? Why didn't you say so in the first place?*"

"Because you wouldn't let me."

"Let's move, father!"

"Hold on for just a moment. I have to warn the twins." I concentrated and sent out my thought. "*Brothers!*" I called to them.

"*Belgarath?*" Beltira replied, sounding a little startled. "*What's the matter?*"

"*There's going to be an attempt on the life of the Rivan King. Pol and I are going there right now. We'll be falcons if you need to reach us. Get word to Beldin. Tell him to get back home right now.*"

"*At once, Belgarath. Hurry!*"

"All right, Pol," I said then. "Let's go to Riva."

We both slipped into the forms of those fierce hunting birds, spiraled upward, and then struck out to the northwest across Ulgoland. At one point, a few leagues to the east of Prolgu, we encountered a flock of Harpies. I've a few suspicions about that. I've traveled around in Ulgoland quite a few times over the years, and that's the only time I've ever seen Harpies. I wouldn't be at all surprised to discover that they'd been put in our path deliberately to delay us. Harpies, however, don't fly all that well—certainly not well enough to catch a pair of streaking falcons. Pol and I simply swooped clear of them and flew on, leaving them floundering around in the air behind us.

The incident's hardly worth even noting, except that it was a clear indication that *somebody* out there was doing his best to delay us. I started to keep an eye out for the dragon at that point. *That* could have been a problem.

We didn't see her, however, and we managed to reach the western border of Ulgoland without any further incident.

It was growing dark, but Pol and I kept flying. I was hungry and tired, but that urgent voice in my head kept pushing me on. Pol flies better than I do, but I'm sure that our frantic pace was wearing her down almost as much as it was exhausting me. We kept going, however.

The sky behind us was starting to turn pale with the approach of dawn when we passed over Camaar and flew out across the dark waters of the Sea of the Winds.

It must have been almost noon before we saw the Isle of the Winds ahead of us to the west. We began a long, shallow descent, and the harbor at Riva seemed to come rushing up at us as we streaked down toward the city.

We'd nearly killed ourselves getting there, but we still arrived about ten minutes too late.

It was as we were crossing the choppy waters of the harbor when I discovered why Polgara had absolutely *had* to come along. I didn't even see the little boy floundering around in the chill waters of the bay, but Pol did. We must have been about thirty feet above the water and streaking in as fast as we could fly when she suddenly flared her wings and blurred back into her own form in midair. She arched herself forward effortlessly and plunged headfirst down toward the water, her arms stretched above her head. I've seen a lot of young men dive headfirst into pools and rivers and even into the sea from time to time—usually to impress young women—but I've never seen a dive like that one. She cut into the water like a knife, and it seemed to me that she was down forever. Fortunately, the harbor at Riva is very deep. You don't want to make that kind of dive unless you've got a *lot* of water under you.

She finally popped to the surface no more than ten feet from the struggling child, and with a few strokes, she had him.

"YES!" the previously silent intruder in my head exulted.

"*Oh, shut up!*" I told it.

There was absolute chaos in the commercial enclave on the beach. One glance told me that Gorek and his son and the other members of his family were all dead. The Rivans, of course, were busy butchering a group of Nyissan merchants. I swooped in, flared my wings, and changed. "Stop!" I thundered at the vengeful Rivans.

"They killed our king!" a burly fellow screamed at me. Tears were running down his face, and he was clearly hysterical.

"Don't you want to find out why?" I shouted, but I saw immediately that it was useless even to try to talk to him—or to any of the others who had been there to guard the king. I was exhausted, but I still had a little bit left in me. I drew in my Will and put an impenetrable shield around the last two Nyissans. Then, as an afterthought, I put the pair of them to sleep. I knew Salmissra well enough to realize that her assassins probably had been ordered to kill themselves once their mission had been accomplished. They were armed with poisoned knives, and they undoubtedly had little vials of toxic substances tucked into every pocket.

"*Polgara!*" I sent out my thought. "*Is the boy all right?*"

"*Yes, father. I've got him.*"

"*Stay out of sight! Don't let anybody see you!*"

"*All right.*"

Then Brand came running toward the commercial enclave from the city gate. I've never fully understood why the Rivan Warder always takes the name Brand. By the time I got around to asking somebody, the origins of the custom had long since been forgotten. In Arendia, where castles are commonplace, the Rivan Warder would have been called a seneschal. In some of the other kingdoms of the west—and even in some of the semiautonomous kingdoms in Mallorea—he'd have been called the prime minister. His duties were approximately the same, no matter what he was called. He was supposed to handle the administrative details that kept the kingdom running. Like most of the men who've held the position, this one was a solid, competent man with a deep sense of loyalty. He was, however, still an Alorn, and the news that Gorek had been murdered made him go all to pieces. His eyes were steaming tears, and he was bellowing with rage. He had his sword out, and he ran at my invisible barrier swinging with all his might. I let him chop at it for a while, and then I took his sword away from him.

Yes, I *can* do that if I have to. When it's necessary, I can be the strongest man in the world.

"Gorek's dead, Belgarath!" he sobbed.

"People die. It happens all the time." I said it in a flat, unemotional voice.

His head came up sharply, and he stared at me in disbelief.

"Pull yourself together, Brand," I told him. "We've got things to do. First off: order your soldiers *not* to kill those two murderers. I need some answers, and I can't get answers out of dead men."

"But—"

"These are just hirelings. I want to find out who hired them." I already had a fair idea, of course, but I wanted confirmation. More than that, though, I needed to jolt Brand back to his senses.

He drew in a long, shuddering breath. "Sorry, Belgarath," he said. "I guess I lost my head."

"That's better. Tell your men to back away from those two. Then get somebody here you can depend on to follow orders. I want those two reptiles put into a safe place and guarded very closely. As soon as I let them wake up, they'll try to kill themselves. You'd better strip them. I'm sure they've got poison somewhere in their clothes."

He straightened, and his eyes went flinty. He turned. "Captain Vant!" he said sharply to a nearby officer. "Come here!" He then proceeded to give the teary-eyed officer some very crisp orders.

Vant saluted and gathered up about a platoon of men. Then I spoke briefly with the soldiers. I must have made an impression on them, because they did as they were told.

"All right, Brand," I said then. "Let's walk down the beach a ways. I don't want anybody to hear what I'm going to tell you."

He nodded, and we walked off toward the south. The beach at Riva

is gravel, and the waves make quite a bit of noise when they come crashing in. I stopped at the water's edge about a quarter of a mile away from
the enclave. "What's the name of Gorek's youngest grandson?" I asked.

"Prince Geran," he replied.

I'm sure that most of you recognize the name. Pol and I have sort of kept
it alive over the centuries.

"All right," I said. "Keep a tight grip on yourself. I don't want you to start
dancing for joy. There are people watching. Prince Geran is alive."

"Thank the Gods!"

"Well, thank my daughter, actually. She's the one who rescued him.
He's a very brave little boy. He got away from the assassins by swimming
out into the harbor. He doesn't swim all that well, but at least he got
away."

"Where is he?"

"Polgara's got him. She's keeping him out of sight."

"I'll send soldiers to escort him back to the Citadel."

"No, you won't. *Nobody's* going to find out that he's still alive. Pol
and I are going to take him into hiding, and you're going to give me your
word never to mention this to anybody."

"Belgarath! The Rivan King is the keeper of the Orb! He *must* be
here."

"No, actually he doesn't. Everybody in the world knows that the
Orb's here, and as long as the Rivan King's here, too, everybody in the
world knows where to find him. That's why we're going to have to separate them."

"Until the boy grows up?"

"It might be a little longer than that. The time *will* come, however,
when the Rivan King will return, and that'll be when the fun starts. The
next Rivan King who sits on that throne is going to be the Child of Light,
and *he's* the one we've been waiting for."

"The Godslayer?"

"We can hope so."

"Where are you going to take Prince Geran?"

"You don't need to know that, Brand. He'll be safe. That's all you
need to know." I looked up at the murky sky. "How much longer until it
gets dark?"

"A couple of hours anyway."

I swore.

"What's the matter?"

"My daughter and your king are out there in the bay, and that's very cold water. Excuse me a moment." I sent out my thought again. *"Polgara, where are you?"*

"We're at the end of the wharf, father. Is it safe to come out yet?"

"No. Stay where you are, and keep out of sight."

"The boy's getting very cold, father."

"Heat the water around you, Pol. You know how to do that. You've been heating your bathwater for centuries."

"What are you up to, Old Wolf?"

"I'm hiding the Rivan King. Get used to it, Pol, because we'll be doing it for quite a long time." Then I pulled my thought away from her. "All right, Brand," I said aloud. "Let's go up to the Citadel. I want to have a long talk with those Nyissans."

We went back up the beach and then on to the city gates.

"Who's going to guard the Orb if you take our king away, Belgarath?" Brand asked me as we started up the stairs.

"You are."

"Me?"

"Of course. You're also going to stand in for the king while he's away, *and* you're going to pass all of this on to your successor. From now on, the Rivan Warder's going to be the only man alive who knows what we're doing—normal man, anyway. Pol and I and my brothers don't quite qualify as normal. We're counting on you, Brand. Don't let us down."

He swallowed hard. "You have my word, Ancient One."

"Good man."

The pair of Nyissan "merchants" who had lured Gorek and his family out of the Citadel by sending word that they had gifts from Queen Salmissra were still comatose, and a number of grim-faced Rivans were sharpening knives as they stood guard over them. "I'll do it," I announced. I said it very firmly in order to head off any protests.

I'll be the first to admit that I'm not as good at interrogation as my daughter is. If you're really interested in her methods, go talk with King Anheg of Cherek. He was present when she interrogated the earl of Jarvik. All she seems to have to do is show somebody something—something that must be pretty awful, because they start talking immediately. My methods are a bit more direct. I've always had a fair amount of success with pain. The only difference between *my* approach and that of your run-of-the-mill torturer lies in the fact that I can hurt people without causing them any physical injury. I can keep a man in agony for a week without killing him.

As it turned out, it didn't take me a week. After I'd erased the effects of the assorted narcotics swarming around in their blood, they became very tractable. Evidently there's a certain amount of discomfort involved when your favorite narcotic runs out. I added a few *other* discomforts, and they started begging me to let them talk.

"It was the queen!" one of them blubbered. "We did it because the queen commanded us to do it!"

"It wasn't her idea, though!" The other one overrode his companion. "A foreigner came to Sthiss Tor and spoke with Eternal Salmissra. It was only then that she summoned us to the throne room."

"Have you any idea of who this foreigner might have been?" I asked him.

"N-no!" he stammered. "Please don't hurt me any more!"

"Relax," I told him. "Is there anything else you'd like to share with me?"

"One of the young princes escaped us," the first one blurted. "He swam out into the harbor."

"And drowned?" one of the Rivan guards demanded before I could head off that question.

"No. A bird saved him."

"A bird?"

"I wouldn't pay too much attention to him," I said quickly. "Nyissans see things that aren't there all the time."

The Rivan gave me a suspicious look.

"Have you ever been really drunk?" I asked him.

"Well, maybe once or twice."

"Nyissans have found ways to get in that condition without beer."

"I've heard about that," he admitted.

"Now you've seen it. These two were still so drunk when I woke them up that they were probably seeing blue sheep and purple goats." I looked at Brand. "Do we need anything else?"

"*I* don't. Do you?"

"No, I guess that just about covers it." I waved one hand and put the two assassins back to sleep. I *didn't* want that one to talk about birds any more.

Certain versions of *The Book of Alorn* mention that story about the bird. Now you know where it came from. I've ridiculed the idea every time it came up, but there were still Rivans who believed it.

"What should we do with these two?" the fellow with the quick questions asked me.

I shrugged. "That's entirely up to you. I've got what I needed out of them. Coming, Brand?"

The two of us left the prison cell and went directly to Brand's private quarters. "You realize that this means war, don't you, Belgarath?" he said.

"I suppose so," I agreed. "It'd look suspicious if we didn't mount a punitive expedition against Nyissa at this point. Let's not do anything out of character. I don't want people to start making wild guesses right now."

"I'll send messages to Val Alorn, Boktor, and the Algarian stronghold."

"Don't bother. I'll take care of that myself. Now let's go fish my daughter and your king out of the bay. I want a ship moved to the end of the main wharf. Have the sailors tie it up there and then go ashore. I don't want anybody at all on board. Then you and I are going to take a little trip."

"Belgarath! I can't leave now!"

"You'll have to. I don't know how to sail a ship. We've got to get Polgara and Prince Geran to the coast of Sendaria, and we can't let anybody else know they're on board."

"I can sail the ship, Belgarath, but I'm going to need a crew."

"You've got one. Pol and I'll take care of manning your sails. We'll drop anchor a few miles north of Camaar. Pol will take the prince into hiding, I'll go to Val Alorn, and you'll go to Camaar to commandeer a crew from any Rivan ships in the harbor and get back here as quick as you can to start mobilizing. Let's go down to the harbor."

When the ship had been moved and the sailors had gone down the wharf, to the city, I sort of sauntered out to the end and stood looking ostentatiously out to sea. "Pol," I said quietly, "are you still there?"

"Where else *would* I be, you old fool?"

I let that slide by. "Stay where you are," I told her. "Brand's coming around with a small boat."

"What took you so long?"

"We had to wait until it got dark. I don't want anybody to see what we're doing."

"What were you talking about earlier—that business about hiding the Rivan King?"

"We don't have any choice, Pol. The Isle of the Winds isn't safe for the boy. We have to get him away from the Orb. Torak knows exactly where it is, and if the boy stays anywhere near it, we'll be able to count on a steady stream of assassins coming here to try to kill him."

"I thought Salmissra sent the assassins."

"She did, but somebody else put her up to it."

"Who?"

"I'm not sure. The next time I see her, I'll ask her."

"Under the circumstances, you might have a little trouble getting into Sthiss Tor."

"I rather doubt that, Pol," I answered grimly. "I'm going to take a few Alorns with me."

"A few?"

"The Chereks, the Rivans, the Drasnians, and the Algars. I'm going to take all of Aloria with me when I go, Pol. I don't think I'll have any trouble getting into Sthiss Tor at all." I glanced over my shoulder and then looked back out to sea. "Here comes Brand with the boat. We'll get you and the boy safely aboard ship, and then we'll sail."

"Sail? Where?"

"Sendaria, Pol. We'll decide what we're going to do when we get there."

PART
FIVE

THE SECRET

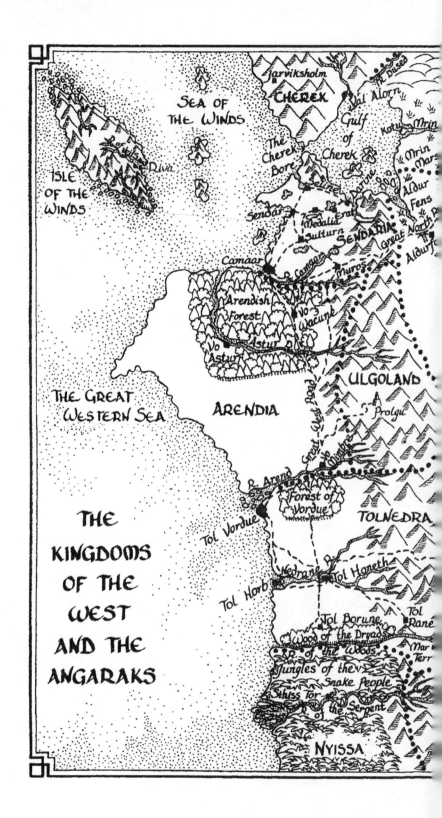

THE

KINGDOMS

OF THE

WEST

AND THE

ANGARAKS

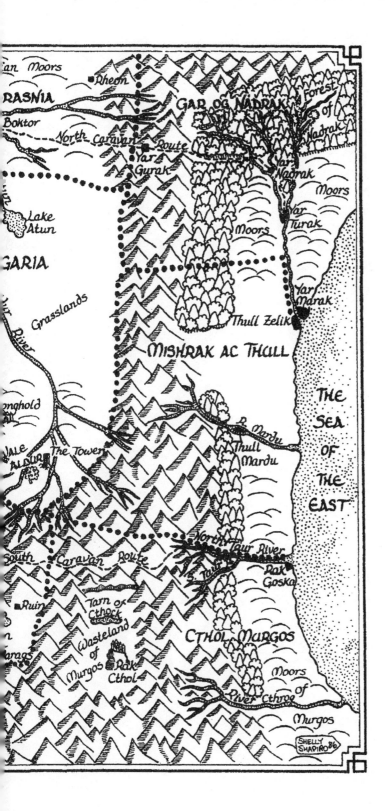

an Moors
■Rheon
RASNIA
Boktor
North Caravan
Route
Yar
Gurak
Lake
Atun
GARIA
Grasslands
r River
GAR OG NADRAK
Forest
of
Nadrak
Yar
Nadrak
Moors
Yar
Turak
Moors
Yar
Marak
Thull Zelik
MISHRAK AC THULL
THE
SEA
OF
THE
EAST
nghold
all
VALE
ALDUR
The Tower
R. Mardu
Thull
Mardu
South
Caravan
Route
North
Taur River
Taur
Rak
Goska
■Ruin
Tarn of
Cthok
Wasteland
of
Murgos
Rak
Cthol
CTHOL MURGOS
Moors
of
arags
River Cthrog
Murgos

SHELLY
SHAPIRO 86

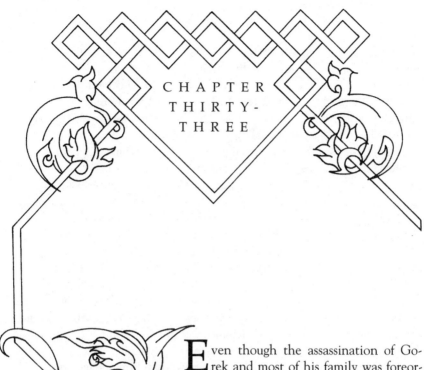

CHAPTER THIRTY-THREE

Even though the assassination of Gorek and most of his family was foreordained and necessary, I still have twinges of guilt about it. Maybe if I'd been just a bit more alert, I'd have interpreted that passage in the Mrin an hour—even a half hour—sooner, and Pol and I could have reached Riva in time. Maybe if Pol hadn't argued with me for quite so long—

Maybe, maybe, maybe. Sometimes it seems when I look back on my life it's nothing but a long string of regretful maybes. The maybe that really stands out, though, is the one that suggests that I'm not emotionally equipped to deal with predestination. It makes me feel helpless, and I don't like that. I always seem to think that there might have been something I could have done to change the outcome. A turnip can just sit there saying "What will be will be." I'm supposed to be a little more resourceful.

Ah, well . . .

It took us the usual two days to reach the Sendarian coast. Brand's eyes got a little wild the first time I reset his sails without even getting up from where I was sitting. That happens fairly often, you know. Despite the fact that people are *intellectually* aware of sorcery, when the real thing happens right in front of their eyes, it tends to upset them. I'm not sure what he'd expected, though. I had told him that Polgara was going to be lending a hand with the mechanics of sailing that ship, but he should have known better. Prince Geran was only about six years old, and he'd just watched his entire family being murdered. He needed Pol far more than I did. I'd only said it to Brand to head off one of those tiresome arguments about the possible and the impossible.

Have you ever had that peculiar feeling that what's happening now has happened before? One of the reasons you have is because it's really true. The interruption of the Purpose of the universe had locked every-thing in one spot, and time and events were simply marching in place. This might help to explain those "repetitions" Garion and I used to talk about. In *my* case, though, I get not only the feeling that something's happened before, but also a slightly different feeling that something's go-ing to happen again. I got that feeling with bells on it as we approached the Sendarian coast.

It was a blustry morning in early summer with the clouds playing ducks and drakes with the sun, and Polgara and the young prince had just come up on deck. It wasn't particularly warm, and Pol drew the little boy protectively close and half enclosed him with her blue cloak just as the sun momentarily broke through. Somehow that brief image seemed to freeze and lock itself in my mind. I can still call it back with absolute clarity—not that I really have to. I've seen Polgara hovering over a long succession of sandy-haired little boys with that obscure pain in her eyes once or twice in every generation for the past thirteen hundred years and more. Protecting those little boys wasn't the *only* reason she'd been born, but it was certainly one of the important ones.

We dropped anchor in a secluded cove about five miles north of Camaar and then we went ashore in the ship's longboat. "Camaar's that way," I told Brand, pointing south.

"Yes, Ancient One, I know." Brand was polite enough not to take of-fense when somebody pointed out the obvious.

"Round up a crew and get back to Riva," I instructed. "I'll go to Val Alorn and tell Valcor what's happened. He'll be along with his fleet to pick you and your army up in a couple of weeks, I'd imagine. I'll talk it over with him when I get to Val Alorn. Then I'll go talk with the Drasnians and the Algars. I think we might want them to go overland while you and Valcor sail south. I want to come at Nyissa from both sides. We'll probably all get there about midsummer."

"Good time for a war," he noted bleakly.

"No, Brand. There's *no* good time for a war. This one's necessary, though. Salmissra needs to be persuaded to keep her nose out of things that don't concern her."

"You seem to be taking this very calmly." It was almost an accusation.

"Appearances can be deceiving. I can get angry later. Right now I've got to map out this campaign."

"Will you be coming down with Valcor?"

"I haven't exactly decided yet. In any case, we'll all get together again in Sthiss Tor."

"See you there, then." He went over and dropped to one knee in front of Geran. "I don't think we'll see each other again, your Majesty," he said sadly. "Good-bye."

The little boy was red-eyed from weeping, but he straightened and looked his Warder full in the face. "Good-bye, Brand," he said. "I know I can count on you to take care of my people and to guard the Orb." He was a brave little boy, and he'd have made a good king if things had turned out differently.

Brand rose, saluted, and started off down the beach.

"Are you going back to your mother's cottage?" I asked Pol.

"I don't think so, father. Zedar knows where it is, and I'm sure he's told Torak about it. I don't want visitors showing up when I'm not expecting them. I still have that manor house at Erat. That should be safe enough until you get back from Nyissa."

"You haven't been there for a long time, Pol," I objected. "The house probably collapsed years ago."

"No, father. I asked it not to."

"Sendaria's a different country now, Pol, and the Sendars don't even remember the Wacite Arends. An abandoned house almost invites somebody to move in."

She shook her head. "The Sendars don't even know it's there. My roses have seen to that."

"I don't follow you."

"You wouldn't believe how big a rosebush can get if you encourage it just a bit, and I had *lots* of roses planted around the house. Trust me, father. The house is still there, but no one's seen it since the fall of Vo Wacune. The boy and I'll be safe there."

"Well, maybe—for the time being, anyway. We'll come up with something else after I've dealt with Salmissra."

"If it's safe, why move him?"

"Because the line has to be continued, Pol. That means he has to get married and produce a son. We might have a little trouble persuading some girl to break through a rose thicket to get to him."

"Are you leaving now, grandfather?" Geran asked me, his small face very serious. For some reason *all* of those little boys have called me that. I think it's in their blood.

"Yes, Geran," I told him. "You'll be safe with your Aunt Pol. There's something I have to attend to."

"I don't suppose you'd care to wait a little while?"

"What did you have in mind?"

"I'd sort of like to go along, but I'm too little right now. If you could wait a few years, I'll be old enough to kill Salmissra myself."

He was an Alorn, all right.

"No, Geran. I'd better take care of it for you. Salmissra might die of natural causes before you grow up, and we wouldn't want that, would we?"

He sighed. "No, I suppose not," he agreed reluctantly. "Would you hit her once or twice for me, grandfather?"

"You have my absolute word on that, boy."

"Hard," he added fiercely.

"*Men!*" Polgara muttered.

"I'll keep in touch, Pol," I promised her. "Now get off this beach. There might be more Nyissans lurking about."

And so Polgara took the grieving little prince up past Lake Sulturn toward Medalia and Erat, and I changed form once again and flew due north toward Val Alorn.

In the hundred and seventy-five years or so since Ran Horb II had founded the kingdom of Sendaria and a former rutabaga farmer named Fundor had been elevated to the throne, the Sendars had been busy—mostly cutting down trees. I don't entirely approve of that. The notion of killing something that's been alive for a thousand years just so you can plant turnips seems a little immoral to me. Sendars, however, are compulsively neat, and they just adore straight lines. If the Sendars start building a road and a mountain gets in their way, the notion of going around it never occurs to them. They'll cut through it instead. The Tolnedrans tend to be the same way. I suppose it stands to reason, though. The Sendars are a peculiar mixture of all races, so a few Tolnedran characteristics were bound to be a part of their nature.

Don't get me wrong here. I *like* Sendars. They're a little stuffy sometimes, but I think they're the most decent and sensible people in the world. Their mixed background seems to have purged them of the obsessions that infect other races.

How did I get off on that? You really shouldn't let me digress that way. We'll be at this forever if I don't stick to the point.

Anyway, when you view it from above, the kingdom of Sendaria resembles nothing quite so much as a checkered tablecloth. I flew over the capital city of Sendar and continued on toward Lake Seline. Then there was a cluster of mountains, and Sendaria finally came to an abrupt end at the Cherek Bore. I won't repeat the dreadful pun some witty fellow came up with by playing around with the ambiguity implicit in the word "bore."

The tide was rushing out of the Gulf of Cherek when I flew over the Bore, and the Great Maelstrom was whirling around, joyously trying to pick boulders up off the bottom. It doesn't take much to make a whirlpool happy.

Then I flew along the east coast of the peninsula past Eldrigshaven and Trellheim, and I finally reached Val Alorn.

Val Alorn had been there for a very long time. I think there was a village in that general vicinity even before Torak cracked the world and formed the Gulf of Cherek in the process. The Chereks settled down to make a real city out of it after I divided Aloria. Bear-shoulders needed something to keep his mind occupied and off the fact that I'd just relieved him of most of his kingdom, I guess. To be perfectly honest about it, I've always found Val Alorn to be just a bit on the bleak side. The sky over the Cherek Peninsula is nearly always cloudy and grey. Did they *have* to make their city out of grey rock as well?

I settled to earth just south of the city and went around to the main gate that faced the harbor. Then I navigated the narrow streets where piles of dirty snow still lay in the shady places and eventually reached the palace and was admitted. I found King Valcor carousing with his earls in the great throneroom. Most of the time the throne room of the Kingdom of Cherek resembles nothing so much as a beer hall. Fortunately, I arrived about midday, and Valcor hadn't had time yet to drink himself into insensibility. He was boisterous, but there's nothing very unusual about that. Chereks, drunk or sober, are always boisterous. "Ho, Belgarath!" he bellowed at me from the throne, "come in and join us!" Valcor was a burly fellow with muddy brown hair and a vast beard. Like so many overly muscular men I've known, he'd gone to flab as middle age crept up on him. He wasn't exactly fat, but he was working on it. Despite the fact that he was the king, he was wearing a peasant smock with beerstains down the front.

I walked past the blazing firepit in the center of the hall and approached the throne. "Your Majesty," I greeted him perfunctorily. "You and I need to talk."

"Any time, Belgarath. Pull up a seat and have some beer."

"Privately, Valcor."

"I don't have any secrets from my earls."

"You will have in just a few minutes. Get up off your behind, Valcor, and let's go someplace where we can talk."

He looked a little startled. "You're serious, aren't you?"

"War does that to me." I chose the word carefully. It's one of the few words that'll get an Alorn's attention when he's been drinking.

"*War?* Where? With whom?"

"I'll tell you about it just as soon as we're alone."

He stood up and led me to a nearby room.

Valcor's reaction to the news I brought him was fairly predictable. It took me a little while to calm him down, but I finally persuaded him to stop swearing and chopping up furniture with his sword long enough to listen to me. "I'm going on to talk with Radek and Cho-Ram. Get your fleet ready and call in the clans. I'll either come back or send word to let you know when to start. You'll have to stop by the Isle of the Winds to pick up Brand and the Rivans on your way south."

"I'll deal with Salmissra myself."

"No, you won't. Salmissra's insulted the whole of Aloria, and the whole of Aloria's going to do something about it. I don't want you to offend Brand, Radek, and Cho-Ram by taking things into your own hands. You've got work to do, Valcor, so you'd better sober up and get cracking. I'm going on to Boktor. I'll be back in a couple of weeks."

It was about dawn of the following day when I reached Boktor. Since there were very few people about, I settled on the battlements of King Radek's palace. The sentry up there was noticeably startled when he turned around and saw me standing in a place he'd just passed. "I need to talk with the king," I told him. "Where is he?"

"I think he's still asleep. Who are you? And how did you get up here?"

"Does the name Belgarath ring any bells for you?"

He gaped at me.

"Close your mouth and take me to Radek," I told him. I get *so* tired of having people gawk at me when I'm in a hurry.

King Radek was snoring when I reached the royal bedchamber. The royal bed was seriously mussed up, and so was the royal playmate, a busty young woman who immediately dived under the covers when I entered. I jerked open the drapes at the window and turned around. "All right, Radek," I barked, "Wake up!"

His eyes popped open. Radek was a fairly young man. He was tall and lean, and he had a decidedly hooked nose. Drasnian noses seem to go off in all directions for some reason. Silk's nose is so pointed that from certain angles he looks like a stork, and Porenn's husband had a little pug nose that wasn't much bigger than a button. I hadn't had much chance to look at the nose of the young lady who'd burrowed under the covers when I'd entered. She'd moved fairly fast, and I'd been more interested in other things.

"Good morning, Belgarath," the king of Drasnia greeted me with un-ruffled calm. "Welcome to Boktor." Fortunately, he was an intelligent man and not nearly as excitable as Valcor, so he didn't waste time try-ing to invent new swearwords when I told him what had happened at Riva. I didn't mention the fact that Prince Geran had survived the mas-sacre on the beach, of course. Nobody except Brand needed to know about that. "What are we going to do about it?" he asked after I'd finished.

"I thought we might all visit Nyissa and have a little talk with Salmissra."

"I don't have any problem with that."

"Valcor's gathering his fleet, and he'll pick up the Rivans on his way south. How far can your pikemen march in a day?"

"Twenty leagues, if it's important enough."

"It is. Round them up and get them started. Go down through Algaria and the Tolnedran Mountains. Stay out of Maragor, though. It's still haunted, and your pikemen won't be of much use if they all go crazy. I'll talk with Cho-Ram, and he'll join you as you go south. Do you know Beldin?"

"I've heard of him."

"He's dwarfed, he's got a hump on his back and a foul temper. You can't miss him. If he's made it back from Mallorea by the time you reach the Vale, he'll go with you. It's five hundred leagues from here to Sthiss Tor. Let's say it'll take you two months to reach the eastern border of Nyissa. Don't take any longer. The rainy season comes on down there in the fall, and we don't want to bog down in the swamps."

"Amen to that."

"Beldin and I can stay in touch with each other, so we'll be able to coordinate things. I want to hit Nyissa from both sides at the same time. We don't want *too* many Nyissans to escape, but whatever you do, don't kill all of them. That'd make Issa almost as unhappy as Mara is, and we don't need another war between Gods."

"Issa let Salmissra kill Gorek, didn't he?"

"No, he didn't. He's hibernating, so he had no idea of what Salmissra was doing. Be very careful, Radek. Issa's the Serpent God. If you offend him, you might come back and find all of Drasnia infested with poisonous snakes. Now get your pikemen together and start south. I've got to go talk with Cho-Ram."

I started toward the door. "You can tell the girl to come out now, Radek," I threw back over my shoulder. "She'll smother if she stays under there too long." I stopped. "Don't you think it's about time for you to stop all this playing?" I asked him.

"There's no real harm in it, Belgarath."

"Not unless it gets out of hand. I think it's time for you to get married and settle down."

"I can do that later," he replied. "Right now I've got business to take care of in Nyissa."

I flew south to Algaria and it only took me two days to find Cho-Ram. The chief of the Clan-Chiefs of Algaria was fairly old, and his hair and beard were almost as white as mine. Old or not, though, you wouldn't have wanted to fight him. Age hadn't slowed his saber-hand in the slightest. I honestly believe he could have cut off both a man's ears so quickly that the man wouldn't notice that they were gone for a day or so.

We met in one of those rolling houses Fleet-foot had designed, so I was fairly sure we'd have some privacy. Cho-Ram and I were neighbors and old friends, so I didn't have to bully him the way I had Valcor and Radek. He listened carefully as I told him about the assassination of Gorek and of what we were going to do about it.

When I finished, he leaned back, his black horsehide jacket creaking. "We'll be violating Tolnedran territory, you know," he pointed out.

"That can't be helped," I said. "Somebody put Salmissra up to this, and I want to find out who he is before he gets too much of a running head start on me."

"Ctuchik, maybe?"

"It's possible. Let's see what Salmissra has to say before we lay siege to Rak Cthol, though. Radek should be along soon. Join forces with him when he gets here. I'm going down to the Vale. If Beldin's made it back from Mallorea, I'll send him along with you. If he hasn't, I'll send the twins. If Ctuchik *was* behind this and he's still in Nyissa, you'll need someone along to counter anything he throws at you. I think I'd better go with Valcor and Brand. The Rivans are enraged, and you know how the Chereks are."

He smiled. "Oh, yes," he agreed. "The whole world knows how the Chereks are."

"Gather your clans, Cho-Ram. Radek should be along in a bit. If you have to, go on ahead of his infantry. I want to be in Sthiss Tor before the rainy season sets in."

"I appreciate that, Ancient One. Wading through swamps in the rain is very hard on the horses."

Then I left for the Vale.

My luck was holding up, because Beldin had made it back from Mallorea two days earlier. I love the twins, but they're too gentle for the plans I had for Nyissa. Beldin can be appropriately ungentle when the occasion arises.

Let me set something straight here. There's no denying the fact that I was very angry about the murder of Gorek and his family. They *were* relatives, after all, but the campaign I'd mapped out had very little to do with vengeance and a great deal to do with deliberate terrorism. Things in the world were already complicated enough without the Nyissans dabbling in international politics. They had access to too many poisons and narcotics for my taste, so the Alorn invasion of that swamp was designed almost entirely to persuade the Serpent People to stay home and mind their own business. I suppose that says a few uncomplimentary things about me, but that can't be helped.

"What are you going to do if the Murgos decide to play, too?" Beldin asked me after I'd laid out my plan for him.

"I don't think we need to worry about that," I replied with more confidence than I really felt. "Ctuchik controls Cthol Murgos, no matter who's sitting on the throne in Rak Goska, and Ctuchik knows that it's not time for a confrontation with the Alorns yet. A lot more has to happen before we get to that." I scowled at the floor of Beldin's tower for a moment. "You'd better stay clear of Murgo territory, though, just to be on the safe side."

"You've got a peculiar idea of 'safe,' Belgarath. If I can't go through Cthol Murgos, I'll have to go through Tolnedra, and the legions won't like that very much."

"I'll swing over to Tol Honeth before I go back to Val Alorn. The Vorduvians are back in power again, but Ran Vordue the First has been on the throne only for about a year. I'll talk with him."

"Inexperienced people make mistakes, Belgarath."

"I know, but they usually hesitate before they make them. We'll be finished in Nyissa before he makes up his mind."

Beldin shrugged. "It's your war. I'll see you in Sthiss Tor."

I flew to Tol Honeth then and went to the Imperial Compound. Some forged documents identified me as a special emissary of the Alorn kings, and I got in to see the emperor immediately.

Emperor Ran Vordue I of the Third Vorduvian Dynasty was a youngish man with deep-sunk eyes and a gaunt face. He was seated on a marble throne, and he was wearing the traditional gold-colored mantle. "Welcome to Tol Honeth, Ancient One," he greeted me. He knew in a general sort of way who I was, but like most Tolnedrans, he thought my name was some kind of hereditary title.

"Let's skip the pleasantries and get to the point, Ran Vordue," I told him. "The Nyissans have assassinated the Rivan King, and the Alorns are mounting a punitive expedition."

"*What?* Why wasn't I told?"

"You just were. There's going to be a technical violation of your borders. I strongly advise you just to let it slide. The Alorns are feeling belligerent just now. Their business is with the Nyissans, but if your legions
get in their way, they'll plow them under. The Algars and Drasnians are
going to march south through the Tolnedran Mountains. Pretend you
don't see them."

"Can't this be settled without war?" he asked me rather plaintively. "I
have some very good negotiators at my disposal. They could persuade
Salmissra to pay reparations or something."

"I'm afraid not, your Majesty. You know how Alorns are. Halfway
measures won't satisfy them. Just stay out of it."

"Couldn't your Alorns go through Murgo territory instead? I'm new
on the throne, Belgarath. If I don't take *some* kind of action, I'll be
viewed as a weakling."

"Send letters of protest to the Alorn kings. I'll make them apologize
after it's all over." Then an idea came to me. "Here's a thought," I told
him. "If you want to do something muscular to impress the Honeths and
the Horbites, send your legions down to your southern border and seal it
off. Don't let *anybody* come across."

He squinted at me. "Very clever, Belgarath," he said. "You're using
me, aren't you? If *I* seal that border, *you* won't have to."

I grinned at him. "You're going to have to do *something*, Ran Vordue.
The politics of the situation almost demands it. The Honeths will start
calling you Ran Vordue the Chicken-Livered if you don't march your legions off in *some* direction. I guarantee that the Alorns won't cross that
border, and the other great families might accept the notion that it was
your show of force that kept them out. We'll both get something we want
that way."

"You've got me over a barrel, Old Man."

"I know," I replied. "It's up to you, though. You know what's coming,
and you know what you'd probably better do about it. Oh, one other
thing. Who's the most deeply involved in the Nyissan trade?"

"The Honeths," he replied shortly. "They're in it up to their ears.
They've got millions invested down there." Then a slow, evil smile came
over his gaunt face. "A disruption of the Nyissan economy would push
the Honeths to the verge of bankruptcy, you realize."

"Wouldn't that be a shame? You see, Ran Vordue? Every cloud has its
silver lining. All you have to do is look for it. Well, we've both got things
to do, so I won't bother you any more. Think it over. I'm sure you'll come
to the right decision." Then I bowed perfunctorily and left him to his
amusements.

Another one of those early summer storms swept in out of the Great
Western Sea to batter the coast, so it took me almost a week to get back

to Val Alorn. By the time I got there, Valcor had assembled his fleet and gathered his army. I contacted Beldin, and he advised me that the Algars and Drasnians had joined forces at the Algarian stronghold and were marching south. Everything seemed to be on schedule, so I unleashed Valcor and his berserkers.

The storm had finally passed, and we sailed from Val Alorn under a bright blue sky. I had a few tense moments when we went through the Cherek Bore, but otherwise the voyage to the Isle of the Winds was uneventful.

The meeting between Valcor and Brand there on the wharf was emotional. Brand had lost his king, and Valcor had lost a brother Alorn monarch. Valcor suggested a few memorial tankards, but I headed that off immediately. "We're running behind, gentlemen," I told them crisply. "Radek and Cho-Ram are already in the Tolnedran Mountains, and it's a long way to the mouth of the River of the Serpent. We can do our drinking after the war. Let's get the Rivans on board and get started."

We sailed southward past Arendia and Tolnedra and anchored just off the mouth of the River of the Woods. For any number of reasons, Ran Vordue had followed my suggestion, and his legions were patrolling the north bank of the river.

We waited there for a couple of days. It was only a short run on down to the delta of the River of the Serpent, but I didn't want to alert the Nyissans by dropping anchor in their coastal waters while we waited for Radek and Cho-Ram to get into position.

I'd just come up on deck on the morning of the third day when Beldin's voice came banging on the side of my head. *"Belgarath! Are you awake?"*

"Don't shout. I can hear you."

"We're in place, but let's give the Drasnian pikemen a day or so to catch their breath. We ran them pretty hard coming down through the mountains."

"It'll take us a few days to get to the mouth of the River of the Serpent anyway. Stay clear of the Tolnedran border. Ran Vordue has it sealed off, and we don't want any incidents with the legions."

"How did you get him to do that?"

"I pointed out certain advantages to him. Send a strike force south to block off any escape routes going in that direction. I'll do the same from this side, and when those two columns meet, we can get started with this."

"Right."

And that was more or less the way we did it. I'll be the first to concede that the Tolnedran Legions were very useful, although they didn't really do anything except stand there.

The Nyissans have always believed that their jungles would protect them. This time they were wrong. We'd run Radek's pikemen to the verge of exhaustion, but we'd reached Nyissa before the rains set in. The swamps had nearly dried up, and the trees were parched. The Nyissans took to the woods, and we simply burned the woods out from under them. I'm told that the vast clouds of smoke drifting northward bothered the Honethites a great deal. They could almost smell their money burning. The Vorduvians, Borunes, and Horbites were able to view the matter philosophically, however.

Wars are never pretty, but the Alorn campaign in Nyissa was particularly ugly. The Algar cavalry drove the Nyissans ahead of them like a herd of terrified cows, and when the Nyissans tried to climb trees to escape them, the Drasnian pikemen came along and speared them out of the branches. The Chereks and Rivans set fires, and when the panic-stricken Nyissans tried to flee, Valcor's berserkers simply drove them back into the flames. Frankly, the whole business sickened me, but we pushed on anyway.

It was a short, nasty war, and it left Nyissa a smoking wasteland. It accomplished its purpose, however. Centuries passed before the Nyissans came out of their hiding places, and that effectively kept them from meddling in international affairs.

Eventually we encircled Sthiss Tor, and after a couple of days we captured the city.

Beldin and I ran on ahead and reached Salmissra's gaudy palace about three jumps ahead of the vengeful Rivans. We definitely didn't want anybody to kill the Serpent Queen—at least not until we'd had a chance to ask her some questions. We sprinted down the corridor that led to her throne room, burst into that huge, dimly lighted hall, and closed and barred the door behind us.

Salmissra was alone and unguarded. The palace eunuchs were sworn to protect her, but evidently a eunuch's oath doesn't mean all that much to him if it's going to involve bleeding. The Serpent Queen was in her usual place, lounging on her throne and admiring her reflection in the mirror as if nothing untoward were happening. She looked very vulnerable somehow. "Welcome to Sthiss Tor, gentlemen," she said in a dreamy sort of voice. "Don't come too close," she warned, pointing negligently at the small green snakes nervously clustered around her throne. "My servants have all deserted me, but my little pets are still faithful." Her words were slurred, and her eyes seemed unfocused.

"We're not going to have much luck here, Belgarath," Beldin muttered to me. "She's so drugged that she's almost comatose."

"We'll see," I replied shortly. I stepped a little closer to the throne, and the little green snakes hissed warningly. "Things haven't turned out too well here, have they, Salmissra?" I said to her. "You should have known what the Alorns would do, though. What possessed you to have Gorek murdered?"

"It seemed like a good idea at the time," she murmured.

There was a heavy pounding on the barred door.

"Keep those enthusiasts off my back," I told Beldin.

"All right," he replied, "but don't be all day at this." I could feel his Will building.

"Do you know who I am?" I asked the dreamy queen.

"Of course. There's a whole body of literature in my library devoted to you and your exploits."

"Good. Then we won't have to go through all those tiresome introductions. I spoke with a couple of your assassins at Riva. One of them told me that this stupid business wasn't entirely your idea. Would you care to elaborate on that for me?"

"Why not?" Her indifference chilled me for some reason. "About a year ago a man came to Sthiss Tor, and he had a little proposition for me. His offer was very attractive, so I took him up on it. That's really about all there was to it, Belgarath."

"What could he possibly have offered you to lure you into exposing yourself to the vengeance of the Alorns?"

"Immortality, Ancient One, immortality."

"No man can offer that, Salmissra."

"The offer didn't come from a man—or so I was led to believe."

"Who was this fellow who made you such a ridiculous proposal?"

"Does the name Zedar ring any bells for you, Belgarath?" She actually looked a bit amused.

A number of things fell into place for me—including the reason for my instructions not to kill Zedar. "Why don't you start at the beginning?" I suggested.

She sighed. "That would be a long and tedious story, Old Man." Her eyelids drooped shut.

I started to have some suspicions at that point. "Why don't you summarize it, then?" I suggested.

She sighed again. "Oh, very well," she replied. Then she looked around. "Does it seem to be getting chilly in here?" she asked with a slight shudder.

"Will you get on with it, Belgarath?" Beldin demanded irritably. "I can't keep those Alorns out much longer without hurting them."

"I don't think we've got too much longer," I told him. Then I looked at the Serpent Queen. "You've taken poison, haven't you, Salmissra?" I asked her.

"Naturally," she replied. "It's the Nyissan sort of thing to do, isn't it? Convey my apologies to your Alorns. I know they'll be terribly disappointed."

"Exactly what did Zedar say to you?"

"You're a tiresome old man, Belgarath. All right, listen carefully. I don't think I'll have time to repeat this. Zedar came to me and said that he was speaking for Torak. He said that the Rivan King was the only thing standing between Torak and something he wanted, and that he'd give *anything* to the person who removed him. The offer was fairly simple. If I'd kill the Rivan King, Torak would marry me, and we'd rule the world jointly—forever. Zedar also told me that Torak would protect me from your Alorns. Did you happen to see the Dragon God on your way to Sthiss Tor?"

"We must have missed him."

"I wonder what can be keeping him."

"Surely you weren't gullible enough to *believe* all that?"

She straightened slightly and lifted her chin. She was a remarkably beautiful woman. "How old would you say I am?" she asked me.

"That's impossible to tell, Salmissra. You take drugs that keep you from aging."

"It may *look* that way, but it's not really true. Actually, I'm fifty-seven, and none of my predecessors has lived much past sixty. There are twenty little girls out in the jungle training to take my place when I die. I believed Zedar because I *wanted* to believe him. I suppose we never outlive our belief in fairy stories, do we? I didn't want to die, and Zedar seemed to be offering me a chance to live forever. I wanted that so much that I chose to believe what he told me. When you get right down to it, this is all *your* fault, you know."

"Mine? Where did you get *that* weird idea?"

"If it hadn't been for the fact that you're a million years old, I wouldn't have been so gullible. If *one* person can live forever, others can, as well. You and your brothers are the disciples of Aldur, and Aldur made you all immortal. Zedar, Ctuchik, and Urvon serve Torak, and they'll live forever, as well."

"Not if *I* can help it, they won't," Beldin threw back over his shoulder.

She smiled faintly, and her eyes seemed glazed. "The notion of conferring immortality on his handmaiden doesn't seem to have occurred to Issa, so I've only got about three more years to live. Zedar knew that, of course, and he used it to dupe me. I wish there were some way I could pay him back for that. He got everything he wanted from me, and all I got was a cup of foul-tasting poison."

I looked around to make certain that nobody was hiding in one of the corners. "Zedar got nothing, Salmissra," I told her very quietly. "Your assassins missed somebody. The Rivan line's still intact."

She stared at me for a moment, and then she actually laughed. "What a wonderful old man you are," she said warmly. "Are you going to kill Zedar?"

"Probably," I replied.

"Tell him that the survivor you mentioned is my last gift to him before you put him away, would you? It's a petty sort of vengeance, but it's all that's available to a dying old lady."

"Did Zedar tell you what Torak planned to do once the Rivan King was dead?" I asked her.

"We didn't get into that," she murmured, "but it shouldn't be hard to guess. Now that he believes that the Guardian of the Orb is dead, he'll probably be paying you a call shortly. I wish I could be in a corner somewhere to watch the rest of his face crumble when he finds out that Zedar's scheme didn't work." Her head drooped, and her eyes went closed again.

"Is she dead?" Beldin asked me.

"Close, I think."

"Belgarath?" Her voice was only a whisper now.

"Yes?"

"Avenge me, would you please?"

"You've got my word on that, Salmissra."

"Please don't call me that, Ancient One. Once, when I was a little girl, my name was Illessa. I was very happy with that name. Then the palace eunuchs came to our village, and they looked at my face. That was when they took me away from my mother and told me that my name was Salmissra now. I've always hated that name. I didn't want to be Salmissra. I wanted to keep on being Illessa, but they didn't give me any choice. It was either become one of the twenty twelve-year-old Salmissras or die. Why couldn't they let me keep my real name?"

"It's a lovely name, Illessa," I told her gently.

"Thank you, Ancient One." She sighed a long quavering sigh. "Sometimes I wish—"

We never found out what she wished, because she died before she could tell us.

"Well?" Beldin said to me.

"Well what?"

"Aren't you going to hit her?"

"Why would I want to do that?"

"Didn't you promise Prince Geran you would?"

"Some promises can't be kept, Beldin."

"Sentimentalist!" He snorted. "She wouldn't mind now."

"*I* would." I translocated the little green snakes to the far side of the throne room, stepped up onto the dais, and arranged the body of the Serpent Queen on her throne in a position that had some dignity. Then I patted her gently on the cheek. "Sleep well, Illessa," I murmured.

Then I stepped down from the dais. "Let's get out of here, Beldin," I suggested. "I *hate* the smell of snakes."

You're disappointed, aren't you? You wanted a lurid description of my dreadful retribution on the body of the Serpent Queen. Well, I'm a pretty good storyteller, so if that's the kind of story you really want, I suppose I could make it up for you. After you've calmed down a bit, though, I think you'll be just a little ashamed of yourself.

Actually, I'm not very proud of what we did in Nyissa. If I'd been filled with rage and a hunger for vengeance, the things we did down there might have been understandable—not particularly admirable, maybe, but at least understandable. But I did it all in cold blood, and that makes it fairly monstrous, wouldn't you say?

I suppose I should have known that Zedar had been behind the whole thing right from the start. It was all too subtle to have come from Ctuchik. Every time I start feeling uneasy about what I ultimately did to Zedar, I run over the long list of his offenses in my mind, and the fact that he duped Illessa into murdering Gorek and then left her to face the Alorns all alone stands fairly high on that list.

Enough of all this tedious self-justification.

The Alorns were still happily dismantling the city when Beldin and I came out of the palace. Most of the houses were made of stone, since wood decays rather quickly in the middle of a tropical swamp. The Alorns set fire to everything that *would* burn, and they took battering rams to the rest. Lurid orange flame seemed to be everywhere, and the streets were almost totally obscured by clouds of choking black smoke. I looked around sourly. "That's ridiculous!" I said. "The war's over. There's no need for all of this."

"Let 'em play," Beldin said indifferently. "We came here to wreck Nyissa, didn't we?"

I grunted. "What's Torak been up to?" I asked him. "We didn't get much chance to talk about that when I passed through the Vale."

"Torak's still at Ashaba—"

A howling Cherek, dressed in bearskins despite the climate, ran past us waving a torch. "I'd better have a talk with Valcor," I muttered. "The Bear-cult's been yearning to invade the southern kingdoms for the past twenty-five centuries. Now that they're here, they might decide to expand the hostilities. Is Mal Zeth quiet? I mean, are they making any preparations?"

Beldin laughed that short, ugly laugh of his and scratched vigorously at one armpit. He shook his head. "The army's in turmoil—there's a new emperor shaking things up. But Torak isn't mobilizing. He didn't know anything about this." He squinted off down a smoky street where flames were belching out of windows. "I hope Zedar's found himself a very deep hole to hide in. Old Burnt-face might get a little peevish when he finds out what's happened."

"I suppose we can worry about that later. Do you want to take the Alorns home?"

"Not particularly. Why?"

"It won't really take you very long, Beldin, and I've got something else to do."

"Oh? What's that?"

"I think I'd better go back to the Vale and dig into the Mrin Codex. If Torak *does* decide to exploit this, we'll want to know that he's coming. It'll be one of those EVENTS, and the Mrin's bound to cover it."

"Probably so, but you'll have to make sense out of it first. Why not just let the Alorns find their way home by themselves?"

"I want to make sure they go home. That means that somebody's going to have to herd the Bear-cult out of the South. Tell Brand what we found out from Illessa. Sort of hint around that you and I are going to take care of Zedar. Don't get too specific about how long it's likely to take us."

"Are you going to look in on Pol before you go back to the Vale?"

"She can take care of herself. If anybody can, she can."

He gave me a sly, sidelong look. "You're very proud of her, aren't you?"

"Of course I am."

"Have you ever considered telling her so?"

"And spoil over a thousand years of bickering? Don't be silly. Stop by the Vale before you go back to Mallorea. I might have dredged a few useful hints out of the Mrin by then."

I left him standing on the palace steps and went on out of the wrecked and burning city to the edge of the jungle. I found a clearing, climbed up on a stump, and changed into a falcon again. I was actually getting rather fond of that shape.

Flying through all the smoke from the burning jungle wasn't particularly pleasant, so I kept climbing until I got above it. I'd received reports about the fires, naturally, and I'd passed through some smoldering burned-off areas on the way to Sthiss Tor myself, but I don't think I'd fully grasped the extent of the fires until I got a mile or so above them. It actually appeared that the whole of Nyissa was burning.

When I got back to the Vale, I told the twins about what had happened in Nyissa. Great tears of sympathy welled up in their eyes when I described Illessa's last hour. The twins are very sentimental sometimes.

All right, I sympathized with her, too. Do you want to make something out of it? Zedar had tricked Illessa and then left her hanging out to dry. Of *course* I felt sorry for her. Use your head.

I spent the next couple of weeks floundering my way through the Mrin. I'm rather proud of the self-control I exhibited there. I didn't once hurl those stupid scrolls out the window.

The core of the difficulty with the Mrin lies in the way it jumps around. I think I've mentioned that before. As I struggled with that long display of incoherence, I began to see where Garion's friend had blundered. The Mrin prophet wasn't a very good choice as a spokesman. Regardless of what we may think about the power of that Necessity, the prophecies had to be filtered through the minds of the prophets, and the Mrin prophet had no conception of time. He lived in a world of eternal now, and the words of Necessity all came out together with "now" and "then" and "sometime next week" scrambled together like an omelette.

It was pure luck when I stumbled across a possible solution. I'd pushed the Mrin aside in disgust and turned to the Darine simply to clear my head. Bormik had been crazy, but at least he'd known the difference between yesterday and tomorrow. I don't think I was actually reading it, just unrolling and looking at it. Bormik's daughter had made fair copies of the hen-scratchings of her scribes, and she'd had beautiful penmanship. Her letters were graceful and her lines well balanced. Bull-neck's scribes should have gone to Darine and taken lessons from her. The Mrin was filled with blotches, scrubbed-out words, and crossed-out lines. A twelve-year-old just learning his letters could have produced a neater page. Suddenly my eyes stopped, and a familiar passage jumped out at me. "Be not dismayed, for the Rivan King *shall* return."

I quickly laid a couple of books on the scroll to keep the place. That's one of the reasons I don't like scrolls. Left to their own devices, they'll roll themselves back up without any outside assistance as soon as you let go of them.

I picked up the Mrin again and rolled my way through it until I came to the place I'd just remembered. "Behold," it said, "all shall seem lost, but curb thy despair, for the Rivan King *shall* return."

They weren't identical, but they were very close. I stared at the two passages with my heart sinking like a rock. A rather horrid prospect was looming in front of me. I knew how to wring coherence out of the Mrin now, but the sheer size of that job made me weak just thinking about it. There were matching passages in those documents. The Mrin had no sense of time, but the Darine did. All I had to do to get a coherent time sequence for the Mrin was to compile a comparative concordance.

Then I read the next line of the Mrin. "I had fullest confidence in thee, Ancient and Beloved, knowing full well that the solution would come to thee—eventually."

Now that was *really* offensive, even though it confirmed my discovery. The Necessity knew the past and the present and the future, so it *knew* that I'd ultimately break its code. The clever remark was there for no reason other than to draw my attention to the fact so that I wouldn't dismiss it out of hand. Evidently it thought I was stupid.

Incidentally, Garion, the next time your friend pays you a visit, you might tell him that I've occasionally taken advantage of his clever little trick. Why should *I* wrack my brains trying to make sense of that solid wall of gibberish we call the Mrin Codex when he's speckled it with those very obvious signals? I'm not above letting somebody else do my work for me. Then you might ask him who got in the last laugh. I'm sure he won't mind. He has an absolutely wonderful sense of humor.

I went back to the place in the Darine that more or less matched the warning in the Mrin that'd sent Pol and me flying off to the Isle of the Winds; then I settled down to work. It was very slow going, since I had to virtually memorize the Mrin in the process. The Darine usually gave only a brief summary of an event, and the Mrin expanded on it. Certain key words linked the two, and after I'd matched up a couple of those passages, I got a little better at pinpointing those keys. I devised a system of index marks that I'd put in the margins to correlate matching passages. Once I'd found a match, I didn't want to lose it. The more I worked on it, the more I came to realize that the Darine was little more than a map to the Mrin. Neither of them was very useful by itself, but when you put them together, the message started to emerge. It was subtle and very complex, but it almost absolutely guaranteed that nobody'd accidentally get his hands on information that was none of his business.

I slogged along for the better part of a year, and then Beldin came back to the Vale. "Did you get the Alorns back where they belong?" I asked him when he came stumping up the stairs to my tower.

"Finally," he said. "You were right about the Bear-cult. They *really* wanted to stay in the South. You'd better keep an eye on Valcor. He's not quite a cultist, but his sympathies sort of lean in that direction. Radek and Cho-Ram finally managed to bring him to his senses, though."

"Cultists don't *have* any sense, Beldin."

"They're not quite suicidal, though. Radek and Cho-Ram chained up all the cultists in their own ranks and started for home. The Chereks are savages, but they're no match for the legions all by themselves. Once the Drasnians and Algars left, Valcor didn't have any choice but to go home, too."

"Did Brand take sides?"

"He was in complete agreement with Radek and Cho-Ram. He's got responsibilities at home, so he wasn't about to get involved in an extended war in the South." He looked at the scrolls on my work table. "Are you making any progress?"

"Some. It's very slow going, though." I explained the concordance I'd been working on.

"Cunning," he noted.

"Thank you."

"Not you, Belgarath; the Necessity."

"It's not quite as easy as it sounds. You wouldn't believe how long it takes to match up some of those passages."

"Have you talked with the twins about it?"

"They're busy with something else."

"Maybe they'd better put it aside. I think this is more important."

"I can handle it, Beldin."

"A little professional jealousy there, old boy? A prophecy isn't really a prophecy if you don't unravel it until after the fact, you know. To all intents and purposes, the twins have a single mind, don't they?"

"I suppose so."

"When *you* try to do this, you have to keep hopping back and forth, but they wouldn't. Beltira could read the Darine, and Belkira the Mrin. When they hit these correspondences, they'll both know it instantly. They'll be able to do in minutes what takes you days."

I blinked. "They *could*, couldn't they? I never thought of that."

"Obviously. Let's go drop your project into their laps. Then you'll be able to do something useful—like cutting firewood or digging ditches. Have you looked in on Pol?"

"I've been busy. Did it really take you a whole year to take the Alorns home?"

"No. I made a quick trip to Mallorea to see if anything was stirring yet."

"Is there?"

"Not so far. Maybe word of what happened at Riva hasn't reached Torak yet. Let's go get Pol. I think we'd all better get together and make some plans before I go back and take up permanent residence in Mal Zeth."

"That might not be a bad idea. I've picked up a few hints about the next couple of centuries while I was putting the concordance together. I don't *think* anything significant's going to happen for a while, but let's all put our heads together on it. Sometimes I miss things."

"*You?* Impossible."

"Quit trying to be clever, Beldin. I'm not in the mood for it. Let's turn the concordance over to the twins and then go to Erat and talk to Pol."

The twins understood the idea behind the concordance immediately, and Beldin had been right. With two sets of eyes, one reading Darine and the other reading Mrin, they definitely could make headway faster than I could. Then Beldin took the form of the blue-banded hawk he's so fond of, I converted myself into the falcon again, and we winged off to the northwest to drop in on Polgara.

There's an old fairy tale about a princess who's locked up in a lonely castle that's completely surrounded by a dense thicket of thorny trees. Pol's manor house in north-central Sendaria is very much like that— except that her thicket has roses all over it. Those rosebushes had been untended for centuries. The canes were as thick as tree trunks, and they were covered with thorns that were at least four inches long. Their ten-drils were so interwoven that *nobody* was going to get through them with-out ripping off most of his skin. Since the house was totally concealed, nobody'd have any reason to take the trouble, so Pol's privacy was guaranteed.

We settled on her doorstep, changed back, and I pounded on the door, sending echoes booming back into the house.

After a few moments, I heard Pol's voice just inside. "Who's there?"

"It's me, Pol. Open up."

She was wearing an apron, and she'd tied a kerchief around her head in a kind of turban. She was holding a cloth-wrapped broom that had cobwebs all over it.

"What are you doing, Pol?" Beldin asked her.

"Cleaning house."

"By *hand?* Why don't you do it the other way?"

"It's my house, uncle. I'll clean it any way I choose."

He shook his head. "You're a strange person, Polgara," he noted. "You spend centuries learning all the shortcuts, and then you refuse to use them."

"It's a matter of principle, uncle. You don't have any principles, so you wouldn't understand."

He bowed to her. "Score one for you, Pol," he said. "An' would y' be willin' t' offer the hospitality of yer splendid house t' a couple o' weary travelers, great lady?"

She ignored his attempt at humor. "What do you two want?" She wasn't very gracious about it.

"We're having a little family get-together at the Vale, Pol," I told her. "It wouldn't be the same without you."

"Out of the question."

"Don't be difficult, Polgara," Beldin said. "This is important. We need you." He pushed his way past her into the hallway.

"Did you chop a road right to my doorstep?"

"No," he replied. "We flew in."

I looked around. The light was subdued because all of the windows in the house were covered with rose vines, but I could see that the entryway to my daughter's house had a highly polished marble floor and glowing wooden wainscoting. "Are you just now getting around to tidying up, Pol?" I asked her.

"No. Geran and I've been at it since we got here. We're on the third floor now."

"You've turned the crown prince of Riva into a cleaning boy? It's very democratic, Pol, but isn't it a little inappropriate?"

"It won't hurt him, father. Besides, he needs the exercise."

Then Geran came warily down the stairway. He was wearing a dust-stained peasant smock, and he was holding a sword. It wasn't a very big sword, but he handled it as if he knew how to use it. "Grandfather!" he exclaimed when he saw me. He ran the rest of the way down the stairs. "Did you kill Salmissra?" he asked eagerly.

"She was dead the last time I looked," I replied evasively.

"Did you hit her for me the way I asked you to?"

"That he did, lad," Beldin stepped in to cover my tail feathers. "That he did."

Geran looked a bit apprehensively at the gnarled dwarf.

"This is Uncle Beldin, Geran," Pol introduced them.

"You aren't very tall, are you?" Geran noted.

"It has its advantages, lad," Beldin replied. "I almost never hit my head on a low-hanging limb."

Geran laughed. "I like him, Aunt Pol."

"That wears off fairly soon."

"Don't carry tales, Pol," Beldin chided. "Let the boy draw his own conclusions."

"I think we'd better bring Brand in on this," I said. "We've got a lot of things to talk about, and Brand's the one who's going to have to stand watch over the Orb, so he'll need to know what's coming."

"*Do* we know what's coming, father?" Pol asked.

"Yer unspeakably clever old father's actually devised a way t' make sense outta th' Mrin, me darlin'."

Geran giggled. "I *really* like him, Aunt Pol," he said.

"I was afraid you might feel that way." She sighed. "Try not to let it get ahead of you."

"You go with Pol back to the Vale," I told Beldin. "Between the two of you, you can hold off anything this side of Torak himself, and Torak's turning to stone at Ashaba. I'll go get Brand, and we'll get down to business." Then I went outside, blurred into feathers, and flew off toward the Isle of the Winds.

It took Brand and me about three weeks to travel from the Isle of the Winds to the Vale, largely because nobody in his right mind goes through Ulgoland. When we arrived, we found that they'd started without us. The twins had picked up where I'd left off, and they'd roughed in the next several centuries. "Nothing much seems to be happening, Belgarath," Beltira told me. "So far as we can tell, the prophecies are concentrating on events in Mallorea. Are you and Brand hungry? Pol and I can fix something to eat if you'd like."

"A light snack, maybe. Something to tide us over till suppertime."

Pol rose and went over to the kitchen area. I looked around for Prince Geran. He was sitting quietly on a chair in the corner. I've noticed that characteristic again and again in his family. Some children absolutely *must* be the center of attention. The long line of little boys in Garion's family, though, are so self-effacing that you hardly notice them. They watch and listen, but they keep their mouths shut. It's a very good trait. You seldom learn anything while your mouth's flapping. He was wearing very ordinary clothes. Polgara was already beginning to come up with ways to make the heirs to the Rivan throne as inconspicuous as possible.

"Oh, something else," Belkira added. "The Third Age has ended. We're in the Fourth Age now. Evidently a Dal went to Ashaba, and the minute he laid eyes on Torak, the Third Age ended."

"That's a relief," I replied.

"How so?"

"It means that we've got all our instructions. The Third Age was the Age of Prophecy. If it's ended, it means that we've been told what's going to happen and what to do about it. Nothing else is going to come along to confuse the issue. What's been going on in Mallorea that's so interesting?"

He picked up his copy of the Mrin, referred to the concordance, and unrolled the scroll until he found the index mark he wanted. "The Darine simply says that one man will gain ascendancy over all Mallorea. Here's what the Mrin says: 'And it shall come to pass that children shall be exchanged in the Kingdoms of the East, and one such child shall ascend the throne of one kingdom by marriage and shall achieve dominion over the other by threat of force. And he shall make one of that which was once two. And in the joining of the two shall the way be cleared for the EVENT which shall take place in the Lands of the Bull God.' That's about as far as we've gotten so far."

"What's *that* to do with anything?" I demanded.

"The one it's talking about was a young Angarak named Kallath," Beldin explained, "and his name made a very loud noise in Mallorea. The Angaraks and the Melcenes had been stepping around each other rather carefully for a long time—the Angaraks had more manpower, but the Melcenes had elephant cavalry. Neither side wanted war. That exchange of children was a Melcene idea. It was supposed to promote greater understanding between the two races. When Kallath was about twelve or so, he was sent to the island of Melcena to grow up in the house of the Minister of Foreign Affairs at the Emperor's court. He got to know the daughter of the Melcene Emperor, and they got married. That technically made Kallath the heir to the Melcene throne. He was ambitious, and he was an Angarak, so the other candidates started having fatal accidents. He was also the youngest member of the Angarak General Staff at Mal Zeth *and* the Governor General of the District of Delchin in eastern Mallorea proper. He had a sort of capital at Maga Renn, which just *happened* to be snuggled up against the Melcene border—and he already had a power base in Angarak territory. If anybody could unite all of Mallorea, it was Kallath."

"Evidently that's what happened," Brand noted.

"Excuse me," Prince Geran said politely. "What's supposed to happen in Arendia?"

"An EVENT, your Highness," Beltira told him.

"What kind of event?"

"The Mrin uses that word when it's talking about a meeting between the Child of Light and the Child of Dark."

"A battle?" The young Alorn's eyes brightened.

"Sometimes it is," I told him, "but not always. I was involved in one of those EVENTS, and there were only two people there."

Polgara was busy in the kitchen area, but she was obviously not missing very much. "It's peculiar that this Kallath came along so recently," she mused, wiping her hands on her apron. "I don't suppose it's just a coincidence, is it?"

"Not very likely, Pol," I said.

"Excuse me again, please," Prince Geran said in that diffident, self-effacing tone. "If we're coming up on one of those EVENTS you mentioned, wouldn't Torak know about it, too?"

"Inevitably," Beldin growled.

"We can't really surprise him then, can we?"

"Not really," Beltira said. "We're all more or less guided by our instructions."

"Do you know what I think?" Geran said. "I don't think that what happened to my family had anything to do with the Orb or where it is, or who's taking care of it. This Kallath person was doing something that Torak wants to happen. He knows that we know about it—because of those prophecies. We'd have tried to stop Kallath, so Torak sent Zedar out to do something to distract us. You all ran off to Nyissa to punish Salmissra for killing my family, and that left Kallath—or whoever came after him—free to finish up the job that Torak needed to have done. Killing my family was a . . ." He paused, groping for a word.

"Diversion," Belkira supplied. "You know, Belgarath, I think this boy's hit the nail square on the head. We all know Zedar, and he knows us. He knew exactly how we'd react to the murder of Gorek and his family. Something crucial was going on in Mallorea, and you and Beldin and the Alorns were down in Nyissa when it happened. We were all looking one way, and Torak and his people were slipping something past us while our attention was distracted."

Beldin swore. "It fits, Belgarath," he said to me. "It fits Torak, and it fits Zedar. How could we have been so stupid that we didn't see it?"

"Natural talent, I suppose," I replied glumly. "I think we've been had. Congratulations, Prince Geran. You came up with an answer we'd have pounded our heads on the wall for weeks to discover. How did you manage to pick it out so quickly?"

"I can't take any credit, grandfather," the boy replied modestly. "My tutors had started to teach me history before the Nyissans murdered my family. They were telling me about some of the things that used to happen in Tolnedra. As I understand it, the Vorduvians were very good at this sort of thing, and so were the Honeths."

"What a mind this boy has!" Beltira marveled. "He put it all together in the blink of an eye!"

"And we'll have to protect that mind—and what's going to come after it," Polgara said, with that steely glint coming into her eyes. "Zedar might have hoped that the assassination would extinguish the Rivan line, but the Ashabine Oracles obviously told Torak otherwise."

"Does that mean that my prince has to stay in hiding?" Brand asked.

"It seems to point that way doesn't it?" Beldin replied.

"Who's going to protect him?"

"That's *my* job, Brand," Polgara told him, removing her apron.

Then something happened that very rarely has. "Dost thou accept this responsibility freely, my daughter?" It was Aldur's voice, and we all turned around quickly, but he wasn't there—only his voice and a peculiar blue light.

Polgara immediately understood the implications of the question. The element of conscious choice has always been rather central to the things we do. I'll admit that I sort of blunder into things now and then, but there always comes that moment when I'm required to choose. Pol had come face to face with one of those choices, and she knew it. She crossed the tower room and laid her hand on Geran's shoulder. "Freely, Master," she replied firmly. "From this day hence, I shall protect and guide the Rivan line."

And in the moment that she said it, I felt one of those peculiar clicks inside my head. Pol's choice had been one of those things that had to happen. I'm not sure exactly why, but I felt a sudden urge to leap into the air with a wild cry of exultation.

Looking back at it now, I realize that Pol's choice was one of those EVENTS we keep talking about. Her choice ultimately led to Garion, and Garion in turn led to Eriond. At the time, we'd all assumed that our Necessity had given something up when it'd agreed to the separation of Geran from the Orb. I think we were wrong there. That separation was a victory, not a defeat.

Don't look so confused. I'll explain it to you—all in good time.

———

After she'd freely accepted her responsibility, Polgara started giving orders. She does that all the time, you know. "The Master has laid this task upon *me*, gentlemen," she told us firmly. "I don't need any help, and I don't need any interference. I'll hide Geran, and I'll make such decisions as need to be made. Don't hover over me, and don't try to tell me what to do. And don't, *please*, don't stand around staring at me. Just stay away. Do we agree?"

Of course we agreed. What else could we do?

CHAPTER
THIRTY-
FIVE

There was no denying that Polgara's interdiction made sense, so I didn't see her very often during the next five centuries or so—or at least so she thought. I managed to keep track of her, however, even though she moved around a lot. Her general strategy was to submerge herself and the heir to the Rivan throne in the general population—usually in Sendaria. Sendaria's a great place for anonymity, because racial differences don't mean anything there, and Sendars are too polite to question people about their backgrounds. But even the politest Sendar's going to start getting curious about someone who doesn't age, so Pol seldom stayed in the same place for more than ten years.

That habit of hers gave me all sorts of entertainment. Finding someone who doesn't want to be found isn't the easiest thing in the world, and Pol became very skilled at misdirection. If she told her neighbors that there was a "family emergency" in Darine, you could be fairly sure that she was actually bound for Muros or Camaar. Once during the forty-third century, it took me eight years to track her down. Her elusiveness didn't really bother me much. If she could hide from *me*, she certainly could hide from anybody else.

She'd ordered me to stay away from her, so I grew quite proficient at disguises, although in my case I didn't have to rely on wigs and false noses. A man who can change himself into a wolf or a falcon doesn't have much trouble modifying his face or general physique.

Usually after I'd located her, I'd just drift into whatever town or village she was currently living in, snoop around a bit, and then drift back on out again without even talking to her.

I've always had a great deal of admiration for the Tolnedran system of highways: it makes traveling much easier, and I had to travel a great deal during the early centuries of the fifth millennium. I did *not*, however, approve of Ran Horb's treaty with the Murgos that opened the South Caravan Route.

At first, the Tolnedran trade with the Murgos was a one-way sort of business. Tolnedran merchants followed the caravan route to Rak Goska, conducted their business, and then came home with their purses filled to overflowing with that reddish-colored gold that comes out of the mines of Cthol Murgos.

Following the Alorn invasions of Nyissa, however, the Murgos developed an absolute passion for trade, and after a century or so it seemed that I couldn't turn around any place in Tolnedra, Arendia, or Sendaria without seeing a scarred Murgo face.

The Tolnedrans spoke piously about the "normalizing of relations" and the "civilizing influence of commerce," but I knew better. The Murgos were coming west because Ctuchik had told them to come west, and commerce had nothing to do with it. The fact that the Rivan line was still intact loomed rather large in *all* the prophecies, and Ctuchik sent his Murgos to look for Polgara and the heirs she spent that part of her life protecting.

It finally came to a head early in the forty-fifth century. Polgara was in Sulturn in central Sendaria with the current heir and his wife. The young man's name just happened to be Darion.

I'm sure you noticed the similarity. It's Polgara's fault, really. Polgara *adores* traditions, so she speckled the Rivan line with repetitions and variations of about a half-dozen names. Polgara can be creative when she has to be, but she'd really rather not if she can possibly avoid it.

Anyway, Darion was a cabinetmaker, and quite a good one. He had a prosperous business on a side street down near the lake, and he lived upstairs over his shop with his wife, Selana, and with his aunt.

Does that sound at all familiar?

I was in Val Alorn when word reached me that the old Gorim of Ulgo had died and that there was a new Gorim in the caves under Prolgu. I decided that it might be a good idea for me to go to Ulgoland and introduce myself. I always like to stay on good terms with the Ulgos. They're a little strange, but I rather like them.

Anyway, it was midautumn when I heard about it. I was going to have to hurry if I didn't want to get snowbound in the mountains, and so I took the first ship that left Val Alorn for Sendaria—a ship that just "happened" to be bound for the capital at the city of Sendar rather than the port at Darine. I probably could call that pure luck, but I've got some doubts about that.

The weather was blustery, so it was four days later when I wound up on a stone wharf in Sendar on a grey, cloudy afternoon. I bought a horse and took the Tolnedran highway that ran southeasterly toward Muros. About midway between Sendar and Muros, the highway just "happened" to pass through Sulturn. Sometimes I get very tired of being led around by the nose. Garion's friend can be so obvious at times.

Since I was there anyway, and since I was getting a little saddle sore, I decided to disguise myself and take a couple days off to do a little constructive snooping. I rode back into a grove of trees on a hill just outside Sulturn, dismounted, and formed an image in my mind that was about as far from my real appearance as I possibly could make it and then flowed into it. The horse seemed a little startled. His new owner was quite tall, and he had coal-black hair and a bushy beard of the same color.

I rode down into Sulturn, took a room in a rundown inn on the west side of town, and nosed around until evening. I asked innocuous questions and kept my eyes open. Pol and her family were still here, and all seemed normal, so I went back to the inn for supper.

The common room of the inn was a low-ceilinged place with dark beams overhead. The tables and benches were plain, utilitarian, and unvarnished, and the fireplace smoked. There were perhaps a dozen people there, a few locals drinking beer from copper-bound wooden tankards, and several travelers eating the unappetizing stew that's the standard fare in Sendarian inns from Camaar to Darine. Sendaria produces a lot of turnips, and turnip stew isn't one of my favorite dishes.

The first face I really noticed when I entered belonged to a Murgo. He was wearing western-style clothes, but his angular eyes and the scars on his cheeks left no doubt about his race. He sat near the fireplace plying a rather tipsy Sendar with beer and talking about the weather.

Since he wouldn't be able to recognize me anyway, I strode over, took a seat at the table next to his, and told the serving wench to bring me some supper.

After the Murgo'd exhausted the conversational potentials of the weather, he got down to business. "You seem well acquainted here," he said to the half-drunk Sendar across the table from him.

"I doubt that there are ten people in all of Sulturn that I don't know," the Sendar replied modestly, draining his tankard.

The Murgo bought him another. "It seems that I've found the right man, then," he said, trying to smile. Murgos don't really know how to smile, so his expression looked more like a grimace of pain. "A country-man of mine was passing through here last week, and he happened to see a lady that took his eye." A Murgo even *looking* at a non-Murgo woman? Absurd!

"We have some real beauties here in Sulturn," the Sendar said.

"My friend was in a hurry, so he didn't have time to introduce himself to the lady in question, but when he found that I was coming here, he begged me to find out what I could about her—where she lives, what her name is, whether she's married—that sort of thing." He tried to smile again, and this one wasn't any better than the first had been.

"Did he describe her to you?" the Sendar asked. What a dunce! Even if the Murgo's transparent fiction had been true, he'd have had a descrip-tion. In his case, however, he had no problem at all. Ctuchik had prob-ably engraved a portrait of Polgara on the inside of his eyeballs.

"He said that she was quite tall and very beautiful."

"That describes a lot of the ladies here in Sulturn, friend. Did he give you any other details?"

"She has very dark hair," the Murgo said, "but the thing that really stood out in my friend's mind was the fact that she's got a white streak in her hair—just above her brow."

The Sendar laughed. "That's easy," he said. "Your friend's been taken with Mistress Pol, the aunt of Darion the cabinetmaker. He's not the first, but you might as well tell him to try his luck somewhere else. Mistress Pol's not interested, and she goes out of her way to let people know that. She can blister the bark off a tree from half a mile away."

I swore under my breath. I was going to have to have a talk with Pol about that. What good did it to do hide if she didn't change her name, her appearance, or her temperament?

I didn't really need to stay any longer. The Murgo had what he wanted, and so did I. I pushed back my bowl of watery turnip stew, got up, and left.

The streets of Sulturn were nearly deserted, and a chill, gusty autumn wind howled around the corners of the solid stone houses. Heavy clouds covered the moon, and the few torches that were supposed to illuminate the streets were flaring and guttering as the wind tore at them. I didn't re-ally pay too much attention to the weather, though. I was more interested in whether there might be another Murgo following me. I doubled back several times, circled around through the narrow, nearly dark streets, and came to Darion's cabinet shop from the far side.

It was after nightfall, so the shop was closed, but the lights in the windows of the living quarters upstairs clearly announced that Darion and his family were home. I didn't pound on the door. There wasn't any point in disturbing the neighbors. I picked the lock instead, went inside, and blundered around in the dark until I found the stairs. I went up them two at time, fumbled around until I found the lock on the door at the top, and picked that one, as well.

The door opened into the kitchen, and I'd have recognized it as Polgara's even if I'd entered it somewhere on the far side of the moon. It was warm and cheerful, and it was arranged in that familiar way all of Polgara's kitchens have been arranged. Pol and her little family were eating supper at the kitchen table when I slipped into the room. "Pol!" I hissed sharply. "We've got to get you out of here!"

She came quickly to her feet, her eyes blazing. "What are you doing here, Old Man?" she demanded. So much for disguises, I guess.

Darion stood up. I hadn't seen him since he was a child. He was quite tall, and there was a certain bulkiness to his shoulders that reminded me of Dras Bull-neck. "Who is this man, Aunt Pol?" he demanded.

"My father," she replied shortly.

"Holy Belgarath?" His voice was startled.

"That 'holy' might be open to some question," she said dryly. "I told you to stay away from me, father."

"This is an emergency, Pol. We've got to leave Sulturn right now. Have you ever thought of hiding that white lock? It makes you awfully conspicuous, you know."

"What are you talking about?"

"There's a Murgo at an inn not a half mile from here. He's been asking after you. Worse yet, he's been getting answers. He knows exactly where you are. Gather up what you need, and let's get out of here. I don't know if he's alone or not, but even if he is now, he won't be for long."

"Why didn't you kill him?"

Darion's eyes went very wide. "Aunt Pol!" he gasped.

"How much does he know?" I asked, pointing at Darion.

"As much as he needs to know."

"That's a little vague, Pol. Does he know who he is?"

"In a general sort of way."

"I think it's time for a few specifics. You'd better pack a few things. We can buy more in Kotu."

"*Kotu?*"

"There are too many Murgos snooping around here in Sendaria. It's time for you to move to one of the Alorn kingdoms. Throw some things together while I explain the situation to Darion and his wife."

"I still think you should have killed the Murgo."

"This is Sendaria, Pol, not Cherek. Dead bodies attract attention here. As soon as you're ready, I'll go buy some horses."

"Get a wagon instead, father. Selana's pregnant. I'm not going to let you bounce her around in a saddle."

"Congratulations, your Majesty," I said to Darion.

"What did you say?"

"Congratulations."

"No, the other—that 'your Majesty' business?"

"Oh, *Polgara!*" I said irritably. "This is ridiculous! How many other facts haven't you told him? Start packing, and I'll explain things to him." I turned back to the heir. "All right, Darion, listen carefully—you, too, Selana. I won't have time to repeat this." I glossed over a number of things. As you may have noticed, this is a *very* long story. After about fifteen minutes, though, Darion and his wife at least knew that he was the heir to Iron-grip's throne and why we had to avoid Murgos.

"I can't just leave my shop behind, Ancient One," he protested.

"I'll set you up in business again once we get to Kotu. You'll have to abandon this one, I'm afraid."

"Go get a wagon, father," Pol told me.

"Where am I going to be able to buy a wagon at this time of night?"

"Steal one, then." Her eyes had gone flinty.

"I've got a two-wheeled cart," Darion said. "I use it as a handcart to deliver furniture. It's a little rickety, but it's got two shafts. I suppose we could come up with some way to hitch a horse to it. It might be a bit crowded, but the four of us should fit in it."

I suddenly laughed. "How very appropriate," I said.

"I didn't quite follow that."

"A very old friend of mine used to travel around in a rickety two-wheeled cart." Then I had an idea—a very good one, even if I do say so myself. "I think a fire might be useful here," I suggested.

"A fire?"

"You're going to have to leave all this behind anyway, Darion, but we can still get some use out of it. A burning house causes a lot of confusion and attracts crowds of gawkers. That might just be the thing to distract the Murgo long enough to give us the time to get away."

"All my things are here!" Selana protested. "All my furniture, my bedding, my clothes!"

"That's the nice thing about leaving town in a hurry, dear child," I told her gaily. "You get all new things when you get to where you're going. I'll buy you whatever you want when we get to Kotu. Frankly, I'd burn down this whole town if it'd help us evade that Murgo."

"I don't think it'll work, Ancient One," Darion said dubiously. "I'm fairly well known here in Sulturn, and somebody's bound to see us leaving."

"I'll hide you three in the back of the cart," I told him. "The only thing people are going to see is a humorous fellow in a rickety cart."

"Would that work?"

"It always has in the past. I'll go get my horse while you three finish packing." I went back downstairs and up the street to the inn. I stopped briefly to glance into the common room on my way to the stables. My Murgo was still there, and the tipsy Sendar was still talking to him. The Murgo evidently didn't intend to follow up on the information he'd received until morning. This was all working out better and better.

Polgara had improved on my plan during my absence. She had been very subtle about it, since I hadn't heard a thing, and if *I* hadn't heard it, I was sure that the Murgo—or Grolim, or whatever he was—hadn't heard her either. Three complete human skeletons were huddled together near one of the windows.

"Nice touch, Pol," I congratulated her.

"Just a little more confusion for your Murgo, father. If he believes that Darion, Selana, and I all died in the fire, he won't come looking for us."

"I'm sure Ctuchik'll be delighted to hear the news—at least until he goes back and rereads his prophecies. Then he'll probably turn our Murgo inside out."

"Wouldn't that be a shame?"

I put the three of them in the back of the cart and covered them with some blankets, and then I drove the cart out into the deserted street. I waited until we'd almost reached the north gate before I set fire to Darion's shop. I didn't start a big fire—just a baby one in a back corner. The shop had large stacks of seasoned lumber in it and wood shavings piled up in the corners, so my little fire had plenty to eat. It took awhile, but eventually it grew up.

The gates of Sulturn were unguarded. Sendars tend to be a little relaxed about security measures, so we were able to leave town unnoticed. We were well out of town on the road toward Lake Medalia before a sudden column of flame announced that my baby fire had finally reached adulthood and broken through the roof of Darion's house.

As I said earlier, it was midautumn, and it was a cloudy, blustery night as I drove the cart north toward Medalia and on beyond that to Darine, where we'd be able to take a ship for Kotu in Drasnia.

There's another repetition for you, Garion. Remember the night when we left Faldor's farm? Except for the turnips, this trip was almost identical.

It took us perhaps two weeks to reach Darine, largely because we stayed off the main roads and because I didn't particularly hurry. I'd learned that from my Master. If you want to stay inconspicuous, don't make any quick moves. He'd used that disguise many times, and I doubt that anyone had ever remembered him for more than ten minutes after he'd passed.

When we reached Darine, Darion sold the horse and cart, and we took passage on a Sendarian merchantman bound for Kotu.

There weren't any Murgos in Drasnia, but trade along the North Caravan Route had resumed—once the Nadraks recovered from their disastrous adventure on the frontier during the twenty-fifth century—so there were occasional Nadrak merchants in Kotu. Nadraks didn't concern me as much as Murgos did, but I was still rather cautious. Darion objected when I set him up in business as a woodcarver instead of a cabinetmaker until I explained it to him. "If you can make furniture, you can certainly carve wood, Darion," I told him. "That fellow we evaded back in Sulturn is very likely to tell all his friends everything he found out about you, so a lot of unfriendly eyes are going to be investigating every cabinet shop in the Western Kingdoms. For your safety, your wife's, and your Aunt Pol's, it's time for you to go into another line of work."

"I suppose you're right, Ancient One," he agreed glumly.

"Look on the bright side, Darion," I told him. "You can sell good wood carvings for almost as much as furniture, and you don't have to buy as much lumber."

I'd also changed their names and bullied Polgara into putting some dye on that conspicuous lock in her hair, although it didn't really work that well.

Then I decided that it was time for me to leave Kotu. I can't even whittle, so my presence in a woodcarver's shop might have been a little hard to explain. I said good-bye and sailed back to Darine, then proceeded to Muros and sat out the winter there before venturing into Ulgoland. I still wanted to meet the new Gorim, but not so much that I was willing to break my way through twelve-foot snowdrifts for the pleasure of his company.

I avoided the assorted monsters in Ulgoland the following spring by the usual expedient of going wolf. I suppose I could have gone falcon and flown instead, but there was no particular hurry, and I'm more comfortable as a wolf.

When I reached the ruins of Prolgu—although Prolgu isn't really ruined, only abandoned—I went to one particular house, announced my presence, and the Ulgos took me down into their dimly lighted caves and

418

to the house of their new Gorim. The traditional home of the Gorim of Ulgo lies in a gloomy cavern. It's an oddly truncated, pyramid-shaped house on a small eyot in the center of a shallow lake where small trickles of water fall down from above, echoing through that great cavern with the melancholy sound of eternal regret. I think the regret may be that of UL Himself. The Ulgos have lived in the dark for so long that daylight frightens them and the sun is an agony to their eyes. That island with its marble columns and pale, sunless shore seems more appropriate for a gathering of ghosts than for humans. Add to that the fact that the perpetual echoes in those caves makes it necessary for Ulgos to speak very softly. It makes a visit to Ulgoland much like a vacation in a mausoleum.

I liked the new Gorim, though. He was a gentle, saintly man, and he and I got on well together. As it turned out, however, I wasn't the only visitor in Prolgu just then. A fellow named Horban, a member of the Tolnedran diplomatic corps, had arrived a bit earlier. The Second Horbite Dynasty was in power in Tol Honeth, and the persistent rumors that Ulgoland actually had people living in it as well as the monsters had piqued the curiosity of Ran Horb XVI. He'd sent his cousin Horban to investigate and to explore the possible opportunities for trade. You know how Tolnedrans are.

"He's woefully uneducated, Belgarath," Gorim told me. "He has absolutely no sense of what's really happening in the world. Would you believe that he didn't even know of the existence of UL when he got here?"

"The Tolnedrans are a worldly people, Holy Gorim," I explained. "Their Nedra's the most secular of all the Gods."

The Gorim sighed. "Truly," he agreed. "What should we do with this man, Belgarath? All he can talk about is exchanging useless trinkets. He calls it 'trade,' and it seems to be a part of his religion."

I laughed. "I suppose you might as well humor him, Gorim. You'll never get any peace if you don't. Let the Tolnedrans come to that valley at the foot of your mountain, and then have your people go down there once in a while and exchange a few trinkets with them. If I'm reading the prophecies right, the time's going to come when we'll all be fighting Angaraks. The Tolnedran legions are going to be involved, so we'd better let them get used to the idea that you're here. The discovery of an untapped market might distract them."

"Oh," he said then, "before I forget, I have a message for you."

"A message?"

"From the Seers of Kell." He smiled a bit wryly. "We'd thought that all connection with our Dallish cousins had been severed long ago, but the Dals aren't like other people. Eons have passed since our last contacts, but they reminded us that we're still kinsmen."

"Are you saying that one of the Seers actually came here to Prolgu? Kell's half a world away."

He shook his head. "It was an illusion, Ancient One. The Seers have abilities we cannot even comprehend. I woke up one morning to find a blindfolded man sitting at my table with a huge mute hovering behind him. The blindfolded man told me to advise you that the unification of Mallorea's nearly complete. The emperors are Angaraks, and their throne's in Mal Zeth, but the continent's largely ruled by the bureaucracy in Melcene. Even the Dals are being gathered into the affairs of the Mallorean Empire. The Seer told me to warn you that the time's coming closer when Torak will come out of his seclusion to resume his old authority."

I nodded. "We'd more or less worked that out for ourselves. It's good to have some confirmation, though. We were baffled when Torak didn't invade right after the assassination of the Rivan King, but the One-eyed God evidently thinks long range. He's been biding his time at Ashaba, letting the Angarak emperors consolidate their hold on Mallorea. As soon as that's complete, he'll take command and mount an invasion."

"Are you making preparations?"

"My friend, I've been making preparations for Torak since the day he cracked the world. I've got a few surprises up my sleeve for him."

"The Seer also told me to warn you that Ctuchik's left Rak Cthol. What can *he* possibly be up to?"

"He's looking for Polgara. He's had his Murgos out scouring the West in search of her for centuries. Apparently the old Hound's going to give it a try himself. You know what she's doing, don't you?"

He nodded. "UL keeps me advised."

"I rather thought he might." I frowned. "Why are we suddenly getting all this help from the Dals? They've maintained a position of strict neutrality since the beginning of time."

"We must assume that it's in furtherance of *their* task. In some way, they're going to be involved in the final EVENT."

I nodded glumly. "That's *all* I need—somebody else to muddy the waters. They're muddy enough as it is."

I stayed in Prolgu for about a month, and then I went on over to Arendia to look in on several families I'd been watching for centuries. Prophecy being what it is, I probably didn't need to bother, but I always like to keep an eye on things. Even the best machine breaks down once in a while, and I'm the only mechanic around who knows how to fix this one.

Following the destruction of Vo Astur, the Mimbrate Duke had proclaimed himself king of all Arendia, but proclamations have very little to do with reality. The Mimbrate "royalty" were little more than puppet kings, their foreign policy dictated from Tol Honeth and their highways patrolled by Tolnedran legionnaires. They had very little time to brood about that, however. Although the Asturian cities and towns had been destroyed, the Asturian nobility and yeomanry remained intact— although greatly diminished. They simply retreated into their forests and took up archery for fun and profit. They shot at trees; they shot at deer; mostly they shot at Mimbrate tax collectors. They ate the deer, but they just let the Mimbrates lie where they fell. As you might expect, the Wildantor family participated enthusiastically.

I looked around a bit, and after I'd assured myself that Lelldorin's family was in the right place and doing more or less what it was supposed to be doing, I bought a horse and rode south toward Vo Mandor.

It was early summer, and once I got beyond the gloomy stretches of that forest that blankets northern Arendia, traveling was pleasant. The Great West Road simplified matters enormously. The helpful Tolnedrans had even bridged the River Mallerin, so I was able to cross without getting my feet wet.

The Arendish Fair stood at the juncture of the Great West Road and the high road that skirted the western edges of Ulgoland. The fair had been there since the time of the First Horbite Dynasty, and its position astride the Great West Road meant that it was policed by Tolnedran legionnaires, which sort of kept down the bloodshed. Tolnedrans won't let *anything* interfere with commerce, not even an ongoing civil war. I decided that it might not be a bad idea to stop over for a few days to rest my horse and pick up some information.

The Arendish Fair looked like a temporary collection of brightly colored tents, but it'd been there for something like a thousand years and was a commercial center rivaling the cattle fair at Muros in Sendaria. Since I wanted information, I went looking for Drasnians.

Yes, even back then. The Drasnian intelligence service had been established not long after the Alorn expedition into Nyissa, and, even as today, it relied heavily on merchants. Anytime you see a Drasnian merchant outside the borders of Drasnia itself, you can safely wager that he has *some* contacts with the intelligence service. He's interested in making money, of course, but he's *also* interested in information. The kings of Drasnia shrewdly have stressed the fact that gathering information is a Drasnian's patriotic duty, so in most cases the spymasters in Boktor don't even have to pay for it. That's very helpful when it comes time to balance the budget.

In many ways the Arendish Fair is like a city. It has its shops, its taverns, and even inns for those merchants who don't want to bother bringing their own tents. It's laid out like a city, too, with muddy streets and, in much the same fashion as in Muros, various districts. The Tolnedrans who police the fair are wise enough to segregate the races. Doing business with someone you hate is one thing; camping right next to him is something else.

The Drasnian enclave lay in the northeast quadrant of the fair, so I went there. I didn't look like a merchant, so the Drasnians *seemed* to ignore me, but nothing really escapes a Drasnian. Of course, the fact that I was scattering recognition signals like a bridesmaid scattering rose petals at a wedding might have helped a little, too.

Eventually a small, sharp-faced merchant with a long, pointed nose emerged from his tent with a feigned expression of surprise on his face. "Garath!" he exclaimed. "Can that really be you? I haven't seen you in ten years! What are you doing in Arendia?" His fingers were very busy telling me that he was a professional spy rather than an amateur and that his name was Khaldan.

I reined in my horse. "Why, strike me blind if it isn't my old friend Khaldan!" I said with a certain enthusiasm. I'd never met him in person, but I definitely knew his father, since I had some plans for his family. Ultimately, a marriage between Khaldan's family and the royal house of Drasnia was going to produce a sharp-nosed little fellow with some rather remarkable talents. Now that I think about it, that sharp-nosed fellow very closely resembled Khaldan—which probably isn't much of a coincidence.

"Come inside," Khaldan invited me. "We'll have a few tankards, and you can tell me what you've been up to for all these years."

I dismounted and followed him into his tent. "Garath?" I asked him incredulously. "Where did you learn about *that* name?"

He touched one finger slyly to his nose—evidently a family trait. "State secret," he replied. "The Service knows a great deal about you, Ancient One. How can I help you?"

"It's nothing very specific, Khaldan," I replied. "I'm going south is all, and I just stopped by to see if there was anything I ought to know about."

He shrugged. "Nothing unusual for Arendia, Ancient One."

I looked meaningfully at his half-open tent flap.

"Not to worry, Garath," he assured me. "Nobody's going to get near my tent who isn't supposed to. We can talk safely."

"Maybe, but let's not bandy that 'Ancient One' around too much. Is anything major happening between here and the Tolnedran border?"

"You might want to go around the barony of Vo Mandor," he suggested. "The Baron's having an argument with one of his neighbors just now."

I swore.

"What's the matter?"

"He's the very man I have to see."

"Stay here for a few weeks, then. It won't take him very long to finish up. The Mandor family has quite a reputation here in Mimbre. They're incapable of anything resembling caution, but they've been lucky enough so far that they haven't come up against anything they can't handle."

"I know," I agreed, "and that's not going to change very much in the foreseeable future. Are there very many Murgos here at the fair?"

"Funny you should ask. I was just going to bring it up myself. A Murgo nobleman of some sort rode into the fair a couple days ago. His rank must be fairly exalted, because the other Murgos are falling all over themselves to do what he asks."

"Have you picked up his name, by any chance?"

"I have, and it wasn't by chance. I *am* a professional, old friend. He calls himself Achak, but I've been getting a faint smell of deception there."

"What's he look like?"

"Tall, thinner than most Murgos, and he's got white hair and a long beard that's kind of yellowish. I don't think he's very clean. From what I hear, he smells bad."

"Well, well, well," I said. "How very convenient. Now I won't have to go looking for him."

"You know him?"

"I've known him for centuries. The Gorim of Ulgo told me that he'd come down from Rak Cthol. I've been curious about what he's doing."

"Rak Cthol? You're not saying that this Achak fellow is Ctuchik, are you?"

"Well, I hadn't yet, but I'd have gotten to it eventually, I guess."

"Now *that's* a name to reckon with." His eyes brightened. "Would you like to have him killed?"

"Forget it, Khaldan. You wouldn't be able to get an assassin near him. Besides, I might need him later on. Is he doing anything here—aside from terrorizing all the Murgos?"

"He's been holding some extended conferences is about all—Murgos, Nadraks, even a few Thulls. What's he doing here?"

"He's looking for something."

"Oh? What's that?"

I slyly touched my nose. "State secret," I replied, throwing his own clever remark back in his teeth. "Where's the Murgo enclave? I think maybe I'd better go have another little talk with the disciple of Torak."

"I'll send some men along to guard you."

"That won't be necessary. Ctuchik's not here for a confrontation— not with me, anyway. As soon as he finds out that I know he's here, he'll probably go back to Rak Cthol where he belongs. Did he come here alone?"

"No. He's got a Grolim priest with him—a sycophant, obviously. If Ctuchik decides to get belligerent, you'll be up against two of them, so I'd be a little careful."

"Numbers don't really mean all that much to me, Khaldan. Where's the Murgo enclave?"

"Over on the west side of the fair. Murgos live in black tents, so you can't miss it."

"Good." I stood up. "I'll be back in a little while." I went outside his tent, remounted, and rode on across the fair to the Murgo enclave. "You there," I said to the first Murgo I encountered. "I need to talk with Achak. Where do I find him?"

"Achak doesn't talk to foreigners," he replied insolently.

"He'll talk to *me*. Go tell him that Belgarath's here to see him."

His face went visibly pale, and he hurried off to a large tent in the middle of the enclave. He came back a moment or so later, and his manners had improved noticeably. "He'll see you," he said.

"Somehow I thought he might. Lead the way, friend."

He did that, though he didn't seem to care much for the idea. I got the feeling that he didn't want to be within five miles of what he expected to happen when I went into "Achak's" tent.

Ctuchik wasn't alone. The Grolim Khaldan had mentioned was hovering in the background with a servile expression on his face. "Awfully good to see you again, old boy," Ctuchik said with one of those bleak smiles pasted to his too-thin face. "It's been a long time, hasn't it? I was beginning to think I might have offended you."

"Your very existence offends me, Ctuchik. What persuaded you to come down off your mountaintop? Did the stink of your temple finally start to turn your stomach?"

"Blasphemy!" the hovering Grolim gasped.

"Is *he* serving any purpose?" I asked Ctuchik, jerking my thumb at the Grolim.

"He's my apprentice, Belgarath. I'm teaching him the business."

"Aren't you getting a little above yourself, old boy? Are you taking your own disciples now? Torak might not approve."

"He's a servant, Belgarath, not a disciple, and Torak more or less allows us to do as we please. You might think about that the next time

Aldur sends you off on some fool's errand. If you'd like to change Masters, I could put in a good word for you."

"One turncoat in the family's quite enough, Ctuchik, and I'm not going to change sides when I'm winning."

"*Are* you winning, Belgarath? How strange that I hadn't noticed that. You might as well get to know my servant here. I expect you'll be seeing a lot of him from now on." He looked at the Grolim. "Chamdar, this is Belgarath, first disciple of the God Aldur. Don't let his foolish exterior deceive you. He can be troublesome at times."

"One does one's best," I said with a little smirk. I looked more closely at the Grolim. He had scarred cheeks like a Murgo, but there was something a bit different about him. There was a certain boldness about him, and a burning ambition in his eyes that I don't think Ctuchik was aware of. "You're wasting your time here, Ctuchik," I said then. "You're *not* going to find my daughter, no matter how many Murgos you send west, and you're certainly not going to find her yourself. Something like that would have shown up in our instructions."

"We'll see," he replied distantly. "It was awfully good of you to stop by, old chap. I could have shown Chamdar here a picture of you, but a picture wouldn't have captured the real you."

I actually laughed. "You're sending a boy to do a man's work, Ctuchik," I told him. "I'm not going to lead your underling anywhere near Polgara."

"We'll see about that, too. Sooner or later, something's bound to come up that'll force you to go to where she is."

"You've never met my daughter, Ctuchik. Believe me, she can take care of herself. Why don't you take your Grolim and go home? The Godslayer *is* coming, and there's not a thing you can do about it."

"That particular EVENT hasn't been decided yet, old boy."

"It *will* be, *old* boy, and I don't think you're going to like the way it turns out. Are you coming, Chamdar?"

"Coming?" he demanded, sounding baffled. "Coming where?"

"Don't be childish. As soon as I'm outside this tent, your Master's going to tell you to follow me. It'll be much easier for both of us if we just ride along together."

"That's for my Master to decide," he replied coldly.

"Suit yourself. I'll be riding south from here. If you happen to lose track of me, I'll be in Tol Honeth in a couple of weeks. Ask around when you get there. I shouldn't be too hard to find."

Then I turned and left the tent.

CHAPTER THIRTY-SIX

Polgara looked upon the centuries she was obliged to spend in the boisterous Alorn kingdoms as a period of exile. Pol's fond of individual Alorns, but as a race they tend to set her teeth on edge. She yearned to go back to Sendaria. The Sendars aren't as courtly as the Wacite Arends were, but they're a polite, civil people, and civility's very important to my daughter.

I devoted quite a bit of time during those years providing entertainment for the ambitious Chamdar. Every so often, I'd come out of the Vale, randomly select some obscure village in Sendaria or northern Arendia, and kill several Murgos there. Chamdar, of course, would leap to the conclusion that I'd killed them because they were getting too close to Polgara. He'd rush to the place and spend five or six years following the various false trails I'd laid down for him. Then the trails would peter out on him, and we'd start all over again someplace else. I'm sure he knew exactly what I was doing, but he didn't have any choice but to respond. The fact that he didn't age over the centuries was an indication of *some* status in Grolim society. He wasn't exactly a disciple, but he was the next thing to it, I suppose.

In the meantime, Polgara remained safe—if not content—in Cherek, or Drasnia, or Algaria. Her common practice during those years was to apprentice a youthful heir to some artisan in a village or small town; and then when the young man reached maturity, she'd set him up in business—much in the way she had with Darion in the forty-fifth century. I never did find out where she got the money for all those business ventures. She invariably posed as a member of the young man's family, an older sister, a cousin, very frequently an aunt, and even once or twice as the young man's mother. The families she thus created were so ordinary that random travelers—or random Angaraks—probably didn't even notice them. I'm sure it was all very tedious for her, but she'd taken on the chore of hiding the heirs of her own free will, and Pol has a very strong sense of responsibility.

My contribution—keeping Chamdar away from her—was fairly peripheral, but I like to think that it helped, if only a little bit. I'd also periodically look in on all those families I was juggling, and every now and then I'd ease on down into Cthol Murgos to see what the opposition was up to.

Murgo society is unlike any other on the face of the earth, largely because it's built along military lines. They don't have principalities down there; they have military districts instead, each with its own general. Because of the Murgo obsession with racial purity, Murgo women are kept closely confined, so you never see any women on the streets—just men, all in chain mail. Over the course of the centuries, the various military commanders have passed the spurious crown of Cthol Murgos around, so there've been Goska Dynasties, Cthan Dynasties, Hagga Dynasties, and recently, Urga Dynasties. It didn't really matter who sat on the throne in Rak Goska, however, because Ctuchik has always ruled Cthol Murgos from his turret in Rak Cthol.

The twins continued to work on their concordance, and Beldin maintained his surveillance in Mallorea. Everything sort of plodded along until the middle of the forty-ninth century with nothing very much happening. It was one of those quiet periods that crop up from time to time in the history of the world. Then there was a total eclipse of the sun in the spring of 4850. An eclipse isn't all that unusual, so we didn't pay much attention to it—at least not at first. This one was fairly unique, in that it seemed to trigger a significant climate change. Would you *believe* that it rained off and on for twenty-five years? We almost never saw the sun.

Several months after that eclipse, Beldin came back from Mallorea with some news we'd all been waiting for. He clumped, dripping, up the stairs to my workshop. "Miserable weather," he muttered. "I haven't been really dry for the last three months. Have you got anything to drink? I think I'm chilled all the way to the bone."

"I don't happen to have anything right now," I told him. "Why don't you go call on the twins?"

"Later, maybe." He slumped down in a chair by the fire and pulled off his soggy shoes. "It's finally happened, Belgarath," he told me, wriggling his toes.

"What has?"

"Old Burnt-face has finally come out of Ashaba."

"Where did he go?"

"Mal Zeth. Where else? He's deposed the current emperor and taken personal command of the Mallorean Empire." He sneezed. "You're the expert on Old Angarak. What does the word 'Kal' mean?"

"King and God. It's a Grolim usage that was fairly prevalent at Korim. It's sort of fallen into disuse—probably because Torak's been holed up at Ashaba for the last three eons or so."

"Burnt-face has a long memory, then. He calls himself 'Kal Torak' now, and he's making sure that everybody in Mallorea recognizes the name."

"Is he mobilizing?"

"Not yet. At the moment, he's busy desecularizing Mallorea. He's reintroduced the joys of religion. Urvon's having a field day. His Grolims are butchering everybody they can lay their hands on. The temples from Camat to Gandahar are running knee-deep in blood."

"Let's go talk with the twins. We'd better see what the Mrin has to say about this."

"You'd also better hustle your tail feathers north to warn the Alorns."

"In a bit. I want to look at the Mrin first."

"I don't have much time, Belgarath. I've got to go back to Mallorea. I don't want Kal Torak to sneak up on you with several million Malloreans."

"I'm almost sure I'll hear him coming."

"Where's Pol now?"

"At Aldurford in northern Algaria."

"You'd better tell her to come home."

"We'll see. I'm not going to do anything until I find out what the Mrin has to say."

The twins became very excited when Beldin told them that Torak had finally come out of Ashaba, and they immediately went to work. Beldin stumped around, growing increasingly impatient.

"Please, brother," Beltira told him, looking up from his copy of the Mrin, "sit down someplace. We're trying to concentrate." It was one of the few times I've ever seen either of the twins display anything remotely resembling irritability.

After about an hour, Belkira slapped his hand down on the Darine triumphantly. "Here it is!" he exclaimed. "I *thought* I remembered it."

"What does it say?" Beltira demanded.

"It's that passage about the eclipse. It says, 'Behold! The sun shall fall dark, and the sky shall endlessly weep, and it shall be a sign that the King returneth, and the God, also."

"It got the part about the sky weeping pretty close," Beldin noted.

"We misread it," Beltira confessed. "It's only talking about one of them, not both."

"Will you two *please* try to make sense?" Beldin exploded.

"We've been looking in the wrong direction," Beltira explained. "We thought the passage meant that the Rivan King would reemerge and that Torak would come out of Ashaba at the same time. It doesn't have anything to do with the Rivan King, though. It's only talking about Torak, since he's both King and God in Angarak. That eclipse and the foul weather we've had since then warned us that this was coming, but Irongrip's heir's over fifty years old right now, so we discounted the possibility. We're sorry, Belgarath."

"I'd have probably missed it, as well, Beltira. Don't blame yourselves. Where's the corresponding passage in the Mrin?"

Belkira checked their concordance, took up the third scroll of the Mrin, and unrolled it until he found the index mark he was looking for. "It's right here," he said, handing me the scroll and pointing at the mark.

" 'Behold!' " I read it aloud. " 'In the day that the sun falls dark at noon and the skies are veiled shall the King reemerge, and shall he journey to the seat of power and put aside the one who hath stood in his stead.' "

"I can see how you missed that one, brothers," Beldin said to the twins. "It's ambiguous enough so that it could very well mean the Rivan King. What does it say next, Belgarath?"

" 'And he shall confer with his tributary kings,' " I read on, " 'instructing all in that which they must do, and in the fullness of time shall he gather his forces and shall move to confront the other Child. And the one of them shall be a God, and the other shall be like unto a God, and the jewel shall decide the outcome in the lands of the children of the Bull-God.' "

"Arendia?" Beldin said. "Why Arendia?"

"There've been hints of that before," Beltira said. "*Something* important's going to happen in Arendia."

"What else does it say?" Beldin asked me.

I read the next line, and then I started to swear.

"What's wrong?" Beldin demanded.

"It just broke off. Now it's talking about 'the Mother of the Race That Died.' "

"Beltira and I'll work with it some more," Belkira told me.

"We know enough to get started, Belgarath," Beldin said. "You and I both have things to do, and the twins can work better without the two of us hanging over their shoulders. I'm going back to Mallorea. You'd better go alert the Alorns—*and* find a safer place to hide Polgara. There's nothing at Aldurford but the river and a lot of open grassland."

I grunted and stood up. "You're probably right," I agreed. "I don't care much for running off on just a few hints, but there's no help for it, I guess."

"We'll stay in touch," Beltira promised. "We'll let you or Pol know just as soon as we pinpoint anything else that seems significant."

"I'd really appreciate that, brother," I replied.

I flew north from the Vale to the Algarian Stronghold and found out from the caretakers there that Cho-Ram XIV, the current chief of the Clan-Chiefs of Algaria, was in the vicinity of Lake Atun up near the Drasnian border.

I'm sure that name rings a bell. Royal families habitually repeat names. It's a silly custom, but at least it doesn't strain anybody's creativity.

It took me only two days to locate the fourteenth Cho-Ram. He was a fairly young man, and he customarily wore clothing made of horsehide and shaved his head—except for a flowing scalp-lock that hung down his back like the tail of a horse. Now that I think back on it, he looked a great deal like Cho-Hag's adopted son, Hettar.

"It's about time" was all he said when I told him that Torak was coming. He was obviously a true descendant of the close-mouthed Algar Fleet-foot.

"He isn't coming to pay a social call," I said acidly.

"I know." Then he grinned wolfishly at me.

Alorns!

"You'd better gather your clans," I advised.

"How long have we got?"

"I'm not sure. Mallorea's a big place, and it's going to take Torak a while to gather his forces. Beldin's there, though, so he'll be able to give us a little advance notice."

"That's all we really need, isn't it? I'll call the clans in, and we'll all go down to the Stronghold. I'll be there when you need me."

"Is Khalan still king in Drasnia?"

"No. He died last fall. His son Rhodar wears the crown."

"I'd better go to Boktor and talk with him. Keep a sharp eye on the Eastern Escarpment. Something important's going to happen in Arendia, so the Murgos might come down the cliff to try to soften you up before Torak gets here. You're sitting on his logical invasion route."

"Good."

"*Good?* What do you mean, good?"

"I won't have to go looking for him."

"Was your grandmother an Arend, by any chance?"

"*Belgarath!* What a thing to suggest!"

"Never mind. Get to work. I'll go talk with Rhodar, and then go to Val Alorn and see Eldrig."

Notice that I'd already broad-jumped my way to an erroneous conclusion. Both Mishrak ac Thull and Algaria were open grasslands, and Torak was going to be leading a very large army. It didn't even occur to me that he'd try to take all those troops through the Nadrak Forest.

Rhodar I of Drasnia was not nearly as corpulent as his namesake five centuries later, but he was still fairly stout. He was a descendant of Bull-neck, though, so a certain bulk was understandable. We ran a lot of that off him during the next twenty or so years. I alerted him to what was happening in Mallorea and then left him mapping out his defenses with his generals while I flew on to Val Alorn.

King Eldrig of Cherek was not exactly what you'd call a true representative of his race. More often than not his tankard held water instead of beer, for one thing, and he was a scholarly man, for another. He was a great deal like Anheg in that respect. About the only difference is the fact that Anheg *will* take a drink on occasion.

"Arendia?" he said when I told him what was coming.

"That's what the Mrin says."

"Are you sure? Torak's coming west to get the Orb, isn't he? The Orb's not in Arendia; it's at Riva."

"The twins are still hammering at the Mrin. They might be able to dig out an explanation. All we've got so far is the fact that the EVENT's going to take place in the lands of the children of the Bull God. Unless something's changed, that means Arendia."

Eldrig scratched at his iron-grey hair and stared at his map. "I suppose Torak *could* swing through Mimbre and then turn north to the hook of Arendia to come at the Isle from the south. If we just happened to be in his way, there *could* be some kind of confrontation down there."

I also looked at his map. "There's no real point in running off there until Torak makes his move," I said. "You'd better get word to Brand. Tell him that I'll come to the Isle in a little bit. I've got a couple of other things to attend to first."

"Do you think I should seal off the Isle?" he asked.

"We'll have to do that eventually, but let's not upset the Tolnedrans by making them shut down their shops on the beach at Riva just yet. We'll need the legions before this is over, so we don't want Ran Borune's nose getting out of joint. We'll have plenty of time to fill the Sea of the Winds with war-boats when Torak starts to move, and Beldin'll give us plenty of warning when that happens."

"I wish we had more to work with."

"So do I, but for right now, we've got enough to get started. Oh, you might want to warn Ormik of Sendaria, as well."

"You're not serious!"

"The Sendars live here, too, Eldrig."

"Cabbage farmers won't be much good in a fight."

"Maybe not, but if all this shapes up the way I think it's going to, we'll probably have to go through Sendaria from time to time, so let's stay on Ormik's good side."

"Anything you say, Ancient One." He leaned back in his chair. King Eldrig had grey hair, but the grin he suddenly flashed at me was surprisingly youthful. "This is the one we've been waiting for, isn't it, Belgarath?" he said.

"One of them, I suppose. I think there'll be others, as well."

"One's enough for right now. I wouldn't want to seem greedy. This is the one we've been expecting since the days of Bear-shoulders, so that's good enough for me."

"Talk to me about how lucky you are after the war, Eldrig. The last one wasn't too pleasant, as I recall. Start getting your people ready, and dip into your treasury so that you can hire shipbuilders. I might need more war boats."

He winced. "Maybe I can float a loan from Ran Borune."

"I wouldn't bet on it, and you wouldn't care for his interest rates. Get started, Eldrig. I'll be in touch."

I left Val Alorn and flew southeast to Aldurford in northern Algaria to talk with Polgara. Her house was near the ford itself, so I strolled on down through the town to the river. With the exception of the Stronghold, Aldurford is just about the only town in Algaria, and it shows. Algars have a rather haphazard idea about what a town ought to look like. The notion of regular streets hasn't really caught on, and the citizens of Aldurford have built their houses wherever it suited them. It makes finding your way around a bit challenging.

Eventually I located Pol's house and knocked on the door. She opened it almost immediately. As usual, she was dressed all in blue, and she greeted me in her usual gracious fashion. "Where have you been?" she demanded. "I've been expecting you for two weeks now."

"I had to go talk with some Alorns." I looked past her into her kitchen. There was a boy of about eleven sitting at the table. It wasn't hard to recognize him, since all of Iron-grip's descendants have looked much the same. He had sandy-colored hair and that same serious expression they've all had. There was a melancholy Algar woman with long dark hair shelling peas at the table with him. I was never certain just how much Pol had told the various heirs she raised, so I thought it might be best if she and I spoke privately. "Let's take a little walk, Pol," I suggested. "We've got some fairly important decisions to make."

She glanced over her shoulder, nodded, fetched a shawl, and came outside.

"What happened to his father?"

"He died," she replied shortly, and that same old sorrow was in her voice.

"What's the boy's name?"

"Garel. He's the heir."

"Obviously."

I could see that she didn't want to talk, so we walked on in silence. We went along the riverbank until we were well beyond the last of the houses. The perpetual clouds that had obscured the sky for months had broken for a brief period, and it was actually sunny. A breeze was rippling the surface of the water. I looked out across the broad river and had one of those peculiar little shocks of recognition. I was almost positive that it had been on the far bank that the funny old man in the rickety cart had given me instructions about the breakup of Aloria after Cherek and the boys and I had returned from Cthol Mishrak about twenty-nine centuries back.

"What's the matter?" Pol asked curiously.

I shrugged. "Nothing important. I've been here before, that's all. I gather you know what's happened?"

She nodded. "The twins told me. They couldn't locate you, so they asked me to pass a few things on to you."

"Oh?"

"They've managed to extract some more information out of the Mrin. Brand's going to be the Child of Light during this particular EVENT."

"*Brand?*"

"That's what the Mrin says. The passage reads, 'And let him who stands in the stead of the Guardian meet the Child of Dark in the domain of the Bull God.' That has to mean Brand, doesn't it?"

"I don't see how it could mean anybody else. Evidently there's going to be a suspension of the rules—enough to allow Brand to take up Riva's sword, at any rate."

"The twins didn't say. They're still working on that part, I guess. There's more."

"There almost has to be. Give me your hand, Pol. I think I'd better talk with the twins directly, and we both need to hear what they say."

She nodded and held out her hand to me. For any number of reasons, Pol and I have rarely touched each other over the years, and we've even more rarely linked our minds in order to do something. Once again I was startled by the breadth and depth of my daughter's mind, and by its exquisite subtlety. What struck me the most, however, was her deep sadness. I think we all overlooked the fact that the task she'd freely accepted involved rearing a long series of little boys, watching them grow up, get married, and then grow old and die. The vaults of her mind echoed with an unremitting sorrow that nothing could ever dispel.

Once our minds were linked, we sent out our combined voices. *"Brothers."*

"Belgarath?" Beltira's voice came back to us. *"Where are you?"*

"I'm at Aldurford. Pol's with me. Could you clarify a few things for us?"

"Of course."

"Have you found out how Brand's supposed to use the Orb yet?"

"No. It's very difficult going here, Belgarath. I think this is going to be a major EVENT. The Mrin always gets very obscure when we come to one of those."

"Any hints about what I'm supposed to do?"

"You and Pol are supposed to go to Riva to meet with the Alorn kings. Oh, something else, too. You're supposed to take Iron-grip's heir to the Stronghold before you go to Riva."

"Out of the question!" Pol's voice overrode mine. "The Stronghold's directly in Torak's path."

"I'm just passing on what the Mrin says, Pol," Beltira replied. *"It says, 'And the Guardian shall take refuge in the fortress of the Horse People, for all the might of the Dark Child shall not prevail against its walls.' You're probably right. Torak's going to lay siege to the Stronghold, but he's not going to be able to storm it under."*

"I don't like it," she fumed.

"It does make sense, Pol," I told her, speaking aloud. "You and I have to go to Riva, and that wouldn't be a safe place for Garel and his mother. The whole point of this last eight hundred years has been to keep the heirs and the Orb separated. If we take Garel to Riva, *he'll* have to take up the sword, and he's a little young yet." Then I sent my thought out to the twins again. *"Have you been able to get any kind of time frame on all of this?"*

"From the Mrin? You know that there's no such thing as time in the Mrin."

"Have you heard from Beldin?"

"Once or twice. Torak's still at Mal Zeth, and he's got Zedar and Urvon with him."

"We've still got plenty of time then."

"We'll see. We'll keep working on this, but you two had better get started."

Pol and I started back along the riverbank toward Aldurford. "I don't like this, father," she told me again.

"I don't very much myself. We're playing a game, Pol, and we don't know all the rules yet, so I guess we'll just have to make one of those great leaps of faith. We have to believe that the Purpose knows what it's doing."

"I still don't like it."

"Sometimes we have to do things we don't like, Pol. That's what we get paid to do."

"Paid?"

"Figuratively speaking."

Garel and his mother didn't really know too much about their real situation, and Pol and I decided that it might be best to leave it that way. The heirs to Iron-grip's throne have all been what we've come to call "talented"—some more, some less—and it's a little dangerous to have a novice sorcerer in possession of *too* much information. Garion, who's far more than marginally talented, probably will remember any number of times while he was growing up on Faldor's farm when either Pol or I skillfully sidestepped his questions. The decision to do it that way was Pol's, of course, but after I thought about it for a bit, I wholeheartedly approved. It headed off all sorts of unpleasant possibilities.

We circulated the usual "family emergency" story around Aldurford for a day or so, and then we bundled up Garel and Adana and left for the Stronghold. When we got there, I had a talk with Cho-Ram, and then the three of us left for Riva.

The weather on the Isle of the Winds is so miserable most of the time anyway that we scarcely noticed the rather profound climate change brought on by that eclipse. The rain was seething across the harbor when we arrived, the stairway leading up to the Citadel looked like a waterfall, and the eaves of the slate-roofed stone houses spilled sheets of water into the cobbled streets. I found it all moderately depressing.

Eldrig and Rhodar hadn't arrived yet, so Pol and I met with Brand

and Cho-Ram high in one of those towers that loom up over the Citadel. I'd been roaming around quite a bit during the past several years, so I didn't really know the current Rivan Warder all that well. Even though the Warder's office isn't hereditary, there's always been a certain continuity of character in the men who've held the position. The Rivans don't quite go as far as the Nyissans do in selecting Salmissra, but they come fairly close when choosing Brand. The Rivan Warders have all been solid, sensible men that we've been able to rely on. *This* one, though, was a truly remarkable man. The putative Child of Light was a big man, but Alorns generally are quite large. Tolnedrans, who are racially small, try to make some issue of an old Tolnedran proverb contrasting physical size with mental capacity. I'm not all that large myself, but I've been jerked up short any number of times when I've come across brilliant giants. This particular Rivan Warder was intelligent, introspective, and he had a low, deep, quiet voice. I liked him right at the outset, and I grew to like him even more as the years drew us inexorably toward that meeting he was going to have in Arendia. "Are you certain that King Garel's going to be safe at the Stronghold?" he asked.

"That's what the Mrin Codex says," I replied.

"Don't worry, Brand," Cho-Ram assured him. "Nobody's going to get over the walls of the Stronghold."

"We're talking about my king, Cho-Ram," Brand said. "I *won't* throw dice for his safety."

"I'll go there myself, Brand, and I'll stand on top of the wall for twenty years and let Torak throw everything he's got at me."

"No, you won't, Cho-Ram," I told him firmly. "I'm not going to let you get locked up inside the Stronghold. Any colonel can defend that place. I need the Alorn kings where I can get my hands on them."

"I'd still feel better if my Lord Garel were here," Brand said.

"That wouldn't be a good idea. If he comes anywhere near the Orb, Torak'll know about it immediately. If he stays at the Stronghold, he'll still be anonymous, and Torak won't even know he's there."

"He'll have to come here eventually, Belgarath."

"Oh? Why's that?"

"To get his sword. If he's going to meet Torak, he's going to need that sword."

"You're getting ahead of yourself, Brand," Pol told him. "Garel's *not* the one who's going to meet Torak in Arendia."

"He's the Rivan King, Polgara. He *has* to meet Torak."

"Not this time."

"Well, if he isn't, who is?"

"You are."

"*Me?*" To his credit, Brand didn't add that inevitable "Why me?" His eyes were a little wild, though.

I recited the passage to him. "It looks like you've been elected, Brand," I added.

"I didn't even know I was a candidate. What am I supposed to do?"

"We're not sure. *You* will be when the time comes, though. When you come face to face with One-eye, the Necessity's going to take over. It always does in these situations."

"I'd be a lot more comfortable if I knew what was supposed to happen."

"We all would, but it doesn't work that way. Don't worry, Brand. You'll do just fine."

Eldrig and Rhodar joined us at Riva a month or so later, and we started mapping out our strategy. Beldin advised us that Torak didn't seem to be in any hurry to start west. He was concentrating instead on consolidating his hold on the hearts and minds of the subject races in Mallorea. I wasn't really worried about any surprises. Torak was far too arrogant to try to sneak up on us. He *wanted* us to know that he was coming.

After our first few meetings, we invited King Ormik of Sendaria to join us. Ormik's mother had been an Alorn, so his inclusion was right and proper. The fact that we were all spending a lot of time at Riva didn't go unnoticed. Ran Borune's intelligence service wasn't as good as Rhodar's, but even the most half-witted spy in the world could hardly miss the fact that *something* was in the wind.

Torak spent a dozen years or so establishing his absolute domination of Mallorea—all unaware that Garel had married an Algar girl, Aravino, in 4860, and that a year later she had given birth to her son, Gelane. Then in the fall of 4864 the Murgos and Nadraks closed the caravan routes to the east. The howls of anguish in Tol Honeth echoed from the jungles of Nyissa to the arctic wastes of Morindland. Ran Borune sent diplomatically worded protests to Rak Goska and Yar Nadrak, but they were generally ignored. Ad Rak Cthoros, the King of the Murgos, and Yar Lek Thun of the Nadraks were taking their orders from Ctuchik, and neither one of them was going to cross that walking corpse just because Ran Borune had his feelings hurt. I don't know if Ctuchik even bothered to tell Gethel Mardu of the Thulls about the planned invasion of the West, since Gethel probably didn't even know which way west was.

The closing of those trade routes was a clear signal that Torak was about to move, so Brand declared the port of Riva closed "for renovations," and Eldrig's war-boats enforced that declaration. Things were definitely going downhill for the merchant princes of Tol Honeth.

After the sealing of the port of Riva, we gathered once more in the

Citadel. "Things are coming to a head, father," Polgara noted. "I think it's time for you to go have a talk with Ran Borune."

"Maybe you're right," I conceded glumly.

"Why so long a face, Belgarath?" Brand asked me.

"Have you ever met Ran Borune?"

"I've never had the pleasure."

"That's not the right word, Brand. The Borunes are stubborn and contentious, and they absolutely refuse to believe in anything the least bit out of the ordinary."

"Shouldn't we alert the Arends, too?" the leather-clad Cho-Ram suggested.

"Not yet," I replied. "It's probably a little premature. If Torak's more than two days from their eastern frontier, they'll forget that he's coming."

"The Arends aren't *that* stupid, father," Pol protested.

"*Really?* Oh, Cho-Ram, see if you can get word of what's afoot to the Gorim of Ulgo, and Ormik, why don't you move your supply dumps down to the north bank of the Camaar River? If we're going to have a war in Arendia, we'll need groceries."

"We can live off the land if we have to," Rhodar said.

"Of course—for maybe a week. After that, we'll be eating our shoes, and you wouldn't care for that."

I left for Tol Honeth the following morning and arrived there two days later. Ran Borune IV was a young man who'd been on the imperial throne only for a few years. The Third Borune Dynasty was still in its infancy, and the Borunes hadn't yet shaken all the Honethites and Vorduvians out of the government. The Honeths in particular were *very* upset about the closing of the trade routes to the East and the "renovations" at Riva. A day without profit sends a Honethite into deep mourning, and so a steady stream of officials, high and low, were beating on Ran Borune's door imploring him to do something. As a result, it was several days before I got in to see him.

Over the centuries, the various imperial families in Tol Honeth have devised a fiction that makes them comfortable. They sagely assure each other that the names "Belgarath" and "Polgara" are hereditary titles. Accepting an alternative would have been out of the question for them, so I came at Ran Borune rather obliquely to avoid a long argument about something that wasn't really that important. "Have you heard about what's happening in Mallorea, your Majesty?" I asked him.

"I understand that they have a new emperor." Like most members of his family, Ran Borune was a small man—probably the result of their Dryad heritage. The Imperial Throne of Tolnedra had been designed to be impressive, so it was quite large and draped in imperial crimson. Ran

Borune IV looked a great deal like a child sitting on a piece of grown-up furniture.

"How much do you know about that new emperor in Mal Zeth?" I asked him.

"Not all that much. Mallorea's a long way away, and I've got things closer to home to worry about."

"You'd better *start* worrying about Kal Torak, because he's coming this way."

"What makes you think so?"

"I have sources of information that aren't available to you, Ran Borune."

"More of *that* tired old nonsense, Belgarath? That might impress Alorns, but it certainly doesn't impress me."

I sidestepped that rather smoothly. "I'm not referring to that, Ran Borune. The information comes from Rhodar's intelligence service. *Nobody* can hide things from a Drasnian spy."

"Why didn't Rhodar let me know?"

"He *is* letting you know. That's why I'm here."

"Oh. Why didn't you say so? I'll send emissaries to Mal Zeth to ask the Mallorean Emperor what his intentions are."

"Don't waste your time, Ran Borune. He'll probably be on your doorstep in a few months, and then you'll be able to talk to him in person."

"What sort of man is he? And why did he choose that particular name?"

"He's arrogant, implacable, and driven by an overwhelming ambition. The word 'Kal' means *King* and *God* in Old Angarak. Does that give you any clues about him?"

"A madman?" Ran Borune looked startled.

"*He* probably wouldn't see it that way—and the Angaraks *certainly* don't. He's convinced them that he's really Torak—largely by having the Grolims gut anybody who *didn't* believe. He's coming west, and he'll be driving all of Mallorea in front of him."

"They'll have to get past the Murgos first. Murgos despise Malloreans, and they certainly won't bow down to a Mallorean Emperor."

"The Murgos do what the Grolims tell them to do, Ran Borune, and the Grolims have accepted this Kal Torak as the *real* Torak."

He began to gnaw on one of his fingernails. "I think we might have a problem," he conceded. "Have Rhodar's spies found out why he wants to invade us?"

"To rule the world, I suppose," I said with a shrug. "We don't know exactly why, yet, but his ultimate destination seems to be Arendia."

"*Arendia?* That doesn't make any sense at all!"

"I know, but that's what Drasnian intelligence is picking up. If we don't do something to stop him, you're going to have a very large, un-friendly army camped on your northern border."

"He'll have to come through Algaria to get to Arendia."

"That's our best guess, too."

"Are the Algars ready for him?"

"The Algars have been getting ready for an Angarak invasion for the past three millennia. So have the Chereks and the Drasnians. Alorns and Angaraks don't get along at all."

"So I've heard. I think maybe I'll put the legions on standby alert."

"I'd go a little further than 'standby,' Ran Borune. I had a look at some of your legionnaires on my way here. They're pitifully out of condi-tion. You'd better toughen them up a bit. I'm going back to Riva now. I think it's time to beef up the defenses of Algaria. We'll keep you advised if Rhodar's spies pick up anything else." Then I bowed and left.

I've used that ploy many times in dealing with Tolnedrans. The sup-posed omniscience of Drasnian Intelligence can be very useful at times. It's easier to lie to them than to tell them where I'm *really* getting my information.

In the spring of 4865, Kal Torak led his Malloreans across the land-bridge to Morindland, and then he started south along the coast. After he'd passed the mountains of Gar og Nadrak, however, his entire army disappeared into that vast primeval forest that blankets the North.

I've been involved in a lot of wars over the years, and I think that might have contributed to my failure to predict what Torak was going to do. A human general will take the shortest, easiest route to get to a bat-tlefield. He doesn't want to waste the lives of his troops, and he doesn't want them to be exhausted when the fighting starts. Torak, however, was most definitely *not* a human general. The lives of his troops meant noth-ing to him, and he had ways to make them fight, no matter how ex-hausted they were.

At any rate, the Alorn kings and I were so convinced that Torak would continue down the coast to Mishrak ac Thull that we were taken completely by surprise when he led his army of northern Murgos, Nadraks, Thulls, and Malloreans down out of the mountains in western Gar og Nadrak and out onto the moors of eastern Drasnia early in the summer of 4865.

Torak himself made the journey in a silly-looking iron castle, com-plete with useless towers and ostentatious battlements. It had wheels on it, but it still took a herd of horses and about a thousand Grolims to pull it. I shudder to think of the amount of labor it took to clear a road through the forests of Gar og Nadrak for that ridiculous thing.

It became clear almost immediately that Kal Torak came not as a conqueror, but as a destroyer. He was not interested in occupying Drasnia and enslaving the people. He wanted to kill them all. Such Drasnians as *were* captured were immediately sacrificed by the Grolim priests.

In retrospect, I can understand what he was doing. He had to reach Arendia, of course, but he gave himself enough time to exterminate the Drasnians before he proceeded into Algaria or Cherek to do the same thing there. Arendia was secondary in his thinking. He wanted to wipe out the Alorns before he got there.

Our mistaken assessment of his probable strategy had pulled us seriously out of position, and his hordes had destroyed Boktor before we could get enough forces north to offer any serious resistance. Since we were hopelessly outnumbered, we didn't even pretend that we were making war. We rushed north on a rescue mission instead, gathering such refugees as we were able to find. Eldrig's war-boats took large crowds of terror-stricken Drasnian civilians off the islands at the mouths of the Aldur and Mrin rivers, and Algar cavalry rounded up those who had fled south toward Lake Atun and escorted them to the relative safety of the Algarian Stronghold. A large column of refugees from Boktor made a truly astounding trek north from their burning city to reach the valley of the River Dused, where it forms the border between Drasnia and the Cherek peninsula. For the rest of the population, the only escape was into the fens. Very few of them survived.

Once it became clear that there was no way that we could match the army Kal Torak had hurled at us, we concluded that Drasnia was lost. I had to do some fairly brutal things at that point to salvage as much of the superb Drasnian army as I could. I didn't even bother trying to argue with the grief-stricken Rhodar. I simply drove him and his pikemen south onto the plains of Algaria. I was fairly sure I was going to need them later.

And so, by the midsummer of 4866, Drasnia had perished. When we went back there after the war, we couldn't find so much as a single house still standing, and there were only a few thousand survivors hiding out in the fens.

When it was over, Kal Torak paused to regroup. Our problem at that point was trying to guess which way he'd go next. Would he sweep across the north and invade Cherek? Would he go southwest in an attempt to reach Arendia by marching across Sendaria? Or would he lead his hordes south into Algaria? The most frightening prospect of all was the distinct possibility, given the size of his army, that he'd simply divide his forces and do all three at the same time.

That strategy would have defeated us. I'm really rather surprised that he didn't think of it himself.

CHAPTER
THIRTY-
SEVEN

K ing Eldrig of Cherek was an old man with hair gone white and a long white beard. He stood at the window looking out over the rain-slashed harbor at Riva. It was about two weeks after we'd managed to extract the last survivors out of Drasnia. "You know him, Belgarath," he said. "How does he think? What's he going to do next?"

"I think you're asking the wrong man, Eldrig," Rhodar said bitterly. In many ways, Rhodar of Drasnia was a broken man now. He lived only for vengeance. "Holy Belgarath hasn't had much luck with his guesses lately."

"That'll do, Rhodar," Brand said firmly in that deep quiet voice of his. "We're not here to chew old soup. We're here to decide what we're going to do now, not what we should have done last month." The revelation that Brand was going to be the Child of Light during this particular EVENT had given him a great deal of authority, and the Alorn kings all automatically deferred to him.

"We know that he'll ultimately wind up in Arendia," Ormik of Sendaria said. Ormik was one of the most ordinary-looking men I've ever known. Even people who knew him probably couldn't have picked him out of a crowd. "Doesn't that mean that he'll turn south once he's regrouped his forces?"

"And leave his rear exposed?" Eldrig scoffed. "Not very likely. I think he'll be at the gates of Val Alorn before the month's out."

"Don't expect him to do what's rational," I told them. "I think that what happened to Drasnia more than proves that. He had no business coming through the Nadrak Forest, but he did it anyway. He doesn't think the way a human general would."

"Why did he destroy Drasnia?" Rhodar demanded with tears in his eyes.

I shrugged. "Revenge, most likely. The Drasnians almost wiped out the Nadraks in that battle during the third millennium."

"That was nearly twenty-five hundred years ago, Belgarath," Rhodar protested.

"Torak's got a very long memory."

"The main question right now is whether he'll divide his forces or not," Cho-Ram said. Cho-Ram was idly sharpening his saber, and the sound of his whetstone on steel set my teeth on edge.

"It's out of character for him," I said, "but we can't really be sure this time."

"I'm not sure I follow that," Cho-Ram said, laying his saber and whetstone down on the table in front of him.

"Torak doesn't like it when his people get out from under his thumb. Back before the War of the Gods, the Angaraks were the most tightly controlled people on earth. Things have changed a bit since then, though. Torak's got disciples now, and he leaves a lot of things up to them. Ctuchik might suggest a division of forces, and Zedar certainly would."

"Would Torak listen to them?" Polgara asked me.

"I can't really be sure. He wouldn't *like* the idea, but he might be able to see the necessity for it." I squinted out through the rain-spattered window. "This is only a hunch," I admitted, "but I *don't* think he'll divide up his army. If he were going to do that, he'd have done it when he came out of the mountains onto the moors of Drasnia. That would have been the logical time for him to send a column south into Algaria, but he didn't. He tends to have a one-track mind. Obsessive people are like that, and maybe obsessive Gods are, as well. I just don't think he'll divide his forces. Whichever way he decides to go, he'll take all his people with him. He's not really here to win battles. He's here to destroy, and that takes a lot of troops."

"Then the only real question is who he'll destroy next," Eldrig said. "I think he'll attack Cherek."

"What for?" Cho-Ram demanded. "All your men are on your warboats where he can't get at them. *I* think he'll invade Algaria next. He's got an appointment he has to keep in Arendia, and that means he's got to get past me first."

"Or me," Ormik added quietly, "and my people aren't very warlike. If he wants to get to Arendia in a hurry, he'll come through Sendaria."

"Isn't this all a little contemptible?" Rhodar asked pointedly. "You gentlemen saw what happened to *my* kingdom, and now you're all coming up with reasons why we should mass our forces inside *your* borders."

"Aloria is one, Rhodar," Eldrig told him. "We are *all* aggrieved for what happened to Drasnia."

"Where were you when I needed you, then?"

"That was *my* fault, Rhodar," I told him. "If you want to throw rocks at somebody, throw them at me and leave your brother kings out of it. The Mrin Codex tells us that Torak's going to lay siege to the Algarian Stronghold—eventually. It *doesn't* tell us if he's going to go someplace else first."

"When does he have to be in Arendia?" Eldrig asked.

"We don't know," I replied sourly.

"Does *he* know?"

"Probably. He's the one who's moving this time. We're making countermoves. When Cherek and his boys and I went to Cthol Mishrak, we knew when we had to be there. Torak didn't know when we were coming. *We* had the advantage that time. *He's* got it this time."

"Then about all we can do is wait," Brand said. "We'll have to watch him and stay mobile. Once he starts to move, we have to be able to respond immediately."

"That's not much of a strategy, Brand," Cho-Ram objected.

"I'll be happy to listen to alternatives."

"There *is* something else we can do," Polgara told them. "I think it's time for us to bring in the other kingdoms—Tolnedra in particular. We're going to need the legions."

"Ran Borune doesn't like Alorns, Polgara," Eldrig told her. "I don't think he'll even listen to our diplomats."

"Maybe not, but I think he *will* listen to me—and to my father. We'll talk to the Arends, as well—and the Nyissans."

"I wouldn't waste my time on the Nyissans," Cho-Ram said disdainfully. "They're so drugged most of the time that they wouldn't be any good in a fight."

"I wouldn't be so sure, Cho-Ram," I told him. "If I can get one good Nyissan poisoner anywhere near Torak's field kitchens, he'll kill more Angaraks than an entire Tolnedran legion could."

"*Belgarath!*" Cho-Ram exclaimed. "That's *horrible!*"

"So was what happened to Drasnia. Torak's got us outnumbered, so we've got to come up with ways to even things out." I stood up. "Stay flexible, gentlemen. Polgara and I are going south for a while."

It took Pol and me more than a week to locate the encampment of the Asturian duke and his green-clad archers. In part that was due to the weather. The endless, accursed rain wreathed down through the trees like mist, obscuring everything on the ground. Even when Pol and I resumed our own forms for brief periods, she smelled like a bagful of wet feathers, and I imagine that I reeked like a sodden dog. Neither of us mentioned it, but we sat on opposite sides of our campfire each night.

I hesitate to use the word, but it was only by chance that we finally found the Asturian encampment. A very brief break in the weather cleared away the prevailing mist, the wind dropped, and Pol was able to see the smoke rising from their campfires.

The Asturian duke's name was Eldallan, and he was a lean, youngish man dressed, as were his men, all in green—people who hide out in a forest usually do choose that color. The Asturian encampment was quite extensive. There were a few tents scattered about, but most of the archers lived in crudely built huts that closely resembled the homes of the serfs. I suppose there's a certain justice there. Eldallan's archers were young noblemen for the most part, and sleeping in mud-and-wattle huts gave them a chance to see how the other half lived.

Eldallan was less than cooperative—at least right at first. He'd had his men build him a crude chair, and he sat in it as if it were a throne with his eight-year-old daughter, Mayaserana, playing with a doll at his side. "That's an Alorn problem." He rejected our appeal. "My problem's the Mimbrates." In what had probably been an effort to distinguish themselves from their countrymen to the south, the Asturians had discarded the "thees" and "thous" and "foreasmuches."

"I'm sure you'll have second thoughts about that when you're stretched out on an altar with two or three Grolims carving out your heart, your Grace," I told him bluntly.

"That's just a fairy story, Belgarath," he scoffed. "I'm not gullible enough to believe Alorn propaganda."

"Why don't you let me talk with him, father?" Pol suggested. "I know Arends a little better than you do."

"Gladly," I agreed. "This skeptic's right on the verge of irritating me."

"Please forgive my father, your Grace," she said sweetly to the duke. "Diplomacy's not one of his strong points."

"I'm no more inclined to accept your horror stories than I am his, Lady Polgara. Your one-time affiliation with the Wacites is well-known. You have no reason to love Asturians."

"I'm not going to tell you horror stories, your Grace. I'm going to *show* you what the Angaraks did to Drasnia."

"Illusions." He dismissed her proposal with a shrug.

"No, your Grace. Reality. I speak as the duchess of Erat, and no true gentleman would question the word of a noblewoman—or have I erred in assuming that there *are* gentlemen in Asturia?"

"You question my honor?"

"Aren't you questioning mine?"

He struggled with it. "Very well, your Grace," he agreed reluctantly. "If you give me your word of honor that what you propose to show me really happened, I'll have no choice but to accept it."

"Your Grace is too kind," she murmured. "Let's go back in time, and north to Drasnia. This is what *truly* happened when Kal Torak came down onto the moors." I heard—or felt—the surge of her Will, and she made a small, curious gesture in front of his face as she released it.

I didn't see a thing, naturally; but the duke did.

"Why, father," the little girl at his side said when he cried out in horror, "whatever's the matter?"

He wasn't able to answer her. Polgara held him frozen in place for about a quarter of an hour. His eyes grew wider and wider, and his face turned deathly pale. After a few minutes, he was begging her to stop.

But she didn't.

He began to weep, and his daughter stared at him incredulously. I'm sure he wanted to cover his eyes with his hands, but his limbs were frozen, and he couldn't move. He groaned. He even screamed a few times, but Pol refused to relent. She kept him locked in place until he'd been forced to witness the entire horror.

He fell out of his chair when she finally released him, and he lay on the ground, sobbing uncontrollably.

"What did you do to my father, bad Lady?" the little girl demanded.

"He'll be fine in a few minutes, dear," Pol told her gently. "He just had a nightmare, that's all."

"But it's daytime—and he isn't even asleep."

"That happens sometimes, Mayaserana. He'll be all right."

It took Eldallan about a half an hour to regain his composure, and when he did, he was ready to listen.

"I'm not going to insist on a direct meeting between you and the Mimbrate King," I told him. "That might be pushing things a bit."

"He's not the king," Eldallan corrected me almost absently.

"*He* thinks he is, but that's beside the point. My daughter and I'll go to Vo Mimbre and talk with him. We'll hammer out the details of a truce between the two of you, and I'll arrange for some Sendars to act as messengers. Sendars are neutral, and they're honorable people, so there won't be any danger of trickery. Tell your archers to quit wasting arrows on Mimbrates. You're going to need every arrow you can lay your hands on when the Angaraks come."

"It shall be as you say, Ancient One." He was suddenly a very agreeable fellow. He definitely didn't want Polgara to show him anything else.

Pol and I went on to the yellow-walled city of Vo Mimbre. Mimbrate poets have written all sorts of nonsense about their "City of Gold," but the plain truth of the matter is the fact that the quarries of the region produce yellow building stones. There wasn't anything mystic or even significant about it at all.

After the destruction of Vo Astur in 3822, the Mimbrate dukes had taken to calling themselves "the kings of All Arendia," but that was a fiction. The authority of that throne in Vo Mimbre stopped at the edge of the Arendish Forest.

Arends aren't quite as stubborn as Tolnedrans are about certain peculiar things, so when Pol and I reached Vo Mimbre and identified ourselves, we were immediately escorted to the throne room of "King" Alodrigen XII. Aldorigen was a bit older than Duke Eldallan, and quite a bit bulkier. Mimbrates start wearing full armor when they're still children, and the sheer dead weight of all that steel puts muscle on them. It doesn't noticeably add brain capacity, however.

Once again, I'll resist using the word "coincidence." It just "happened" that Aldorigen *also* had a child of about eight years—a son named Korodullin.

Isn't *that* interesting?

Aldorigen was no less stubborn than Eldallan had been, so Polgara was obliged to repeat her performance. The king came around as quickly as his Asturian counterpart had. The Asturians and Mimbrates have always claimed that they're completely different from each other. To be honest with you, though, I've never been able to really tell them apart, even though Mimbrates still use archaic speech and Asturians don't.

After Polgara'd brought Aldorigen to his senses, I spoke with the Sendarian ambassador and arranged for several go-betweens to carry information back and forth between Mimbre and Asturia, and then Pol and I proceeded—damply—to Tol Honeth.

Ran Borune's skepticism about Torak's intentions had been evaporated by what had happened in Drasnia, and he was willing at least to listen to us. "I assume the Alorns have a plan," he said after we had explained the situation to him.

"A tentative one," I replied. "Kal Torak's invasion of Drasnia taught us not to lock our thinking in stone. We *do* know that this is going to be settled one way or another someplace in Arendia, but we can't be certain which route Torak's going to take to get there. What he did in Drasnia suggests that he wants to obliterate the Alorns before he gets to Arendia. Eldrig expects him to invade Cherek, but I'm not so sure. We *do* know that he's going to lay siege to the Algarian Stronghold, but we're not sure what he'll do before that. He might even try to attack the Isle of the Winds. That's his ultimate goal, and he might try to go there and retake the Orb of Aldur *before* he goes to Arendia."

"I thought you could see the future, Belgarath."

"Sort of," I replied, making a sour face. "There are a couple of prophecies, but they're very obscure."

"Are your Alorns going to want help in the north?"

"I think they can manage. If Torak *does* decide to go directly to the Isle, he'll run head-on into the Cherek fleet, and the entire war could be settled in the Sea of the Winds. If it happens that way, I *know* who's going to win. No navy on earth is a match for Eldrig's war-boats."

"Are you and Lady Polgara planning to stay here for long?"

"As long as it takes."

"I want to talk with my generals, but we'll need to coordinate our strategy. Can I offer you the hospitality of the palace here?"

"We appreciate the thought, Ran Borune," Polgara said, "but it might cause you some problems. The Honethites and Vorduvians would probably make a very big issue of the fact that you're consorting with 'heathen sorcerers.' "

"*I'm* the emperor here, Lady Polgara, and I'll consort with whomever I bloody well please."

"Isn't he a dear man?" Pol said to me.

"She's right, Ran Borune," I told the emperor. "We've got enough trouble with Kal Torak. Let's not go out of our way to pick fights with the other great families. We'll stay at the Cherek embassy. The ambassador's got a war-boat at his disposal, and I need to send the Alorn kings a report about what we accomplished in Arendia. Who's the current Nyissan Ambassador?"

"A reptilian sort of fellow named Podiss," Ran Borune replied with obvious distaste.

"I'll need to talk with him, as well," I said. "I want to let Salmissra know that we're coming."

"Why bring her into it at all?"

"She has certain resources I might need later on. If something comes up, I'll get word to you."

He smiled faintly. "My door's always open to you, Belgarath."

Polgara and I went to the Cherek embassy, and I composed a dispatch for the ambassador's courier ship to take to Riva. Then I went across town to the Nyissan embassy.

After I returned, Pol and I had a quiet supper and retired for the night. I was just getting ready for bed when Beltira's voice came at me from out of nowhere. *"Belgarath!"* He sounded excited.

"Yes, I'm here. What's happening?"

"Torak's made his move! He's invading Algaria!"

"Has he committed all his forces?"

"Evidently so. There's a small occupation army holding the ground in

Drasnia—mostly to guard his rear, we think, but the rest of his troops are marching south."

I breathed a very large sigh of relief. The possibility of Torak selecting one of his other options had been worrying me more than a little. *"How far has he penetrated?"*

"As far as Lake Atun. It's slow going for him. The Algar cavalry's been slicing large pieces out of his flanks."

"Good. Keep an eye on him and let me know if he changes direction. I don't want to commit any troops until I'm sure this isn't a feint."

"I don't think so, Belgarath. We've heard from Beldin, and he says that the army that invaded Drasnia's only about half of Torak's force. He's gathered a huge fleet at Dal Zerba on the west coast of the Dalasian protectorates. Urvon's in charge there, and Beldin's positive that he's going to ferry that army across the Sea of the East to march across Southern Cthol Murgos to attack us from that direction. We've got two armies coming at us."

I started to swear. Torak *had* divided his forces, after all, but he'd done it before he even left Mallorea. *"I'll get back to you,"* I told Beltira. *"Pol and I'd better go to the palace and let Ran Borune know what's afoot."*

I went down the hall to Pol's room and knocked on her door. "It's me, Pol," I said. "Let me in."

"I'm bathing, father. Go away."

"You can do that later. Torak just invaded Algaria."

I heard some splashing and, a moment or two later, Pol opened the door. She'd thrown on a robe, but her hair was still dripping. "He *what?*" she demanded.

"I just told you. Torak's on the move, and he's coming south."

"Garel's at the Stronghold, father. I'd better move him."

"He's safe there, Pol. We *know* that the Stronghold won't fall, and Torak can't stay there forever. He's got an appointment he has to keep in Arendia. There's some other bad news, though. Beldin told the twins that Urvon's commanding a second Mallorean army. They're crossing the Sea of the East. They'll be coming at us from southern Cthol Murgos. Torak's going to try to put us in a vise. We'd better go back to the palace and alert Ran Borune."

"I'll get dressed."

It was almost midnight when we reached the palace, and it took us a while to persuade the servants to wake the emperor. He was sleepy-eyed and tousled when we were finally admitted to his private quarters. "Don't you people ever sleep?" he asked in a grouchy tone of voice.

"Only when there's nothing better to do, your Majesty," I told him. "Torak's invaded Algaria."

That woke him up. "I'll start the legions north immediately," he said.

"I'd hold off on that, Ran Borune," Pol suggested. "I think you're going to need them someplace else."

I told him about the second army gathering at Dal Zerba, and it was one of the few times I've ever heard a Borune swear. "How many people does that madman *have?*" he demanded.

"They don't call it 'Boundless Mallorea' for nothing," I replied.

"What are we going to do?"

"We still have some time, I think," I said. "Urvon's not going to be able to ferry his army across the Sea of the East in a single day, and it's a long way across southern Cthol Murgos."

"What about Kal Torak? He could be on my eastern frontier in a week."

"Not very likely, Ran Borune. He has to get past the Algars first."

"Drasnia didn't slow him down very much."

"There's a world of difference between Drasnia and Algaria," Pol told him. "The Algars don't have towns to defend, for one thing, and they've got the finest horses in the world, for another. Kal Torak's going to find a trip into Algaria *very* expensive."

"You *do* realize that the second Mallorean army means that I won't be able to lend you a hand in Arendia, don't you?" he said. "I'm going to have to put my legions on my southern border."

"We were fairly certain you'd feel that way about it," Pol murmured.

I scratched at my beard. "It's still not a disaster," I told them. "We probably could use the help of the legions in Arendia, but I'd much rather they concentrated on keeping that second Mallorean column away from the battlefield. As I said before, we've still got time. Urvon won't get here overnight, and Kal Torak's going to have his own problems in Algaria. I think Pol and I'd better go to Sthiss Tor and have a talk with the Snake Woman. We don't want her to just open her borders to Urvon and stand aside while he marches through. I want to do everything I possibly can to upset Kal Torak's timetable."

"Good luck," the emperor said. "I'd better summon my generals. We've got a lot of planning to do."

"And Pol and I'd better leave for Nyissa. We'll see how things stand when we get back."

My daughter and I reached Sthiss Tor two days later, long before the Nyissan Ambassador's message did, so there was a bit of delay before we were escorted into Salmissra's throne room. The Serpent Woman's response to our information was profoundly unenthusiastic. "Why should I involve myself in your war with the Angaraks?" she said, hardly bothering to take her eyes off her mirror.

"It's not just *our* war, Salmissra," Pol told her. "It concerns all of us."

"Not me, it doesn't. One of my predecessors discovered the folly of becoming involved in this private feud between the Alorns and the Angaraks. I'm not going to make that same mistake. Nyissa will remain neutral."

"That option isn't open to you, Salmissra," I told her. "Urvon's army's going to show up on your southern border before very long, and Nyissa stands between him and Tolnedra."

"So?"

"He'll march right straight through your country."

She shrugged. "Let him. I won't do anything to hinder him, so he won't have any reason to do to Nyissa what Kal Torak did to Drasnia."

"Oh, yes he will," Pol disagreed. "Issa participated in the War of the Gods, remember? Torak has a very long memory, and he holds grudges. Urvon's army *won't* just march through. They'll destroy Nyissa as they go along. You're Issa's handmaiden, so I'd imagine Urvon's going to take special pains to find you so that the Grolims can cut out your heart."

Salmissra's colorless eyes grew worried. "He wouldn't do that—not if I don't offer any resistance."

"It's your heart, Snake Woman," Pol replied with a chilling kind of indifference.

"What you do is your affair, Salmissra," I told her then. "We've told you what's coming. Deal with it in any way you see fit. If you *do* decide to fight, you might get in touch with Ran Borune. It's to his advantage to keep Urvon away from his southern border, so he might just lend you a few legions."

"Would he do that?"

"It wouldn't hurt to ask. Now, if you'll excuse us, my daughter and I have some business in Maragor."

That turned out to be a complete waste of time. Pol and I flew to Mar Amon, hoping that the news of Torak's invasion would shake Mara out of his grief to some small degree, but I don't think the weeping God even heard us. He refused to listen, and his wails continued to echo from the mountains surrounding haunted Maragor.

Finally we gave up and went on to Prolgu to talk with the Gorim. "He'll almost have to cross Ulgoland to reach Arendia, Holy One," I told the ancient man after Pol and I had explained the situation. "I know that your people are very religious, and they might be opposed to shedding blood, but this is an unusual situation."

"I shall consult with Holy UL," he promised. "The circumstances might prompt him to set aside his distaste for violence."

"That's entirely up to him, Gorim," I said with a faint smile. "I'm *definitely* not going to try to tell UL what to do. We'll keep you advised of what's happening. If you *do* decide to stay out of it, we'll give you enough warning so that you can seal up the mouths of your caves."

"I appreciate that, Ancient One."

Then Pol and I went back up through the caves to the ruins of Prolgu. "Now what?" she asked me.

I considered it. "Since we're this close anyway, why don't we fly over and see how far Torak's managed to penetrate before we go back to Riva? And I'd also like to get some idea of just how big this army of his really is."

"Whatever you say, father." It always makes me a little nervous when Pol agrees with me without any arguments.

It was cloudy over Algaria, but at least it wasn't raining. You have no idea of how difficult it is trying to fly with wet feathers, and I've never really been comfortable as a duck. Ducks are probably no sillier than other birds, but they *look* so ridiculous.

Beltira had told me that Torak had penetrated as far as Lake Atun in northern Algaria. That had been almost a week ago, however, and he'd come quite a bit farther south. He'd crossed the Aldur River upstream from Aldurford, and his army was spread out on the grasslands of central Algaria now. They weren't very hard to find, since there were quite a lot of them.

They weren't moving very fast, however. Pol and I saw a number of engagements down there. As Beltira had said, Algar cavalry units were slashing at the flanks of that huge army, and their attacks went quite a bit farther than simple harassment. Algars are the finest horsemen in the world, and their long centuries of patient breeding had produced superb horses. In addition to the Malloreans, Torak's army also included Murgos, Nadraks, and Thulls, and those were the units that were bearing the brunt of the Algar attacks.

They weren't very good at it, from what I saw. The Algars were simply too fast for them. Central Algaria is rolling country, and there are a lot of hills and grassy ravines that provide cover for the cavalry units. In most cases, the Angaraks didn't see the Algars coming until it was too late. Torak's army was moving slowly south, and the trail behind them was littered with their dead. That didn't mean anything to Kal Torak, of course, but it *did* seem to concern his generals. They weren't moving very fast, and they had whole platoons of scouts ranging out ahead and along the flanks. From what I was able to see, those scouts weren't getting very much information back to the generals. Like all cavalry units the world over, the Algars carried short bows in addition to their lances and sabers. A cavalry bow doesn't have the range that the longbows of the Asturian Arends have, but a man on a fast horse doesn't need range. He can get close enough to do the job. Not very many Angarak scouts returned.

In effect, what was happening down there was a running battle, and it was very one-sided. Torak was taking appalling casualties, but he pressed on firmly. In addition to the scouts, the army had foragers out, looking for cows to feed that horde. The foragers were having an even worse time of it than the scouts were, since every herd of cattle they came across had dozens of Algar bowmen concealed in it. The Algars *also* amused themselves by stampeding cattle herds through the Mallorean ranks, and that slowed the advance even more.

It was going to take Kal Torak a long time to reach the Stronghold.

Those stampedes were effective, I'll grant you, but they goaded Torak's generals into an action that ultimately caused an economic disaster in the West. At first, the foragers had gone out to round up the cows, intending to drive them along as a moving food source. After a few of those stampedes, though, they started to kill every cow they came across. It was a long time after the war was over before the Algarian herds even reached a fraction of their former numbers. Beef was very scarce in the west for years.

After we'd seen enough of that slow-moving battle, Pol and I turned and flew west toward Sendaria and the coast. I wanted to get back to Riva so that I could have a talk with Cho-Ram. The Mrin clearly stated that the Stronghold wouldn't fall, but it never hurts to be careful. Garel *was* inside that fortress, after all.

It was raining in Riva when we got there. Isn't *that* a surprise? The foul weather triggered by that eclipse had been very unusual elsewhere, but it's *always* raining in Riva.

Ran Borune had sent word to the Alorn kings about Urvon's army, and they were very concerned about it. "Where are they right now?" Rhodar asked me when Pol and I joined them in our customary conference room.

"I'm not sure," I replied. "Pol and I've been moving around quite a bit. The twins always stay in the Vale, so Beldin usually makes his reports to them. I'll talk with them about it later, but right now we've got some things to discuss and a few decisions to make. Then I want to go check out the defenses of the Stronghold."

"The Stronghold's secure, Belgarath," Cho-Ram assured me. "You don't have to go there."

"Just a precaution, Cho-Ram. What kind of a force have you got inside?"

"Three clans and the Drasnian pikemen we managed to rescue. There are plenty of people inside to hold it. Besides, the walls are thirty feet thick, and no scaling ladder in the world could reach the top of them."

"I think that's what Fleet-foot had in mind when he designed the place," I told him. "We know that the Stronghold won't fall, but Torak's probably going to keep hammering at it for several years before he gives up. That gives us some time to get ready for his next move. The Mrin says that the final battle's going to be in Arendia, so it might not be a bad idea for us to move these sessions to Tol Honeth."

"Why Tol Honeth?" Brand asked.

"It's closer to the battleground, for one thing, and that's where the Tolnedran generals are, for another."

"The Tolnedrans aren't going to be much use, Belgarath," Eldrig protested. "Ran Borune's going to be concentrating on his southern border. He's *not* going to send any legions to Arendia."

"We're planning a campaign, Eldrig, and those Tolnedran generals know just about all there is to know about strategy and tactics. Their advice could be useful."

"We're not *completely* incompetent, Belgarath," he objected. "We've won every war we've ever been in so far, haven't we?"

"That's been pure luck, Eldrig. I don't want to hurt your feelings, but you Alorns have a habit of just making your wars up as you go along. Let's do this one professionally—just for the sake of novelty, if nothing else."

It took Pol and me a little while to persuade the Alorn kings to go to Tol Honeth to seek the advice to the Tolnedran High Command, but they eventually agreed. Then my daughter and I left the Isle and flew across Sendaria, over Ulgoland, and on to the Algarian Stronghold. This time we didn't really have any choice. We *had* to use the form of ducks.

I've referred to the Stronghold as a man-made mountain, and that comes fairly close. It looks like a walled city from the outside, but it's not, since there aren't any buildings inside. Such Algars as live there have constructed rooms and halls and corridors inside the walls themselves. The open space inside those walls is nothing more than an elaborate maze.

A tragedy, however, had occurred. It was one of those stupid accidents that crop up from time to time. Garel, heir to the Rivan throne, had gone out horseback riding, and his horse had stumbled; Iron-grip's heir fell and broke his neck when he hit the ground. *Idiocy!* What in the name of all seven Gods was he doing on a horse?

Fortunately, he'd already secured the succession; the line was still intact, although Gelane was only five years old. But that was all right. Everybody grows up—eventually.

I spoke with the boy and found, that like all the rest, he had uncommonly good sense. We've been lucky in that. If stupidity had cropped up in the Rivan line, we'd have been in a great deal of trouble.

"Can't I do something, grandfather?" the earnest little boy asked me. "This *is* my responsibility, after all." That startled me.

"What did you tell him, Pol?" I asked suspiciously.

"Everything, father," she replied calmly. "He's entitled to know what this is all about."

"He doesn't *need* that information, Pol! I thought we agreed to that."

She shrugged. "I changed my mind. He *is* the Rivan King, father. If all our elaborate plans fall apart, he might have to take up the sword."

"He's only a child, Pol. He couldn't even *lift* that sword."

"We've got time, father. Torak hasn't even begun the siege yet."

"The Mrin says that Brand's going to confront Torak. Gelane's not supposed to get involved."

"The Mrin's very obscure, father, and sometimes things change. I want to be ready for any eventuality."

"I really think I could handle it, grandfather," Gelane assured me. "I've got an Algar friend who's been teaching me how to use a sword."

I sighed, and then I buried my face in my hands for a while.

There wasn't really very much to do at the Stronghold except to wait for Torak. I suppose Pol and I could have left at any time, but I wanted to be absolutely certain that One-eye didn't change direction on me again. The invasion of Drasnia had caught me completely off guard, and I wasn't going to let that happen again. I wanted to make sure that he was completely committed before I went off and left him to his own devices. I *also* wanted to watch the defenders crush the first few assaults, just to make sure they knew what they were doing.

Riders from the outlying clans came by frequently during the next two weeks to keep us posted. Torak was still advancing, and he showed no signs of veering off.

Then, early one morning when dawn was turning the rain silver, Polgara's voice woke me from my fitful sleep. *"I think you'd better come up here, father."*

"Where are you?"

"I can't understand you, father. Just come up to the parapet on top of the north wall. There's something you'd better have a look at."

I grumbled a bit, but I climbed out of bed and pulled on my clothes. What was she up to now? The fact that she couldn't understand me was a clear sign that she'd changed form. I went out into the torchlit corridor outside my room and on up those interminable staircases that lead to the top of the Stronghold.

There was a snowy owl perched on the rain-swept battlements.

"I've asked you not to do that, Pol," I reminded her.

She blurred and shimmered back into her own form. "I'm sorry, father," she said. "I'm not doing it to upset you. I'm following instructions. I think you'd better look at that," she told me, gesturing toward the north.

I looked out over the battlements. The clouds overhead were dirty grey and dawn-stained. The rain had slackened to some degree, so it wasn't that solid curtain I'd been staring at for the past several weeks. At first I couldn't really see anything, but then a movement caught my eye about a mile out on that half-obscured plain. Then, as I looked harder, a mass of humanity seemed to grow out of the mist, a huge, faceless mass that stretched from horizon to soggy horizon.

Kal Torak had reached the Stronghold.

"Are you sure Torak's with them?" I asked, still staring out at that slow-moving army.

"Yes, father. I went out and looked. That iron pavilion of his is right in the center of the crowd."

"You did *what*? Polgara, that's *Torak* out there! Now he knows you're here!"

"Don't get excited, Old Man. I was *told* to do it. Torak had no way of even knowing I was there. He's inside his pavilion, and Zedar's with him."

"How long has this been going on?"

"Since he left Mallorea, I'd imagine. Let's go alert the Algars, and then I think we'll have time for some breakfast. I've been up all night, and I'm positively ravenous."

It was midmorning by the time the Angaraks had completed their encirclement of the Stronghold and noon before they tried their first tentative assault. The Algars and the Drasnian pikemen stayed out of sight, and I think that unnerved Kal Torak's generals just a bit. They'd hauled their siege-engines into place, and they started out by trying to loft boulders into the city. That didn't work out very well, because the walls were too high. I could see their engineers feverishly trying to adjust the catapults to change their trajectory.

Then, more I think to get some sort of response from the defenders than out of any hope of success, they mounted an attack on the front gate. They rolled up battering rams, but that wasn't really necessary. The gate wasn't locked. The first troops through the gate were Thulls. Thulls always seem to get the dirty jobs in Angarak society.

I'm not even sure that the Thulls realized what they'd encountered when they burst through the gate. As I've said before, the Stronghold isn't a city in the usual sense. Those enormous walls don't enclose houses and public buildings, they enclose an elaborate maze of narrow, high-walled corridors without a roof in sight. The Thulls rushed in, and all they found was geometry. They found corridors laid out in straight lines, in curved lines, in lines so complex that they turned back on themselves and almost seemed to dissolve off into unimaginable dimensions.

The defenders allowed the Thulls to mill around inside that maze for about an hour, and then they rose from their places of concealment atop those twenty-foot-high interior walls and obliterated the intruders.

And the Mallorean generals and the kings of the western Angarak nations still hadn't seen a single defender. They didn't see the horde of Thullish soldiers again either. They'd sent several thousand men through the gate, and not one of them ever came back out again—at least not through the gate.

During the following night, however, they *did* start seeing the men they had ordered inside. The Algar catapultists atop the walls began lofting dead Thulls into the middle of the Angarak encampment. It's *very* hard to get any sleep when it's raining Thulls.

The next day, the second siege got under way. There were three Algar clans inside the Stronghold. The rest of them were outside. Kal Torak had encircled the Stronghold, and then the free-roving Algar horsemen encircled *him*. They didn't take up positions or dig in fortifications the way besiegers usually do, because cavalry doesn't work that way. The Algars kept moving, and Kal Torak's generals and subordinate kings never knew where or when they'd strike next. It was almost as dangerous for them outside the walls as it was inside.

After a few days, I concluded that Cho-Ram's tactics were working out fine, and Pol and I said good-bye to Gelane, his mother, and the Algar Clan-Chiefs defending the fortress. And then we flew off to the west through the rainy, wind-swept gloom that seemed to have settled in perpetually. We had other things to attend to.

With Kal Torak effectively pinned down in Algaria, we had some time to expand and polish our plans. We moved our discussions from Riva to Tol Honeth so that we could take advantage of the expertise of the Imperial War College and the Tolnedran General Staff. I found working with professional soldiers to be something of a novelty. Despite their fearsome reputation, Alorns are at best only gifted amateurs, largely because their rank is hereditary. A man who's born a general doesn't have nearly the grasp of things a man who's worked his way up through the ranks has. Tolnedran officers work out contingency plans to deal with surprises. The customary Alorn approach to a battlefield emergency is simply to go berserk and kill everything in sight—including trees and bushes.

Although Ran Borune had by now tentatively—and very reluctantly—conceded that Pol and I might *possibly* have capabilities he wasn't prepared to admit actually existed, she and I remained largely in the background during those meetings. As I told the emperor, "There's not much point in distracting your generals by telling them things they're not philosophically prepared to accept. If we announce that I'm sneaking up on my seven thousandth birthday, they'll spend so much time trying to prove that we're lying that they won't be able to pay attention to what they're supposed to be doing. Let's just tell them that Pol and I are Rivans and let it go at that."

The thing that baffled us the most was the fact that Urvon wasn't moving. He'd brought his army across the Sea of the East, right enough, but then he'd settled down in the Hagga Military District on the southern coast of Cthol Murgos as if he planned to put down roots. Finally I sent word to the twins that I needed to talk with Beldin face to face. You can only do so much at a distance.

My brother arrived a few days later and came to my room in the Cherek embassy. It wasn't a particularly large room, but I'm a plain sort of person, so I don't really need luxurious quarters. My first question to him was fairly simple. "What's holding him up?"

"The Murgos," he replied. "What else? That and the fact that he hasn't received his marching orders from Burnt-face yet."

"What's Ctuchik's problem?"

"He doesn't like Urvon."

"Who does? I don't think even Torak likes him very much. But Urvon's following orders, and Torak's likely to rip Ctuchik's heart out of his skinny chest if he interferes."

"You weren't listening, Belgarath," my stumpy brother told me. "I didn't say it was *Ctuchik* who was blocking Urvon. It's the Murgos—and somewhat more specifically, the Murgo Grolims."

"What's the difference? Ctuchik rules Cthol Murgos, doesn't he?"

"That he does, brother, but he's sort of looking the other way at the moment. Let's see if I can explain it. If Urvon reaches Arendia with his army, Torak's very likely to promote him to Most Favored Disciple, or whatever you want to call it. Ctuchik doesn't want that to happen, but he doesn't dare interfere—at least not overtly. That doesn't keep him from slipping around behind the scenes, though. He's spent centuries instilling an obsession with racial purity in the collective Murgo mind, and Malloreans aren't pure Angaraks. The average Mallorean's part Angarak, part Karand, part Melcene, with maybe a pinch of Dal thrown in for good measure. Murgos look on Malloreans as mongrels, and they don't hesitate to say so."

"Yes, I know all about that, but Murgos take their orders from the Grolims, and no Grolim alive is likely to do anything to offend Torak."

"You don't really know that much about Grolims, I see. Grolim politics are very involuted. No matter what Torak might think, there's a great schism in the Angarak religion, and it's based on the hatred that exists between Ctuchik and Urvon. Ctuchik dropped a few hints to his Grolims after Urvon landed in Hagga, and his priests have been spreading wild stories all over southern Cthol Murgos about drunken Mallorean soldiers breaking into Murgo houses and raping Murgo women. That's the sort of thing almost guaranteed to make a Murgo go up in flames. Ctuchik's official position is that he'll help Urvon's army in any way he can, but his Grolims are out there spreading atrocity stories for all they're worth. Murgo generals are very polite to Mallorean officers in the daytime—but every night disorganized mobs of common soldiers come out of their barracks and butcher every Mallorean they can lay their hands on. Ctuchik piously sits in Rak Cthol going 'Tsk, tsk, tsk,' and pretends that he can't do anything about it, and all Urvon can do is squat in Rak Hagga wringing his hands while Murgo lynch mobs decimate his army. I know it's an unnatural thing to suggest, but in this particular situation, Ctuchik might turn out to be our most valuable ally."

"That'll all come to an end once Torak gives Urvon his marching orders, won't it?"

"I doubt it. Ctuchik's probably going to obediently order his southern Murgos to join Urvon's army, but all that'll do is give the Murgos an opportunity to get in close to the Malloreans—with knives. The trek across southern Cthol Murgos is likely to be very interesting, and Urvon'll be lucky if he's got a regiment left by the time he reaches the southern Tolnedran border."

"What an absolutely beautiful notion."

"I thought you might like it."

"Why don't I take you to the palace and introduce you to the Tolnedran generals so you can fill them in on this? Oh, incidentally, Pol and I haven't made an issue of who we really are. I'll just tell them that you're a Drasnian spy and let it go at that. Let's not upset the generals just yet."

He shrugged. "If that's the way you want it," he agreed.

The officer commanding the Tolnedran general staff was named Cerran, and he was a member of the Anadile family in southern Tolnedra. The Anadiles had never had sufficient land or power to aspire to the Imperial Throne, so they usually joined the army. They had traditionally been closely allied with the Borunes, so when the Borunes were on the throne, you would normally find an Anadile general in command of the military. General Cerran was a thoroughgoing professional in his early fifties. He was a Tolnedran, so he wasn't as tall as the Alorns, but he was a blocky sort of man with broad shoulders and large hands. He and Brand got along together very well.

I'm not really all that competent with the Drasnian secret language, but I managed to advise Pol and Rhodar that Beldin was posing as a member of Drasnian intelligence, and Rhodar greeted him warmly and introduced him as "one of our most valuable agents." Then Beldin repeated what he'd told me earlier.

"How long would you say it'll take Urvon to march across southern Cthol Murgos, Master Beldin?" General Cerran asked after my brother had finished his account.

Beldin shrugged. "Half a year at least. He'll have to stop every so often to put down riots, I expect."

"That tells us one of the things we've needed to know, then. Your friend and his daughter told us that this Kal Torak of Mallorea has to be in Arendia on a certain date. As I understand it, it has something to do with the Angarak religion."

"I suppose you could put it that way, yes. So what?"

"We don't know what that date is, but Kal Torak does. He'll want Urvon in place when that date approaches, so as soon as Urvon starts marching, we'll know that we've got just about a year until we've got to be ready to meet the Angaraks somewhere in Arendia."

"That's a little imprecise, Cerran," Ran Borune objected.

"It's a lot more specific than anything we've been able to come up with so far, your Majesty," Cerran replied. "King Cho-Ram assures us that his Stronghold's impregnable, so Kal Torak's going to get more and more frustrated as the time for him to be in Arendia approaches. Eventually he'll be forced to break off his siege and march west. Angaraks take their religious obligations very seriously." Cerran rose from his chair and went to the large map hanging on the wall of the war room. "An army the size of Kal Torak's won't move very fast," he noted, "particularly not once it gets up into the mountains of Ulgoland. It's a hundred and fifty leagues from the Stronghold to central Arendia. At ten miles a day, it'll take him forty-five days. Give him another fifteen days to regroup, and we're talking about two months. Our first signal will come when Urvon marches. The second will be Kal Torak's abandonment of the siege of the Stronghold. That's all we really need, isn't it? The Murgos may or may not try to stop Urvon's Malloreans, but *we* definitely will. I rather think that General Urvon's going to be late getting to Arendia. Kal Torak's a foreigner, so he doesn't know all that much about the legions. I fully intend to educate him. I'll stop Urvon dead in his tracks at Tolnedra's southern border."

Now you see why Pol and I insisted that we coordinate our planning with the Tolnedran generals.

Once we knew that we'd have plenty of warning, we turned our attention to the campaign in Arendia. General Cerran's staff had carefully prepared plans for the defense of just about every location in the country. I'd spoken privately with Brand about that. Very few battles have ever been won from defensive positions. The methodical Tolnedrans, however, had compared Torak's numbers with ours and concluded that our taking the offensive without the legions to help us was absolutely out of the question, and the legions were going to be busy somewhere else.

The Tolnedran generals didn't know why the Alorn kings all deferred to Brand, but they weren't stupid. They recognized respect when they saw it, and after a few months of those ongoing strategy sessions, they also recognized Brand's tactical genius. Tolnedrans don't normally have much use for Alorns, but in Brand they could see an altogether different sort of man. His genius lay in his ability to assess the strengths and weaknesses of the various elements that were to be a part of the army that was going to face Kal Torak when the final battle took place.

Our decision not to tell the Tolnedran generals that we were basing a number of our decisions on the ravings of a madman was probably sound. The least hint of mysticism in an associate makes a Tolnedran nervous. There were times when we had to talk very fast, of course. We knew that certain things were going to happen, but we couldn't tell the Tolnedrans *how* we knew. Rhodar took care of most of that for us. The skills of the Drasnian Intelligence Service were already legendary, and after a couple of years, the generals had come to believe that there were Drasnian agents hidden in just about every element of the Angarak armies. Every time the inevitable "How do you know that?" came up, Rhodar would look sly, take out a piece of paper, and lay it on the table with an insufferably smug expression. The implications were obvious.

Even Rhodar's cunning was strained to the limit when, after the siege of the Stronghold had plodded on for an interminable six years, the twins finally isolated the passage in the Mrin that told us where the battle was going to take place. The reference was obscure, but that's normal for the Mrin. All it really said was "The Child of Light and the Child of Dark shall meet before the walls of the golden city." The key word in that passage is "golden." Those of you who've seen Vo Mimbre's yellow walls know where it comes from.

Anyway, we had to lead General Cerran and his colleagues rather gently until Cerran himself finally made the right decision. Rhodar, pretending to have received the information from his spies, laid out Torak's probable invasion route, and the rest of us found all sorts of things wrong with the other potential battle sites. Finally Cerran stabbed the map with one blunt finger. "There," he said. "You should prepare your forces to meet Kal Torak at Vo Mimbre."

"The ground around there *looks* to be all right, I guess," King Eldrig said, trying to sound a little dubious.

I stepped in at that point. "Isn't it awfully flat?" I objected. "Don't we want the advantage of high ground?"

"We don't really need it, Old One," Cho-Ram told me. "The city itself is high enough to slow Kal Torak's army down. They'll come down the valley of the River Arend and take up positions around Vo Mimbre in preparation for another siege. Then we'll hit them from all sides and grind them up against the walls. General Cerran's right. It's the perfect place for the kind of battle we want."

Eldrig and I raised a few more feeble objections, then Brand and Rhodar sided with Cho-Ram, and that settled the matter. It was a cumbersome way to do business, but we really didn't have much choice.

Polgara came to my room in the Cherek embassy a few nights after we'd decided where we were going to meet Kal Torak, and she found me muttering swear words at my copy of the Mrin Codex. "What *is* the matter with you, father?" she asked me. "You've been as cross as a bear with a sore paw for the past week."

I slammed my fist down on the Mrin. "*This* is what's the matter!" I yelled at her. "It doesn't make any sense!"

"It's not supposed to. Wasn't that the whole idea? It's *supposed* to sound like gibberish. Why don't you tell me about your problem, father? Maybe I can help."

I drew in a deep breath. "All right. Brand's the Child of Light, isn't he—at least in this particular EVENT? If I'm reading this right, he'll have to be in several places at the same time."

"Read it to me, father," she said patiently. "You don't make all that much sense when you start to splutter."

"All right, let's see what *you* make of it." I unrolled the scroll, found the index mark, and read that cursed passage to her. " 'And the Child of Light shall take the jewel from its accustomed place and shall cause it to be delivered up to the Child of Light before the gates of the golden city.' That clearly implies a paradox, doesn't it? And paradoxes just don't happen."

"I don't see it that way, father. How long does one of these EVENTS last?"

"As long as it takes, I suppose."

"Centuries, maybe? Years? Days? Or could it be just a few minutes, or perhaps even a single instant? How long did it take you to put Zedar to sleep in Morindland? That was one of these EVENTS, wasn't it? How long did it *really* take you, father?"

"Not too long, I guess. What are you driving at, Pol?"

"I get a strong feeling that the EVENTS are instantaneous. The Necessities are just too powerful for these confrontations to last for more than a few seconds at the very most. Any longer might rip the universe to pieces. The prophecies tell us what we have to do to get ready, and that can take eons, but the actual EVENT is something as simple as a decision—or even a single word. 'Yes,' maybe, or 'No.' The Mrin says that the final confrontation's going to be settled one way or the other by a choice, and choosing takes only an instant. I think that the last EVENT's not the *only* one that's going to involve choice. I think they *all* are. When you met Zedar in Morindland, you chose not to kill him. I think *that* was the EVENT. Everything else was just preparation."

Now do you see what I mean about the subtlety of Polgara's mind? It might be pushing things a bit, but I chose to believe her explanation, and that turns that little conversation into an EVENT, doesn't it? It also implies that the EVENTS don't always involve face-to-face confrontations between the agents of the two Necessities. Now *there's* a concept almost guaranteed to give you a perpetual headache.

"I'm going to have to go to Riva," I told her.

"Oh? Why?"

"I have to pick up Iron-grip's sword. Brand's going to need it when the time comes. The Mrin says that the Orb's going to be the deciding factor, and that means the sword."

"Then you think the passage you read to me means that *you're* going to be the Child of Light who's supposed to take the Orb to Brand?"

"It won't be the first time I've been saddled with it." I shrugged. "If it turns out that I'm wrong, I won't even be able to get the sword off that wall. That's the nice thing about dealing with the Orb. It won't let you do something you're not supposed to do."

I decided not to make an issue of my little errand. No, it wasn't one of those choices Pol had been talking about. It was based entirely on a desire not to embarrass myself. If it turned out that I *couldn't* get the sword off the wall, I'd wind up looking a bit foolish if I'd been pompously announcing my intentions. Vanity's ridiculous, but we all fall prey to it from time to time.

I spoke with the Cherek ambassador and arranged to sail on the next courier ship to Riva. I suppose I could have gone there on my own, but if all went well, I'd be bringing something heavy with me when I came back.

It wasn't a pleasant voyage. I don't like Cherek war boats to begin with, and the foul weather that had plagued us for all those years didn't make things any better.

We tied up to the wharf at Riva, and I climbed up those steep, dripping stairs to the Citadel.

Brand's eldest son Rennig was in charge during his father's absence. The position of the Rivan Warder was not, strictly speaking, hereditary, but I was fairly certain that this time it would be passed on to Rennig. He was as solid and dependable as his father.

He was a bit wild-eyed when I was admitted into Brand's study, though. "Thank the Gods!" he said, rising to his feet. "You got my message!"

"What message?"

"You mean you didn't? Why did you come, then?"

"I've got something to attend to. What's happening, Rennig? I haven't seen you *this* excited since you were a little boy."

"You'd better come and see for yourself, Ancient One. I don't think you'd believe me if I told you. I'll send for the guards who saw it happen. I'm sure you'll want to talk with them." He led me out into the corridor, and we went to the Hall of the Rivan King. That hall, the throne room, hadn't been used much during the centuries since Gorek's assassination, and it was damp and musty and not very well lighted. Rennig took a torch from one of the rings set in the wall just outside the door, and we went inside, marching down past the firepits to the throne. As we drew nearer, I could see Iron-grip's sword hanging point down on the wall, but I could also see that there was something terribly wrong with it.

My Master's Orb was not on the pommel.

"What's going on here, Rennig?" I demanded. "Where's the Orb?"

"It's over here, Ancient One," he told me. He pointed at a large round shield leaning against the wall about ten feet off to the right of the throne. It was a fairly standard Alorn shield, big, round, and heavy, with those thick steel straps Alorns always rivet to their shields. What was definitely *not* standard was the fact that my Master's Orb was embedded in the exact center of it.

"Who did this?" My voice was shaking.

"We don't know. The guards who were here that night had never seen her before."

"*Her?* A woman did this?"

He nodded. "I'd have had some doubts about it myself, Belgarath, but

I've known both of those men since childhood. They're honest men, and they'd never lie about something like this."

"No one can touch the Orb except—" I broke off as that passage in the Mrin started echoing in my head. "And the Child of Light shall take the jewel from its accustomed place—" I'd thought that it meant that this interim Child would take down the Sword and deliver it to Brand. I'd even believed that the passage was a set of instructions to *me*—that *I* was the one who was supposed to take it down off the wall and carry it back to Tol Honeth. But the passage wasn't talking about the sword. This woman, whoever she was, had removed it and set it in the center of the shield instead. Pol had been right. Since no one could touch the Orb except the Child of Light, that particular position was being passed around—but a woman?

Then the two off-duty guardsmen came into the hall and walked rather hesitantly toward us. I suppose that someday I'm going to have to do something about my reputation for being bad-tempered. "Oh, come here," I told them shortly. "I'm not going to bite you. You couldn't have done anything to stop her. When did this happen?"

"About a week ago, Ancient One," the taller of the two replied.

How convenient—and how predictable. The incident had occurred at almost exactly the same time as when I'd decided to come to Riva.

"It was sorcery, Holy One," the other guard asserted. "We were standing guard outside the door late at night, and a woman came down the corridor."

"We knew that something strange was happening," the tall guard added, "particularly since she was on fire."

"On fire?"

"Well, glowing, actually. There was bright blue light coming from her."

That got my attention.

"She was a pretty woman," the other guard put in. "At least she would have been if she hadn't been all blue. She opened the door to the hall and went inside. We followed her down to the throne. When she got there, she raised her hand and said, 'Come to me.' It was almost as if she was calling a pet dog."

"This was all pretty strange," the other man said, "but we've talked it over, and we both saw what happened next. The pommel stone on that big sword just came loose and floated down to her hand—and it was glowing, too. Then she walked over to that shield—and I've never seen that shield in here before—and she set the stone against the middle of it, and it sort of melted its way right into the steel."

"Did she leave then?" I asked them.

"She said something first."

"Oh? Did she say who she was?"

"She only said, 'One will come, and he will know what to do.' Then she sort of smiled and went back to the door. We followed her, but when we got out into the corridor, she was gone. That's all we saw, Ancient One. There wasn't a thing we could do to stop her."

"You've got that part right," I told him. "*Nobody* could have stopped her—whoever she was."

I picked up the heavy shield with both hands. "This 'ghost,' or whatever, was right about one thing. I *do* know what to do with this."

"That's the Orb, Holy Belgarath," Rennig objected. "It's supposed to stay here on the Isle."

"Yes, it is," I replied, "right up until the time we need it. And unless my calculations are off, your father's going to need it fairly soon."

On my trip back to Tol Honeth, I brooded about the fact that the Orb was now part of a shield rather than a sword. That obviously meant that Brand wasn't going to *kill* Torak. A shield by its very nature is defensive, and that began to change my thinking about the strategy the Tolnedran generals had put together for the battle that was going to be fought at Vo Mimbre. Maybe we *could* win from a defensive position.

Just about the only really significant thing I did during the return voyage was to notify the twins about the alteration in the Orb's location. I was definitely going to need some instruction here.

The Angarak siege of the Algarian Stronghold dragged on for another year. Then in the late spring of 4874, Beldin came back from southern Cthol Murgos to advise us that Urvon had assembled his army on the plains of Hagga and begun his march to the west. If General Cerran's calculations were correct, we had about one more year before the final battle. We'd know for certain when Torak broke off his siege of the Stronghold and also started west.

I spent much of the following summer scurrying around to make certain that everything was in place. Inevitably, hostilities broke out periodically between the warring factions in Arendia, and Polgara and I had to rush north from Tol Honeth to quiet things down again.

Although the twins labored mightily, we weren't able to get very many clues from the Mrin. That concerned me a great deal until I finally realized that the whole business of the fight between Brand and Torak was completely out of my hands. That particular revelation came to me in the early autumn when we all saw a marked change in Brand's behavior.

"A word with you, Belgarath?" he said to me one rainy afternoon as our meeting with the Tolnedran generals was breaking up.

"Of course," I replied.

"Let's go outside," he suggested. "I think this needs to be sort of private, and I'd rather not have some Tolnedran spy carrying word of what we say to Ran Borune. He's a good man, I suppose, but he gets nervous when things he doesn't understand start cropping up."

I smiled faintly. "Nervous" was a gross understatement. Brand and I went out of the army headquarters building and strolled across the sodden lawns of the imperial compound. "You've been the instrument of Necessity in the past, haven't you?" he asked me once we were certain that no one was near us.

"I'm not sure I follow you, my friend," I replied. "I've spent my whole life running errands for it."

"I'm talking about something a little more specific. As I understand it, you and the Necessity were fairly close when you and Bear-shoulders and the others went to Cthol Mishrak."

"Yes. So what?"

"Did it talk to you?"

"Oh, yes, that it did."

"I'm glad to hear that. I thought that my reason might be slipping. It has a peculiar way of talking, doesn't it?"

"It's got a warped sense of humor. What's it been saying?"

"Nothing all that specific. I've been a little edgy about what I'm supposed to do when we all get together at Vo Mimbre, and it's been telling me not to worry so much." He stopped and looked directly at me. "Did you know what you were going to do before you did it? I mean, when something came up, did the knowledge of how to respond just pop into your head?"

I nodded. "That's part of the way it works," I replied. "The friend you've got inside your head usually doesn't bother to explain things, he just builds the correct responses into your mind. You don't even have to think about it. What's he got you doing right now?"

"I'm supposed to persuade the Tolnedrans that the threat of Urvon's army isn't all that great. I'm going to need the legions at Vo Mimbre."

"That might take a bit of doing. General Cerran's completely committed to the idea that he's going to have to defend his southern border."

"He'll find out that it won't be necessary. Urvon and Ctuchik are going to make a mistake. They won't even reach Nyissa."

"What kind of mistake?"

"I have no idea. The problem's going to be that Cerran won't find out about it until Torak's almost right on top of Vo Mimbre. He won't have time to march his legions from southern Tolnedra to the battlefield."

"We aren't going to march them," I told him.

"How are they going to get there, then?"

"The Chereks are going to sail them there."

"How do you know that?"

I made a face. "Our mutual friend stuck the idea in my brain several thousand years ago."

"You mean you've known all along?"

"Not consciously. You'll get used to that, Brand. The instructions don't surface until you need them. I think that's part of the agreement between our Necessity and Torak's. As soon as you told me about this 'mistake' that Urvon and Ctuchik are going to make, I knew exactly how we were going to get the legions to Vo Mimbre."

He smiled a wry sort of smile. "I guess it makes sense—in a peculiar sort of way. Apparently our friend doesn't want our minds cluttered up with these things until we absolutely need to know them. I just hope he isn't late with the information when Torak and I get started."

"Amen to that. Have you got any clues about why the Orb's set in that shield now instead of on the hilt of the sword?"

"All I know is that I'm not supposed to hit Torak with it—or with anything connected to it. Somebody else is going to do that. All I'm supposed to do is show it to Torak."

"Show it to him? He's seen it before, Brand."

"All right, Belgarath, keep your nose out of it." I recognized the voice, of course. *"You do your work and let Brand do his."*

The startled look on Brand's face clearly showed that he'd also heard what our friend had just said. "Does he always talk to you that way?" he asked.

I nodded glumly. "All the time. There must be something about me that sets his teeth on edge. I think we'd better get General Cerran off to one side and start him to thinking about contingency planning."

"Why not just tell him who you really are? And where we're getting our instructions from?"

"No, Brand, not yet. I want him to have his legions at Vo Mimbre before I spring any surprises on him. Cerran's a good, solid man, but he's still Tolnedran. We'll tell him that there'll be a Cherek fleet at the mouth of the River of the Woods, 'just in case he needs it.' He'll know what to do when the time comes."

It was spring of 4875 when Torak finally threw up his hands in disgust, broke off his siege of the Stronghold, and started marching west with what was left of his army. The Algars and the vengeful Drasnians harried his rear as he moved westward. There are always stragglers trailing along behind any army on the march, but in this situation, those stragglers never caught up with their main force.

When Kal Torak reached Ulgoland, things went even further downhill for him. Every night the Ulgos came out of their caves like hunting cats to cut up the sentries posted around the fringes of the Angarak army.

On a number of occasions they even managed to get into the midst of the encampment to kill large numbers of Torak's soldiers. Torak tended to ignore those inconveniences but his troops grew *very* nervous, and most of them gave up on sleeping altogether.

The maimed God of Angarak grimly pressed on, taking dreadful casualties as he went, and eventually he reached the headwaters of the River Arend.

The Alorn kings and I'd deployed our forces around Vo Mimbre as soon as the twins advised me that Torak was on the move, and all was in readiness—except that we didn't have any Tolnedran Legions.

Torak paused to regroup, but we still had no word of what was happening in southern Cthol Murgos. If something didn't happen down there, and very soon, we were going to have to fight without the aid of the legions. This wasn't turning out very well.

Then, late one night when I'd just fallen into a fitful sleep, Beldin's voice woke me up again. *"Belgarath!"* he chortled. *"You can stop worrying about Urvon! He isn't going to make it!"*

"What happened?"

"The Murgos were cutting his army to pieces, and he wanted some open ground to fight them off. He went out into the Great Desert of Araga, and the Murgos followed him."

"They exterminated each other?" I asked gleefully.

"No, something else did. Is it still raining there?"

"Beldin, it's been raining almost steadily since 4850. It's never going to let up."

"It probably will now. The reason for it just went through the Desert of Araga. There's been a blizzard raging in that wasteland for the last five days. There are fifteen-foot snowdrifts piled all over the top of Urvon and the Murgos who were chasing him. Nobody down here is going to go anyplace. Torak's going to have to fight you with just the men he's got."

I went down the hallway, woke Pol, and passed Beldin's news on to her.

"Fortuitous," she noted, brewing herself a cup of tea. I've never cared that much for tea myself, but Pol had picked up a taste for the stuff during her years in Vo Wacune.

"I think it goes a little further than that, Pol," I disagreed. "The foul weather we've endured for the past quarter century was all in preparation for that blizzard, so we can hardly call it a stroke of luck. Even then, Urvon wouldn't have gone out into that waste and got himself trapped if Ctuchik hadn't been playing games."

"How big is that desert?"

"The Great Desert of Araga? It's about the size of Algaria. There's no way Urvon can dig himself out of those snowdrifts in time to make any difference at Vo Mimbre."

"Unless Torak decides to stop and wait for him."

"He can't. The EVENT has to take place at a specific time."

"I think we've still got a problem, though."

"Oh? Things seem to be going along rather well from where I sit."

"Don't smirk like that, father. We know that Urvon's bogged down, but how are we going to convince Ran Borune and General Cerran that he's no longer a danger to their southern border? We're used to these manipulations of the natural order of things, but they aren't. This blizzard doesn't mean a thing if it doesn't free up the legions."

Trust Polgara to take the shine off things. I scowled at the floor for a few moments. "We'd better talk with Rhodar," I decided. "A dispatch from one of his spies might turn the trick."

"That ploy's wearing a bit thin, father. Ran Borune and Cerran both know that we want the legions at Vo Mimbre. A dispatch that just 'happens' to arrive in the nick of time's going to make them *very* suspicious. Why not just tell them the truth? Show them your copy of the Mrin and point out the number of times it's been right in the past."

"I don't think it'll work, Pol. We might persuade Ran Borune. He's seen enough in the past few years to realize that there's more going on here than he can explain rationally. But we've made such a point of giving the generals reasonable explanations for things that a sudden jump into reality's going to jerk Cerran up short. It'd take months to persuade him, and we don't *have* months. Torak's marching down the River Arend toward Vo Mimbre right now, and it's going to take the Chereks a while to ferry the legions north to Arendia. Cerran's learned that Rhodar's information's usually correct. Let's try it that way before we jump off into something exotic. I want those legions at Vo Mimbre, and I don't have time to educate the Tolnedran General Staff."

"This isn't going to be settled by armies, father. Brand and Torak are going to fight a duel, and *that's* the EVENT we're waiting for. All this maneuvering around isn't anything but preparation."

"*Necessary* preparation, Pol. Torak outnumbers us if we don't have the legions. He won't have any reason to accept Brand's challenge unless the issue's in doubt. We're going to have to bloody his nose a bit before he'll even consider coming out of that iron pavilion of his to engage in single combat with the Child of Light. Torak might be crazy, but he's not foolish enough to risk something like that unless we force him into it."

"We still have to get past General Cerran."

"I know. Let's get Rhodar and go to the palace. We might as well get started with this."

As I'd more or less expected, Ran Borune was inclined to accept Rhodar's story about a dispatch from the South. The Tolnedran Emperor was shrewd enough to realize that Pol and I had ways to get information that he couldn't fully understand, and as long as we gave him a graceful way to take what we told him on faith, he was willing to go along with us. General Cerran, however, dug in his heels. "I'm sorry, your Majesty," he apologized to his emperor, "but I simply can't advise leaving our southern border undefended without some verification of this report. I'm not trying to be offensive, King Rhodar, but I'm sure you can see my position. All I've got to go on here is an encrypted message that I can't even read, from a man I don't even know. His dispatch might be exaggerated, or it might be that he was captured and *forced* to send the message. Nothing would suit Urvon better than tricking us into pulling the legions out of the south. If the report's inaccurate, Urvon could be camped in the streets of Tol Borune before we could get back into position."

"How long would it take you to get some verification, Cerran?" Ran Borune asked him.

"A couple of weeks at least, your Majesty," the general replied. "I've got three legions on the north bank of the River Borgasa in southern Nyissa. They're functioning primarily as scouts to give us a warning when Urvon approaches the Nyissan border. If I can get orders to them to go have a look, a mounted patrol could cut across the southwestern tip of Goska to the desert and be back again in a week or ten days." He spread his hands helplessly. "I'm sorry, your Majesty, but that's about the best I can do. You can move information only as fast as a man on a good horse can carry it. That's always been the problem with large campaigns. I wish there were a faster way, but there isn't."

He was wrong about that, of course. There *is* a faster way, but I couldn't explain it to him—not in terms that he'd understand, anyway.

"I think you're in a bit of a quandary, General Cerran," Polgara said. "If Rhodar's report isn't accurate, Urvon could still come at you from the south, but if Kal Torak wins at Vo Mimbre, he'll be sitting on your northern border with nothing between him and Tol Honeth but a few unarmed peasants. At that point, you'll be looking at a repetition of what happened in Drasnia."

That worried him a little bit, and it worried Ran Borune even more. The shrewd little emperor thought about it for a few moments. "How about a compromise here?" he asked finally.

"I'm willing to listen, Ran Borune," Rhodar said.

"Why don't we send half the legions to Arendia and leave the other half where they are?"

"Will that be enough, Belgarath?" Rhodar asked.

"It'll be touch and go," I replied dubiously.

"Is that your Majesty's decision?" Cerran asked his emperor. "It covers both borders, but . . ." He left it in the air.

"I don't see that we've got much choice, Cerran. We're going to have to protect ourselves on both sides."

"I *hate* two-front wars," Cerran muttered. He scowled at the ceiling for a while. "Numerical superiority's largely a matter of appearances," he mused. "Less than half the troops are actually engaged, in most cases. The rest are held in reserve—usually where the opposing general can see them."

"That's the way it normally works, yes," Rhodar agreed.

"I *do* have some additional forces available," Cerran told us. "They aren't very well trained, they aren't in good condition, and I wouldn't want to venture any guarantees about how well they can fight, but they'll *look* impressive to Kal Torak."

"Where did you come up with this phantom army of yours, Cerran?" Ran Borune asked him.

"There are eight legions in the Imperial Garrison right here in Tol Honeth, your Majesty. They're fat and lazy, and they're mostly Honeth-ites. No man's ever come up with a way to make real soldiers out of Honeths, but at least they'll swell our ranks at Vo Mimbre."

"It's a start," Rhodar conceded.

"I think I can go a little further," Cerran added. "There are twelve le-gion training camps here in the vicinity of Tol Honeth and seven more up near Tol Vordue. Those recruits probably can't even march in a straight line yet, but they *have* got uniforms. That'd give us the appear-ance of twenty-seven additional legions to beef up our reserves. If we pull half of the regular legions off the southern border and reinforce them with these pseudosoldiers, Kal Torak's going to look out and see some-thing in excess of seventy-five legions—*and* King Eldrig's berserkers—on his right flank. I think that'll get his attention."

"General Cerran, you're a genius!" Ran Borune enthused.

"You know, Belgarath," Rhodar said to me, "it might just work at that. Kal Torak's probably crazy, but Ad Rak Cthoros of Cthol Murgos isn't, and neither's Yar Lek Thun of the Nadraks. They're *not* going to let their armies be exterminated as long as there's a Mallorean presence on this continent. They might bow down to Kal Torak, but they aren't stupid enough to trust him. If it starts to look as if they're seriously outnum-bered, I think they'll try to defect—or escape. I'll talk with Cho-Ram about it. If the Murgos and Nadraks start getting homesick, I don't think we should get in their way when they start back east."

"What about the Thulls?" Cerran asked him.

"The Thulls couldn't find their way home without guide dogs, Gen-eral," Rhodar replied, laughing. "Thulls have what you might call a very limited sense of direction. Thulls have a very limited grasp of just about anything. It takes the average Thull a half a day just to tie his shoes."

"You gentlemen *do* realize that you're basing the fate of the world on an elaborate trick, don't you?" Polgara asked us.

"It's a gamble, Lady Polgara," Rhodar admitted gaily, "but gambling's a lot of fun sometimes, and the higher the stakes, the more exciting it is."

She sighed and rolled her eyes upward, but she didn't say anything.

"It's about the best we can do, Belgarath," Ran Borune apologized. "The legions are all spread out along the River of the Woods. General Cerran can get the ones closest to the coast down to the mouth of the River of the Woods and the Cherek fleet in fairly short order. Those that are farther east would take too long to reach the coast to be of any use at Vo Mimbre anyway."

"I'll take personal command of our forces in Arendia," Cerran added. "I might be able to persuade the Honeths to earn their pay for a change."

"Well," I said, "if it's the best we can do, it'll have to be enough." I'm sure I sounded a little dubious, but I was actually quite pleased. Cerran's phantom army might very well be enough to persuade Kal Torak to accept Brand's challenge when the time came.

Torak wasn't moving very fast. The weather still hadn't really returned to normal, and his army was slogging through foot-deep mud. He also stopped frequently to crush every fortified house, every castle, and every serfs' village he came across. The prisoners he took were turned over to the Grolims, of course. There were other things slowing him down, as well—little things like the Algars, the Drasnians, the Ulgos, and the Asturian bowmen. The upper reaches of the River Arend are heavily forested, so there were lots of opportunities for ambushes. I'd had some doubts about the enthusiasm of the Asturians, to be honest with you. Kal Torak was invading *Mimbre*, after all. But after Eldallan's bowmen had seen a few Angarak atrocities, their archery improved to the point that no place in the horde was truly safe from Asturian arrows, and Kal Torak of Mallorea took horrid casualties as he marched west toward Vo Mimbre.

Beldin had flown north from the Desert of Araga, and he was with King Eldrig at the mouth of the River of the Woods. The Tolnedran Legions were drifting in, but it didn't seem to me that they were moving very fast. I didn't make an issue of that with General Cerran, though. I needed him, so I was careful not to be offensive.

Eldrig was in the South with his fleet when the twins arrived in Tol Honeth with some additional clues they'd dredged out of the Mrin, but the rest of us still gathered in the Cherek embassy. If anyplace in Tol Honeth was secure from the prying eyes and ears of Ran Borune's spies, it was the Cherek embassy, and we were going to be talking about things that were none of Ran Borune's business. I rather like the Cherek embassy in Tol Honeth anyway. It's a homey, Alorn sort of place that's a welcome relief from marble-encased Tolnedran stuffiness. The chairs are rough-hewn and covered with fur, and the fireplaces are always going, even in the summertime. Chereks are convinced that they discovered fire, so blazing fireplaces are a sort of religious observance for them.

Once we'd gathered in a fairly standard Alorn council chamber and the ambassador had sent his bully-boys through the building to weed out any spies, we got down to business. Beltira uncased one of the scrolls of the Mrin and read to us from it. " 'Behold!' " he read. " 'It shall come to pass that the Dragon God shall be engaged before the golden city for three days, and then the Child of Light shall issue his challenge. And on the third day shall all be decided by the EVENT.'"

"At least it won't be a protracted siege," Cho-Ram noted.

"I'd been sort of hoping that it might be," I said. I went to the map and measured off some distances. "I think we'd better stop harassing Torak's rear and pull those troops back a bit. If we keep crowding him, he might not stop to regroup. He'll just rush out onto that plain around Vo Mimbre and start the assault on the city. Whether we like it or not, that'll be the first day of that three-day battle the Mrin talks about, and I want Eldrig and Cerran to be a lot closer before things get that far along."

"He might just go ahead and attack anyway, Belgarath," Rhodar pointed out. "He's the one with the calendar, so he knows when he has to be there. We don't. If he's running behind, he won't stop."

"Logic suggests that he gave himself plenty of time, Rhodar," Pol disagreed. "A lot of things have to happen before the EVENT, and Torak knows that—probably even better than we do. Certain things are going to have to be in place before Brand can issue his challenge, and if Torak does anything to disrupt any of that, we'll have an entirely different EVENT—one that's probably not even mentioned in the Mrin *or* the Ashabine Oracles. At that point, *nobody'll* know what's going to happen."

"We could just go ahead and throw everything we've got in his path," Rhodar suggested. "*That* should delay him a bit."

"But that'd put the battle someplace *other* than at Vo Mimbre," Brand objected, "and the EVENT *must* take place there."

"Well, father," Pol said to me, "are you going to make one of those great leaps of faith you keep talking about?"

"I think I'm going to have to. You and I should probably go to Vo Mimbre and give Aldorigen some instructions. I don't want the Mimbrate knights to start feeling muscular and invincible. If they come charging out of the gates of Vo Mimbre before the legions and the Chereks are in place, they'll be obliterated. I think we're only going to have one chance at this, so we'd better get it right the first time. We've done all we can here, so you gentlemen had better take your leave of Ran Borune and go join your forces. We all know the signals and what we're supposed to do when they come. Pol and I'll go to Vo Mimbre and put a leash on Aldorigen. Then we'll just sit tight and wait for the Cherek fleet. Don't provoke any confrontations, but don't let Kal Torak lure you out of position, either."

We all rose to our feet. "Good luck, gentlemen," Pol said gravely. Then the meeting broke up. The kings went across town to the Imperial Palace to advise Ran Borune that they were leaving, and then Cho-Ram and Rhodar rode west to swing around Kal Torak's left flank to join their armies in the mountains, while Brand and Ormik of Sendaria rode north to join theirs at the verge of the Arendish Forest.

Pol and I lingered while I had a few words with the twins. "Try to keep Ran Borune from getting hysterical," I told them. "If he loses his nerve at this point, we'll be in trouble." Then Pol and I left the embassy, crossed the north bridge across the Nedrane, and went into a birch grove to change form.

"I'm going to do something you aren't going to like, father," Pol told me. "I have to use Mother's form during all of this. I'm acting on instructions, so don't waste your time getting indignant."

"I'll try to control myself," I replied. I knew a great deal more about what was going on than Ran Borune did, but there were still many things happening that I *didn't* know about. It was probably just as well, I suppose. If I'd known everything, *I'd* have been the one going into hysterics.

The weather had begun to moderate—slightly. At least it wasn't perpetually raining anymore. The forces that had been building since Kal Torak had left Ashaba had reached their climax in the blizzard that had buried Urvon, but it would still take a while for things to settle back down to normal. The skies over northern Tolnedra and southern Arendia were still cloudy, and even though it was early summer, it wasn't really warming up very much.

Pol and I reached Vo Mimbre in the middle of the night, and we settled down on the battlements of Aldorigen's palace. We waited until the steel-clad sentry had clanked past, and then we changed back into our own forms and descended to the dimly lighted throne room.

"Why don't you let me handle this, father?" Polgara suggested. "I know Arends much better than you do, and I can explain things to Aldorigen in a way that won't offend him. You just sit there looking impressive and let me do the talking."

"Gladly," I agreed. "Trying to talk with an Arend makes my teeth itch."

"Oh, *father!*" Strangely enough, she said it almost affectionately.

Dawn was murkily starting to peep through the windows of the throne room when the great doors opened and Aldorigen and his seventeen-year-old son, Korodullin, entered. Pol and I were sitting back in a corner, so they didn't see us right at first. "He is a miscreant, sire," Korodullin was saying hotly, "an outlaw. His presence here would profane the most sacred place in all Arendia."

"I know that he is a scoundrel and a rogue, Korodullin, but I have given mine oath. Thou shalt not speak disparagingly unto him, nor offer him any impertinence whilst he is within the confines of Vo Mimbre. If thou canst not restrain thine ire, remain in thy chambers until he doth

depart. He will be here ere noon, and he and I must speak of diverse matters concerning the forthcoming battle. He will be here under safe-
conduct, and no man—not even thou—shall stain mine honor by word
or deed. I will have thy pledge to that effect, or I shall have thee
confined."

Korodullin drew himself up. He was a handsome young devil, I'll give
him that, but his face was filled with anger, and it was frighteningly devoid of anything even remotely resembling good sense. "It shall be as my
king commands," he grated out from between tightly clenched teeth.

What was going on here?

I'd have eavesdropped a bit longer, but Polgara was already moving down toward the dais where the two were standing. "Good morrow,
your Majesty," she greeted Aldorigen with an exquisitely graceful curt-
sey. "Mine agèd father and I have but recently arrived from Tol Honeth, and, though all bemused by the splendor of this most renowned of
cities, have we come hither to consult with thee and to divulge unto thee
certain information concerning that which hath come to pass which doth
concern thee and thy realm most poignantly."

How could she possibly manage to get all of that into one sentence?

Aldorigen bowed deeply to her. "My poor city is honored by thy presence, divine Lady Polgara," he responded, "for thou, like the sun itself, do
bring light and joy to all that thou lookst upon." If you give a couple of
Arends a little bit of leisure, they'll keep on exchanging involuted and increasingly complicated compliments for days on end. Once Polgara lapsed
into the "thees" and "thous," her good sense went out the window, and
she became an Arend to her fingertips. I knew that I'd just be wasting my
breath if I tried to hurry them along, so I pulled a small, tightly wound
scroll out from under my tunic, sat down in a chair not far from the dais,
and tried to look studious and preoccupied.

After about a half hour or so, during which my daughter and the so-
called king of Arendia compared each other to suns, moons, rainbows,
summer mornings, stars, eagles in flight, roaring lions, and gentle doves,
Polgara got down to the point. She impressed the necessity of waiting for
the signal to attack upon the witless Aldorigen by the simple expedient
of repeating it over and over and over again, couching it in different sim-
iles or metaphors with each repetition. Gradually the light of understanding began to flicker, dimly, in his eyes.

"Prithee, my Lord King," she protested, "I would not dare presume to
give instruction to the paramount monarch of all this world . . ." And *that*
went on for about another half hour as the two of them tried to outdo
each other in a cloying display of humility. Then finally Pol got around
to asking him what he and his son had been arguing about when they'd
entered the throne room.

"The miscreant Asturian, Eldallan, hath besought me that I provide him safe-conduct that he and I might confer at some length on diverse matters of concern to us both in regard to the forthcoming battle. Methinks, however, that there is some faint odor of subterfuge in his request. Our battle plans are clear, and they are not complex. There is no need for this meeting."

"The rogue hath seized this opportunity to spy out our defenses," Korodullin asserted hotly. "He is Asturian, and therefore a knave by definition. Should the battle exhaust us, Eldallan will descend upon Vo Mimbre with all his might. Moreover, since he is Asturian, it is well within the realm of possibility that he hath concluded some secret accord with Kal Torak to betray us at a crucial moment during the battle."

I sent my thought out to my daughter. *You'd better head that off immediately, Pol. This entire alliance is teetering in the balance here.*

"*Right,*" she replied. She looked at the two of them with artfully feigned astonishment. "I can scarce believe mine ears," she told them. "Are ye *truly* so timid? Is the legendary bravery of Mimbrates no more than a sham? Doth the antagonism of a few Asturian outlaws so greatly concern ye? Fie, gentlemen, fie! These womanish suspicions bring shame upon the both of ye!"

I almost choked. That *wasn't* the way *I'd* have done it. If *that* was Polgara's idea of the best way to smooth things over, she and I needed to have a long talk.

Astonishingly, it worked. She continued to berate them until she had them squirming like a couple of embarrassed schoolboys, and then she let the matter drop.

Duke Eldallan arrived on the stroke of noon, and he had his daughter, Mayaserana, with him. The implications of that were obvious. He was offering himself and his daughter up as hostages as proof of his good faith. Rather astonishingly, Aldorigen got his point immediately. Mayaserana had grown considerably since I'd last seen her. She was almost eighteen now, and astonishingly beautiful, a fact that Korodullin noticed right away. Her beauty was only slightly marred by the fact that her large, dark eyes were as hard as agates.

"I'll get right to the point here, Aldorigen," Eldallan said briskly after he and his daughter had been escorted into the throne room under heavy guard. "You and I aren't particularly fond of each other, so there's no point in dragging it out. I've given my word to her Grace, the Duchess of Erat, that I'll come to your aid when Kal Torak assaults your city, and I'll do that. In return, however, I want your oath that when the battle's done, my people will be permitted to return to Asturia unmolested by Mimbrate knights."

"Asturia no longer exists," Korodullin asserted.

"Come up to our forest and say that, foolish boy," Mayaserana told him. "Mimbrate bones are turning green and mossy under every bush. One more set won't seriously add to the clutter."

They were getting along just splendidly.

Polgara stepped in at that point and badgered Eldallan and Aldorigen into exchanging oaths. Eldallan swore to take his assigned place beside the Rivans and Sendars on Kal Torak's north flank, and Alodrigen vowed that the Mimbrate knights wouldn't interfere with the Asturians on their way home. The entire matter *could* have been resolved by the Sendarian intermediaries, of course, but Eldallan had another reason for coming to Vo Mimbre. He broached it after he and Aldorigen had exchanged oaths. "It occurs to me that we've got too good an opportunity to pass up, Aldorigen," he said in an insolent tone of voice.

"I will hear thy words, Eldallan." Aldorigen's tone was cool and offensively superior.

"Whole generations are likely to pass before the rulers of Mimbre and Asturia are so conveniently close to each other, wouldn't you say?"

Aldorigen's eyes brightened. "A most acute perception, my Lord," he replied. It was the first time either of them had addressed the other with any kind of respect.

"Why not seize the day, my Lord?" Eldallan suggested. "Once we've eliminated the annoyance of Kal Torak, you and I could go to some private place and discuss our differences—at length." He laid his hand suggestively on the hilt of his sheathed rapier. "I'm sure you'll find my arguments very pointed."

An almost beneficent smile came over Aldorigen's face. "What a splendid suggestion, my Lord," he said warmly.

"Until that day, then, my Lord," Eldallan said with a deep bow.

"Stay out of it, Pol!" I sent the thought out sharply. *"This is supposed to happen!"*

The thought she threw back at me doesn't bear repeating.

"And *you*, rash youth, will stay away when our fathers meet," Mayaserana said to Korodullin. "I'm Asturian, and my hand was built to hold a bow. Your bones can turn green here in Mimbre just as well as they can in Asturia."

"Come not within bow-shot of my father, outlaw wench," he replied, "not if thou wilt have further need of thine head."

Then Eldallan and his feisty daughter were escorted out.

"Now is my day complete!" Aldorigen exulted. "Were it not so unnatural, I could almost embrace that foul villain, Eldallan!"

Arends, I sighed, rolling my scroll back up.

It took Kal Torak another week to reach the upper end of that large plain that surrounds Vo Mimbre, and he stopped there to regroup and to send out scouts. I started getting nervous at that point. *"What's keeping you?"* I threw the thought at Beldin.

"I've still got ten legions coming down the river," he replied.

"Beldin, Torak's almost in my lap here! Can't you send the ones you've already got on hand?"

"Didn't we decide not to do it that way? Torak's not going to be very intimidated by the legions if I just dribble them in. The whole force has to arrive at the same time."

"How much longer before you'll be able to sail?"

"A couple of days. Then Eldrig's got to pick up the Imperial Guard at Tol Honeth and those training legions there and at Tol Vordue. Give us a week."

"If Torak starts his attack in the next day or so, you'll get here after it's all over. The Mrin says that the battle's going to last for three days. The first two days will probably only be skirmishes, but you absolutely must be here on that third day."

"You've got your work cut out for you, then. All you've got to do is keep him away from the walls of Vo Mimbre for five days. Then fight him for the first two days of the battle. I'll be there on the third day, and we can get down to business."

"Don't be late."

"Trust me."

I went to the door of my room in Aldorigen's palace. "I need a large current map of southern Arendia," I told the sentry patrolling the hallway.

"At once, Holy Belgarath," he replied, clashing one steel-gauntleted fist against his breastplate. Mimbrates are so *noisy!*

When he returned with the map, I spread it out on the table and got down to work. The more I studied the map, the more feasible the half-formed plan in my mind began to seem. *"Polgara,"* I silently called my daughter. *"I need you."*

It only took her a couple of minutes to reach my door. "Yes, father?" she said.

"I want you to go have a talk with Eldallan," I instructed. "I need a thousand or so of his archers. Beldin's still a week away, so we've got to delay Torak for five days."

"I don't think a thousand bowmen could quite manage that, father."

"They can if the people they're shooting at are out in the middle of a river trying to rebuild a bridge." I showed her the map. "There are a dozen tributaries feeding down into the River Arend," I pointed out, "and twenty-five years of steady rain has them all running bank-full. I'm going to have Aldorigen send out a force of Mimbrates to destroy the bridges.

I want archers on the west banks of those streams. It's very hard to concentrate on building bridges when it's raining arrows. That *might* just delay Torak for the five days we need."

"I'd imagine so, yes. You can be a very nasty old man when you set
your mind to it."

"I try." I scowled at the map for a moment. "You'll have to stay with
those archers," I decided, "and I'll be with the Mimbrates. The two forces
have to be coordinated, and direct contact between Mimbrates and Asturians isn't a very good idea. Get started, Pol. I'll go explain the plan to
Aldorigen."

It just so happened that the commander of the Asturian archers Pol
brought down onto the eastern side of the plain of Mimbre was a fiery
young nobleman, the Baron of Wildantor, and the knight who led my
Mimbrate bridge-wreckers was the Baron of Vo Mandor. Garion's friend
can be very obvious at times. Pol and I were careful to keep Mandorallen's ancestor some distance away from Lelldorin's. I'd devoted a lot of
time to those two families, so I didn't want any accidents.

Our strategy wasn't particularly profound. We advanced eastward until we began encountering Kal Torak's scouts. The Mimbrate knights
trampled them under, and we pressed on, crossing bridges every few miles.
When we began to encounter stiffer resistance, the archers raked the opposing force with arrows, and *then* the Mimbrates charged.

It doesn't sound very complicated, but it kept Pol and me hopping.
I had to go through the ranks of the Mimbrate knights each and every
time, pointing out the fact that they were supposed to charge the
Angaraks rather than the Asturians. At the same time, Pol had to remind
the archers that they weren't supposed to shoot at Mimbrates.

We eventually reached a wide tributary that had several thousand
Murgos camped on its east bank. I called Pol and the two barons in to
discuss strategy. "This is about as far east as we need to go," I told them.
"Let's wreck the west end of the bridges crossing this river and then pull
back to the next stream."

"I will delay their pursuit," Wildantor declared.

"No, actually you *won't*," I told him firmly. "You're not going to start
doing that until we've crossed two more rivers."

"I'm sworn to delay them!" The young baron had red hair—and all
that implies.

"Listen carefully, Lord Baron," I told him. "I don't want the Murgos
to even know that you're here for a while yet. Mandor's Mimbrates will
destroy the bridges here; then we'll pull back to the next river, and he'll
do it again. Then we'll do it for the third time on the next river to the
west. The Murgos will have developed a pattern by then. They'll rush forward in a mass carrying timbers with them to repair the bridges. When

they come to the fourth river, you'll have *lots* of targets out there in the water. I want the surface of that river absolutely covered with the floating bodies of dead Murgos. After that, they're going to be *very* cautious when they come to a river."

He frowned and thought it over. It took him a while. Then his eyes brightened, and his face broke into a broad grin. "I *like* it!" he exclaimed.

"Though it seemeth me a most unnatural thing, my Lord of Wildantor," the Baron of Vo Mandor said, "I find myself growing fond of thee. Thine exuberance is contagious, methinks."

"You're not so bad yourself, Mandor," the Asturian admitted. "Why don't we agree not to kill each other when this is over?"

"Doth that not violate the precepts of our religion?" Mandor said it with an absolutely straight face, and that sent Wildantor off into gales of laughter.

It wasn't much, but it was a start in the right direction.

My rudimentary plan worked surprisingly well—although, given the limited mentality of Murgos, I don't know why I was surprised. Lulled into a sense of security by the lack of any opposition to their bridge-building operations, the Murgos, as I'd predicted, rushed whole regiments carrying timbers to the east bank of the fourth river. Wildantor held his archers in check until the Murgos had their spans reaching out to the middle of the river. Then he sounded his horn as a signal to his hidden archers.

The Asturian arrows arched overhead like a slithering rainbow, and the Murgos quite literally melted off their half-completed bridges to fill the river with floating corpses.

Then Wildantor waited, exercising remarkable self-control for an Arend.

The Murgos left on the banks crept forward fearfully, their shields held protectively over their heads.

Still Wildantor waited.

Eventually the Murgos decided that the archers had withdrawn, and they resumed their construction.

Then the second rainbow of arrows swept the bridges clean again.

The surviving Murgos gathered on the east bank, screaming curses at the still-unseen archers.

It was at that point that the Baron of Wildantor gave the shrieking Murgos a pointed demonstration of the incredible range of the Asturian longbow. His third rainbow piled heaps of dead Murgos along the east bank of a river that was fully two hundred paces wide.

"Splendid!" Mandor cheered. "Capital!"

Then we withdrew again, retreating back to the fifth tributary of the River Arend. Wildantor and his archers brought up the rear, pausing every few hundred paces to rake the pursuing Murgos with yard-long arrows, thus giving the Mimbrate knights time to tear down all the bridges except one. Then the Asturians sprayed the Murgos with a prolonged arrow-storm, closed up shop, and retreated across the lone remaining bridge.

As you might expect, Wildantor stood his ground at the east end of the bridge until all his men were safely across. His hands seemed almost to blur as he loosed arrow after arrow into the faces of the advancing Murgos. Then he ran out of arrows, turned, and started across the bridge.

The Mimbrate knights had weakened the bridge timbers to the point that a good healthy sneeze would have made the whole thing collapse, and somewhere up in the mountains to the northeast, Garion's friend sneezed. A cloudburst, one of the last gasps of that quarter-century-long rainstorm, had filled every ravine and gully with rushing water; it all came down that tributary in a ten-foot wave.

The bridge dissolved under Wildantor's feet.

I rushed to the west band, drawing in my Will.

"Stay out of it, father!" Pol snapped at me.

"But—"

"It's already been taken care of."

The Baron of Vo Mandor set his spurs to his horse's flanks, galloped down to the next bridge, and rolled out of his saddle with a vast clanking of armor. He ran out on the shattered remnants of that wrecked bridge to its very teetering end, knelt, and stretched his arm down toward the seething water. *"Wildantor!"* he bellowed in a voice they probably heard in Vo Mimbre. *"To me!"*

The red-haired Asturian was being carried downriver at a ferocious speed, but he angled across the current and reached up his arm as he was swept past the splintered end of the ruined bridge. The hands of the two men came together with a resounding smack, and the Mimbrate leaned back, literally jerking the Asturian up out of the current. Then he caught hold of the back of Wildantor's tunic and swung him up to safety.

Wildantor lay facedown for a minute or two, spluttering, coughing, and spitting out a quart or so of muddy water. Then he raised his face with a broad grin. "You've got a nice firm grip there, Mandor," he said. "You could probably break rocks without using a hammer." He sat up, massaged the hand the Mimbrate had nearly crushed, and looked around. "I guess I'd better get my bowmen in place," he said as if nothing had happened. "We'll hold off the Murgos while you and your knights go tear down some more bridges."

"Right," Mandor said. He rose, clanking, pulled Wildantor to his feet, and went back to his horse.

Neither of them ever spoke of the incident again, but the sound of that resounding smack when their hands met still seemed to echo in my mind, and it somehow gave me hope for the future.

We continued our slow withdrawal, but after that fifth tributary, where Wildantor's archers took a dreadful toll on the advancing Murgos, King Ad Rak Cthoros of Murgodom found something very pressing for his soldiers to do elsewhere, and the Thulls were given the chore of rebuilding bridges. Somehow it always seems to work out that way in Angarak society.

All right, our little exercise wasn't really very creative, but it slowed Kal Torak's advance for the requisite five days. Always look for the simplest solution to any problem. It's when you start getting exotic that things begin to go wrong.

The clouds began to blow off during the afternoon of the day when the Thulls finished repairing the bridges crossing the last remaining tributary of the River Arend. Pol and I decided that there wasn't much point in wasting lives trying to hold back the advancing Angaraks any more. We'd achieved the delay we needed, so we took our forces inside the walls of Vo Mimbre and closed the gates behind us.

The sunset that evening was glorious, and it promised that we would have clear, sunny skies for the first day of the Battle of Vo Mimbre.

CHAPTER
FORTY

The southern wall of the city of Vo Mimbre rises out of the River Arend, and the seemingly endless rains of the past quarter century had filled the river to over-flowing. That made an attack from that front highly unlikely, so we only had three sides to defend.

I went along the top of the golden walls as dusk gathered over Vo Mimbre to check the defenses before I settled in for the night. I'm sure the Mimbrates knew what they were doing, but it never hurts to make sure, particularly when you're dealing with Arends. I found my two barons, Mandor and Wildantor, standing on the parapet over the main gate looking out gravely at the gradually darkening plain. "Is One-eye moving at all?" I asked them.

"A few advance parties is all," the green-tuniced Wildantor replied. "He'll probably wait until after dark to take up his positions. If we get a decent moon tonight, my archers can make camping right under our wall very expensive for him."

"Save your arrows," I told him. "There'll be plenty of targets when the sun comes up."

"We've got lots of arrows, Belgarath. Mandor here's got Mimbrate fletchers turning them out for us by the barrelful."

"I did note that Asturian arrows are much longer than ours by reason of the extreme length of the Asturian bow." Mandor noted, shifting his armor. "Since we are temporarily allies, it seemed to me provident to give our friends an ample supply."

486

"Isn't he a *nice* boy?" Wildantor said outrageously, flashing his friend that infectious grin of his.

Mandor laughed. The impudent young redhead seemed to charm him to the point that he was willing to lay aside two eons of hereditary enmity. I approved of that. Their friendship was a good sign of things to come. "You gentlemen might as well get some sleep," I told them. "Tomorrow's going to be a long day." Then I left them and went on down to my room.

Polgara was sitting by the fire waiting for me. "Where have you been?" she asked me.

I shrugged. "Having a look at the defenses."

"The Mimbrates have been preparing for a siege of this city for over two thousand years, father. They know what they're doing. I'm going to be gone for a look around."

"Be careful out there."

"Of course. Are you going to bed?"

"Why bother? I'm not going to be able to sleep. I want to talk with Beldin anyway. Don't be out all night." How many fathers have ever said that?

She nodded a bit distantly, and then she left.

"Beldin," I sent out the thought, "*are you making any progress?*"

"*We're at Tol Honeth,*" he replied. "*We'll start downriver in the morning. How are things going there?*"

"We managed to delay Torak. We're inside the city now. I expect he'll try to pay us a call first thing in the morning. Are you going to make it in time?"

"*It shouldn't be any problem. It's only forty leagues down the river and another forty to Tol Vordue. We should reach the mouth of the River Arend sometime day after tomorrow.*"

"*You won't be able to count on a following wind when you start up the river, you know.*"

"*Then we'll row. That's why oars were invented. Do me a favor and keep Torak out of Vo Mimbre. We're working on a tight schedule, so I won't have time to take the city back from him. Don't pester me any more, Belgarath. I'm busy.*"

I grunted and wandered down the hall to talk with the twins. I didn't really have anything important to say to them, but I was feeling edgy, and I needed some company.

It was well past midnight when Polgara returned. "He's bringing up his siege engines," she informed us.

"Do you think the walls'll hold?" Beltira asked me.

"Probably," I replied. "Vo Mimbre's not quite as impregnable as the Algarian Stronghold, but it comes fairly close. I think it's secure—as long as Torak doesn't start getting exotic. He could knock down a mountain if he really wanted to."

"That's forbidden," Belkira assured me. "The Necessities have agreed on that point."

"I think we're relatively safe on that score, father," Pol said. "If Torak were going to knock down mountains, he'd have knocked down the Stronghold. He hasn't once been out of that iron pavilion since his army crossed the land bridge."

"How do you know that?" I asked her.

"He and Zedar were talking about it this evening, and I was eaves-dropping." She smiled faintly. "I definitely wouldn't want to be in Urvon's shoes—or Ctuchik's. Torak's really put out with both of them. He was *re-ally* counting on Urvon's second army. Zedar seems fairly smug, though. Now that Urvon and Ctuchik are in disfavor, he's the cock of the walk." She paused reflectively. "I think we'll have to keep an eye on Zedar, fa-ther. *Torak* might abide by the prohibition, but Zedar might not. If things start going badly, Zedar's probably going to break a few rules."

"My brother and I'll keep an eye on him," Beltira promised.

"What else were the two of them talking about?" I asked Pol.

"Their instructions, for the most part," she replied. "Evidently the Ashabine Oracles gave Torak far more in the way of details than the Mrin Codex gives us. He knows that Eldrig's bringing the legions, for ex-ample, and he knows that there's not a great deal he can do about it. He also knows that the EVENT's going to take place in three days. He's known about that for a long time now. He doesn't really want to meet Brand. Apparently there's some bad news for him in the Oracles. When he came across the land-bridge and gathered up the western Angaraks, there was no way we could have matched his numbers, but his campaigns in Drasnia and Algaria and his trek across Ulgoland have cost him at least half his army. I guess Zedar went out and counted noses. If the le-gions get here in time, the numbers are going to be fairly even. At that point, Torak won't have any choice but to accept Brand's challenge."

"Well, now," I said, "isn't *that* interesting?"

"Don't start gloating, father. Torak's ordered Zedar to throw every-thing they've got at Vo Mimbre here. If they can take the city, the advantage swings back his way, and he'll be able to ignore Brand's chal-lenge. Once we go past that third day, we go into an entirely different EVENT. Torak knows what it is, but we don't. He seemed a bit smug about it, though."

"That suggests that he'll win if this goes into the fourth day," Belkira said.

"And the corollary to that is that *we'll* win if the EVENT takes place on the third day," Beltira added. He frowned. "Did they talk at all about trying to delay the war-boats on their way upriver, Pol?"

"Zedar suggested it," she replied, "but Torak said no. He's not going to split his forces. He wants Vo Mimbre, and that's going to take every man he's got. How long is it until morning?"

"Three or four hours," I told her.

"I'll have time for a bath, then. If you gentlemen will excuse me, I'll go see to that."

The night seemed to drag on forever. I wound up prowling the tops of the walls and staring out into the darkness. The stars overhead were very bright, but there was no moon. Poets rhapsodize about starlight, but you really can't see very much by it.

Then, after what seemed an eternity, a faint stain of light touched the eastern horizon. It grew and gradually began to wash out the stars with its steely luminescence. At first, all I could see on the plain before the walls of Vo Mimbre were dark masses. Far out on the rim of Kal Torak's army, twinkling watchfires glowed like fireflies. Torak's generals had just come through Ulgoland, and the cat-eyed Ulgos made them nervous.

I joined Mandor and Wildantor on the wall above the massive main gate, and we waited.

"It looks like we'll have good weather," Wildantor observed in that quiet voice men use when it's very early in the day.

"If it doth not rain," Mandor added. I don't think he was trying to be funny, but his remark set Wildantor to laughing.

The dawn light grew gradually stronger, and details began to emerge. The siege engines Pol had mentioned looked very much like large, spindly black insects with slender limbs; long, arched-back necks; and small, bucket-shaped heads. They encircled the city about a hundred and fifty paces out from the walls, and the dark bulky forms of the Thulls who manned them swarmed around them like clusters of fleas.

Wildantor chuckled.

"Something funny?" I asked him.

"I don't think the Thulls are going to laugh very much," he replied. "They've set up their siege engines within bow-shot of the walls. Thulls seem to have trouble learning from experience, don't they? When we were coming down the valley, we were picking them off at half again that range. Give the word, Belgarath, and I'll have my archers educate them some more."

I considered it. "Let's hold off on that," I decided. "When they start shooting rocks at us, their assault troops are likely to start massing up behind the engines. That's going to impede escape routes for the Thulls manning the engines and create a great deal of confusion."

The sky gradually began to take on some color. It was blue off to the
east above the mountains of Ulgoland now.

"Why do they wait?" Mandor asked.

"Time's a part of the EVENT, my friend," I explained. "Torak's waiting for a specific moment to begin. The first rock he throws at us starts
the battle, and if he's off by so much as a second, he'll lose."

"Methinks he will lose anyway," Mandor said.

"We can hope, I guess."

Then, just as the upper rim of the sun rose above the mountains of
Holy Ulgo, a deep-toned horn sounded from the black iron pavilion that
headquartered Kal Torak of Mallorea, the siege engines all lashed forward
like striking snakes, and a veritable cloud of large rocks arched upward to
crash against the golden walls of Vo Mimbre.

The battle had begun.

There was a lot of confusion, of course—people shouting and cursing
and running for cover. A fair number of the rocks those engines were
hurling at us *did* fall inside the city, but that was only incidental, and
probably the result of poor aim. Torak wasn't trying to kill people with his
engines; he was trying to batter down the walls. After the first few volleys,
his engineers adjusted their aim, and the whole business settled down to
the clash and rattle of large rocks striking the outer walls of the city. It
was noisy, but it didn't really accomplish much. The walls held.

As I'd anticipated, masses of assault troops began to move battering
rams, assault towers, and scaling ladders up into position just behind the
siege engines in preparation for an attack on the walls. It was about midmorning, after four hours or so of steady pounding, when I turned to
Wildantor. "I think this might be a good time for you to give our Thullish
friends out there some idea of the range of your longbows," I suggested.

"I thought you'd never ask."

The fact that the Asturian archers were shooting from the top of a
very high wall added more distance to the range of their bows, and the
effect of their arrows devastated the Thulls manning the siege engines.
The bombardment stopped immediately. The air between the engines and
the walls had been littered with rocks coming our way all morning. Now
it was filled with a glowing arch of slender arrows, all going the other way.
The survivors of those engine crews turned and fled back into the very
teeth of the assault forces massed behind them with the arrows relent-
lessly following them. Kal Torak's army flinched in on itself and pulled
back about a quarter of a mile. The insectlike siege engines stood silent
and unmoving with windrows of dead Thulls heaped around them.

"What thinkest thou will be their next move, Ancient One?" Mandor asked me.

"They're going to have to retrieve those engines," I speculated.

"They're not going to be able to tear down these walls with their bare hands."

"My very thought," he agreed. Then he raised that horn he always carried at his side and blew a strident note on it.

The main gate crashed open and a couple thousand armored Mimbrate knights mounted on huge horses charged out.

"What are you *doing?*" I almost screamed at him.

"The Angaraks have withdrawn in fearful confusion, Holy One," he explained in an infuriatingly reasonable tone of voice. "Their engines stand unmanned and unguarded. I find those engines irritating. 'Twere best, methinks, to seize this opportunity to destroy them."

I couldn't fault his reasoning, but I *wished* that he'd told me about his plan before he'd opened those gates. I was getting older, and my veins weren't as good as they used to be.

The Mimbrate knights were armed with battle-axes, and they swept out of that gate like two great scythes, one cutting to the left and one to the right. They didn't exactly reduce the Angarak siege engines to kindling wood, but they came close, then they circled back; pounded, cheering, along the foot of the walls; reentered the city; and slammed the gates behind them.

"Nice job, Mandor," Wildantor complimented his friend.

Mandor smiled with becoming modesty.

Kal Torak, however, probably *wasn't* smiling. His iron pavilion was at least a mile out on the plain, but the sound of his raging came to us quite clearly.

"What'll he do now?" Wildantor asked me.

"Something foolish, most likely," I replied. "Kal Torak doesn't think very clearly when he's angry."

With the loss of his siege engines, Torak's chances of broaching the walls of Vo Mimbre were reduced to almost zero. He really didn't have any choice but to try a frontal assault on the main gates at that point. The battering rams crept forward, and the tall, swaying assault towers came lumbering toward us. Hordes of Murgos, Nadraks, and Malloreans ran at the walls carrying scaling ladders. The Asturian archers picked them off in droves as they rushed forward, and when they got closer, Mimbrates joined in with their shorter-limbed bows. When the Angaraks reached the walls, we dropped boulders on them and poured boiling pitch on their heads. Fire arrows into the pitch added confusion and smoke.

It was a very expensive afternoon for Kal Torak of Mallorea, and his demoralized army withdrew as a smoky sunset decorated the western sky.

We'd survived the first day. Kal Torak had lost thousands of men, and he was still outside the walls.

We dumped heaps of dried brush and stacks of cordwood off the top of the walls, doused the resulting jumble with naptha, and set fire to it. The smoke was a little inconvenient, but that ring of fire surrounding the city made sure that there wouldn't be any surprises during the night.

Then we all gathered in the throne room. King Aldorigen was almost beside himself with glee. "A most fruitful day!" he gloated. "I salute thee, my Lord baron of Wildantor. Thine archers have saved the day for us."

"I thank your Grace," Wildantor replied with a modest bow, "but much of the credit should go to my friend Mandor here. All my men did was drive the Angaraks away from their engines. Mandor sent the axemen out to hack the silly things to pieces."

"There's credit enough to go around, gentlemen." It was Mergon, the Tolnedran ambassador to the court at Vo Mimbre. He was a weedy-looking little fellow, whose short stature proclaimed him to be a Borune, a fact confirmed by his silver-trimmed blue mantle. Tolnedrans have an elaborate color code to identify members of the various families. "All in all, I'd say that it was a fairly successful day," he continued.

"It's only the first day of the battle, Mergon," I warned him. "I'm not going to start gloating until we get through tomorrow." I looked around. "Where's Polgara?"

"She left just after sunset," Belkira told me. "She thought it might be a good idea to listen in on Torak and Zedar this evening."

"You can stand on the walls and listen to Torak, brother," I said. "He gets very loud when he's angry. When Cherek and I went to Cthol Mishrak and stole back the Orb, we could hear him from ten miles off."

Mergon's face grew pained. "*Please* don't say things like that, Belgarath," he pleaded. "You know it's a violation of my religion to listen to that sort of thing."

I shrugged. "Don't listen, then."

"What can we expect tomorrow?" Wildantor asked me.

"I haven't the faintest idea," I admitted. "Why don't we wait until Pol gets back with some solid information rather than waste time on wild guesses."

It was shortly after midnight when Polgara returned, and we gathered in the throne room again to listen to her report. "Zedar seems to have fallen out of favor," she told us with a faint smile. "He was supposed to take the city yesterday, and Torak said any number of highly uncomplimentary things to him about his failure."

"It wasn't entirely Zedar's fault, Lady Polgara," Mergon told her. "We had a little bit to do with it, after all."

"Torak's not known for his forgiveness, your Excellency," Beltira said. "He tends to hold grudges."

"That he does," Pol added. "He made quite an issue of the fact that

Zedar's failed before. He raised the point that it was Zedar's failure in Morindland that made it possible for father to retrieve the Orb, and that was almost three thousand years ago."

"That's a *very* long time to hold a grudge," Wildantor noted.

"Torak's like that," I said. "Were you able to pick up any hints about what we should expect tomorrow, Pol?"

"Torak didn't say anything specific, father, but I think I can make a few guesses. He told Zedar that he *would* be inside the walls by nightfall, and Zedar's supposed to use *any* means to accomplish that."

"Sorcery?" Mandor guessed.

"Torak didn't say it in so many words, but the implications were there. I think we can expect Zedar to resort to his gifts to try to get inside. Tomorrow's his last chance. If he fails again, Torak'll probably incinerate him."

"I can face the prospect with a certain equanimity," I said. Then I looked at Beltira. "Would it violate the rules of this particular EVENT if Zedar tries to use sorcery?"

"That's not too clear," he replied. "*Torak* isn't supposed to, but the Mrin doesn't say anything about his disciples."

"If the prohibition's absolute, Zedar might be in for a nasty shock," Belkira added. "I'm not sure what it'd do to one of us if nothing happened when we spoke the Word to release the Will, but I'm fairly sure I wouldn't care to find out."

"Zedar's probably desperate enough to try it," Polgara told him. "Torak gave him an ultimatum." She frowned. "We all know Zedar well enough to know that he'd rather not risk his own skin, but there *are* Grolims out there. He might order *them* to try to use Will and Word against us. If a few Grolims get turned to stone, Zedar could use that as an excuse when Torak called him to account."

"We could speculate all night about that," I told them. "To be on the safe side, we're going to have to assume that they'll try it and that it'll work. If it doesn't, fine; if it does, we'd better be ready."

Mergon's expression was very pained.

"We're just talking shop, your Excellency," Pol told him. "It's a family trait, and it doesn't really concern you. I'm sure Nedra won't be angry with you if you happen to hear some things you aren't supposed to."

"My cousin might be, though," he replied.

"Ran Borune's not entirely unreasonable, Mergon," I said. "A lot of things have happened recently that he doesn't understand. A few more won't unhinge him." I looked around. "I think we've covered just about everything," I told them. "We might as well try to get some sleep. I think we'll all need to be alert tomorrow."

I didn't follow my own advice, of course, but I've learned to get along without sleep when I have to. I caught Pol in the dim corridor outside the throne room. "I think we'd better start moving people," I told her. "I'll go tell Cho-Ram and Rhodar to start closing up the gap between them and Torak's east flank. Then I'll go talk with Brand and Ormik and have them ease down from the north. I want those soldiers to be in place and fresh when Beldin gets here day after tomorrow."

"Do you want me to do it?" she offered.

"No. I'll take care of it. I couldn't sleep tonight anyway. Keep an eye on things here, Pol. Zedar might decide to get an early start."

"I'll take care of it, father. Would a suggestion offend you?"

"That depends on the suggestion."

"Use the form of an owl. That falcon of yours doesn't see all that well in the dark, and Zedar might have alerted his troops to keep an eye out for wolves."

"I'll think about it. I'll try to be back by morning, but if I'm not, you'll have to handle things here for a while. *Don't* let Mandor open that gate again."

"I'll see to it. Have a nice flight, father." I think that Polgara's the only person in the world who can say something like that without sounding ridiculous.

I took her advice about the owl, but I did not assume Poledra's favorite form. I used an ordinary horned owl instead. Once I got out past the Angarak armies, though, I went wolf. Owls don't really fly very fast, and I was in a hurry.

I woke Cho-Ram and Rhodar, and they sent for the Ulgo, Brasa, who commanded the Gorim's forces. "Don't make any contact with Kal Torak's army," I cautioned them. "He knows you're here, but he isn't going to do anything about it unless you force him to."

"Can Vo Mimbre hold?" Rhodar asked.

"I think so. The Mrin says that Torak's going to be engaged *before* the golden city for three days. It doesn't say anything about him getting inside."

"That could be open to interpretation, Belgarath," Cho-Ram objected.

"Just about everything in the Mrin's open to interpretation, Cho-Ram, but I think it'd mention it if Vo Mimbre were going to fall. That'd probably be an EVENT, and the Mrin doesn't miss very many of those. Get your people together, gentlemen. Move out at first light, but stay at least five miles back from Torak's left. The Mimbrates are going to have to hold out alone for one more day."

I went northwesterly from their encampment, and it was very close to morning when I found the Rivans, Sendars, and Asturian archers. "It's time to move, gentlemen," I told Brand, Ormik, and Eldallan. "I want you to be within striking distance of Kal Torak's rear by this evening. Don't engage him, though. I'll need every man I can get when tomorrow rolls around."

Brand was holding the shield with my Master's Orb embedded in the center of it, and, probably without even being aware that he was doing it, he was idly stroking the glowing jewel almost as if it were a puppy. "Don't play with it, Brand," I cautioned him. "It'll do some strange things to your mind if you keep your hand on it for too long. Has your friend told you what you're supposed to do yet?"

He shook his head. "Not yet. I imagine he'll get around to it when the time comes."

"You seem to be taking this all very calmly," Ormik accused him.

"It won't do me any good to get excited." Brand looked at me. "You've been the Child of Light once or twice, haven't you, Belgarath?" he asked.

"Once," I said. "At least once that I know about. Your friend might have slipped a couple of others in on me without bothering to tell me about it. Why do you ask?"

"Did you feel—well—sort of distant from what was going on? I've been feeling just a bit abstracted for the past few days. It's almost as if I weren't going to be personally involved when I meet Torak."

"That's the Necessity working. And you're at least partly right: when you get right down to it, your friend'll sort of take over."

"And Torak's friend will take *him* over, as well?"

"I'm not too sure about that, Brand. The two Necessities are different, and they might do things differently. Ours just steps in and takes charge. Torak's might not do it that way. Torak's not the sort to take something like that philosophically anyway. Maybe we'll find out when the EVENT rolls around. Start your men south, gentlemen. I'd better get back to Vo Mimbre and see what Zedar's up to."

Zedar evidently had been up to no good. There were a dozen or so mangonels emplaced just beyond the range of Asturian arrows as I flew back to the city, and they were already hurling huge rocks at the walls. A mangonel's an oversized catapult, about the size of a small house, and it can throw thousand-pound rocks for a long distance. There hadn't been any of them among the other engines the previous day, and their sudden appearance this morning was a fair indication that Zedar'd had a busy night. He hadn't thrown the Will and the Word directly at the city or its defenders, so I couldn't be certain whether he was breaking the rules yet. He was pushing at the edges of them, though, and that gave me an idea. If *he* could do it without getting himself exploded, then so could I.

I settled onto the battlements, resumed my own form, and went looking for the twins. "When did the mangonels start?" I asked them.

"Just before dawn," Beltira replied. "They're doing a lot of damage to the walls, Belgarath. There are several places where the foundations are starting to crack. We'd better do something—and soon."

"I was just getting to that. Did you hear Zedar working during the night?"

"Quite clearly," Belkira replied. "He was in a hurry, so he didn't even try to hide the fact that he was using his Will. What are we going to do?"

"The same thing he did. He got away with it, so we can—I think. Let's go build some mangonels of our own."

"They take a long time to aim, Belgarath," Beltira objected. "And thousand-pound rocks would be very hard to move, even for us."

"A thousand one-pound rocks should be manageable, though," I said. "We'll be shooting at the engine crews, not at a solid wall. We won't have to be too accurate if all we're trying to do is fill the sky with smaller rocks to rain down on the Thulls manning Zedar's mangonels. Then, once we've got the range, we can start dropping burning pitch on them. I think they'll lose interest at that point. Let's go get started."

I had some of the same reservations about the idea as Belsambar'd had during the War of the Gods. I *didn't* like the idea of burning people alive, but I had to neutralize those engines. If the walls of Vo Mimbre fell, Torak'd be in the city by nightfall, and he'd win. I *wasn't* going to let that happen if I could possibly stop it.

It didn't take the twins and me very long to manufacture our mangonels. Zedar's engines were sitting out in plain sight, so we plagiarized. Aiming them wasn't a particular problem either. Among his other talents, Belmakor had been a mathematician, and he'd given the twins several centuries of instruction. It took them only about fifteen minutes to compute angles, trajectories, proper tension, and weights. Our first throw dropped half a ton of fist-size rocks directly on top of one of Zedar's engines. The second one engulfed that monstrosity in fire.

Did you know that people almost always run when they're on fire? It doesn't do any good, of course, but they do it anyway. Burning Thulls fell back into the ranks of Torak's other troops, causing a great deal of confusion, and after an hour or so, we'd eliminated the problem. Zedar'd lost a whole night's sleep for nothing.

At that point, he didn't really have any choice but to mount another frontal assault. I knew that something was coming, because I could feel his Will building even as his troops were forming up for the charge. When he released it, a howling wind-storm struck the walls of Vo Mimbre.

No, he wasn't trying to blow us off the top of the walls. He was trying to deflect the arrows of our archers. I shudder to think of the effort his wind-storm caused him. Moving that much air's a great deal like trying to pick up a mountain.

The twins took steps without even bothering to consult with me. Working in tandem, they erected a barrier of pure Will about a mile out from the walls, neatly dividing Zedar's wind-storm and sending it streaming off to either side of the city. The air around Vo Mimbre became dead calm, and the Asturian archers cut down whole battalions of charging Malloreans. The attack faltered, stopped, and then reversed.

Polgara came up and joined us on the walls late in the morning. "You three *have* been busy, haven't you?" she observed. "You're making so much noise that I can't even hear myself think. Zedar's right on the verge of exhaustion, you know."

"Good," I said. "I'm getting tired of playing games with him."

"Don't start gloating yet, father. Zedar's not the only one out there, you know. I'm getting the sense of a lot of other minds at work. Zedar's called in the Grolims to help him."

"Can you get any idea of what he'll try next, dear sister?" Belkira asked her.

"Nothing specific," she replied. "They seem to be thinking about dirt."

"*Dirt?*" Belkira exclaimed. "What's dirt got to do with anything? All that's out there right now is mud."

"They're drying it out. Zedar's got his Grolims concentrating on extracting the last trace of moisture out of that plain."

"What on earth for?"

"I'm not privy to that information, uncle," she told him. "Zedar doesn't confide in me, for some reason."

"Zedar's always been a tacky sort of person," Belkira said. "I don't want to hurt your feelings, Belgarath, but I've never really liked him all that much. Are you sure you didn't leave a few things out when you were educating him?"

Beltira would never have said that. My brothers weren't exactly identical, I discovered. It's very easy to miss these subtle little variations. Identical twins look alike, but no two people are ever really the same.

Pol's left eyebrow was already up before she even looked at me. "Yes?" she said. "Was there something?"

"Never mind," I said. *I've* never been entirely sure just how deeply Polgara can reach into my thoughts, and I think I'd like to keep it that way. Durnik doesn't have any secrets from Pol, but I've got secrets that I don't even want to look at myself. If you're going to maintain any kind of self-respect, you're going to have to keep secrets from yourself.

It was late afternoon before we discovered why Zedar had been spending so much time and effort drying out dirt. The wind-storm he'd kicked up earlier in the day to deflect the Asturian arrows was still blowing harmlessly off to either side of the city, but it changed direction and came swirling across that now bone-dry plain picking up great clouds of dust. After a few minutes, it was impossible to see anything out there. The duststorm obviously was meant to conceal another assault. Wildantor's archers would have to shoot blind, and that's not particularly effective.

"We'd better do something, Belgarath!" Beltira shouted over the scream of the wind.

"I'm working on it," I told him, but try as I might, I couldn't come up with a thing.

Polgara was already ahead of me, though. "We've got a river right here, father," she said, "and Zedar's half killed himself raising this windstorm for us. What does that suggest to you?"

"Nothing in particular. What does it suggest to you?"

"Oh, father, have your brains gone to sleep?"

"Don't be coy, Pol. Out with it."

"We need to lay all that dust, don't we? I think a waterspout would probably take care of it, don't you?"

"Pol, that's brilliant! Get the twins to help you. They stirred up all kinds of bad weather during the War of the Gods."

"We could probably use a little help from you, father."

"You'll get it, Pol."

"Oh?"

"I think brother Zedar needs a quick lesson in good manners."

"You're going to reach out and stop his heart?"

"No. I've been told not to do anything permanent to him. But I can distract him, and don't think making him extremely uncomfortable will violate any rules."

"Have fun," she told me, and then she and the twins went on around the top of the wall to the side that faced the river.

I considered a number of options and finally settled on one that not only would make him extremely uncomfortable, but would also humiliate him. I went looking for him with my mind, and I eventually found him on top of a hill about five miles away. Trust Zedar to stay as far away from the fighting as he possibly could. I gathered in my Will and then released it very slowly. I didn't want him to know what I was doing until it was too late.

He was looking out over his duststorm with a sense of smug satisfaction.

He absently scratched his nose.

Then he vigorously dug his fingernails into one armpit. After that he moved his attention to other parts of his body. His scratching grew more and more feverish even as Polgara and the twins broke off a piece of his windstorm and sent it whirling down the River Arend.

In a burst of sheer, fiendish creativity, I even made his toenails itch. After a few minutes, he was actually dancing, and he was digging at his skin so hard that he was bleeding from a dozen different places.

When the wind Pol and the twins had borrowed came swirling back up the River Arend, it was carrying tons of water with it, and that was more than enough to settle the dust Zedar'd spent hours carefully drying out.

The attack force that had been creeping through the duststorm was largely comprised of Murgos, and once Wildantor's archers could see them, King Ad Rak Cthoros led a much smaller army back out of the range of those far-reaching arrows.

Pol's brief rainstorm had passed, but the setting sun sparkled on the wet grass, and Torak was still outside the walls.

We had survived another day, and if all went well tomorrow we'd see the end of all this.

CHAPTER FORTY-ONE

I'm sure you noticed that Zedar's ploys on that second day really weren't very effective. I'd always thought he was strong on planning, but Zedar tended to get rattled in emergencies, and he'd frequently try the first thing that popped into his head without thinking his way completely through it. Add the fact that Torak left everything up to him, but expected results, and you can see his problem. Zedar didn't work well under pressure.

Anyway, we'd survived the first two days of the battle. Vo Mimbre had withstood everything the Angaraks had thrown at it, and if we were reading the Mrin Codex right, things should start turning in our favor now.

There was an Arendish poet known as Davoul the Lame at the Mimbrate court during Aldorigen's reign, and he'd been working on his prose epic, "The Latter Days of the House of Mimbre," for about ten years when Torak invaded Arendia. The invasion gave him something important to include in his epic, and he was forever limping around the outskirts of our discussions feverishly scribbling notes. I didn't care much for him. He was technically the official court poet, and that seems to have gone to his head. The epic he was producing was cast in "high style," and it was pompous, windy, and without too much in the way of literary merit. The Mimbrates adore that shop-worn convention, however, and even to this day they'll quote long passages of Davoul's epic every time they get a chance. I've got a copy of the silly thing, if you want to borrow it, but I wouldn't waste my time, if I were you.

By the evening of the second day of the battle, I had everyone in position, and all we were doing was waiting for Beldin. Pol flew out to have a look just before dawn of the third day, and she reported back that Eldrig's war-boats were coming upriver. The River Arend was in flood stage because of all the rain, however, and the current was definitely slowing him down.

Pol, the twins, and I had decided that there wasn't much point in remaining in the city now. The Mimbrates knew what they were supposed to do, and they didn't need guidance. Beltira went east to march with the Algars, Drasnians, and Ulgos while Belkira went up into the fairly extensive forest lying to the north to join Brand.

Don't waste your time looking for those woods. They aren't there anymore. We chopped them down shortly after the battle was over. I disapprove of chopping down trees as a general rule, but we needed a lot of firewood in a hurry.

We still weren't entirely certain just how stringent the prohibitions the Necessities had imposed on us really were, so we rather tentatively nibbled around the edges of them. We were fairly sure that we wouldn't be permitted to turn all the Angaraks into frogs, but there didn't seem to be anything preventing the one thing we *really* needed. As long as I could speak with the twins and Beldin, we'd be able to coordinate things, and we didn't need anything else. This third day was going to be settled on the ground, so we didn't need exotic displays of our talents to confuse matters.

Pol and I flew north and perched in a tree at the edge of Brand's woods to keep an eye on the Angaraks while we all waited for it to get light. As dawn slowly crept up the eastern sky, we were able to make out more and more details of Zedar's deployment. He'd moved his people around during the night. Torak knew what was coming as well or better than we did, and Zedar'd made preparations for it.

Ad Rak Cthoros, the bulky, grim-faced king of Cthol Murgos, was now on the left flank. A lot of the soldiers in the world wear chain mail the same as the Murgos do, so Ad Rak Cthoros had ordered his men to paint their mail shirts red for purposes of identification on the battlefield. It made them look as it they'd been dipped in blood, but I guess it served its purpose.

The Malloreans, who were by far the most numerous members of Kal Torak's army, were solidly planted in the center, and they were commanded by generals from Mal Zeth, although it was Zedar who was giving all the orders, and Zedar was getting *his* orders from Torak himself. Torak liked to think of himself as a military genius, but how much intelligence does it take to overwhelm your opponents with sheer numbers?

Yar Lek Thun of Gar og Nadrak and Gethel Mardu of Thulldom held the right flank. I don't think I'd have done it that way. The legions and Eldrig's Chereks were going to be coming from that direction, and, although the Nadraks are fairly good warriors despite the fact that they're a bit high strung, Thulls aren't very dependable once the fighting starts.

"Why don't you wake everybody up, father?" Pol suggested.

"I guess we might as well," I agreed. *"Belkira,"* I sent out my thought. *"Let's get started. Tell Brand to blow his horn."*

He didn't bother to answer, but I'm sure he got my message, because a moment or so later, Brand's deep-toned horn sounded a long, haunting note. Then, a minute later, Cho-Ram's silver-voiced trumpet answered from the east, and then Mandor's horn sang out from inside the walls of Vo Mimbre. Pol and I listened carefully for several minutes, but Beldin didn't respond. He wasn't in place yet.

A scholar at the University of Tol Honeth once wrote a long dissertation about the mythic significance of those horn blasts, but they weren't really anything but announcements that the various forces were in place and ready. Nothing was going to happen until Beldin answered. We certainly weren't going to start without him.

I'm sure that Zedar knew what the horn blasts meant. We'd used those same signals during the War of the Gods. The sounds, coming just as it was starting to get light, made the leaders of the various Angarak forces nervous, though, and the Malloreans began to bang their swords against their shields and shout war cries. I guess that noisy racket was supposed to hearten everybody. It sounded just a little desperate to me, though. Horn blasts are a traditional signal to attack, but nobody was attacking. I can see where that might get on somebody's nerves, can't you?

We waited for about another half hour. Then, just as the sun was coming up, I called to Belkira. *"Have him try it again, brother,"* I said.

Brand blew his horn again, and Cho-Ram and Mandor answered. Then we waited. Still no sound from Beldin. I could have called out to him, but Zedar certainly would have heard me, and, far more important, he'd have heard my twisted brother's reply, and that would have pinpointed Beldin's location. If he were still several leagues away, Zedar might decide to attack, either to the east or the north, and that'd have started things before I was ready.

Nadraks, as I said, are high-strung people, and Yar Lek Thun reached the point that he absolutely *had* to know what was going on. He sent a cavalry troop pounding toward the woods to the north. They galloped in among the trees about a half mile from where Pol and I waited.

Most of their horses came back after a while, but none of the Nadraks did. It's not a good idea to ride into a forest where Asturian archers are lying in wait.

Then, probably not to be outdone, since Murgos don't much care for Nadraks, Ad Rak Cthoros *also* sent out scouts. The Murgo horsemen rode up into the foothills to the east.

They didn't come back, either. Riding into the teeth of Algarian cavalry is almost as stupid as riding in among trees where Asturians are hiding.

We kept on waiting. After another half hour or so, I tried once more. *"Have him tootle again, Belkira,"* I sent out the thought.

"Tootle?" Belkira sounded slightly offended, but Brand tried it again.

Cho-Ram and Mandor answered immediately, and then after a moment that seemed to last for a year or so, a veritable fanfare of trumpets replied from the west. It was probably excessive, but some of those legions were ceremonial troops from the garrison in Tol Honeth, and I guess there were a couple of military bands in their ranks.

That was what I'd been waiting for. "Sit tight, Pol," I told my daughter. "I'm going to go have a look. I don't want to start anything until I've seen for myself that Beldin's in place."

"Don't be too long, father. The morning's wearing on, and I don't think we want Brand to issue his challenge after the sun goes down."

I spread my wings and swooped down off my limb to gain momentum, and then I started up into the air, flapping vigorously.

When I got a up a couple hundred feet, I could see just about everything. Eldrig's war-boats were moored to the north bank of the River Arend no more than a couple of miles downstream from Vo Mimbre. The high water had slowed their progress upriver, but it had also made it possible for them to row over the shallows that lie some distance west of the city. If he'd really wanted to, Beldin could have rowed right up to the south wall of Vo Mimbre itself.

The legions, their burnished breastplates glinting in the morning sun, were spread out impressively, and they were marching in perfect order as they advanced on the Nadraks and Thulls. Eldrig's berserkers *weren't* marching. They were running on ahead of the legions. Chereks hate sharing a good fight with anybody.

"All right, Belkira." I passed the word. *"Tell Brand to give the signal."*

This time Brand blew his horn twice. Cho-Ram answered in the same way. Mandor, however, almost blew his heart out. The note from his horn went on and on and on.

Then the gates of Vo Mimbre crashed open, and the knights came charging out.

The charge of the Mimbrate knights is probably the most famous cavalry charge in history, so I don't really need to describe it in detail, do I?

I probably couldn't give you a very good description anyway, because something else caught my eye just then. Kal Torak's black iron pavilion was in the center of the horde, and I saw a raven spiraling up from one of its spires. I was fairly certain it wasn't an ordinary raven. Either Zedar wanted to see the Mimbrates for himself, or he'd concluded even as I had that the best place to direct a battle was from over the top of it.

There was a surprise waiting for him, though. Far above the battlefield, a single white speck plummeted down toward the raven that was spiraling upward. That particular form of attack is highly unusual for the snowy owl, and no ordinary owl should have been out hunting in the daytime. . . .

There was a puff of black feathers when the owl struck, and Zedar fled, squawking in terror.

Kal Torak's Malloreans were good soldiers, I'll give them that much, but *nobody* could have met the charge of those Mimbrate knights. I'd estimate that there were at least ten thousand of them. The front ranks charged with leveled lances, and the crash when they struck the Malloreans was thunderous. So far as I could tell, the charge didn't even falter as the front ranks of the Malloreans were ridden under.

We'd spent months discussing this particular tactic at the Imperial War College in Tol Honeth. The charge of the Mimbrate knights had one purpose and one only: it was designed to keep the Malloreans in place so that they couldn't rush to the aid of the armies on their flanks. Mimbrates are enthusiasts, though, and Mandor, who led the charge, gave every indication that he fully intended to ride up to Kal Torak's iron pavilion and start banging on his door.

There were casualties among those knights, of course, but not as many as you might expect. I guess full body armor has its good points, after all. Even beyond that, though, the ferocity of the charge demoralized the Malloreans. They hadn't expected it, for one thing, since there was no real reason for it. Vo Mimbre had stood like a rock in the face of two days of furious assaults, and there was no cause to believe that this day would be any different. We'd taken that element of surprise into our planning. The startled Malloreans gave way as the Mimbrates charged right into their faces, and the charge cut a wide swath through their ranks.

"*Father!*" Polgara's voice sounded inside my head. "*Zedar's trying something else! He just came out of the pavilion again!*"

"*Which way's he going?*"

"*East. He's taken the form of a deer.*"

"*I'll chase him back.*" I veered off toward the Murgo lines and saw Zedar running swiftly through the red-armored ranks. I've never really understood why he chose that form. He knew what my favorite form was, and taking the form of a deer wasn't the best choice he could have made. I got out some distance ahead of him, settled to earth among the foothills, and went wolf. He was running hard when he approached the place where I was concealed, bounding up the hill with his antlers flaring above his head. He stopped abruptly when I stepped, snarling, out from behind a clump of bushes. He tried to dodge around me, but that didn't work. I was just too close to him. Zedar's day wasn't going at all well.

I didn't really try to kill him, though I suppose I could have. I bit him a number of times in some fairly sensitive spots, and he turned and bolted back toward the Murgo lines. It's not really a good idea to turn your back on a wolf. I ran along behind him savaging his hindquarters as he fled. He wouldn't be sitting down very much when he resumed his own form. I made sure of that.

I broke off the chase when I was a hundred yards or so from the Murgo lines, and then I trotted back up into the hills. "*Beltira,*" I called the twin who was with Cho-Ram and Rhodar, "*the Mimbrates are fully engaged now. You'd better come on down here and distract the Murgos.*"

"*If you wish,*" he replied, and a moment later Cho-Ram's trumpet signaled the charge. There was a thunder of hooves as the Algar cavalry closed the distance between the place where they'd lain concealed during the night and the Murgo lines. I'd taken cover among a cluster of boulders, and I watched Cho-Ram lead his horsemen down the hill to engage the Murgos.

The Algar tactics were quite a bit different from those of the Mimbrates. Heavy cavalry rushes in to crush the enemy, but light cavalry slashes at him. Ad Rak Cthoros had his own cavalry units of course, but they were no match for the Algars. Soon there was a running battle taking place out in front of the Murgo lines, and the Murgo horsemen were definitely coming out second best. Then, when the mounted Murgos were badly out of position, Rhodar arrived with his pikemen, and Brasa's Ulgo irregulars were artfully concealed among their ranks. The combination worked out quite well. You really can't get too close to a man with a twenty-foot-long pike, and keeping him from slicing you to pieces with it is going to take all your attention. The Ulgos are a short-statured people, and they move very quickly, as a large number of Murgos found out that day. Ulgo weapons are very unpleasant things. There are a lot of hooks and saw-edges involved in them. A wave of screaming rose from the Murgo ranks, since those Ulgo knives aren't designed to kill people instantly. Ulgos probably hate Angaraks even more than Alorns do, so they tend to take their time killing Murgos. The Murgos they killed were only incidental, though. Brasa's instructions were to take his people through the Murgo front and to deal with Grolims. We'd provided the Ulgos with black, hooded robes, and that permitted them to move around among the Murgos almost at will. If Zedar grew desperate enough, he'd probably try to call on the priests of Torak to assist him in breaking the rules. Brasa was making sure that when he tried that, not very many Grolims would be around to answer the call.

I watched from the top of that outcropping of boulders, and when I saw that the Murgos were fully engaged, I sent my thought out in search of Beldin. *"Where are you?"* I called to him.

"About a half mile from the Nadrak lines," he replied. *"The Chereks are already working on them."*

"You might as well take Cerran's legions in. The Mimbrates have got the Malloreans pinned down, and Cho-Ram and Rhodar have got the Murgos' full attention on this side. It's time to hit the Nadraks and Thulls. See if Cerran can break through them with some of his legions. I think the Mimbrates could use some help."

"I'll get right on it."

"Polgara!" I said then.

"I'm busy, father. Don't pester me."

"What are you doing now? I told you to stay out of this!"

"I'm at Torak's pavilion. We ought to know what he and Zedar are up to."

"Get away from there, Pol! It's too dangerous!"

"I know what I'm doing, father. Don't get so excited. What did you do to Zedar? He's limping around and groaning."

"I nipped him a few times. Is feeling sorry for himself about all he's doing?"

"No. He's trying to persuade Torak to go outside and take command of his army. He isn't having much luck, though. Torak refuses to move."

"He's probably waiting for Brand's challenge. I don't suppose there's anything I can say to persuade you to get away from there, is there?"

"I'm perfectly fine, father."

"Torak probably can hear you, Pol."

"He can't hear a thing, it's taken care of. He can't see me, and he can't hear me. I'll let you know when he decides to come out."

I muttered a few swear words, but my heart wasn't really in it. The fact that Polgara was practically in the same room with Torak and Zedar gave us an enormous advantage. I trotted back in among the boulders and slipped into the form of my falcon again.

You wouldn't believe how well you can direct a battle when you're flying over the top of it. We were coming at Torak's forces from all sides now—except from the north. I didn't want to spring *that* little surprise on Zedar until *after* he'd committed his reserves. I wanted the Angarak armies fully engaged before I brought in the Rivans, Sendars, and Asturians. Their situation was grave at the moment, but it wouldn't grow desperate until Cerran's legions broke through the Nadraks and Thulls to attack the Mallorean right.

There's always a lot of confusion during a battle, and this was probably the biggest battle in history. Our years of planning and preparation were beginning to pay off. The Angaraks were confused, but we knew exactly what we were doing and what was going to come next. All the Angaraks could do was to try to respond.

"*Belgarath!*" It was Beltira. "*Ad Rak Cthoros is down.*"

"*Is he dead?*"

"*Not yet, but he's working on it. He's got an Ulgo knife in his belly.*"

"*Good. Stay on top of his Murgos. I want them to break and run, if you can possibly manage it.*" I glanced off to the west. The legions were methodically chopping their way through the Nadraks, and the Thulls were already fleeing. "*The legions are starting to break through,*" I reported to Beltira. "*If you can break the Murgos, Zedar's going to have to commit his reserves, and that's what I'm waiting for.*"

I'm probably not the best general in the world, but I had certain advantages at Vo Mimbre. I was several hundred feet above the battle, so I could see everything that was going on. I was also in constant contact with my brothers, so I could exploit anything that happened down below. To top it all off, Polgara could keep me advised of everything Kal Torak and Zedar could come up with to counter what we were doing to them. With those advantages, any sergeant could have directed the Battle of Vo Mimbre. I think that when you get right down to it, we won the battle at the Imperial War College in Tol Honeth long before our advance forces even started to march. Planning—that's all it really takes. You might want to make a note of that before you declare war on somebody. I've spent centuries trying to pound that notion into the heads of any number of very thick-skulled Alorns.

The charge of the Mimbrate knights had slowed by now. After the Malloreans' initial dismay had passed, their resistance stiffened and elements of their army had flanked the knights and closed in behind them. The tide of that part of the battle was inexorably turning. The Mimbrates were surrounded now, and their horses were nearing exhaustion. Their lances had long since been shattered, and they'd fallen back on their broadswords and battle-axes. Their numbers were being whittled down gradually, and Mandor had been forced to draw his men into that circle that usually signals the beginning of what is romantically called "the last stand." Arendish poets love to describe last stands. It gives them the opportunity to extol lavishly unspeakable bravery and to exaggerate outrageously the exploits of individual knights. The outcome is almost always the same, however. The standees ultimately are swarmed under. It makes for exciting poetry, but from a tactical standpoint, it's a futile and useless waste of lives.

"Beldin!" I shouted. "I need those legions! Now! The Mimbrates are surrounded! If they go under, you're going to be neck deep in Malloreans!"

"We're coming, Belgarath! Keep your feathers on!"

I've never fully understood the significance of some of the tactics of Tolnedran Legions. Quite often it appears to me that their changes of formation would be more appropriate for a parade ground than a battlefield. Cerran had been advancing on a broad front with about forty legions. He issued a few sharp commands, which were passed on by some great-voiced sergeants, and his force rapidly coalesced into a solidly massed spearhead. The Nadraks had been spread out to face a more generalized advance, and they simply could not respond fast enough to that sudden change of formation. The legions, their shields interlocked, advanced at a trot, cutting through the Nadrak lines like a hot knife slicing through butter. Once they were through the Nadraks, they came at the Mallorean rear, since the Malloreans had been concentrating on Mandor's knights. In a matter of minutes the legions and the knights had joined forces.

There wasn't any last stand that day.

To make Kal Torak's situation even more desperate, the Chereks had exploited the corridor Cerran had cut through the Nadraks and had joined with the growing force in the very center of the Mallorean army, and the Murgo lines were beginning to break on Torak's left.

At that point Zedar didn't have any choice but to commit his reserves, and that's what I'd been waiting for. I held off for about a quarter of an hour to give the Angarak reserves enough time to rush down from their positions just to the north of the main battlefield. I wanted Torak's rear only lightly defended, and I also wanted to give Rhodar's pikemen time to break through the crumbling Murgo lines to link up with my main force. The death of Ad Rak Cthoros had broken the Murgos' spirit, and their resistance grew less and less effective. Finally the Drasnians crashed through, and the Algar cavalry kept the Murgos from closing ranks behind them.

"All right, Belkira," I sent out the thought. "You can join us now."

Brand sounded a single long note on his horn, and I waited—a little anxiously, I'll admit. Then the edge of those woods on the north side of the plain suddenly began to erupt Rivans, Sendars, and Asturian archers. They were coming very fast, and there weren't any Angarak forces on that side of the plain to slow them down.

"Father!" Polgara's voice was a little shrill. "Torak's coming out!"

"Of course he is, Pol," I replied. "That was the whole idea." I said it quite calmly, as if I had never had any doubts at all. That was a pose, of course. I was far enough up in the sky above the battlefield so that she couldn't see me—at least not clearly enough to see my wild triumphant swoops of sheer exultation. I'm fairly certain that she couldn't hear any shrill cries of triumph, either. Our desperate strategy had worked!

Zedar's reserves had not yet engaged, and after a few moments of confusion, they turned and tried desperately to run back to defend their former positions. By then, however, the Asturians were close enough to intercept them with a solid wall of arrows, and the Rivans and Sendars were charging down to meet them head on.

Kal Torak's original strategy had been to crush us between two armies. Now the tables had been neatly turned. *His* army was in the middle, and *mine* was coming at him from both sides. The Malloreans were trapped, the Thulls had run away, and the Murgos and Nadraks were demoralized and largely out of action. I had him! Then I suddenly knew what I was supposed to do.

"*All right, Pol,*" I called to my daughter, "*get out of there. It's time for you and me to join Brand.*"

"*What?*"

"*We're supposed to be with him during the EVENT.*"

"*You've never told me about that.*"

"*I didn't know about it until just now. Don't dawdle, Polgara. We don't want to be late.*"

I flew up to the northern edge of the battlefield, settled to earth, and resumed my own form. That noticeably startled a platoon of Sendars. I didn't have time to explain it to them, though, and some very wild stories have been circulating in Sendaria for the last five hundred years as a result.

It took me a little while to find Brand, and Polgara had already joined him by the time I reached them. "You know what you're supposed to do?" I asked the Rivan Warder.

"Yes," he replied.

"And do you know *when* to do it?"

"I will when the time comes." The calm, almost indifferent attitude of the Child of Light—whoever he is—has always sort of unnerved me. I guess it's understandable, since he's totally under the control of the Necessity, but it seems sort of unnatural to me. Garion's told me that he felt much the same way on that dreadful night in Cthol Mishrak when he and Torak finally met. As I remember it, though, I didn't feel that way when Zedar and I had our little get-together up in Morindland. Of course, I had a certain amount of personal animosity toward Zedar at the time, and that might have had something to do with it.

Then there was a slight change in Brand's expression. His calm indifference faded, and it was replaced by a look of almost inhuman resolution. He straightened, and when he spoke, his voice didn't even sound like his own, and the language that came out of his mouth was certainly not in the Rivan idiom.

"In the name of Belar I defy thee, Torak, maimed and accursed," he said. His voice didn't sound all that loud to me, but I was told later that it was clearly audible inside the walls of Vo Mimbre. "In the name of Aldur, also," he went on, "I cast my despite into thy teeth. Let the bloodshed be abated, and I will meet thee—man against God—and I shall prevail against thee. Before thee I cast my gage. Take it up or stand exposed as craven before men and Gods!"

Now *that* got Torak's immediate attention. He'd armed himself before he had emerged from that silly iron castle, and he was wearing that same archaic armor he'd worn during the War of the Gods. His huge shield was strapped to his maimed left arm, his high-plumed and visored helmet covered the polished mask that hid his ruined face, and he had that black sword he called Cthrek Goru clenched in his right fist. Brand's insulting challenge enraged him, and he shattered a dozen or so large boulders with the sword before he got control of himself. The Angaraks in his immediate vicinity pulled back several hundred yards, and Zedar bolted like a rabbit.

"Who among mortal kind is so foolish as to thus defy the King of the World?" Torak roared. "Who among ye would contend with a God?"

You have to admire the cunning of the Necessity that spoke through Brand's lips. Torak had been very reluctant to meet Brand in single combat, but his rage overcame his better judgment. Torak, always the sublime egomaniac, absolutely *had* to respond to those insults.

"I am Brand, Warder of Riva," the Child of Light replied, "and *I* defy thee, foul and misshapen Godling, and all thy putrid host. Bring forth thy might. Take up my gage or slink away and come no more against the Kingdoms of the West."

That was *really* pushing things. Torak was still a God, and prohibition or no prohibition, that particular speech might very well have pushed him over the edge. I had a momentary vision of a repetition of the cracking of the world at that point. He didn't do it again, however, but he *did* bash a few more boulders with his sword.

"*Behold!*" he roared in a voice that probably broke windows in Tol Honeth "I am Torak, King of Kings and Lord of Lords! I fear no man of mortal kind nor the dim shades of long-forgotten Gods! I will come forth and destroy this loud-voiced Rivan fool, and mine enemies shall fall away before my wrath, and Cthrag Yaska shall be mine again and the world, also!"

In spite of everything that had warned him against it, he had accepted Brand's challenge.

The exchange between the two of them had caused a vast silence to fall over the battlefield. Many soldiers, both mine and Zedar's, seemed paralyzed by the sheer sound of those two thundering voices. The fighting stopped, and the only sounds were the groans of the wounded and the dying. The challenge and its acceptance laid the full burden of the Battle of Vo Mimbre on Brand's shoulders—and on Torak's.

Torak strode north, and his Malloreans melted out of his path as he came. Brand, equally implacable, marched south to meet him. I went wolf, and I trotted along at his side. There was also a snowy owl drifting above him.

Brand was a big man with heavy shoulders and powerful arms. In many ways he closely resembled Dras Bull-neck, though he wasn't quite as tall. His shield was strapped to his left arm, and he'd taken some pains to rivet a grey Rivan cloak to the face of it to conceal my Master's Orb. The sword he was carrying wasn't *quite* as large as Iron-grip's sword, but it was large enough that I wouldn't have wanted to swing it.

Torak was wearing that antique black armor, and he was brandishing Cthrek Goru as he came. The agreement between the Necessities kept him from swelling into immensity as he did at Cthol Mishrak when he met Garion, but he was every bit as big as Brand. So far as I could tell, the two of them were evenly matched. Since neither of them had any particular advantage—either in size or weaponry—this promised to be a very interesting duel.

They advanced on each other until they were about twenty yards apart, and then they both stopped, evidently acting on instructions. Brand spoke once more at that point. "I am Brand, Warder of Riva," he introduced himself in a civil tone of voice. "I am he who will contend with thee, Torak. Beware of me, for the spirits of Belar and Aldur are with me. I alone stand between thee and the Orb for which thou hast brought war into the West."

Torak didn't answer him, but spoke to me instead. "Begone, Belgarath," he told me. "Flee if thou wouldst save thy life. It occurs that I may soon have the leisure to give thee that instruction I so long ago promised thee, and I doubt that even thou wouldst survive *my* instruction."

I've never been sure why he bothered with that. He should have known what my answer would be. I bared my teeth and snarled at him.

Then he spoke to the owl hovering in the air over Brand's head. "Abjure thy father, Polgara, and come with me," he said in an oddly wheedling tone of voice. "I will wed thee," he continued, "and make thee Queen of all the world, and thy might and thy power shall be second only to mine."

That marriage proposal has given Polgara nightmares for five centuries now. It also seriously confused the Grolims; they've stepped rather carefully around Pol ever since. They did *not* want to offend the chosen bride of Torak. I suspect that he'd gotten the idea from the Ashabine Oracles, and it was probably that same passage that had given Zedar the idea for his cruel deception of Illessa.

The scream of an owl is usually just a scream, but Pol managed to fill the one she threw into Torak's teeth with all sorts of defiance and scorn to let him know just what she thought of his proposal of marriage.

"Prepare then to perish all," Torak roared at us, rushing forward with his black sword upraised.

That made me a little nervous. I'd just seen him shatter a number of large boulders with that sword.

Brand didn't even change his expression when he raised the shield to ward off that massive blow.

If you've ever seen a fight between a couple of men armed with broadswords and shields, you know how badly the shields get dented and gashed. Brand's shield, however, showed no visible effects as Cthrek Goru bounced harmlessly off its face. Torak's huge blow didn't even cut through the grey cloth that covered the shield. My Master's Orb was clearly taking steps.

Torak's shield, however, didn't seem to be quite so impervious, because Brand's return blow sliced deep into its rim.

Torak struck again, and his second blow had no more effect than the first.

Then it was Brand's turn, and his stroke left a deep dent in the face of Torak's shield.

That went on for quite a while. They banged at each other with those huge broadswords, raising a dreadful amount of noise and spraying sparks in all directions every time their sword-edges met. They reeled back and forth, struggling to keep their balance on the uneven ground. Brand still seemed to be in the grip of that unnatural calmness, but Torak grew increasingly enraged. He bellowed at the grave-faced Rivan facing him, and his sword-strokes came faster and faster. Despite the huge weight of Cthrek Goru, Torak was swinging it almost as rapidly as an Algar horseman might swing a saber. The sheer fury of his attack was driving Brand backward.

Then, with a stroke that changed direction in midswing, Torak gashed open Brand's left shoulder.

"*Well, finally!*" that familiar voice said. "*I thought they were going to be at it all day. Go ahead and give the signal, Belgarath. Let's finish this right now.*"

I did it without even thinking. I didn't *have* to think. The instructions had been floating around in my head for almost three thousand years. I dropped to my haunches, lifted my muzzle, and howled. And, at exactly the same instant, the white owl screamed a piercingly shrill scream.

Brand jumped back and scraped the edge of his sword down over the face of his shield, ripping off the grey cloth that had covered it.

Kal Torak flinched back violently as my Master's Orb blazed forth its baleful blue fire. The smoldering fire that always glowed behind the left eye-slit of his steel mask suddenly blazed forth like a small sun.

He screamed, and Cthrek Goru fell out of his violently trembling hand. He shook away his shield and tried to clutch at his face. His right hand covered his right eye, but he had no left hand to cover the other.

Then Brand struck the final blow of their duel, and it was *not* an overhand stroke. It was a thrust. He seized his sword hilt in both hands and lunged forward, and his thrust wasn't aimed at Torak's chest or throat or belly.

It was aimed directly at Torak's burning left eye.

Brand's sword made a terrible sound as it slid through the visor of Torak's helmet and an even worse sound as it crunched through that flaming eye and on into the brain of the maimed God of Angarak.

Torak screamed again, and it was not so much a scream of pain as it was one of unutterable loss. He clutched at the blade protruding from his eye and jerked it away. Then he threw away his helmet and clawed away that steel mask.

It was the first time I'd seen his face since the day when he had cracked the world. The right side was still unmarred and beautiful.

The left side was hideous. The revenge of my Master's Orb had been too horrible to imagine. There were still inflamed scars, of course, but there were parts of Torak's face where the flesh had been burned away and bone showed through.

His left eye no longer flamed. It wept blood instead.

Most of the epic of Davoul the Lame is very badly written, but its climax isn't too bad, so I'll quote it here.

. . . and raised he up and pushed his arms even into the sky and cried out again. And cried he out one last time as he beheld the jewel which he had named Cthrag Yaska and which had caused him to be smitten again, and then, as a tree hewn away at the ground, the Dark God fell, and the earth resounded with his fall.

CHAPTER
FORTY-
TWO

And that's what *really* happened at Vo
Mimbre. Whole libraries have been
written about the battle, but with only a
few exceptions—mostly written by Alorn
scholars—those lurid accounts miss the
truly significant events that led up to the duel between Brand and Torak.
Everything we did was designed to force Torak to accept Brand's challenge. Once we put him in a situation where he didn't have any choice,
the outcome was inevitable.

The fall of their God totally demoralized the Angaraks; and the
Ulgos and various others had killed their kings and generals, so there
wasn't anybody around to give them orders. Angaraks don't function well
independently. Someone very wise once said, "It's all very well to put the
government in the hands of the perfect man, but what do you do when
the perfect man gets a bellyache?" That's the major argument against any
kind of absolutism.

The Malloreans, of course, were doomed. They were surrounded by
people who had every reason to hate them, and forgiveness and mercy
weren't very evident as the armies of the West fell on the luckless invaders like the wrath of a whole pantheon of Gods.

The Murgos on the left flank really didn't see any reason to rush to
the aid of their Mallorean cousins. Murgos don't like Malloreans in the
first place, so there weren't any strong ties between the two races—not
without Torak ramming brotherhood down their throats. There weren't

really any orders given. The Murgos simply turned, fled south to the banks of the River Arend on the east side of the city, and tried to swim across. The current was very swift there, and the river was deep. A few Murgos made it across, but not very many.

The Thulls had already bolted to the river just to the west of Vo Mimbre. Thulls aren't bright, but they're strong, and they weren't weighted down with mail shirts the way the Murgos were, so a surprising number of them made it across to the Tolnedran side. The Nadraks tried to follow them, but Nadraks don't swim very well, so probably no more of them reached safety than did Murgos.

The slaughter continued until dark, and then the Alorns lit torches and kept on killing Malloreans.

Finally General Cerran came to Brand. "Isn't that enough?" he demanded in a sick voice.

"No," Brand replied firmly, adjusting the sling cradling his bandaged left arm. "They came here to butcher us. I'm going to make sure they don't do it again. No seed nor root is going to escape this cleansing."

"That's barbaric, Brand!"

"So was what happened to Drasnia."

And after midnight when the torches had burned down, Brasa's Ulgos went around and killed all the wounded. I didn't care for that kind of savagery any more than Cerran did, but I kept my nose out of it. Brand was in charge now, and I still had things for him to do. Those things were very important, and he might start getting stubborn and uncooperative if I started giving him orders he didn't like.

The dawn the following morning was bleary with smoke, and the only Angaraks left on the field were the dead ones. Malloreans, Murgos, Nadraks, Thulls, and black-robed Grolims lay scattered or piled in heaps on that blood-soaked field. Brand's cleansing was complete.

The Rivan Warder had slept for an hour or two at the end of that awful night, but he came out of his tent when the sun rose to join my brothers, my daughter, and me. "Where is he?" he demanded.

"Where's who?" Beldin said shortly.

"Torak. I want to have a look at the King of the World."

"You can look for him if you want to," Beldin told him, "but you're not going to find him. Zedar spirited him off during the night."

"*What?*"

"Didn't you tell him?" Beldin asked me.

"He didn't need to know about it," I replied. "If he *had* known, he'd probably have tried to stop it."

"He couldn't have, you dunce—any more than you or I could have."

"Does somebody want to explain this?" Brand's voice had a testy edge to it.

"It was part of the agreement between the Necessities," I told him. "Those agreements get very complicated sometimes, and they appear to involve a lot of horse-trading. After they'd agreed that you'd win if the duel took place on the third day, our Necessity was forced to agree that you wouldn't be permitted to keep Torak's body. This wasn't the last EVENT, you know. We haven't seen the last of Torak."

"But he's dead!"

"No, Brand," Polgara told him, "actually, he's not. You didn't *really* think that sword of yours could kill him, did you? There's only one sword in the world that can do that, and it's still hanging on the wall behind the throne of the Rivan King. That was another part of the agreement, and it's why the Orb was set in your shield instead of left where it was. You *aren't* the one who's supposed to use that sword."

"Hang it all, Polgara," he burst out. "*Nobody* survives a sword thrust through the head!"

"Torak can—and has. Your thrust rendered him comatose, but the time's going to come when he'll wake up again."

"When?"

"When the Rivan king returns. He's the one who's supposed to take down that sword. When he does, Torak'll wake up, and there'll be another EVENT."

"Will that be the last one?"

"Probably, but we're not entirely sure," Beltira replied. "There are several things in the Mrin that don't seem to match up."

"Is Gelane going to be able to handle it?" Brand asked Pol. "He doesn't seem all that muscular to me, and Torak's a very serious opponent."

"I didn't say it was going to be Gelane, Brand," she corrected him. "It probably won't be, if I'm reading the signs correctly. It might be his son—or somebody twenty generations out in the future."

Brand's shoulders slumped, and he winced and put his hand on his wounded arm. "Then all of this has been for nothing," he sighed.

"I'd hardly call it nothing, Brand," I disagreed. "Torak was coming after the Orb, and he didn't get it. That counts for something, doesn't it?"

"I suppose," he conceded glumly. Then he looked out over the corpse-littered battlefield. "We'd better get rid of all these dead Angaraks," he said. "It's summer, and there'll be pestilence if we just leave them lying there to rot."

"Are you going to bury them?" Beltira asked him.

"No, I think we'll burn them instead. I wouldn't be very popular if I took everybody's sword away from him and handed him a shovel."

"Where are you going to get that much wood?" Beldin asked.

"There's a sizable forest on the northern edge of this plain," Brand replied with a shrug. "As long as it's so close, we might as well use it."

And *that's* what happened to those woods. We had a lot of dead Angaraks on our hands, so we needed some very large bonfires.

It took several days to clean up the battlefield, and while we were all concentrating on that, Aldorigen of Mimbre and Eldallan of Asturia went off a ways to have that private discussion Eldallan had proposed before the battle. Neither of them survived that discussion. The symbolic significance of that useless meeting wasn't lost on the older nobles of both duchies. The Arendish civil wars had lasted for eons, and if they were permitted to continue, it was very probable that Mimbre and Asturia would follow their rulers into extinction.

Mandor and Wildantor led the deputation that came to Brand with a rather surprising proposal. "Our hatreds run too deep, Lord Brand," Wildantor noted glumly. "Mandor and I've learned to get along, but we're a couple of unusual fellows. We can't really hope that other Arends might be willing to follow our lead."

"You all cooperated fairly well during the battle," Brand replied. "Couldn't you build on that?"

Mandor sighed and shook his head. "Our uneasy truce doth already begin to show signs of strain, Lord Brand," he said. "Some ancient grievance will surely arise to rend us apart again."

"Our problem's fairly simple, my Lord," Wildantor said with a rueful smile. "Arendia needs to be unified, but who's going to rule once we get it pasted together? No Asturian alive will bow to a Mimbrate king, and the Mimbrates feel the same way about Asturians."

"Where are we going with this, gentlemen?" Brand asked.

"We needs must have a king who will unify poor Arendia, my Lord," Mandor replied gravely, "and our mutual animosities suggest that this king cannot be Arendish. Thus, after extended consultation, have we come to offer the crown of Arendia unto thee."

Brand blinked. Fortunately, he was wise enough not to laugh. "I'm honored, gentlemen, but I've got responsibilities on the Isle of the Winds. I can't very well rule Arendia from the city of Riva."

Mandor sighed. "Then is poor Arendia doomed to endless civil strife," he mourned.

Brand scratched at his cheek. "Maybe not," he said. "Didn't Aldorigen have a son?"

"Prince Korodullin, yes," Mandor replied.

"And didn't Eldallan have a daughter?"

"Mayaserana," Wildantor said. "Now that her father's dead, she's the Duchess of Asturia. She's a very strong-willed girl—pretty, though."

"Would you say that the two of them are patriots?"

"Everybody in Arendia's a patriot, Lord Brand," Wildantor replied. "That's part of our problem."

"Doesn't that suggest a solution to your quandary? A king who was either Mimbrate or Asturian wouldn't be able to rule, but how about a joint rulership? If we could persuade these two young people to get married and rule jointly . . ." He left it hanging.

The two Arends looked at each other, and then they both burst out laughing, and the laughter spread through the rest of the Arends.

"Did I say something funny?" Brand asked them.

"You don't know those two, my Lord," Wildantor said gaily.

Mandor was still chuckling. "Thy proposal *doth* have some merit, my Lord. A marriage between Korodullin and Mayaserana might well serve to quiet dissention in the rest of Arendia, but methinks our civil war will continue, though it will be confined to one household."

"Is it *that* bad?"

"Worse, my Lord," Wildantor assured him. "We *might* be able to keep them from killing each other—if we chained them to opposite walls of the royal bedchamber, but anything less probably wouldn't work. Their fathers just killed each other, remember?"

"Why don't you bring the two of them here and I'll talk with them. Maybe if I appeal to their sense of patriotism, they'll go along with the idea."

Wildantor looked skeptical. "What do you think, Mandor?" he asked his friend. "Is it worth a try? We could search them both for weapons before we brought them here."

"Gladly would I brave anything to heal our poor Arendia," Mandor swore fervently.

"Stout fellow," Wildantor murmured.

"That's the most ridiculous proposal I've ever heard!" Mayaserana screamed when Brand presented his idea to her and Korodullin. "I'd sooner die than marry a Mimbrate butcher!"

"Gladly would I help thee to accomplish that end, outlaw wench!" Korodullin offered.

It all went downhill from there—quite rapidly.

"I really think you children ought to think this over," Pol suggested smoothly, cutting across the screaming. "You both need to calm down and talk about it—someplace private, I think. Tell me, my Lord of Mandor, thinkest thou that there might be some secluded room where our youngsters here might hold their discussions without interruption or distraction? At the top of some tower, perhaps?"

"There *is* a secure room at the top of the south tower of the palace, your Grace," he replied a bit dubiously. "It hath ofttimes in the past served as a prison for miscreants of noble birth whose rank forbade their being incarcerated in the dungeon."

"Barred windows?" she asked. "And a stout door that can be locked from the outside?"

"Yes, your Grace."

"Why don't we all go have a look at this room?" she suggested.

"It couldn't hurt to look," Brand replied.

I took my daughter by the arm and drew her aside. "They'll kill each other if you lock them in the same room, Pol," I muttered.

"Oh, I don't think they'll go that far, father," she assured me. "They might yell at each other, but I don't think they'll get violent. There are certain rules of behavior in Arendia that prohibit violence between men and women."

"But not between Mimbrates and Asturians."

"We'll see, father. We'll see."

And so Mayaserana and Korodullin became cellmates. There was a lot of screaming and yelling at first, but we didn't really mind that. The yelling proved that they were both still alive, after all.

I've always meant to ask Polgara if the notion of imprisoning those two together was her own or if Garion's friend had suggested it to her. Given his twisted sense of humor, it might very well have been his idea. On the other hand, Pol's very wise about the peculiarities of the human heart, and she knows what's likely to happen when two young people are alone together for any extended period of time. Polgara's arranged a long series of marriages; she's very good at it.

Anyway, after we'd locked the two of them in the south tower of the palace, we moved on to other things. No war or major battle is ever complete without an extended conference after the fighting's over. We were all a little surprised when the Gorim of Ulgo came to join us in our discussions. The various Gorims have almost never come out of the caves. Ran Borune was tied up with affairs of state in Tol Honeth, so Mergon represented him, and Podiss came north to speak for Salmissra.

We usurped Aldorigen's throne room for our conference, largely at Mandor's insistence, and after we'd spent a couple of hours complimenting each other, we got down to business. Ormik, the king of the ever-practical Sendars, spoke first. Ormik was a rather dumpy, unassuming sort of fellow, but he was a lot shrewder than he looked. "Gentlemen," he started, "and Lady Polgara—it seems to me that we've got too good an opportunity here to pass up. This is one of those rare occasions when most of the rulers of the Western Kingdoms are gathered in one place, and the recent unpleasantness put us all on the same side for a change. Why don't we take advantage of this temporary sense of brotherhood to smooth over all the little disputes that have cropped up over the years? If we can hammer out a set of accords, we might have some reason to be grateful to Kal Torak." He smiled faintly. "Wouldn't it be ironic if he came to bring war and the result of his little adventure was peace?"

"We've still got a few little odds and ends to take care of, Ormik," Rhodar said. "There's an Angarak army occupying Drasnia, and I'd like to persuade them to pack up and go home."

"And I've still got some Murgos camped around the Stronghold," Cho-Ram added.

Then Eldrig took the floor, and I think he got a little carried away. "Aloria can deal with the few rags and tatters of Angarak still inside her borders," he told us. *That* made me prick up my ears. I've used the word "Aloria" periodically myself, usually to rally the Alorns when I needed them to do something, but Eldrig's rather casual introduction of a name that hadn't really meant anything since the time of Bear-shoulders made me more than a little nervous. When some Alorn starts talking about Aloria, it's usually a sign that he's a member of the Bear-cult, and there was a sizable army of Alorns camped right on Tolnedra's northern border.

"We've got something a little more momentous to discuss here," the aged king of Cherek continued. "We've seen something happen here that's never happened before. A God was overthrown right before our eyes. I'm sure the other Gods had a hand in that, and Brand was their instrument. I don't know about the rest of you gentlemen, but that suggests something very interesting to me. My copy of the Mrin Codex speaks of a Godslayer who'll become Overlord of the West. Very well, then. I watched Brand kill Torak with my own eyes, and I'm ready to take the next step. Cherek acknowledges Brand's Overlordship. If we've all got one ruler, those disputes Ormik spoke of will evaporate."

"He's got a point there," Cho-Ram said thoughtfully. "Brand and I get along fairly well, so I think Algaria can join Cherek in this. I'll acknowledge Brand's Overlordship, too."

Those *idiots*! Brand wasn't the one the Mrin was talking about! It was Garion, and he hadn't even been born yet!

"I suppose we might as well make it unanimous," Rhodar chimed in. "The Children of the Bear God speak as one. Brand is Overlord."

"Aren't we going a little fast here?" Ormik protested. "I'm part Alorn myself, and I'd be more than willing to accept Brand as Overlord. I'll go wherever he tells me to go, but I think I'd like to hear from Tolnedra, Ulgo, Arendia, and Nyissa before I start making plans for a coronation. We've got all the armies of the West camped right here. If those of us who happen to be Alorn rush into something exotic and offend the non-Alorn rulers, we could have a second Battle of Vo Mimbre before the blood even dries off the grass from the first one."

Then the oily, reptilian Podiss, the emissary of Queen Salmissra, rose. "The king of the Sendars speaks wisely. Much have I marveled at the readiness of sovereign kings to submit to the Overlordship of a man of no known heritage. Brand isn't even the king of the Isle of the Winds. He's nothing more than a caretaker. I don't even have to send to Sthiss Tor for instructions about this. Eternal Salmissra will *never* swear fealty to a nameless Alorn butcher."

"You Nyissans have very short memories, Podiss," Eldrig said angrily. "If you haven't got a history book with you, I'll send for one. You might want to look over the chapter that deals with what happened to Nyissa in the year four thousand and two after Salmissra murdered King Gorek."

Then Mergon stood up. "Let's not start threatening each other, gentlemen. This is supposed to be a peace conference, remember?" He paused thoughtfully. "I yield to no one in my admiration for the Rivan Warder. I greet Lord Brand in the name of my emperor, and extend him an invitation to come to Tol Honeth so that Ran Borune may honor him as befits the foremost warrior of the West. Let us not, however, rush into unchangeable decisions in the first flush of admiration and gratitude. I'm sure that noble Brand would be the first to agree that the arts of war and the arts of peace have little in common, and they're seldom linked in one man. A battle is soon over, but the burdens of peace grow heavier with each passing year." He paused again, and then he spoke rather firmly. "I'm troubled by this talk of Aloria, gentlemen. I've heard of Cherek and Drasnia and Algaria, and all the world knows about the Isle of the Winds and unassailable Riva. But where is this Aloria? What are its boundaries? Where is its capital? There hasn't been a place called Aloria since the days of Cherek Bear-shoulders. I'm startled by this sudden reemergence of a kingdom long buried in the mists of antiquity. Imperial Tolnedra must deal with mundane reality. We can't send emissaries to the court of the king of the Fairies. We can't conclude a treaty with the Emperor of the Moon. We can only have commerce with earthly kingdoms. Myth and legend, however grand, can't enter into the affairs of the empire; not if we want to keep any kind of stability in the world."

I could see Eldrig's face getting redder and redder. Mergon was definitely pushing his luck.

"I'm puzzled about something else, as well," Ran Borune's spokesman went on. "Why have you all suddenly decided to disregard long-standing covenants and treaties? You've all signed those treaties with the empire, and now you're just throwing them out the window. Is it really wise to offend Ran Borune? Particularly in view of the size of his army?"

"Listen to me, Mergon," Eldrig growled pugnaciously. "Aloria's where I say it is, and I've got a big enough army to back me up. If you want to go back to Tol Honeth to report what we've decided here, go right ahead. My war-boats move fast enough that I'll probably be there before you make it. If I have to, I'll explain the situation to Ran Borune myself. Then I'll go on to Sthiss Tor and do the same for Salmissra."

"That should do, Eldrig," the Gorim said at that point. "We're starting to approach that second Battle of Vo Mimbre that King Ormik mentioned. One battle here is quite enough, wouldn't you say? You Alorn kings want to appoint Brand Overlord of the West—because he's an Alorn. Tolnedra and Nyissa don't mind honoring him, but they're not really interested in submitting to his Overlordship—*also* because he's an Alorn. Let's back away from this incipient war. We've managed to get enough people killed already. The plain fact is that no one man can rule the entire West, so let's just drop that notion right here and now. I think I know Brand well enough to know that he wouldn't accept that crown if you offered it to him."

"Well put, Holy Gorim," Brand agreed fervently. "I hate to disappoint you, Eldrig, but I'm *not* this Overlord of yours. Go find somebody else to saddle with the title."

"We can't just do *nothing*, Brand!" Eldrig protested. "You killed Torak. We've got to find *some* way to honor you for that. How about a contribution from all our treasuries or something?"

"A suggestion, perhaps?" Gorim interposed. "Why not give Brand an Imperial Tolnedran Princess to be his wife? That's probably the greatest honor Tolnedra can bestow."

"I've already got a wife, Holy One," Brand told him, "and only a madman wants more than one. I don't need a crown; I don't need a Tolnedran princess; and I don't need the treasuries of the other kingdoms. What do Rivans need with treasure?" He put his hand on his shield. "In case you hadn't noticed, we've already got one, and our race has guarded it with our lives for over two thousand years now. Would you inflict another treasure on us to guard? How many lives do we have? The Gorim's right. I can't sit in Riva and run the world. If something came up somewhere in Nyissa or down in the Caves of Ulgo, it'd be months before I even heard about it. Not only that, I serve Belar. I think we might offend Nedra and Issa and Chaldan if I assumed some kind of Overlordship, not to mention that UL might object. If there *is* going to be an Overlord, the appointment's going to have to come from the Gods, not from men."

It was at that point that I decided to put down this nonsense for good and all. I stood up.

"Gladly will we hear the counsel of the Eternal Man," Gorim murmured.

"Glad or not, you're going to get it," I said bluntly. "What in the names of all the Gods possessed you to come up with this absurd idea, Eldrig? Brand's not the one who's going to be the Overlord. Surely you realize that."

Eldrig looked a little embarrassed. "Well, he *did* beat Torak, didn't he? I thought I could take it one step further, is all." Then he threw up his hands. "All right, I was pushing. I'll admit it. I was hoping that this was the final EVENT. I wanted it to happen during my lifetime, so I thought I might be able to bend the prophecy a little. I was probably wrong. I'm sorry. The Mrin *could* mean Brand, though, couldn't it?"

"Absolutely not," Beltira told him. "The Rivan King is going to be Overlord, not the Rivan Warder."

"Well," Eldrig floundered weakly, "I thought that Brand was almost the same as a king."

"Not from where *I* sit, I'm not," Brand told him.

"Just forget that I even mentioned it," Eldrig gave up.

"You can count on that," I said.

"The Overlord *will* come, though, Belgarath," the Gorim reminded me.

"I know."

"Will you be here to guide him?"

"Probably so. I don't feel any symptoms of incipient mortality coming over me yet. Pol and I'll take care of it when the time comes. We've been at it for a long time now."

"The Mrin *does* say that the Overlord's going to marry a Tolnedran Princess, you know."

"I know all about it, Gorim. I'm the one who introduced the Dryad strain into the Borune line to get ready for it."

"What *is* this Mrin thing you people keep talking about?" Mergon demanded. "I thought that the Mrin was a river in Drasnia."

"It's an Alorn holy book, your Excellency," Pol told him. "It foretells the future."

"I'm sorry, Lady Polgara, but nothing foretells the future."

"It hasn't been wrong yet, your Excellency," Beltira disagreed.

"That's probably because it's so general that it doesn't really mean anything," Mergon scoffed.

"No, actually it's very specific. It's hard to read, but once you unravel it, it tells you exactly what's going to happen."

"Only if you believe, Master Beltira. I've seen the holy books of other races, and they mean absolutely nothing to me."

"That's probably Nedra's doing, Mergon," I said. "Nedra doesn't like mysticism of any kind. You've got a very practical God. Let's move along, gentlemen. If we're going to come up with a set of accords here, we'd better get at it—unless you'd all like to just sign blank pieces of parchment. I could fill in the contents later, if you'd rather do it that way."

"Nice try, Belgarath." Beldin chuckled. "Just exactly what has to be in these accords?"

I turned to the twins. "You two are the experts. What does the Mrin say? How much should we nail down, and how much can we just leave open?"

"I think we'll want to establish the marriage of the king and the princess," Beltira replied. "That almost has to be agreed upon."

"And the Overlordship, as well," Belkira added. "That *must* be in the accords so that there won't be any question about it when the time comes. The Rivan King's going to have to give certain orders, and the kings of the other nations are going to have to obey them. Otherwise Torak's going to win next time."

"*Will* you people talk sense?" Mergon burst out. "There *is* no Rivan King. That line died with King Gorek."

"Oh, just tell him, Belgarath," Rhodar said disgustedly. "He'll argue about it for a week if you don't."

"And have him spread the information all over Tol Honeth? Be serious, Rhodar."

"I'm a diplomat, Belgarath," Mergon said in an offended tone of voice. "I know how to keep secrets."

"You might as well go ahead and tell him, father," Polgara told me. "He's going to start making some educated guesses anyway before we go much further with this."

I looked around at the assembled kings and emissaries. "I'll have an oath of silence on this, gentlemen," I said. "Those of you with ambassadorial rank can tell your rulers, but I don't want this going any further." I gave them all a hard look, and they mumbled their agreement. "To put it very shortly," I told them, "the Rivan line did *not* die out when Gorek was killed. One of his grandsons survived. The line's still intact, and someday one of that line will return to Riva and resume his throne. *That's* the information that doesn't leave this room. We've had enough trouble protecting those heirs without their existence becoming general knowledge."

I'm not really positive that Mergon believed me, but Eldrig and the other Alorns were feeling muscular, so he *behaved* as if he believed. He really didn't have anything to lose, after all. If I was lying to him, there'd never be a Rivan King to marry one of those precious Imperial Princesses, nor would anyone ever become Overlord of the West, so he went along with us, largely to pacify the Alorns, I believe.

Podiss, however, was another matter. Nyissans tend to be a little touchy about the fact that their kingdom is the only one ruled by a

woman, and any kind of disparagement of Salmissra, real or imagined,
raises screams of outrage. To put it rather bluntly, however, Nyissa doesn't
loom very large in the family of nations. It's a swampy backwater with a
small population and, aside from the slave trade, it doesn't have much in
the way of commerce. When it became more and more obvious that the
accords weren't even going to mention Nyissa, Podiss lost his temper.
"And what of my queen, Eternal Salmissra?" he demanded. "What voice
will *she* have in this ordering of the world?"

"Not a very loud one," Eldrig said, "at least not if I can help it, she
won't. She won't have to do anything except sign the document, Podiss—
that and keep her nose out of matters that don't concern her." Eldrig
wasn't exactly what you'd call the soul of diplomacy.

"I'll have no further part in this," Podiss said, rising to his feet. "And
I won't insult my queen by carrying this absurdity to her. Write down
anything you wish, gentlemen, but Salmissra won't sign it."

This was the point in his account of the conference where Davoul
the Lame lost his head entirely. His epic blandly asserts that Polgara
sprang to her feet, turned Podiss into a snake, changed herself into an
owl, and carried him off into the sky. I think it was the fact that Davoul
suddenly realized that he'd gone for ten whole pages without any magic
that pushed him over the edge. Polgara *did* do something to Podiss, but
it didn't involve anything like that. It was probably a lot worse, but nobody else at the conference saw it. She simply went to where Podiss was
standing and did much the same thing to him as she'd done to Eldallan
in the Asturian Forest. I haven't any idea at all of what she showed
him—he didn't scream at all—but whatever it was made him pale and
very cooperative.

It *also* persuaded Mergon to keep his objections to himself from
then on.

It took us another day or so to finish the Accords of Vo Mimbre, and
yet another day for a Mimbrate scribe to cast them into "high style."
Since the Mimbrates were our hosts, it was only polite to let them produce the final version. When that was all finished, the Gorim took up his
copy, rose to his feet, and read to us.

These then are the Accords which we have reached here at Vo
Mimbre. The nations of the West will prepare themselves for the
return of the Rivan King, for in the day of his return shall Torak
awaken and come again upon us, and none but the Rivan King
may overcome him and save us from his foul enslavement. And
whatsoever the Rivan King commands, that shall we do. And he
shall have an Imperial Princess of Tolnedra to wife and shall have
Empire and Dominion in the West. And whosoever breaketh

these accords, will we do war upon him and scatter his people and pull down his cities and lay waste his lands. We pledge it here in honor of Brand, who hath overthrown Torak and bound him in sleep until the One comes who might destroy him. So be it.

Eldrig leaned back in his chair. "Well," he said, "now that's taken care of. I guess we can all go home."

"Not quite yet, your Majesty," Wildantor disagreed. "There's still a royal wedding in the works."

"I'd almost forgotten about that," Eldrig said. "Are those two still screaming at each other?"

"No," Pol told him. "The screaming stopped a few days ago. The last time I listened at the door, there was a lot of giggling going on. Evidently Mayaserana's a bit ticklish."

"I wonder what they can be doing," the Gorim said mildly.

"We probably can start our armies marching toward home," Rhodar put in. "Ordinary soldiers aren't really very interested in royal weddings, and I'd like to have my pikemen at the Drasnian border before the end of summer."

"I can have my war boats take them to Kotu, if you'd like," Eldrig offered.

"Thanks all the same, Eldrig, but Drasnians aren't very good sailors. I'm fairly sure that my pikemen would rather walk."

Then Brand sent for Korodullin and Mayaserana. They were both blushing when they were escorted into his presence. "Have you two more or less settled your differences?" he asked them.

"We really should apologize, Lord Brand," Mayaserana said in a tone of sweet reasonableness and a rosy blush. "We both behaved very badly when you made that suggestion."

"Oh, that's all right, Mayaserana," Brand forgave her. "I take it you've had a change of heart."

"The sweet light of reason hath opened our eyes, Lord Brand," Korodullin assured him, also blushing, "and our duty to Arendia hath touched our hearts and caused our animosity to fade. Though we still have our differences, we are both willing to set them aside for the sake of our homeland."

"I was almost certain you'd see it that way," Polgara said with a faint smile.

Mayaserana blushed again. "And when would you like to have us married, Lord Brand?" she asked.

"Oh, I don't know," Brand replied. "Have either of you got anything urgent to take care of tomorrow?"

"What's wrong with today?" she countered. Patience, it appeared, wasn't Mayaserana's strong suit, and she had things on her mind.

"I think we could arrange that," Brand told her. "Somebody go get a priest of Chaldan."

"There might be a problem there, Lord Brand," Wildantor said dubiously. "Our priests are just as partisan as the rest of us. The priest might refuse to perform the ceremony."

"Not for very long, my friend," Mandor disagreed, "not if he values his continued good health."

"You'd actually hit a priest?" Wildantor asked.

"My duty to Arendia would compel it of me," Mandor said, "though it would, of course, rend mine heart."

"Oh, of course. Let's go find one, shall we? And you can explain things to him while we're dragging him back here."

And so Korodullin and Mayaserana were married, and Arendia was technically united. There was still a certain amount of bickering between Mimbrates and Asturians, of course, but the open battles more or less came to an end.

After the wedding, the kings of the West dispersed. We'd all been away from home for a long time, after all. Pol and I rode north with Brand as far as the great Arendish Fair, and then we said our good-byes and took the road leading toward the Ulgo border. "Will you be taking Gelane back to Aldurford?" I asked her after we'd gone several miles.

"No, father. I don't think that'd be a good idea. A lot of Algar soldiers saw the two of us at Vo Mimbre, and some of them came from Aldurford. Someone might make the connection. I think we'd better start fresh somewhere."

"Where did you have in mind?"

"I think I'll go back to Sendaria. After Vo Mimbre, there aren't going to be any Grolims around to worry about."

"That's your decision, Pol. Gelane's *your* responsibility, so whatever you decide is all right with me."

"Oh, *thank* you, father!" she said with a certain amount of sarcasm. "Oh, one other thing."

"Yes?"

"Stay out of my hair, Old Wolf, and this time I mean it."

"Whatever you say, Polgara." I didn't really mean it, of course, but I said it anyway. It was easier than arguing with her.

PART
SIX

GARION

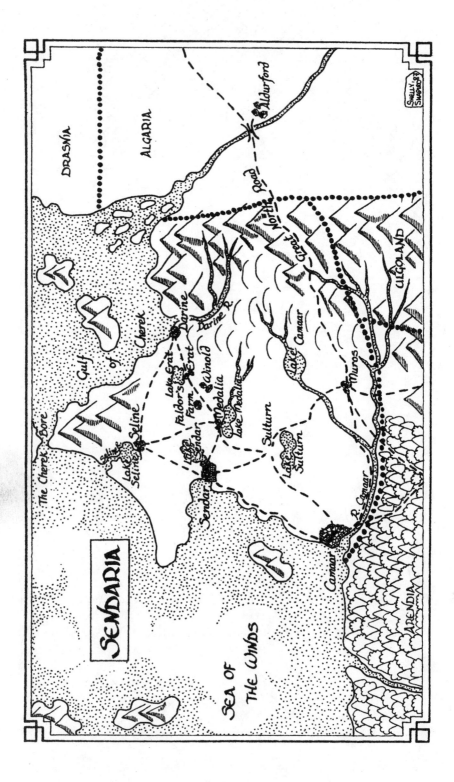

CHAPTER
FORTY-
THREE

There's a peculiar dichotomy in the nature of almost anyone who calls himself a historian. Such scholars all piously assure us that they're telling us the real truth about what really happened, but if you turn any competent historian over and look at his damp underside, you'll find a storyteller, and you can believe me when I tell you that no storyteller's ever going to tell a story without a few embellishments. Add to that the fact that we've all got assorted political and theological preconceptions that are going to color what we write, and you'll begin to realize that no history of any event is entirely reliable—not even this one. What I've just told you about the Battle of Vo Mimbre is more or less true, but I'll leave the business of separating truth from the fiction up to you. It'll sharpen your mind.

When you get right down to the bottom of the matter, the accords we reached at Vo Mimbre were more important than the battle itself. The war with the Angaraks was the climax of particular set of events, and the word "climax" means "end." The Accords of Vo Mimbre set up a new set of events, so in a certain sense they could be called a beginning.

The formalized summary of the accords that the Gorim read to us as our conference came to a close was just that—a summary. The meat of the thing lay in the specific articles, and we didn't let the creative Mimbrate scribes who prepared our summary anywhere near those. Over the years I've seen too many absurdities enacted into law or appearing in royal proclamations because some half-asleep scribe missed a line—or transposed a couple of words—for me to take chances. Those accords were *very* important. The articles we'd hammered out covered such things as how the Rivan King would issue his call to arms, how the various kingdoms were supposed to respond, and other logistical details. I'll concede that the presence of Brand, who'd just struck down Kal Torak and shaken the world by that act, made slipping a few things in much easier for me. Those things absolutely *had* to be included, but trying to explain exactly *why* would have taken years, I expect.

It was Polgara who dictated the specifics of the little ceremony that's become a ritual for the past five hundred years, and I use the word "dictated" advisedly here, since my imperious daughter refused to hear of any amendments or revisions. Mergon, the Tolnedran ambassador, almost had apoplexy by the time she was finished, and I'm not entirely certain that Ran Borune didn't.

"This is the way it's going to be from now on," she declared, and that's not really the best way to introduce a subject at a peace conference. "From this day forward, each Princess of Imperial Tolnedra shall present herself in her wedding gown in the Hall of the Rivan King on their sixteenth birthday. She'll wait there for three days. If the Rivan King comes to claim her during those three days, they'll be wed. If he doesn't, she'll be free to return to Tolnedra, and her father can choose another husband for her."

It was at that point that Mergon began to splutter, but Pol overrode his objections, and the Alorn kings backed her to the hilt, threatening invasions, the burning of cities, the scattering of the Tolnedran population, and other extravagances. I made a point of going to Tol Honeth a year or so later to apologize to Ran Borune for her behavior. The presence of the legions at Vo Mimbre had turned the tide of battle, and Polgara's ultimatum had a faint odor of ingratitude about it. I know that she was following instructions, but her cavalier attitude almost suggested that Tolnedra was a defeated enemy.

When the conference ended, Pol and I rode north, and it was late summer by the time we reached the border of Ulgoland. We were met there by a fairly large detachment of leather-clad Algars. Cho Ram had sent an honor guard to escort us through the Ulgo Mountains. I didn't want to insult him by refusing, so we plodded on across those mountains with his Algars rather than doing it the other way—which would have been much faster, of course. There wasn't anything pressing that needed to be done, though, and it was the courteous thing to do.

When we came down out of the mountains of Ulgoland onto the plains of Algaria, Pol and I separated. She went on to the Stronghold with the Algars, and I rode on south to the Vale. I had it in my mind that some fairly serious loafing might be in order. I'd been on the go for a quarter century, and I felt that I owed myself a vacation.

Beldin had other ideas, though. "What are your feelings about a little trip to Mallorea?" he asked when I got home.

"Profoundly unenthusiastic, if you want the truth. What's in Mallorea that's so important?"

"The Ashabine Oracles, I hope. I thought that you and I could go to Ashaba and ransack Torak's house there. He might just have left a copy of the Oracles lying around, and those prophecies could be very useful, don't you think? Zedar, Urvon, and Ctuchik aren't going to let this slide, Belgarath. We bloodied their noses quite thoroughly at Vo Mimbre, and they'll almost certainly try to get back at us. If we can get our hands on a copy of the Oracles, it might give us a few clues about what to expect from them."

"You can burglarize a house without any help from me, brother," I told him. "I don't feel any great yearnings to visit a deserted castle in the Karandese Mountains."

"You're lazy, Belgarath."

"Has it taken you this long to realize that?"

"Let me put it to you another way," he said. "I need you."

"What for?"

"Because I can't read Old Angarak, you ninny!"

"How do you know that the Oracles are written in Old Angarak?"

"I don't, but it's the language that'd come most naturally to Torak, especially since he was probably in a sort of delirium when the voice came to *him*. If the Oracles *are* written in Old Angarak, I wouldn't be able to recognize them if they were out in plain sight."

"I could teach you how to read the language, Beldin."

"And by then Urvon will have gotten to Ashaba first. If we're going, we'd better go now."

I sighed. It looked as if I was going to have to postpone my vacation.

"Did I just hear the sound of a change of heart?" he asked.

"Don't push it, Beldin. I *am* going to sleep for a couple of days first, though."

"You old people do that a lot, don't you?"

"Just go away for a while, brother. You're keeping me up past my bedtime."

Actually, I slept for only about twelve hours. The possibility that there might be a copy of the Oracles hidden somewhere at Ashaba intrigued me enough so that I got up, fixed myself some breakfast, and then went on over to Beldin's tower. "Let's get started," I told him.

He was wise enough not to make any clever remarks. We went to the

window of his tower, pulled on our feathers, and left. We flew in a generally northeasterly direction and soon crossed the Eastern Escarpment to
Mishrak ac Thull. Thulldom had been devastated by the war, but that
hadn't been our idea. Kal Torak's Malloreans had enlisted the Thulls by
the simple expedient of destroying all their towns and villages and burning their crops. This left the Thulls with no alternatives. They had to
join the army or starve. The women, children, and aged were left to fend
for themselves in a land with no houses and nothing to eat. My opinion
of Torak hadn't been high in the first place, and it went down precipi-
tously when I saw the plight of the Thulls.

When we reached the coast, Beldin veered north. Hawks and falcons
have a great deal of stamina, but not so much so that we were willing to
try crossing the expanse of the Sea of the East in one jump. Gar og
Nadrak wasn't *quite* as devastated as Thulldom, but conditions there were
also fairly miserable.

We winged our way north along the coast of Morindland and crossed
over to Mallorea, following the string of islands that formed the land-
bridge. Then Beldin led the way across the Barrens to the Karandese
Mountains and then on south to Ashaba.

Ashaba's not a town in the ordinary sense of the word. It's really
nothing more than a very large castle with a number of Karandese villages in the surrounding forest. The villages were there to support the
Grolims who'd lived in the palace. Torak himself probably didn't have to
eat, but Grolims get hungry once in a while, I guess, and the ground
around the castle, like the ground at Cthol Mishrak, was dead and unpro-
ductive. Even the soil rejected Torak.

The house at Ashaba was black basalt, naturally. It was Torak's favorite color—or lack of it. It stood on the east side of a sterile plateau that
seemed incapable of sustaining any kind of vegetation except for leprous
grey lichens and dead-white toadstools, and it was backed up against a
lowering cliff.

The place was immense, and it was surmounted with ugly, graceless
towers and spires that stabbed up toward the scudding clouds roiling overhead. It was walled in, naturally. It was an Angarak building, and
Angaraks put walls around everything—even pigpens. Our simplest
course would have been to come to roost inside the wall, but Beldin
veered off and settled to earth just outside the main gate. I swooped in
and dropped to the ground beside him even as he was shimmering back
into his own form.

I also changed back. "What's the problem?"

"Let's probe around a bit before we go blundering in. Torak may have
left a few surprises behind."

"I guess that makes sense."

Beldin concentrated, his ugly face twisting with the effort. "There's nobody home," he said after a moment.

"Any sign of Hounds?"

"Look for yourself. I'm going to poke around and see if there are any traps lurking inside."

I sensed nothing at all. There weren't even any rats inside. So far as I could tell, there weren't even any bugs.

"Anything?" Beldin asked.

"Nothing at all. Did you find anything?"

"No. The place is safe." He squinted at the gate, and I felt his Will building. Then he released it, and the huge iron gate burst inward with a thunderous detonation.

"What did you do that for?" I demanded.

"Just me quaint way o' leavin' my callin' card, don't y' know," he replied in that tired old Wacite brogue he was so fond of. "Old Burnt-face might come back someday, an' I'd like fer him t' know that we stopped by."

"I think you're getting senile."

"Well, *you're* the expert on that. Let's go inside."

We went through the shattered gate, crossed the courtyard, and warily approached a huge, nail-studded black door surmounted by the inevitable polished steel mask. Evidently Torak had felt that any house he lived in was by definition a temple.

"Be my guest," Beldin offered, pointing at the door.

"Don't be ridiculous." I took hold of the massive iron door handle, twisted it, and opened the door.

The house of Torak had an entryway that was about the size of a grand ballroom, and there was a majestic staircase just opposite the door.

"Should we start down here?" Beldin asked me.

"No, let's go up to the top and work our way down. You *would* recognize Old Angarak script if you saw it, wouldn't you?"

"I think so. It looks kind of spidery, doesn't it?"

"More or less. We'll split up. Look into any book you find in a language you can read, and gather up any in Old Angarak script. I'll sort through them later."

The place was vast—more for show, I think, than out of any real need for that much room. Many of the chambers on the upper floors didn't even have furniture in them. It still took us weeks to thoroughly investigate the house, though, since it was at least as big as Anheg's palace at Val Alorn.

At first, Beldin grew very excited each time he found a book or scroll written in Old Angarak, but most of them turned out to be nothing more than copies of the *Book of Torak*. Most of the people at Ashaba had been

Grolims, and every Grolim in the world owns a copy of the Holy Book of the Angaraks. After the first few times he came running down a hallway waving one of those books in the air, I sat him down and patiently gave him some instruction in the Old Angarak alphabet. After that he was able to recognize copies of the *Book of Torak* and to discard them.

We finally found Torak's library on the second floor of the castle, and it was there that we spent so much time. There *might* be more books at the University of Tol Honeth or the one in Melcene, but not very many.

A pair of ordinary scholars would have taken decades to examine all those books, but Beldin and I have certain advantages. We can identify the contents of a book without too great an exertion.

Finally, after we'd worked our way through the last shelf, way back in one of the corners, Beldin hurled a book across the room and swore for about a quarter of an hour. "This is ridiculous!" he roared. "There *has* to be a copy here!"

"There might be," I agreed, "but I don't think we're going to find it. Zedar was the one who ultimately wound up taking down Torak's ravings, and Zedar's a master at hiding things. For all we know, the Oracles are concealed inside some other book—or inside dozens of other books, a page here and a page there. There could be a complete copy someplace, but I don't think it'll be right out in the open. It might even be hidden under the floor or in the wall of some room we've already searched. I don't think we're going to have any luck, brother. We can check out the ground floor if you want, but I think we're just wasting our time. If there *does* happen to be a copy here and Zedar's the one who hid it, we aren't going to find it. He knows you and me well enough to have thought up a way to counteract anything we might come up with to locate it."

"I guess you're right, Belgarath," he admitted glumly. "Let's rip the ground floor apart and then go home. This place stinks, and I need some fresh air."

And so we abandoned our search and went home. For the time being, at least, we were going to have to rely on our own prophecies without any help from Torak's.

I took that vacation I'd been promising myself, but after a month or so, I started to get bored. I went on over to Sendaria to check in with Polgara and to tell her about the little expedition to Ashaba. She'd set Gelane up in business as a cooper in the town of Seline in northern Sendaria, and the heir to Iron-grip's throne spent most of his time making barrels and kegs. When he wasn't doing that, he was "walking out" with a pretty little blonde girl, the daughter of a local blacksmith.

"Are you sure she's the right one?" I asked Pol.

She sighed. "Yes, father," she replied in that long-suffering tone of voice.

"Just exactly *how* do you know, Pol? There's nothing in the Mrin or the Darine that identifies these girls—at least nothing *I've* ever come across."

"I'm getting instructions, father."

I wandered around in the Western Kingdoms for the next couple years, looking in on the assorted families I'd been nurturing for centuries. The Angarak invasion of Algaria and the wholesale slaughter of the Algarian cattle herds had brought the Kingdoms of the West to the verge of an economic disaster. It was generations before there were any more cattle drives to Muros. The Tolnedrans went into deep mourning, but the always-practical Sendars came up with a partial solution. All of Sendaria turned into one vast pig ranch. Pork has certain advantages over beef. I suppose you *could* smoke and cure beef if you really wanted to, but the Algars didn't bother. It might have been because there weren't that many trees in Algaria, so the woodchips required to smoke meat weren't readily available. The Sendars didn't have that problem, and wagonloads of cured hams and bacon and sausages were soon trundling along every Tolnedran highway in all the Western Kingdoms.

There was a tentative, nervous kind of peace in Arendia when I came back through there on my way north after a visit to Tol Honeth where I'd presented my apologies for Polgara's bad manners to Ran Borune and General Cerran. I reached Vo Mandor in the autumn of 4877, and I spent a pleasant winter with my friend, the baron. I really liked Mandor. He had a rudimentary sense of humor, a rarity in Arendia, and he set a very nice table. I put on a few pounds during that visit.

In the spring of the following year, baron Wildantor came down from Asturia to visit. The friendship that had sprung up between the two of them during the Battle of Vo Mimbre had deepened, and they were now almost like brothers. The addition of the boisterous, red-haired Wildantor turned our little reunion into an extended party, and I was enjoying myself immensely. Then one evening when we'd stayed up late savoring our reminiscences, Beldin finally located me. It was a glorious spring night, and I'd thrown open the windows of my third-floor bedroom to let in the flower-scented spring breeze. The familiar blue-banded hawk appeared out of the night, settled on my windowsill, and shimmered back into my ugly little brother. "I've been looking all over for you," he rasped.

"I've been right here for six months. Is there something I ought to know about?"

"I've found out where Zedar's got Torak's body hidden, is about all."

"About *all*? That's fairly momentous, Beldin. Where is it?"

"Southern Cthol Murgos—about fifty leagues south of Rak Cthol. There's a cave in the side of a mountain down there, and Zedar's got Torak tucked away inside of it."

"He's *that* close to Ctuchik? Is he insane?"

"Of course he's insane. He always has been. Ctuchik doesn't know he's there, though."

"Ctuchik's a Grolim, Beldin. He can sense Zedar's presence."

"No, actually he can't. Zedar's using some of the tricks *you* taught him before he turned bad on us. That's what makes Zedar so dangerous. He's the only one of the lot of us who's had instruction from *two* Gods."

"How did *you* find him, then?"

"Sheer luck. He came out of the cave for firewood and I just happened to be flying over."

"Are you sure Torak's inside?"

"Well, of *course* I am, Belgarath! I went into the cave to make sure."

"You did *what?*"

"Don't get excited. Zedar didn't know I was there. He was even nice enough to carry me inside."

"How did you manage that?"

He shrugged. "I used a bug—a flea, actually." He laughed. "That's *really* challenging. You wouldn't *believe* what that kind of compression does to your innards. Anyway, Zedar's none too clean these days, so he's pretty well flea-bitten, and he's got lice, as well. I hopped onto his head and burrowed into his hair while he was bent over picking up some sticks for his fire. He took me inside, and there was old Burnt-face all laid out on a flat rock with ice all around him. Zedar's put the mask back on him—probably because Torak's face makes him as sick as it makes the rest of humanity. I stayed where I was until Zedar went to sleep. Then I bit him a few times and hopped out of the cave."

I suddenly burst out laughing. I couldn't help it.

"What's so funny?"

"You *bit* him?"

"Under the circumstances, it was the best I could do. I wasn't big enough to bash out his brains. He's going to have a very itchy scalp for the next week or so, though. I'll stop by that mountain of his from time to time to make sure he stays put. Mallorea's gone all to pieces, you know."

"Oh?"

"When word got back that Torak wasn't functioning any more, independence movements started springing up all over the continent. The old emperor—the one Torak deposed—is back on the throne at Mal Zeth now, but he's not really very effective. He's got a grandson—Korzeth, I think his name is. The old emperor's grooming *him* for the task of reuniting Mallorea. I was going to slip into the palace and slit the little monster's throat, but the Master told me not to—very firmly. Evidently

Korzeth's line's going to produce somebody we're going to need eventually. That's about it, Belgarath, so pass all this on to the twins and to Pol. I'm going back to Cthol Murgos. I think I'll graze on Zedar's head for a while longer." Then he blurred back into feathers and went out the window.

I made my apologies to Mandor and Wildantor the next morning and rode north, intending to go to Seline to advise Pol of these developments, but I hadn't gone five miles when I heard the sound of a galloping horse behind me. I was more than a little startled when I saw that it was General Cerran.

"Belgarath!" he shouted before he'd even caught up with me. "Thank Nedra I caught up with you before you vanished into the Asturian Forest! Ran Borune wants you to come back to Tol Honeth!"

"Have you run out of couriers, Cerran?" I asked, a little amused to see a middle-age Tolnedran general reduced to a messenger boy.

"It's a sensitive matter, old friend. Something's going on in Tol Honeth that might involve you. The emperor doesn't even want you to come to the palace. I'm supposed to take you to a certain place and then leave you to your own devices. His Majesty thinks it might be one of those things a Tolnedran wouldn't understand, but you would."

"You've managed to arouse my curiosity, Cerran. Can you give me any details?"

"There's a member of the Honethite family who's a thoroughgoing scoundrel."

"I thought they all were."

"This one's so bad that his *family's* disowned him. There are some things so rancid that even the Honeths can't stomach them, but this fellow, Olgon, will do *anything* for a price. He does business out of a low tavern that's frequented by pickpockets and hired killers. We like to keep an eye on him, so a couple of our agents have wormed their way in among the regular patrons. We're fairly sure that the Drasnian ambassador's got some people in there, as well."

"You probably could make a safe bet on that," I agreed.

"Truly. To cut this short, a couple of weeks ago, this Honethite Olgon was approached by a Nyissan who said that his employer would pay a great deal of money to find out where you are—and much more to find out where Lady Polgara is."

"Pol's not in Tolnedra."

"We were fairly sure she wasn't, but Olgon's got people scattered all over the Western Kingdoms, and he has contacts with just about every thief and outlaw on this side of the escarpment."

"Why would a Nyissan be trying to find us?"

"His employer isn't Nyissan. One of our agents was close enough to eavesdrop when the Nyissan told Olgon his employer's name. The man who's looking for you is called Asharak the Murgo."

"I can't say that I've ever heard of him."

"It's an assumed name. Our intelligence service has quite an extensive file on this particular Murgo. He uses about a half-dozen names, but there's one report about twenty years old that identifies him as somebody named Chamdar. Does that name mean anything to you?"

I gaped at him for a moment, and then I wheeled my horse and spurred him toward the south and Tol Honeth.

CHAPTER
FORTY-
FOUR

General Cerran and I very nearly killed our horses getting to Tol Honeth. I'm sure Cerran thought I'd gone crazy until I told him of some of my previous encounters with Ctuchik's ambitious underling. When we finally reached Tol Honeth, we went immediately to the Drasnian embassy. Ran Borune's Intelligence Service was good, I suppose, but it was no match for Rhodar's. The Drasnian ambassador was a stout fellow named Kheral, and he didn't seem very surprised to see us when we were escorted into his red-draped office. "I rather thought you might be stopping by, Ancient One," he said to me.

"Let's get down to business, Kheral," I said, cutting across the pleasantries. "How much can you tell me about this fellow who calls himself Asharak the Murgo?"

Kheral leaned back, clasping his pudgy hands on his paunch. "He was fairly active here in Tolnedra back before the war, Belgarath—all the usual things, spies, corrupting government officials, and the like. There were dozens of Murgos doing that sort of thing back in those days. We routinely kept an eye on all of them, but Asharak wasn't doing anything so radically different from the others that he stood out."

"Didn't your home office in Boktor make the connection?"

"Evidently not. Asharak's name was in our reports, but it was mixed in with the names of all the other Murgo agents, so it didn't ring any bells. Then Kal Torak invaded Drasnia, and the Intelligence Service had to move out of Boktor in a hurry. They set up shop in Riva, but the files were an absolute shambles. That might explain why later reports on Asharak didn't attract attention until just recently. Murgo operatives were still functioning here in Tolnedra even after the South Caravan Route was closed, but when the war started getting serious, they all left the country."

"Good riddance," Cerran noted.

"No, General, not really," Kheral disagreed. "Murgos sort of stand out in the Western Kingdoms, so they're easy to identify. Ctuchik's using Dagashi now instead, and it's much more challenging to try to identify *them*. We *did* manage to locate one a few months back, though, so I put some people to watching him. Then, about two weeks ago, this Dagashi was speaking with a fellow who looked like a Sendar, but probably wasn't, and one of my agents was close enough to them to hear them talking about some orders they'd received from Asharak the Murgo. I sent a report to our temporary headquarters in Riva, and a clerk who was a little more alert than the one who's been mishandling my correspondence made the connection. He checked the dossier we've kept on Asharak for years now, and he found some documents that were cross-referenced to the file we keep on Chamdar. The Chief of Service alerted me, and I arranged to leak information to Ran Borune's spies. I knew that you'd recently visited the palace, Belgarath, and there was a good chance that the emperor would know where you'd gone. I felt that it'd be easier—and cheaper—to let his people find you rather than sending out my own."

Cerran was looking speculatively at Kheral. "I'm getting the distinct impression that you wear two hats, your Excellency," he observed.

"Didn't you know that, Cerran?" I asked him. "Every Drasnian ambassador in the world's a member of the Intelligence Service."

Kheral made a slight face. "It's a budgetary consideration, General," he explained. "King Rhodar's a very thrifty fellow, and this way he only has to pay one salary rather than two. The savings *do* mount up after a while."

Cerran smiled. "How typically Drasnian," he murmured.

"How does this renegade Honethite, Olgon, fit into all of this, Kheral?" I asked.

"I was just getting to that, Ancient One. The Dagashi we've been watching is currently posing as a Nyissan—shaved head, silk robe, and all of that. He's been spending a lot of time in that tavern Olgon frequents. I've got a couple of agents close to Olgon, and we're fairly sure Tolnedran intelligence does, as well. This so-called Nyissan was the one who enlisted Olgon to aid in the search for you and Lady Polgara."

I stood up. "I think maybe I'd better go to this tavern and have a look at Olgon for myself. Exactly where is the place?"

"On the southern end of the island," Cerran told me, "but would that be wise? You *are* fairly well known, and I'm sure that Asharak's Dagashi would recognize you."

"I can disguise myself, Cerran," I assured him. "Nobody's going to recognize me." I looked him straight in the face. "You don't really want to know how I do that, do you?"

He looked uncomfortable. "No, I guess not, Belgarath," he said.

"I didn't think so. Kheral, why don't you have one of your people show me where this tavern is? I'll take it from there. You two wait here. I'll be back in a little bit."

When you enter the city of Tol Honeth, you get the impression that it's all stately houses and marble-sheathed public buildings, but, like every other city in the world, it has its share of slums. The tavern to which Kheral's spy took me was decidedly shabby, and it was identified by a crude sign that supposedly represented a cluster of grapes. I think that every tavern in the West has the same sign out front. The sun was just going down when the Drasnian spy pointed out the tavern and then went off down the street. I stepped back into a reeking alleyway, formed the image of a tall, lean fellow dressed in rags in my mind, and then fitted myself into that image. Then I half staggered out of the alley, crossed the street, and went into the dimly lighted, stale-smelling tavern. I plopped myself down on a bench at one of the wobbly tables and loudly announced, "I'll have beer!"

"I'll see your money first," the tavernkeeper replied in a bored tone of voice.

I fumbled around in the pocket of my shabby smock and produced a Tolnedran halfpenny. The tavernkeeper took my coin and brought me a tankard of definitely inferior beer.

Then I looked around. Olgon wasn't too hard to pick out. He was far and away the best-dressed man in the tavern, and his face was locked in that arrogant expression that all Honeths are born with. He was holding court at a large table near the back wall, and he was surrounded by thieves and cutthroats. His face had that pouchy look that comes only after years of serious dissipation. "All you have to do is say that you saw her in the street, Strag," he was patiently explaining to an evil-looking fellow with a purple scar on the side of his face.

"What good will that do?" Strag retorted.

"If he doesn't get *some* kind of information that she's still in Tol Honeth, he might take his money to Tol Borune—or even up into Arendia. We could lose him altogether."

"I don't know about you, Olgon," Strag replied, "but I value my own skin. I'm *not* going to lie to a Dagashi and then take his money for it."

"You're a coward, Strag," Olgon accused.

"Maybe so, but I'm a live one. I've seen what the Dagashi do to people who cross them. Get somebody else to do your lying for you—or do it yourself."

Olgon sneered. "All right," he said to the other scoundrels at the table, "who wants to earn a silver half-mark?"

He didn't find any takers. Evidently the reputation of the Dagashi was well known in this shabby society.

Olgon glowered around at his hirelings, and then he let the matter drop. That little snatch of conversation revealed worlds about his character. I couldn't for the life of me understand how a Dagashi could possibly put any faith in anything Olgon told him.

It was about ten minutes later, and I'd been nursing that tankard of lukewarm, watered-down beer for about as long as I cared to, when the tavern door opened and a shaved-headed man wearing a Nyissan silk robe came in. He went directly to Olgon's table. "Have you anything for me?" he asked abruptly.

"I've got everybody out looking," Olgon replied a bit evasively. "This is costing me a great deal of money, Saress. Can you see your way clear to give me a little bit of an advance?"

"Asharak doesn't pay in advance, Olgon," the man in the silk robe said with a sneer. "He pays only on delivery."

Olgon muttered something, and the other man leaned over the table. "What was that?" he asked ominously. Since he was bent over, I could clearly see the outline of the triangular object he had nestled against the small of his back under that robe.

"I said that this Asharak of yours is a cheapskate," Olgon retorted.

"I'll pass that on to him," Saress replied. "I'm sure he'll be charmed."

"I'm not asking for the whole sum, Saress," Olgon said plaintively. "Just enough to cover my expenses."

"Look upon those expenses as an investment, Olgon. If you can produce the woman Asharak's looking for, he'll make you rich. If you can't, you'll just have to stay poor." Then he turned on his heel and left the tavern.

Something wasn't right here. They were all just a little too obvious. I knew that *my* disguise was impenetrable, but it was entirely possible that Olgon and the fellow in the Nyissan robe had recognized one of the Drasnian or Tolnedran agents here and that what I'd just seen had been carefully staged to deceive *them*. I started to get very suspicious about this whole business at that point. I waited for another few minutes, and then I stood up and dumped my tankard out on the floor. "That's enough of this swill," I announced loudly. "If I want a drink of river water, I can go down to one of the wharves and drink my fill without paying for it." Then I stormed out. I kept my disguise in place until I was certain that I wasn't being followed. Then I stepped into another alleyway, resumed my own form, and went back to the Drasnian embassy as evening settled over Tol Honeth.

"Have any of your people actually *seen* Asharak?" I asked Kheral.

"Not yet, Ancient One," the ambassador replied. "We've tried to track that Dagashi back to his employer, but he always manages to evade us."

"I'm not surprised. That's no run-of-the-mill Dagashi. He's carrying an adder-sting. He bent over a table in that tavern, and I saw the outline of the thing under his silk robe."

Kheral whistled.

"What's an adder-sting?" Cerran asked.

"It's a triangular throwing knife," Kheral replied. "It's about six inches across and razor sharp. The tips are usually dipped in poison. Only the most elite among the Dagashi use them."

"It doesn't make sense," I fumed. "Those elite Dagashi are *very* expensive. Why would Asharak pay that much for an errand boy? I'm starting to get a strong odor of rotten fish here. Somebody's paying a lot of money to get us to believe that Asharak's here in Tol Honeth, but until somebody actually sees him, I won't be convinced."

"Why would Asharak go to all the trouble and expense to do something like this?" Cerran seemed baffled.

"Probably because he wants me to believe that he's here when he's actually someplace else," I replied. I didn't say so, but I was fairly certain that I knew where Chamdar really was. "Well," I said then. "Two can play that game. I'm looking for Chamdar, and he's looking for somebody else. I think I can come up with a way to make him come back to Tol Honeth at a dead run."

"What are you going to do, Ancient One?" Kheral asked me.

"Chamdar's got people out looking for Polgara. I'm going to make sure that they find her—several times a day, actually, and right here in Tol Honeth. Let's go to the palace. I need to talk with Ran Borune."

The three of us went to the Imperial Compound and were admitted into the emperor's private quarters almost immediately.

"Good evening, gentlemen," Ran Borune said, laying aside the lute he had been strumming. "I gather that something's come up."

"I need a favor, your Majesty," I told him.

"Of course."

"This Chamdar you've been hearing about is a Grolim priest who does a lot of Ctuchik's dirty work for him."

Ran Borune's eyes narrowed. "He's more significant than we thought, then. What's he doing in Tolnedra? I'd have thought that what happened at Vo Mimbre would have completely demoralized the Grolims."

"It probably did, your Majesty, but Chamdar's no ordinary Grolim.

Ctuchik gave him an assignment a long time ago, and Chamdar's a dog-ged sort of fellow. My daughter's protecting something that's important, and Chamdar's been trying to find her for years now. He's so obsessed with locating her that I don't think he even noticed Vo Mimbre."

"Why's he looking here, then? Your daughter's not in Tolnedra, is she?"

"Not at the moment, no, but I don't think Chamdar is, either. This whole business with that renegade Honethite's a trick to lure me into thinking that he is. He definitely wants my attention locked on Tol Honeth. Now I'm going to turn the tables on him and see to it that he comes running back here where Kheral can keep an eye on him for me."

"How do you plan to manage that?"

"Kherel's going to have his people start letting some false information filter through to this Olgon fellow. I'd appreciate your having your agents do the same. Tell them to be very careful about it, though. Chamdar's people aren't Murgos now. He's using the Dagashi instead. Murgos aren't bright, and they're easy to pick out of a crowd. The Dagashi are very clever, though, and they're almost impossible to recognize."

"Who are these Dagashi?"

"They're members of a semireligious order based in the Araga Mili-tary District in southwestern Cthol Murgos, your Majesty. They're primar-ily assassins, but they're also very good spies. They can cause us a lot of problems, because they don't look like Murgos."

"How did they manage that?"

"Interbreeding. The Nyissans sell them slave women from all over the world, and the male children those slave women produce are trained and then admitted to the order. They're fanatically loyal to their elders, and they're very dangerous, since to all intents and purposes, they're practi-cally invisible. Now we get to that favor I was talking about."

"What can I do for you, old friend?"

"I'd like to see a new ladies' hairstyle become fashionable."

He blinked. "Have we suddenly changed the subject?"

"Not really. You've met my daughter. Would you be willing to con-cede that she has a striking appearance?"

"You won't get any argument from me there."

"What's the first thing you notice about her?"

"That white streak in her hair, of course."

"Exactly."

He suddenly grinned at me. "Oh, you *are* a sly old fox, Belgarath," he said admiringly. "You want me to blanket Tol Honeth with imitation Polgaras, don't you?"

"For a start, yes. I want to jerk Chamdar back to Tol Honeth. I'll let him run around here for a while, and then I'll start expanding the ruse.

I think I'll be able to arrange for him to get word of Polgara sightings about a dozen times a day—starting here in Tol Honeth."

"If Polgara really wants to stay out of sight, why doesn't she just dye her hair?"

"She's tried that, and it doesn't work. The dye won't adhere to that white lock. It washes right out, and Polgara washes her hair at least once a day. Since I can't make her look like every other woman, I'll do it the other way around and make every dark-haired woman in the West look like her. Tol Honeth's the fashion center of the Western World, so if the ladies here start painting a white stripe in their hair, the ladies in the other kingdoms will follow suit in six months or so. I'll pull Chamdar back to Tol Honeth for a start, and then I'll circulate around in the other kingdoms and encourage all the ladies I come across to follow the new fashion. I'll keep Chamdar running from the fringes of Morindland to the southern border of Nyissa for the next ten years with this little trick. To make things even worse, the Dagashi expect payment for each and every service. Chamdar's going to pay very dearly for all those false reports. If nothing else, I'll bankrupt him."

I stayed in Tol Honeth for about a month while the new fashion caught on. I made no effort to conceal the fact that I was there, either. If Chamdar's agents reported that *I* was there, the Polgara sightings would be far more credible. I sort of hate to admit that it was Olgon's conversation with the evil-looking Strag that gave me the idea in the first place. I embellished it, though. I *always* embellish other people's ideas. It's called "artistry"—or sometimes "plagiarism."

It was at that point in my long and speckled career that I assumed a guise that's worked out rather well for the past five hundred years. I became an itinerant storyteller. Storytellers are welcome everywhere in a preliterate society, and literacy wasn't very widespread in those days.

People who've known me over the past five centuries always have assumed that my somewhat shabby appearance is the result of a careless indifference on my part, but nothing could be further from the truth. I spent a great deal of time designing that costume, and I had it made for me by one of the finest tailors in Tol Honeth. Those clothes *look* as if they're right on the verge of falling off my back, but they're so well made that they're virtually indestructible. The patches on the knees of my hose are purely cosmetic, since there aren't any holes under them. The sleeves of my woolen tunic are frayed at the cuffs, but not from wear. The fraying was woven into the cloth of the tunic before I ever put it on. The rope belt is a touch of artistry, I've always thought, and the yoked hood gives me a distinctive and readily identifiable appearance. I added a stout grey Rivan cloak and a sack for my assorted belongings. Then I spent a full day arguing with a cobbler about the shoes. He absolutely could *not* understand why I didn't want them to match. They're very well-made shoes, actually, but they look as if I'd found them in a ditch somewhere. The entire costume made me look like a vagabond, and it hasn't changed substantially for five centuries.

I left Tol Honeth on foot. A vagabond storyteller probably couldn't afford a horse in the first place, and a horse is largely an encumbrance anyway, since I have other means of transportation available to me.

I wouldn't have made such an issue of all that except to correct a widely held misconception. Regardless of what people may think, I'm not really all that slovenly. My clothes look the way they do because I *want* them to.

Does it surprise you to discover that I'm not really a tramp? Life's just filled with these little disappointments, isn't it?

I stopped by Vo Mimbre on my way north, and I was quite surprised when Queen Mayaserana immediately fell in with my scheme. Sometimes we misjudge Arends. It's easy to dismiss them as simply stupid, but that's not entirely true. Their problem isn't so much stupidity as it is enthusiasm. They're an emotional people, and that clouds their judgment. The fiery Mayaserana saw the meaning of my ploy almost as quickly as Ran Borune had, and she'd added that white lock to her hair before the sun went down. It was very becoming, and the following day I was pleased to note that all the dark-haired ladies at court had rushed to follow suit. The blonde ladies did a lot of sulking, as I recall.

I discovered something about the female nature as I made my way north. No matter where I stopped, in whatever village or small town or isolated farmstead, sooner or later some woman was going to ask me "What's the current fashion at court? How long are the gowns? How are the ladies wearing their hair?"

Nothing could have suited my purposes better. I left a wake of white locks behind me like the wake of a Cherek war boat with a good following wind.

I rather carefully avoided the families I'd been nurturing over the centuries. It occurred to me that Chamdar might just be shrewd enough to realize that he could seriously disrupt the course of what the Mrin had laid out for us if he managed to kill a few key ancestors. My primary concern, however, was still the safety of Gelane, so I avoided Seline as if it were infected with the pox.

As it turned out, though, the danger to Gelane wasn't physical; it was spiritual instead.

I'd drifted into Medalia in central Sendaria, and I was telling stories for farthings in the town square and advising the ladies on the latest fashions. I was sleeping in a stable on the outskirts of town, and after I'd been in Medalia for about a week, Pol's distressed voice woke me up in the middle of the night.

"Father, I need you."

"What's the matter?"

"We've got a problem. You'd better get here as soon as you can."

"What is it?"

"I'll tell you when you get here. Somebody might be eavesdropping. Wear a different face." Then her voice was gone.

Now *there's* a cryptic message for you. Unless she loses her temper, Polgara's probably the most unexcitable person in the world. Almost *nothing* upsets her, but she definitely sounded upset this time. I stood up, shook the straw out of my cloak, and left Medalia immediately.

I was on the outskirts of Seline before the sun came up, and I mentally leafed through my catalog of disguises and assumed the form of a bald-headed fat man. Then I went to the shop where Gelane spent his time building barrels.

Polgara was out front vigorously sweeping off the doorstep, despite the fact that it was still very early. "Where have you been?" she demanded when I approached her. Somehow she always sees through my disguises.

"Calm down, Pol. What's got you so worked up?"

"Come inside." She led me into the shop. "Gelane's still asleep," she whispered. "I want to show you something." She led me to what appeared to be a broom closet at the back of the shop. She opened the door and took out a shaggy fur tunic. My heart dropped into my shoes.

The tunic was made of bearskin.

"How long's this been going on?" I whispered to my daughter.

"I can't be entirely sure, father. Gelane's been sort of distant and evasive for about the last six months. He goes out almost every night and doesn't come back until quite late. At first I thought he might be cheating on Enalla."

"His wife?"

She nodded and carefully put the bearskin tunic back in the broom closet. "Let's go outside," she whispered. "I don't want him to come down and find us in here."

We went back out into the street and walked down to the corner. "Anyway," she took up her account, "Gelane's mother's been quite ill of late, so I've had to stay with her. She seems to be recovering now, and last evening I finally had a chance to follow him. He went down into the shop and stuck that tunic into a sack. Then he went on down to the lakeshore and followed the beach to a large grove of trees about a mile east of town. There were a dozen or so other Alorns standing around a fire in the center of the grove, and they were all dressed in bearskins. Gelane put on that tunic, and he fit right in. It's fairly obvious that he's become a member of the Bear-cult."

I started to swear.

"That's not accomplishing anything, father," Pol told me crisply. "What are we going to do?"

"I'm not sure. Who seemed to be in charge of that little get-together last night?"

"There was a bearded man wearing the robe of a priest of Belar who did most of the talking."

"Did he say anything significant?"

"Not really. Mostly he just repeated all those worn-out old slogans. 'Aloria is one,' 'Cursed be the children of the Dragon God,' 'Belar rules'—that sort of thing."

"Pol, you're supposed to be keeping an eye on Gelane. How did you let this happen?"

"I didn't expect it, father. He's always been so sensible."

"Is this priest attached to the local Alorn church?"

"No. As far as I can tell, he's not from Seline."

"What does he look like?"

"He's fairly bulky, but that could be the robe. I couldn't really see very much of his face. That beard of his seems to start just underneath his lower eyelids."

"Is his hair blond? I mean, does he look like an ordinary Alorn?"

"No. He's very dark. His hair and beard are almost coal black."

"That doesn't really mean anything. There are a lot of dark-haired Drasnians and Algars. Does Gelane go there often?"

"Almost every night."

"I'll follow him this evening, then. I want to have a look at this shaggy priest of Belar. Go on back home, Pol. I'll stay away from Gelane's shop today. Suspicion's built into Bear-cultists, and if Gelane gets any hint that I'm around, he might decide to skip this evening's meeting."

I loafed around Seline for the rest of the day, keeping my eyes and ears open and my mouth shut. Now that I knew what I was looking for, picking out members of the Bear-cult wasn't too hard. They were all Alorns, of course, and they had that shifty-eyed, nervous suspicion and overdramatic caution about them that stupid people with secrets to hide all seem to share.

The thing that baffled me was the fact that there was a chapter of the cult anywhere at all in Sendaria. Sendars, no matter what their racial background, are just too sensible to get caught up in that kind of fanaticism.

I loitered in the street outside Gelane's barrel works as evening descended on Seline. It was just getting dark when he emerged furtively from the shop with a canvas sack over his shoulder. Gelane was in his late thirties by now, and the slenderness he'd shown as a child had been replaced by a stocky muscularity. Inevitably, he was now sporting a beard. All Bear-cultists wear beards, for some reason. He started down the street toward the lakeshore, and I went off in the other direction. I knew where he was going, so I didn't really have to follow him every step of the way.

I went out one of the other gates, chose the form of a barn owl, and flew on ahead, so I reached the meeting place in that grove of trees a quarter of an hour before Gelane did. The cultists who were already there were shambling around the fire in that peculiar swaying walk that Bear-cultists seem to think approximates the walk of a bear. I've seen a lot of bears in my time, and I've never seen one walk that way. Actually, you very seldom see a bear trying to walk on its hind feet at all.

The Alorns were chanting all the usual slogans in unison. I guess idiocy's more fun when it's shared, and there's nothing in this world that's more idiotic than the Bear-cult. I've never understood the idea behind choral chanting, but it always seems to comfort religious fanatics of whatever stripe.

When Gelane, now wearing his own bearskin tunic, arrived, the other cultists all bowed low to him, proclaiming—again in unison—"All hail the Rivan King, Godslayer, and Overlord of the West. Where he leads us, we will follow."

The secret that Pol and I had so carefully kept for almost nine hundred years was obviously out of the bag now. I started muttering curses, savagely biting them off with my hooked beak.

When I finally got my anger under control, I carefully probed the minds of the individual cultists gathered around their hero. Most of them were just the usual dimwitted Alorns that have always filled the ranks of the cult. A couple of them, however, were not. I picked the word "Kahsha" out of their thoughts, and Kahsha is the mountain in the Desert of Araga that's the headquarters of the Dagashi. Chamdar had finally gotten ahead of me. I started swearing again.

Then the Priest of Belar arrived. As Pol had told me, his shaggy beard covered most of his face, but it didn't hide his eyes—those angular-shaped eyes of the typical Angarak. How could Gelane and the other Alorns around that fire have been so stupid that they hadn't noticed that? When the robed priest reached the fire and I could make out his face more clearly, I redoubled my swearing.

The Priest of Belar who'd led Iron-grip's heir astray was Chamdar himself.

It all fell in around my ears at that point. The Dagashi in the Nyissan robe back in Tol Honeth had known exactly what he was doing. Chamdar would *not* have gone running off to Tol Honeth or to any other city in the West in response to my carefully arranged fashion statement, because Chamdar had known where Pol and Gelane were all the time. I'd just wasted better than half a year persuading ladies all over the Western Kingdoms to duplicate Pol's distinctive trademark, and it hadn't accomplished a thing. This time Chamdar had tricked *me!*

"You'd better get here right away, Pol." I sent the thought out as a whisper—largely because Chamdar was no more than twenty feet from the tree where I was perched. Fortunately, he was talking to the cultists at the time, so he didn't hear me.

He was in the process of pronouncing a benediction on the Rivan King, "who shall lead us into the Kingdoms of the South, where all whom we meet shall be converted to the worship of the Bear God."

Then Gelane started to talk, and I saw no evidence whatsoever of that self-effacing modesty that's been the predominant characteristic of his family since the time of Prince Geran. Gelane was obviously very full of himself. "Behold!" he declaimed. "I am the Godslayer of whom the prophecies speak. I, Gelane, am the Rivan King, and Overlord of the West, and I call upon the Kingdoms of the West to submit to me. Where I lead, you *will* follow, and all of Angarak will tremble before me."

That went on for quite some time, and he was still admiring himself when Pol arrived.

Just to set the record straight here, let me say at this point that Gelane's descent into idiocy wasn't his own idea. Garion can give you a very detailed description of just how subtly Chamdar can take over somebody else's mind. At Faldor's farm when he was growing up, Garion probably saw Asharak the Murgo about every other week, and he was prevented from telling anyone about it. The process is an old Grolim trick that's been kicking around in Angarak societies since before the cracking of the world. The absurdities implicit in the Angarak religion almost demand that the Grolims have *some* means to control the thoughts of others. Now that I think about it, though, *all* religions do that—except mine, of course.

Polgara had wisely chosen the form of the brownish-colored spotted owl when she came to that grove to join me. White birds *do* tend to stick out in the dark. She settled onto the limb beside me and listened to Gelane's extended self-congratulation without comment.

"The so-called Priest of Belar is Chamdar, Pol," I whispered to her.

"So *that's* what he looks like," she replied, her hooked beak clicking. "What now, father?"

"I was hoping *you* could come up with an idea. I'm at my wits' end on this one. Chamdar's got Gelane totally under his control at this point. We *have* to break him clear of that control."

"There's something that *might* work," she said. She sat looking at Gelane with those huge, unblinking eyes. "Are you willing to gamble?"

"My whole life's been a gamble, Pol."

"Yes. I've noticed. I used something back at Vo Wacune once when an Asturian spy had wormed his way into the duke's confidence. Chamdar's a Grolim, though, so there might be some way he can counter it. If Gelane's completely under Chamdar's domination, he won't believe anything we tell him about his Master, will he?"

"Probably not. What have you got in mind?"

"Chamdar's got to expose himself, then."

"How do you plan to manage that?"

"All I have to do is make Chamdar's thoughts audible. That's how I persuaded the Wacite duke that his new friend wasn't all he seemed to be. The Asturian spy was only an ordinary man, though. This might not work on a Grolim."

"You'd better give it a try, Pol. Otherwise I'm going to have to do something fairly serious to Gelane."

"Just how serious, father?"

"We *can't* have Iron-grip's heir under Chamdar's control. That's unthinkable. I might have to erase most of Gelane's mind. He won't be able to make barrels any more, but he'll still be able to father children."

"You can *do* that?"

"Yes, I can. I wouldn't like it much, though."

"That's going too far, father."

"We don't have any choice, Pol. We've lost heirs before. It's the line that's important, not individuals, and the line must *not* be under Grolim domination."

I think *that* notion made Pol concentrate all the harder. There are some limitations on what you can do when you're not in your natural form, so she swooped to earth behind the tree we'd been perched in and changed back.

I tend to be a little noisy when I use the Will and the Word—out of sheer arrogance, most likely—but Pol's always been very subtle. Even though I knew in a general sort of way what she was going to do, I could scarcely hear so much as a whisper when she released her Will with a single murmured Word.

Gelane was still spouting gibberish, telling his fellow cultists what a great fellow he was, when a new voice overrode his. He faltered, and then he stopped talking entirely.

The voice was Chamdar's, but Chamdar's lips weren't moving. The sound of that voice seemed to come from just over his head, and he appeared not to realize that his thoughts had just become audible. "Ctuchik will reward me if I kill this dolt," that hollow-sounding voice mused, "but Torak himself will reward me even more if my plan works. As soon as I have this feebleminded Alorn completely in my power, I'll take him to Riva, and he can seize Cthrag Yaska. Then I'll chain him and deliver him to the Dragon God to kneel and deliver that accursed jewel to Torak as a sign of his submission. So great a service *must* be rewarded. I will become the Dragon God's fourth disciple—and his most favored. I *will* be first disciple, and Ctuchik and Urvon and Zedar will be compelled to bow down to me. Torak will gain Lordship and dominion over all the world as the result of my gift, and I shall sit at his right hand for all of eternity as my just reward."

I actually heard the sound when Chamdar's hold on Gelane's mind was broken. We'd had a few hints in the past that Gelane was moderately talented, and Chamdar's audible musings were enough to bring him to his senses. With a great wrench, Gelane tore his mind free, and the full significance of what had happened came crashing in on him. The noise was absolutely awful.

Then, since he was Alorn, Gelane's reaction was fairly predictable. He advanced on the startled Grolim with blazing eyes and with murder in his heart.

"What are you *doing?*" Chamdar's voice was shrill.

Gelane answered with his fist. He struck Ctuchik's underling with a blow that would have felled an ox.

I've speculated any number of times about how the course of history might have been changed if Gelane had been carrying an axe that night. In the long run, though, I guess the fact that he wasn't worked out for the best.

Chamdar reeled back, his eyes glazed and his Will evaporating. He fell heavily to the ground, and the pair of pseudo-Alorns from Ashaba immediately jumped in to protect their employer. I was just about to take steps, but the other cultists beat me to it. They'd sworn fealty to Gelane, and that's a religious obligation in the Bear-cult. They swarmed all over the two Dagashi. The confusion, however, gave Chamdar time to recover his senses and make good his escape. He translocated himself to the edge of the grove, took wing, and flew off into the night.

"We've been tricked!" Gelane roared. "That was no Priest of Belar!"

"What are we to do, Godslayer?" a cultist demanded in a helpless voice.

"Don't *ever* call me that again!" Gelane screamed at him. "I'm *not* the Godslayer! This was all a trick! I've dishonored my name!" He tore off his bearskin tunic and threw it into the fire. "The Bear-cult is a lie and a deception! I'll have no further part in it!"

"Let's find that false priest and kill him!" one big fellow shouted, and, since they were Alorns, they tried to do that. They floundered around in the woods for a half an hour or so, but Chamdar was miles away by then.

Finally they gave up and returned to the fire. "What do we do now, your Majesty?" the big Alorn demanded.

"First off, we'll all forget about that 'your Majesty' business," Gelane replied. "I'm *not* the Rivan King, so don't any of you ever call me that again." He straightened. "I'll have your oaths on that. No word of this must ever leak out. From now on, I'm just Gelane the cooper, and nothing else. Will you swear?"

Naturally they swore. What else could they do?

"Now go home to your families!" he commanded. "Get rid of those stinking bearskins, go back to your lives, and forget that any of this ever happened."

"What about that Grolim?" the big belligerent fellow demanded. "The one who pretended to be the Priest of Belar?"

"My family will deal with him," Gelane replied. "Now go home."

And then, when they were all gone, Iron-grip's heir fell facedown on the ground, weeping uncontrollably in shame and remorse.

Now that Gelane had recovered his senses, he was so overcome with guilt that he was virtually incoherent. "How could I have been so foolish, grandfather?" he wept. "I'm unworthy! I'm unfit to bear my name! I've betrayed everything we stand for!"

"Oh, stop that!" I told him. "It doesn't accomplish a thing."

"Who *was* that man, grandfather?"

"His name's Chamdar, and he's a Grolim priest. Couldn't you tell from the shape of his eyes that he's an Angarak?"

"This is Sendaria, father," Polgara told me. "People don't pay that much attention to race here."

"Perhaps, but Gelane should have realized that somebody with an Angarak heritage couldn't possibly be a Priest of Belar." I looked rather sternly at my grandson. "How did he get such a hold on you, Gelane?" I demanded.

"Flattery," he replied in a tone of self-contempt. "Sometimes I wish that Aunt Pol had never told me about who I really am. That's what made it so easy for that Grolim to get his hands on my soul."

"What's your identity got to do with it?" I demanded.

"I'm not really a very important person here in Seline, grandfather. People who come into my shop to buy barrels treat me like some kind of servant. Back during the war, when Mother and Aunt Pol and I were at the Stronghold and Kal Torak was besieging the place, some of the people there treated me with a great deal of respect because they knew that I was really the Rivan King. Here in Seline, I'm just another tradesman. Who respects a barrel-maker? When some brewer or wine merchant starts putting on airs, I sort of wrap myself in my real identity. It keeps me from feeling small and insignificant. That's how the Grolim captured me."

"You didn't tell him, did you?"

"He already knew. He came into my shop one day, and he bowed to me and hailed me as the Rivan King. He told me that he was a Priest of Belar and that the auguries had told him who I really was. Nobody'd called me 'your Majesty' since we all left the Stronghold, and it went to my head."

"That's the way it usually works, Gelane," I told him. "More people have been tripped up by their own hubris than you could possibly imagine."

"Hubris?"

"Overweening pride. It's when you get so impressed with yourself that your head stops working. That little speech you were making here this evening was a fair indication of it. You're not the first to be infected with it, and you probably won't be the last. How did Chamdar get you involved with the Bear-cult?"

"He worked his way up to it gradually. At first all he talked about was how I ought to go to Riva to claim my throne. He said that all of Aloria was waiting for me."

"That's probably true, Gelane," Pol told him, "but Aloria doesn't know that it's waiting. We've kept your family fairly well hidden for a long time now."

"*He* seemed to know all about it."

"Naturally," I replied. "The Grolims have prophecies of their own. We've been able to hide you, but we couldn't keep your existence a secret. Chamdar's been tearing the world apart looking for your family for about three centuries."

"I'll kill him!" Gelane said fiercely, stretching forth his hands in a hungry sort of gesture.

"No," I disagreed, "actually you won't. That's my job, not yours. Your job is to stay out of sight. What you're going to do right now is go back to town and start packing. You're going to take your wife and your mother and go down the deepest hole your Aunt and I can find for you." I thought about it for a moment. "Val Alorn, I think."

"You're not *serious!*" Pol objected.

"Val Alorn isn't so bad, Pol, and Chamdar can't hide his race from the Chereks the way he hid it from the Sendars. Chereks are usually blond, and with that black beard and those funny-shaped eyes, Chamdar'd definitely stick out on the streets of Val Alorn. King Eldrig's got a standing reward for the head of any Angarak found in his kingdom.

It's a sizable amount of money, and that encourages the Chereks to keep their eyes open for foreigners. I'll have a talk with Eldrig, and we'll pick some village where no veterans of the war in Arendia live."

Gelane looked puzzled.

"Your grandfather and I were a little conspicuous at Vo Mimbre, Gelane," Pol explained. "Someone who'd been there might recognize me, and Chereks talk too much when they get drunk—which happens almost every night, I've noticed."

"Let's go back a bit here," I said to Gelane. "Exactly how did Chamdar enlist you in the Bear-cult?"

"He started out by warning me that I have to be very careful, because there are all sorts of people looking for me, and they don't all look like Angaraks. He said that the only people I can really trust are Alorns. Then he said that there was a religious order in the Alorn kingdoms that's sworn to protect me and to see to it that I can take my rightful place on the throne in the Hall of the Rivan King. My head was so swollen up by then that I even made it easy for him. I said that I wanted to meet these people who were so devoted to me, but he told me that Bear-cultists are forbidden to reveal their affiliation with the cult to anybody who wasn't a member. Would you believe that I actually volunteered to join at that point?"

"He led you into it rather carefully, Gelane," I replied. "Every time you accepted something he told you, his hold on you grew stronger. Grolims are very good at that. By the time you volunteered to join the cult, he'd have been able to get you to do almost anything."

"Were the other Alorns from Seline really cult members?"

"They probably thought they were, but I doubt that any real cultists even knew that they existed. The cult doesn't have much of a following here in Sendaria. This little group in Seline was living in a vacuum, totally isolated from the rest of the cult, and I'd imagine that Chamdar added quite a few items that aren't a part of standard cult dogma. Just to be on the safe side, though, I think I'll have a talk with the Alorn kings. I think it might be time for the cult to be put down again." I looked around at the trees. "We've got things to do. Why don't we go back to town?"

"In a moment, father," Pol said. "Chamdar had Gelane almost totally under his control for several months. I want to make sure that his hold's completely broken."

"That's probably not a bad idea, Pol," I agreed.

"This won't hurt, Gelane," she assured him. Then she reached out and took his right hand—the one with that characteristic mark on the palm—and touched it to the white lock in her hair. Her eyes grew momentarily distant, and Gelane's went very wide. I got the distinct impression that their minds had never overtly touched before. Then Polgara lightly kissed his cheek. "A few hints is about all, father," she told me, "and they're already fading. I doubt that Chamdar could compel him to raise even one finger right now."

"Good. Let's head back to town and start getting you packed. We'll set out for the capital at Sendar first thing in the morning. I'll find some Cherek sea captain and arrange passage to Val Alorn."

"Through the *Bore?*" Pol said with some distaste.

"It's the shortest way to get there, Pol, and I want to get back as soon as I can. I'd like to run Chamdar to ground someplace and get him out of our hair once and for all."

"*Yes!*" Gelane said fervently.

It didn't work out that way, of course. Asharak the Murgo had something very important still left to do. His death was the thing that opened Garion's mind and set him on the course to where he is right now.

This is not to say that I didn't spend a couple of years looking for the elusive Grolim. I finally gave up in disgust and went back to the Vale. Pol, Gelane, and their little family took up residence in a small farming village about ten miles outside Val Alorn, and they were fairly safe there—if anyplace in the world was truly safe for Iron-grip's heir.

Beldin had returned from Mallorea during the course of my search for Ctuchik's underling, and he stopped by my tower on the morning after I finally got back home. He said some very uncomplimentary things to me after I told him about how Chamdar'd tricked me, but I didn't really take offense—I'd already said things to myself that were far worse. I let him ramble on until he started repeating himself, and then I cut in. "What's happening in Mallorea?" I asked him.

"Do you remember that young man in Mal Zeth that I told you about?" he replied. "The grandson of the old emperor Torak deposed when he left Ashaba?"

"Vaguely. His name's Korzeth, isn't it?"

"That's the name they gave him when he was born. There are a lot of people in Mallorea who are calling him other names right now, though. When he turned fourteen, he set his grandfather aside and took the crown for himself. In some ways, he's as cold-blooded as Torak himself. I don't know why he wanted the throne. He never sits on it. He's spending all his time in the saddle now, and he's reunifying Mallorea. The whole continent's running ankle-deep in blood. Korzeth doesn't even bother to ask people if they want to accept his rule. He just kills everybody in sight. He'll have an empire when he's done. There won't be very many people in it, but he'll own all the ground, at least."

"I'd say that sort of diminishes the Mallorean threat," I noted approvingly. "Is Zedar still holed up in that cave with Torak's body?"

"He was, the last time I looked. I flew over there on my way home."

"Are the Murgos doing anything worth mentioning?"

"Fortifying the walls of their cities is about all. I think they're expecting an invasion."

"Why would we want to do that? We accomplished everything we needed to at Vo Mimbre."

"The Murgos aren't so much worried about us as they are about Ran Borune. After those two disasters, there aren't really very many Murgos left, and they *do* have all those gold mines. I guess they expect Ran Borune to start biting large chunks out of the middle of Cthol Murgos."

"Any idea of what Ctuchik's up to?"

"Haven't got a clue. As far as I know, he's holed up at Rak Cthol. Urvon's made it back to Mal Yaska, and he's sitting tight, as well. I think that Vo Mimbre persuaded the Angaraks to give peace a chance."

"Good. I need a rest anyway. Have you got any definite plans?"

"I think I'll go back to southern Cthol Murgos and keep an eye on Zedar. If he decides to move old Burnt-face, I'd like to know about it."

After Beldin left, I loafed around my tower, intermittently cleaning up several decades' worth of dust and debris. I didn't make a major project out of it, though. I usually can find something more interesting to do than housecleaning.

I'd been home for about a month when the twins came over to my tower one fine morning in late spring. "We've found something rather puzzling in the Darine, Belgarath," Beltira told me.

"Oh?"

"It mentions a couple of 'helpers.' They won't be as significant as the Guide or the Horse-Lord or any of the others, but they *will* be making a contribution."

"I'll take all the help I can get. What's so puzzling about them?"

"As closely as we can make out, they're going to be Nadraks."

"Nadraks?" I was a bit startled by that. "Why would any Angaraks want to help us?"

"The Darine doesn't say, and we haven't found the corresponding passage in the Mrin yet."

I thought about it for a few moments. "Nadraks have never really been all that fond of Murgos or Thulls," I mused. "Now that Torak's been put to sleep, they might decide to strike out on their own. I'm not doing anything right now, anyway. Maybe I ought to go have a look."

"These 'helpers' won't have emerged yet," Belkira pointed out. "And we don't know anything at all about the families they'll descend from."

"You're probably right there," I admitted, "but if I nose around a bit, I might be able to get a sense of the general sentiments among the Nadraks."

"It couldn't hurt, I suppose," Beltira agreed.

"I'll check in with you from time to time," I promised. "Let me know if you find anything in the Mrin. A few more details might help me to locate those families."

There wasn't anything particularly urgent about this project, as far as I could tell, so I stopped by the Stronghold as I went north and bought a horse. There's quite a bit of effort involved in traveling the other way, and I was feeling a little lazy.

It took me several weeks to reach Boktor, which the Drasnians were busy rebuilding. In a certain sense, Kal Torak had done the Drasnians a favor when he destroyed all their cities. Alorn cities have always tended to sprawl out, and the streets follow whichever cowpath happens to be handy. Now the Drasnians had the chance to start fresh and actually plan their cities. I found Rhodar conferring with a number of architects. They were having a fairly heated discussion about boulevards, as I recall. One school favored wide, straight streets. The other preferred narrow, crooked ones, justifying the inconvenience with the word "coziness."

"What do you think, Belgarath?" Rhodar asked me.

"It all depends on whether you want to build another Tol Honeth or another Val Alorn, I guess," I replied.

"Tol Honeth, I think," Rhodar said. "Tolnedrans have always looked down their noses at us because of the way our cities look. I get very tired of being referred to as 'quaint.' "

"Have you had any contacts with the Nadraks since the war?" I asked him.

"Nothing official. There's a little bit of trade along the border, and there are always gold hunters in the Nadrak Mountains. The gold deposits aren't as extensive as the ones in southern Cthol Murgos, but there's enough gold up there to attract people from other countries."

That gave me an idea. "I think you've just solved a problem for me, Rhodar."

"Oh?"

"I need to have a look around over there in Gar og Nadrak, and I'd like to be sort of inconspicuous. The Nadraks are probably used to seeing foreigners up in those mountains, so I think I'll get a pick and shovel and go looking for gold."

"That's very tedious work, Belgarath."

"Not the way I'm going to do it."

"I didn't quite follow that."

"I'm not really all that interested in gold. All I'm going to do is wander around asking questions. The tools will explain why I'm there."

"Have fun," he said. "Now, if you'll excuse me, I've got a city to build."

I bought some tools and a pack mule and set out across the moors toward the Nadrak border. It was early summer by now, and the usually dreary Drasnian moors were all abloom, so travel was actually pleasant.

The Angaraks had been so soundly defeated at Vo Mimbre that their societies had virtually disintegrated, so there weren't any guards at the border crossing. I was fairly sure that I was being watched, but my pack mule with all those tools on its back explained my presence, so the Nadraks let me pass without any interference.

I followed the North Caravan Route, and the first town I came to was Yar Gurak, which isn't really a town but more in the nature of a mining camp. It squats on either side of a muddy creek, and most of the buildings are slapdash affairs, half log and half canvas tenting. I've passed through it several times in the past five centuries, and it hasn't really changed very much. Silk goes there quite often, and he and Garion and I passed through on our way to Cthol Mishrak for Garion's meeting with Torak. Nobody really lives in Yar Gurak for any extended period of time, so they aren't civic-minded enough to bother with building more permanent structures. I set up my tent at the far end of a muddy street, and without very much effort I blended into the population. The mining camps in the mountains of Gar og Nadrak are very cosmopolitan, and it's considered bad manners to ask personal questions.

There were certain frictions, of course. We *had* just come through a war, after all, but aside from a few tavern brawls, things were relatively peaceful. The people living in Yar Gurak were looking for gold, not for fights. After I'd been there for a few days and my face had become fairly well known, I began to frequent the large tavern that was the center of what passed for social life in Yar Gurak. I passed myself off as a Sendar, since Sendars are so racially mixed that my peculiar background and slightly alien features didn't attract much attention.

While there were a fair number of solitary gold hunters operating out of Yar Gurak, it was far more common for the adventurers living there to set out for the mountains in twos and threes. There weren't any laws in that part of the world, and it was safer to have friends around—just in case you happened to be lucky enough actually to find gold. There are always people around who feel that stealing is easier than digging.

I struck up an acquaintanceship with a bluff, good-natured Nadrak named Rablek. Rablek had returned to Yar Gurak for supplies, then he lingered awhile for beer and companionship. He'd been in partnership with a Tolnedran the previous year, but he and his friend had strayed up into Morindland and a passing band of Morinds had rather casually removed his partner's head. After we'd gotten to know each other, he finally made the offer I'd been waiting for. We were sitting in the tavern drinking that rather fruity-tasting Nadrak beer, and he looked across the table at me. He was a rangy fellow with coarse black hair and a scruffy-looking beard. "You seem like a sensible sort of fellow, Garath," he said. "What would you say to the notion that we team up and go out looking for gold together?"

Notice that I'd reverted to my original name. I've done that from time to time. Assumed names can be awkward, particularly if you forget which one you're using. I squinted at him. "Do you snore?" I asked him.

"Can't say for sure. I'm usually asleep when that's supposed to happen. I've never had any complaints, though."

"We could give it a try, I suppose," I said. "If it turns out that we can't get along, we can always break off the partnership and go our separate ways."

"Are you any good in a fight? I'm not trying to pry, understand, but sometimes we might need to defend whatever we find out there."

"I can usually handle my own end of a fight."

"That's good enough for me. Equal shares?"

"Naturally."

"That's it, then. I'm willing to give it a try if you are. I'll come by your tent tomorrow morning, and we can get out of this place. I've just about satisfied my hunger for civilization."

I'd picked up a few hints about Rablek during the course of our conversations. He'd been pressed into military service during the recent war, and he'd been one of the few Nadraks to escape the carnage at Vo Mimbre. He'd opinions, and he wasn't the sort to keep them to himself. After we'd been in the mountains for a few days, he started to open up, and I picked up a great deal of information about him—and about other Nadraks, as well. He assured me that all Nadraks despised Murgos, for one thing, and that they felt much the same way about Malloreans. Rablek habitually spat every time he mentioned the name of Kal Torak. Though my partner didn't come right out and say it in so many words, I got the impression that he'd had some disagreements with Grolims in the past, and Rablek was quick with his knife when somebody irritated him. Ctuchik might have thoroughly cowed the Murgos and Thulls, but his Grolims had at best an only tenuous hold on the Nadraks. From what Rablek told me, I could see that it really wouldn't pay a Grolim to go anywhere in Gar og Nadrak by himself. Rablek suggested that all sorts of accidents had a way of happening to lone Grolims in the forests and mountains of that northernmost Angarak kingdom.

The more I talked with Rablek, the more I came to understand that curious passage in the Darine Codex. Angarak society was not nearly as monolithic as it appeared to be, and if anybody was going to break away, it was almost certain to be the Nadraks.

And then, if you can believe it, we found gold! We were up at the northern end of the mountains, not far from that indeterminate boundary of Morindland, and we were following a turbulent mountain stream that boiled and tumbled over large boulders and formed deep swirling pools of frothy green water. It was at that point that I discovered a hitherto un-realized aspect of what my brothers and I routinely refer to as "talent." I could *feel* the presence of gold!

I looked around. It was there; I knew it was there. "It looks to be coming on toward evening," I said to my partner. "Why don't we set up camp here and rinse out a few shovelfuls of gravel before it gets dark?"

Rablek looked around. "It doesn't look all that promising to me," he said.

"We'll never know for sure until we try it."

He shrugged. "Why not?"

I let *him* find the first few nuggets. I didn't want to give away *too* much, after all. What we'd found were some fairly extensive deposits of free gold the stream had carried down from farther up in the mountains and deposited in those pools of relatively calm water.

We made a fortune there. It's one of the few times in my life I've ever actually been rich. We settled in and built a crude shack, and we worked that merry little creek from one end to the other. Winter came, but we didn't move. We couldn't do much work during that season, but we weren't about to go off and leave our diggings. We got snowed in, natu-rally, and Rablek opened up more and more during those long months. I picked up a great deal of information from him during that winter, and the gold was in the nature of a bonus.

Then spring came, and with it came a band of marauding Morindim. We'd put out the usual pestilence-markers and curse-markers as a precau-tion, but this particular band had a young apprentice magician with them, and he knew enough about his trade to neutralize our markers.

"This isn't turning out very well, Garath," Rablek said somberly, star-ing out through a crack in the wall of our cabin at the twenty or so fur-clad Morindim advancing on us. "We're going to have those savages inside here with us before long."

We both had bows, of course, but a winter of hunting deer had se-verely depleted our supply of arrows.

I started to swear. "How broad-minded are you feeling, Rablek?" I asked.

"Not so much so that I'm ready to welcome twenty Morind houseguests."

"I think I'd draw the line there myself. I'm going to do something a little out of the ordinary. Don't get excited."

"If you can come up with a way to run those animals off, I think I'll be able to control myself."

I didn't have time to explain, and there was no way I could hide what I was doing from my partner. I carefully formed the image of a medium-size demon in my mind and crammed myself into it.

Rablek jumped back, his eyes bulging.

"Stay here!" I growled at him in that soul-chilling voice of the demon. "Don't come outside, and you'd better not watch. This is going to get worse." Then I crashed out through our crude door to face the advancing Morindim.

As I think I've indicated, the Morind magician was an inexperienced and callow youth. He might have been able to raise an imp the size of a mouse, but anything beyond that was far beyond his capability. Just to add to his chagrin, I expanded the image in which I was encased until I had the appearance of a full-grown Demon-Lord.

The Morindim fled, screaming in terror. The magician, I noticed, led the flight. He was young, and he ran very fast.

Then I resumed my own form and returned to the shack.

"Just who *are* you, Garath?" Rablek demanded in a trembling voice as I came through the splinters of our door.

"I'm your partner, Rablek. That's all you really need to know, isn't it? You and I came up here to get rich. Why don't we get at that before we lose any more daylight?"

He started to shake violently. "Where's my mind been for all these months? I should have recognized the name. You're not just Garath. You're *Bel*garath, aren't you?"

"It's no great thing, partner." I tried to calm him. "It's only a name, after all, and I haven't done anything to harm *you*, have I?"

"Well—not yet, I guess." He didn't sound very convinced. "I've heard a lot of stories about you, though."

"I can imagine. Most of them are just Grolim propaganda, partner. I've had occasion to disrupt Grolim schemes now and then in the past, and they've had to invent some very wild stories to explain their failures."

"Are you really as old as they say you are?"

"Probably older."

"What are you doing in Gar og Nadrak?"

I grinned at him. "Getting rich, I hope. Isn't that why we're both out here in this wilderness?"

"You've got that part right."

"We're still partners then?"

"I wouldn't have it any other way, Belgarath. Did you just conjure up all this gold we've been finding?"

"No. It's a natural deposit of real gold, and it's just laying there waiting for us to pick it up."

He grinned back at me. "Well, then, partner, why don't we get back to picking?"

"Why don't we?" I agreed.

CHAPTER FORTY-SIX

There's a kind of irresistible lure about gold—and I'm not just talking about the red-tinted gold of Angarak that the Grolims use to buy the souls of men like the Earl of Jarvik. By midsummer, Rablek and I had accumulated more gold than our horses could carry, but we still lingered beside that tumbling mountain stream "for just one more day."

I finally managed to clamp a lid on my own hunger for more, but it took me another week to persuade my partner that it was time to leave. "Be reasonable, Rablek," I told him. "You've already got more gold than you can possibly spend in a lifetime, and if you're really all *that* desperate, you know how to find this place again. You can come back and dig up more, if you really want to."

"I just hate to leave any behind," he replied.

"It's not going to go anyplace, Rablek. It'll be here forever, if you happen to need it."

I know that it sounds unnatural, but I liked my Nadrak partner. He was a bit crude and rough-hewn, but I'm no angel myself, so we got along well together. He wasn't afraid of work, and when the sun went down and we'd laid aside our tools, he could talk for hours, and I didn't mind listening. He'd been a little wild-eyed and standoffish after our encounter with the Morindim, but he got over that, and the pair of us went back to just being a couple of fellows out to make our fortunes. We both forgot about the fact that we were supposed to be natural enemies and concentrated instead on getting rich.

Anyway, we tore down our shack, concealed the traces of our diggings as best we could, and started back to Yar Gurak. "What do you plan to do with all your money?" I asked my partner on the night before we reached the shabby mining camp.

"I think I'll go into the fur trade," he replied. "There's a lot of money to be made there."

"You've already got a lot of money."

"Money doesn't mean very much unless you put it to work for you, Belgarath. I'm not the sort to just lie around getting fat, and I know some fur traders who double their money every year or two."

"If you've already got more than you can spend, why bother?"

"It's the game, Belgarath," he said with a shrug. "Money's just a way of keeping score. I'm going into the fur trade for the sake of the game, not for the money."

That opened my eyes and gave me a profound insight into the Nadrak character. At last I understood why Nadraks dislike Murgos so much.

Never mind. It's much too complicated to explain.

Rablek and I parted company on the outskirts of Yar Gurak. I saw no real reason to go back into that ugly place. Moreover, I had a great deal of gold in my pack-saddle, and I didn't want any curious people rifling through it while I was asleep.

"It was fun, wasn't it, Belgarath?" Rablek said just a bit wistfully as we were saddling our horses.

"That it was, my friend."

"If you ever get bored, look me up. The mountains'll always be there, and I can be ready to go again any time you say the word."

"Be well, Rablek," I said, clasping his hand warmly.

The Nadrak border was still unguarded, and I entered Drasnia with a certain sense of relief. I was a bit surprised to discover that my sudden riches had made me nervous and apprehensive. What a peculiar thing! When I was no more than a poor vagabond, I'd been willing to go anywhere without a second thought. Now that I was rich, my whole attitude had changed.

I rode on down through Algaria at the tag end of the summer of the year 4881, and I reached the Vale just as autumn was turning all the leaves golden. The color suited my mood and reflected the cargo in my pack-saddle. Rablek and I had put the fruits of our labors into stout canvas bags, and I had forty of those bags. It took me hours to carry them all up into my tower.

The next day I built a makeshift kind of forge and cast my gold into bars. Forty bags of gold sounds like a lot, but gold's so heavy that the bars weren't really all that big, and when I'd stacked them all in one corner, the pile was disappointingly small. I sat looking at it, idly wondering if I could catch up with Rablek before he left Yar Gurak. There was still a lot of gold left in our creek up there near the border of Morindland, after all.

Well, of *course* I was greedy. I've told you about the kind of person I was before I entered my Master's service, and some things never change. I've thought about that a lot over the years. Every so often I get a powerful urge to return to that nameless little stream. Then, however, usually in the cold grey light of morning, rationality rears its ugly head. What on earth does a man in my situation need with money? If I really want something, I can usually get it somehow—or make it. In the long run, that'd be much easier than digging gold out of the ground. But gold's so pretty to look at, and so exciting when you find it.

Over the years, I've spent a few bars of my horde, but not very many. Most of it's still around here—someplace.

Excuse me a moment. I think I'll root around and see if I can find it.

About a year after I'd returned from Gar og Nadrak, Pol sent word to me that Gelane's wife, Enalla, had finally given birth to a son. They'd been married for about twenty years at that point, and Gelane was approaching his fortieth birthday. Enalla's childlessness had caused all of us quite a bit of concern. In the light of the significance of that particular family, I'm sure you can see why. Considering the forces at work, we probably shouldn't have worried, but we did all the same. I journeyed up to Cherek to have a look at my new grandson, and I found that he looked very much as his father had as a baby—another indication of those forces I just mentioned.

I'm sure you noticed that in my own mind I'd long since discarded all those tedious "great-great's." To me, that long string of sandy-haired little boys were simply grandsons. I loved them all in just about the same way.

Polgara, however, loved each of them a bit differently, some more, some less. For any number of reasons, she was particularly close to Gelane, and she was absolutely devastated when he died in the year 4902, exactly nine hundred years after the murder of King Gorek. The twins felt the date to be highly significant, and they tore the Mrin apart trying to find something hinting at what it meant. Garion's silent friend, however, had remained just that—silent.

I don't think any of us fully realized just how much Polgara had suffered during those seemingly endless centuries and losses. My primary concern had been with the line, not the individuals. My relationship with those heirs had been sketchy at best, and their passings hadn't really touched me all that much. I could be fairly philosophical about it. I'd grown used to the fact that people are born, they grow up, and then they die. Everybody loses a few family members if he lives long enough, but Pol's situation was unique. She'd been intimately involved with all those little boys, and she'd lost them by the score in the course of those nine centuries; grief's not something you're *ever* going to get used to.

I went back to Cherek after Gelane died and took a long, hard look at his son. Then I sighed and went away. He wasn't the one we'd been waiting for.

The years continued their stately, ordered procession, and things were quiet in the West for a change. That disastrous defeat at Vo Mimbre had subdued the Angaraks, and they largely left us alone. Chamdar was still lurking around somewhere, but he wasn't making enough noise to attract my attention, and I was fairly certain that he wouldn't appear in Cherek to give Polgara any problems. Chereks are, almost by definition, the most primitive, archetypical Alorns. Drasnians have established a somewhat wary relationship with the Nadraks, and Algars can tolerate the Thulls, but Chereks steadfastly maintain a stiff-necked racial prejudice against *all* Angaraks. Occasionally I've tried to explain to any number of Chereks why prejudice isn't particularly commendable, but I don't believe I've ever gotten through to any of them, largely because I think that Belar got to them first. Don't get me wrong here, I *liked* Belar, but, ye Gods, he was stubborn! I sometimes think that the Cherek hatred of all Angaraks is divinely inspired. It suited our purposes during those years, however, since it most definitely kept Chamdar away from Polgara.

The Third Borune Dynasty went on and on; that, all by itself, strongly hinted that something important was in the wind. The Mrin was fairly specific about the fact that the Godslayer's wife was going to be a Borune princess.

Things had begun to deteriorate in Arendia. The peace we'd imposed on Asturia and Mimbre by marrying Mayaserana to Korodullin began to come apart at the seams, largely, I think, because the Mimbrates refused to recognize the titles of the Asturian nobility. That offended the hot-headed Asturians, and there were any number of ugly incidents during the fiftieth century.

Prosperity returned to Sendaria when the yearly Algar cattle drives to Muros resumed. The limited trade on the Isle of the Winds was reestablished, but foreign merchants still were not allowed inside the city of Riva. The Ulgos didn't change at all, but Ulgos never do. The Tolnedran merchant princes in Tol Honeth had looked upon the Ulgo participation in the war against Kal Torak as a good sign, hoping that the Ulgos might loosen some of their restrictions on trade. The Ulgos, however, went back to Prolgu, descended into their caves, and slammed the door behind them.

The Nyissans grew increasingly sulky, since their economy was largely based on the slave trade, and when there are no battles, there aren't any new slaves. Nyissans *always* pout during an extended period of peace.

Korzeth had completed the reunification of Mallorea—sort of. He delivered a nominally unified empire to his son, but the actual business of welding Mallorea together was accomplished by the Melcene bureaucracy and its policy of including *all* the subject people in the government.

Kell, like Ulgoland, didn't change.

Since nothing was really going on, I had the chance to return to my studies, and I rediscovered something that's always aggravated me. It takes a considerable amount of time to reactivate your brain after you've been away from your studies for a while. Study is a very intensive activity, and if you lay it aside for a bit, you have to learn how all over again. I know that it's going to happen every time, and that's why I get irritable when something comes up that drags me away from what is, after all, my primary occupation. The long period of relative peace and tranquility gave me about three hundred and fifty years of uninterrupted study time, and I accomplished quite a bit.

Did you really want me to break off at this point to give you an extended lecture on number theory or the principles of literary criticism?

I didn't really think you would, so why don't we just lay those things aside and press on with this great work that we are in?

I think it was sometime in the middle of the fifty-third century—5249 or 5250—when I completed something I'd been working on for twenty years or so and decided that it might not be a bad idea for me to go out and have a look around. I slipped down into Cthol Murgos and looked in on Ctuchik.

That's all I did—just look. He appeared to be busy with his assorted amusements—some obscene and some merely disgusting—so I didn't bother him.

Then I went on south from Rak Cthol to see if I could locate the cave where Zedar was keeping his comatose Master. I didn't have much trouble finding it, because Beldin was sitting on top of a ridge just across the rocky gorge from it. It didn't look as if he'd moved for several decades. "Did you kill Ctuchik yet?" he asked me after I'd shed my feathers.

"Beldin," I said in a pained tone of voice, "why is that always your first answer to any problem?"

"I'm a simple man, Belgarath," he replied, reaching out his gnarled hand with surprising swiftness, snatching up an unwary lizard, and eating it alive. "Killing things is always the simplest answer to problems."

"Just because it's simple doesn't mean that it's the best way," I told him. "No, as a matter of fact, I didn't kill Ctuchik. The twins have been getting some hints out of the Mrin that we'll need him later, and I'm not going to do anything to get in the way of things that have to happen." I looked across the gorge. "Is Zedar still in that cave with One-eye?"

"No. He left a few years back."

"Why are you setting down roots here, then?"

"Because it's altogether possible that Torak'll be the first to know when the Godslayer arrives. That might be all the warning we'll get when things start coming to a head. I'll let you know when the side of that mountain over there blows out."

"Have you any idea of where Zedar went?"

"I can't do *everything*, Belgarath. I'll watch Torak; Zedar's *your* problem. What have you been up to lately?"

"I proved that three and three make six," I replied proudly.

"*That* took you three centuries? I could have proved that with a handful of dried beans."

"But not mathematically, Beldin. Empirical evidence doesn't really prove anything, because the investigator might be crazy. Certainty exists only in pure mathematics."

"And if you accidentally turn your equation upside down, will that make all of us suddenly fly off the face of the earth?"

"Probably not."

"Forgive me, brother, but I'd much rather trust empirical evidence. I might be a little crazy now and then, but I've *seen* some of the answers you come up with when you try to add up a column of figures."

I shrugged. "Nobody's perfect." I moved around to the upwind side of him. "How long's it been since you've had a bath?"

"I couldn't say. When's the last time it rained around here?"

"This is a desert, Beldin. It can go for years without raining here."

"So? I've always felt that too much bathing weakens you. Go on home, Belgarath. I'm trying to work something out."

"Oh? What's that?"

"I'm trying to distinguish the difference between 'right' and 'good.' "

"Why?"

He shrugged. "I'm interested, that's all. It keeps my mind occupied while I'm waiting for my next bath. Go find Zedar, Belgarath, and quit pestering me. I'm busy."

To be quite honest about it, though, I wasn't particularly interested in Zedar's location. Torak's condition made Zedar largely irrelevant. I circulated around in the Kingdoms of the West instead, looking in on those families I'd been nurturing for all these centuries. Lelldorin's family was at Wildantor, and they were deeply involved in various crackpot schemes against the Mimbrates. The baron of Vo Mandor, Mandorallen's grandfather, was busy picking fights with his neighbors, usually on spurious grounds. Hettar's clan was raising horses, preparing, although they didn't realize it, for the coming of the Horse-Lord. Durnik's grandfather was a village blacksmith, and Relg's was a religious fanatic who spent most of his time admiring his own purity. I had no idea of where Taiba's family was, and I lost a lot of sleep about that. I knew that her family was *someplace* in the world, but I'd completely lost track of them after the Tolnedran invasion of Maragor.

I stopped by Tol Honeth before I went north to visit Drasnia and Cherek. I always like to keep an eye on the Borunes. The man on the throne at that time was Ran Borune XXI, who, as it turned out, was Ce'Nedra's great-grandfather. I've mentioned the tendency of Tolnedrans to marry their cousins several times in the past, I think, and Ran Borune XXI was no exception. The Dryad strain in the Borune family always breeds true in female children, and the men of the family are absolutely captivated by Dryads. I think it's in their blood.

Anyway, Ce'Nedra's great-grandfather was forty or so when I stopped by the palace, and his wife, Ce'Lanne, had flaming red hair and a disposition to match. She made the emperor's life very exciting, I understand.

Tolnedrans were still keeping alive the fiction that my name was some obscure Alorn title, and the scholars of history at the university had concocted a wild theory about a "Brotherhood of Sorcerers" out of whole cloth. Some chance remark by Beldin or one of the twins probably had given rise to that, and the creative historians expanded on it. We were supposed to be some sort of religious order, I guess. One imaginative pedant even went so far as to suggest that the enmity between my brothers and me and Torak's disciples was the result of a schism within the order at some time in the distant past.

I never bothered to correct all those wild misconceptions because they helped me to gain access to whichever Borune or Honethite or Vorduvian currently held the throne, and that saved a lot of time.

It was winter when I reached Tol Honeth and presented myself at the palace. Winters are not particularly severe in Tol Honeth, so at least I hadn't been obliged to plow through snowdrifts on my way to the imperial presence.

"And so you're Ancient Belgarath," Ran Borune said when I was presented to him.

"That's what they tell me, your Majesty," I replied.

"I've always wondered about that title," he said. Like all the Borunes, he was a small man, and his massive throne made him look just a bit ridiculous. "Tell me, Ancient One, is the title 'Belgarath' hereditary, or were you and your predecessors chosen by lot or the auguries?"

"Hereditary, your Majesty," I replied. Well, it was *sort* of true, I guess, depending on how you define the word "hereditary."

"How disappointing," he murmured. "It'd be much more interesting if all those Belgaraths had been identified by some sign from on high. I gather that you've come to bring me some important news?"

"No, your Majesty, not really. I happened to be in the vicinity, and I thought I might as well stop by and introduce myself."

"How very courteous of you. One of my ancestors knew one of yours, I'm told—back during the war with the Angaraks."

"So I understand, yes."

He leaned back on that red-draped throne. "Those must have been the days," he said. "Peace is all right, I guess, but wars are much more exciting."

"They're greatly overrated," I told him. "When you're at war, you spend most of your time either walking or sitting around waiting for something to happen. Believe me, Ran Borune, there are better ways to spend your time."

Then his wife burst into the throne room. "What *is* this idiocy?" she demanded in a voice they could probably have heard in Tol Vordue.

"Which particular idiocy was that, dear heart?" he asked quite calmly.

"You're *surely* not going to send my daughter to the Isle of the Winds in the dead of winter!"

"It's not *my* fault that her birthday comes in the wintertime, Ce'Lanne."

"It's as much your fault as it is mine!"

He coughed, looking slightly embarrassed.

"The Rivans can wait until summer!" she stormed on.

"The treaty states that she has to be there on her sixteenth birthday, love, and Tolnedrans *don't* violate treaties."

"Nonsense! You cut corners on treaties all the time!"

"Not *this* one. The world's peaceful right now, and I'd like to keep it that way. Tell Ce'Bronne to start packing. Oh, by the way, this is Ancient Belgarath."

She flicked only one brief glance at me. "Charmed," she said shortly. Then she continued her tirade, citing all sorts of reasons why it was totally impossible for her daughter, Princess Ce'Bronne, to make the trip to Riva.

I decided to step in at that point. I knew that Princess Ce'Bronne wasn't the one we were waiting for, but I didn't want the Borunes getting into the habit of ignoring one of the key provisions of the Accords of Vo Mimbre. "I'm going to Riva myself, your Imperial Highness," I told Ran Borune's flaming little wife. "I'll escort your daughter personally, if you'd like. I can guarantee her safety and make sure that she's treated with respect."

"How very generous of you, Belgarath," Ran Borune stepped in quickly. "There you have it, Ce'Lanne. Our daughter will be in good hands. The Alorns have enormous respect for Ancient Belgarath here. I'll make all the arrangements personally." He was *very* smooth, I'll give him that. He'd lived with his empress long enough to know how to get around her.

And so I escorted her Imperial little Highness, Princess Ce'Bronne, to the Isle of the Winds for her ritual presentation in the Hall of the Rivan King as the Accords of Vo Mimbre required. Ce'Bronne was as fiery as her mother and as devious as her grandniece. What she couldn't get by screaming, she usually got by wheedling. I rather liked her. She sulked for the first few days on board the ship that carried us north, and I finally got tired of it. "What *is* your problem, young lady?" I demanded at breakfast on our fourth day out from Tol Honeth.

"I *don't* want to marry an Alorn!"

"Don't worry about it," I told her. "You won't have to."

"How can you be so sure?"

"The Rivan King hasn't arrived yet. He won't be along for quite some time."

"*Any* Alorn can show up at Riva and claim to be Iron-grip's descendant. I could be forced to marry a commoner."

"No, dear," I told her. "In the first place, no Alorn would do that, and in the second, an imposter couldn't pass the test."

"What test?"

"The *true* Rivan King's the only one who can take Iron-grip's sword down off the wall in the throne room. An imposter couldn't get it off the stones with a sledgehammer. The Orb will see to that."

"Have you ever seen this mysterious jewel?"

"Many times, dear. Trust me. You're not going to be forced to marry an Alorn."

"Because I'm not good enough?" she flared. She could change direction in the blink of an eye.

"That has nothing to do with it, Ce'Bronne," I told her. "It's just not time yet. Too many other things have to happen first."

Her eyes narrowed, and I'm sure she was trying to find some insult in what I'd just told her. "Well," she said finally in a somewhat ungracious manner, "all right—I guess. But I'm going to hold you to your word on this, Old Man."

"I wouldn't have it any other way, Princess."

And so I got the Imperial Princess Ce'Bronne to Riva on time, and the Alorn ladies in the Citadel pampered and flattered her into some semblance of gracious behavior. She made her obligatory appearance in the throne room and waited the required three days, and then I took her home again.

"There now," I said to her as we disembarked on one of the marble wharves at Tol Honeth, "that wasn't so bad, was it?"

"Well," she replied, "I *guess* not." Then she laughed a silvery laugh, threw her tiny arms around my neck, and kissed me soundly.

I waited around Tol Honeth until spring arrived, and then I commandeered a Cherek war-boat to take me north. I went to Trellheim to look in on Barak's grandfather, who was every bit as big and red-bearded as the "Dreadful Bear" turned out to be, and quite nearly as intelligent. Everything seemed in order at Trellheim, so I went on to the village where Polgara was watching over the family of Garion's great-grandfather, another one of those Gerans. Pol likes to slip that name in about every other generation. I think it has something to do with her sense of continuity. This particular Geran had just married a blonde Cherek girl, and things seemed to be going along the way they were supposed to.

After we'd done all the usual things people do at family reunions, I finally got the chance to talk privately with my daughter. "I think we're going to have some problems with the Dryad princess when the time comes," I warned her.

"Oh? What sort of problems?"

"They're not particularly docile. We've been marrying all these young men to Alorn girls, and Alorn women are fairly placid. The Dryads in the Borune family are anything *but* placid. They're willful, spoiled, and very devious." I told her about Princess Ce'Bronne and our trip to Riva.

"I'll take care of it, father," she assured me.

"I'm sure you will, Pol, but I thought I ought to warn you. I think you're going to find the Rivan Queen quite a handful. Don't *ever* make the mistake of believing anything she tells you."

"I can handle her when the time comes, father. Where are you going from here?"

"Drasnia. I want to look in on the family of the Guide."

"Are we getting at all close to the time?"

"The twins think we are. They're starting to see some of the signs and omens. They seem to think that what we've been waiting for is going to happen in the next century or so."

"Then I'll be out of a job, won't I?"

"Oh, I think we'll be able to find *something* for you to do, Pol."

"Thanks awfully, Old Man. If we're getting that close, I'd better think about relocating to Sendaria, shouldn't I?" She looked directly at me. "I can read the Darine and the Mrin as well as you can, father." She told me. "I know where the Godslayer's supposed to be born."

"I guess we'd better start thinking about it," I agreed. "After I'm finished in Drasnia, I'll go back to the Vale and talk with the twins. Maybe they've picked up something more definite. This *wouldn't* be a good time to start making mistakes."

"When are you leaving for Drasnia?"

"Tomorrow ought to be soon enough. Do you suppose you could make one of those cherry tarts for breakfast, Pol? I haven't had one of your cherry tarts for over a century now, and I've *really* missed them."

She gave me a long, steady look.

"Yours are the very best, Pol," I said without even smiling. "There's an idea for you. After we get the Godslayer on his throne, you could open a pastry shop."

"Have you lost your mind?"

"You said you were going to be looking for a job, Pol. I'm just making a few suggestions, is all."

She even had the grace to laugh.

The next morning I left for Drasnia. Silk's grandfather was in the import business, dealing mainly in spices, and working for Drasnian intelligence on the side. There's nothing very unusual about that, though. *All* Drasnian merchants work for Drasnian intelligence on the side. Once again, everything was on schedule, so I went on back to the Vale.

I was a bit surprised to find that the twins weren't around when I got home. They'd left a rather cryptic note for me—something about an urgent summons from Polgara. I tried to reach out to them with my mind, but for some reason I couldn't get them to answer. I swore a little bit, and then I turned around to go back to Cherek. I was starting to get just a little tired of all this traveling.

It was late in the summer when I reached Val Alorn again, and I went on out to the village where Pol lived with her little family. She wasn't there, however. The twins were minding things instead. They were just a bit evasive when I asked them where she was. "She asked us not to tell you, Belgarath," Beltira said with a slightly pained expression.

"And I'm asking you to ignore her," I told him flatly. "All right, you two, give. I don't have time to tear the world apart looking for her. Where'd she go?"

They looked at each other. "She's a long way ahead of him by now," Belkira said to his brother. "I don't think he could catch her, so we might as well tell him."

"You're probably right," Beltira agreed. "She's gone to Nyissa, Belgarath."

"Nyissa? What for?"

"Pol's got ways to get information—and instructions. You knew about that, of course, didn't you?"

I'd known for quite a long time now that Pol received her own instructions. It simply never occurred to me that hers might come from a different source than mine. I nodded.

"Anyway," Beltira went on, "Pol received a warning that Ctuchik's been following up on something Zedar did back at the beginning of the fifth millennium. He's been in contact with the current Salmissra, and he's just about persuaded her to join with him. Pol was instructed to go to Sthiss Tor to talk her out of it."

"Why Pol?" I asked him. "I could have taken care of that."

"Pol didn't go into too much detail," Belkira replied. "You know how she can be sometimes. Evidently it's something that requires a woman's touch."

"We aren't the only ones who have prophecies, Belgarath," Beltira reminded me. "The Salmissras have their own ways to see into the future. They've all been far more afraid of Polgara than they have been of you. Pol's going to do something pretty awful to one of the Serpent queens, I guess, and she's gone to Sthiss Tor to ask the current Salmissra if she's volunteering to be the one it happens to. That all by itself should be enough to persuade Salmissra to break off her contacts with Ctuchik."

"All right, but why all this subterfuge? Why didn't she just tell *me* about it? Why did she sneak around behind my back?"

Belkira smiled. "She explained it to us," he said. "You don't *really* want us to repeat what she said, do you?"

"I think I can probably live with it. Go ahead and tell me."

He shrugged. "It's up to you. She said that you're tiresomely overprotective and that every time she sets out to do something, you argue with her about it for weeks on end. Then she said that she was going to do this whether you liked it or not, and that things would go more smoothly if you kept your nose out of it." He grinned at me.

"I don't think that's particularly funny, Belkira."

"It was when *she* said it. I've glossed over some of the words she used. Pol's got quite a vocabulary, hasn't she?"

I have him a long, steady look. "Why don't we just drop it?" I suggested.

"Anything you say, brother."

"The next time she talks with you, ask her to stop by the Vale on her way home. Tell her that I'm looking forward to a little chat."

Then I turned around and went on back to the Vale.

About a month later, Pol obediently came to my tower. I'd calmed down by then, so I didn't berate her—at least not *too* much.

"You seem to be taking this very well, Old Man," she noted.

"There's not much point in screaming about something after it's over. Exactly what was Ctuchik up to?"

"The usual," she replied. "He's trying to subvert enough people in the West to help him when the time comes. The Murgos have reopened the South Caravan Route, and they're flooding into the West again. I think we'd all better start concentrating on the Mrin Codex. Ctuchik seems to believe that things are coming to a head. He's doing everything he can to drive the Western Kingdoms apart. He *definitely* doesn't want us to be unified next time the way we were at Vo Mimbre. Angarak alliances are tenuous at best, and it seems that Ctuchik wants to sow dissention in the West to offset that."

"You're getting very good at this, Pol."

"I've had a good teacher."

"Thank you," I said, and for a minute there, I felt unaccountably grateful to that unpredictable daughter of mine.

"Don't mention it." She grinned at me.

"Why don't you get back to Cherek and send the twins home? If anybody's going to get anything definite out of the Mrin, they'll be the ones who'll do it."

"Whatever you say, father."

It took the twins until the turn of the century to start getting what we needed out of the Mrin Codex. In the spring of the year 5300 they came to my tower bubbling over with excitement. "It's just about to happen, Belgarath!" Beltira exclaimed. "The Godslayer will arrive during this century!"

"It's about time," I said. "What took you two so long to dig it out?"

"We weren't supposed to find it until now," Belkira replied.

"Would you like to clarify that?"

"The Necessity's got a much tighter control than we've ever realized," he said. "The passage that told us that *this* is the century when it's all going to happen is right out there in plain sight. We've all read it dozens of times, but it didn't make any sense until now. Last night, though, the meaning of it just fell into place in our minds. We've talked it over, and we're both sure that no matter how much we struggle with the Mrin, we're not going to understand what any given passage means until the Necessity's ready for us to understand it. In a peculiar sort of way, the understanding itself is a part of the EVENT."

"That's a mighty cumbersome way to do business," I objected. "Why would the Necessity play those kind of games with all of us?"

"We talked about that, too, Belgarath," Beltira told me. "It almost seems designed to keep *you* from tampering. We think that the Necessity's rather fond of you, but it knows you too well to give you enough time to step in and try to change things."

"You *do* try to do that a lot, you know," Belkira said, grinning at me.

CHAPTER
FORTY-
SEVEN

I suppose I should have been offended by the twins' insulting line of speculation, but I guess I really wasn't. I'd known Garion's friend for long enough now to have a pretty clear idea of his opinion of me, and I *have* tried to tamper with things on occasion. I guess it goes back to something I've said before; I'm not temperamentally equipped just to sit back and let destiny take its course. No matter how clever I think I am, though, Garion's friend is always about two jumps ahead of me. I should be used to that by now, I guess, but I'm not.

A part of the reason that I didn't get *too* excited about those unflattering observations was the fact that I was much *more* excited by the information that we'd finally reached the century during which the Godslayer would be born. I pestered poor Polgara unmercifully during the first three decades of the fifty-fourth century. I'd stop by every two or three months to find out if the heir's wife was pregnant, and I insisted on being present at every birth in that little family.

Pol was living in Medalia in central Sendaria at the time, and the current heir's name was Darral. I was very disappointed when, in 5329, Darral's wife, Alara, gave birth to a baby boy and the infant's birth wasn't accompanied by any of necessary signs and portents. He wasn't the Godslayer. Pol named him Geran, and it somehow seemed very right.

Maybe it was the fact that Darral was a stone-cutter that moved my daughter to relocate the family to the mountain village of Annath, just

on the Sendarian side of the Algarian border, in 5334. There were extensive stone quarries in the area, so Darral could find steady work.

I had a few qualms about that. The name Annath seemed to send a
chill through me for some reason. It wasn't that Annath was such a bad
little town. It was much like every mountain village in the world. It had
one street, which is normal for a town built at the bottom of a steep valley, and as it had grown, the houses of the new arrivals were simply added
onto each end of that street. That made the town a little strung out, but
that didn't bother anybody. People who live in the mountains are used to
walking. The sides of the valley were covered with aspens, and that gave
Annath a light and airy atmosphere. Some mountain towns are up to
their ears in fir and spruce, and they're perpetually gloomy as a result.
Annath wasn't like that, but it chilled me all the same.

I didn't have time to stand around shivering, though, because I had
to go to Boktor for the birth of one of the members of the extended royal
family of Drasnia. They named him Prince Kheldar, though he was far
down in the line of succession, but his birth and his name filled the air
around him with those signs and portents that I'd so sorely missed at the
birth of Geran. The Mrin refers to him as the Guide, but the rest of the
world knows him by the nickname his classmates at the academy
of the Drasnian Intelligence Service gave him when he was a student
there—Silk.

I was kept running for the next few years. The Guide was born in
5335, and so was the Blind Man—Relg the Ulgo zealot. Then, in 5336,
the son of the Earl of Trellheim was born. They named him Barak, but
the Mrin calls him the Dreadful Bear. In the following year, the Horse-
Lord and the Knight Protector—Hettar and Mandorallen—came along.
The Companions were sprouting all around me, but where was the
Godslayer?

Then in the spring of 5338, I received an urgent summons from
Polgara. I hurried on up to Annath, thinking the worst, but there wasn't
any emergency that I could see. Pol seemed quite calm when she met me
near a stone quarry on the edge of town.

"What's the problem here, Pol?" I asked her.

"No problem, father," she replied with a slight shrug. "I just need
somebody to fill in for me for a few months. I have something to take
care of."

"Oh? What's that?"

"I'm not at liberty to discuss it."

"Are we going to play *that* tired old game again, Pol?"

"It's not a game, father, and if you're tired of it, I'll call the twins
instead."

"You *can't* pull them out of the Vale now, Pol! There's too much going on at the moment for them to go off and leave the Mrin!"

"And Uncle Beldin's keeping watch over Torak. That's important, too. I guess you're elected, father—whether you like it or not. You're not *really* doing anything important right now, are you? The midwives can deliver these various babies without your supervision. Look after Darral and the little boy, Old Man—and if you say 'Why me?' I'll snatch out your beard."

"I'm not your servant, Pol."

"No, you're not. You're the servant of something far more important, and so am I. I have an errand to take care of, and you're supposed to take over here while I'm gone."

"The Master didn't say anything to *me* about this."

"He's busy right now, so I'm passing the instructions on for him. Just do it, father. Don't argue with me."

Before I could think up any kind of reply, she blurred and was gone.

I swore for a while, and then I stamped down into the village. Geran, who was about nine or so, was waiting for me outside the solid house his father had built at the east end of Annath's single street. "Hello, Grandfather," he greeted me. "Did Aunt Pol talk with you?"

"Talk *to* would come closer, Geran," I replied sourly. "Did she happen to mention to *you* where she's going?"

"Not that I remember, no, but there's nothing unusual about that. Aunt Pol hardly ever tells us what she's going to do—or why."

"You've noticed that, I see. Where's your mother?"

"She stepped down to the baker's shop for a minute. Aunt Pol said that you'd be staying with us for a while, and Mother knows how fond you are of pastries."

"We all have our little weaknesses, I suppose."

"Mother should be back fairly soon," he said, "but as long as we're waiting anyway, do you suppose you could tell me a story?"

I laughed. "I might as well," I said. "Your aunt's nailed me to the ground here until she gets back, so we'll have lots of time for stories." I looked at him a bit more closely. Although, like most of the members of his family, he'd been born with that sandy-colored hair, Geran's hair was beginning to turn dark. He'd never be as big as Iron-grip had been, but I could already see certain resemblances.

A little word of caution here, if you don't mind. When you know that something's going to happen, you'll start trying to see signs of its approach in just about everything. Always try to remember that most of the things that happen in this world *aren't* signs. They happen because they happen, and their only real significance lies in normal cause and effect. You'll drive yourself crazy if you start trying to pry the meaning out of every gust of wind or rain squall. I'm not denying that there might actually be a few signs that you won't want to miss. Knowing the difference is the tricky part.

I've always enjoyed the company of my grandsons. There's a peculiarly earnest quality about them that I find appealing. I'm not trying to say that they don't occasionally do things that are a bit foolish and sometimes downright dangerous—Garion's encounter with the wild boar in the woods outside Val Alorn sort of leaps to mind—but if you're willing to follow their occasionally faulty reasoning, you'll find that, in their own minds at least, most of the things they do are fully justified. The descendants of Iron-grip and Beldaran always have been very serious little boys. A sense of humor might have rounded out their personalities, but you can't have everything.

Despite the fact that Polgara had ruthlessly dragooned me into watching over Geran, I'll admit that I enjoyed those months I spent with him. I'll never be the kind of fisherman Durnik is, but I know the basics—which is to say that I can bait a hook. But Geran was at that age in a young boy's life when catching fish becomes an all-consuming passion. Years of observation have taught me that this particular passion crops up just before the boy suddenly realizes that there are two kinds of people in the world—boy-people and girl-people. In a general sort of way, most boys approve of that.

If only they wouldn't behave as if they thought they'd invented it.

Anyway, Geran and I spent that spring and summer in search of the wily trout. There are other kinds of fish in the world, of course, but it's always seemed to me that trout are the most challenging. Moreover, if you're not *too* noisy about it, you can have some fairly serious conversations while you're waiting for the fish to start biting.

I particularly remember one truly miserable, but at the same time absolutely wonderful day my grandson and I spent huddled on a makeshift raft in the center of a small mountain lake with a drizzling rain hissing into the water around us. I'm not sure exactly why, but the trout were in a positive frenzy. Geran and I caught more fish that day than we'd normally catch in a week.

About midafternoon, when we were both soaked to the skin and the wicker basket we'd brought along "just in case we got lucky" was filled almost to the brim with silvery-sided trout, things began to slow down a bit. "This is really a lot of fun, grandfather," my fishing partner noted. "I wish we could do it more often."

"Geran," I replied, "we've been out fishing every day for the past three weeks. You can't *get* much more often than that."

"Yes, but today we're *catching* them."

I laughed. "That always seems to help," I agreed.

"We're not the same as other people, are we?" He asked then.

"Because we both like to fish? There are a lot of fishermen in the world, Geran."

"That's not what I mean. I'm talking about our family. It seems to me that there's something sort of different about us—something a little odd and . . . special." He made a small face and wiped the water off his nose on his sleeve. "I didn't say that very well, did I? I'm not trying to say that we're really important or anything like that, but we're just not like other people—at least that's the way it seems to me. Aunt Pol never talks to *me* about it, but sometimes at night I can hear her talking with my father down in the kitchen before I go to sleep. She knows a *lot* of people, doesn't she?"

"Your aunt? Oh, yes, Geran. Your Aunt Pol knows people in just about every Kingdom in the West."

"What I can't understand is *how* she got to know all those kings and nobles and such. She almost never goes anywhere. You know what I think?"

"What's that, boy?"

"I think Aunt Pol's a lot older than she looks."

"She's what they call 'well preserved,' Geran. I wouldn't make a big issue of it, if I were you, though. Ladies are a little sensitive about how old they are."

"*You're* old, and it doesn't seem to bother *you*."

"That's because I never really grew up. I still know how to have fun. That's what keeps you young. Your aunt thinks that having fun isn't important."

"She's very strange, isn't she? Sometimes I think she's the strangest woman in the world."

I broke down and laughed at that point.

"What's so funny?"

"Someday I'll explain it to you. You're right, though. Our family *is* special, but it's important for us all to behave as if we were ordinary. Your aunt will explain it to you when you're a little older."

"Does it make you feel good? Being special, I mean?"

"Not really. It's just something else that you have to carry around with you. It's not all that complicated, Geran. There's something very important that our family has to do, and there are people in the world who don't want us to do it."

"We'll do it anyway, though, won't we?" His boyish face was very determined.

"I think we probably will—but that's still a ways off yet. Are you going to pull that fish in? Or are you planning to just keep him on the line for the rest of the day?"

My grandson gave a small whoop and pulled in a trout that probably weighed about five pounds.

I think back on that day fairly often. All things considered, it was one of the better ones.

It was almost winter when Polgara returned. The leaves had changed color and then fallen to the ground, the sky had turned grey, and there was the smell of approaching snow when she came walking down the single street of Annath with a blue cloak wrapped about her and a look of satisfaction on her face.

I saw her coming and I went out to meet her. "Back so soon, Pol?" I bantered. "We hardly even had time to miss you. *Now* do you suppose you could tell me where you went and what you were doing?"

She shrugged. "I had to go to Nyissa again. There were some people there I had to meet."

"Oh? Who?"

"Zedar, for one, and the current Salmissra, for another."

"Pol, stay away from Zedar! You're good, but not *that* good."

"It was required, father. Zedar and I *have* to know each other. It's one of *those* things."

"What's Zedar up to?" I demanded.

"I can't see why you've all been so excited about Zedar. Actually, he's rather pathetic. He's terribly shabby, he's not eating right, and he looks awfully unhealthy."

"Good. I wish him all the pleasures of ill-health. I'll even invent some new diseases for him, if what's currently available starts to bore him."

"You're a barbarian, father."

"You've noticed. What's he doing in Nyissa?"

"As far as I can tell, he's turned into a vagabond. He's sort of wandering around the world desperately looking for something—or somebody."

"Let's all hope that he doesn't find whatever or whomever it is."

"On the contrary, he absolutely has to. If *he* doesn't find it, you're going to have to find it yourself, and you wouldn't even know where to begin looking."

"Does *he?*"

"No. What he's looking for is going to find him."

And that was the first hint we had that Eriond was coming. Beldin and I talked about it once, and we sort of agreed that Eriond and Torak were mirror images of each other—Torak on one side, and Eriond on the other. Each of them was the exact opposite of his counterpart.

Sometimes I wonder if Torak knew that he was a mistake.

That in itself would justify my entire existence.

"Why did you have to talk to Salmissra?" I asked.

"To warn her," my daughter replied. "She'll do something in a few years, and I'll have to do something to her in return. She won't like it much—and neither will I." Polgara sighed. "It's going to be fairly dreadful, I'm afraid, but I won't have any choice." She suddenly threw her arms around me and buried her face in my shoulder. "Oh, father," she wept, "why do I have to be the one who has to do it?"

"Because you're the only one who can, Pol." Then I patted her shoulder. "There, there," I said. "There, there."

The next couple of years were quiet, and that made me very edgy. The most momentous event in the history of the world was right on the verge of happening, and I wanted to get on with it. I'm not really very good at waiting.

Then, in 5340, Ran Borune XXIII was crowned Emperor of Tolnedra, and not long thereafter he was married to one of his cousins, a red-haired Dryad named Ce'Vanne. The twins found that highly significant, and they assured me that the marriage would result in the birth of the Queen of the World. If they were right, and they almost always were, this meant that when Geran reached adulthood and married, he'd become the father of the one we'd all been waiting for.

Not long after that, Beldin came back to the Vale. "I see that you finally got tired of watching that cave," I said to him after he had come up the stairs to my tower.

"Not really," he replied. "Some things have been happening, haven't they?"

"A few. We're getting closer to the birth of the Godslayer."

"I thought it might be something like that. A few months back I suddenly got a powerful urge to go out and have a look around. The Murgos have a new king, Taur Urgas, and he's as crazy as a loon. There's nothing new or startling about that; all the Urgas are crazy. Taur Urgas carries it to extremes, though. I saw him once in Rak Goska, and I think he's going to figure in events."

"Is there any sign of his Mallorean counterpart yet?"

He nodded. "His name's Zakath. He hasn't been crowned emperor yet, but I don't think it's going to be much longer. His father's in failing health. For an Angarak, Zakath's a remarkably civilized man. From what I gather, he's extremely intelligent, and his tutors were able to persuade his father to let him attend the university in Melcene. An educated Mallorean Emperor's going to be a novelty. How many of the companions have showed up so far?"

"Six that I know of. The Guide and the Blind Man were born in 5335, the Dreadful Bear in '36, and the Horse-Lord and the Knight Protector in '37."

"That's only five."

"I thought you already knew about the Man with Two Lives. He was born earlier—5330, I think. He's apprenticed to a blacksmith in Erat in central Sendaria."

"Any hints about the others?"

"The twins think that the present Tolnedran Emperor's going to produce the Godslayer's wife."

"That sort of nails things down, doesn't it? How's Pol?"

"Difficult, the same as always. She went to Nyissa a couple of years ago, and she met Zedar down there."

"And you *let* her?"

"*Let* is a term that doesn't apply when you're talking about Pol. You should know that by now, Beldin. Actually, she didn't bother to tell me where she was going. She told me afterward that she and Zedar *have* to know each other. She's getting instructions from someplace other than the Mrin."

"I'm sure she is. Oh, I almost forgot. There's a new king in Gar og Nadrak, too. His name's Drosta lek Thun, and he was only twelve when they put him on the throne."

"Did you see him?"

"No. I heard about it when I was in Rak Goska. Are the Algars going to do anything about their Crown Prince?"

"What do you mean, 'do anything about him'?"

"He's a cripple, isn't he? I don't think the Algars are very likely to accept a defective as king."

"He'll probably be all right. Once he's on a horse, he's as good as any Algar alive." I scratched at my beard. "I'm a little concerned about it, though. The Mrin says that the Horse-Lord's going to be his son, and the Horse-Lord's already been born—into another clan. The twins are working on it. The Mrin's being very stubborn right now. Are you going to be around for a while?"

"No. I think I'd better go back to southern Cthol Murgos and keep an eye on Burnt-face. We're getting close to the birth of the Godslayer, and that might be the thing that wakes Torak up."

"I'm not so sure about that. If it *does*, we're going to be in trouble. An infant wouldn't pose all that much threat to Torak One-eye."

"I still think we should be ready—just in case. If it *does* wake Torak, you might have to take the baby out into the woods someplace and hide him. Is Chamdar still poking around?"

"He's in Tolnedra right now. Drasnian intelligence is keeping an eye on him."

"I thought *you* were supposed to do that."

"It's better this way. Chamdar knows me a little too well. He can feel it when I'm in his general vicinity."

"It's up to you, I guess. I'm going to go talk with the twins for a bit, and then I'd better get back to Cthol Murgos." Then he turned around and clumped back on down my stairs. It was only after he'd left that I realized that he hadn't once asked me for something to drink. Our growing sense of anticipation was making us all behave a little strangely.

The following year, the lame Cho-Hag was elevated to the position of Chief of Clan-Chiefs of Algaria, and that gave me a lot of trouble. I knew that Hettar would one day take that position, and I couldn't for the life of me see how that could happen—short of another clan war. Considering what lay ahead, a clan war in Algaria was the *last* thing we needed.

Everything was happening very fast now, with events piling on top of each other everywhere I turned, and yet in a very real sense, I was just marking time, waiting for Geran to grow up and get married. I tend at times to get impatient, and just sitting around waiting drives me right up the wall, so, though there wasn't really any need for it, I dusted off my storyteller costume and went out to have a look around.

My first stop was Annath, naturally. Geran was twelve or so now, and he was growing like a weed. His hair had grown even darker, and his voice was changing, sometimes coming out as a rich baritone and at other times cracking and squeaking. Quite often he sounded like a young rooster trying to crow.

"Has he started to notice girls yet?" I asked Pol when I had gotten her off to one side.

"Give him time, father," she replied. "Ildera's only nine. Let's not rush things."

"Ildera?"

"The girl he's going to marry."

"That doesn't sound like a Sendarian name."

"It's not. Ildera's the daughter of a Clan-Chief of Algaria. Their pastures are just over on the other side of the border."

I frowned. "Are you sure, Pol? I'd always assumed that the Godslayer's mother was going to be a Sendar."

"Whatever gave you that idea?"

"I'm not sure. He's supposed to be born here in Sendaria, so I guess I just jumped to the conclusion that his mother'd be a Sendar."

"All you had to do was ask me, father. I could have told you she'd be an Algar about six generations ago."

"You're sure she's the right one?"

"Of course I'm sure."

"Have you told Geran yet?"

"I don't do that, father. You should know that by now. If you start telling young people whom they're supposed to marry, they tend to get mule-headed about it."

"The Godslayer's going to know."

"Not until I'm ready for him to know, he won't."

"Pol, it's written down in the Accords of Vo Mimbre. It's right there in black and white that he'll marry a Tolnedran Princess."

"It won't mean a thing to him, father."

"How do you plan to keep it from him?"

"I'm not going to teach him how to read, that's how."

"You can't do that! He *has* to know how to read! How's he going to know what he's supposed to do if he can't read the Mrin?"

"There'll be time enough for him to learn to read later, Old Man. I didn't start learning until after Beldaran got married, remember? If he's the kind of person we think he's going to be, he won't have any trouble picking it up."

I had my doubts about that, but I kept them to myself. "How much have you told Geran?" I asked her.

"Not very much. Young people have a tendency to blurt things out when they get excited. I'd rather that the people here in Annath didn't know that they have royalty in their midst. Darral knows, of course, but he knows how to keep his mouth shut."

"Where *is* the boy this morning?"

"He's at the stone quarry with his father—learning the trade."

"Working in a quarry can be dangerous, Pol," I objected.

"He'll be fine, father. Darral's keeping an eye on him."

"I think I'll go on over there."

"Why?"

"I want to see if Darral might give his apprentice the rest of the day off."

"What for?"

"So the boy and I can go fishing."

"Don't you be getting him off alone and telling him things he doesn't need to know yet."

"That wasn't what I had in mind."

"Why *do* you want to take him fishing then?"

"To catch fish, Pol. Isn't that why people usually go fishing?"

She rolled her eyes upward. *"Men!"* She said.

Geran and I spent a pleasurable afternoon working a mountain stream that tumbled down out of that little lake I mentioned before. We didn't have much time to talk, because the fish were biting, and that kept us quite busy.

The next morning, I told them all good-bye and left for Erat. I wanted to look in on Durnik. I knew that he was the Man with Two Lives, but I didn't realize at the time exactly what that was going to mean, or just how important Durnik was going to be in all our lives. Now, of course, he's my son-in-law and the most recent disciple of my Master.

Isn't it strange how these things turn out?

Durnik was about a year younger than Geran, but he was already very strong. He was apprenticed to a blacksmith named Barl, and working around a forge is one of the fastest ways I know of to develop muscles.

Durnik was already a very serious young fellow, and he was growing up to be a typical Sendar: sober, industrious, and steadfastly moral. I seriously doubt that Durnik's had an unclean or salacious thought in his entire life.

I broke a buckle on my pack—quite deliberately—and I stopped by Barl's shop to get it fixed. Barl was busy shoeing a horse, so Durnik repaired my buckle. We talked for a little bit, and then I moved on.

I frankly doubt that my son-in-law even remembers that meeting. *I* do, though, because that brief conversation told me all I really needed to know about him.

After I left Barl's smithy, I turned south and proceeded down into Arendia to look in on the Wildantors. The most typical of the family was a young count, Reldegen, who seemed fully intent on going through his life with his rapier half drawn. Reldegen was sort of what they had in mind when they came up with the term "hothead." He wasn't *quite* as prone to disaster as his nephew, Lelldorin, would become, but he ran him a close second. I liked him, though.

When I left Arendia, I hurried on back to the Vale. Winter was coming anyway, and I wanted to find out if the twins had discovered anything new. Events were plunging ahead, and scarcely a day went by that they didn't crack open another passage in the Mrin.

It wasn't until 5344 that the problem in Algaria was resolved. Young Hettar and his parents had been traveling alone near the Eastern Escarpment, and they were attacked by Murgos. The Murgos killed the boy's parents and then dragged him behind a horse for several miles and left him for dead. Cho-Hag found him a couple of days later and, in time, adopted him. Hettar *would* be the next Chief of the Clan-Chiefs, and it wouldn't take a clan war to get him there. *That* was a relief.

In the spring of the following year, the twins strongly suggested that I take Polgara to meet those young Alorns who would become so important to us later. "They really ought to get to know her, Belgarath," Belkira told me. "The time's going to come when you'll all be doing important things together, so they should be able to recognize her on sight. Alorns have some peculiar prejudices where women are concerned, so you'd better get them used to the idea that Pol's no ordinary woman while they're still young. We'll go up to Annath with you and keep an eye on things while the two of you are gone."

I couldn't fault their reasoning, since they were Alorns themselves. Besides, Pol was vegetating in Annath, and I thought it might not be a bad idea for her to get away for a while.

You have no idea of how quickly she agreed with me about that.

We went on over to Algaria first, since it was right next door—so to speak—and we finally ran Cho-Hag down. Algars *do* move around a lot. Even at the age of eight, Hettar was a grim-faced little boy who spent almost every waking moment practicing with his weapons and his horses. His eyes went absolutely flat every time anyone even mentioned the word "Murgo." He obviously already had plans for what would become his life's work. I don't like Murgos all that much myself, but Hettar takes it to extremes.

All Alorns have heard of me and my daughter, of course, so Cho-Hag greeted us royally. I saw to it that Pol got the chance to talk with Hettar at some length, and she was very dubious about him when we left for Drasnia. "I think he's hovering right on the verge of insanity, father," she told me. "He'll be an absolute monster when he grows up, and he'll eventually become King of the Algars."

"That's a problem for the Murgos, isn't it?" I replied.

"Don't be so smug, Old Man. Hettar's got all the makings of a berserker, and I think there'll be times when that could put us *all* in danger. You *do* know that he's a Sha-Dar, don't you?"

"Yes. I sensed that the first time I saw him. Does he know yet?"

"He might. He knows that he's a lot closer to horses than other Algars are. He may not have made the connection yet. Are the other two Alorns as wild as this one seems to be?"

"I haven't seen either of them in a while. Kheldar should be fairly civilized. He's Drasnian, after all. I can't make any promises about Barak. He's Cherek, and that whole country's full of wildmen."

Prince Kheldar, the nephew of Rhodar, crown prince of Drasnia, was a small, wiry boy with a long, sharp nose, and he was already too clever by half. Even at ten, he was smarter than most full-grown men. He flattered Pol outrageously and won her over in about ten minutes. She *liked* him, but she was wise enough not to trust him.

You should always keep that firmly in mind if you happen to have any dealings with Silk. It's perfectly all right to like him, but don't ever make the mistake of trusting him. He's married now, but his wife's at least as devious as he is, so I wouldn't trust her, either.

After we'd visited with Kheldar's family for a few days, Pol and I went down to Kotu and took ship for Val Alorn. When we got there, I borrowed some horses at the palace, and we rode to Trellheim. Barak was nine years old or so, and his cousin, Anheg, the crown prince of Cherek, was about a year older. Anheg was visiting his cousin, and the two of them were already almost as big as full-grown men. Barak had flaming red hair, but Anheg's hair was coarse and black. They were a couple of rowdies, but that was to be expected. They *were* Chereks, after all.

I introduced Pol to them, and she managed to get them to stay in one place long enough for a talk.

"Well?" I said to her as we were riding back to Val Alorn. "What do you think?"

"They'll work out just fine," she replied. "They're noisy and boastful, but they're both very intelligent. Anheg's going to make a very good king, I think, and he already relies on Barak."

"Did you get any sense of what that 'Dreadful Bear' business is all about?"

"Not entirely. It's got something to do with the Godslayer. It *could* simply mean that Barak's going to go berserk if the Godslayer's in any kind of danger, but it might go even further. Maybe it'll get clearer by the time Barak's full grown."

"Let's hope so. I'd like to know about it a little in advance if there's going to be an actual change."

We sailed back to Darine from Val Alorn, and then went on to Annath. The twins went back to the Vale, and I said good-bye to Pol and took the Great North Road back to Boktor. I wanted to have a look at Prince Kheldar's uncle, Rhodar, the crown prince of Drasnia. I talked with him a bit, and I wasn't disappointed. Even as a young man, Rhodar was decidedly chubby, but what a mind he had! The three of them, Rhodar, Anheg, and Cho-Ram, were all going to be outstanding kings, and I was fairly sure we were going to need all their talents when things started to come to a head.

I was on the go almost continually then, so I seldom got back to the Vale to talk with the twins. We stayed in touch, though.

Then, in the spring of 5346, they told me that Pol had gone off on another of those mysterious errands of hers and that they were filling in for her at Annath.

I hurried back there so that I could talk with them face to face. Our means of communication was convenient, I'll grant you, but there were Murgos in the West again, and where you've got Murgos, you've also got Grolims, and Grolims have ways to pick random conversations out of the air. I *definitely* didn't want some Grolim locating Polgara and tracking her back to Annath.

"I *wish* she'd let me know what she's going to do before she just runs off like this!" I fumed when I met with the twins. "Where's she gone to *this* time?"

"Gar og Nadrak," Beltira replied.

"She's gone *where?*"

"Gar og Nadrak. This time it was the Mrin that told her to go there. You remember those Nadrak 'friends' we told you about back in the forty-ninth century? And you went there to have a look?"

"Yes." Of course I remembered. That was the time I'd picked up all that gold.

"These 'friends' are out and about now, so Pol's gone to Gar og Nadrak to identify them."

"I could have done that!" I shouted in a sudden fury.

"Not as well as Pol can," Belkira disagreed. "Don't yell at *us*, Belgarath. We just passed on the instructions to her, we didn't make them up."

I got control of myself. "Where exactly is she?"

"She and her owner are in Yar Nadrak."

"Her *owner?*"

"Didn't you know? Women are considered property in Gar og Nadrak."

CHAPTER FORTY-EIGHT

I t was in that same year, 5346, that a re-curring pestilence broke out once again in western Drasnia. The disease appears to be endemic in that part of the world, and I rather think that the fens might have something to do with it. It's a virulent kind of disease that's usually fatal, and those who survive it are generally grotesquely disfigured.

Since Pol was off in Yar Nadrak, I was obliged to spend a year or so pinned down in Annath. I kept an eye on Geran, but we seldom had time to do any fishing, since he had other things on his mind. He was in the process of building his own house, and every time Ildera's clan was near the border, he spent just about every waking moment with her. Ildera was a tall blonde girl and very lovely. Geran seemed quite taken with her, not that he really had any choice in the matter. It appeared that the Necessity could handle those arrangements all by itself even when Pol wasn't around to guide the young people into those marriages. That made me feel rather smug, for some reason.

It was about midsummer in the year 5347 when a bone-thin Drasnian named Khendon came to Annath with a message for me. Khendon was a margrave, I think, but he had better things to do than sit around pol-ishing his title. Since spying seems to be Drasnia's national industry, most members of the Drasnian nobility routinely attend the academy of the In-telligence Service, and Khendon had been no exception. It's while they're at the academy that they pick up those distinctive nicknames, and Khendon had been dubbed "Javelin," probably because he was so thin.

Though he wasn't really very old, Javelin was already one of the best in the service. I've always rather liked him. He's one of the few men in the world who can keep Silk off balance. That in itself makes him extremely valuable.

He leaned back in his chair in Darral's kitchen while Geran's mother was fixing supper. Darral and Geran were still hard at work in the stone quarry. "I chanced to be in Yar Nadrak, Ancient One," Javelin told me, "and your daughter looked me up. She gave me a message for you." He reached inside his doublet, drew out a folded and sealed sheet of parchment, and held it out to me. "She said that you'd understand why she chose to do it this way instead of what she called 'the other way.' What did she mean by that?"

"It's one of those things you don't need to know about, Javelin," I told him.

"I need to know about *everything*, Ancient One," he disagreed.

"Curiosity can get you into a lot of trouble, Javelin. There are two worlds out there that sort of coexist. You take care of yours, and I'll take care of mine. We'll try not to step on each others' toes too often. Believe me, it's smoother that way. I've been at this for a long time, so I know what I'm doing." I broke the wax seal—which I'm sure Javelin had carefully replaced after he'd browsed through the message—and read the note from my daughter.

"Father," it began, "I'm ready to come home now. Come to Yar Nadrak, and bring plenty of money. My owner will probably expect a sizable price for me."

"What's the going price for a slave woman in Gar og Nadrak, Khendon?" I asked the skinny Drasnian.

"That depends on the woman, Holy One," he replied, "and upon how good a bargainer the buyer is. Bear in mind the fact that there are three parties involved in the bargaining."

"Would you like to explain that?"

"The woman's interested in the price, too, Belgarath—since she gets half, and since the price is an indication of her value. As a matter of pride, your daughter's going to insist on a very high price."

"Even from *me?*"

"It's a quaint custom, Holy One. You *do* want her back, don't you?"

"That depends on how much it's going to cost me."

"*Belgarath!*" He actually sounded shocked.

"I'm joking, Khendon. Just give me a round number. I've got some ten-ounce gold bars knocking around in my tower somewhere. How many should I take with me?"

"A dozen or so, at least. Anything less would be insulting."

"You're enjoying this, aren't you?"

"You're the one who asked the question, Belgarath. I'm just trying to give you my best guess."

"Thanks," I said in a flat tone of voice. "What's her owner's name?"

"Gallak, Holy One. He's a merchant who's involved in the fur trade. The fact that he owns your daughter gives him a certain amount of prestige, so he probably won't sell her cheaply. Take my advice and bring plenty of money to the bargaining table."

I stood up. "Keep an eye on things here, Khendon. I'll send the twins up to relieve you as soon as I get back to the Vale."

"It shall be as you say, Holy Belgarath."

I walked on out of Annath, went falcon, and flew directly to the Vale. I spoke briefly with the twins, then I hunted through my tower and finally located my stack of gold bars—behind a bookshelf, if you can imagine that. I tucked about twenty of them—twelve and a half pounds or so—into a saddlebag, and then I went north in search of an Algar clan to provide me with a horse. I've imposed on the Algars that way any number of times over the years.

I skirted the Sendarian border, and I reached Aldurford in a couple of days. Then I followed the Great North Road up along the causeway that crosses the fens to Boktor. I stopped there only long enough to purchase a suit of Drasnian clothes. Then I crossed the moors to the Nadrak border.

"What's your business in Gar og Nadrak?" one of the border guards demanded suspiciously after he'd stopped me.

"My business is just that, friend," I told him bluntly. "My business. I'm going to Yar Nadrak to buy something. Then I'm going to take it back to Boktor and sell it. I've got all the necessary documents, if you want to see them."

"A certain gratuity's customary," he suggested hopefully.

"I try not to be a slave to custom," I told him. "I should probably tell you that King Drosta's a personal friend of mine." Actually I'd never even met Drosta, but dropping names can be useful.

The guard's face grew slightly apprehensive.

"I wonder how your king's going to react when I tell him that his border guards are accepting bribes," I added.

"You wouldn't actually tell him, would you?"

"Not if you let me go across the border without any more of this nonsense."

He sullenly raised the gate and let me pass. I suppose I *could* have paid him, but Rablek and I had worked very hard digging up that gold, so I didn't feel like squandering any of it.

I followed the North Caravan Route eastward, and it took me about a week to reach Yar Nadrak, the capital. Yar Nadrak's a particularly ugly town. It lies at the juncture of the east and west forks of the River Cordu, and the land around it is marshy and dotted with charred snags, since Nadraks habitually clear forests by setting fire to them. I think the thing that makes the capital so unappealing is the fact that just about everything inside the walls is smeared with tar. It keeps wood from decaying, I guess, but it doesn't add much in the way of beauty—or fragrance.

I rode directly to the fur market and asked around for the fur merchant, Gallak. I was directed to a nearby tavern, which is probably the last place I'd have expected to find Polgara. It was a rowdy sort of place with a low ceiling held up by tar-smeared beams, and as soon as I entered I saw something that *really* surprised me.

Polgara was dancing.

She might not have been *quite* as good as Vella, but she came very close. She was wearing soft leather boots of a Nadrak design, and the hilt of a dagger protruded from the top of each one. Two more daggers were tucked into her belt. She was wearing a rather flimsy dress made of Mallorean silk—blue, naturally—and all sorts of interesting things were going on under that dress as she spun on flickering feet through the intricate steps of the dance.

The patrons of the tavern were cheering her on, and I started feeling belligerent. Sometimes it feels as if I've spent eons feeling belligerent when men have started paying too much attention to Polgara. But aren't fathers supposed to feel that way?

Anyway, she concluded her dance with that challenging strut that's the traditional finale of the dance of the Nadrak woman, and the patrons cheered, whistled, and stamped their feet in approval. Then she returned to the table where the man I guessed to be her owner sat basking in reflected glory. He was a lean-faced Nadrak of middle years, and the cut and quality of his garments proclaimed him to be a man of some substance. I noticed that he very carefully kept his hands to himself when Pol sat down. It was fairly clear that she knew how to use those daggers.

I pushed my way through the crowd to his table. "That's quite a woman you've got there, friend," I said to him. "Would you care to sell her?" It was a little blunt, but Nadraks tend to get right to the point in these matters.

He looked me up and down. "You're a Drasnian, aren't you?" he judged from my clothes.

"Right," I replied.

"I don't think I'd care to sell her to a Drasnian."

"Business is business, Gallak," I told him, "and my money's as good as anybody else's." I hefted the saddlebags I'd brought.

"How did you come to know my name?" he asked me.

"I asked around," I replied.

"Aren't you a little old to be buying women?"

"I'm not buying her for myself, Gallak. I want to give Crown Prince Rhodar a special gift when the time comes for him to assume the throne of Drasnia. It never hurts a businessman to have his king obligated to him."

"That's very true," he conceded, "but Rhodar's an Alorn. What makes you think he'd be interested in a Nadrak woman?"

"You don't know Rhodar, I see. He's got a very large appetite—for lots of things."

"He might start to lose that appetite after Polanna here cuts out his tripes for getting too familiar. She's *very* quick with her daggers."

"Is that her name?"

He nodded. "Just for the sake of argument, what would you be willing to offer me for her?"

I reached inside my saddlebags, took out one of my bars of gold and laid it on the table in front of him.

Polgara had been watching us rather closely. "Absolutely out of the question," she snapped. "You'd need twenty of those to buy me. Tell him to go away, Gallak."

Gallak, however, was examining the bar rather closely. "Don't be in such a rush, Pol," he told her. "This is very good quality. I'd say that it's almost pure." He squinted at me. "How'd you come by this, friend?"

"I did some prospecting a few years back," I replied. "My partner and I found a stream that was running bank-full of this stuff."

His eyes grew very bright at that point. "I'd like to see that stream," he said.

"A lot of people would, but I think I'll just keep its location to myself. Well? Are you going to make a counteroffer?"

"Polanna just did. Twenty bars."

"Five," I countered.

"I could go as low as fifteen, I suppose."

"Ridiculous!" I retorted. "I could buy this whole tavern and everybody in it for fifteen bars. Let's be realistic here, friend. She's only a woman, after all."

We haggled about it for an hour or so, and Pol's eyes got flintier by the moment. We finally settled on twelve. Then we each spit on our hands, smacked our palms together, and the deal was struck. I stood up. "All right, girl," I said to my daughter, "let's go to Drasnia."

"I have some things I need to pick up," she replied, gathering up her share of the gold.

"Leave them behind."

"Not on your life, Old Man. You bought *me*. You didn't buy my possessions. It's just a short way to Gallak's house. It won't take me long."

She turned and strutted out of the tavern with every eye upon her as she went.

"Spirited, isn't she?" I noted mildly.

"Indeed she is," Gallak agreed. "To be honest with you, friend, I'm just as happy to be rid of her. You know your future king better than I do, but you might want to consider some other gift. His gratitude might go downhill after a few weeks with Polanna."

"She'll be just fine, Gallak. It's been a pleasure doing business with you." I picked up my much-lighter saddlebags and went back out into the street.

Polgara's eyes were steely when she returned. "I wasn't particularly amused by your performance in there, Old Man." She said. "It was *very* insulting."

"I thought I pulled it off fairly well. Do you want to give me back my gold?"

"Oh, no, father. That gold is *mine* now."

I sighed. "All right, Pol." I gave up. "If that's the way you feel about it. Let's find a stable. I'll buy you a horse and we can get started."

After we rode out of Yar Nadrak, Pol and I were able to speak more freely. "Did you find the people you were looking for?" I asked her.

"Of course I did," she replied. "I wouldn't have sent for you if I hadn't."

"Who are they?"

"One of them is Drosta lek Thun himself."

"The Nadrak King?" *That* was surprising.

She nodded. "Drosta's a very complicated fellow, and he seems bent on getting out from under the thumb of the Grolims. He wants to turn his kingdom into a secular society. He's devious and has no principles whatsoever, but he *does* want what's best for his country."

"Who's the other one?"

"A fellow named Yarblek. He's a descendant of someone you used to know, I believe."

"You mean Rablek?"

"Of course. Nothing ever really happens by chance, father."

I made a face. "I get *so* tired of that," I said.

"I'd have thought you'd be used to it by now. Yarblek's a businessman—of sorts. He's young, but he's already so unscrupulous that he's building quite a reputation. I think that when the time comes, he'll help us—if the price is right. You *do* have more of that gold, don't you, father?"

We followed the North Caravan Route westward toward the Drasnian border. It was autumn by now, and the leaves of the birch and aspen groves had begun to turn golden. That's always very pretty, but it *does* sort of hint at the onset of winter, and we still had to go through the mountains up around Yar Gurak.

Pol and I hurried right along, but when we reached the mountains, our luck ran out. An early blizzard swept down out of Morindland and buried us in about five feet of snow. I put together a crude sort of shelter in a thick grove of jack-pines, and we sat out the storm. It blew itself out after three days, and we set out again. It was very slow going, and Pol's temper began to deteriorate about midmorning. "This is ridiculous, father!" She snapped. "There are other ways for us to get to where we're going, you know."

I shook my head. "We're in Angarak territory, Pol, and that means Grolims. Let's not make any noise if we don't have to. We'll get through all right—if the weather holds."

But of course, it didn't. Another blizzard came along right on the heels of the first one, and I had to build us another shelter.

It must have been about midmorning of the following day when we had a visitor. The gale was howling around our makeshift shelter, and the snow was coming down so thickly that we couldn't see ten feet. Then a voice came out of the snow. "Hello, the camp," it said. "I'm coming in. Don't get excited."

He seemed to be a fairly old man, lean and stringy, and his tangled hair was as white as the snow around him. He was bundled to the ears in furs, and his face was tanned, weatherbeaten, and deeply wrinkled. His blue eyes didn't seem to be all that old, however. "Got yourself in trouble, didn't you?" he observed as he came trudging through the driving snow. "Didn't you smell this storm coming?"

I shrugged. "We thought we could outrun it."

"Not much chance of that up in these mountains. Which way were you bound?"

"Toward Drasnia."

"You'll never make it. You started out too late. I expect you'll have to winter up here."

"That's impossible," Pol told him.

"I know these mountains, girl. This is just about as far as you're going to get until spring." He squinted at us, then he sighed. "I guess there's no help for it. You'd better come with me." He didn't sound too happy about it.

"Where are we going?" I asked him.

"I'm wintering in a cave about a mile from here. It's not much of a cave, but it's better than this lean-to you've got here. I guess I can put up with a little company for one winter. At least it'll give me somebody to talk to. My donkey listens pretty good, but he don't answer very often when I say something to him."

I'm sure that Garion and Silk remember that old fellow. We ran across him in those same mountains years later while we were on our way to Cthol Mishrak.

He never did tell us what his name was. I'm sure that he'd had a name at some time, but it's entirely possible that he'd forgotten it. He talked a great deal during that seemingly endless winter, but there was very little in the way of information in what he said. I gathered that he'd spent his life looking for gold up in these mountains, but I got the impression that he didn't really look that hard for it. He just liked being in the mountains.

I don't think I've ever known anybody who could see as much in a single glance as that old man did. He'd realized almost as soon as he saw us that Pol and I weren't ordinary people, but if he had any opinions about that, he kept them to himself.

I liked him, and I think Polgara did, too. She *didn't* like the fact that he kept his donkey and our horses in the cave with us, though. They talked about that quite a bit that winter, as I recall.

As he'd predicted, the blizzards kept rolling in out of Morindland, and the snowdrifts just kept growing. He and I hunted, of course, and I grew more than a little tired of a steady diet of venison. Pol had taken over the cooking, but even Pol began to run out of recipes before winter was over.

I didn't say anything about it, but despite Pol's aversion to the little beast, the old man's donkey grew very fond of her, and he showed his affection by butting at her with his head, usually when she wasn't expecting it. Maybe he thought it was funny to surprise her.

Then, after it seemed that the winter would last forever, our host went to the mouth of the cave one morning and sniffed at the air. "It's just about over," he told us. "We'll get a warm wind out of Drasnia before the day's out, and it'll cut off all this snow before you know it. The river'll run bank-full for a few days, but it'll be safe to travel by the end of the week. I've enjoyed your company, you two, but it's coming on time for us to go our separate ways."

"Which way will you go after the weather clears?" Pol asked him.

He scratched at his head. "Haven't decided yet," he replied. "South maybe, or maybe back up toward Morindland. Maybe I'll just see which way the wind's blowing when the time comes to start out—or maybe I'll just let the donkey decide. It don't really matter none to me—as long as we stay in the mountains."

His prediction about the change in the weather turned out to be very accurate, and about at the end of that week, Pol and I said good-bye and set out again. There were still snowbanks back under the trees, but the trails were mostly clear. We reached the Drasnian border in about four days, and a week later we reached Boktor.

The pestilence I mentioned earlier had run its course in western Drasnia, but among its victims were Rhodar's father and Silk's mother. The king died, but Silk's mother didn't. The disease had disfigured her horribly, but it also had taken her sight, so she couldn't look into a mirror to see her ruined face. Silk and his father *could*; neither of them ever mentioned it to her, though.

Pol and I stayed in Boktor to attend Rhodar's coronation, and then I bought a boat so that we could go on down the Mrin River and through the fens. I don't really like the fens, but the Great North Road had too many travelers on it at this time of year for my comfort.

Winters can be miserable, but there are times when spring's even worse—particularly in the fens. It started raining on the day when Pol and I set out from Boktor, and it rained steadily for at least a week. I started to wonder if there might have been another eclipse to disturb the weather patterns.

At one time or another, most of you probably have gone through the fens, since you almost have to if you want to get to Boktor from the west. For those of you who haven't, though, all you really need to know about them is the fact that it's all one vast marsh lying between the Mrin and Aldur rivers. It's filled with rushes, cattails, and stringy willow trees that trail their limbs in the water. The two rivers that feed it insure that the water's not stagnant, but their currents are so slow that it comes fairly close. The customary way to get a boat through the fens is to pole it along. Rowing doesn't really work very well, since many of those channels are too narrow to give oars much play. I don't *like* poling boats, but in the fens there isn't much choice.

"I think we should have booked passage on some merchantman in Boktor," I said moodily one rainy morning. "We could be halfway to Darine by now."

"Well, it's too late to turn back now, father," Pol said. "Just keep poling."

We began to see fenlings—quite a few of them—and then, to my absolute amazement, we came around bend in the channel we were following and there was a house!

Actually, it was more in the nature of a cottage built of weathered logs and surmounted by a thatched roof. It stood in the middle of a grove of sad-looking willows on a small island that rose in a gentle slope out of the surrounding water.

As I poled the boat closer, one of the fenlings we'd noticed swam on ahead, climbed up on the muddy bank of that little island, and loped like an otter up to the door of the cottage, chittering urgently.

Then the door opened, and a woman stood there looking gravely out at us through the drizzling rain. "Welcome to the house of Vordai," she said to my daughter and me, but there wasn't much welcome in her tone of voice.

"I'm a little surprised to see anyone living in a place like this," I called to her.

"There are reasons," she replied. "You might as well come inside—at least until the rain lets up."

I've had more gracious invitations in my time, but something seemed to come together in my head, and it told me that I was supposed to accept this one, no matter how ungracious it was.

I poled our boat up to the island, and Pol and I stepped out on the shore.

"So you're Vordai," Polgara said to the woman at the cottage door.

"And you would be Polgara," the woman replied.

"I seem to be missing something here," I told them.

"We know each other by reputation, father," Pol told me. "Vordai's the one they call the Witch of the Fens. She's an outcast, and this is the only place in all of Drasnia that's safe for her."

"Probably because the firewood here is too wet to make burning people at the stake practical," the owner of the cottage added with a certain bitterness. "Come in out of the rain, both of you." The Witch of the Fens was a very old woman, but there were still traces of what must have been a luminous beauty in her face—marred, I'll admit, by the bitter twist to her lips. Life hadn't been good to Vordai the witch.

No one who's spent any time in Drasnia hasn't heard of the Witch of the Fens, but I'd always assumed that the stories I'd heard were no more than fairy tales, and most of them probably were. She was most definitely not a hag, for one thing, and I'm fairly sure that she didn't go out of her way to lure unwary travelers into quicksand bogs, for another. Certain events in her past had made her absolutely indifferent to other humans.

The interior of her cottage was scrupulously neat. The ceiling was low and heavily beamed, and the wooden floor had been scrubbed until it was white. There was a pot hanging in her fireplace; there were wild-flowers in a vase on her table, and curtains at the window.

Vordai wore a plain brown dress, and she limped slightly. She looked worn and tired. "So this is the famous Belgarath," she said, taking our wet cloaks and hanging them on pegs near her fire.

"Disappointing, isn't he?" Pol said.

"No," Vordai replied, "not really. He's about what I'd have expected."
She gestured toward her table. "Seat yourselves. I think there's enough in
the pot for us all."

"You knew that we were coming, didn't you, Vordai?" Pol suggested.

"Naturally. I *am* a witch, after all."

A fenling came in through the open door and stood up on its short
hind legs. It made that peculiar chittering sound that fenlings all
make.

"Yes," Vordai said to the little creature, "I know."

"It's true, then," Pol said cryptically, eyeing the fenling.

"Many unusual things are true, Polgara," Vordai replied.

"You shouldn't really have tampered with them, you know."

"I didn't hurt them, and I've found that tampering with *humans* can
be very dangerous. All in all, I much prefer the company of fenlings to
that of my fellow man."

"They're cleaner, if nothing else," Pol agreed.

"That's because they bathe more often. The rain should let up soon,
and you and your father will be able to continue your journey. In the
meantime, I'll offer breakfast. That's about as far as I'd care to stretch my
hospitality."

There were a lot of things going on that I didn't completely understand. Evidently Polgara's studies had taken her into an examination of
witchcraft, an area I'd neglected, and there were things passing back and
forth between Pol and the Witch of the Fens that were incomprehensible
to me. The one thing that I *did* perceive, however, was the fact
that this lonely old woman had been treated very badly at some time in
the past.

All right, Garion, don't beat it into the ground. Yes, as a matter of fact,
I *did* feel sorry for Vordai—almost as sorry as I had felt for Illessa. I'm not
a monster, after all. Why do you think I did what I did when you and Silk
and I passed through the fens on our way to Cthol Mishrak? It certainly
wasn't because I couldn't think of any alternatives.

As Vordai had suggested it might, the sky cleared along about noon, and
Pol and I put on our now-dry cloaks and went back to our boat.

Vordai didn't even bother to see us off.

I poled the boat around another bend in that twisting channel we
had been following, and as soon as we were out of sight of that lonely
cottage there in the middle of that vast swamp, Pol's eyes filled with tears.
I didn't really think it would have been appropriate for me to ask her

why. When the occasion demands it, Pol can be absolutely ruthless, but she's not inhuman.

We came out of the fens near Aldurford and continued on foot along the eastern border of Sendaria until we reached the rutted track that led to Annath. It was midafternoon when we crossed the frontier, and Geran was waiting for us near the stone quarry on the outskirts of town when we finally arrived. "Thank the Gods!" he said fervently. "I was afraid you wouldn't make it back in time for the wedding!"

"What wedding?" Pol asked sharply

"Mine," Geran replied. "I'm getting married next week."

CHAPTER FORTY-NINE

The wedding of Geran and Ildera took place in the late spring of the year 5348, and the entire village of Annath took the day off work to attend. Not to be outdone, Ildera's leather-clad clansmen also came across the border to participate.

There'd been a certain amount of squabbling about who was going to officiate at the ceremony. Since Ildera was an Algar, the Priest of Belar who attended to the spiritual needs of her clan assumed that *he* should be the one to conduct the ceremony, but the local Sendarian priest had objected strenuously. Polgara had stepped in at that point and smoothed things over—on the surface, at least—by suggesting the simple expedient of having *two* ceremonies instead of one. It didn't matter to me one way or the other, so I kept my nose out of it.

Some frictions had arisen between Geran's mother, Alara, and Ildera's mother, Olane. Ildera's father, Grettan, was a Clan-Chief, after all, and that's about as close as you're going to get to nobility in Algar society. Geran, on the other hand, was the son of an ordinary stone-cutter, so Olane didn't make any secret of the fact that she felt that her daughter was marrying beneath her. That didn't set at all well with Alara, and Pol had been obliged to speak with her firmly to prevent her from blurting out some things about her son's heritage that others didn't need to know about. These periodic outbreaks of animosity between mothers have caused Pol more concern over the centuries than Chamdar himself, I think.

Country weddings are normally rather informal affairs. The bride-groom usually takes a bath, and most of the time he'll put on a clean shirt, but that's about as far as it goes. Olane's superior attitude in this sit-uation, however, had moved Alara to tear the village of Annath apart in search of finery in which to dress her son. Quite by chance she discovered that the local cobbler had a dust-covered old purple doublet hanging in his attic, and she'd badgered the poor man unmercifully until he'd finally agreed to lend it to Geran. She'd washed it and almost forcibly compelled my grandson to put it on for the happy occasion.

It didn't fit him very well, though, and he kept reaching up under it trying to adjust it. "Just leave it alone, Geran," his father told him while the three of us were waiting for the ceremony to begin. "You'll rip it."

"I don't see why I have to wear this silly thing anyway, father," Geran complained. "I've got a perfectly good tunic."

"Your mother wants you to look a bit more dressed up in front of the Algars," Darral told him. "Let's not go out of our way to disappoint her. She's having a little problem right now, so let's humor her. Do it as a fa-vor to your poor old father, Geran. *You* might be eating in your own kitchen from now on, but I still have to eat what your mother prepares. Just wear the doublet, boy. You can endure it for a few hours, and it'll make *my* life a lot easier."

Geran grumbled a bit and then went back to that nervous pacing that all bridegrooms seem to find entertaining.

Since the weather was fine and there were a lot of guests in atten-dance, the wedding took place in a pleasant flower-strewn meadow on the outskirts of Annath. When the time came, Darral and I escorted our ner-vous bridegroom to the altar that'd been erected in the center of the field and where the two priests who were to officiate stood glowering at each other. I could see from their expressions that Pol's suggestion hadn't quite ironed out all the wrinkles.

The immediate families of the bride and groom were seated on benches just in front of the altar while the rest of the guests stood. The Sendars were all dressed in sober, serviceable brown, and they stood on one side. The Algars wore black horsehide and they stood on the other. There were some hard looks being exchanged, I noticed. The hostility be-tween Olane and Alara had obviously polarized the wedding guests into two opposing camps.

Most of the residents of Annath were stone-cutters by trade, so there weren't any competent musicians among the Sendarian contingent; and Algars are so unmusical that most of them couldn't carry a tune in a bucket. Pol had considered this and had wisely decided to forgo the tra-ditional bridal march. There was enough trouble in the wind already.

Some chance remark by a budding music critic might well have set off the fights even before the ceremony.

Ildera was escorted to the alter by her father, Grettan, whose expression indicated that he was devoutly wishing that this day would end. The bride, dressed all in white and with a garland of spring flowers encircling her pale, blonde head, was radiant. Brides always are—or had you noticed that? Brides are radiant, and bridegrooms are nervous. Does that suggest to you who *really* runs the world?

Polgara—dressed in blue, naturally—came immediately behind Ildera and Grettan. Though this was supposed to be a happy event, Polgara's face was stern. There was an enormous potential for violence in the air, and Pol wanted everybody to understand that she'd brook no nonsense here.

The double ceremony seemed to go on for hours. I'm fairly sure that Geran felt it did, at any rate. The Algar priest invoked the blessing of Belar at some length, and the Sendarian priest responded by invoking the blessing of each of the other six Gods in turn. I tried not to show any visible signs of amusement when he got to Torak. I was almost positive that even if he'd been awake, Torak wouldn't have responded, since this particular wedding and its ultimate outcome was most definitely not the sort of thing to fill the One-eyed God with rejoicing and goodwill. The Sendars are broadly ecumenical, however, so they habitually include all seven Gods in their religious observances.

At any rate, the ceremony was finally completed, and the bride and groom exchanged a chaste kiss. Then came the wedding banquet, which Pol herself had prepared, and there were many toasts to the bride and groom. Along about sunset, the happy couple was escorted to the front door of the house Geran had built for them by everyone still sober enough to walk.

Then, as a soft and luminous evening settled over Annath, the fights got under way.

All in all, it was a fairly successful wedding.

I spent the night in Darral's house, and the next morning, Pol woke me up just as the sun was rising. "What was all the shouting and noise last night?" she asked me.

"The wedding guests were celebrating."

"Really? It didn't sound exactly like a celebration to me."

"Weddings are emotional events, Pol, and all sorts of emotions were floating around last evening."

"It sounded like a general brawl, father."

"No wedding's complete without a few fights. They make the occasion memorable."

"Were there many fatalities?"

"None that I know of. That windy Priest of Belar won't be giving any long sermons for a while, though—at least not until his broken jaw heals."

"No cloud's without its silver lining, I suppose. What are your plans?"

"I think I'll go back to the Vale. This wedding's been a kind of EVENT, and it might have shaken a few more things out of the Mrin. Besides, I'd better get away from Annath. Chamdar's in Tolnedra right now, but I'm sure he's got Grolims out scouting around, and I don't want to attract attention to this place."

"Wise decision. Give my best to the twins."

"I'll do that."

And so I got up and dressed. I ate a rather hasty breakfast and rambled down to the other end of the single street of the village of Annath to pay my respects to the bride and groom. Geran had that somewhat startled look on his face that new husbands always seem to have, and Ildera spent a lot of time blushing, as new wives almost always do. I took that to be a good sign. Then I left Annath and went on back to the Vale.

I didn't really do much when I got home. Something very important was about to happen, and my anticipation made it a little hard for me to concentrate. Despite their best efforts, the twins had been unable to dig anything else significant out of the Mrin. Garion's friend, like the rest of us, seemed to be just biding his time.

Sometimes it seems that I've spent most of my life biding my time.

It was just after Erastide the following winter when Beldin came home. I don't really like to travel in the wintertime myself, but Beldin has always ignored the seasons—one of the results of his peculiar childhood, I'd imagine. Just to pass the time, I'd been rereading an ancient Melcene epic that recounted the probably mythic adventures of one of their national heroes, the halfwit who'd blundered out to sea in a small boat and had discovered the Melcene Islands off the east coast of Mallorea.

"Belgarath!" my distorted brother bellowed up to me from down below. "Open your stupid door!"

I went to the head of the stairs. "Open!" I told the flat boulder that kept most of the weather out of the vestibule of my tower. It rolled smoothly off to one side, and Beldin came in. "Why do you keep that silly thing closed?" he demanded, stamping the snow off his feet.

"Habit, I suppose," I replied. "Come on up."

He clumped up the stairs. "Aren't you ever going to clean this place?" he asked, looking around at clutter I've grown so accustomed to that I didn't even notice it any more.

"I'll get to it—one of these days. What finally persuaded you to come down off the top of that ridge in southern Cthol Murgos?"

"An earthquake, actually. Did something significant happen last spring?"

"Oh, Geran and Ildera got married."

"If the twins are right, that's probably the most significant thing to happen since Vo Mimbre. That explains the earthquake, I guess."

"Did it wake up Torak?"

"Not as far as I could tell. He didn't blow out the side of his cave, anyway. How was the wedding?"

"Not bad. The ceremony itself was tedious, but the fights afterward were fairly exciting."

"Sorry I missed it, then," he said with that short, ugly laugh of his. "Is Ildera pregnant yet?"

"Not that I've heard."

"What's taking them so long?"

"The Necessity, I'd imagine. The birth of the Godslayer's going to be one of those EVENTS, and time's rather crucial in those. Ildera won't get pregnant until the Necessity decides that it's the proper moment. Has Zedar ever come back to that cave?"

"Not yet. He's probably still wandering around. Have the twins found out what he's looking for?"

"No. At least they haven't said so to me."

"Are you sure that Geran's going to be the father of the one we've been waiting for?"

"The twins seem to think so. It's going to happen in this century, anyway."

"Well, it's about time!"

"Patience was never one of your strong points, brother mine. What took you so long to get here from Cthol Murgos?"

"I went out and had a look around. There's trouble in Mallorea."

"Oh?"

"Zakath's been crowned emperor, and that terrified Taur Urgas for some reason, so he decided to take steps."

"Why's Taur Urgas so afraid of Zakath?"

"Taur Urgas is crazy, Belgarath, and crazy people don't need reasons for the things they do—or for the way they feel. Zakath's a very ambitious young man, though, and Taur Urgas has agents in Mallorea keeping an eye on him. Mallorea's a big place, but the notion of being Overking of All of Angarak seems to appeal to Zakath for some reason, and word of that's been filtering back to Rak Goska. I guess it's making Taur Urgas very nervous. Mallorea's at least twice the size of Cthol Murgos, and it's got about five times as many people. If Zakath decides that he wants to rule the Angarak world, there wouldn't be very much Taur Urgas could do to prevent it."

"If we're lucky, we might see a repetition of what happened in the Desert of Araga just before Vo Mimbre."

"I wouldn't get my hopes up, Belgarath. Torak's going to wake up before too much longer, and Old Burnt-face is at least as crazy as Taur Urgas is, but he *does* have a long memory. He's *not* going to permit Taur Urgas and Zakath to repeat what Ctuchik and Urvon did to disrupt his plans last time."

"You said that Taur Urgas was taking steps. What did he do?"

"I think I told you that Zakath went to Melcena to study at the university. He was *very* impressed with Melcena. When you get right down to it, Mal Zeth's not much more than an army camp, but Melcena's very civilized and sophisticated. Zakath was the crown prince of Mallorea, so he was customarily invited into the best homes in town. He was introduced to a high-ranking Melcena girl of his own age, and she absolutely took his breath away." He sighed. "If that'd been allowed to run its course, it probably would have changed the course of history. The girl was beautiful and brilliant. Her influence on Zakath would have been enormous."

"What happened?"

"I was just getting to that. It was at that point that Taur Urgas stepped in. His agents reported the connection between Zakath and the Melcene girl, and they *also* reported that the girl was a member of a high-ranking family that was in debt up to its eyebrows. Taur Urgas is crazy, but he's not stupid. He saw the possibilities of the situation immediately. He sent orders to his people in Melcena to quietly buy up those debts. Once he owned their obligations, he was in a position to put quite a bit of pressure on the girl's family."

"What did he hope to gain from that?"

"Zakath came to the throne when he was eighteen or so, and it was fairly common knowledge in Melcena that there was a marriage proposal in the wind. Taur Urgas is a Murgo, so he's abysmally ignorant of the nature of the Melcenes. Murgo women are kept penned up and ignorant, so they do what their families tell them to do. Obedience is beaten into them from the cradle. A Murgo girl would cut her own throat if her father told her to. Melcene girls are more spirited, but Taur Urgas didn't know that. He just assumed that the girl would do whatever her family ordered her to do. He sent word to his people in Melcene to give the girl's family some very specific instructions and to threaten to call in their debts if they didn't obey. The family had been scrambling round trying to raise enough money to pay off those debts, but they needed more time, so they *seemed* to go along with the plot."

"This is starting to sound like a bad Arendish tragedy, Beldin," I observed.

"Oh, it gets even worse. Taur Urgas had a very simple plan to delete a potential rival. He sent one of the more potent Nyissan poisons to a nephew of his in the city of Melcene—along with some very blunt instructions. The girl was supposed to encourage Zakath's attentions and then to poison him at the first opportunity. A nice obedient Murgo girl would have done exactly that, but a Melcene girl would have refused. Taur Urgas is so crazy that he couldn't tell the difference. The girl's family was still playing for time, so they pretended to agree. Unfortunately, there are always a few black sheep in any flock, and an unscrupulous fellow in one of the minor branches of the family saw a chance to make a killing." Beldin made a sour face. "Bad choice of words there, perhaps."

"I think I see where this is going."

"I thought you might. Anyway, this devious scoundrel sold the details of the plot to some government officials, and the word filtered up to Zakath himself. Despite his civilized manner, Zakath's still an Angarak, so he immediately went up in flames. Without even thinking, he ordered the extermination of every member of that Melcene family. His underlings— also Angaraks—followed his orders to the letter. The girl was among the first to fall. When the information came to light later that she'd been totally innocent, Zakath quite nearly went mad with grief and remorse. He locked himself in his room for about six months, and when he came out, he was an entirely different man. Before the incident, he seemed to be a civilized, enlightened sort of fellow who probably would have made a good emperor. Now he's an absolute monster who rules Mallorea with an iron fist, and he's obsessed with the idea of doing some *very* unpleasant things to Taur Urgas."

"More power to him." I approved. "If I weren't so busy right now, I might offer to lend him a hand."

"You can be nasty when you set your mind to it, Belgarath, but you're no match for Zakath. He sent Taur Urgas a letter after he came out of seclusion, and he ordered copies of the letter widely circulated—just to add to the insult, I'd imagine. I got my hands on a copy." He reached inside his ragged tunic and brought out a folded piece of paper. "Would you like to read the most insulting letter one reigning monarch has ever sent to another?"

I took the paper, unfolded it, and read.

"To His Majesty, Taur Urgas of Murgodom," it began.

I was unamused by your recent attempt to influence Mallorean internal affairs, you Murgo dog. Were it not for current world conditions, I would bring the entire weight of my empire down upon your head for your offense.

To insure that there will be no recurrence of this affair, I

have taken all Murgos within my boundaries into custody to
serve as hostages to your continued good behavior. I am advised
that several of these internees are closely related to you. Should
you instigate further adventures in my realm, I shall return your
kinsmen to you—piece by piece.

In the past, your madness has filled your world with imagined
enemies. Rejoice, Taur Urgas, and put aside your insanity, for you
now have a *real* foe, far more deadly than any of the phantoms
of your lunacy. You may be assured that as soon as world conditions permit, I will descend upon you and that stinking wasteland
you rule. It is my firm intention to destroy you and your entire
vile race. It will be my pleasure to exterminate every last Murgo
from the face of the world and to expunge every mention of your
people from the record of human history.

Keep a watchful eye over your shoulder, you madman, for as
surely as the sun rises tomorrow, one day I will be there to ad-
minister the punishment you so richly deserve.

Zakath.

I whistled and handed the letter back. "That comes very close to being an open declaration of war," I said.

"Impressive, wot?" Beldin agreed with a broad grin. "I may just frame
it and hang it on the wall in my tower. I've heard that Taur Urgas was
frothing at the mouth and chewing up the carpet before he even finished
reading it. Zakath's been carrying out his threat, too. He's been sending
bits and pieces of assorted Murgos to Rak Goska for the edification of the
Murgo King. Urvon's been trying to make peace between the two of
them, but he's not making much progress. Zakath's heart's been turned to
stone, and Taur Urgas is getting crazier by the minute."

"I'll pass this on to Rhodar," I said. "Drasnian intelligence might be
able to keep the pot boiling. Is Ctuchik doing anything?"

"Ctuchik's *your* responsibility, Belgarath. I *did* hear that he'd formed
a Council of Hierarchs, though. I don't know that they'll ever be very
significant, Grolim politics being what they are. I saw several Murgo car-
avans on the south trail as I came across. Are they up to something?"

I nodded. "They're coming west in droves, pretending to be interested in trade. It's probably Chamdar's idea. He can read the signs as well
as we can, so he knows we're getting close. Evidently he want *lots* of
help."

"Where is he now?"

"In Tolnedra, last I heard. Drasnian intelligence is keeping track of
him for me."

"You've got just about everybody in the West doing your work for you, haven't you, Belgarath?"

"It's called 'delegating responsibility,' brother. There's a lot going on right now, so I have to stay flexible."

"Somehow I knew you'd have some facile explanation for the fact that you're loafing. Don't get *too* comfortable, Belgarath. When the time comes, you might just have to be in six or eight places all at the same time. Let's go see the twins. This business between Zakath and Taur Urgas might have shaken a few more clues out of the Mrin."

It hadn't, though. The Mrin Codex remained as intractable as always. I could only assume that the Necessity knew what it was doing and that it was deliberately keeping me in the dark.

I don't think any of us have ever given full credit to the twins for their patient centuries of labor. That pair of gentle Alorn shepherds have been so vital to what the rest of us have done that in a rather special way, they've been our guides. *We* run around the world in response to what *they* discover. The Necessity usually doesn't bother to talk to *us*. It talks to the twins instead. They've worn out six or eight copies of the Mrin and the Darine over the years, and the Gods know that *I* wouldn't have had that kind of patience, and neither would Beldin. To this very day, if the twins told me to jump, I'd be about four feet up in the air before I even bothered to ask "Which way?" That's probably what Aldur had in mind when he first sent for them. The Master's at least as much a slave to the Necessity as the rest of us are. That's why we're all here, I guess.

Beldin remained in the Vale for a week or so, and then he returned to southern Cthol Murgos to take up his lonely vigil over our Master's sleeping brother. Not long after he left, I went to Boktor to advise Rhodar of the contention between Zakath and Taur Urgas, King Rhodar wasn't getting any slimmer, but his mind seemed to be growing even faster than his waistline. He squinted at me shrewdly after I'd told him of the recent events in Mallorea. "This isn't natural, Belgarath. A Murgo king wouldn't be interested enough in what's happening in Mallorea to take all that much trouble. There's a whole ocean between the two countries. Some EVENT's about to happen, isn't it? The reports I've been getting are raising a strong odor of something momentous in the wind."

There wasn't really any point in trying to hide things from Rhodar. his spies were too good, and his mind was too quick. "Why don't we just say that we're living in interesting times and let it go at that, Rhodar?"

I suggested. "You deal with the ordinary world and let me take care of the other one."

"Is there going to be a war involved? If so, I'd better start recruiting more men for my army."

"That'd be premature, and don't be too obvious about going to a war footing. Concentrate on this enmity between the Murgos and the Malloreans instead. If it *does* get down to a war, I don't want the Angaraks to be all cozy with each other." Then I changed the subject. "When are you going to get married?"

"Not for a while yet." His tone was evasive and his expression slightly embarrassed. Now that I think back on it, I'm almost certain that he already had his eye on Porenn, who was only about thirteen at the time, as I recall.

I went on to Val Alorn and from there to the Isle of the Winds. I didn't really have any specific reasons for those trips, but I always like to keep an eye on the Alorns. They have a tendency to get into trouble if you don't watch them rather closely.

Then, in 5349, my grandson Darral was killed by a rockslide in the quarry where he worked, and I rushed back to Annath. There wasn't anything I could do about it, of course, but I went all the same. A death in the family's not the sort of thing you just let slide, and Polgara's always taken these things very hard. You'd think Pol and I would have grown philosophical about the notion of human mortality by now, but we hadn't. I'd loved Darral, naturally. He *was* my grandson, after all, but I'd steeled myself to the idea that one day he'd grow old and die. It happens, and there's nothing you can do about it. Polgara, however, isn't temperamentally equipped to take this sort of thing philosophically. She always seems to take the death of a loved one as a personal insult of some kind. Maybe her medical studies have had something to do with that. For a physician, death is the ultimate enemy.

I tried to console her with the usual platitudes, but she wanted no part of that. "Just go away and leave me alone, father," she told me flatly. "I'll deal with this in my own way."

So I went on down the street to talk with Geran. "What really happened?" I asked him.

"There must have been some hidden flaw in that rock-face, grandfather," he replied somberly. "Father and I had both checked it from top to bottom. It seemed completely sound, and there hadn't been any hints of weakness. The workmen were cutting blocks off the top of the face, and the whole thing just gave way and collapsed. Father was down in the quarry at the bottom of the face, and there was no way he could get out from under it when it came down." His face grew angry, and he slammed his fist down on the table. "There was no reason for it, grandfather! That face should *not* have broken away! I'm going to tear that mountain apart until I find out why it happened!"

I know now why it happened—and who was responsible. That's one of the reasons that I take an enormous satisfaction in what Garion did to Chamdar down in the Wood of the Dryads.

Polgara remained inconsolable. There was nothing I could do or say to comfort her. She locked herself in her room and refused to talk to any of us. For a time I was about half afraid that she would go mad with grief.

Darral's wife did.

It wasn't too obvious at first. After her initial outburst of grief, she seemed to grow abnormally calm. Two weeks after the funeral, she went back to her normal routine of cleaning house, sweeping off her doorstep, and preparing meals as if nothing had happened. Quite frequently, she even sang while she was cooking.

I'm sure that there are people out there who'll say that this is a healthy way to deal with grief, but they're wrong. The death of a wife or husband is a wound that takes years to heal. Believe me, I know. If my own grief hadn't been so profound, I'd have recognized the fact that something wasn't right.

Alara cooked the usual meals, and she always set a place for Darral at her table. Then, as evening descended, she'd keep going to the door to look out anxiously into Annath's single street as if she were waiting for someone to come home to supper. The signs of her madness were all there. I can't believe that Pol and I missed them.

If I'd been just a bit more alert, I'd have realized who'd been responsible for Darral's death and Alara's madness. At that point, I'd have torn the world apart looking for Asharak the Murgo, and when I caught him I'd have cut his throat all the way back to the neck bone—with a dull saw. It might have taken me awhile, but I'd have enjoyed every minute of it.

Of course I'm a savage. Haven't you realized that yet?

I'm not saying here that Alara went stark-staring mad. She just got vague—which is probably even worse, when you get right down to it. As

Polgara recovered from her own sorrow, she was obliged to keep a more or less continual watch over Alara, and that turned out to be fairly significant as time went on.

I took my own sorrow out on the road. Walking thirty miles a day or so will numb almost any emotion, and I definitely didn't think that a return to the waterfront dives of Camaar would have been a good idea right then. I drifted back to the Vale in the last spring of 5351, and Javelin was there, waiting for me. "We lost him, Ancient One," he confessed with a certain degree of shame. "I've had people watching him from every possible angle, and one day he simply wasn't there any more. Chamdar's a Murgo, and they're not supposed to be that clever."

"He's deceptive, Khendon." I sighed. "It looks as if I'm going to have to put on my walking shoes again. I'd better go find him."

"Aren't you getting a little old for this kind of thing, Holy One?" he asked me with surprising directness. "Keeping track of Chamdar was *my* job. Why don't you let *me* locate him?"

"I may be old, Javelin, but I can still run *you* into the ground any day in the week. Just don't get in my way. If you do, I'll run right up your back." I hate having people make an issue of my age. Don't they realize by now that it doesn't mean anything?

"It shall be as you say, Ancient One," he replied with a curt bow. At least he had sense enough to know when to back away.

I went directly to Tol Honeth to take up the search. As closely as the twins were able to determine, we were within a couple of years of the birth of the Godslayer, and I vividly remembered Chamdar's audible ruminations back when Gelane had fallen in with the Bear-cult. Ctuchik had ordered his Grolim underling to *kill* Iron-grip's heir, but Chamdar had come up with an alternative to that. He was looking for the chance to be elevated to disciple status and thus to step over Ctuchik to deliver the Godslayer and the Orb directly to Torak. He was ambitious, I'll give him that. I quite literally tore Tolnedra apart, but I couldn't put my hands on him. He'd stolen a page out of my own book and had laid down various hints and false clues that kept me running from one end of Tolnedra to the other. I didn't find out exactly how he'd done it until after the tragedy in Annath.

Lelldorin, the Archer mentioned in the Mrin, was born in 5352, but I didn't have time to look in on the Wildantor family, since I was too busy ripping up the paving stones in Tol Honeth looking for my elusive Grolim adversary. After a while I started to get irritable.

Javelin returned to Tol Honeth to help me, and he shrewdly prevailed on the Drasnian Ambassador to try to enlist the aid of Ce'Nedra's father in the search. Tolnedran intelligence isn't really a match for what the Drasnains can come up with, but it would have put more eyes out there on the streets. Ran Borune XXIII wasn't having any of that, though. He was involved in some rather delicate trade negotiations with the representatives of Taur Urgas, and he wasn't inclined to do anything at all to disrupt those negotiations, so he withheld the services of his assorted spies and informers. I *liked* Ran Borune, and I adore his daughter, but he was greedy, and the prospect of getting his hands on all that red Murgo gold turned his head, so Javelin and I got no help whatsoever from Tolnedran intelligence.

Finally, in the late summer of 5354, I was ready to give up entirely. It was obvious by then that the various clues I'd been frantically chasing up and down the length and breadth of Tolnedra were no more than false trails. For once Chamdar had outsmarted me. I was absolutely certain that he wasn't in Tolnedra any more, so I gave Javelin the thankless task of chasing down all the fictitious "Chamdars" that the Grolims were inventing for our entertainment and took myself off to Arendia.

And the Grolims there were as busy as the ones in Tolnedra had been. I'll give Chamdar credit here. He'd learned all the lessons I'd given him over the centuries very well. I heard stories about Asharak the Murgo every time I turned around, and the stories got wilder and wilder every day. Grolims are schemers, to be sure, but there's no sense of art in their schemes. They always go to extremes. I think it's a racial flaw.

Then, when I was riding north out of Vo Mimbre, I encountered a handsome young fellow in full armor sitting astride a prancing war-horse. I recognized the crest of the Mandor family on his shield. "Well met, Ancient Belgarath!" Mandorallen greeted me in that booming voice of his. "I have been in search of thee!" Mandorallen was only about seventeen at that time, but there was already an impressive muscularity about him.

"What is it this time, Mandorallen?" I demanded.

"I have been, as thou doubtless know—for certes, all things are known to thee—at Vo Ebor, where my dear friend and guardian, the baron of that fair domain, hath been providing instruction unto me in the knightly arts, and—"

"Mandorallen, get to the point!"

He looked a little injured by that. "In short," he said—as if a Mimbrate could ever say *anything* in short, "thy brethren Beltira and Belkira came but recently to Vo Ebor and besought me that I should seek thee out. Straightaway I went to horse, and, thinking that thou wert still in Tol Honeth, I posted southward that I might bring thee news that thy gentle brethren felt might be of interest unto thee."

"Oh? What news is this?"

"I confess that I have no understanding of the true import of their message, but I am instructed to advise thee that a certain kinswoman of thine is with child, and that thy daughter, whom I have not yet had the

pleasure of meeting—though I yearn for the day when I shall be privi-
leged to greet her and respectfully bend my knee unto her—"

"All right, Mandorallen, I get the message."

"This news, I presume, is of some significance?"

"Moderately so, Sir Knight."

"Might I know its import?"

"No, you might not. You don't need to know what it means. Turn
around and go back to Vo Ebor. You have performed your duty, Sir
Knight, and I thank you. Now go home."

I'll take this opportunity to apologize for my abruptness to the Knight
Protector. All I really wanted him to do was to get out of sight so that
I could go into paroxysms of exultation. Ildera was pregnant! The
Godslayer dozed beneath her heart!

I broke off my fruitless search for Chamdar at that point, since it was
fairly obvious that I wasn't going to find him. I went on up to Asturia to
have a look at Lelldorin, and I came away with the knowledge that he
was indeed the Wildantor we had been waiting for. Everything was
coming together the way it was supposed to, so I crossed Ulgoland to
the Vale.

When I got home, the twins advised me that Ildera would be delivered about midwinter.

"Polgara's going to move the family not long after the child's birth,"
Beltira told me.

"That's probably not a bad idea," I said. "We've all been in and out
of Annath quite frequently for about fifteen years now, and Chamdar's on
the loose out there somewhere. It'll be safer if Pol moves on. Is Alara improving at all?"

Belkira shook his head sadly. "She still refuses to accept the fact that
her husband's dead. Polgara's tried everything she can think of to bring
her out of it, but nothing's worked yet."

"A change of scene might bring her around," I suggested.

"It's hard to say." He didn't sound very hopeful about it.

The twins and I talked about it at some length, and we agreed that
I probably should go to Sendaria and let myself be seen in places other
than Annath. The Grolim prophecies, and probably the Ashabine Oracles, as well, were certainly keeping Ctuchik advised, so I was sure that
he knew of the Godslayer's imminent birth *and* the fact that he'd be born
in Sendaria. It was time for me to start pulling Chamdar out of position,
so I put on my storyteller's costume and went to Sendaria.

I stopped by the city of Sendar to look in on the new king, Fulrach, and his giddy wife, Layla. Don't misunderstand me here. I love Layla. She's probably got the biggest heart in the world, but she was awfully silly as a girl—and almost perpetually pregnant. I sometimes wonder how Fulrach found time to run his kingdom.

Then I went out into the countryside. I tramped the back roads and country lanes of central Sendaria all during the autumn and early winter of that year, and I'm positive that Chamdar's Grolims were watching my every move. I didn't go out of my way to make it difficult for them.

It was almost Erastide by now, and my sense of anticipation was growing stronger. Erastide is a major holiday in Sendaria, since it fits so neatly into the traditional ecumenicism of the Sendars. The date of the holiday—midwinter—is really quite arbitrary. The creation of the world didn't happen on a single day, but I guess the clergy just picked a day at random for the yearly celebration. As the holiday approached, I moved from Darine to Erat to Winold with a growing conviction that Erastide *this* year was going to be something rather special. It was the kind of thing Garion's friend would do.

I was completely out of touch, of course. We'd had evidence in the past that the Grolims have ways of listening when we communicate with each other in our rather peculiar way, and the upcoming EVENT was so important that we didn't want to give Chamdar anything to work with inadvertently. In retrospect, I can say that our extreme cautiousness was probably a mistake.

Polgara and I have gone over what happened in Annath that winter again and again and again, and we can now see exactly where we both made our mistakes. The death of Darral should have alerted us, for one thing. As Geran had suspected, that rockslide that had killed his father had *not* been a simple accident. In some way that we've never been able to determine, Chamdar *had* located my daughter and the family she'd protected for over thirteen centuries, and Darral's death—murder, I can call it—was just the first step in his elaborate plan.

Alara's insanity was the second step, I'm afraid, and Pol and I both missed it.

My daughter tells me that Alara's condition had worsened that fall and that she'd taken to wandering off into the surrounding mountains in search of her husband. I'm sure that Chamdar had a hand in that, too; the Grolims are expert at tampering with the minds of others, after all.

At any rate, it was on the day before Erastide when Ildera went into false labor, and Polgara had gone from Darral's house to the far end of the village to examine her, and Alara—at Chamdar's instigation, I'm sure— had seized the opportunity to go off into the nearby mountains in search of her husband. Pol returned to Darral's house and found that Alara was gone. It'd happened several times before, and Pol, quite naturally, went out to look for her.

And that's how Chamdar got Pol out of the way. She's blamed herself about that for years, but it wasn't her fault.

I'm convinced now that Ildera's false labor was also Chamdar's doing. You almost have to admire how carefully he orchestrated the events during those dreadful two days. Once Pol had left the village, Ildera's false labor turned into the real thing. There were other women in the village who knew what to do, of course, and Garion was born shortly after midnight on Erastide.

And Polgara, searching for Alara, was miles away!

That was when that familiar voice inside my head alerted me. "Belgarath!" It almost shouted, "Go to Annath immediately! The Child of Light is in danger!"

It didn't have to tell me twice. I was in Muros at the time, and it took me about a quarter of an hour to get out of town and sprout feathers. I almost tore my wings off trying to make good time, but I got there too late.

Following Ildera's delivery, the village women had done what women do after the birth of a child, and then they'd gone home. It was a holiday, after all, and there was cooking to be done. You see how shrewdly Chamdar'd planned everything?

It was just about dawn, and I was still winging my way in from Muros. Geran, Ildera, and Garion were alone in their little house, and that was when Chamdar made his move.

He set fire to the house.

It was a stone house, but Chamdar was a Grolim—and stone will burn if you make the fire hot enough.

To this day, I can't be entirely certain if Chamdar knew what Geran would do once he realized that there was no way he and Ildera could escape. It's entirely possible that he'd given up his wild notion of delivering the Rivan King to Torak and had decided instead to follow Ctuchik's instructions simply to kill Iron-grip's heir.

The doors and windows of the house were all engulfed in flames, and Geran, probably already in agony, realized that there was no possible way he could save himself or his wife, but there was a faint chance that he could save their son. His tools were in the house, and he was a stone-cutter. As closely as I can determine, he took up his hammer and chisel and chopped a small hole through the wall down close to the ground. Then, even as he was dying, he seized up the blanket-wrapped baby and pushed that precious bundle out through the hole he'd made.

And that was when I got there, just as dawn was breaking.

Either Chamdar had known what was going to happen, or he simply seized an opportunity when it presented itself. He dashed in, picked up the blanket-protected infant, and fled back out of range of the fire.

. Even as I was changing form in that snow-clogged street, I took in everything that was happening. I came very close at that point to doing something that's absolutely forbidden. I was right on the verge of obliterating Chamdar with the sheer force of my Will. I think that the only thing that pulled me back from that fatal mistake was the fact that I wanted to kill that murderous Grolim with my bare hands. I howled in fury as I ran through the snow at him, and that gave him just the moment of warning he needed. I'd often wished that I'd kept my mouth shut.

Chamdar spun around, his eyes wide with fright. "You!" he cried as I bore down on him with murder written all over my face. And then he did the only thing he could think of to save his own life.

He threw the baby at me.

CHAPTER
FIFTY

Chamdar's panic-stricken response at that point altered the course of history. In order to save his own life, he threw the infant Garion to safety. Had he been just a little more dedicated, he'd have turned and thrown the baby back into the fire.

My own dedication was a little stronger. I choked back my homicidal rage long enough to snatch the hurtling little bundle out of the air, and that gave Chamdar enough time to escape. I made a desperate leap to catch Garion, rolling in the dirt in the process, and by the time I looked back, Chamdar was gone. My howl of frustration woke everyone in the still-sleeping village, I think.

I have it on fairly good authority that it was precisely at that moment that Barak underwent his first metamorphosis up there in Cherek. It was momentary, but he *did* change over into the Dreadful Bear for a while. Garion *was* in danger at that point, and, all unthinking, Barak responded in the way he was supposed to. He was boar-hunting at the time, and he'd spent the night carousing with some friends. He was still fairly drunk, so all that he really remembers is waking up out in the woods standing over the half-eaten carcass of a wild pig.

Several of his hunting companions, however, were a bit more sober. I'm told that most of them took the pledge at that point and lived out the rest of their lives in total and absolute sobriety.

"*Father!*" Polgara's voice came to me.

"*You'd better get back here, Pol! Right now!*"

Then I knelt on the ground and unwrapped the baby I'd just grabbed out of midair. So far as I could tell, Garion was all right. He wasn't even crying. His expression was grave as he looked at me, and when our eyes met for the first time, I felt a powerful jolt at the very center of my being. I was suddenly filled with a kind of wonder; there was no question whatsoever that he was the one we'd all been waiting for.

Then I looked at the burning house, hoping that there still might be a chance to save Geran and Ildera, but it was clearly hopeless. I felt no signs of life in the midst of that fire. I broke down and wept.

Pol found me kneeling in tears beside the baby. "What happened, father?" she demanded.

"It was Chamdar!" I almost shouted at her. "Use your eyes, Pol! What were you thinking of? Why did you go off like that?" I've always regretted that outburst.

Pol's eyes grew stricken as my accusation struck her full in the face. She looked at the blazing house. "Is there any hope at all?" she asked me.

"None. They're both dead."

And that was when Polgara broke down. "I've failed, father!" she wailed. "I had the most important task in history, and I failed!"

I choked back my own grief. "There's no time for that now, Pol!" I told her sharply. "We have to get the baby away from here. Chamdar got away from me, and he could be almost anywhere."

"Why did you let him escape?"

"I didn't have any choice. I had to save the baby. There's nothing we can do here. Let's move!"

She bent and picked up Garion with that peculiar tenderness she's always demonstrated in caring for a long series of infants that were not really her own. When she straightened, her eyes were steely. "Chamdar's got a lot to answer for."

"That he does, Pol, and I'll do my best to make sure that his answering takes at least a week. What happened to Alara?"

"She walked off the edge of a cliff. She's dead, father."

My rage flared up again. "I'll add another week to what I'm going to do to Chamdar for that," I promised.

"Good! I'll take the baby. You go after Chamdar."

I shook my head. "Not a chance, Pol. I've got to get you two to safety first. Our main responsibility's wrapped up in that blanket. Let's go."

Pol and I left the village and took to the woods, avoiding all the roads and anything even remotely resembling a path. It wasn't a pleasant trip at that time of year, and I solved the problem of feeding Garion by the simple expedient of stealing a she-goat from an isolated farmstead.

Eventually we made our way down out of the mountains, and I took Pol back to her house at Erat. Then I went some distance away and summoned the twins, speaking so cryptically that I wasn't entirely positive that they'd understand what I was saying. I could only hope that they'd get the point when I told them that I needed them at "the rose garden."

Then I went back to Pol's thicket-enclosed house. "They should be along shortly," I told her. "I'll stay until they get here."

"I'll be all right, father. Don't let Chamdar get away."

"It's more important not to let him get behind me. I'll stay. Don't argue with me about it." I looked out the window at her winter-browned rose thicket. "I think your house here is too isolated to be entirely safe. Wait out the winter and then go find some remote village or farmstead and submerge yourself among the Sendars. Don't do anything to attract attention until I've dealt with Chamdar."

"Whatever you say, father."

It always makes me nervous when Pol takes that submissive attitude.

The twins had deciphered my message, and they arrived the next morning. I spoke with them briefly, and then I left Erat and went north to Boktor to speak with Hunter. The position, if you can call it that, was held at that time by an obscure filing clerk in the intelligence headquarters, a nondescript fellow named Khonar. "I need Prince Kheldar," I told him abruptly. "Where is he?"

Khonar carefully laid down the sheaf of documents he'd been reading. "May I ask why, Ancient One?"

"No, you may not. Where's Silk?"

"In Tol Honeth, Holy One. He's working for Javelin at the moment." He pursed his lips. "This is Kheldar's first assignment in the field, you know. He's not very experienced."

"Is he any good?"

"We have rather high hopes for him—as soon as he settles down. If it's important, I could go with you. I'm the best, after all."

"No. I think I'll need you here. Silk's the one I need. There are reasons."

"Oh," he said. "One of *those* things."

"Exactly. Have you heard anything at all about Asharak the Murgo lately?"

"He was in Arendia no more than a week ago, Ancient One. An agent of ours saw him at the Great Fair."

I heaved a very large sigh of relief. At least Chamdar wasn't poking around in Sendaria. "Which way did he go from the fair?"

"Southeast—toward the Tolnedran Mountains. Our agent reports that he seemed a little nervous about something."

"I can imagine," I said grimly. "He's done something that offended me. I want to talk with him about it, and he'd rather avoid that conversation—since it's very likely to involve my hanging his entrails on a fence someplace."

"That's fairly graphic." Nothing startles Hunter. "If any of my people come across him, do you want them to kill him?"

"No. I'll do that myself. Just locate him for me, if you can. Your people are good, but they're no match for Asharak."

His look grew shrewd. "You're being inconsistent, Ancient One. First you ask specifically for a man of twenty or so—no more than a year out of the academy—and then you say that my most experienced agents are no match for the man you're after."

"Consistency's the defense of small minds, Khonar. Get word to your people in Arendia and Tolnedra. I'll be there long before your messages arrive, and I'll have a look around first. Then I'll want every scrap of information about Asharak that they can lay their hands on."

He shrugged. "If that's the way you want it, Ancient One."

"It is. I'll be leaving now—and don't waste time trying to have me followed."

He counterfeited an innocent look. "Would I do that, Holy Belgarath?"

"You wouldn't be doing your job if you didn't."

I left Boktor that same afternoon, rather ostentatiously going southwest along the Great North Road, and I'm positive that at least one of Hunter's spies was following me. As soon as it grew dark, however, he lost my trail—unless he knew how to fly.

Although it was midwinter, the weather had cleared over the snow-choked mountains, and I flew over the southeastern edge of Sendaria and went on to Prolgu to advise the Gorim that the Godslayer had come. Then I flew on to the Great Fair on the plains of Mimbre to confer with Hunter's chief agent there, a lean Drasnian named Talvar.

Just by way of clarification here, Hunter's always been the most secret of Drasnian intelligence agents, and he—or she—frequently has a little private agency—a kind of secret service within a secret service. Drasnians are like that. They absolutely *love* secrets.

"We think this Asharak fellow might have doubled back, Ancient One," Talvar advised me. "When he left here, he was going southeasterly toward the Tolnedran Mountains, but there are some things going on in Vo Mimbre that seem to have his distinctive footprints all over them."

"Oh?"

"There's a Murgo trade delegation there, and they're spending a lot of money bribing assorted Mimbrate knights. Mimbrates aren't very bright, and they usually go into debt in order to make an impression on their fellows. Asharak's always been very free with his gold. When you start seeing blood-red coins, you know where they're coming from. It may be something he set in motion in the past, but I personally don't think so. The sudden influx of Murgo gold suggests a new ploy. Track the money, Ancient One. You'll get more information from that than from anything else."

"You're a Drasnian to the bone, Talvar," I told him.

"That's why Hunter put me here, Ancient One. Anyway, the whole thrust of all of this is to subvert the crown prince, who's probably deeper in debt than anybody else in all of Arendia." He made a face. "If I weren't working for my government, I could make a fortune down here. Some of these Mimbrate idiots would pay exorbitant interest just to clear their debts."

"Keep your eyes on what we're doing, Talvar," I told him. "Don't get sidetracked. Make money on your own time, not on mine. Does Asharak have his hands around the crown prince's heart yet?"

"Probably not. Young Prince Korodullin still has a sense of honor, despite all his debts. He's resisting the Murgo blandishments, but I think he's starting to waver. He needs somebody to stiffen his backbone."

"I think I know just the man. Get me some names, Talvar. I need to know just who these bought-and-paid-for Mimbrate knights are. I'll send the man I've got in mind to Vo Mimbre to deal with the matter."

"Now I know why they call you Holy Belgarath," he said.

"Don't mix 'Holy' and 'money,' Talvar. You'll get in trouble if you do."

Then I went on to Vo Ebor, where Mandorallen was in training under the tutelage of the baron. The baron of Vo Ebor had recently married a young noblewoman, Nerina by name. The baron's duties were such that he had very little time for his new wife, but there was a handsome and honorable young knight handy who sort of filled in for him—nothing improper, you understand, but it did create an interesting situation.

I got straight to the point when I arrived. "Just how good is your pupil, my Lord Baron?" I asked the older man.

"He doth far exceed our expectations, Ancient One," the baron replied. "I doubt that any knight in all Arendia is his match."

"Good." I looked at Mandorallen. "I want you to go to Vo Mimbre," I said. "There are some people there who need chastisement. They've been taking money from the Murgos to lead Prince Korodullin astray. Make them stop. The Drasnian ambassador to the old King's court will know who they are. Issue a few challenges and break a few bones. Try not to kill too many of them in the process, though. There are things you have to do later on, and I don't want you embroiled in any blood feuds when the time comes for you to do them."

"I shall strive to mine utmost to do as thou hast commanded me, Holy Belgarath," the young man replied. "My lance, my sword, and my good right arm stand ever at thy service, and, forasmuch as I am—as all the world doth know—the mightiest knight on life, I doubt not that the overthrow of these miscreant knights shall be but a light task, which I gladly undertake, and my skill and my prowess are such that, barring accident, I may confidently assure thee that their overthrow shall not do them permanent injury."

Lord, Mandorallen can be windy once he dives headlong into a sentence!

As I recall, though, the face of the Baroness Nerina positively glowed at his modest announcement of his invincibility. Arendish ladies are like that.

I never did get the full details of the scheme Chamdar had set in motion at Vo Mimbre. I suppose it might have been nothing more than a delaying tactic to keep me from snapping at his tail feathers. Chamdar'd seen my face at Annath, and I'm sure that he'd have done almost anything to avoid seeing it at close range again.

A report from the Drasnian ambassador at Vo Mimbre caught up with me a couple of months later, and I gather that Mandorallen had more than fulfilled his promise. Windy or not, Mandorallen—once he'd shut his mouth and got started—was something on the order of a natural disaster. A fair number of the knights he met in the lists that day actually had to be cut out of their armor before their injuries could be tended.

By the time Mandorallen had finished talking and got down to business, however, I was already at the Drasnian embassy in Tol Honeth.

"How good is he?" I asked Javelin, pointing at Silk. It probably wasn't very polite to ask the question right there in front of the rat-faced little spy, but recent events had eroded my good manners noticeably.

"He shows a certain amount of promise, Ancient One," Javelin replied. "He has a slight tendency to get sidetracked, though. Honesty's not one of his strong points. He's got the soul of a thief, and he can't seem to be able to pass up the opportunity to steal things."

"Javelin!" Silk protested. Prince Kheldar was wearing the typical Drasnian black doublet and hose. He was a wiry little fellow with a sharp face and a long, pointed nose. He was only about twenty at the time, but his eyes were already cynical and intelligent far beyond his years.

"All right then, gentlemen," I said, "let's get down to business. There's a Grolim named Chamdar who usually goes by the name of Asharak the Murgo. He was in Sendaria recently, and he did some things there that seriously irritated me. As closely as I can determine, he recently passed through Arendia, and he was coming this way. I want him. Find him for me."

"He gets right to the point, doesn't he?" Silk said to his friend. Then he gave me that impudent little grin that's always irritated me for some reason. "Just out of curiosity, Ancient One, why have *I* been selected for the great honor of assisting you in this quest of yours? I'm a relative novice, after all."

"Because Chamdar knows me, and he probably can also recognize most of Javelin's more experienced agents on sight. You're new enough in this business that your face isn't widely known. *That's* why I've looked you up specifically. I'm hoping that your anonymity's going to make it possible for you to search him out for me."

"Do you want me to kill him?" Silk's eyes grew bright.

"No. I just want you to find him. I'll take it from there."

"Spoilsport."

"Is he always like this?" I asked Javelin.

"Usually, yes. Sometimes it's worse."

"What would the location of this Asharak be worth to you, Ancient One?" Silk asked in a sly tone of voice.

"*Silk!*" Javelin snapped.

"I was only joking." The little fellow grinned. "I've known Holy Belgarath since I was a boy. He knows that I like to tweak his beard now and then." He looked at me. "In point of fact, Asharak the Murgo's in Tol Rane right now. I can give you the name of the inn where he's staying, if you'd like. Now, is there anything else I can do for you?"

"Are you *sure* he's in Tol Rane?" I demanded.

"As sure as we can be about anything in our peculiar business. Tolnedran intelligence isn't really very good, but they *do* have a lot of people out in the streets, and they've always kept an eye on this Asharak fellow."

"How did *you* find out about it?" Javelin asked him.

"I have some contacts inside Tolnedran intelligence," Silk replied with a lofty expression as he buffed his fingernails on the front of his doublet. "Anyway, Ran Borune's involved in trade negotiations with the Murgos right now, and the Murgo trade delegation reports directly to Asharak. They've had messengers burning up the road between here and Tol Rane for the past two weeks."

"How did you find out about *that?*" Javelin demanded.

Silk smirked at him. "I have my sources," he replied.

"More to the point, why didn't you report it to me?"

"I'd have gotten around to it—eventually. I wanted a few more details before I laid it on your desk. You always ask so many questions, Javelin. I've got it under control, and you've got other things on your mind."

"You're an absolute gold mine of information, Prince Kheldar," Javelin said sarcastically. "At least you are once I manage to pry your jaws open." Then he moved on rather quickly. "What's Ran Borune trying to sell to the Murgos?"

Silk shrugged. "A bit of this, a bit of that," he replied evasively.

"Describe the 'this' and the 'that,' Silk."

Silk winced. "All right, if you're going to be *that* way about it. Ran Borune's got a nephew who's in business in the commercial enclave at Riva. The nephew's come very close to cornering the market in the spring shearing on the Isle of the Winds, and he'll be able to make a very tidy profit if he can find a way to sell all that wool to the Murgos. I've got a friend on the Isle who's trying to outbid the nephew, though. If Ran Borune *does* manage to strike a deal with the Murgos, he may very well make my friend rich instead of his own nephew."

"And you're getting a commission from your friend, aren't you?" Javelin demanded.

"Naturally. I *am* supplying him with information on the trade negotiations, after all. Fair's fair, Javelin."

"If your uncle finds out that you're using the resources of the intelligence service for your personal enrichment, he'll have apoplexy. You *do* know that, don't you?"

"Then we'll just have to make sure he doesn't find out, won't we?" Silk replied blandly. "My uncle's the king of Drasnia, Javelin. He's got enough on his mind already without concerning himself with something like this." The little swindler looked at me. "Did you want me to go with you to Tol Rane?" he asked.

"I think so, yes. You have contacts there, I assume?"

"Old friend, I have contacts *everywhere*. Did you want to know what Salmissra had for breakfast this morning?"

"Not particularly. Why don't you go throw a few things together? We'll be leaving for Tol Rane tomorrow morning."

"I don't have to throw things together, Belgarath. My bags are *always* packed."

The next morning Silk came down into the courtyard of the embassy wearing a maroon velvet doublet and a baglike black velvet hat cocked over one ear.

"Isn't that a little fancy for a long trip on horseback?" I asked him.

"One must look the part, Ancient One," he replied. "I'm known in Tol Rane as Radek of Boktor. I do business there on occasion, and I've found it useful not to use my real name. That 'prince' my family tacked onto me has a tendency to make various merchants think that I'm an easy mark. Believe me, *nobody* tries to swindle Radek of Boktor. I've cut some very sharp deals in this particular guise."

"I'm sure you have. Let's get started."

We took the high road to Tol Rane and arrived in that snow-clogged city about a week later. Since Tol Rane's right up against the border of what used to be Maragor, it's high up in the mountains, and it gets almost as much snow as Val Alorn or Boktor do each winter. We went to the inn where Silk usually stayed when he was in town and took a fairly opulent suite of rooms on the top floor, "for the sake of appearances," as he put it.

Not long after we arrived, one of the local Drasnian agents stopped by to pay a visit, and he and Silk held an extended conversation in the secret language. It wasn't really necessary to do it that way, of course, but I think Silk was showing off.

After the other Drasnian had left, my little companion filled me in on some of the details of their discussion. There were a number of large gaps, but I didn't bother to correct him. He didn't really need to know that I understood all that finger-waving.

"Asharak's been here, right enough," the little man concluded, "but no one's seen him in the past several days. I'll nose around a bit and see if I can turn up anything more specific."

"Do that," I told him. "I'll stay here. There's no point in announcing the fact that I'm in Tol Rane, and Chamdar knows me on sight. If he catches so much as a glimpse of me, he'll be across the border into Cthol Murgos before the sun goes down."

Silk nodded, and then he left.

No sooner had the door closed behind him, though, than I altered my appearance enough to be unrecognizable and followed him. I didn't do it because I didn't trust him, although Silk's not the most trustworthy man in the world, but I wanted to see him in action. He didn't know it yet, but the Guide was going to be very important as time went on, and I wanted to be sure that he would be able to handle the things he'd come up against.

He didn't disappoint me. Prince Kheldar was already as smooth as his nickname implied. He hadn't shaved in the week or so that we'd been on the road from Tol Honeth, and that hint of a beard gave him the appearance of being older than he really was, and he was able to assume mannerisms that reinforced that perception in the eyes of others. I'm convinced that if Silk had really wanted to—and if the business of being a spy hadn't been so exciting for him—he might very well have been able to make a fortune as an actor. I've assumed various disguises over the years, so I'm in a position to recognize genius when I see it.

All right, Silk, don't let it go to your head. I'll freely admit that you're very good, but isn't that what I hired you for?

"Radek of Boktor" drifted around the snowy streets of Tol Rane, and he concluded a fair number of business transactions as he went. I stayed in the background, so I couldn't actually hear any of the details, but I get the strong impression that "Radek" sold a lot of things that he didn't actually own that day. He glibly promised delivery, however, and I'd imagine that he probably made good on most of those promises. Silk isn't above swindling people on occasion, but he was still working very hard to establish "Radek's" reputation.

Eventually he worked his way across town to the district where the Murgos normally stayed, and in the common room of an inn there he got down to business. After he'd sold some things that he didn't really have title to, he made a few discreet inquiries. He was sitting at a table with three scar-faced Murgos, and he leaned back, idly toying with his tankard. "If any of you happen to know a man named Asharak, you might pass the word along that Radek of Boktor's got a business proposition for him," he declared.

"Why should I go out of my way to make Asharak richer?" one of the Murgos countered.

"Because Asharak pays good commissions," Silk replied. "I'm sure he'll make it worth your while. The proposition promises to be very lucrative."

"If it's that good, I might be interested myself."

"I don't want to insult you, Grachik," Silk said with a thin smile, "but you don't have the resources for this particular transaction. It involves a commodity, and we all know how expensive commodity transactions can be."

"What kind of commodity?"

"I'd prefer to tell Asharak about that privately. Sometimes things have a way of leaking out, and I have some competitors I'd sort of like to keep in the dark. If they find out that Radek's coming into the market, prices are going to start climbing. That wouldn't do either me or Asharak much good."

"Asharak isn't here in Tol Rane," Grachik told him. "He left for Tol Borune two days ago."

One of the other Murgos kicked the talkative Grachik under the table.

"Well," Grachik amended quickly, "that's what I heard, anyway. With Asharak, you never really know. He has dealings all over Tolnedra, you realize. For all I know, he could be in Tol Horb by now." It was pitifully transparent. Grachik had let something slip that he was supposed to keep to himself.

"Asharak's an elusive one, all right," Silk agreed. "I've been trying to track him down for two months now. The proposition I have in mind is *very* large, and Asharak's probably the only man around who can afford it. If you happen to know anybody who can get word to him, let him know that I'll be going back to Tol Honeth in a day or so. Tell him that I usually stay in that large inn near the Drasnian embassy, and that if he wants to double his money, he should look me up. I'm not going to waste any more of my time looking for him."

Silk talked with the Murgos for about another half hour, and then he left. I stayed around long enough to hear the other two Murgos berate Grachik for his slip of the tongue *and* long enough to see Grachik try to cover his blunder by sending a pair of burly hirelings after my little friend. The Murgos were obviously willing to go to any lengths to keep Asharak's location a secret.

The pair of hired assassins caught up with Silk in a dark, snow-clogged side street, but Silk clearly knew that he was being followed, and he seemed to be confident that he could deal with the situation. I wasn't all that sure myself, so I stayed close enough to be able to lend a hand if it became necessary.

It wasn't. I've never seen *anyone* quite as agile as Silk can be in tight quarters. The assassins were a pair of knockabout Tolnedran footpads, and they were no match at all for my little Drasnian friend. He spun on the two of them, pulled one dagger out of his boot and another from down the back of his neck, and killed the pair of them in the space of about six heartbeats. Then he kicked snow over the two bodies and continued on his way. This boy was good!

I managed to reach our lodgings a couple of minutes before he did, and I was sitting before the fire when he arrived. "Well?" I said when he came in. "Did you find anything?"

"The word I'm getting is that Asharak's in Tol Borune right now. It's probably fairly accurate, because the Murgo who let it slip tried to cover his mistake by having me waylaid on my way back here. That's all the confirmation we really need, isn't it?"

"Probably so, yes. I guess we'd better go to Tol Borune, then."

"*Tonight*, Belgarath. By morning that talkative Murgo's going to realize that his hired killers failed, and I don't want to be looking back over my shoulder every step of the way. Let's get a running head start, if we can."

It took us about four days to reach Tol Borune, since Silk insisted that we stay off the main highway. I thought that I knew most of the country lanes in all the Western Kingdoms, but my sharp-nosed little companion led me along roads I'd never even seen before. Just outside Tol Borune, he reined in and changed clothes. "New identity," he explained. "Word's probably reached Asharak by now that a fellow named Radek is looking for him."

"Who are you this time?"

"Ambar of Kotu. Ambar's a little less conspicuous than Radek, and they don't move in the same circles."

"How many of these mythical Drasnians have you got up your sleeve?"

"I've lost count. I'm partial to Radek and Ambar, though. I've spent more time with them, so I know them better. I dust off one of the others now and then, though—just to keep in practice."

"Is this what they teach you people at the academy?"

"They bring it up now and then, but I developed most of it on my own even before I went there. I was born for this work, Belgarath. Shall we press on?"

Since "Ambar of Kotu" is a much shabbier-looking fellow than "Radek of Boktor" is, we took a room in one of the rundown quarters of Tol Borune, and Silk immediately took to the streets with assorted fictions to conceal his real purpose. He came back late that night with that pointed nose twitching. "Something isn't right here, Belgarath," he told me.

"Oh?"

"Are you sure that Asharak knows that you're after him?"

"Oh, yes. I'm like the wrath of God at this point, and he knows that I'll hunt him down, no matter where he tries to hide."

"Then why isn't he hiding? I located him in about two hours. I'm good, but I don't think I'm *that* good."

I gave him a sharp look. "Maybe we'd better go have a look at this fellow," I said. "I think I know you well enough by now to trust your instincts. If you're getting a whiff of something that doesn't smell right, we'd probably better investigate."

He bowed with outrageous flamboyance. "I live but to serve, Ancient One," he told me.

It was nearly midnight, and a raw wind was blowing through the deserted streets of Tol Borune as we went to the southern end of town where the Murgos usually gathered. Silk led me to a blocky sort of inn, and then we crept around to a bleary window made of cheap glass.

"That's the one they tell me is Asharak the Murgo," the little thief whispered, pointing at a scar-faced fellow sitting back in a corner.

The man *looked* like Chamdar, and I'll concede that the resemblance was almost uncanny, but when I sent out a carefully probing thought to make sure, my heart sank. The Murgo sitting in that corner was *not* Chamdar. I started to swear.

"What's the matter?" Silk whispered.

"That man's not the one I'm looking for."

"Belgarath, there are people in this town who know him, and they're all convinced that he's Asharak the Murgo."

"I'm sorry about that, but they're wrong. We've been chasing an imposter." I swore some more. "We'd better get back to Tol Honeth. I want to fill Javelin in on this. The man everybody's been watching isn't Chamdar."

"How can you be so sure?"

"Chamdar's a Grolim. That fellow at the table's just an ordinary Murgo. The resemblance is very close, but that fellow's not the one we want to find." I thought about it as we returned to our lodgings. The startling discovery explained a lot of things. I'm ashamed to admit that I hadn't thought of it before. I should have known that *something* had made Chamdar so hard to keep track of. My brains must have been asleep.

"What gave that Murgo back there away?" Silk asked.

"His thoughts. I can recognize Chamdar's mind when I encounter it. We're just wasting time here in Tol Borune. I want to be on the road to Tol Honeth when the sun comes up."

"Javelin's going to be *very* upset about this, you know. He's devoted a lot of time and money to watching this imposter."

"It's not his fault. It's probably mine. For all we know, there could be a half dozen or so of these imitation Asharaks knocking around here in the West. Chamdar's working for Ctuchik, and I'm sure that Ctuchik knows how to alter another man's features enough to lead us astray."

"What's Chamdar supposed to do?"

"He's looking for something. I've been trying to keep him from finding it."

"Oh? What's he looking for?"

"You don't need to know that, Silk. When we get back to Tol Honeth, I want you to go to Cherek."

"*Cherek?* At *this* time of year?"

"The time of year doesn't make any difference. You know Barak, don't you?"

"The Earl of Trellheim? Of course. He and I got drunk together at the last meeting of the Alorn Council. He's a bit of a braggart, but I sort of like him."

"Hold that thought. You two are going to be working together for quite a long time."

"How do you know that?"

I couldn't resist it. "I have my sources." I threw his clever remark back into his own teeth. "I want you to go to Trellheim and take Barak in hand. He'll never be a really competent spy, but he needs to know what's going on in the world. He's only nineteen, and he needs educating."

"I'll have to clear this with Javelin first."

"Forget about Javelin. I'll tell him what he needs to know. From now on, you're working for *me*. When I call you, I want you to come immediately, and when I tell you to do something, I want you to do it. No arguments. No questions. What we're involved in is the most important thing since the cracking of the world, and you're going to be in it up to your pointed nose."

"Well, now," he said. Then he gave me a shrewd look. "It's finally come, then, hasn't it?"

"That it has, my young friend."

"Are we going to win?"

"We're certainly going to try."

When we got to Tol Honeth, Beldin was waiting for me at the Drasnian embassy. "What are *you* doing here?" I demanded of him. I wasn't particularly gracious about it.

"You're in a sour mood," my brother noted.

"I got a nasty surprise a few days ago. Ctuchik's devised a way to make ordinary Murgos resemble Chamdar. I've been counting on Drasnian intelligence to keep an eye on him for me, but that was a mistake. They've spent centuries watching the wrong people."

Beldin whistled. "*That's* something we didn't expect. I told you that you ought to do your own work. You *do* realize that you've given Chamdar an absolutely free rein with this laziness of yours, don't you?"

"Don't beat it into the ground, Beldin. I blundered. It happens."

"You'd better hustle your behind back to Sendaria. Pol's out there all alone, and you haven't got the faintest idea of where Chamdar really is."

"Where is she?"

"I was just getting to that—it's why I'm here, actually. The twins called me back to the Vale and sent me out to find you. She left that house of hers at Erat last week."

"Where'd she go?"

"There's a village called Upper Gralt south of Erat. Pol's at the farm of a man named Faldor about ten leagues west of there. She's working in his kitchen, and she's got the baby there with her. You'd better get up there and warn her that Chamdar's on the loose."

"You're probably right," I agreed glumly. "I've made a pretty thorough mess of things so far, haven't I?"

"You haven't exactly covered yourself with glory. Is the Guide as good as the Mrin says he's going to be?"

"Close. I'll probably have to hone his edge a bit, though."

"Does he know what's really going on?"

"He's made some educated guesses that aren't too far off the mark."

"Are the rest of them in place?"

"I'm missing the Mother of the Race That Died, but I'm sure she'll turn up when we need her."

"Optimism's all well and good, Belgarath, but sometimes you carry it to extremes."

"Are you going back to the Vale?"

"No. I'd better get back to southern Cthol Murgos. Torak could be waking up at any time now, and somebody's got to keep an eye on him."

"Right, and I'll get on up to Sendaria."

"Have a nice trip."

I dusted off my storyteller's costume once again, and I left Tol Honeth as soon as the gates opened the following morning. I'd passed through the village of Upper Gralt a number of times over the years, so I knew exactly where it was.

My search for Chamdar had proved to be a serious waste of time, but it *had* led to the discovery of the ruse that had made it possible for him to elude me so many times. I suppose that counts for something. I didn't really worry too much about the fact that he'd escaped me. I was fairly certain that he'd show up again someday and that I'd be able to deal with him once and for all.

I put all that behind me, though, and I took the Imperial Highway north toward Sendaria and a place called Faldor's Farm.

Captain Greldik was swinishly drunk when the one-armed General Brendig and his men finally tracked him down to the waterfront dive in Camaar. "Ho, Brendig!" Greldik bellowed. "You'd better come over here and get started! I'm already a long way ahead of you!"

"What's the fastest way to sober him up?" Brendig asked the bulky sergeant standing just behind him.

"We could throw him in the bay, I suppose, sir. It's winter, and the water's pretty cold. That might work." The sergeant didn't sound very hopeful about it, though.

"Be sure you don't drown him."

"We'll be careful, sir."

The sergeant and his four Sendarian soldiers crossed the straw-covered floor of the tavern, picked Greldik up bodily, and carried him outside, ignoring his squirming and outraged howls of protest. Then they took him out to the end of the wharf, tied a rope to one of his legs, and threw him into the icy water.

Greldik was spluttering curses when he came to the surface. He still seemed fairly drunk to Brendig. "Let him swim around for a while," he instructed the sergeant.

"Yes, sir." The sergeant was a veteran of the Battle of Thull Mardu, a solid, practical man who always seemed able to get things done.

They let Greldik flounder around in the bay for about five minutes and then they unceremoniously hauled him out. "What do you think you're doing, Brendig?" Greldik demanded. His lips were turning blue and his teeth were chattering.

"Getting your attention, Greldik," Brendig replied calmly. "We'll be sailing for Riva in the morning, so I want you to be sober enough to hold the right course."

"And just why are we going to Riva?"

"Prince Hettar of Algaria brought some documents from Holy Belgarath to the palace in Sendar a few days ago. We have to take them to King Belgarion."

"Couldn't you find a ship in the harbor at Sendar?"

"Prince Hettar told me that Belgarath specifically asked for you. I can't for the life of me think why, but he seems to believe that you're dependable."

Greldik was shivering violently. "Can we go back inside?" he asked. "It seems a little chilly tonight." Water was dripping out of his beard.

"All right," Brendig agreed, "but no more drinking."

"You've got a cruel streak in you, Brendig," Greldik accused.

"So I've been told, yes."

It took most of the rest of the night to round up Greldik's sailors, and they all seemed to be as drunk as their captain had been.

The ship was battered and none too clean. The sails were patched and frayed, but General Brendig judged that she was sound. She was a Cherek war-boat, but she had been modified slightly to carry cargo. Brendig had a few suspicions about just where and how Greldik obtained those cargoes; piracy was second nature to Chereks, he'd observed. The crew wasn't particularly spritely that morning, but they managed to row out beyond the breakwater and then they set the sails. Greldik himself, red-eyed and trembling, stood at the tiller. He held his course, despite the fact that they were sailing almost into the teeth of a howling gale.

General Brendig was a Sendar, so he admired professionalism, and he was forced to admit that, despite his bad habits, Captain Greldik might just be the finest sailor in the world. A Sendarian sea captain wouldn't have ventured out of port in this kind of weather, but Greldik had a tendency to ignore the elements.

They'd been three days at sea when they raised the port at Riva. Greldik smoothly brought his battered ship up to one of the wharves. The instructions he gave his crew were couched in language that made even the professional soldier Brendig turn pale. Then the two of them crossed to the wharf and made their way up the steep stairs that mounted through the city to the fortress that was the home of the Rivan King.

No one approaches Riva without being observed, so, despite the weather, King Belgarion and his tiny Queen, Ce'Nedra, were waiting in the shallow square before the great hall. *"Brendig!"* Ce'nedra squealed delightedly, rushing forward to embrace her old friend.

"You're looking well, your Majesty," he replied, wrapping his single arm about her shoulders.

"Brendig, can't you *ever* smile?"

"I *am* smiling, your Majesty," he said with an absolutely straight face.

"Hello, Garion," the bearded Greldik said to the Rivan King. Captain Greldik was probably the least formal of all men. He *never* used titles when speaking to anyone.

"Greldik," Garion responded as they shook hands.

"You look older."

"I hope so. If I went the other way, people might begin to suspect things. What brings you to Riva at this time of year?"

"Brendig here," Greldik replied, giving the Sendarian general a hard look. "He rooted me out of a perfectly comfortable tavern in Camaar, threw me into the bay, and then insisted that I bring him here to Riva. Brendig's just a little too used to giving orders. If he'd been civil enough to get drunk with me, I'd probably have agreed to bring him here without his giving me my annual bath."

"Captain Greldik!" Ce'Nedra said sharply. "Are you sober?"

"More or less," Greldik replied with a shrug. "It was a little stormy out there, so I sort of had to pay attention to what I was doing. I see that you've filled out a bit, girl. You look better. You were kind of scrawny before."

The Rivan Queen actually blushed. The blunt-spoken Greldik always seemed to catch her off guard. Free as a bird, Greldik usually said exactly what was on his mind with no regard for propriety or even common courtesy.

"What was so important to make you venture out into the Sea of the Winds in the dead of winter, General?" Garion asked the Sendarian soldier.

"Prince Hettar brought a package of documents to the palace at Sendar, your Majesty," Brendig replied. "They're from Holy Belgarath, and he wanted them delivered to you immediately. There are a couple of letters, as well."

"Well, *finally!*" Ce'Nedra said. "I thought it was going to take that old dear *forever* to finish up! He's been at it for almost a year now!"

"Is it really all that important, your Majesty?" Brendig asked Garion.

"It's a history book, General," Garion replied.

"A history book?" Brendig seemed startled.

"It has a certain special meaning for our family. My wife's been particularly interested in it, for some reason. Of course, she's Tolnedran, and you know how they are. Let's go inside out of the weather."

"Tell me, Garion," Greldik said as they crossed the square to the broad gateway to the Rivan Citadel, "do you think you might possibly have something to drink lying around somewhere?"

Belgarion of Riva, Godslayer and Overlord of the West, read the last page of his grandfather's text with a certain awe and a kind of wonder as his entire perception of the world subtly shifted. So much had happened that he hadn't known about. The meaning of events that had passed almost unnoticed suddenly came sharply into focus as he reflected on what he had just read. He remembered any number of conversations with Belgarath during which he and his grandfather had discussed the "possible" and the "impossible," and now the true meaning of these seemingly casual discussions became clear. Belgarath may have taken the world in his hands and shaken it to its foundations, but he was first and foremost a teacher.

Garion was ruefully forced to concede that he hadn't really been a very good pupil. Belgarath had patiently told him time and again what was *really* happening, and he'd totally missed the point. "Maybe I'd better pay a little more attention to my studies," he muttered, half aloud, looking up at the shelves filled with books and scrolls that lined the walls of his cramped little study. "And I think that maybe I'm going to need a little more room," he added. The image of Belgarath's tower suddenly came to him, and it seemed so perfectly right that it filled him with a kind of yearning. He needed a private place where he could come to grips with what he'd just learned. There was an unused tower on the west side of the Citadel. It was cold and drafty, of course, but it wouldn't take much to make it habitable—a little mortar to fill the chinks in the walls, decent glass in the windows, and a bit of repair to the fireplace was about all.

Then he sighed. It was an impossible dream. He had a wife and family, and he had a kingdom to rule. The scholarly life simply wasn't available to him as it had been to Aldur's first disciple, and Garion was forced to admit that he wasn't that good a scholar in the first place. Of course, with a little time—a few centuries at most—

That thought brought him up short. The text he had just read had casually dismissed time. To Belgarath the Sorcerer centuries meant no more than years to normal men. He'd spent forty-five years studying grass and the Gods only knew how much time trying to discover the reason for mountains. Garion realized that he didn't even know what questions to ask, much less how to go about finding the answers. He *did* know, however, that the first question was, "Why?"

It was at that point that he took up the letter from his grandfather. It wasn't really very long.

"Garion," he read. "There you have it, since you and Durnik were so insistent about this ridiculous project. This is the beginning and the middle. You already know the end—if something like this can really be said to have an end. Someday, when you've got some time, stop by, and we'll talk about it. Right now, though, I think I'll go back and look over my notes on mountains. Belgarath."

Garion started violently as the door of his study burst open. "Haven't you finished *yet*!" Ce'Nedra demanded. Though they had been married for quite some time now, Garion was always slightly startled by just how tiny his wife really was. When he was away from her for more than a few hours, she seemed to grow in his mind's eye. She was perfect, but she was very, very small. Maybe it was that flaming red hair that seemed to give her added stature.

"Yes, dear," he said, handing over the last couple of chapters, which she eagerly snatched out of his hand.

"Well, *finally*!"

"You're going to have to learn patience, Ce'Nedra."

"Garion, I've gone through two pregnancies. I know all about patience. Now hush and let me read." She pulled a chair up to the side of his desk, seated herself, and started in. Ce'Nedra had received the finest education the Tolnedran Empire could provide, but her husband was still startled by just how quickly she could devour any given text. It took her no more than a quarter of an hour to reach the end. "It doesn't *go* anyplace!" she burst out. "He didn't finish the story!"

"I don't think the story's over yet, dear," Garion told her. "We all know what happened at Faldor's Farm, though, so grandfather didn't think he'd have to go over it again for us." He leaned back reflectively. "An awful lot was going on that none of us were even aware of, you know. Grandfather doesn't even live in the same world with the rest of us. He let it slip a few times in there toward the end. I wish I had time to go to Mal Zeth and talk with Cyradis. There's another world out there that we don't even know about."

"Well, of *course* there is, you ninny! Don't pester Cyradis. Talk with Eriond instead. *He's* what this was all about!"

And that rang some bells in the Rivan King's mind. Ce'Nedra was right! Eriond had been at the center of everything they'd done! Torak and Zandramas had been error. Eriond was truth. The struggle between the two Necessities had been that simple. Torak had been the result of a mistake. Eriond was the correction of that mistake. Ce'Nedra, perhaps instinctively, had seen that. The Godslayer had somehow missed it. "Sometimes you're so clever that you almost make me sick," he told his wife with just a hint of spite.

"Yes," she replied blandly, "I know. But you still love me, don't you?" She gave him that winsome little smile that always made his knees go weak.

"Of course," he replied, trying to look stern and regal. "What did grandfather have to say in the letter he sent you?"

"I thought it was pure nonsense, but now that I see how he ended this thing, I can see what he was driving at. Here." She handed him a folded sheet of paper.

"Yes, Ce'Nedra," the letter began, "I *know* that the story's not complete. You all got together and bullied me into doing this. You've got this much out of me, and that's as far as I'm willing to go. If you want the rest, go bully Polgara. I wish you all the luck in the world with *that* little project. Don't expect much help from *me*, though. I'm old enough to know when I'm well off. Belgarath."

"I'd better start packing," Ce'Nedra said after her husband had finished reading the letter.

"Packing? Where are we going?"

"To Aunt Pol's cottage, of course."

"That went by me a little fast, Ce'Nedra. This isn't *that* urgent is it? Do we *really* have to dash off to the north end of the Vale in the dead of winter?"

"I want the rest of the story, Garion. I don't really care about how drunk Belgarath got after he lost his wife—I want to know about Polgara. *That's* the part of the story that your disreputable old grandfather left out." She slapped her hand rather disdainfully down on Belgarath's manuscript. "This is only half of it. I want Polgara's half—and I *am* going to get it, even if I have to drag it out of her."

"We've got responsibilities here, Ce'Nedra, and Aunt Pol's busy with her children. She doesn't have time to write her life story just for your entertainment."

"That's just too bad, isn't it? Is Greldik still sober?"

"I doubt it. You know how Greldik is when he makes port. Can't we talk this over a bit?"

"No. Go find Greldik and start sobering him up. I'll go pack. I want to leave on the morning tide."

Garion sighed. "Yes, dear," he said.

ABOUT THE AUTHOR

DAVID EDDINGS was born in Spokane, Washington, in 1931, and was raised in the Puget Sound area north of Seattle. He received a Bachelor of Arts degree from Reed College in Portland, Oregon, in 1954 and a Master of Arts degree from the University of Washington in 1961. He has served in the United States Army, has worked as a buyer for the Boeing Company, has been a grocery clerk, and has taught college English. He has lived in many parts of the United States.

His first novel, *High Hunt* (published by Putnam in 1973), was a contemporary adventure story. The field of fantasy has always been of interest to him, however, and he turned to THE BELGARIAD in an effort to develop certain technical and philosophical ideas concerning that genre.

Eddings and his wife, Leigh, currently reside in the Southwest, where they work together on these bestselling fantasy epics.

═══ **DEL REY® ONLINE!** ═══

THE DEL REY INTERNET NEWSLETTER (DRIN)

The DRIN is a monthly electronic publication posted on the Internet, America Online, GEnie, CompuServe, BIX, various BBSs, our Web site, and the Panix gopher. It features:
- hype-free descriptions of new books
- a list of our upcoming books
- special announcements
- a signing/reading/convention-attendance schedule for Del Rey authors
- in-depth essays by sf professionals (authors, artists, designers, salespeople, and others)
- a question-and-answer section
- behind-the-scenes looks at sf publishing
- and much more!

INTERNET INFORMATION SOURCE

Del Rey information is now available on our Web site (http://www.randomhouse.com/delrey/) and on a gopher server—gopher.panix.com—including:
- the current and all back issues of the Del Rey Internet Newsletter
- a description of the DRIN and content summaries of all issues
- sample chapters of current and upcoming books—readable and downloadable for free
- submission requirements
- mail-order information

New DRINs, sample chapters, and other items are added regularly.

ONLINE EDITORIAL PRESENCE

Many of the Del Rey editors are online—on the Internet, GEnie, CompuServe, America Online, and Delphi. There is a Del Rey topic on GEnie and a Del Rey Folder on America Online.

WHY?

We at Del Rey realize that the networks are the medium of the future. That's where you'll find us promoting our books, socializing with others in the sf field, and—most important—making contact and sharing information with sf readers.

FOR MORE INFORMATION

The official e-mail address for Del Rey Books is
delrey@randomhouse.com

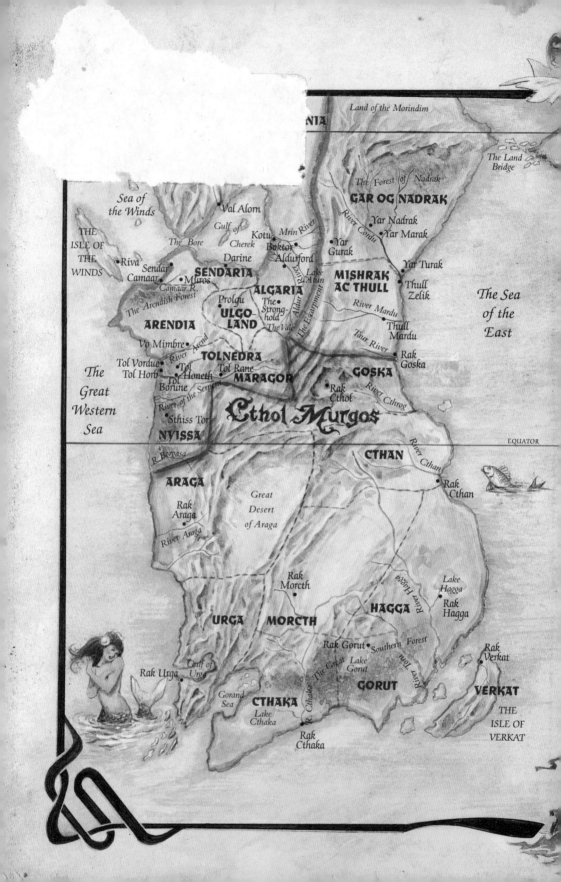

Land of the Morindim

...NIA

The Land Bridge

Sea of
the Winds

The Forest of Nadrak

GAR OG NADRAK

• Val Alorn

Gulf of
Cherek

THE
ISLE OF
THE
WINDS

The Bore

Kottu

Mrin River

• Yar Nadrak

• Yar Marak

River Cordu

• Yar
Gurak

• Riva
Sendar
Camaar

Boktor
Darine
Aldurford

Muros

• Yar Turak

SENDARIA

MISHRAK
AC THULL

Thull
Zelik

Camaar R.

ALGARIA

The Arendish Forest

Prolgu •

ULGO
LAND

The
Strong-
hold

The Vale

The Escarpment

Aldur River

Lake
Altun

River Mardu

The Sea
of the
East

ARENDIA

Vo Mimbre •

• Asend

River

Thull
Mardu

Taur River

Rak
Goska

Tol Vordue •
Tol Horb

TOLNEDRA

• Tol
Honeth

• Tol Rane

GOSKA

Tol
Borune

MARAGOR

Rak
Cthol

River Cthrog

River of the Serpent

The
Great
Western
Sea

• Sthiss Tor

Ethol Murgos

NYISSA

R. Borgasa

EQUATOR

ARAGA

CTHAN

River Cthan

Rak
Araga

Great
Desert
of Araga

River Araga

Rak
Cthan

Rak
Morcth

Lake
Hagga

Rak
Hagga

River Hagga

HAGGA

URGA

MORCTH

Rak Gorut •

Southern Forest

Rak
Verkat

Rak Urga

Gulf of
Urga

Gorand
Sea

CTHAKA

Lake
Cthaka

R. Cthaka

Lake
Gorut

The Great

GORUT

River Torn

VERKAT

THE
ISLE OF
VERKAT

Rak
Cthaka